EPIC

NORSE MYTHS & TALES

ANTHOLOGY OF CLASSIC TALES

Foreword by Dr Brittany Schorn

FLAME TREE PUBLISHING

TALES

This is a FLAME TREE Book

Publisher & Creative Director: Nick Wells
Project Editor: Catherine Taylor

FLAME TREE PUBLISHING
6 Melbray Mews, Fulham,
London SW6 3NS, United Kingdom
www.flametreepublishing.com

First published 2018

21 20
5 7 9 10 8 6

ISBN: 978-1-78664-769-6

The cover image is created by Flame Tree Studio
based on artwork by Slava Gerj and Gabor Ruszkai.

A copy of the CIP data for this book is available from the British Library.

Printed and bound in China

EPIC

NORSE MYTHS & TALES

ANTHOLOGY OF CLASSIC TALES

Foreword by Dr Brittany Schorn

FLAME TREE PUBLISHING

TALES

Contents

FOREWORD BY DR BRITTANY SCHORN 8

PUBLISHER'S NOTE 9

NORSE MYTHOLOGY: INTRODUCTION 12

THE CREATION MYTHS

Introduction...23
The Creation of the Universe...................................24
The Creation of the Earth.......................................26
Night and Day...27
The First Humans..28
Asgard..29
Yggdrasil...30

LEGENDS OF ODIN AND FRIGGA

Introduction... 31
Odin and Frigga in Asgard.....................................32
Mimir's Well, or How Odin Lost His Eye.................36
Kvasir's Blood..39
Bragi..43
Geirrod and Agnar..44
The Valkyrs..46
Volund and the Valkyrs..47
Frigga's Attendants..49
The Discovery of Flax...51
The Magic Apples...52
Skadi's Choice..58

LEGENDS OF LOKI

Introduction... 61
Loki's Character...62
Loki's Children...64
Loki and the Necklace..67
Skrymsli and the Peasant's Child............................68

The Giant Builder...69
Balder and the Mistletoe.. 73
The Punishment of Loki.. 78

LEGENDS OF THOR

Introduction..83
The Dwarf's Gifts...84
Thor's Fishing...89
Thor's Visit to the Giants..94
The Quest of the Hammer.. 101
Thor's Duel..107
In the Giant's House.. 112

FREYIA AND OTHER GODS

Introduction.. 117
Freyia and Odur.. 118
Ottar and Angantyr... 120
Frey.. 121
Niord.. 124
Aegir.. 126
Heimdall in Midgard.. 129
Tyr's Sword... 131
How Tyr Lost His Hand.. 134
The Norns' Web... 136
The Story of Nornagesta... 137
Hermod... 139
Vidar.. 141
Vali.. 143
Forseti.. 145
Uller.. 147

GIANTS, DWARFS AND ELVES

Introduction.. 149
The Giants... 150
The Dwarfs.. 154
The Elves.. 157

The Sigurd Saga

Introduction 159
The Sword in the Branstock 160
Siggeir's Treachery 162
The Story of Sinfiotli 164
The Birth of Sigurd 167
The Treasure of the Dwarf King 169
The Fight with the Dragon 171
The Sleeping Warrior Maiden 173
The Niblungs 175
The Death of Sigurd 178
Atli, King of the Huns 180

The Story of Frithiof the Bold

Introduction 182
Part One (Chapters 1–10) 183
Part Two (Chapters 11–15) 198

The Story of Gunnlaug the Worm-Tongue and Raven the Skald

Introduction 204
Part One (Chapters 1–6) 205
Part Two (Chapters 7–11) 212
Part Three (Chapters 12–18) 220

The Story of Grettir the Strong

Introduction 230
Part One (Chapters 1–13) 231
Part Two (Chapters 14–95) 244

The Laxdaela Saga

Introduction 356
Part One (Chapters 1–31) 357
Part Two (Chapters 32–56) 394
Part Three (Chapters 57–78) 435

The End of the World

Introduction.. 464
The Death of Balder 465
Revenge of the Gods.. 469
Ragnarok 471
Regneration 474

Biographies & Text Sources 476

Foreword

MEDIEVAL SCANDINAVIANS are perhaps as well known for their storytelling as their Viking raids, and rightly so. The huge body of literature they have left us is full of engrossing tales at times so realistic they feel like modern novels, and at others so utterly strange they transport the reader to a world dark and forbidding. In Old Norse mythology the lines between the earthly and the supernatural, and the human and the divine, are blurred, so as to be easily and frequently crossed. These stories are populated by gods, giants, dragons, dwarfs, and heroic men and women from a bygone age who struggle with the most profound questions of existence: mortality, the clash between nature and the trappings of civilization, the often conflicting social bonds of family, friendship and love, and the battle to survive and pursue one's own destiny in an often hostile world.

Indeed, practically the first thing we learn about the world of Old Norse mythology is that it is going to end. *V luspá* ('the Seeress's Prophecy') gives a synoptic history of the cosmos from creation to the destruction, when all life will perish at Ragnarok (Old Norse *Ragnar k* – 'the doom of the gods'). It is the opening poem in the *Poetic Edda* (sometimes called the *Elder Edda*) a collection of poems upon which the thirteenth-century Icelander Snorri Sturluson, the first great re-teller of Old Norse myths, based his *Prose Edda* (sometimes called the *Younger Edda*). The desire to escape his own mortality drives Odin (Old Norse Óðinn) to dangerous encounters in which he faces hostile giants, sacrifices himself on Yggdrasil (the world tree) and gives up his own eye as a pledge. When he cannot avert the final battle at Ragnarok, he prepares for it by sending his Valkyrs to round up the best human warriors to join his army. Gods and humans find common purpose as allies against the destructive forces represented by the giants. Odin's son Thor (Old Norse Þórr) is their champion in the present, keeping the enemies at bay with his hammer Mjǫllnir.

But the greatest threats the men and gods of legend face come from within. The gods owe many of their greatest triumphs, as well as their problems, to Loki's unscrupulous methods and deceit. As he reminds them in the poem *Lokasenna* ('Loki's Quarrel'), however, the other gods aren't so different. Odin in particular is a fickle and treacherous patron, ultimately motivated by his own self-interest. Good and evil are rarely absolute concepts in Old Norse mythology. Human heroes like Sigurd (Old Norse *Sigurðr Fáfnisbani* – 'the slayer of Fafnir') are ultimately as guilty as the gods of breaking oaths, and often strict adherence to the heroic code causes even more heartbreak and destruction. It is their choice to fight on in the face of futility that ultimately allows them to transcend fate and makes their stories timeless. Thus Odin advises:

> *Cattle die, kinsmen die,*
> *oneself must also die;*
> *but the glory of reputation never dies,*
> *for the man who can earn himself a good one.*

At the end of *V luspá*, the earth rises again and some of the younger gods come back. A shadow-dark dragon flies overhead signalling new troubles to come. Perhaps it will be different this time, perhaps not. That's where the poem ends.

Dr Brittany Schorn

Publisher's Note

Norse mythology has its roots in the oral tradition of storytelling across the northern Germanic and Scandinavian lands from paganism through to Christianity, with tales telling of mythological characters and stories, along with family sagas relating pseudo-historical events. These were all written down in Old Norse in manuscripts mostly around the thirteenth century, and have been translated and re-told many times since. This collection aims to present a curated selection of introductions, summaries and stories for you to enjoy uncluttered, for their innate power to inform, entertain and enthrall. They have been drawn from various sources (*see* Biographies & Text Sources), and some alterations have been made in terms of spellings and presentation – including the removal of most accents, which are often used inconsistently – in order for the reader to have a more accessible experience.

EPIC

NORSE MYTHS & TALES

ANTHOLOGY OF CLASSIC TALES

Foreword by Dr Brittany Schorn

FLAME TREE PUBLISHING

TALES

NORSE MYTHOLOGY

Introduction

EVIDENCE FOR THE MYTHOLOGY of Northern Europe is fragmentary, relying heavily on a few sources, but there is no doubt that to the ancient peoples of the North, gods and myths were hugely important. What we do know reveals a colourful and lively mythology, and a pantheon of fascinating characters.

After the decline of the Roman Empire by the fifth century AD, Germanic tribes settled in Northern Europe in territories formerly claimed by the Romans. They brought with them their languages – the predecessors of English, German, Dutch, Flemish, Danish, Swedish, Norwegian and Icelandic – as well as their religion and mythology.

In mainland Europe and England, early conversion to Christianity means that little evidence for the ancient beliefs has survived, so we have to turn to Scandinavia and Iceland, where Christianity took hold much later, to discover the details. Nevertheless, the importance of their gods to the Northern peoples, and the far-reaching influence of this mythology as part of a European heritage, is witnessed by the fact that in English, and other languages descended from Germanic, we still recall the Northern deities in the days of the week: Tuesday is Tyr's day; Wednesday is Odin/Woden's day; Thursday is Thor's day and Friday is Frigga's day.

Mythology of the North

The Vikings (vikingar) were men of the north, the inhabitants of Scandinavia who were best known in Europe for their raids throughout the ninth and eleventh centuries. Across history, Vikings have been portrayed as blood-thirsty, passionate and violent savages who looted and plundered England and the coasts of Europe for their own gain. Indeed, the English monk Alcuin wrote, 'Never before has such a terror appeared in Britain as we have now suffered from a pagan race.' The Vikings were a fierce people, and as well as having an intense desire for wealth, power and adventure, they were encouraged by King Harold I to look for foreign conquests. As 'Norsemen' their impact was particularly profound in Northern France, where they began to sail up French rivers, looting and burning the cities of Rouen and Paris, among others, destroying what navigation and commerce they could find. Their ships were spectacular, the finest ever built, and they were able to travel great distances – in the end their quest for adventure and the overpopulation and internal problems in Scandinavia drove them as far as North America and Greenland, where they raided and then settled, showing little regard for existing cultures and religions.

It was these activities which gave the Vikings their reputation, one which has shifted little since the tenth century. Even in 1911, G.K. Chesterton, wrote:

> *Their souls were drifting as the sea,*
> *And all good towns and lands*
> *They only saw with heavy eyes,*
> *And broke with heavy hands.*

> *Their gods were sadder than the sea*
> *Gods of a wandering will,*
> *Who cried for blood like beasts at night,*
> *Sadly from hill to hill.*

These heavy-handed, great men spoke a strange language and their brutality and lack of regard for Christianity in Europe gave them a reputation as being men of little culture, and certainly men of no religion. Very few Vikings were able to write, and most religious, spiritual and cultural documents were transmitted by word of mouth, or through their art. Because they carried with them little that explained their origins and their beliefs, and because they did not have an obvious pantheon and system of belief and scripture, it was many years before their new countries developed any real understanding of the Viking religions and mythology.

The myths and legends of the Vikings have come down to us from three major sources, although what we have is incomplete, and bare of theology, which must have existed in partnership with their mythological beliefs. Jones writes, '... [the religion] accounted for the creation of the world, and charted the doom to come. It provided mysteries as transcendent as Odin hanging nine nights on a windswept tree as a sacrifice to himself, and objects of veneration as crude as the embalmed penis of a horse. Like other religions it rejoiced the devout with hidden truth, and contented mere conformers with its sacral and convivial occasions. There was a god for those who lived by wisdom and statecraft, war and plunder, trade and seafaring, or the land's increase. Poet, rune-maker, blacksmith, leech, rye-grower, cattle-breeder, king, brewer, each had a god with whom he felt secure; warlocks, men on skis, barren women, brides, all had a deity to turn to. Best of all the powers, attributes, and functions of the gods overlapped so generously that Odin's man, Thor's man, Frey's man and the like could expect to be looked after in every aspect of life and death.'

The first main source of Viking myths and legends is the *Poetic Edda*, a work in old Icelandic that constitutes the most valuable collection in old Norse literature. Also called the *'Elder' Edda*, it is made up of thirty-four mythological and heroic lays, of various lengths. It was written in the second half of the thirteenth century, after the Vikings had accepted Christianity, and therefore the mythology may be influenced by other cultures and beliefs. Although the *Poetic Edda* was written after Christianity, it is not as easy to ascertain when the poems that make it up were actually composed. Some are clearly pre-Viking, and others relate to the period after Scandinavian civilization moved into the Middle Ages.

As the name suggests, the works are all poetic, stanzaic in nature, but other than that there is very little linking the various works that comprise it, and many of the poems included in it are obscure. Guerber writes, 'The religious beliefs of the north are not mirrored with any exactitude in the *Elder Edda*. Indeed, only a travesty of the faith of our ancestors has been preserved in Norse literature. The early poet loved allegory and his imagination rioted among the conceptions of his fertile muse ... We are told nothing as to sacrificial and religious rites, and all else is omitted which does not pride material for artistic treatment ... regarded as a precious relic of the beginning of Northern poetry rather than a representation of the religious beliefs of the Scandinavians, and these literary fragments bear many signs of the transitions stage wherein the confusion of the old and new faiths is easily apparent.'

Many of the poems are narrative, many taking the form of a parable or proverb. There are also works surrounding rite, mysticism and magic, describing chants and spells and healers.

The second great collection of mythological material is the *Prose Edda*, probably written around 1222 by Snorri Sturluson, who was a wealthy farmer in the service of the Norwegian king Hakon Hakonarson. He was also a poet, and a widely educated man, and the Prose Edda forms a treatise on the art of Icelandic poetry and a compendium of Viking mythology. There are four main sections to the book, but it is the second, the *Skáldskaparmál*, or 'The Language of Poetry', which has provided such a wealth of information on the mythology, for it explains the mythological allusion common in traditional verse, to help poets who wish to recreate it get the facts straight.

R.I. Page, in *Norse Myths*, writes: '... Snorri too was a Christian, and could hardly tell such tales as though they were truth, particularly tales that related adventures of the pagan gods. So he distanced himself from the subject in a number of ways. He composed a prologue full of early anthropological observation: how in primitive times men realized there was order in the universe, and deduced it must have a rule; how the most splendid of early communities was Troy in Turkey, with twelve kingdoms each with a prince of superhuman qualities, and one high king above all ...'

Snorri often quotes from the *Poetic Edda*, and in many cases expands ideas and philosophies introduced but never carried to term in the first book. The major failing of the work is the fact that Snorri never manages to place the mythology of the Vikings in any kind of real religious context, by explaining theology or worship. His accounts are very much tainted by his Christianity, and he often takes an orthodox Christian position, identifying the pagan gods and heroes deified by their pagan and therefore ignorant followers.

But the work is lively, witty and full of splendid details; much of the information takes the form of an inventive narrative, in which a chieftain called Odin leads a conquering army into Sweden, where he is welcomed by a king called Gylfi. Gylfi has a series of questions for the

Aesir, as the conquerors were called, and these questions and answers are recounted in the *Prose Edda*, in the form of a fascinating account of lore, folktale and legend.

The third major source for Viking mythology is the work of the court poets or 'skalds'. Skaldic verse comprise a confusion of contemporary events interspersed with works from the Viking ages into the Middle Ages and the advent of Christianity. Again, because these works were written after the conversion to Christianity, there have undoubtedly been alterations to the fabric of the myths and it is unlikely that the transmission of the oral tradition has been entirely accurate. But there are many mythological tales which form the subject of the skalds' verse, and there are several notable writers; however, the poetry was normally very elaborate and often technically pretentious, making it difficult to follow in parts.

The best-known of the Northern European deities were Odin, Thor, Loki, Balder, Niord, Frey and Freyia. These had the most distinct and vivid personalities, though there were other, more shadowy figures such as Tyr, fearless god of war. Niord, Frey and Freyia belonged to a sub-group of fertility gods known as the Vanir, while the others belonged to the main group of gods known as the Aesir.

The myths deal in conflict between the gods and giants, representing the constant struggle between chaos and order. An intense sense of fate also permeates Northern mythology: Odin chose those who would die in battle; and Ragnarok, the final great battle between the gods and the giants, was unavoidable. The people believed that their destiny was not within their own control and their myths helped them accept this, following the example of their gods. Mirroring the strong family ties of Northern society, the gods were a close-knit group that helped and supported each other, with very clear loyalties to their own kind.

Northern mythology takes us from the formation of life from the fusion of extremes – ice and fire – to the end of the world, when fire and water will again claim the life they have engendered.

Yet existence does not finish there completely: the earth will reappear after Ragnarok has passed, washed clean and renewed, when the sons of the gods will pick up where their fathers left off and life will begin again.

Worship of Northern gods was conducted in many different ways, ranging from huge statues of Thor, Odin and Frey in the magnificent temple at Uppsala in Sweden, where sacrifices included humans, to the simple sacrifices of foodstuffs brought to groves, rocks and stones in which patron gods were thought to reside. Altars of piled stones were also created in the open air for such sacrifices.

Natural features of the landscape might also be chosen for worship or veneration. An example is Helgafell (Holy mountain) in western Iceland. Thorolf Mostur-Beard, a devoted follower of Thor, held this mountain to be so sacred that no one could look at it unwashed, and no living creature could be harmed there. He was an early settler in Iceland whose story is related in the first chapters of the Icelandic saga *Erbyggja saga*. He lived in the late ninth century, the time of settlement of the newly discovered Iceland, and died in AD 918. The sagas are important sources of evidence of the practices involved in worship and this one is particularly rich in evidence for the worship of Thor. However, the fact that the sagas were written down in the Middle Ages (twelfth or thirteenth centuries) – *Erbyggja saga* is thought to have been written in the mid-thirteenth century – and contain what was then still known, understood or had been passed down of religious practices three or more centuries earlier, shows how our picture of early Scandinavian worship is a delicate web constructed from piecing together disparate and fragmented clues.

Creation

In answer to the question every culture asks – how did everything we see and experience come to be? Northern creation myths are complex and evocative. They cover the construction of the cosmos, the engendering of life, the establishment of the heavenly bodies and the population of the world.

In the beginning there was a gaping void: Ginnungagap. To its south was flaming Muspell; to the north lay freezing Niflheim, where a spring, Hvergelmir, gave rise to the eleven rivers of Elivagar. As the rivers flowed along, poisonous substances accompanying them hardened and turned to ice. Vapour from the poison froze into rime, and layer upon layer of rime increased until it had spread right across Ginnungagap. When the rime met hot gusts emanating from Muspell it began to melt and drip and there was a quickening from the drops – the first signs of life.

The drops formed the shape of a giant, Ymir. While Ymir slept he sweated, and from the sweat in his left armpit two beings were formed, a male and a female. Ymir's two legs mated with each other, producing a monstrous son. These beings began the race of frost-giants.

Next, a cow called Audhumla came into being from the dripping rime, who nourished Ymir with four rivers of milk from her udder. For her own sustenance Audhumla licked the salty rime stones. As she licked, by the evening of the first day, a man's hair was visible, on the second day a man's head, and by the end of the third day a complete man had emerged. This man was called Buri. He begot a son, Bor, who married Bestla, daughter of a giant called Bolthorn. They produced three sons: the gods Odin, Vili and Ve, who killed the huge primeval giant Ymir. When he fell, the whole race of frost-giants was drowned in his blood (except one, Bergelmir, who became the progenitor of a new race of giants).

Odin and his brothers then used Ymir to create the world. Carrying his enormous body out into Ginnungagap they formed the earth from his flesh and rocks from his bones. They made stones and gravel from his teeth and any bones that had been broken. They made his blood into the lakes and sea. Ymir's skull they formed into the sky and set it up over the earth, placing one of four dwarfs, Nordri, Sudri, Austri and Vestri (North, South, East and West), at each corner to hold it up. They created plants and trees from Ymir's hair and threw his brains up into the sky to form the clouds.

The earth was circular, and the gods arranged the sea around it. Along the shore they gave land to the giants, while inland they made a fortification from Ymir's eyelashes within which they placed Midgard, the realm of men.

Then the gods created people to inhabit the world. They took two tree trunks and created a man and a woman. Odin gave the new beings breath and life, Vili gave consciousness and movement and Ve gave them faces, speech, hearing and sight. The man was called Ask (ash tree – a fitting name for a person made from a tree trunk) and the woman Embla (of more obscure meaning, possibly elm, vine or creeper). From these two the human race descended.

Cosmology – the Structure of the Universe

The dramas of Northern myths were played out against the background of a complicated cosmology, peopled with diverse races of beings. In the course of the mythological narratives, the gods would travel from land to land over differing terrains and vast distances, and a rich and varied picture of the world emerges.

The Northern cosmic structure consisted of three different levels, one above the other like a series of plates. On the top level was Asgard, the stronghold of the gods, where the Aesir lived in their magnificent halls, as well as Vanaheim, home to the Vanir, and Alfheim, land of the elves.

On the level below lay Midgard, the world of men, and Jotunheim, mountainous realm of the giants. Svartalfheim, where dark elves lived, and Nidavellir, home of the dwarfs, were also here. Asgard and Midgard were connected by a flaming bridge, Bifrost, which was very strong and built with more skill than any other structure. Humans knew Bifrost as the rainbow.

The lowest level was cold Niflheim, which included Hel, the dwelling place of those who died of sickness, old age or accident. Warriors who died in battle were received into Odin's hall, Valhalla, or Freyia's hall, Sessrumnir, on the top level in Asgard, where they became part of Odin's personal army. Those dying at sea went to another place again: the hall of the sea gods Aegir and Ran, at the bottom of the sea.

The axis and supporting pillar of the universe was an enormous ash tree, Yggdrasil, also known as the World Tree. This gigantic tree formed a central column linking the worlds of gods, men, giants and the dead, and also protected and sheltered the world. Yggdrasil's fortunes mirrored those of the universe it sheltered; it suffered alongside the world at the same time as sustaining it under its protection.

Besides gods and men, the Northern cosmos was also inhabited by dwarfs, elves and giants. There were two types of elf in Northern myth. Light elves, living in Alfheim, were thought to be more beautiful than the sun. Dark elves were blacker than pitch, and unlike their light counterparts in nature. The dark elves lived underground in Svartalfheim, and appear to have been similar to, and perhaps interchangeable with, dwarfs.

Dwarfs were not in fact thought to be particularly small, but were believed to be ugly. They were famous for their extraordinary craftsmanship, particularly in working precious metals, especially gold. They were able to fashion remarkable objects with magical powers. Most of the treasures belonging to the gods, including Miolnir, Thor's hammer, were made by dwarfs. Dwarfs were thought to have been generated from the soil: they first took form as maggots in the flesh of Ymir, the primeval giant whose body became the earth, and the gods then gave them consciousness and intelligence.

Giants, certainly thought to be of great size, played a significant part in the mythology. They represented the forces of chaos and negativity, and were usually hostile. The gods continually strove to maintain the order of their universe against these unpredictable external forces. The relationship between gods and giants was not always straightforward, however. Giants were not invariably the enemy – many gods had affairs with or even married giantesses, or were descended from them – but more often than not dealing with them involved the crashing down of Thor's hammer, which could both punish and protect gods and ordinary mortals.

Odin

Odin was the most complex of the Northern Gods. Although known as 'Allfather', he was not a benevolent father god, but a powerful and fickle character, as treacherous as he could be generous. He was respected and worshipped – particularly by kings and nobles – but was not entirely to be trusted.

Odin, head of the Northern pantheon, was a terrifying figure. The awesome god of magic, war and wisdom, he was invoked for victory in battle, but could be faithless and was often accused of awarding triumph unjustly. Bloody sacrifices would sometimes be necessary to appease him.

Odin's mastery of magic was legendary. He could change his shape at will, or be transported instantly to distant lands while his body lay as if asleep. His magical abilities made him a formidable opponent; with mere words he could calm or stir up the sea, extinguish fires or change the winds.

Odin went to great lengths to acquire magical learning. He had only one eye, as he had pledged the other as payment for a drink from the well of Mimir, which gave inspiration and knowledge of the future. Another story relates how Odin gained this wisdom and information from the decapitated head of Mimir, the wisest of the Aesir, which he kept after it was cut off by the Vanir, a group of fertility gods. Odin preserved the head with herbs and chanted incantations over it, making it able to speak to him.

While he was particularly favoured by kings, Odin was also god of poetry, which perhaps explains the prominence the poetic sources accord him. It was said that Odin himself spoke only in poetry and that poetic inspiration was his gift. Odin was also god of the dead, particularly of those who died in certain ways. Casualties of battle, especially those killed by the spear – a weapon sacred to Odin – were seen as an offering to him, and fallen enemies could also be dedicated to him. Hanged men were also sacred to Odin; he could bring them back to life. Hanging and gashing with a spear were sacrificial rites associated with Odin, and a mysterious and fascinating myth concerning the god tells of his own self-sacrifice, hanging on the World Tree for nine nights without food or water, slashed with a spear and "given to Odin, myself to myself", to win the sacred runes, source of wisdom and magical lore.

Odin owned two particular treasures that had been forged by dwarfs: his mighty, unstoppable spear, Gungnir, and a gold arm-ring, Draupnir, from which eight other rings of equal weight and value would drip every ninth night. Odin also possessed an extraordinary horse named Sleipnir, which had eight legs and was the fastest of horses, able to carry Odin on his errands through the sky and over the sea.

Odin was regularly portrayed walking amongst men as a sinister, one-eyed old man, cloaked and wearing a broad-brimmed hat or hood. He was married to Frigga, queen of the gods and goddesses, who shared with him the ability to foresee the future, although she did not make pronouncements. Frigga was beautiful, gracious, stately and possessed of deep wisdom. She was highly respected, both in Northern mythology and by the population, and as a maternal figure was invoked by women during childbirth and by those wishing to conceive.

Thor the Thunder God

The best-loved of the Northern gods, the mighty figure of Thor, strode the cosmos, fighting the forces of evil: giants and trolls. He was the protector of Asgard and the gods could always call upon him if they were in trouble – as could mankind – and many relied on him.

Ordinary people put their trust in Thor, for Thor's concerns were with justice, order and the protection of gods and men. Ancient inscriptions on rune stones, such as 'may Thor bless these runes' or 'may Thor bless this memorial', or sometimes just 'may Thor bless' are common. Sometimes Thor's protection was invoked merely with a carving of a hammer. Thor's hammer as a symbol of protection is also seen in miniature version in the form of little hammers of silver or other metals which were placed in graves alongside the buried bodies.

Thor's mighty strength excelled that of all other gods. He was huge, with red hair and beard and red eyebrows that sank down over his face when he was angry. Thunder was thought to be the sound of Thor's chariot driving across the sky, and his fierce, red, flashing eyes befitted the god of thunder and lightning. Thor also had an enormous appetite, regularly devouring more than a whole ox at one sitting.

Thor's most important possession was his hammer, Miolnir, which could never miss its mark, whether raised up or thrown, and would always return to Thor's hand. With this weapon Thor kept the forces of evil at bay, protecting the gods and mankind. Furthermore, Miolnir held the power to sanctify and could be raised for the purpose of blessing. As well as Miolnir, Thor owned a belt of strength which doubled his already formidable might when buckled on, and a pair of iron gloves, without which he could not wield Miolnir.

Thor's main occupation was destroying giants, a constant threat to the worlds of gods and men. Thor actively sought them out, with the express intention of their annihilation, and seldom hesitated to raise his hammer when he encountered one. If any gods were threatened, Thor would instantly appear. Famous stories tell how Thor defeated the giant Hrungnir, strongest of all giants, in a duel; and how he destroyed the giant Geirrod, in spite of Geirrod's attempts to attack him. The situation was not always clear-cut, however. Giants were occasionally helpful – although Geirrod and his two daughters made many attempts to defeat Thor, another giantess, Grid, chose to forewarn Thor and lent him a staff and some iron gloves. Thor even had two sons, Modi and Magni, with a giantess, Jarnsaxa. Nevertheless, Giants were usually Thor's hostile adversaries.

Many tales of Thor are affectionately humorous, attesting to the fondness the populace had for him. When Thor's hammer was stolen by a giant demanding Freyia as his wife, Thor, to his horror, had to agree to be dressed up as the bride and delivered to the giant in order to destroy the giant and thus reclaim his hammer. Gentle humour is also evident in the tale of Thor's encounter with a magical giant king, Utgard-Loki. Thor's brute strength is not enough when pitted against Utgard-Loki's magical wiles, but even so the giants have to retain a healthy respect for Thor for trying.

Thor's ultimate adversary at Ragnarok – which according to the myths is yet to happen – will not be a giant, but the World Serpent, and one myth (*see* 'Thor's Fishing', page 89) tells of an encounter before this final one.

Loki the Trickster

One of the most extraordinary characters in Northern mythology, the strange figure of Loki was not a god, yet he was ranked among the Aesir, and was the blood brother of their chief Odin. There is no evidence that Loki was worshipped as a god, but he appears to be an essential character within the mythological kinship. His presence is pivotal to many of the mythical events. He was both the constant companion and great friend of the gods, and at the same time an evil influence and a deadly enemy.

Loki was handsome, witty and charming, but was also malicious and sly. He was descended from giants – his father was the giant Farbauti – but his wife Sigyn was a goddess, and they had two sons, Narfi and Vali. Loki plays a crucial role in Northern myth, although he is not one of the gods. He takes part in most of the gods' escapades and it is his presence that causes many of the events in the myths to happen.

Loki was full of mischief, and often caused the gods great trouble with his tricks, but equally as often it was Loki's artfulness that saved them again. Loki caused the theft of Idunn's apples, yet also reversed the disaster. To keep from ageing, the gods had to eat golden apples guarded by the goddess Idunn. At the behest of a giant, Loki lured Idunn out of Asgard, where the giant abducted the goddess together with her apples. Without the apples the gods quickly grew old and grey, but Loki found Idunn and brought her home, and enabled the Aesir to kill the pursuing giant.

Loki could take on the shapes of animals, birds and, in particular, insects, reflecting his insidious nature. He became a fly when trying to distract dwarfs from their work during the making of Thor's hammer and a flea in an attempt to steal the Necklace of the Brisings from Freyia. He used the form of a fly to enter Freyia's house and when he found Freyia asleep with the clasp of the necklace beneath her, Loki became a flea and bit the goddess. She turned over and Loki stole the necklace.

The conflict between Loki and the gods was serious and far-reaching, however. When Loki brings about the death of Balder, most beloved of the gods, his true malevolence shows through, and the gods no longer tolerate him. They shackle him until Ragnarok, when he will break free and is destined to show his true colours – fighting on the side of the giants.

Loki also produced three monstrous children with a giantess, Angrboda: Jormungand, the World Serpent; Hel, guardian of the realm of the dead, and a huge wolf, Fenrir. These three terrifying creatures all played significant roles in the myths and it was believed the wolf and World Serpent would ultimately destroy Odin and Thor at Ragnarok.

The gods were all afraid when they discovered Loki's three children were being brought up in Jotunheim (Giantland). Odin had to decide their fate and sent gods to bring the monsters before him. He threw the serpent into the ocean, where it grew until it encircled the world, biting on its tail. Hel, Loki's hideous half-dead, half-alive daughter, Odin cast into Niflheim, the land of the dead, charging her with giving food and lodgings to all those sent to her – those who died of sickness or old age. The wolf, Fenrir, the Aesir decided to restrain in Asgard, to keep an eye on it, though only the god Tyr was brave enough to tend it.

The Fertility Deities

In the constant struggle with difficult terrain and climate there was much cause in Northern mythology to rely heavily on fertility deities. A group of gods known as the Vanir were especially associated with fertility, peace and prosperity. The population looked to these gods for bountiful harvests, plentiful fish, wealth, increase and peace.

The most prominent of the Vanir were the sea god Niord and his twin children, Frey and Freyia. These were the offspring of Niord's union with his sister. She is not named, but such unions were apparently permitted amongst the Vanir. When Niord and his children later came to live amongst the Aesir, Niord married a giantess, Skadi, in a myth that has been seen as the joining of a fertility deity with the cold and dark of winter represented by Skadi, who lived high up in the mountains, wore skis or snowshoes and was known as the ski goddess.

Niord was worshipped in his own right, but relatively little information about him has survived. Best known as god of the sea, he was invoked for sea travel and success in fishing as he controlled the bounty of the sea and the wind and waves. Like the other Vanir, Niord was closely associated with wealth. It was thought he could grant land and possessions to any who prayed to him for them, and a rich man was said to be 'as rich as Niord'.

Frey, Niord's son, was the principal god of fertility and plenty. A radiant god of sunshine and increase, Frey ruled the Sun and the rain, holding sway over the harvests. Marriages were also occasions to invoke Frey, as he was not only responsible for increase in the produce of the earth, but for human increase too – an important aspect of fertility gods. Furthermore, Frey was considered to be the bringer of peace. Weapons were banned in his temples and the shedding of blood or sheltering of outlaws in his sacred places was taboo. Peace and fertility appear to have been closely linked in the Northern psyche: sacrifices were often made for fruitfulness and peace together, and the fertility gods had special responsibilities regarding peace.

Frey owned two treasures made by dwarfs. The first was Skidbladnir, a ship which was large enough to hold all the gods, yet could be folded up and kept in a pouch when not in use. It would always have a fair wind when launched and so could travel anywhere at will. The other was a golden boar, Gullinbursti (golden bristles), which travelled through the air and over the sea faster than any horse and would light up its surroundings, however dark, with the light shed from its bristles.

Famous myths tell of both Frey and Niord's marriages. Frey's union is the productive relationship between a fertility god and the earth. Frey saw the beautiful Gerda, who had giantess blood on her mother's side and whose name is related to 'gard' (field), from afar and fell hopelessly in love. Gerda was in the clutches of the giants, representing winter, but eventually Frey's servant Skirnir, 'the shining one', personifying the Sun, brought them together.

Niord's marriage was not so successful, demonstrating the incompatibility of a fertility god and the barren cold of winter. Niord and the giantess Skadi tried to live alternately for nine nights in her mountain home, and nine nights at Niord's home, Noatun, (enclosure of ships, harbour), but eventually had to admit irreconcilable differences, just as winter must give way to fertile spring.

Ragnarok – the End of the World

The concept of inescapable fate informs all Northern mythology: destiny is preordained and unavoidable. It culminates in Ragnarok, the expected destruction of the world, of which all the details were known. This apocalypse must be faced, but will not be the end of everything; afterwards a new world will begin.

For the gods, and perhaps for the population as well, Ragnarok was both a cataclysmic event in the future and, because all the elements were understood and anticipated, something they lived with in the present.

The gods could not stop Ragnarok – it had to come to pass as prophesied – and their spirited bravery in the face of inevitable annihilation reflects the Northern sensibility concerning pre-destiny. Fate was a fact of life, something that could not be avoided or changed. Even one's death was already decreed and must be faced with calm and brave acceptance. To laugh in the face of death was one of the greatest achievements a Northern warrior could attain, and such a warrior would be long remembered by his peers.

Ragnarok will be preceded by fierce battles raging throughout the world for three years. Brothers will kill each other and no ties of kinship will prevent slaughter. Next a bitter winter, Fimbul-winter, will last for another three years with no summer in between. The sky will darken and the sun will not shine. The wolf chasing the sun will finally swallow it and the other wolf will catch the moon. A terrible earthquake will uproot all trees and bring the mountains crashing to the ground. All fetters and bonds will break. Fenrir, the huge wolf, will become free, and so will Loki. The World Serpent, Jormungand, will fly into a giant rage and come up onto the shore, causing the ocean to surge over the land.

A ship made from dead men's fingernails, Naglfar, will ride the wild ocean, filled with giants, with Loki at the helm. Fenrir will advance with his mouth gaping, one jaw against the sky and the other against the earth, his eyes and nostrils spouting flames. Jormungand, spitting poison, will bespatter the sky and the sea. The sky will open and from it will ride Muspell's sons, led by Surt, the fire-flinging guardian of Muspell, holding aloft his flaming sword, surrounded by burning fire. They will all advance to the plain, Vigrid, where the last battle will take place.

Sensing Ragnarok's approach, the watchman of the gods, Heimdall, will then stand up and blow mightily on Gjallarhorn, the horn used to awaken all the gods and alert them to danger, so that they can hold counsel together. The ash Yggdrasil will shake – and all heaven and earth will be terrified. The gods will arm themselves and, with the Einherjar, will advance onto the plain. Odin will ride in front brandishing his spear, Gungnir, and attack Fenrir. Thor will be unable to help him for he must fight the World Serpent. He will vanquish it, but will step away only nine paces before succumbing to the poison it will spit at him. Fenrir will swallow Odin whole. After a fierce fight, Frey will succumb to Surt, and Loki and Heimdall will slay each other.

Then Surt will fling fire over the whole earth. Flames, smoke and steam will shoot up from the burning earth to the firmament. The sky will turn black and the stars will disappear. The earth will sink down into the engulfing sea.

THE CREATION MYTHS

Introduction

THE DRAMATIC CONTRADICTIONS of the Viking landscape and the constant battle with the elements; the spectacular backdrop of perpetual darkness and then perpetual light provide a mythology of profound contrasts. The creation myths are no exception. It was believed that cold was malevolent, evil, and that heat was good and light; when the two meet – when fire meets ice – there comes into existence a cosmos from which the universe can be created. The myths are filled with frost and fire; they are allusive and incomplete; the images and events are impossible and unlinked. But the creation myths of the Viking people are supremely beautiful, and explain, in a way that only a people in a wilderness could conceive, how we came to be.

The Creation of the Universe

IN THE BEGINNING, before there was anything at all, there was a nothingness that stretched as far as there was space. There was no sand, nor sea, no waves nor earth nor heavens. And that space was a void that called to be filled, for its emptiness echoed with a deep and frozen silence. So it was that a land sprung up within that silence, and it took the place of half the universe. It was a land called Filheim, or land of fog, and where it ended sprung another land, where the air burned and blazed. This land was called Muspell. Where the regions met lay a great and profound void, called Ginnungagap, and here a peaceful river flowed, softly spreading into the frosty depths of the void where it froze, layer upon layer, until it formed a fundament. And it was here the heat from Muspell licked at the cold of Filheim until the energy they created spawned the great frost-giant Ymir. Ymir was the greatest and the first of all frost-giants, and his part in the creation of the universe led the frost-giants to believe that they should reign supreme on what he had made.

Filheim had existed for many ages, long before our own earth was created. In the centre was a mighty fountain and it was called Vergelmir, and from that great fountain all the rivers of the universe bubbled and stormed. There was another fountain called Elivagar (although some believe that it is the same fountain with a different name), and from this bubbled up a poisonous mass, which hardened into black ice. Elivagar is the beginning of evil, for goodness can never be black.

Muspell burned with eternal light and her heat was guarded by the flame giant, Surtr, who lashed at the air with his great sabre, filling it with glittering sparks of pure heat. Surtr was the fiercest of the fire giants who would one day make Muspell their home. The word Muspell means 'home of the destroyers of the world' and that description is both frightening and accurate because the fire giants were the most terrifying there were.

On the other side of the slowly filling chasm, Filheim lay in perpetual darkness, bathed in mists which circled and spun until all was masked. Here, between these stark contrasts, Ymir grew, the personification of the frozen ocean, the product of chaos. Fire and ice met here, and it was these profound contrasts that created a phenomenon like no other, and this was life itself. In the chasm another form was created by the frozen river, where the sparks of the Surtr's sabre caused the ice to drip, and to thaw, and then, when they rested, allowed it to freeze once again. This form was Audhumla, a cow who became known as the nourisher. Her udders were swollen with rich, pure milk, and Ymir drank greedily from the four rivers which formed from them.

Audhumla was a vast creature, spreading across the space where the fire met the ice. Her legs were columns, and they held up the corners of space.

Audhumla, the cow, also needed sustenance, and so she licked at the rime-stones which had formed from the crusted ice, and from these stones she drew salt from the depths of the earth. Audhumla licked continuously, and soon there appeared, under her thirsty tongue, the form of a god. On the first day there appeared hair, and on the second, a head. On the third day the whole god was freed from the ice and he stepped forth as Buri, also called the Producer. Buri was beautiful. He had taken the golden flames of the fire, which gave him a warm, gilded glow, and from the frost and ice he had drawn a purity, a freshness that could never be matched.

While Audhumla licked, Ymir slept, sated by the warmth of her milk. Under his arms the perspiration formed a son and a daughter, and his feet produced a giant called Thrudgemir, an evil frost-giant with six heads who went on to bear his own son, the giant Bergelmir. These were the first of the race of frost-giants.

Buri himself had produced a son, called Bor, which is another word for 'born', and as Buri and Bor became aware of the giants, an eternal battle was begun – one which is to this day waged on all parts of earth and heaven.

For giants represent evil in its many forms, and gods represent all that is good, and on that fateful day the fundamental conflict between them began – a cosmic battle which would create the world as we know it.

Buri and Bor fought against the giants, but by the close of each day a stalemate existed. And so it was that Bor married the giantess Bestla, who was the daughter of Bolthorn, or the thorn of evil. Bestla was to give him three fine, strong sons: Odin, Vili and Ve and with the combined forces of these brave boys, Bor was able to destroy the great Ymir. As they slayed him, a tremendous flood burst forth from his body, covering the earth and all the evil beings who inhabited it with his rich red blood.

The Creation of the Earth

YMIR'S BODY WAS CARRIED by Odin and his brothers to Ginnungagap, where it was placed in the centre. His flesh became the earth, and his skeleton the rocky crags which dipped and soared. From the soil sprang dwarfs, spontaneously, and they would soon be put to work. Ymir's teeth and shards of broken bones became the rocks and pits covering the earth and his blood was cleared to become the seas and waters that flowed across the land. The three men worked hard on the body of Ymir; his vast size meant that even a day's work would alter the corpse only slightly.

Ymir's skull became the sky and at each cardinal point of the compass was placed a dwarf whose supreme job it was to support it. These dwarfs were Nordri, Sudri, Austri and Westri and it was from these brave and sturdy dwarfs that the terms North, South, East and West were born. Ymir's hair created trees and bushes.

The brow of Ymir became walls which would protect the gods from all evil creatures, and in the very centre of these brows was Midgard, or 'middle garden', where humans could live safely.

Now almost all of the giants had fallen with the death of Ymir, drowned by his surging blood – all, that is, except Bergelmir, who escaped in a boat with his wife and sought asylum at the edge of the world. Here he created a new world, Jotunheim, or the home of the giants, where he set about the creation of a whole new breed of giants who would carry on his evil deeds.

Odin and his brothers had not yet completed their work. As the earth took on its present form, they slaved at Ymir's corpse to create greater and finer things. Ymir's brains were thrust into the skies to become clouds, and in order to light this new world, they secured the sparks from Surtr's sabre and dotted them among the clouds. The finest sparks were put to one side and they studded the heavenly vault with them; they became like glittering stars in the darkness. The stars were given positions; some were told to pass forward, and then back again in the heavens. This provided seasons, which were duly recorded.

The brightest of the remaining stars were joined together to become the sun and the moon, and they were sent out into the darkness in gleaming gold chariots. The chariots were drawn by Arvakr (the early waker) and Alsvin (the rapid goer), two magnificent white horses under whom were placed balls of cool air which had been trapped in great skins. A shield was placed before the sun so that her rays would not harm the milky hides of the steeds as they travelled into the darkness.

Although the moon and the sun had now been created, and they were sent out on their chariots, there was still no distinction between day and night, and that is a story of its own.

Night and Day

THE CHARIOTS WERE READY, and the steeds were bursting at their harnesses to tend to the prestigious task of setting night and day in place. But who would guide them? The horses would need leadership of some sort, and so it was decided that the beautiful children of the giant Mundilfari – Mani (the moon) and Sol (the sun) would be given the direction of the steeds. And at once, they were launched into the heavens.

Next, Nott (night), who was daughter of one of the giants, Norvi, was provided with a rich black chariot which was drawn by a lustrous stallion called Hrim-faxi (frost mane). From his mane, the frost and dew were sent down to the earth in glimmering baubles. Nott was a goddess, and she had produced three children, each with a different father. From Naglfari, she had a son named Aud; Annar, her second husband, gave her Jord (earth), and with her third husband, the god Dellinger, a son was born and he was called Dag (day).

Dag was the most radiant of her children, and his beauty caused all who saw him to bend down in tears of rapture. He was given his own great chariot, drawn by a perfect white horse called Skin-faxi (shining mane), and as they travelled, wondrous beams of light shot out in every direction, brightening every dark corner of the world and providing much happiness to all.

Many believe that the chariots flew so quickly, and continued their journey round and round the world because they were pursued by wolves: Skoll (repulsion) and Hati (hatred). These evil wolves sought a way to create eternal darkness and like the perpetual battle of good and evil, there could be no end to their chase.

Mani brought along in his chariot Hiuki, who represented the waxing moon, and Bil, who was the waning moon. And so it was that Sun, Moon, Day and Night were in place, with Evening, Midnight, Morning, Forenoon, Noon and Afternoon sent to accompany them. Summer and Winter were rulers of all seasons: Summer was a popular and warm god, a descendant of Svasud. Winter, was an enemy for he represented all that contrasted with Summer, including the icy winds which blew cold and unhappiness over the earth. It was believed that the great frost-giant Hraesvelgr sat on the extreme north of the heavens and that he sent the frozen winds across the land, blighting all with their blasts of icy death.

The First Humans

ODIN, ALLFATHER, was king of all gods, and he travelled across the newly created earth with his brothers Vili and Ve. Vili was now known as Hoenir, and Ve had become Lothur, or Loki. One morning, the three brothers walked together on the shores of the ocean, looking around with pride at the new world around them. Ymir's body had been well distributed, and his blood now ran clear and pure as the ocean, with the fresh new air sparkling above it all. The winds blew padded clouds across a perfect blue sky, and there was happiness all around. But, and there was no mistaking it, there was silence.

The brothers looked at one another, and then looked out across the crisp sands. There lay on the shore two pieces of driftwood which had been flung onto the coast from the sea, and as their eyes caught sight of them, each brother shared the same thought. They raced towards the wood, and Hoenir stood over the first piece, so that his shadow lay across it and the wood appeared at once to have arms and legs. Loki did the same with the second piece of wood, but he moved rather more animatedly, so that the wood appeared to dance in the sunlight. And then Odin bent down and blew a great divine breath across the first piece of wood. There in front of them, the bark, the water-soaked edges of the log began to peel away, and there the body of a pale, naked woman appeared. She lay there, still and not breathing. Odin moved over to the next piece of wood, and he blew once more. Again, the wood curled back to reveal the body of a naked man. He lay as still as the woman.

Odin had given the gift of life to the man and woman, and they had become entities with a soul and a mind. It was now time for Loki to offer his own gifts. He stood at once over the woman and as he bent over her, he transferred the blush of youth, the power of comprehension, and the five senses of touch, smell, sight, hearing and taste. He was rewarded when the woman rose then and smiled unquestioningly at the three gods. She looked around in wonder, and then down at the lifeless body by her side. And Loki leaned across the body of man this time, and gave to him blood, which began to run through his veins. He too received the gifts of understanding, and of the five senses, and he was able to join woman as she stood on the beach.

Hoenir stepped forward then, and offered to both man and woman the power of speech. At this, the two human beings turned and walked together into the new world, their hands held tightly together.

"Stop," said Odin, with great authority.

Turning, the two humans looked at him and nodded. "You are Ash," said Odin to the man, which represented the tree from which he had been created. "And you are Elm," he said to the woman. Then Odin leaned over and draped his cloak around the shoulders of the first human woman and sent her on her way, safe in the care of man, who would continue in that role until the end of time – or so the Vikings said.

Asgard

ASGARD IS ANOTHER WORD for 'enclosure of the gods'. It was a place of great peace, ruled by Odin and built by Odin and his sons on Yggdrasil, above the clouds, and centred over Midgard. Each of the palaces of Asgard was built for pleasure, and only things which were perfect in every way could become part of this wondrous land. The first palace built was Gladsheim, or Joyous home, and it was created to house the twelve thrones of the principal deities. Everything was cast from gold, and it shone in the heavens like the sun itself. A second palace was built for the goddesses, and it was called Vingof, or Friendly Floor. Here, too, everything was made from gold, which is the reason why Asgard's heyday became known as the golden years.

As Asgard was conceived, and built, a council was held, and the rules were set down for gods and goddesses alike. It was decreed at this time that there would be no blood shed within the limits of the realm, and that harmony would reign forever. A forge was built, and all of the weapons and tools required for the construction of the magnificent palaces were made there. The gods held their council at the foot of Yggdrasil, and in order to travel there, a bridge was erected – the rainbow bridge, or Bifrost as it became known. The bridge arched over Midgard, on either side of Filheim, and its colours were so spectacular that one could only gaze in awe upon seeing them for the first time.

The centre of Asgard displayed the plan of Idavale, with hills that dipped and soared with life. Here the great palaces were set in lush green grasses. One was Breibalik, or Broad Gleaming, and there was Glitnir, in which all was made gold and silver. There were palaces clustered in gems, polished and shimmering in the light of the new heavens. And that beauty of Asgard was reflected by the beauteous inhabitants – whose minds and spirits were pure and true. Asgard was the home of all the Aesir, and the setting for most of the legends told here. But there was another family of gods – and they were called the Vanir.

For many years the Vanir lived in their own land, Vanaheim, but the time came when a dispute arose between the two families of gods, and the Aesir waged war against the Vanir. In time, they learned that unity was the only way to move forward, and they put aside their differences and drew strength from their combined forces. In order to ratify their treaty, each side took hostages. So it was that Niord came to dwell in Asgard with Frey and Freyia, and Hoenir went to live in Vanaheim, the ultimate sacrifice by one of the brothers of creation.

Yggdrasil

YGGDRASIL IS THE WORLD ASH, a tree that has been there for all time, and will always be there. Its branches overhang all nine worlds, and they are linked by the great tree. The roots of the Yggdrasil are tended by the Norns, three powerful sisters who are also called the fates. The roots are nourished by three wells. One root reaches into Asgard, the domain of the gods, and feeds from the well of Wyrd, which is the name of the eldest Norn. The second root leads to Jotunheim, the land of the frost-giants. The well at the end of this root is called Mimir, who was once a god. Only the head of Mimir has survived the creation of the world, and it drinks daily from the well and is kept alive by the magic herbs which are scattered in it. Mimir represents great wisdom, and even Odin chose to visit him there to find answers to the most profound questions that troubled his people.

The third root winds its way to Filheim, and the well here is the scum-filled fountain of black water called Vergelmir. Here, the root of the tree is poisoned, gnawed upon, and from it rises the scent of death and dying. In Vergelmir is a great winged dragon called Nithog, and he sits at the base of the root and inflicts damage that would have caused another tree to wither away.

And the magnificent tree stands, as it has always stood, as the foundation of each world, and a point of communication between all. The name Yggdrasil has many evil connotations, and translated it means 'Steed of Ygg' or, 'Steed of Odin'. There once was a time when Odin longed to know the secret of runes – the symbols which became writing, as we know it. The understanding of runes was a cherished one, and in order to acquire it, a terrible sacrifice must be undergone by the learner. Odin had longed for many years to have that knowledge, and the day came when he was prepared to make his sacrifice. Odin was told that he must hang himself by the neck from the bough of the World Ash, and he must remain there, swinging in the frozen anarchy of the dark winds, for nine days. The story has been told that Odin, the bravest of the gods, the father of all, screamed with such terror and pain that the gods held their hands to their ears for each of those nine wretched days.

But Odin's strength of character carried him through the tortuous ordeal and so it was that he was at once the master of the magic runes, the only bearer of the secret along the length of the great tree. His knowledge was shared amongst his friends and his wisdom became legendary.

Odin was at the helm of the nine worlds, which stretched from Asgard in the topmost branches, to the world of Hel down below, at the lowest root. In between were the worlds of the Vanir, called Vanaheim, Midgard, where humans lived, as well as the worlds of the light elves, the dark elves, the dwarfs, the frost and hill giants and, at last, the fire-giants of Muspell. The most magnificent, and the world we hear the most about was Asgard, and it is here that our story begins.

LEGENDS OF ODIN AND FRIGGA

Introduction

IN THE GOLDEN AGE OF ASGARD, Odin reigned at the head of the nine worlds of Yggdrasil. He was a fair man, well-liked by all, and his kingdom of Asgard was a magnificent place, where time stood still and youth and the pleasures of nature abounded. Odin was also called Allfather, for he was the father of all men and gods. He reigned high on his throne, overlooking each of the worlds, and when the impulse struck him, Odin disguised himself and went among the gods and people of the other worlds, seeking to understand their activities. Odin appeared in many forms, but he was often recognized for he had just one eye, and that eye could see all. Odin had many adventures, and before the war of the gods, before Odin began to prepare for Ragnarok, Frigga was Odin's wife and the Queen of Asgard. Asgard was a setting for many of them, as you will see. All of the gods have their stories, and some of the most exciting are recorded here.

Odin and Frigga in Asgard

ODIN WAS THE SON OF BOR, and the brother of Vili and Ve. He was the most supreme god of the Northern races and he brought great wisdom to his place at the helm of all gods. He was called Allfather, for all gods were said to have descended from him, and his esteemed seat was Asgard itself. He held a throne there, one in an exalted and prestigious position, and it served as a fine watchtower from which he could look over men on earth, and the other gods in Asgard as they went about their daily business.

Odin was a tall, mighty warrior. While not having the brawn of many excellent men, he had wisdom which counted for much more. On his shoulders he carried two ravens, Hugin (thought) and Munin (Memory), and they perched there, as he sat on his throne, and recounted to him the activities in the great wide world. Hugin and Munin were Odin's eyes and his ears when he was in Asgard and he depended on their bright eyes and alert ears for news of everything that transpired down below. In his hand Odin carried a great spear, Gungnir, which had been forged by dwarfs, and which was so sacred that it could never be broken. On his finger Odin wore a ring, Draupnir, which represented fertility and fruitfulness and which was more valuable to him, and to his land, than anything in any other god's possession. At the foot of Odin's throne sat two wolves or hunting hounds, Geri and Freki, and these animals were sacred. If one happened upon them while hunting, success was assured.

Odin belonged to a mysterious region, somewhere between life and death. He was more subtle and more dangerous than any of the other gods, and his name in some dialects means 'wind', for he could be both forceful and gentle, and then elusive or absent. On the battlefield, Odin would dress as an old man – indeed, Odin had many disguises, for when things changed in Asgard, and became bad, he had reason to travel on the earth to uncover many secrets – attended by ravens, wolves and the Valkyrs, who were the 'choosers of the slain', the maidens who took the souls of fallen warriors to Valhalla.

Valhalla was Odin's palace at Asgard, and its grandeur was breathtaking. Valhalla means 'hall of the chosen slain', and it had five hundred great wooden doors, which were wide enough to allow eight hundred warriors to pass, breastplate to breastplate. The walls were made of glittering spears, polished until they gleamed like silver, and the roof was a sea of golden shields which shone like the sun itself. In Odin's great hall were huge banqueting tables, where the Einheriar, or warriors favoured by Odin, were served. The tables were laden with the finest horns of mead, and platters of roast boar. Like everything else in Asgard, Valhalla was enchanted. Even the boar was divine and Saehrimnir, as he was called, was slain daily by the cook, boiled and roasted and served each night in tender, succulent morsels, and then brought back to life again the following day, for the procedure to take place once again. After the meal, the warriors would retire to the palace forecourt where they would engage in unmatched feats of arms for all to see. Those who were injured would be healed instantly by the enchantment of Valhalla, and those who watched became even finer warriors.

Odin lived in Asgard with Frigga, who was the mother-goddess and his wife. Frigga was daughter of Fiogyn and sister of Jord, and she was greatly beloved on earth and in Asgard.

She was goddess of the atmosphere and the clouds, and she wore garments that were as white as the snow-laden mountains that gently touched the land of Asgard. As mother of all, Frigga carried about her a heady scent of the earth – blossoming flowers, ripened fruit, and luscious greenery. There are many stories told about Frigga, as we will discover below.

Life in Asgard was one of profound comfort and grace. Each day dawned new and fresh for the passage of time had not been accorded to Asgard and nothing changed except to be renewed. The sun rose each day, never too hot, and the clouds gently cooled the air as the day waned. Each night the sky was lit with glistening stars, and the fresh, rich white moon rose in the sky and lit all with her milky light. There was no evil in Asgard and the good was as pure as the water, as the air, and as the thoughts of each god and goddess as he and she slept.

In the fields, cows grazed on verdant green grass and in the trees birds caught a melody and tossed it from branch to branch until the whole world sang with their splendid music. The wind wove its way through the trees, across the mountains, and under the sea-blue skies – kissing ripples into the streams and turning a leaf to best advantage. There was a peace and harmony that exists for that magical moment just before spring turns to summer, and it was that moment at which Asgard was suspended for all time.

And so it was that Odin and Frigga brought up their young family here, away from the darkness on the other side, far from the clutches of change and disharmony. There were nine worlds in Yggdrasil, the World Ash, which stretched out from Asgard as far as the eye could see. At the top there was Aesir, and in the bottom was the dead world of Hel, at the Tree's lowest roots. In between were the Vanir, the light elves, the dark elves, men, frost and hill giants, dwarfs and the giants of Muspell.

Frigga kept her own palace in Asgard, called Fensalir, and from his high throne Odin could see her there, hard at her work. Frigga's palace was called the hall of mists, and she sat with her spinning wheel, spinning golden threat or long webs of bright-coloured clouds with a marvellous, jewelled spinning wheel which could be seen as a constellation in the night's sky.

There was a story told once of Frigga, one in which her customary goodness and grace were compromised. Frigga was a slim and elegant goddess, and she took great pride in her appearance – something the later Christians would consider to be a sin, but which the Vikings understood, and indeed encouraged. She had long silky hair and she dressed herself in exquisite finery, and Odin showered her with gifts of gems and finely wrought precious metals. She lived contentedly, for her husband was generous, until the day came when she spied a splendid golden ornament which had been fastened to a statue of her husband. As the seamless darkness of Asgard fell one evening, she slipped out and snatched the ornament, entrusting it to dwarfs whom she asked to forge her the finest of necklaces. When the jewel was complete, it was the most beautiful decoration ever seen on any woman – goddess or humankind – and it made her more attractive to Odin so that he plied her with even more gifts, and more love than ever. Soon, however, he discovered that his decoration had been stolen, and he called together all of the dwarfs and with all the fury of a god demanded that this treacherous act be explained. Now Frigga was beloved both by god and dwarf, and although the dwarfs were at risk of death at the hand of Odin, they remained loyal to Frigga, and would not tell Allfather who had stolen the golden ornament.

Odin's anger knew no bounds. The silence of the dwarfs meant only one thing to him – treason – and he swore to find out the real thief by daybreak. And so it was that on that night Odin commanded that the statue be placed above the gates of the palace, and he began to devise runes which would enable it to talk, and to betray the thief. Frigga's blood turned cold when she heard this commandment, for Odin was a kind and generous god when he was happy and content, but when he was crossed, there was a blackness in his nature that put them all in danger. There was every possibility that Frigga would be cast out of Asgard if he were to know of her deceit, and it was at the expense of everything that she intended to keep it a secret.

Frigga called out to her favourite attendant, Fulla, and begged her to find some way to protect her from Odin. Fulla disappeared and several hours later returned with a dwarf, a hideous and frightening dwarf who insisted that he could prevent the secret from being uncovered, if Frigga would do him the honour of smiling kindly on him. Frigga agreed at once, and that night, instead of revealing all, the statue was smashed to pieces while the unwitting guards slept, drugged by the ugly dwarf.

Odin was so enraged by this new travesty that he left Asgard at once – disappearing into the night and taking with him all of the blessings he had laid upon Asgard. And in his absence, Asgard and the worlds around turned cold. Odin's brothers, it is said, stepped into his place, taking on his appearance in order to persuade the gods and men that all was well, but they had not his power or his great goodness and soon enough the frost-giants invaded the earth and cast across the land a white blanket of snow. The trees were stripped of their finery, the sun-kissed streams froze and forgot how to gurgle their happy song. Birds left the trees and cows huddled together in frosty paddocks. The clouds joined together and became an impenetrable mist and the wind howled and scowled through the barren rock.

For seven months Asgard stood frozen until the hearts of each man within it became frosted with unhappiness, and then Odin returned. When he saw the nature of the evil that had stood in his place, he placed the warmth of his blessings on the land once more, forcing the frost-giants to release them. He had missed Frigga, and he showered her once more with love and gifts, and as mother of all gods, once again she took her place beside him as his queen.

Asgard had many happy days before Frigga's necklace caused the earth to become cold. Frigga and Odin had many children, including Thor, their eldest son, who was the favourite of the gods and the people – a large and boisterous god with a zeal for life. He did everything with great passion, and spirit, and his red hair and red beard made him instantly identifiable, wherever he went. Thor lived in Asgard at Thruthvangar, in his castle hall Bilskirnir (lightning). He was often seen with a sheet of lightning, which he flashed across the land, ripening the harvest and ensuring good crops for all. With his forked lightning in another hand, he travelled to the edges of the kingdoms, fighting trolls and battling giants, the great guardian of Asgard and of men and gods.

Thruthvangar had five hundred and forty rooms, and it was the largest castle ever created. Here he lived with the beautiful Sif, an exquisite goddess with hair made of long, shining strands of gold. Sif was the goddess of the fields, and the mother of the earth, like Frigga. Her long, golden hair was said to represent the golden grass covering the harvest fields, and Thor was very proud of her.

Balder was the second son of Odin and Frigga at Asgard, and he was the fairest of all the gods – indeed, his purity and goodness shone like a moonbeam and he was so pale as to be translucent. Balder was beloved by all, and his innate kindness caused him to love everything around him – evil or good. He lived in Breidablik, with his wife Nanna.

The third son of Odin was Hodur, a blind but happy god who sat quietly, listening and enjoying the sensual experiences of the wind in his hair, the sun on his shoulders, the joyful cries of the birds on the air. While all was good in Asgar, Hodur was content, and although he represented darkness, and was the twin to Balder's light, that darkness had no real place and it was kept in check by the forces of goodness.

Odin's fourth son was Tyr, who was the most courageous and brave of the gods – the god of martial honour and one of the twelve gods of Asgard. He did not have his own palace, for he travelled widely, but he held a throne at Valhalla, and in the great council hall of Gladsheim. Tyr was also the god of the sword, and every sword had his rune carved into its handle. Although Odin was his father, Tyr's mother is said to have been a beautiful unknown giantess.

Heimdall also lived in Asgard, and he was called the white god, although he was not thought to be the son of Odin and Frigga at all. Some said he had been conceived by nine mysterious sisters, who had given birth to him together. His stronghold was a fort on the boundary of Asgard, next to the Bifrost bridge, and he slept there with one eye open, and both ears alert, for the sound of any enemy approaching.

There were many other gods in Asgard, and many who would one day come to live there. But in those early days of creation, the golden years of Asgard, life was simple, and its occupants few and wondrous. The gods and goddesses lived together in their palaces, many of them with children, about whom many stories can be told.

But even the golden years of Asgard held their secrets, and even the best of worlds must have its serpent. There was one inhabitant of Asgard who no one cared to discuss, the very spirit of evil. He was Loki, who some said was the brother of Odin, although there were others who swore he could not be related to Allfather. Loki was the very personification of trickery, and deceit, and his mischief led him into great trouble. But that is another story.

Mimir's Well, or How Odin Lost His Eye

IN THE BEGINNING OF THINGS, before there was any world or sun, moon, and stars, there were the giants; for these were the oldest creatures that ever breathed. They lived in Jotunheim, the land of frost and darkness, and their hearts were evil. Next came the gods, the good Aesir, who made earth and sky and sea, and who dwelt in Asgard, above the heavens. Then were created the queer little dwarfs, who lived underground in the caverns of the mountains, working at their mines of metal and precious stones. Last of all, the gods made men to dwell in Midgard, the good world that we know, between which and the glorious home of the Aesir stretched Bifrost, the bridge of rainbows.

In those days, folk say, there was a mighty ash-tree named Yggdrasil, so vast that its branches shaded the whole earth and stretched up into heaven where the Aesir dwelt, while its roots sank far down below the lowest depth. In the branches of the big ash-tree lived a queer family of creatures. First, there was a great eagle, who was wiser than any bird that ever lived – except the two ravens, Thought and Memory, who sat upon Father Odin's shoulders and told him the secrets which they learned in their flight over the wide world. Near the great eagle perched a hawk, and four antlered deer browsed among the buds of Yggdrasil. At the foot of the tree coiled a huge serpent, who was always gnawing hungrily at its roots, with a whole colony of little snakes to keep him company, – so many that they could never be counted. The eagle at the top of the tree and the serpent at its foot were enemies, always saying hard things of each other. Between the two skipped up and down a little squirrel, a tale-bearer and a gossip, who repeated each unkind remark and, like the malicious neighbor that he was, kept their quarrel ever fresh and green.

In one place at the roots of Yggdrasil was a fair fountain called the Urdar-well, where the three Norn-maidens, who knew the past, present, and future, dwelt with their pets, the two white swans. This was magic water in the fountain, which the Norns sprinkled every day upon the giant tree to keep it green, – water so sacred that everything which entered it became white as the film of an eggshell. Close beside this sacred well the Aesir had their council hall, to which they galloped every morning over the rainbow bridge.

But Father Odin, the king of all the Aesir, knew of another fountain more wonderful still; the two ravens whom he sent forth to bring him news had told him. This also was below the roots of Yggdrasil, in the spot where the sky and ocean met. Here for centuries and centuries the giant Mimir had sat keeping guard over his hidden well, in the bottom of which lay such a treasure of wisdom as was to be found nowhere else in the world. Every morning Mimir dipped his glittering horn Gioll into the fountain and drew out a draught of the wondrous water, which he drank to make him wise. Every day he grew wiser and wiser; and as this had been going on ever since the beginning of things, you can scarcely imagine how wise Mimir was.

Now it did not seem right to Father Odin that a giant should have all this wisdom to himself; for the giants were the enemies of the Aesir, and the wisdom which they had been hoarding for ages before the gods were made was generally used for evil purposes. Moreover, Odin longed and longed to become the wisest being in the world. So he resolved to win a draught from Mimir's well, if in any way that could be done.

One night, when the sun had set behind the mountains of Midgard, Odin put on his broad-brimmed hat and his striped cloak, and taking his famous staff in his hand, trudged down the long bridge to where it ended by Mimir's secret grotto.

"Good-day, Mimir," said Odin, entering; "I have come for a drink from your well."

The giant was sitting with his knees drawn up to his chin, his long white beard falling over his folded arms, and his head nodding; for Mimir was very old, and he often fell asleep while watching over his precious spring. He woke with a frown at Odin's words. "You want a drink from my well, do you?" he growled. "Hey! I let no one drink from my well."

"Nevertheless, you must let me have a draught from your glittering horn," insisted Odin, "and I will pay you for it."

"Oho, you will pay me for it, will you?" echoed Mimir, eyeing his visitor keenly. For now that he was wide awake, his wisdom taught him that this was no ordinary stranger. "What will you pay for a drink from my well, and why do you wish it so much?"

"I can see with my eyes all that goes on in heaven and upon earth," said Odin, "but I cannot see into the depths of ocean. I lack the hidden wisdom of the deep, – the wit that lies at the bottom of your fountain. My ravens tell me many secrets; but I would know all. And as for payment, ask what you will, and I will pledge anything in return for the draught of wisdom."

Then Mimir's keen glance grew keener. "You are Odin, of the race of gods," he cried. "We giants are centuries older than you, and our wisdom which we have treasured during these ages, when we were the only creatures in all space, is a precious thing. If I grant you a draught from my well, you will become as one of us, a wise and dangerous enemy. It is a goodly price, Odin, which I shall demand for a boon so great."

Now Odin was growing impatient for the sparkling water. "Ask your price," he frowned. "I have promised that I will pay."

"What say you, then, to leaving one of those far-seeing eyes of yours at the bottom of my well?" asked Mimir, hoping that he would refuse the bargain. "This is the only payment I will take."

Odin hesitated. It was indeed a heavy price, and one that he could ill afford, for he was proud of his noble beauty. But he glanced at the magic fountain bubbling mysteriously in the shadow, and he knew that he must have the draught.

"Give me the glittering horn," he answered. "I pledge you my eye for a draught to the brim."

Very unwillingly Mimir filled the horn from the fountain of wisdom and handed it to Odin. "Drink, then," he said; "drink and grow wise. This hour is the beginning of trouble between your race and mine." And wise Mimir foretold the truth.

Odin thought merely of the wisdom which was to be his. He seized the horn eagerly, and emptied it without delay. From that moment he became wiser than any one else in the world except Mimir himself.

Now he had the price to pay, which was not so pleasant. When he went away from the grotto, he left at the bottom of the dark pool one of his fiery eyes, which twinkled and winked up through the magic depths like the reflection of a star. This is how Odin lost his eye, and why from that day he was careful to pull his gray hat low over his face when he wanted to pass unnoticed. For by this oddity folk could easily recognize the wise lord of Asgard.

In the bright morning, when the sun rose over the mountains of Midgard, old Mimir drank from his bubbly well a draught of the wise water that flowed over Odin's pledge. Doing so, from his underground grotto he saw all that befell in heaven and on earth. So that he also was wiser by the bargain. Mimir seemed to have secured rather the best of it; for he lost nothing that he could not spare, while Odin lost what no man can well part with, – one of the good windows wherethrough his heart looks out upon the world. But there was a sequel to these doings which made the balance swing down in Odin's favor.

Not long after this, the Aesir quarreled with the Vanir, wild enemies of theirs, and there was a terrible battle. But in the end the two sides made peace; and to prove that they meant never to quarrel again, they exchanged hostages. The Vanir gave to the Aesir old Niord the rich, the lord of the sea and the ocean wind, with his two children, Frey and Freyia. This was indeed a gracious gift; for Freyia was the most beautiful maid in the world, and her twin brother was almost as fair. To the Vanir in return Father Odin gave his own brother Hoenir. And with Hoenir he sent Mimir the wise, whom he took from his lonely well.

Now the Vanir made Hoenir their chief, thinking that he must be very wise because he was the brother of great Odin, who had lately become famous for his wisdom. They did not know the secret of Mimir's well, how the hoary old giant was far more wise than any one who had not quaffed of the magic water. It is true that in the assemblies of the Vanir Hoenir gave excellent counsel. But this was because Mimir whispered in Hoenir's ear all the wisdom that he uttered. Witless Hoenir was quite helpless without his aid, and did not know what to do or say. Whenever Mimir was absent he would look nervous and frightened, and if folk questioned him he always answered:

"Yes, ah yes! Now go and consult some one else."

Of course the Vanir soon grew very angry at such silly answers from their chief, and presently they began to suspect the truth. "Odin has deceived us," they said. "He has sent us his foolish brother with a witch to tell him what to say. Ha! We will show him that we understand the trick." So they cut off poor old Mimir's head and sent it to Odin as a present.

The tales do not say what Odin thought of the gift. Perhaps he was glad that now there was no one in the whole world who could be called so wise as himself. Perhaps he was sorry for the danger into which he had thrust a poor old giant who had never done him any wrong, except to be a giant of the race which the Aesir hated. Perhaps he was a little ashamed of the trick which he had played the Vanir. Odin's new wisdom showed him how to prepare Mimir's head with herbs and charms, so that it stood up by itself quite naturally and seemed not dead. Thenceforth Odin kept it near him, and learned from it many useful secrets which it had not forgotten.

So in the end Odin fared better than the unhappy Mimir, whose worst fault was that he knew more than most folk. That is a dangerous fault, as others have found; though it is not one for which many of us need fear being punished.

Kvasir's Blood

ONCE UPON A TIME there lived a man named Kvasir, who was so wise that no one could ask him a question to which he did not know the answer, and who was so eloquent that his words dripped from his lips like notes of music from a lute. For Kvasir was the first poet who ever lived, the first of those wise makers of songs whom the Norse folk named *skalds*. This Kvasir received his precious gifts wonderfully; for he was made by the gods and the Vanir, those two mighty races, to celebrate the peace which was evermore to be between them.

Up and down the world Kvasir traveled, lending his wisdom to the use of men, his brothers; and wherever he went he brought smiles and joy and comfort, for with his wisdom he found the cause of all men's troubles, and with his songs he healed them. This is what the poets have been doing in all the ages ever since. Folk declare that every skald has a drop of Kvasir's blood in him. This is the tale which is told to show how it happened that Kvasir's blessed skill has never been lost to the world.

There were two wicked dwarfs named Fialar and Galar who envied Kvasir his power over the hearts of men, and who plotted to destroy him. So one day they invited him to dine, and while he was there, they begged him to come aside with them, for they had a very secret question to ask, which only he could answer. Kvasir never refused to turn his wisdom to another's help; so, nothing suspecting, he went with them to hear their trouble.

Thereupon this sly pair of wicked dwarfs led him into a lonely corner. Treacherously they slew Kvasir; and because their cunning taught them that his blood must be precious, they saved it in three huge kettles, and mixing it with honey, made thereof a magic drink. Truly, a magic drink it was; for whoever tasted of Kvasir's blood was straightway filled with Kvasir's spirit, so that his heart taught wisdom and his lips uttered the sweetest poesy. Thus the wicked dwarfs became possessed of a wonderful treasure.

When the gods missed the silver voice of Kvasir echoing up from the world below, they were alarmed, for Kvasir was very dear to them. They inquired what had become of him, and finally the wily dwarfs answered that the good poet had been drowned in his own wisdom. But Father Odin, who had tasted another wise draught from Mimir's well, knew that this was not the truth, and kept his watchful eye upon the dark doings of Fialar and Galar.

Not long after this the dwarfs committed another wicked deed. They invited the giant Gilling to row out to sea with them, and when they were a long distance from shore, the wicked fellows upset the boat and drowned the giant, who could not swim. They rowed back to land, and told the giant's wife how the 'accident' had happened. Then there were giant shrieks and howls enough to deafen all the world, for the poor giantess was heartbroken, and her grief was a giant grief. Her sobs annoyed the cruel-hearted dwarfs. So Fialar, pretending to sympathize, offered to take her where she could look upon the spot where her dear husband had last been seen. As she passed through the gateway, the other dwarf, to whom his brother had made a sign, let a huge millstone fall upon her head. That was the ending of her, poor thing, and of her sorrow, which had so disturbed the little people, crooked in heart as in body.

But punishment was in store for them. Suttung, the huge son of Gilling, learned the story of his parents' death, and presently, in a dreadful rage, he came roaring to the home of the dwarfs.

He seized one of them in each big fist, and wading far out to sea, set the wretched little fellows on a rock which at high tide would be covered with water.

"Stay there," he cried, "and drown as my father drowned!" The dwarfs screamed thereat for mercy so loudly that he had to listen before he went away.

"Only let us off, Suttung," they begged, "and you shall have the precious mead made from Kvasir's blood."

Now Suttung was very anxious to own this same mead, so at last he agreed to the bargain. He carried them back to land, and they gave him the kettles in which they had mixed the magic fluid. Suttung took them away to his cave in the mountains, and gave them in charge of his fair daughter Gunnlod. All day and all night she watched by the precious kettles, to see that no one came to steal or taste of the mead; for Suttung thought of it as his greatest treasure, and no wonder.

Father Odin had seen all these deeds from his seat above the heavens, and his eye had followed longingly the passage of the wondrous mead, for Odin longed to have a draught of it. Odin had wisdom, he had drained that draught from the bottom of Mimir's mystic fountain; but he lacked the skill of speech which comes of drinking Kvasir's blood. He wanted the mead for himself and for his children in Asgard, and it seemed a shame that this precious treasure should be wasted upon the wicked giants who were their enemies. So he resolved to try if it might not be won in some sly way.

One day he put on his favorite disguise as a wandering old man, and set out for Giant Land, where Suttung dwelt. By and by he came to a field where nine workmen were cutting hay. Now these were the servants of Baugi, the brother of Suttung, and this Odin knew. He walked up to the men and watched them working for a little while.

"Ho!" he exclaimed at last, "Your scythes are dull. Shall I whet them for you?" The men were glad enough to accept his offer, so Odin took a whetstone from his pocket and sharpened all the scythes most wonderfully. Then the men wanted to buy the stone; each man would have it for his own, and they fell to quarreling over it. To make matters more exciting, Odin tossed the whetstone into their midst, saying:

"Let him have it who catches it!" Then indeed there was trouble! The men fought with one another for the stone, slashing right and left with their sharp scythes until every one was killed. Odin hastened away, and went up to the house where Baugi lived. Presently home came Baugi, complaining loudly and bitterly because his quarrelsome servants had killed one another, so that there was not one left to do his work.

"What am I going to do?" he cried. "Here it is mowing time, and I have not a single man to help me in the field!"

Then Odin spoke up. "I will help you," he said. "I am a stout fellow, and I can do the work of nine men if I am paid the price I ask."

"What is the price which you ask?" queried Baugi eagerly, for he saw that this stranger was a mighty man, and he thought that perhaps he could do as he boasted.

"I ask that you get for me a drink of Suttung's mead," Odin answered.

Then Baugi eyed him sharply. "You are one of the gods," he said, "or you would not know about the precious mead. Therefore I know that you can do my work, the work of nine men. I cannot give you the mead. It is my brother's, and he is very jealous of it, for he wishes it all himself. But if you will work for me all the summer, when winter comes I will go with you to Suttung's home and try what I can do to get a draught for you."

So they made the bargain, and all summer Father Odin worked in the fields of Baugi, doing the work of nine men. When the winter came, he demanded his pay. So then they set out for

Suttung's home, which was a cave deep down in the mountains, where it seems not hard to hide one's treasures. First Baugi went to his brother and told him of the agreement between him and the stranger, begging for a gift of the magic mead wherewith to pay the stout laborer who had done the work of nine. But Suttung refused to spare even a taste of the precious liquor.

"This laborer of yours is one of the gods, our enemies," he said. "Indeed, I will not give him of the precious mead. What are you thinking of, brother!" Then he talked to Baugi till the giant was ready to forget his promise to Odin, and to desire only the death of the stranger who had come forward to help him.

Baugi returned to Odin with the news that the mead was not to be had with Suttung's consent. "Then we must get it without his consent," declared Odin. "We must use our wits to steal it from under his nose. You must help me, Baugi, for you have promised."

Baugi agreed to this; but in his heart he meant to entrap Odin to his death. Odin now took from his pocket an auger such as one uses to bore holes. "Look, now," he said. "You shall bore a hole into the roof of Suttung's cave, and when the hole is large enough, I will crawl through and get the mead."

"Very well," nodded Baugi, and he began to bore into the mountain with all his might and main. At last he cried, "There, it is done; the mountain is pierced through!" But when Odin blew into the hole to see whether it did indeed go through into the cave, the dust made by the auger flew into his face. Thus he knew that Baugi was deceiving him, and thenceforth he was on his guard, which was fortunate.

"Try again," said Odin sternly. "Bore a little deeper, friend Baugi." So Baugi went at the work once more, and this time when he said the hole was finished, Odin found that his word was true, for the dust blew through the hole and disappeared in the cave. Now Odin was ready to try the plan which he had been forming.

Odin's wisdom taught him many tricks, and among them he knew the secret of changing his form into that of any creature he chose. He turned himself into a worm, – a long, slender, wiggly worm, just small enough to be able to enter the hole that Baugi had pierced. In a moment he had thrust his head into the opening, and was wriggling out of sight before Baugi had even guessed what he meant to do. Baugi jumped forward and made a stab at him with the pointed auger, but it was too late. The worm's striped tail quivered in out of sight, and Baugi's wicked attempt was spoiled.

When Odin had crept through the hole, he found himself in a dark, damp cavern, where at first he could see nothing. He changed himself back into his own noble form, and then he began to hunt about for the kettles of magic mead. Presently he came to a little chamber, carefully hidden in a secret corner of this secret grotto, – a chamber locked and barred and bolted on the inside, so that no one could enter by the door. Suttung had never thought of such a thing as that a stranger might enter by a hole in the roof!

At the back of this tiny room stood three kettles upon the floor; and beside them, with her head resting on her elbow, sat a beautiful maiden, sound asleep. It was Gunnlod, Suttung's daughter, the guardian of the mead. Odin stepped up to her very softly, and bending over, kissed her gently upon the forehead. Gunnlod awoke with a start, and at first she was horrified to find a stranger in the cave where it seemed impossible that a stranger could enter. But when she saw the beauty of Odin's face and the kind look of his eye, she was no longer afraid, but glad that he had come. For poor Gunnlod often grew lonesome in this gloomy cellar-home, where Suttung kept her prisoner day and night to watch over the three kettles.

"Dear maiden," said Odin, "I have come a long, long distance to see you. Will you not bid me stay a little while?"

Gunnlod looked at him kindly. "Who are you, and whence do you come so far to see me?" she asked.

"I am Odin, from Asgard. The way is long and I am thirsty. Shall I not taste the liquor which you have there?"

Gunnlod hesitated. "My father bade me never let soul taste of the mead," she said "I am sorry for you, however, poor fellow. "You look very tired and thirsty. You may have one little sip." Then Odin kissed her and thanked her, and tarried there with such pleasant words for the maiden that before he was ready to go she granted him what he asked, – three draughts, only three draughts of the mead.

Now Odin took up the first kettle to drink, and with one draught he drained the whole. He did the same by the next, and the next, till before she knew it, Gunnlod found herself guarding three empty kettles. Odin had gained what he came for, and it was time for him to be gone before Suttung should come to seek him in the cave. He kissed fair Gunnlod once again, with a sigh to think that he must treat her so unfairly. Then he changed himself into an eagle, and away he flew to carry the precious mead home to Asgard.

Meanwhile Baugi had told the giant Suttung how Odin the worm had pierced through into his treasure-cave; and when Suttung, who was watching, saw the great eagle fly forth, he guessed who this eagle must be. Suttung also put on an eagle's plumage, and a wonderful chase began. Whirr, whirr! The two enormous birds winged their way toward Asgard, Suttung close upon the other's flight. Over the mountains they flew, and the world was darkened as if by the passage of heavy storm-clouds, while the trees, blown by the breeze from their wings, swayed, and bent almost to the ground.

It was a close race; but Odin was the swifter of the two, and at last he had the mead safe in Asgard, where the gods were waiting with huge dishes to receive it from his mouth. Suttung was so close upon him, however, that he jostled Odin even as he was filling the last dish, and some of the mead was spilled about in every direction over the world. Men rushed from far and near to taste of these wasted drops of Kvasir's blood, and many had just enough to make them dizzy, but not enough to make them wise. These folk are the poor poets, the makers of bad verses, whom one finds to this day satisfied with their meagre, stolen portion, scattered drops of the sacred draught.

The mead that Odin had captured he gave to the gods, a wondrous gift; and they in turn cherished it as their most precious treasure. It was given into the special charge of old Bragi of the white beard, because his taste of the magic mead had made him wise and eloquent above all others. He was the sweetest singer of all the Aesir, and his speech was poetry. Sometimes Bragi gave a draught of Kvasir's blood to some favored mortal, and then he also became a great poet. He did not do this often, – only once or twice in the memory of an old man; for the precious mead must be made to last a long, long time, until the world be ready to drop to pieces, because this world without its poets would be too dreadful a place to imagine.

Bragi

ALTHOUGH ODIN HAD thus won the gift of poetry, he seldom made use of it himself. It was reserved for his son Bragi, the child of Gunlod, to become the god of poetry and music, and to charm the world with his songs.

As soon as Bragi was born in the stalactite-hung cave where Odin had won Gunlod's affections, the dwarfs presented him with a magical golden harp, and, setting him on one of their own vessels, they sent him out into the wide world. As the boat gently passed out of subterranean darkness, and floated over the threshold of Nain, the realm of the dwarf of death, Bragi, the fair and immaculate young god, who until then had shown no signs of life, suddenly sat up, and, seizing the golden harp beside him, he began to sing the wondrous song of life, which rose at times to heaven, and then sank down to the dread realm of Hel, goddess of death.

While he played the vessel was wafted gently over sunlit waters, and soon touched the shore. Bragi then proceeded on foot, threading his way through the bare and silent forest, playing as he walked. At the sound of his tender music the trees began to bud and bloom, and the grass underfoot was gemmed with countless flowers.

Here he met Idun, daughter of Ivald, the fair goddess of immortal youth, whom the dwarfs allowed to visit the earth from time to time, when, at her approach, nature invariably assumed its loveliest and gentlest aspect.

It was only to be expected that two such beings should feel attracted to each other, and Bragi soon won this fair goddess for his wife. Together they hastened to Asgard, where both were warmly welcomed and where Odin, after tracing runes on Bragi's tongue, decreed that he should be the heavenly minstrel and composer of songs in honour of the gods and of the heroes whom he received in Valhalla.

As Bragi was god of poetry, eloquence, and song, the Northern races also called poetry by his name, and scalds of either sex were frequently designated as Braga-men or Braga-women. Bragi was greatly honoured by all the Northern races, and hence his health was always drunk on solemn or festive occasions, but especially at funeral feasts and at Yuletide celebrations.

When it was time to drink this toast, which was served in cups shaped like a ship, and was called the Bragaful, the sacred sign of the hammer was first made over it. Then the new ruler or head of the family solemnly pledged himself to some great deed of valour, which he was bound to execute within the year, unless he wished to be considered destitute of honour. Following his example, all the guests were then wont to make similar vows and declare what they would do; and as some of them, owing to previous potations, talked rather too freely of their intentions on these occasions, this custom seems to connect the god's name with the vulgar but very expressive English verb 'to brag.'

In art, Bragi is generally represented as an elderly man, with long white hair and beard, and holding the golden harp from which his fingers could draw such magic strains.

Geirrod and Agnar

ODIN, AS HAS ALREADY BEEN STATED, took great interest in the affairs of mortals, and, we are told, was specially fond of watching King Hrauding's handsome little sons, Geirrod and Agnar, when they were about eight and ten years of age respectively. One day these little lads went fishing, and a storm suddenly arose which blew their boat far out to sea, where it finally stranded upon an island, upon which dwelt a seeming old couple, who in reality were Odin and Frigga in disguise. They had assumed these forms in order to indulge a sudden passion for the close society of their protégés. The lads were warmly welcomed and kindly treated, Odin choosing Geirrod as his favourite, and teaching him the use of arms, while Frigga petted and made much of little Agnar. The boys tarried on the island with their kind protectors during the long, cold winter season; but when spring came, and the skies were blue, and the sea calm, they embarked in a boat which Odin provided, and set out for their native shore. Favoured by gentle breezes, they were soon wafted thither; but as the boat neared the strand Geirrod quickly sprang out and pushed it far back into the water, bidding his brother sail away into the evil spirit's power. At that self-same moment the wind veered, and Agnar was indeed carried away, while his brother hastened to his father's palace with a lying tale as to what had happened to his brother. He was joyfully received as one from the dead, and in due time he succeeded his father upon the throne.

Years passed by, during which the attention of Odin had been claimed by other high considerations, when one day, while the divine couple were seated on the throne Hlidskialf, Odin suddenly remembered the winter's sojourn on the desert island, and he bade his wife notice how powerful his pupil had become, and taunted her because her favourite Agnar had married a giantess and had remained poor and of no consequence. Frigga quietly replied that it was better to be poor than hardhearted, and accused Geirrod of lack of hospitality – one of the most heinous crimes in the eyes of a Northman. She even went so far as to declare that in spite of all his wealth he often ill-treated his guests.

When Odin heard this accusation he declared that he would prove the falsity of the charge by assuming the guise of a Wanderer and testing Geirrod's generosity. Wrapped in his cloud-hued raiment, with slouch hat and pilgrim staff.

Odin immediately set out by a roundabout way, while Frigga, to outwit him, immediately despatched a swift messenger to warn Geirrod to beware of a man in wide mantle and broad-brimmed hat, as he was a wicked enchanter who would work him ill.

When, therefore, Odin presented himself before the king's palace he was dragged into Geirrod's presence and questioned roughly. He gave his name as Grimnir, but refused to tell whence he came or what he wanted, so as this reticence confirmed the suspicion suggested to the mind of Geirrod, he allowed his love of cruelty full play, and commanded that the stranger should be bound between two fires, in such wise that the flames played around him without quite touching him, and he remained thus eight days and nights, in obstinate silence, without food. Now Agnar had returned secretly to his brother's palace, where he occupied a menial position, and one night when all was still, in pity for the suffering of the unfortunate captive, he conveyed to his lips a horn of ale. But for this Odin would have had nothing to drink – the most serious of all trials to the god.

At the end of the eighth day, while Geirrod, seated upon his throne, was gloating over his prisoner's sufferings, Odin began to sing – softly at first, then louder and louder, until the hall re-echoed with his triumphant notes – a prophecy that the king, who had so long enjoyed the god's favour, would soon perish by his own sword.

As the last notes died away the chains dropped from his hands, the flames flickered and went out, and Odin stood in the midst of the hall, no longer in human form, but in all the power and beauty of a god.

On hearing the ominous prophecy Geirrod hastily drew his sword, intending to slay the insolent singer; but when he beheld the sudden transformation he started in dismay, tripped, fell upon the sharp blade, and perished as Odin had just foretold. Turning to Agnar, who, according to some accounts, was the king's son, and not his brother, for these old stories are often strangely confused, Odin bade him ascend the throne in reward for his humanity, and, further to repay him for the timely draught of ale, he promised to bless him with all manner of prosperity.

On another occasion Odin wandered to earth, and was absent so long that the gods began to think that they would not see him in Asgard again. This encouraged his brothers Vili and Ve, who by some mythologists are considered as other personifications of himself, to usurp his power and his throne, and even, we are told, to espouse his wife Frigga.

The Valkyrs

ODIN'S SPECIAL ATTENDANTS, the Valkyrs, or battle maidens, were either his daughters, like Brunhild, or the offspring of mortal kings, maidens who were privileged to remain immortal and invulnerable as long as they implicitly obeyed the god and remained virgins. They and their steeds were the personification of the clouds, their glittering weapons being the lightning flashes. The ancients imagined that they swept down to earth at Valfather's command, to choose among the slain in battle heroes worthy to taste the joys of Valhalla, and brave enough to lend aid to the gods when the great battle should be fought.

These maidens were pictured as young and beautiful, with dazzling white arms and flowing golden hair. They wore helmets of silver or gold, and blood-red corselets, and with spears and shields glittering, they boldly charged through the fray on their mettlesome white steeds. These horses galloped through the realms of air and over the quivering Bifrost, bearing not only their fair riders, but the heroes slain, who after having received the Valkyrs' kiss of death, were thus immediately transported to Valhalla.

As the Valkyrs' steeds were personifications of the clouds, it was natural to fancy that the hoar frost and dew dropped down upon earth from their glittering manes as they rapidly dashed to and fro through the air. They were therefore held in high honour and regard, for the people ascribed to their beneficent influence much of the fruitfulness of the earth, the sweetness of dale and mountain-slope, the glory of the pines, and the nourishment of the meadow-land.

The mission of the Valkyrs was not only to battlefields upon earth, but they often rode over the sea, snatching the dying Vikings from their sinking dragon-ships. Sometimes they stood upon the strand to beckon them thither, an infallible warning that the coming struggle would be their last, and one which every Northland hero received with joy.

The numbers of the Valkyrs differ greatly according to various mythologists, ranging from three to sixteen, most authorities, however, naming only nine. The Valkyrs were considered as divinities of the air. It was said that Freyia and Skuld led them on to the fray.

The Valkyrs had important duties in Valhalla, when, their bloody weapons laid aside, they poured out the heavenly mead for the Einheriar. This beverage delighted the souls of the new-comers, and they welcomed the fair maidens as warmly as when they had first seen them on the battlefield and realised that they had come to transport them where they fain would be.

Volund and the Valkyrs

THE VALKYRS WERE SUPPOSED TO take frequent flights to earth in swan plumage, which they would throw off when they came to a secluded stream, that they might indulge in a bath. Any mortal surprising them thus, and securing their plumage, could prevent them from leaving the earth, and could even force these proud maidens to mate with him if such were his pleasure.

It is related that three of the Valkyrs, Olrun, Alvit, and Svanhvit, were once sporting in the waters, when suddenly the three brothers Egil, Slagfinn, and Volund, or Wayland the smith, came upon them, and securing their swan plumage, the young men forced them to remain upon earth and become their wives. The Valkyrs, thus detained, remained with their husbands nine years, but at the end of that time, recovering their plumage, or the spell being broken in some other way, they effected their escape.

The brothers felt the loss of their wives extremely, and two of them, Egil and Slagfinn, putting on their snow shoes, went in search of their loved ones, disappearing in the cold and foggy regions of the North. The third brother, Volund, however, remained at home, knowing all search would be of no avail, and he found solace in the contemplation of a ring which Alvit had given him as a love-token, and he indulged the constant hope that she would return. As he was a very clever smith, and could manufacture the most dainty ornaments of silver and gold, as well as magic weapons which no blow could break, he now employed his leisure in making seven hundred rings exactly like the one which his wife had given him. These, when finished, he bound together; but one night, on coming home from the hunt, he found that some one had carried away one ring, leaving the others behind, and his hopes received fresh inspiration, for he told himself that his wife had been there and would soon return for good.

That selfsame night, however, he was surprised in his sleep, and bound and made prisoner by Nidud, King of Sweden, who took possession of his sword, a choice weapon invested with magic powers, which he reserved for his own use, and of the love ring made of pure Rhine gold, which latter he gave to his only daughter, Bodvild. As for the unhappy Volund himself, he was led captive to a neighbouring island, where, after being hamstrung, in order that he should not escape, the king put him to the incessant task of forging weapons and ornaments for his use. He also compelled him to build an intricate labyrinth, and to this day a maze in Iceland is known as 'Volund's house.'

Volund's rage and despair increased with every new insult offered him by Nidud, and night and day he thought upon how he might obtain revenge. Nor did he forget to provide for his escape, and during the pauses of his labour he fashioned a pair of wings similar to those his wife had used as a Valkyr, which he intended to don as soon as his vengeance had been accomplished. One day the king came to visit his captive, and brought him the stolen sword that he might repair it; but Volund cleverly substituted another weapon so exactly like the magic sword as to deceive the king when he came again to claim it. A few days later, Volund enticed the king's sons into his smithy and slew them, after which he cunningly fashioned drinking vessels out of their skulls, and jewels out of their eyes and teeth, bestowing these upon their parents and sister.

The royal family did not suspect whence they came; and so these gifts were joyfully accepted. As for the poor youths, it was believed that they had drifted out to sea and had been drowned.

Some time after this, Bodvild, wishing to have her ring repaired, also visited the smith's hut, where, while waiting, she unsuspectingly partook of a magic drug, which sent her to sleep and left her in Volund's power. His last act of vengeance accomplished, Volund immediately donned the wings which he had made in readiness for this day, and grasping his sword and ring he rose slowly in the air. Directing his flight to the palace, he perched there out of reach, and proclaimed his crimes to Nidud. The king, beside himself with rage, summoned Egil, Volund's brother, who had also fallen into his power, and bade him use his marvellous skill as an archer to bring down the impudent bird. Obeying a signal from Volund, Egil aimed for a protuberance under his wing where a bladder full of the young princes' blood was concealed, and the smith flew triumphantly away without hurt, declaring that Odin would give his sword to Sigmund – a prediction which was duly fulfilled.

Volund then went to Alfheim, where, if the legend is to be believed, he found his beloved wife, and lived happily again with her until the twilight of the gods.

But, even in Alfheim, this clever smith continued to ply his craft, and various suits of impenetrable armour, which he is said to have fashioned, are described in later heroic poems. Besides Balmung and Joyeuse, Sigmund's and Charlemagne's celebrated swords, he is reported to have fashioned Miming for his son Heime, and many other remarkable blades.

There are countless other tales of swan maidens or Valkyrs, who are said to have consorted with mortals; but the most popular of all is that of Brunhild, the wife of Sigurd, a descendant of Sigmund and the most renowned of Northern heroes.

William Morris, in 'The Land East of the Sun and West of the Moon,' gives a fascinating version of another of these Norse legends. The story is amongst the most charming of the collection in *The Earthly Paradise*.

The story of Brunhild is to be found in many forms. Some versions describe the heroine as the daughter of a king taken by Odin to serve in his Valkyr band, others as chief of the Valkyrs and daughter of Odin himself. In Richard Wagner's story, 'The Ring of the Nibelung,' the great musician presents a particularly attractive, albeit a more modern conception of the chief Battle-Maiden, and her disobedience to the command of Odin when sent to summon the youthful Siegmund from the side of his beloved Sieglinde to the Halls of the Blessed.

Frigga's Attendants

FRIGGA HAD, as her own special attendants, a number of beautiful maidens, among whom were Fulla (Volla), her sister, according to some authorities, to whom she entrusted her jewel casket. Fulla always presided over her mistress's toilet, was privileged to put on her golden shoes, attended her everywhere, was her confidante, and often advised her how best to help the mortals who implored her aid. Fulla was very beautiful indeed, and had long golden hair, which she wore flowing loose over her shoulders, restrained only by a golden circlet or snood. As her hair was emblematic of the golden grain, this circlet represented the binding of the sheaf. Fulla was also known as Abundia, or Abundantia, in some parts of Germany, where she was considered the symbol of the fulness of the earth.

Hlin, Frigga's second attendant, was the goddess of consolation, sent out to kiss away the tears of mourners and pour balm into hearts wrung by grief. She also listened with ever-open ears to the prayers of mortals, carrying them to her mistress, and advising her at times how best to answer them and give the desired relief.

Gna was Frigga's swift messenger. Mounted upon her fleet steed Hofvarpnir (hoof-thrower), she would travel with marvellous rapidity through fire and air, over land and sea, and was therefore considered the personification of the refreshing breeze. Darting thus to and fro, Gna saw all that was happening upon earth, and told her mistress all she knew. On one occasion, as she was passing over Hunaland, she saw King Rerir, a lineal descendant of Odin, sitting mournfully by the shore, bewailing his childlessness. The queen of heaven, who was also goddess of childbirth, upon hearing this took an apple (the emblem of fruitfulness) from her private store, gave it to Gna, and bade her carry it to the king. With the rapidity of the element she personified, Gna darted away, and as she passed over Rerir's head, she dropped her apple into his lap with a radiant smile.

The king pondered for a moment upon the meaning of this sudden apparition and gift, and then hurried home, his heart beating high with hope, and gave the apple to his wife to eat. In due season, to his intense joy, she bore him a son, Volsung, the great Northern hero, who became so famous that he gave his name to all his race.

Besides the three above mentioned, Frigga had other attendants in her train. There was the mild and gracious maiden Lofn (praise or love), whose duty it was to remove all obstacles from the path of lovers.

Vjofn's duty was to incline obdurate hearts to love, to maintain peace and concord among mankind, and to reconcile quarrelling husbands and wives. Syn (truth) guarded the door of Frigga's palace, refusing to open it to those who were not allowed to come in. When she had once shut the door upon a would-be intruder no appeal would avail to change her decision. She therefore presided over all tribunals and trials, and whenever a thing was to be vetoed the usual formula was to declare that Syn was against it.

Gefjon was also one of the maidens in Frigga's palace, and to her were entrusted all those who died unwedded, whom she received and made happy for ever.

According to some authorities, Gefjon did not remain a virgin herself, but married one of the giants, by whom she had four sons. This same tradition goes on to declare that Odin sent her before him to visit Gylfi, King of Sweden, and to beg for some land which she might call her own. The king, amused at her request, promised her as much land as she could plough around in one day and night. Gefjon, nothing daunted, changed her four sons into oxen, harnessed them to a plough, and began to cut a furrow so wide and deep that the king and his courtiers were amazed. But Gefjon continued her work without showing any signs of fatigue, and when she had ploughed all around a large piece of land forcibly wrenched it away, and made her oxen drag it down into the sea, where she made it fast and called it Seeland.

As for the hollow she left behind her, it was quickly filled with water and formed a lake, at first called Logrum (the sea), but now known as Mälar, whose every indentation corresponds with the headlands of Seeland. Gefjon then married Skiold, one of Odin's sons, and became the ancestress of the royal Danish race of Skioldungs, dwelling in the city of Hleidra or Lethra, which she founded, and which became the principal place of sacrifice for the heathen Danes.

Eira, also Frigga's attendant, was considered a most skilful physician. She gathered simples all over the earth to cure both wounds and diseases, and it was her province to teach the science to women, who were the only ones to practise medicine among the ancient nations of the North.

Vara heard all oaths and punished perjurers, while she rewarded those who faithfully kept their word. Then there were also Vor (faith), who knew all that was to occur throughout the world, and Snotra, goddess of virtue, who had mastered all knowledge.

With such a galaxy of attendants it is little wonder that Frigga was considered a powerful deity; but in spite of the prominent place she occupied in Northern religion, she had no special temple nor shrine, and was but little worshipped except in company with Odin.

The Discovery of Flax

THERE WAS ONCE A PEASANT who daily left his wife and children in the valley to take his sheep up the mountain to pasture; and as he watched his flock grazing on the mountain-side, he often had opportunity to use his cross-bow and bring down a chamois, whose flesh would furnish his larder with food for many a day.

While pursuing a fine animal one day he saw it disappear behind a boulder, and when he came to the spot, he was amazed to see a doorway in the neighbouring glacier, for in the excitement of the pursuit he had climbed higher and higher, until he was now on top of the mountain, where glittered the everlasting snow.

The shepherd boldly passed through the open door, and soon found himself in a wonderful jewelled cave hung with stalactites, in the centre of which stood a beautiful woman, clad in silvery robes, and attended by a host of lovely maidens crowned with Alpine roses. In his surprise, the shepherd sank to his knees, and as in a dream heard the queenly central figure bid him choose anything he saw to carry away with him. Although dazzled by the glow of the precious stones around him, the shepherd's eyes constantly reverted to a little nosegay of blue flowers which the gracious apparition held in her hand, and he now timidly proffered a request that it might become his. Smiling with pleasure, Holda, for it was she, gave it to him, telling him he had chosen wisely and would live as long as the flowers did not droop and fade. Then, giving the shepherd a measure of seed which she told him to sow in his field, the goddess bade him begone; and as the thunder pealed and the earth shook, the poor man found himself out upon the mountain-side once more, and slowly wended his way home to his wife, to whom he told his adventure and showed the lovely blue flowers and the measure of seed.

The woman reproached her husband bitterly for not having brought some of the precious stones which he so glowingly described, instead of the blossoms and seed; nevertheless the man proceeded to sow the latter, and he found to his surprise that the measure supplied seed enough for several acres.

Soon the little green shoots began to appear, and one moonlight night, while the peasant was gazing upon them, as was his wont, for he felt a curious attraction to the field which he had sown, and often lingered there wondering what kind of grain would be produced, he saw a misty form hover above the field, with hands outstretched as if in blessing. At last the field blossomed, and countless little blue flowers opened their calyxes to the golden sun. When the flowers had withered and the seed was ripe, Holda came once more to teach the peasant and his wife how to harvest the flax – for such it was – and from it to spin, weave, and bleach linen. As the people of the neighbourhood willingly purchased both linen and flax-seed, the peasant and his wife soon grew very rich indeed, and while he ploughed, sowed, and harvested, she spun, wove, and bleached the linen. The man lived to a good old age, and saw his grandchildren and great-grandchildren grow up around him. All this time his carefully treasured bouquet had remained fresh as when he first brought it home, but one day he saw that during the night the flowers had drooped and were dying.

Knowing what this portended, and that he too must die, the peasant climbed the mountain once more to the glacier, and found again the doorway for which he had often vainly searched. He entered the icy portal, and was never seen or heard of again, for, according to the legend, the goddess took him under her care, and bade him live in her cave, where his every wish was gratified.

The Magic Apples

IT IS NOT VERY AMUSING to be a king. Father Odin often grew tired of sitting all day long upon his golden throne in Valhalla above the heavens. He wearied of welcoming the new heroes whom the Valkyrs brought him from wars upon the earth, and of watching the old heroes fight their daily deathless battles. He wearied of his wise ravens, and the constant gossip which they brought him from the four corners of the world; and he longed to escape from every one who knew him to some place where he could pass for a mere stranger, instead of the great king of the Aesir, the mightiest being in the whole universe, of whom every one was afraid.

Sometimes he longed so much that he could not bear it. Then – he would run away. He disguised himself as a tall old man, with white hair and a long gray beard. Around his shoulders he threw a huge blue cloak, that covered him from top to toe, and over his face he pulled a big slouch hat, to hide his eyes. For his eyes Odin could not change – no magician has ever learned how to do that. One was empty; he had given the eye to the giant Mimir in exchange for wisdom.

Usually Odin loved to go upon these wanderings alone; for an adventure is a double adventure when one meets it single-handed. It was a fine game for Odin to see how near he could come to danger without feeling the grip of its teeth. But sometimes, when he wanted company, he would whisper to his two brothers, Hoenir and red Loki. They three would creep out of the palace by the back way; and, with a finger on the lip to Heimdall, the watchman, would silently steal over the rainbow bridge which led from Asgard into the places of men and dwarfs and giants.

Wonderful adventures they had, these three, with Loki to help make things happen. Loki was a sly, mischievous fellow, full of his pranks and his capers, not always kindly ones. But he was clever, as well as malicious; and when he had pushed folk into trouble, he could often help them out again, as safe as ever. He could be the jolliest of companions when he chose, and Odin liked his merriment and his witty talk.

One day Loki did something which was no mere jest nor easily forgiven, for it brought all Asgard into danger. And after that Father Odin and his children thought twice before inviting Loki to join them in any journey or undertaking. This which I am about to tell was the first really wicked deed of which Loki was found guilty, though I am sure his red beard had dabbled in secret wrongs before.

One night the three high gods, Odin, Hoenir, and Loki, stole away from Asgard in search of adventure. Over mountains and deserts, great rivers and stony places, they wandered until they grew very hungry. But there was no food to be found – not even a berry or a nut.

Oh, how footsore and tired they were! And oh, how faint! The worst of it ever is that – as you must often have noticed – the heavier one's feet grow, the lighter and more hollow becomes one's stomach; which seems a strange thing, when you think of it. If only one's feet became as light as the rest of one feels, folk could fairly fly with hunger. Alas! This is not so.

The three Aesir drooped and drooped, and seemed on the point of starving, when they came to the edge of a valley. Here, looking down, they saw a herd of oxen feeding on the grass.

"Hola!" shouted Loki. "Behold our supper!" Going down into the valley, they caught and killed one of the oxen, and, building a great bonfire, hung up the meat to roast. Then the three sat around the fire and smacked their lips, waiting for the meat to cook. They waited for a long time.

"Surely, it is done now," said Loki, at last; and he took the meat from the fire. Strange to say, however, it was raw as ere the fire was lighted. What could it mean? Never before had meat required so long a time to roast. They made the fire brighter and re-hung the beef for a thorough basting, cooking it even longer than they had done at first. When again they came to carve the meat, they found it still uneatable. Then, indeed, they looked at one another in surprise.

"What can this mean?" cried Loki, with round eyes.

"There is some trick!" whispered Hoenir, looking around as if he expected to see a fairy or a witch meddling with the food.

"We must find out what this mystery betokens," said Odin thoughtfully. Just then there was a strange sound in the oak-tree under which they had built their fire.

"What is that?" Loki shouted, springing to his feet. They looked up into the tree, and far above in the branches, near the top, they spied an enormous eagle, who was staring down at them, and making a queer sound, as if he were laughing.

"Ho-ho!" croaked the eagle. "I know why your meat will not cook. It is all my doing, masters."

The three Aesir stared in surprise. Then Odin said sternly: "Who are you, Master Eagle? And what do you mean by those rude words?"

"Give me my share of the ox, and you shall see," rasped the eagle, in his harsh voice. "Give me my share, and you will find that your meat will cook as fast as you please."

Now the three on the ground were nearly famished. So, although it seemed very strange to be arguing with an eagle, they cried, as if in one voice: "Come down, then, and take your share." They thought that, being a mere bird, he would want but a small piece.

The eagle flapped down from the top of the tree. Dear me! What a mighty bird he was! Eight feet across the wings was the smallest measure, and his claws were as long and strong as ice-hooks. He fanned the air like a whirlwind as he flew down to perch beside the bonfire. Then in his beak and claws he seized a leg and both shoulders of the ox, and started to fly away.

"Hold, thief!" roared Loki angrily, when he saw how much the eagle was taking. "That is not your share; you are no lion, but you are taking the lion's share of our feast. Begone, Scarecrow, and leave the meat as you found it!" Thereat, seizing a pole, he struck at the eagle with all his might.

Then a strange thing happened. As the great bird flapped upward with his prey, giving a scream of malicious laughter, the pole which Loki still held stuck fast to the eagle's back, and Loki was unable to let go of the other end.

"Help, help!" he shouted to Odin and to Hoenir, as he felt himself lifted off his feet. But they could not help him. "Help, help!" he screamed, as the eagle flew with him, now high, now low, through brush and bog and briar, over treetops and the peaks of mountains. On and on they went, until Loki thought his arm would be pulled out, like a weed torn up by the roots. The eagle would not listen to his cries nor pause in his flight, until Loki was almost dead with pain and fatigue.

"Hark you, Loki," screamed the eagle, going a little more slowly; "no one can help you except me. You are bewitched, and you cannot pull away from this pole, nor loose the pole from me, until I choose. But if you will promise what I ask, you shall go free."

Then Loki groaned: "O eagle, only let me go, and tell me who you really are, and I will promise whatever you wish."

The eagle answered: "I am the giant Thiasse, the enemy of the Aesir. But you ought to love me, Loki, for you yourself married a giantess."

Loki moaned: "Oh, yes! I dearly love all my wife's family, great Thiasse. Tell me what you want of me?"

"I want this," quoth Thiasse gruffly. "I am growing old, and I want the apples which Idunn keeps in her golden casket, to make me young again. You must get them for me."

Now these apples were the fruit of a magic tree, and were more beautiful to look at and more delicious to taste than any fruit that ever grew. The best thing about them was that whoever tasted one, be he ever so old, grew young and strong again. The apples belonged to a beautiful lady named Idunn, who kept them in a golden casket. Every morning the Aesir came to her to be refreshed and made over by a bite of her precious fruit. That is why in Asgard no one ever waxed old or ugly. Even Father Odin, Hoenir, and Loki, the three travelers who had seen the very beginning of everything, when the world was made, were still sturdy and young. And so long as Idunn kept her apples safe, the faces of the family who sat about the table of Valhalla would be rosy and fair like the faces of children.

"O friend giant!" cried Loki. "You know not what you ask! The apples are the most precious treasure of Asgard, and Idunn keeps watch over them as if they were dearer to her than life itself. I never could steal them from her, Thiasse; for at her call all Asgard would rush to the rescue, and trouble would buzz about my ears like a hive of bees let loose."

"Then you must steal Idunn herself, apples and all. For the apples I must have, and you have promised, Loki, to do my bidding."

Loki sniffed and thought, thought and sniffed again. Already his mischievous heart was planning how he might steal Idunn away. He could hardly help laughing to think how angry the Aesir would be when they found their beauty-medicine gone forever. But he hoped that, when he had done this trick for Thiasse, now and then the giant would let him have a nibble of the magic apples; so that Loki himself would remain young long after the other Aesir were grown old and feeble. This thought suited Loki's malicious nature well.

"I think I can manage it for you, Thiasse," he said craftily. "In a week I promise to bring Idunn and her apples to you. But you must not forget the great risk which I am running, nor that I am your relative by marriage. I may have a favor to ask in return, Thiasse."

Then the eagle gently dropped Loki from his claws. Falling on a soft bed of moss, Loki jumped up and ran back to his traveling companions, who were glad and surprised to see him again. They had feared that the eagle was carrying him away to feed his young eaglets in some far-off nest. Ah, you may be sure that Loki did not tell them who the eagle really was, nor confess the wicked promise which he had made about Idunn and her apples.

After that the three went back to Asgard, for they had had adventure enough for one day.

The days flew by, and the time came when Loki must fulfill his promise to Thiasse. So one morning he strolled out into the meadow where Idunn loved to roam among the flowers. There he found her, sitting by a tiny spring, and holding her precious casket of apples on her lap. She was combing her long golden hair, which fell from under a wreath of spring flowers, and she was very beautiful. Her green robe was embroidered with buds and blossoms of silk in many colors, and she wore a golden girdle about her waist. She smiled as Loki came, and tossed him a posy, saying: "Good-morrow, red Loki. Have you come for a bite of my apples? I see a wrinkle over each of your eyes which I can smooth away."

"Nay, fair lady," answered Loki politely, "I have just nibbled of another apple, which I found this morning. Verily, I think it is sweeter and more magical than yours."

Idunn was hurt and surprised.

"That cannot be, Loki," she cried. "There are no apples anywhere like mine. Where found you this fine fruit?" and she wrinkled up her little nose scornfully.

"Oho! I will not tell any one the place," chuckled Loki, "except that it is not far, in a little wood. There is a gnarled old apple-tree, and on its branches grow the most beautiful red-cheeked apples you ever saw. But you could never find it."

"I should like to see these apples, Loki, if only to prove how far less good they are than mine. Will you bring me some?"

"That I will not," said Loki teasingly. "Oh, no! I have my own magic apples now, and folk will be coming to me for help instead of to you."

Idunn began to coax him, as he had guessed that she would: "Please, please, Loki, show me the place!"

At first he would not, for he was a sly fellow, and knew how to lead her on. At last, he pretended to yield.

"Well, then, because I love you, Idun, better than all the rest, I will show you the place, if you will come with me. But it must be a secret – no one must ever know."

All girls like secrets.

"Yes – yes!" cried Idunn eagerly. "Let us steal away now, while no one is looking."

This was just what Loki hoped for.

"Bring your own apples," he said, "that we may compare them with mine. But I know mine are better."

"I know mine are the best in all the world," returned Idun, pouting. "I will bring them, to show you the difference."

Off they started together, she with the golden casket under her arm; and Loki chuckled wickedly as they went. He led her for some distance, further than she had ever strayed before, and at last she grew frightened.

"Where are you taking me, Loki?" she cried. "You said it was not far. I see no little wood, no old apple-tree."

"It is just beyond, just a little step beyond," he answered. So on they went. But that little step took them beyond the boundary of Asgard – just a little step beyond, into the space where the giants lurked and waited for mischief.

Then there was a rustling of wings, and *whirr-rr-rr*! Down came Thiasse in his eagle dress. Before Idunn suspected what was happening, he fastened his claws into her girdle and flapped away with her, magic apples and all, to his palace in Jotunheim, the Land of Giants.

Loki stole back to Asgard, thinking that he was quite safe, and that no one would discover his villainy. At first Idunn was not missed. But after a little the gods began to feel signs of age, and went for their usual bite of her apples. Then they found that she had disappeared, and a great terror fell upon them. Where had she gone? Suppose she should not come back!

The hours and days went by, and still she did not return. Their fright became almost a panic. Their hair began to turn gray, and their limbs grew stiff and gouty so that they hobbled down Asgard streets. Even Freyia, the loveliest, was afraid to look in her mirror, and Balder the beautiful grew pale and haggard. The happy land of Asgard was like a garden over which a burning wind had blown, – all the flower-faces were faded and withered, and springtime was turned into yellow fall.

If Idunn and her apples were not quickly found, the gods seemed likely to shrivel and blow away like autumn leaves. They held a council to inquire into the matter, endeavoring to learn who had seen Idunn last, and whither she had gone. It turned out that one morning Heimdall had seen her strolling out of Asgard with Loki, and no one had seen her since. Then the gods understood; Loki was the last person who had been with her – this must be one of Loki's tricks. They were filled with anger. They seized and bound Loki and brought him before the council. They threatened him with torture and with death unless he should tell the truth. And Loki was so frightened that finally he confessed what he had done.

Then indeed there was horror in Asgard. Idunn stolen away by a wicked giant! Idunn and her apples lost, and Asgard growing older every minute! What was to be done? Big Thor seized Loki and threw him up in the air again and again, so that his heels touched first the moon and then the sea; you can still see the marks upon the moon's white face. "If you do not bring Idunn back from the land of your wicked wife, you shall have worse than this!" he roared. "Go and bring her *now*."

"How can I do that?" asked Loki, trembling.

"That is for you to find," growled Thor. "Bring her you must. Go!"

Loki thought for a moment. Then he said:

"I will bring her back if Freyia will loan me her falcon dress. The giant dresses as an eagle. I, too, must guise me as a bird, or we cannot outwit him."

Then Freyia hemmed and hawed. She did not wish to loan her feather dress, for it was very precious. But all the Aesir begged; and finally she consented.

It was a beautiful great dress of brown feathers and gray, and in it Freyia loved to skim like a falcon among the clouds and stars. Loki put it on, and when he had done so he looked exactly like a great brown hawk. Only his bright black eyes remained the same, glancing here and there, so that they lost sight of nothing.

With a whirr of his wings Loki flew off to the north, across mountains and valleys and the great river Ifing, which lay between Asgard and Giant Land. And at last he came to the palace of Thiasse the giant.

It happened, fortunately, that Thiasse had gone fishing in the sea, and Idunn was left alone, weeping and broken-hearted. Presently she heard a little tap on her window, and, looking up, she saw a great brown bird perching on the ledge. He was so big that Idunn was frightened and gave a scream. But the bird nodded pleasantly and croaked: "Don't be afraid, Idun. I am a friend. I am Loki, come to set you free."

"Loki! Loki is no friend of mine. He brought me here," she sobbed. "I don't believe you came to save me."

"That is indeed why I am here," he replied, "and a dangerous business it is, if Thiasse should come back before we start for home."

"How will you get me out?" asked Idunn doubtfully. "The door is locked, and the window is barred."

"I will change you into a nut," said he, "and carry you in my claws."

"What of the casket of apples?" queried Idun. "Can you carry that also?"

Then Loki laughed long and loudly.

"What welcome to Asgard do you think I should receive without the apples?" he cried. "Yes, we must take them, indeed."

Idunn came to the window, and Loki, who was a skillful magician, turned her into a nut and took her in one claw, while in the other he seized the casket of apples. Then off he whirred out of the palace grounds and away toward Asgard's safety.

In a little while Thiasse returned home, and when he found Idunn and her apples gone, there was a hubbub, you may be sure! However, he lost little time by smashing mountains and breaking trees in his giant rage; that fit was soon over. He put on his eagle plumage and started in pursuit of the falcon.

Now an eagle is bigger and stronger than any other bird, and usually in a long race he can beat even the swift hawk who has an hour's start. Presently Loki heard behind him the shrill scream of a giant eagle, and his heart turned sick. But he had crossed the great river, and already was in sight of Asgard. The aged Aesir were gathered on the rainbow bridge watching eagerly for Loki's return; and when they spied the falcon with the nut and the casket in his talons, they knew who it was. A great cheer went up, but it was hushed in a moment, for they saw the eagle close after the falcon; and they guessed that this must be the giant Thiasse, the stealer of Idun.

Then there was a great shouting of commands, and a rushing to and fro. All the gods, even Father Odin and his two wise ravens, were busy gathering chips into great heaps on the walls of Asgard. As soon as Loki, with his precious burden, had fluttered weakly over the wall, dropping to the ground beyond, the gods lighted the heaps of chips which they had piled, and soon there was a wall of fire, over which the eagle must fly. He was going too fast to stop. The flames roared and crackled, but Thiasse flew straight into them, with a scream of fear and rage. His feathers caught fire and burned, so that he could no longer fly, but fell headlong to the ground inside the walls. Then Thor, the thunder-lord, and Tyr, the mighty war-king, fell upon him and slew him, so that he could never trouble the Aesir any more.

There was great rejoicing in Asgard that night, for Loki changed Idunn again to a fair lady; whereupon she gave each of the eager gods a bite of her life-giving fruit, so that they grew young and happy once more, as if all these horrors had never happened.

Not one of them, however, forgot the evil part which Loki had played in these doings. They hid the memory, like a buried seed, deep in their hearts. Thenceforward the word of Loki and the honor of his name were poor coin in Asgard; which is no wonder.

Skadi's Choice

THE GIANT THIASSE, whom Thor slew for the theft of Idunn and the magic apples, had a daughter, Skadi, who was a very good sort of girl, as giantesses go. Most of them were evil-tempered, spiteful, and cruel creatures, who desired only to do harm to the gods and to all who were good. But Skadi was different. Stronger than the hatred of her race for the Aesir, stronger even than her wish to be revenged for her father's death, was her love for Balder the beautiful, the pride of all the gods. If she had not been a giantess, she might have hoped that he would love her also; but she knew that no one who lived in Asgard would ever think kindly of her race, which had caused so much trouble to Balder and his brothers. After her father was killed by the Aesir, however, Skadi had a wise idea.

Skadi put on her helm and corselet and set out for Asgard, meaning to ask a noble price to pay for the sorrow of Thiasse's death. The gods, who had all grown young and boyish once again, were sitting in Valhalla merrily enjoying a banquet in honor of Idun's safe return, when Skadi, clattering with steel, strode into their midst. Heimdall the watchman, astonished at the sight, had let this maiden warrior pass him upon the rainbow bridge. The Aesir set down their cups hastily, and the laughter died upon their lips; for though she looked handsome, Skadi was a terrible figure in her silver armor and with her spear as long as a ship's mast brandished in her giant hand.

The nine Valkyrs, Odin's maiden warriors, hurried away to put on their own helmets and shields; for they would not have this other maiden, ten times as huge, see them meekly waiting at table, while they had battle-dresses as fine as hers to show the stranger.

"Who are you, maiden, and what seek you here?" asked Father Odin.

"I am Skadi, the daughter of Thiasse, whom your folk have slain," answered she, "and I come here for redress."

At these words the coward Loki, who had been at the killing of Thiasse, skulked low behind the table; but Thor, who had done the killing, straightened himself and clenched his fists tightly. He was not afraid of any giant, however fierce, and this maiden with her shield and spear only angered him.

"Well, Skadi," quoth Odin gravely, "your father was a thief, and died for his sins. He stole fair Idunn and her magic apples, and for that crime he died, which was only just. Yet because our righteous deed has left you an orphan, Skadi, we will grant you a recompense, so you shall be at peace with us; for it is not fitting that the Aesir should quarrel with women. What is it you ask, O Skadi, as solace for the death of Thiasse?"

Skadi looked like an orphan who was well able to take care of herself; and this indeed her next words showed her to be. "I ask two things," she said, without a moment's hesitation: "I ask the husband whom I shall select from among you; and I ask that you shall make me laugh, for it is many days since grief has let me enjoy a smile."

At this strange request the Aesir looked astonished, and some of them seemed rather startled; for you can fancy that none of them wanted a giantess, however handsome, for his wife. They put their heads together and consulted long whether or not they should allow Skadi her two wishes.

"I will agree to make her laugh," grinned Loki; "but suppose she should choose me for her husband! I am married to one giantess already."

"No fear of that, Loki," said Thor; "you were too near being the cause of her father's death for her to love you overmuch. Nor do I think that she will choose me; so I am safe."

Loki chuckled and stole away to think up a means of making Skadi laugh.

Finally, the gods agreed that Skadi should choose one of them for her husband; but in order that all might have a fair chance of missing this honor which no one coveted, she was to choose in a curious way. All the Aesir were to stand in a row behind the curtain which was drawn across the end of the hall, so that only their feet were seen by Skadi; and by their feet alone Skadi was to select him who was to be her husband.

Now Skadi was very ready to agree to this, for she said to herself, "Surely, I shall know the feet of Balder, for they will be the most beautiful of any."

Amid nervous laughter at this new game, the Aesir ranged themselves in a row behind the purple curtain, with only their line of feet showing below the golden border. There were Father Odin, Thor the Thunderer, and Balder his brother; there was old Niord the rich, with his fair son Frey; there were Tyr the bold, Bragi the poet, blind Hodur, and Vidar the silent; Vali and Ull the archers, Forseti the wise judge, and Heimdall the gold-toothed watchman. Loki alone, of all the Aesir, was not there; and Loki was the only one who did not shiver as Skadi walked up and down the hall looking at the row of feet.

Up and down, back and forth, went Skadi, looking carefully; and among all those sandaled feet there was one pair more white and fair and beautiful than the rest.

"Surely, these are Balder's feet!" she thought, while her heart thumped with eagerness under her silver corselet. "Oh, if I guess aright, dear Balder will be my husband!"

She paused confidently before the handsomest pair of feet, and, pointing to them with her spear, she cried, "I choose here! Few blemishes are to be found in Balder the beautiful."

A shout of laughter arose behind the curtain, and forth slunk – not young Balder, but old Niord the rich, king of the ocean wind, the father of those fair twins, Frey and Freyia. Skadi had chosen the handsome feet of old Niord, and thenceforth he must be her husband.

Niord was little pleased; but Skadi was heart-broken. Her face grew longer and sadder than before when he stepped up and took her hand sulkily, saying, "Well, I am to be your husband, then, and all my riches stored in Noatûn, the home of ships, are to be yours. You would have chosen Balder, and I wish that this luck had been his! However, it cannot be helped now."

"Nay," answered Skadi, frowning, "the bargain is not yet complete. No one of you has made me laugh. I am so sad now, that it will be a merry jest indeed which can wring laughter from my heavy heart." She sighed, looking at Balder. But Balder loved only Nanna in all the world.

Just then, out came Loki, riding on one of Thor's goat steeds; and the red-bearded fellow cut up such ridiculous capers with the gray-bearded goat that soon not only Skadi, but all the Aesir and Niord himself were holding their sides with laughter.

"Fairly won, fairly won!" cried Skadi, wiping the tears from her eyes. "I am beaten. I shall not forget that it is Loki to whom I owe this last joke. Some day I shall be quits with you, red joker!" And this threat she carried out in the end, on the day of Loki's punishment.

Skadi was married to old Niord, both unwilling; and they went to live among the mountains in Skadi's home, which had once been Thiasse's palace, where he had shut Idunn in a prison cell. As you can imagine, Niord and Skadi did not live happily ever after, like the good prince and princess in the story-book. For, in the first place, Skadi was a giantess; and there are few folk, I fancy, who could live happily with a giantess. In the second place, she did not love Niord, nor did he love Skadi, and neither forgot that Skadi's choosing had been sorrow to them both. But the third reason was the most important of all; and this was because Skadi and Niord could not agree upon the place which should be their home. For Niord did not like the mountain palace of Skadi's people, – the place where roaring winds rushed down upon the sea and its ships. The sea with its ships was his friend, and he wanted to dwell in Noatûn, where he had greater wealth than any one else in the world, – where he could rule the fresh sea-wind and tame the wild ocean, granting the prayers of fisher-folk and the seafarers, who loved his name.

Finally, they agreed to dwell first in one place, then in the other, so that each might be happy in turn. For nine days they tarried in Thrymheim, and then they spent three in Noatûn. But even this arrangement could not bring peace. One day they had a terrible quarrel. It was just after they had come down from Skadi's mountain home for their three days in Niord's sea palace, and he was so glad to be back that he cried:

"Ah, how I hate your hills! How long the nine nights seemed, with the wolves howling until dawn among the dark mountains of Giant Land! What a discord compared to the songs of the swans who sail upon my dear, dear ocean!" Thus rudely he taunted his wife; but Skadi answered him with spirit.

"And I – I cannot sleep by your rolling sea-waves, where the birds are ever calling, calling, as they come from the woods on the shore. Each morning the sea-gull's scream wakes me at some unseemly hour. I will not stay here even for three nights! I will not stay!"

"And I will have no more of your windy mountain-tops," roared Niord, beside himself with rage. "Go, if you wish! Go back to Thrymheim! I shall not follow you, be sure!"

So Skadi went back to her mountains alone, and dwelt in the empty house of Thiasse, her father. She became a mighty huntress, swift on the skees and ice-runners which she strapped to her feet. Day after day she skimmed over the snow-crusted mountains, bow in hand, to hunt the wild beasts which roamed there. "Skee-goddess," she was called; and never again did she come to Asgard halls. Quite alone in the cold country, she hunted hardily, keeping ever in her heart the image of Balder the beautiful, whom she loved, but whom she had lost forever by her unlucky choice.

LEGENDS OF LOKI

Introduction

BESIDES THE HIDEOUS GIANT Utgard-Loki, the personification of mischief and evil, whom Thor and his companions visited in Jotunheim, the ancient Northern nations had another type of sin, whom they called Loki also, and whom we have already seen under many different aspects.

In the beginning, Loki was merely the personification of the hearth fire and of the spirit of life. At first a god, he gradually becomes 'god and devil combined,' and ends in being held in general detestation as an exact counterpart of the medieval Lucifer, the prince of lies, 'the originator of deceit, and the back-biter' of the Aesir.

By some authorities Loki was said to be the brother of Odin, but others assert that the two were not related, but had merely gone through the form of swearing blood brotherhood common in the North.

Loki's Character

WHILE THOR IS THE EMBODIMENT of Northern activity, Loki represents recreation, and the close companionship early established between these two gods shows very plainly how soon our ancestors realised that both were necessary to the welfare of mankind. Thor is ever busy and ever in earnest, but Loki makes fun of everything, until at last his love of mischief leads him entirely astray, and he loses all love for goodness and becomes utterly selfish and malevolent.

He represents evil in the seductive and seemingly beautiful form in which it parades through the world. Because of this deceptive appearance the gods did not at first avoid him, but treated him as one of themselves in all good-fellowship, taking him with them wherever they went, and admitting him not only to their merry-makings, but also to their council hall, where, unfortunately, they too often listened to his advice.

As we have already seen, Loki played a prominent part in the creation of man, endowing him with the power of motion, and causing the blood to circulate freely through his veins, whereby he was inspired with passions. As personification of fire as well as of mischief, Loki (lightning) is often seen with Thor (thunder), whom he accompanies to Jotunheim to recover his hammer, to Utgard-Loki's castle, and to Geirrod's house. It is he who steals Freyia's necklace and Sif's hair, and betrays Idunn into the power of Thiassi; and although he sometimes gives the gods good advice and affords them real help, it is only to extricate them from some predicament into which he has rashly inveigled them.

Some authorities declare that, instead of making part of the creative trilogy (Odin, Hoenir, and Lodur or Loki), this god originally belonged to a pre-Odinic race of deities, and was the son of the great giant Fornjotnr (Ymir), his brothers being Kari (air) and Hler (water), and his sister Ran, the terrible goddess of the sea. Other mythologists, however, make him the son of the giant Farbauti, who has been identified with Bergelmir, the sole survivor of the deluge, and of Laufeia (leafy isle) or Nal (vessel), his mother, thus stating that his connection with Odin was only that of the Northern oath of good-fellowship.

Loki (fire) first married Glut (glow), who bore him two daughters, Eisa (embers) and Einmyria (ashes); it is therefore very evident that Norsemen considered him emblematic of the hearth-fire, and when the flaming wood crackles on the hearth the goodwives in the North are still wont to say that Loki is beating his children. Besides this wife, Loki is also said to have wedded the giantess Angur-boda (the anguish-boding), who dwelt in Jotunheim, and who, as we have already seen, bore him the three monsters: Hel, goddess of death, the Midgard snake Iormungandr, and the grim wolf Fenris.

Loki's third marriage was with Sigyn, who proved a most loving and devoted wife, and bore him two sons, Narve and Vali, the latter a namesake of the god who avenged Balder. Sigyn was always faithful to her husband, and did not forsake him even after he had definitely been cast out of Asgard and confined in the bowels of the earth.

As Loki was the embodiment of evil in the minds of the Northern races, they entertained nothing but fear of him, built no temples to his honour, offered no sacrifices to him, and designated the most noxious weeds by his name. The quivering, overheated atmosphere of summer was supposed to betoken his presence, for the people were then wont to remark that Loki was sowing his wild oats, and when the sun appeared to be drawing water they said Loki was drinking.

The story of Loki is so inextricably woven with that of the other gods that most of the myths relating to him have already been told, and there remain but two episodes of his life to relate, one showing his better side before he had degenerated into the arch deceiver, and the other illustrating how he finally induced the gods to defile their peace-steads by wilful murder.

Loki's Children

RED LOKI, the wickedest of all the Aesir, had done something of which he was very much ashamed. He had married a giantess, the ugliest, fiercest, most dreadful giantess that ever lived; and of course he wanted no one to find out what he had done, for he knew that Father Odin would be indignant with him for having wedded one of the enemies of the Aesir, and that none of his brothers would be grateful to him for giving them a sister-in-law so hideous.

But at last All-Father found out the secret that Loki had been hiding for years. Worst of all, he found that Loki and the giantess had three ugly children hidden away in the dark places of the earth, – three children of whom Loki was even more ashamed than of their mother, though he loved them too. For two of them were the most terrible monsters which time had ever seen. Hel his daughter was the least ugly of the three, though one could scarcely call her attractive. She was half black and half white, which must have looked very strange; and she was not easily mistaken by any one who chanced to see her, you can well understand. She was fierce and grim to see, and the very sight of her caused terror and death to him who gazed upon her.

But the other two! One was an enormous wolf, with long fierce teeth and flashing red eyes. And the other was a scaly, slimy, horrible serpent, huger than any serpent that ever lived, and a hundred times more ferocious. Can you wonder that Loki was ashamed of such children as these? The wonder is, how he could find anything about them to love. But Loki's heart loved evil in secret, and it was the evil in these three children of his which made them so ugly.

Now when Odin discovered that three such monsters had been living in the world without his knowledge, he was both angry and anxious, for he knew that these children of mischievous Loki and his wicked giantess-wife were dangerous to the peace of Asgard. He consulted the Norns, the three wise maidens who lived beside the Urdar-well, and who could see into the future to tell what things were to happen in coming years. And they bade him beware of Loki's children; they told him that the three monsters would bring great sorrow upon Asgard, for the giantess their mother would teach them all her hatred of Odin's race, while they would have their father's sly wisdom to help them in all mischief. So Odin knew that his fears had warned him truly. Something must be done to prevent the dangers which threatened Asgard. Something must be done to keep the three out of mischief.

Father Odin sent for all the gods, and bade them go forth over the world, find the children of Loki in the secret places where they were hidden, and bring them to him. Then the Aesir mounted their horses and set out on their difficult errand. They scoured Asgard, Midgard the world of men, Utgard and Jotunheim where the giants lived. And at last they found the three horrible creatures hiding in their mother's cave. They dragged them forth and took them up to Asgard, before Odin's high throne.

Now All-Father had been considering what should be done with the three monsters, and when they came, his mind was made up. Hel, the daughter, was less evil than the other two, but her face was dark and gloomy, and she brought death to those who looked upon her. She must be prisoned out of sight in some far place, where her sad eyes could not look sorrow into men's lives and death into their hearts. So he sent her down, down into the dark, cold land of Niflheim, which lay below one root of the great tree Yggdrasil. Here she must live forever and ever. And, because she was not wholly bad, Odin made her queen of that land, and for her subjects she was to have all the folk who died upon the earth, – except the heroes who perished in battle; for these the Valkyrs carried straight to Valhalla in Asgard. But all who died of sickness or of old age, all who met their deaths through accident or men's cruelty, were sent to Queen Hel, who gave them lodgings in her gloomy palace. Vast was her kingdom, huge as nine worlds, and it was surrounded by a high wall, so that no one who had once gone thither could ever return. And here thenceforth Loki's daughter reigned among the shadows, herself half shadow and half light, half good and half bad.

But the Midgard serpent was a more dangerous beast even than Death. Odin frowned when he looked upon this monster writhing before his throne. He seized the scaly length in his mighty arms and hurled it forth over the wall of Asgard. Down, down went the great serpent, twisting and twirling as he fell, while all the sky was black with the smoke from his nostrils, and the sound of his hissing made every creature tremble. Down, down he fell with a great splash into the deep ocean which surrounded the world. There he lay writhing and squirming, growing always larger and larger, until he was so huge that he stretched like a ring about the whole earth, with his tail in his mouth, and his wicked eyes glaring up through the water towards Asgard which he hated. Sometimes he heaved himself up, great body and all, trying to escape from the ocean which was his prison. At those times there were great waves in the sea, snow and stormy winds and rain upon the earth, and every one would be filled with fear lest he escape and bring horrors to pass. But he was never able to drag out his whole hideous length. For the evil in him had grown with his growth; and a weight of evil is the heaviest of all things to lift.

The third monster was the Fenris wolf, and this was the most dreadful of the three. He was so terrible that at first Father Odin decided not to let him out of his sight. He lived in Asgard then, among the Aesir. Only Tyr the brave had courage enough to give him food. Day by day he grew huger and huger, fiercer and fiercer, and finally, when All-Father saw how mighty he had become, and how he bid fair to bring destruction upon all Asgard if he were allowed to prowl and growl about as he saw fit, Odin resolved to have the beast chained up. The Aesir then went to their smithies and forged a long, strong chain which they thought no living creature could break. They took it to the wolf to try its strength, and he, looking sidewise, chuckled to himself and let them do what they would with him. But as soon as he stretched himself, the chain burst into a thousand pieces, as if it were made of twine. Then the Aesir hurried away and made another chain, far, far stronger than the first.

"If you can break this, O Fenrir," they said, "you will be famous indeed."

Again the wolf blinked at his chain; again he chuckled and let them fasten him without a struggle, for he knew that his own strength had been increased since he broke the other; but as soon as the chain was fastened, he shook his great shoulders, kicked his mighty legs, and – snap! – the links of the chain went whirling far and wide, and once more the fierce beast was free.

Then the Aesir were alarmed for fear that they would never be able to make a chain mighty enough to hold the wolf, who was growing stronger every minute; but they sent Skirnir, Frey's trusty messenger, to the land of the dwarfs for help. "Make us a chain," was the message he bore from the Aesir, – "make us a chain stronger than any chain that was ever forged; for the Fenris wolf must be captured and bound, or all the world must pay the penalty."

The dwarfs were the finest workmen in the world, as the Aesir knew; for it was they who made Thor's hammer, and Odin's spear, and Balder's famous ship, besides many other wondrous things that you remember. So when Skirnir gave them the message, they set to work with their little hammers and anvils, and before long they had welded a wonderful chain, such as no man had ever before seen. Strange things went to the making of it, – the sound of a cat's footsteps, the roots of a mountain, a bear's sinews, a fish's breath, and other magic materials that only the dwarfs knew how to put together; and the result was a chain as soft and twistable as a silken cord, but stronger than an iron cable. With this chain Skirnir galloped back to Asgard, and with it the gods were sure of chaining Fenrir; but they meant to go about the business slyly, so that the wolf should not suspect the danger which was so near.

"Ho, Fenrir!" they cried. "Here is a new chain for you. Do you think you can snap this as easily as you did the last? We warn you that it is stronger than it looks." They handed it about from one to another, each trying to break the links, but in vain. The wolf watched them disdainfully.

"Pooh! There is little honor in breaking a thread so slender!" he said. "I know that I could snap it with one bite of my big teeth. But there may be some trick about it; I will not let it bind my feet, – not I."

"Oho!" cried the Aesir. "He is afraid! He fears that we shall bind him in cords that he cannot loose. But see how slender the chain is. Surely, if you could burst the chain of iron, O Fenrir, you could break this far more easily." Still the wolf shook his head, and refused to let them fasten him, suspecting some trick. "But even if you find that you cannot break our chain," they said, "you need not be afraid. We shall set you free again."

"Set me free!" growled the wolf. "Yes, you will set me free at the end of the world, – not before! I know your ways, O Aesir; and if you are able to bind me so fast that I cannot free myself, I shall wait long to have the chain made loose. But no one shall call me coward. If one of you will place his hand in my mouth and hold it there while the others bind me, I will let the chain be fastened."

The gods looked at one another, their mouths drooping. Who would do this thing and bear the fury of the angry wolf when he should find himself tricked and captured? Yet this was their only chance to bind the monster and protect Asgard from danger. At last bold Tyr stepped forward, the bravest of all the Aesir. "Open your mouth, Fenrir," he cried, with a laugh. "I will pledge my hand to the trial."

Then the wolf yawned his great jaws, and Tyr thrust in his good right hand, knowing full well that he was to lose it in the game. The Aesir stepped up with the dwarfs' magic chain, and Fenrir let them fasten it about his feet. But when the bonds were drawn tight, he began to struggle; and the more he tugged, the tighter drew the chain, so that he soon saw himself to be entrapped. Then how he writhed and kicked, howled and growled, in his terrible rage! How the heavens trembled and the earth shook below! The Aesir set up a laugh to see him so helpless – all except Tyr; for at the first sound of laughter the wolf shut his great mouth with a click, and poor brave Tyr had lost the right hand which had done so many heroic deeds in battle, and which would never again wave sword before the warriors whom he loved and would help to win the victory. But great was the honor which he won that day, for without his generous deed the Fenris wolf could never have been captured.

And now the monster was safely secured by the strong chain which the dwarfs had made, and all his struggles to be free were in vain, for they only bound the silken rope all the tighter. The Aesir took one end of the chain and fastened it through a big rock which they planted far down in the earth, as far as they could drive it with a huge hammer of stone. Into the wolf's great mouth they thrust a sword crosswise, so that the hilt pierced his lower jaw while the point stuck through the upper one; and there in the heart of the world he lay howling and growling, but quite unable to move. Only the foam which dripped from his angry jaws trickled away and over the earth until it formed a mighty river; from his wicked mouth also came smoke and fire, and the sound of his horrible growls. And when men hear this and see this they run away as fast as they can, for they know that danger still lurks near where the Fenris wolf lies chained in the depths of the earth; and here he will lie until Ragnarok, – until the end of all things.

Loki and the Necklace

ONE EVENING, when Freyia had become part of Asgard, Loki spied her marvellous necklace, a golden symbol of the fruitfulness of the earth which she wore about her slender neck at all times. Loki coveted this necklace, and he found he could not sleep until he had it in his possession. So it was that he crept one night into her chamber and bent over as if to remove it. Finding that her position in sleep made this feat impossible, he turned himself into a small flea, and springing under the bedclothes, he bit the lovely goddess so that she turned in her sleep. Loki returned to his shape and undid the clasp of the necklace, which he removed without rousing Freyia.

Not far from Freyia's palace, Heimdall had heard the sound of Loki becoming a flea – a sound so slight that only the great watchman of the gods could have heard it – and he travelled immediately to the palace to investigate. He saw Loki leaving with the necklace, and soon caught up with him, drawing his sword in order to remove the thief's head. Loki immediately changed himself into a thin blue flame, but quick as a flash, Heimdall became a cloud and sent down a sheath of rain in order to douse the flame. Loki quickly became a polar bear and opened his jaws to swallow the water, whereupon Heimdall turned himself into bear and attacked the hapless trickster. In haste, Loki became a seal, and then, once again, Heimdall transformed himself in the same form as Loki and the two fought for many hours, before Heimdall showed his worth and won the necklace from Loki.

Skrymsli and the Peasant's Child

A GIANT AND A PEASANT were playing a game together one day (probably a game of chess, which was a favourite winter pastime with the Northern vikings). They of course had determined to play for certain stakes, and the giant, being victorious, won the peasant's only son, whom he said he would come and claim on the morrow unless the parents could hide him so cleverly that he could not be found.

Knowing that such a feat would be impossible for them to perform, the parents fervently prayed to Odin to help them, and in answer to their entreaties the god came down to earth, and changed the boy into a tiny grain of wheat, which he hid in an ear of grain in the midst of a large field, declaring that the giant would not be able to find him. The giant Skrymsli, however, possessed wisdom far beyond what Odin imagined, and, failing to find the child at home, he strode off immediately to the field with his scythe, and mowing the wheat he selected the particular ear where the boy was hidden. Counting over the grains of wheat he was about to lay his hand upon the right one when Odin, hearing the child's cry of distress, snatched the kernel out of the giant's hand, and restored the boy to his parents, telling them that he had done all in his power to help them. But as the giant vowed he had been cheated, and would again claim the boy on the morrow unless the parents could outwit him, the unfortunate peasants now turned to Hoenir for aid. The god heard them graciously and changed the boy into a fluff of down, which he hid in the breast of a swan swimming in a pond close by. Now when, a few minutes later, Skrymsli came up, he guessed what had occurred, and seizing the swan, he bit off its neck, and would have swallowed the down had not Hoenir wafted it away from his lips and out of reach, restoring the boy safe and sound to his parents, but telling them that he could not further aid them.

Skrymsli warned the parents that he would make a third attempt to secure the child, whereupon they applied in their despair to Loki, who carried the boy out to sea, and concealed him, as a tiny egg, in the roe of a flounder. Returning from his expedition, Loki encountered the giant near the shore, and seeing that he was bent upon a fishing excursion, he insisted upon accompanying him. He felt somewhat uneasy lest the terrible giant should have seen through his device, and therefore thought it would be well for him to be on the spot in case of need. Skrymsli baited his hook, and was more or less successful in his angling, when suddenly he drew up the identical flounder in which Loki had concealed his little charge. Opening the fish upon his knee, the giant proceeded to minutely examine the roe, until he found the egg which he was seeking.

The plight of the boy was certainly perilous, but Loki, watching his chance, snatched the egg out of the giant's grasp, and transforming it again into the child, he instructed him secretly to run home, passing through the boathouse on his way and closing the door behind him. The terrified boy did as he was told immediately he found himself on land, and the giant, quick to observe his flight, dashed after him into the boathouse. Now Loki had cunningly placed a sharp spike in such a position that the great head of the giant ran full tilt against it, and he sank to the ground with a groan, whereupon Loki, seeing him helpless, cut off one of his legs. Imagine the god's dismay, however, when he saw the pieces join and immediately knit together. But Loki was a master of guile, and recognising this as the work of magic, he cut off the other leg, promptly throwing flint and steel between the severed limb and trunk, and thereby hindering any further sorcery. The peasants were immensely relieved to find that their enemy was slain, and ever after they considered Loki the mightiest of all the heavenly council, for he had delivered them effectually from their foe, while the other gods had lent only temporary aid.

The Giant Builder

AGES AND AGES AGO, when the world was first made, the gods decided to build a beautiful city high above the heavens, the most glorious and wonderful city that ever was known. Asgard was to be its name, and it was to stand on Ida Plain under the shade of Yggdrasil, the great tree whose roots were underneath the earth.

First of all they built a house with a silver roof, where there were seats for all the twelve chiefs. In the midst, and high above the rest, was the wonder-throne of Odin the All-Father, whence he could see everything that happened in the sky or on the earth or in the sea. Next they made a fair house for Queen Frigga and her lovely daughters. Then they built a smithy, with its great hammers, tongs, anvils, and bellows, where the gods could work at their favorite trade, the making of beautiful things out of gold; which they did so well that folk name that time the Golden Age. Afterwards, as they had more leisure, they built separate houses for all the Aesir, each more beautiful than the preceding, for of course they were continually growing more skillful. They saved Father Odin's palace until the last, for they meant this to be the largest and the most splendid of all.

Gladsheim, the home of joy, was the name of Odin's house, and it was built all of gold, set in the midst of a wood whereof the trees had leaves of ruddy gold, – like an autumn-gilded forest. For the safety of All-Father it was surrounded by a roaring river and by a high picket fence; and there was a great courtyard within.

The glory of Gladsheim was its wondrous hall, radiant with gold, the most lovely room that time has ever seen. Valhalla, the Hall of Heroes, was the name of it, and it was roofed with the mighty shields of warriors. The ceiling was made of interlacing spears, and there was a portal at the west end before which hung a great gray wolf, while over him a fierce eagle hovered. The hall was so huge that it had 540 gates, through each of which 800 men could march abreast. Indeed, there needed to be room, for this was the hall where every morning Odin received all the brave warriors who had died in battle on the earth below; and there were many heroes in those days.

This was the reward which the gods gave to courage. When a hero had gloriously lost his life, the Valkyrs, the nine warrior daughters of Odin, brought his body up to Valhalla on their white horses that gallop the clouds. There they lived forever after in happiness, enjoying the things that they had most loved upon earth. Every morning they armed themselves and went out to fight with one another in the great courtyard. It was a wondrous game, wondrously played. No matter how often a hero was killed, he became alive again in time to return perfectly well to Valhalla, where he ate a delicious breakfast with the Aesir; while the beautiful Valkyrs who had first brought him thither waited at table and poured the blessed mead, which only the immortal taste. A happy life it was for the heroes, and a happy life for all who dwelt in Asgard; for this was before trouble had come among the gods, following the mischief of Loki.

This is how the trouble began. From the beginning of time, the giants had been unfriendly to the Aesir, because the giants were older and huger and more wicked; besides, they were jealous because the good Aesir were fast gaining more wisdom and power than the giants had ever known. It was the Aesir who set the fair brother and sister, Sun and Moon, in the sky to give light to men; and it was they also who made the jeweled stars out of sparks from the place of fire. The giants hated the Aesir, and tried all in their power to injure them and the men of the earth below, whom the Aesir loved and cared for. The gods had already built a wall around Midgard, the world of men, to keep the giants out; built it of the bushy eyebrows of Ymir, the oldest and hugest of giants. Between Asgard and the giants flowed Ifing, the great river on which ice never formed, and which the gods crossed on the rainbow bridge. But this was not protection enough. Their beautiful new city needed a fortress.

So the word went forth in Asgard, – "We must build us a fortress against the giants; the hugest, strongest, finest fortress that ever was built."

Now one day, soon after they had announced this decision, there came a mighty man stalking up the rainbow bridge that led to Asgard city.

"Who goes there!" cried Heimdall the watchman, whose eyes were so keen that he could see for a hundred miles around, and whose ears were so sharp that he could hear the grass growing in the meadow and the wool on the backs of the sheep. "Who goes there! No one can enter Asgard if I say no."

"I am a builder," said the stranger, who was a huge fellow with sleeves rolled up to show the iron muscles of his arms. "I am a builder of strong towers, and I have heard that the folk of Asgard need one to help them raise a fair fortress in their city."

Heimdall looked at the stranger narrowly, for there was that about him which his sharp eyes did not like. But he made no answer, only blew on his golden horn, which was so loud that it sounded through all the world. At this signal all the Aesir came running to the rainbow bridge, from wherever they happened to be, to find out who was coming to Asgard. For it was Heimdall's duty ever to warn them of the approach of the unknown.

"This fellow says he is a builder," quoth Heimdall. "And he would fain build us a fortress in the city."

"Ay, that I would," nodded the stranger. "Look at my iron arm; look at my broad back; look at my shoulders. Am I not the workman you need?"

"Truly, he is a mighty figure," vowed Odin, looking at him approvingly. "How long will it take you alone to build our fortress? We can allow but one stranger at a time within our city, for safety's sake."

"In three half-years," replied the stranger, "I will undertake to build for you a castle so strong that not even the giants, should they swarm hither over Midgard, – not even they could enter without your leave."

"Aha!" cried Father Odin, well pleased at this offer. "And what reward do you ask, friend, for help so timely?"

The stranger hummed and hawed and pulled his long beard while he thought. Then he spoke suddenly, as if the idea had just come into his mind. "I will name my price, friends," he said; "a small price for so great a deed. I ask you to give me Freyia for my wife, and those two sparkling jewels, the Sun and Moon."

At this demand the gods looked grave; for Freyia was their dearest treasure. She was the most beautiful maid who ever lived, the light and life of heaven, and if she should leave Asgard, joy would go with her; while the Sun and Moon were the light and life of the Aesir's children, men, who lived in the little world below. But Loki the sly whispered that they would be safe enough if they made another condition on their part, so hard that the builder could not fulfill it. After thinking cautiously, he spoke for them all.

"Mighty man," quoth he, "we are willing to agree to your price – upon one condition. It is too long a time that you ask; we cannot wait three half-years for our castle; that is equal to three centuries when one is in a hurry. See that you finish the fort without help in one winter, one short winter, and you shall have fair Freyia with the Sun and Moon. But if, on the first day of summer, one stone is wanting to the walls, or if any one has given you aid in the building, then your reward is lost, and you shall depart without payment." So spoke Loki, in the name of all the gods; but the plan was his own.

At first the stranger shook his head and frowned, saying that in so short a time no one unaided could complete the undertaking. At last he made another offer. "Let me have but my good horse to help me, and I will try," he urged. "Let me bring the useful Svadilfori with me to the task, and I will finish the work in one winter of short days, or lose my reward. Surely, you will not deny me this little help, from one four-footed friend."

Then again the Aesir consulted, and the wiser of them were doubtful whether it were best to accept the stranger's offer so strangely made. But again Loki urged them to accept. "Surely, there is no harm," he said. "Even with his old horse to help him, he cannot build the castle in the promised time. We shall gain a fortress without trouble and with never a price to pay."

Loki was so eager that, although the other Aesir did not like this crafty way of making bargains, they finally consented. Then in the presence of the heroes, with the Valkyrs and Mimir's head for witnesses, the stranger and the Aesir gave solemn promise that the bargain should be kept.

On the first day of winter the strange builder began his work, and wondrous was the way he set about it. His strength seemed as the strength of a hundred men. As for his horse Svadilfori, he did more work by half than even the mighty builder. In the night he dragged the enormous rocks that were to be used in building the castle, rocks as big as mountains of the earth; while in the daytime the stranger piled them into place with his iron arms. The Aesir watched him with amazement; never was seen such strength in Asgard. Neither Tyr the stout nor Thor the strong could match the power of the stranger. The gods began to look at one another uneasily. Who was this mighty one who had come among them, and what if after all he should win his reward? Freyia trembled in her palace, and the Sun and Moon grew dim with fear.

Still the work went on, and the fort was piling higher and higher, by day and by night. There were but three days left before the end of winter, and already the building was so tall and so strong that it was safe from the attacks of any giant. The Aesir were delighted with their fine new castle; but their pride was dimmed by the fear that it must be paid for at all too costly a price. For only the gateway remained to be completed, and unless the stranger should fail to finish that in the next three days, they must give him Freyia with the Sun and Moon.

The Aesir held a meeting upon Ida Plain, a meeting full of fear and anger. At last they realized what they had done; they had made a bargain with one of the giants, their enemies; and if he won the prize, it would mean sorrow and darkness in heaven and upon earth. "How did we happen to agree to so mad a bargain?" they asked one another. "Who suggested the wicked plan which bids fair to cost us all that we most cherish?" Then they remembered that it was Loki who had made the plan; it was he who had insisted that it be carried out and they blamed him for all the trouble.

"It is your counsels, Loki, that have brought this danger upon us," quoth Father Odin, frowning. "You chose the way of guile, which is not our way. It now remains for you to help us by guile, if you can. But if you cannot save for us Freyia and the Sun and Moon, you shall die. This is my word." All the other Aesir agreed that this was just. Thor alone was away hunting evil demons at the other end of the world, so he did not know what was going on, and what dangers were threatening Asgard.

Loki was much frightened at the word of All-Father. "It was my fault," he cried, "but how was I to know that he was a giant? He had disguised himself so that he seemed but a strong man. And as for his horse, – it looks much like that of other folk. If it were not for the horse, he could not finish the work. Ha! I have a thought! The builder shall not finish the gate; the giant shall not receive his payment. I will cheat the fellow."

Now it was the last night of winter, and there remained but a few stones to put in place on the top of the wondrous gateway. The giant was sure of his prize, and chuckled to himself as he went out with his horse to drag the remaining stones; for he did not know that the Aesir had guessed at last who he was, and that Loki was plotting to outwit him. Hardly had he gone to work when out of the wood came running a pretty little mare, who neighed to Svadilfori as if inviting the tired horse to leave his work and come to the green fields for a holiday.

Svadilfori, you must remember, had been working hard all winter, with never a sight of four-footed creature of his kind, and he was very lonesome and tired of dragging stones. Giving a snort of disobedience, off he ran after this new friend towards the grassy meadows. Off went the giant after him, howling with rage, and running for dear life, as he saw not only his horse but his chance of success slipping out of reach. It was a mad chase, and all Asgard thundered with the noise of galloping hoofs and the giant's mighty tread. The mare who raced ahead was Loki in disguise, and he led Svadilfori far out of reach, to a hidden meadow that he knew; so that the giant howled and panted up and down all night long, without catching even a sight of his horse.

Now when the morning came the gateway was still unfinished, and night and winter had ended at the same hour. The giant's time was over, and he had forfeited his reward. The Aesir came flocking to the gateway, and how they laughed and triumphed when they found three stones wanting to complete the gate!

"You have failed, fellow," judged Father Odin sternly, "and no price shall we pay for work that is still undone. You have failed. Leave Asgard quickly; we have seen all we want of you and of your race."

Then the giant knew that he was discovered, and he was mad with rage. "It was a trick!" he bellowed, assuming his own proper form, which was huge as a mountain, and towered high beside the fortress that he had built. "It was a wicked trick. You shall pay for this in one way or another. I cannot tear down the castle which, ungrateful ones, I have built you, stronger than the strength of any giant. But I will demolish the rest of your shining city!" Indeed, he would have done so in his mighty rage; but at this moment Thor, whom Heimdall had called from the end of the earth by one blast of the golden horn, came rushing to the rescue, drawn in his chariot of goats. Thor jumped to the ground close beside the giant, and before that huge fellow knew what had happened, his head was rolling upon the ground at Father Odin's feet; for with one blow Thor had put an end to the giant's wickedness and had saved Asgard.

"This is the reward you deserve!" Thor cried. "Not Freyia nor the Sun and Moon, but the death that I have in store for all the enemies of the Aesir."

In this extraordinary way the noble city of Asgard was made safe and complete by the addition of a fortress which no one, not even the giant who built it, could injure, it was so wonder-strong. But always at the top of the gate were lacking three great stones that no one was mighty enough to lift. This was a reminder to the Aesir that now they had the race of giants for their everlasting enemies. And though Loki's trick had saved them Freyia, and for the world the Sun and Moon, it was the beginning of trouble in Asgard which lasted as long as Loki lived to make mischief with his guile.

Balder and the Mistletoe

LOKI HAD GIVEN UP trying to revenge himself upon Thor. The Thunder Lord seemed proof against his tricks. And indeed nowadays Loki hated him no more than he did the other gods. He hated some because they always frowned at him; he hated others because they only laughed and jeered. Some he hated for their distrust and some for their fear. But he hated them all because they were happy and good and mighty, while he was wretched, bad, and of little might. Yet it was all his own fault that this was so. He might have been an equal with the best of them, if he had not chosen to set himself against everything that was good. He had made them all his enemies, and the more he did to injure them, the more he hated them, – which is always the way with evil-doers. Loki longed to see them all unhappy. He slunk about in Asgard with a glum face and wrinkled forehead. He dared not meet the eyes of any one, lest they should read his heart. For he was plotting evil, the greatest of evils, which should bring sorrow to all his enemies at once and turn Asgard into a land of mourning. The Aesir did not guess the whole truth, yet they felt the bitterness of the thoughts which Loki bore; and whenever in the dark he passed unseen, the gods shuddered as if a breath of evil had blown upon them, and even the flowers drooped before his steps.

Now at this time Balder the beautiful had a strange dream. He dreamed that a cloud came before the sun, and all Asgard was dark. He waited for the cloud to drift away, and for the sun to smile again. But no; the sun was gone forever, he thought; and Balder awoke feeling very sad. The next night Balder had another dream. This time he dreamed that it was still dark as before; the flowers were withered and the gods were growing old; even Idun's magic apples could not make them young again. And all were weeping and wringing their hands as though some dreadful thing had happened. Balder awoke feeling strangely frightened, yet he said no word to Nanna his wife, for he did not want to trouble her.

When it came night again Balder slept and dreamed a third dream, a still more terrible one than the other two had been. He thought that in the dark, lonely world there was nothing but a sad voice, which cried, "The sun is gone! The spring is gone! Joy is gone! For Balder the beautiful is dead, dead, dead!"

This time Balder awoke with a cry, and Nanna asked him what was the matter. So he had to tell her of his dream, and he was sadly frightened; for in those days dreams were often sent to folk as messages, and what the gods dreamed usually came true. Nanna ran sobbing to Queen Frigga, who was Balder's mother, and told her all the dreadful dream, asking what could be done to prevent it from coming true.

Now Balder was Queen Frigga's dearest son. Thor was older and stronger, and more famous for his great deeds; but Frigga loved far better gold-haired Balder. And indeed he was the best-beloved of all the Aesir; for he was gentle, fair, and wise, and wherever he went folk grew happy and light-hearted at the very sight of him, just as we do when we first catch a glimpse of spring peeping over the hilltop into Winterland. So when Frigga heard of Balder's woeful dream, she was frightened almost out of her wits.

"He must not die! He shall not die!" she cried. "He is so dear to all the world, how could there be anything which would hurt him?"

And then a wonderful thought came to Frigga. "I will travel over the world and make all things promise not to injure my boy," she said. "Nothing shall pass my notice. I will get the word of everything."

So first she went to the gods themselves, gathered on Ida Plain for their morning exercise; and telling them of Balder's dream, she begged them to give the promise. Oh, what a shout arose when they heard her words!

"Hurt Balder! – Our Balder! Not for the world, we promise! The dream is wrong, – there is nothing so cruel as to wish harm to Balder the beautiful!" they cried. But deep in their hearts they felt a secret fear which would linger until they should hear that all things had given their promise. What if harm were indeed to come to Balder! The thought was too dreadful.

Then Frigga went to see all the beasts who live in field or forest or rocky den. Willingly they gave their promise never to harm hair of gentle Balder. "For he is ever kind to us," they said, "and we love him as if he were one of ourselves. Not with claws or teeth or hoofs or horns will any beast hurt Balder."

Next Frigga spoke to the birds and fishes, reptiles and insects. And all – even the venomous serpents – cried that Balder was their friend, and that they would never do aught to hurt his dear body. "Not with beak or talon, bite or sting or poison fang, will one of us hurt Balder," they promised.

After doing this, the anxious mother traveled over the whole round world, step by step; and from all the things that are she got the same ready promise never to harm Balder the beautiful. All the trees and plants promised; all the stones and metals; earth, air, fire, and water; sun, snow, wind, and rain, and all diseases that men know, – each gave to Frigga the word of promise which she wanted. So at last, footsore and weary, she came back to Asgard with the joyful news that Balder must be safe, for that there was nothing in the world but had promised to be his harmless friend.

Then there was rejoicing in Asgard, as if the gods had won one of their great victories over the giants. The noble Aesir and the heroes who had died in battle upon the earth, and who had come to Valhalla to live happily ever after, gathered on Ida Plain to celebrate the love of all nature for Balder.

There they invented a famous game, which was to prove how safe he was from the bite of death. They stationed Balder in the midst of them, his face glowing like the sun with the bright light which ever shone from him. And as he stood there all unarmed and smiling, by turns they tried all sorts of weapons against him; they made as if to beat him with sticks, they stoned him with stones, they shot at him with arrows and hurled mighty spears straight at his heart.

It was a merry game, and a shout of laughter went up as each stone fell harmless at Balder's feet, each stick broke before it touched his shoulders, each arrow overshot his head, and each spear turned aside. For neither stone nor wood nor flinty arrow-point nor barb of iron would break the promise which each had given. Balder was safe with them, just as if he were bewitched. He remained unhurt among the missiles which whizzed about his head, and which piled up in a great heap around the charmed spot whereon he stood.

Now among the crowd that watched these games with such enthusiasm, there was one face that did not smile, one voice that did not rasp itself hoarse with cheering. Loki saw how every one and every thing loved Balder, and he was jealous. He was the only creature in all the world that hated Balder and wished for his death. Yet Balder had never done harm to him. But the wicked plan that Loki had been cherishing was almost ripe, and in this poison fruit was the seed of the greatest sorrow that Asgard had ever known.

While the others were enjoying their game of love, Loki stole away unperceived from Ida Plain, and with a wig of gray hair, a long gown, and a staff, disguised himself as an old woman. Then he hobbled down Asgard streets till he came to the palace of Queen Frigga, the mother of Balder.

"Good-day, my lady," quoth the old woman, in a cracked voice. "What is that noisy crowd doing yonder in the green meadow? I am so deafened by their shouts that I can hardly hear myself think."

"Who are you, good mother, that you have not heard?" said Queen Frigga in surprise. "They are shooting at my son Balder. They are proving the word which all things have given me, – the promise not to injure my dear son. And that promise will be kept."

The old crone pretended to be full of wonder. "So, now!" she cried. "Do you mean to say that *every single thing* in the whole world has promised not to hurt your son? I can scarce believe it; though, to be sure, he is as fine a fellow as I ever saw." Of course this flattery pleased Frigga.

"You say true, mother," she answered proudly, "he is a noble son. Yes, everything has promised, – that is, everything except one tiny little plant that is not worth mentioning."

The old woman's eyes twinkled wickedly. "And what is that foolish little plant, my dear?" she asked coaxingly.

"It is the mistletoe that grows in the meadow west of Valhalla. It was too young to promise, and too harmless to bother with," answered Frigga carelessly.

After this her questioner hobbled painfully away. But as soon as she was out of sight from the Queen's palace, she picked up the skirts of her gown and ran as fast as she could to the meadow west of Valhalla. And there sure enough, as Frigga had said, was a tiny sprig of mistletoe growing on a gnarled oak-tree. The false Loki took out a knife which she carried in some hidden pocket and cut off the mistletoe very carefully. Then she trimmed and shaped it so that it was like a little green arrow, pointed at one end, but very slender.

"Ho, ho!" chuckled the old woman. "So you are the only thing in all the world that is too young to make a promise, my little mistletoe. Well, young as you are, you must go on an errand for me today. And maybe you shall bear a message of my love to Balder the beautiful."

Then she hobbled back to Ida Plain, where the merry game was still going on around Balder. Loki quietly passed unnoticed through the crowd, and came close to the elbow of a big dark fellow who was standing lonely outside the circle of weapon-throwers. He seemed sad and forgotten, and he hung his head in a pitiful way. It was Hodur, the blind brother of Balder.

The old woman touched his arm. "Why do you not join the game with the others?" she asked, in her cracked voice. "Are you the only one to do your brother no honor? Surely, you are big and strong enough to toss a spear with the best of them yonder."

Hodur touched his sightless eyes madly. "I am blind," he said. "Strength I have, greater than belongs to most of the Aesir. But I cannot see to aim a weapon. Besides, I have no spear to test upon him. Yet how gladly would I do honor to dear Balder!" and he sighed deeply.

"It were a pity if I could not find you at least a little stick to throw," said Loki sympathetically. "I am only a poor old woman, and of course I have no weapon. But ah, – here is a green twig which you can use as an arrow, and I will guide your arm, poor fellow."

Hodur's dark face lighted up, for he was eager to take his turn in the game. So he thanked her, and grasped eagerly the little arrow which she put into his hand. Loki held him by the arm, and together they stepped into the circle which surrounded Balder. And when it was Hodur's turn to throw his weapon, the old woman stood at his elbow and guided his big arm as it hurled the twig of mistletoe towards where Balder stood.

Oh, the sad thing that befell! Straight through the air flew the little arrow, straight as magic and Loki's arm could direct it. Straight to Balder's heart it sped, piercing through jerkin and shirt and all, to give its bitter message of "Loki's love," as he had said. With a cry Balder fell forward on the grass.

And that was the end of sunshine and spring and joy in Asgard, for the dream had come true, and Balder the beautiful was dead.

When the Aesir saw what had happened, there was a great shout of fear and horror, and they rushed upon Hodur, who had thrown the fatal arrow.

"What is it? What have I done?" asked the poor blind brother, trembling at the tumult which had followed his shot.

"You have slain Balder!" cried the Aesir. "Wretched Hodur, how could you do it?"

"It was the old woman – the evil old woman, who stood at my elbow and gave me a little twig to throw," gasped Hodur. "She must be a witch."

Then the Aesir scattered over Ida Plain to look for the old woman who had done the evil deed; but she had mysteriously disappeared.

"It must be Loki," said wise Heimdall. "It is Loki's last and vilest trick."

"Oh, my Balder, my beautiful Balder!" wailed Queen Frigga, throwing herself on the body of her son. "If I had only made the mistletoe give me the promise, you would have been saved. It was I who told Loki of the mistletoe, – so it is I who have killed you. Oh, my son, my son!"

But Father Odin was speechless with grief. His sorrow was greater than that of all the others, for he best understood the dreadful misfortune which had befallen Asgard. Already a cloud had come before the sun, so that it would never be bright day again. Already the flowers had begun to fade and the birds had ceased to sing. And already the Aesir had begun to grow old and joyless, – all because the little mistletoe had been too young to give a promise to Queen Frigga.

"Balder the beautiful is dead!" the cry went echoing through all the world, and everything that was sorrowed at the sound of the Aesir's weeping.

Balder's brothers lifted up his beautiful body upon their great war shields and bore him on their shoulders down to the seashore. For, as was the custom in those days, they were going to send him to Hel, the Queen of Death, with all the things he best had loved in Asgard. And these were, – after Nanna his wife, – his beautiful horse, and his ship Hringhorni. So that they would place Balder's body upon the ship with his horse beside him, and set fire to this wonderful funeral pile. For by fire was the quickest passage to Hel's kingdom.

But when they reached the shore, they found that all the strength of all the Aesir was unable to move Hringhorni, Balder's ship, into the water. For it was the largest ship in the world, and it was stranded far up the beach.

"Even the giants bore no ill-will to Balder," said Father Odin. "I heard the thunder of their grief but now shaking the hills. Let us for this once bury our hatred of that race and send to Jotunheim for help to move the ship."

So they sent a messenger to the giantess Hyrrockin, the hugest of all the Frost People. She was weeping for Balder when the message came.

"I will go, for Balder's sake," she said. Soon she came riding fast upon a giant wolf, with a serpent for the bridle; and mighty she was, with the strength of forty Aesir. She dismounted from her wolf-steed, and tossed the wriggling reins to one of the men-heroes who had followed Balder and the Aesir from Valhalla. But he could not hold the beast, and it took four heroes to keep him quiet, which they could only do by throwing him upon the ground and sitting upon him in a row. And this mortified them greatly.

Then Hyrrockin the giantess strode up to the great ship and seized it by the prow. Easily she gave a little pull and presto! it leaped forward on its rollers with such force that sparks flew from the flint stones underneath and the whole earth trembled. The boat shot into the waves and out toward open sea so swiftly that the Aesir were likely to have lost it entirely, had not Hyrrockin waded out up to her waist and caught it by the stern just in time.

Thor was angry at her clumsiness, and raised his hammer to punish her. But the other Aesir held his arm.

"She cannot help being so strong," they whispered. "She meant to do well. She did not realize how hard she was pulling. This is no time for anger, brother Thor." So Thor spared her life, as indeed he ought, for her kindness.

Then Balder's body was borne out to the ship and laid upon a pile of beautiful silks, and furs, and cloth-of-gold, and woven sunbeams which the dwarfs had wrought. So that his funeral pyre was more grand than anything which had ever been seen. But when Nanna, Balder's gentle wife, saw them ready to kindle the flames under this gorgeous bed, she could bear her grief no longer. Her loving heart broke, and they laid her beside him, that they might comfort each other on their journey to Hel. Thor touched the pile gently with his hammer that makes the lightning, and the flames burst forth, lighting up the faces of Balder and Nanna with a glory. Then they cast upon the fire Balder's war-horse, to serve his master in the dark country to which he was about to go. The horse was decked with a harness all of gold, with jewels studding the bridle and headstall. Last of all Odin laid upon the pyre his gift to Balder, Draupnir, the precious ring of gold which the dwarf had made, from which every ninth night there dropped eight other rings as large and brightly golden.

"Take this with you, dear son, to Hel's palace," said Odin. "And do not forget the friends you leave behind in the now lonely halls of Asgard."

Then Hyrrockin pushed the great boat out to sea, with its bonfire of precious things. And on the beach stood all the Aesir watching it out of sight, all the Aesir and many besides. For there came to Balder's funeral great crowds of little dwarfs and multitudes of huge frost giants, all mourning for Balder the beautiful. For this one time they were all friends together, forgetting their quarrels of so many centuries. All of them loved Balder, and were united to do him honor.

The great ship moved slowly out to sea, sending up a red fire to color all the heavens. At last it slid below the horizon softly, as you have often seen the sun set upon the water, leaving a brightness behind to lighten the dark world for a little while.

This indeed was the sunset for Asgard. The darkness of sorrow came in earnest after the passing of Balder the beautiful.

But the punishment of Loki was a terrible thing. And that came soon and sore.

The Punishment of Loki

AFTER THE DEATH of Balder the world grew so dreary that no one had any heart left for work or play. The Aesir sat about moping and miserable. They were growing old, – there was no doubt about that. There was no longer any gladness in Valhalla, where the Valkyrs waited on table and poured the foaming mead. There was no longer any mirth on Ida Plain, when every morning the bravest of earth-heroes fought their battles over again. Odin no longer had any pleasure in the daily news brought by his wise ravens, Thought and Memory, nor did Freyia enjoy her falcon dress. Frey forgot to sail in his ship Skidbladnir, and even Thor had almost wearied of his hammer, except as he hoped that it would help him to catch Loki. For the one thought of all of them now was to find and punish Loki.

Yet they waited; for Queen Frigga had sent a messenger to Queen Hel to find if they might not even yet win Balder back from the kingdom of death.

Odin shook his head. "Queen Hel is Loki's daughter," he said, "and she will not let Balder return." But Frigga was hopeful; she had employed a trusty messenger, whose silver tongue had won many hearts against their will.

It was Hermod, Balder's brother, who galloped down the steep road to Hel's kingdom, on Sleipnir, the eight-legged horse of Father Odin. For nine nights and nine days he rode, through valleys dark and chill, until he came to the bridge which is paved with gold. And here the maiden Modgard told him that Balder had passed that way, and showed him the path northward to Hel's city. So he rode, down and down, until he came to the high wall which surrounded the grim palace where Hel reigned. Hermod dismounted and tightened the saddle-girths of gray Sleipnir, whose eight legs were as frisky as ever, despite the long journey. And when he had mounted once more, the wonderful horse leaped with him over the wall, twenty feet at least!

Then Hermod rode straight into the palace of Hel, straight up to the throne where she sat surrounded by gray shadows and spirit people. She was a dreadful creature to see, was this daughter of Loki, – half white like other folk, but half black, which was not sunburn, for there was no sunshine in this dark and dismal land. Yet she was not so bad as she looked; for even Hel felt kindly towards Balder, whom her father had slain, and was sorry that the world had lost so dear a friend. So when Hermod begged of her to let his brother return with him to Asgard, she said very gently:

"Freely would I let him go, brave Hermod, if I might. But a queen cannot always do as she likes, even in her own kingdom. His life must be bought; the price must be paid in tears. If everything upon earth will weep for Balder's death, then may he return, bringing light and happiness to the upper world. Should one creature fail to weep, Balder must remain with me."

Then Hermod was glad, for he felt sure that this price was easily paid. He thanked Hel, and made ready to depart with the hopeful message. Before he went away he saw and spoke with Balder himself, who sat with Nanna upon a throne of honor, talking of the good times that used to be. And Balder gave him the ring Draupnir to give back to Father Odin, as a remembrance from his dear son; while Nanna sent to mother Frigga her silver veil with other rich presents. It was hard for Hermod to part with Balder once again, and Balder also wept to see him go. But Hermod was in duty bound to bear the message back to Asgard as swiftly as might be.

Now when the Aesir heard from Hermod this news, they sent messengers forth over the whole world to bid every creature weep for Balder's death. Heimdall galloped off upon Goldtop and Frey upon Goldbristle, his famous hog; Thor rumbled away in his goat chariot, and Freyia drove her team of cats, – all spreading the message in one direction and another. There really seemed little need for them to do this, for already there was mourning in every land and clime. Even the sky was weeping, and the flower eyes were filled with dewy tears.

So it seemed likely that Balder would be ransomed after all, and the Aesir began to hope more strongly. For they had not found one creature who refused to weep. Even the giants of Jotunheim were sorry to lose the gentle fellow who had never done them any harm, and freely added their giant tears to the salt rivers that were coursing over all the world into the sea, making it still more salt.

It was not until the messengers had nearly reached home, joyful in the surety that Balder was safe, that they found an ugly old giantess named Thokt hidden in a black cavern among the mountains.

"Weep, mother, weep for Balder!" they cried. "Balder the beautiful is dead, but your tears will buy him back to life. Weep, mother, weep!"

But the sulky old woman refused to weep.

"Balder is nothing to me," she said. "I care not whether he lives or dies. Let him bide with Hel – he is out of mischief there. I weep dry tears for Balder's death."

So all the work of the messengers was in vain, because of this one obstinate old woman. So all the tears of the sorrowing world were shed in vain. Because there were lacking two salty drops from the eyes of Thokt, they could not buy back Balder from the prison of death.

When the messengers returned and told Odin their sad news, he was wrathful.

"Do you not guess who the old woman was?" he cried. "It was Loki – Loki himself, disguised as a giantess. He has tricked us once more, and for a second time has slain Balder for us; for it is now too late, – Balder can never return to us after this. But it shall be the last of Loki's mischief. It is now time that we put an end to his deeds of shame."

"Come, my brothers!" shouted Thor, flourishing his hammer. "We have wept and mourned long enough. It is now time to punish. Let us hasten back to Thokt's cave, and seize Loki as quickly as may be."

So they hurried back into the mountains where they had left the giantess who would not weep. But when they came to the place, the cave was empty. Loki was too sharp a fellow to sit still and wait for punishment to overtake him. He knew very well that the Aesir would soon discover who Thokt really was. And he had taken himself off to a safer place, to escape the questions which a whole world of not too gentle folk were anxious to ask him.

The one desire of the Aesir was now to seize and punish Loki. So when they were unable to find him as easily as they expected, they were wroth indeed. Why had he left the cave? Whither had he gone? In what new disguise even now was he lurking, perhaps close by?

The truth was that when Loki found himself at war with the whole world which he had injured, he fled away into the mountains, where he had built a strong castle of rocks. This castle had four doors, one looking into the north, one to the south, one to the east, and one to the west; so that Loki could keep watch in all directions and see any enemy who might approach. Besides this, he had for his protection the many disguises which he knew so well how to don. Near the castle was a river and a waterfall, and it was Loki's favorite game to change himself into a spotted pink salmon and splash about in the pool below the fall.

"Ho, ho! Let them try to catch me here, if they can!" he would chuckle to himself. And indeed, it seemed as if he were safe enough.

One day Loki was sitting before the fire in his castle twisting together threads of flax and yarn into a great fish-net which was his own invention. For no one had ever before thought of catching fish with a net. Loki was a clever fellow; and with all his faults, for this one thing at least the fishermen of today ought to be grateful to him. As Loki sat busily knotting the meshes of the net, he happened to glance out of the south door, – and there were the Aesir coming in a body up the hill towards his castle.

Now this is what had happened: from his lookout throne in Asgard, Odin's keen sight had spied Loki's retreat. This throne, you remember, was in the house with a silver roof which Odin had built in the very beginning of time; and whenever he wanted to see what was going on in the remotest corner of Asgard, or to spy into some secret place beyond the sight of gods or men, he would mount this magic throne, whence his eye could pierce thick mountains and sound the deepest sea. So it was that the Aesir had found out Loki's castle, well-hidden though it was among the furthest mountains of the world. They had come to catch him, and there was nothing left for him but to run.

Loki jumped up and threw his half-mended net into the fire, for he did not want the Aesir to discover his invention; then he ran down to the river and leaped in with a great splash. When he was well under water, he changed himself into a salmon, and flickered away to bask in his shady pool and think how safe he was.

By this time the Aesir had entered his castle and were poking among the ashes which they found smouldering on the hearth.

"What is this?" asked Thor, holding up a piece of knotted flax which was not quite burned. "The knave has been making something with little cords."

"Let me see it," said Heimdall, the wisest of the Aesir, – he who once upon a time had suggested Thor's clever disguise for winning back his hammer from the giant Thrym. He took now the little scrap of fish-net and studied it carefully, picking out all the knots and twists of it.

"It is a net," said Heimdall at last. "He has been making a net, and – pfaugh! – it smells of fish. The fellow must have used it to trap fish for his dinner, though I never before heard of such a device."

"I saw a big splash in the river just as we came up," said Thor the keen-eyed, – "a very big splash indeed. It seemed too large for any fish."

"It was Loki," declared Heimdall. "He must have been here but a moment since, for this fire has just gone out, and the net is still smouldering. That shows he did not wish us to find this new-fangled idea of his. Why was that? Let me think. Aha! I have it. Loki has changed himself into a fish, and did not wish us to discover the means of catching him."

"Oho!" cried the Aesir regretfully. "If only we had another net!"

"We can make one," said wise Heimdall. "I know how it is done, for I have studied out this little sample. Let us make a net to catch the slyest of all fish."

"Let us make a net for Loki," echoed the Aesir. And they all sat down cross-legged on the floor to have a lesson in net-weaving from Heimdall. He found hemp cord in a cupboard, and soon they had contrived a goodly net, big enough to catch several Lokis, if they should have good fisherman's luck.

They dragged the net to the river and cast it in. Thor, being the strongest, held one end of the net, and all the rest drew the other end up and down the stream. They were clumsy and awkward, for they had never used a net before, and did not know how to make the best of it. But presently Thor exclaimed, "Ha! I felt some live thing touch the meshes!"

"So did we!" cried the others. "It must be Loki!" And Loki it was, sure enough; for the Aesir had happened upon the very pool where the great salmon lay basking so peacefully. But when he felt the net touch him, he darted away and hid in a cleft between two rocks. So that, although they dragged the net to and fro again and again, they could not catch Loki in its meshes; for the net was so light that it floated over his head.

"We must weight the net," said Heimdall wisely; "then nothing can pass beneath it." So they tied heavy stones all along the under edge, and again they cast the net, a little below the waterfall. Now Loki had seized the chance to swim further down the stream. But ugh! suddenly he tasted salt water. He was being swept out to sea! That would never do, for he could not live an hour in the sea. So he swam back and leaped straight over the net up into the waterfall, hoping that no one had noticed him. But Thor's sharp eyes had spied the flash of pink and silver, and Thor came running to the place.

"He is here!" he shouted. "Cast in the net above the fall! We have him now!"

When Loki saw the net cast again, so that there was no choice for him but to be swept back over the falls and out to sea, or to leap the net once more still further up the river, he hesitated. He saw Thor in the middle of the stream wading towards him; but behind him was sure death. So he set his teeth and once more he leaped the net. There was a huge splash, a scuffle, a scramble, and the water was churned into froth all about Thor's feet. He was struggling with the mighty fish. He caught him once, but the salmon slipped through his fingers. He caught him again, and this time Thor gripped hard. The salmon almost escaped, but Thor's big fingers kept hold of the end of his tail, and he flapped and flopped in vain. It was the grip of Thor's iron glove; and that is why to this day the salmon has so pointed a tail. The next time you see a salmon you must notice this, and remember that he may be a great-great-great-grand-descendant of Loki.

So Loki was captured and changed back into his own shape, sullen and fierce. But he had no word of sorrow for his evil deeds; nor did he ask for mercy, for he knew that it would be in vain. He kept silent while the Aesir led him all the weary way back to Asgard.

Now the whole world was noisy with the triumph of his capture. As the procession passed along it was joined by all the creatures who had mourned for Balder, – all the creatures who longed to see Loki punished. There were the men of Midgard, the place of human folk, shouting, "Kill him! kill him!" at the top of their lungs; there were armies of little mountain dwarfs in their brown peaked caps, who hobbled along, prodding Loki with their picks; there were beasts growling and showing their teeth as if they longed to tear Loki in pieces; there were birds who tried to peck his eyes, insects who came in clouds to sting him, and serpents that sprang up hissing at his feet to poison him with their deadly bite.

But to all these Thor said, "Do not kill the fellow. We are keeping him for a worse punishment than you can give." So the creatures merely followed and jostled Loki into Asgard, shouting, screaming, howling, growling, barking, roaring, spitting, squeaking, hissing, croaking, and buzzing, according to their different ways of showing hatred and horror.

The Aesir met on Ida Plain to decide what should be done with Loki. There were Idunn whom he had cheated, and Sif whose hair he had cut off. There were Freyia whose falcon dress he had stolen and Thor whom he had tried to kill. There were Hodur whom he had made a murderer; Frigga and Odin whose son he had slain. There was not one of them whom Loki had not injured in some way; and besides, there was the whole world into which he had brought sorrow and darkness; for the sake of all these Loki must be punished. But it was hard to think of any doom heavy enough for him. At last, however, they agreed upon a punishment which they thought suited to so wicked a wretch.

The long procession formed again and escorted Loki down, down into a damp cavern underground. Here sunlight never came, but the cave was full of ugly toads, snakes, and insects that love the dark. These were Loki's evil thoughts, who were to live with him henceforth and torment him always. In this prison chamber side by side they placed three sharp stones, not far apart, to make an uneasy bed. And these were for Loki's three worst deeds, against Thor and Hodur and Balder. Upon these rocks they bound Loki with stout thongs of leather. But as soon as the cords were fastened they turned into iron bands, so that no one, though he had the strength of a hundred giants, could loosen them. For these were Loki's evil passions, and the more he strained against them, the more they cut into him and wounded him until he howled with pain.

Over his head Skadi, whose father he had helped to slay, hung a venomous, wriggling serpent, from whose mouth dropped poison into Loki's face, which burned and stung him like fire. And this was the deceit which all his life Loki had spoken to draw folk into trouble and danger. At last it had turned about to torture him, as deceit always will do to him who utters it. Yet from this one torment Loki had some relief; for alone of all the world Sigyn, his wife, was faithful and forgiving. She stood by the head of the painful bed upon which the Red One was stretched, and held a bowl to catch the poison which dropped from the serpent's jaws, so that some of it did not reach Loki's face. But as often as the bowl became full, Sigyn had to go out and empty it; and then the bitter drops fell and burned till Loki made the cavern ring with his cries.

So this was Loki's punishment, and bad enough it was, – but not too bad for such a monster. Under the caverns he lies there still, struggling to be free. And when his great strength shakes the hills so that the whole ground trembles, men call it an earthquake. Sometimes they even see his poisonous breath blowing from the top of a mountain-chimney, and amid it the red flame of wickedness which burns in Loki's heart. Then all cry, "The volcano, the volcano!" and run away as fast as they can. For Loki, poisoned though he is, is still dangerous and full of mischief, and it is not good to venture near him in his torment.

But there for his sins he must bide and suffer, suffer and bide, until the end of all sorrow and suffering and sin shall come, with Ragnarok, the ending of the world.

LEGENDS OF THOR

Introduction

THOR WAS ONE OF THE TWELVE principal deities of Asgard, and he lived in the splendid realm of Thrudvang, where he built a palace called Bilskirnir. Here he lived as god of thunder, and his name was invoked more than any other in the age of the Vikings. For Thor was the protector of the land, a fine figure of a man with glowing eyes, firm muscles, and a red beard that made him instantly recognizable. He became known across the worlds for his great hammer, Miolnir (the crusher), which had been forged by the dark elves. This hammer, together with Thor's strength and his terrible temper, made him the fiercest god of Asgard, and the personification of brute force. Thor was also god of might and war, and because of his popularity, he soon grew to embody the forces of agriculture, and became a symbol of the earth itself. He is remembered throughout the world on the fourth day of every week – Thursday, or Thor's day.

The Dwarf's Gifts

RED LOKI HAD BEEN up to mischief again! Loki, who made quarrels and brought trouble wherever he went. He had a wicked heart, and he loved no one. He envied Father Odin his wisdom and his throne above the world. He envied Balder his beauty, and Tyr his courage, and Thor his strength. He envied all the good Aesir who were happy; but he would not take the trouble to be good himself. So he was always unhappy, spiteful, and sour. And if anything went wrong in Asgard, the kingdom of the gods, one was almost sure to find Loki at the bottom of the trouble.

Now Thor, the strongest of all the gods, was very proud of his wife's beautiful hair, which fell in golden waves to her feet, and covered her like a veil. He loved it better than anything, except Sif herself. One day, while Thor was away from home, Loki stole into Thrudheim, the realm of clouds, and cut off all Sif's golden hair, till her head was as round and fuzzy as a yellow dandelion. Fancy how angry Thor was when he came rattling home that night in his thunder-chariot and found Sif so ugly to look at! He stamped up and down till the five hundred and forty floors of his cloud palace shook like an earthquake, and lightning flashed from his blue eyes. The people down in the world below cried: "Dear, dear! What a terrible thunderstorm! Thor must be very angry about something. Loki has been up to mischief, it is likely." You see, they also knew Loki and his tricks.

At last Thor calmed himself a little. "Sif, my love," he said, "you shall be beautiful again. Red Loki shall make you so, since his was the unmaking. The villain! He shall pay for this!"

Then, without more ado, off set Thor to find red Loki. He went in his thunder-chariot, drawn by two goats, and the clouds rumbled and the lightning flashed wherever he went; for Thor was the mighty god of thunder. At last he came upon the sly rascal, who was trying to hide. Big Thor seized him by the throat.

"You scoundrel!" he cried, "I will break every bone in your body if you do not put back Sif's beautiful hair upon her head."

"Ow – ow! You hurt me!" howled Loki. "Take off your big hand, Thor. What is done, is done. I cannot put back Sif's hair. You know that very well."

"Then you must get her another head of hair," growled Thor. "That you can do. You must find for her hair of real gold, and it must grow upon her head as if it were her own. Do this, or you shall die."

"Where shall I get this famous hair?" whined Loki, though he knew well enough.

"Get it of the black elves," said Thor; "they are cunning jewelers, and they are your friends. Go, Loki, and go quickly, for I long to see Sif as beautiful as ever."

Then Loki of the burning beard slunk away to the hills where, far under ground, the dwarfs have their furnaces and their workshops. Among great heaps of gold and silver and shining jewels, which they have dug up out of the earth, the little crooked men in brown blink and chatter and scold one another; for they are ugly fellows – the dwarfs. *Tink-tank! Tink-tank!* go their little hammers all day long and all night long, while they make wonderful things such as no man has ever seen, though you shall hear about them.

They had no trouble to make a head of hair for Sif. It was for them a simple matter, indeed. The dwarfs work fast for such a customer as Loki, and in a little while the golden wires were beaten out, and drawn out, made smooth and soft and curly, and braided into a thick golden braid. But when Loki came away, he carried with him also two other treasures which the clever dwarfs had made. One was a golden spear, and the other was a ship.

Now these do not sound so very wonderful. But wait until you hear! The spear, which was named Gungnir, was bewitched, so that it made no difference if the person who held it was clumsy and careless. For it had this amazing quality, that no matter how badly it was aimed, or how unskillfully it was thrown, it was sure to go straight to the mark – which is a very obliging and convenient thing in one's weapon, as you will readily see.

And Skidbladnir – this was the harsh name of the ship – was even more wonderful. It could be taken to pieces and folded up so small that it would go into one's pocket. But when it was unfolded and put together, it would hold all the gods of Asgard for a sea-journey. Besides all this, when the sails were set, the ship was sure always to have a fair wind, which would make it skim along like a great bird, which was the best part of the charm, as any sailor will tell you.

Now Loki felt very proud of these three treasures, and left the hill cave stretching his neck and strutting like a great red turkey cock. Outside the gate, however, he met Brock, the black dwarf, who was the brother of Sindri, the best workman in all the underworld.

"Hello! what have you there?" asked Brock of the big head, pointing at the bundles which Loki was carrying.

"The three finest gifts in the world," boasted Loki, hugging his treasures tight.

"Pooh!" said Brock, "I don't believe it. Did my brother Sindri make them?"

"No," answered Loki; "they were made by the black elves, the sons of Ivaldi. And they are the most precious gifts that ever were seen."

"Pooh!" again puffed Brock, wagging his long beard crossly. "Nonsense! Whatever they be, my brother Sindri can make three other gifts more precious; that I know."

"Can he, though?" laughed Loki. "I will give him my head if he can."

"Done!" shouted the dwarf. "Let me see your famous gifts." So Loki showed him the three wonders: the gold hair for Sif, the spear, and the ship. But again the dwarf said: "Pooh! These are nothing. I will show you what the master-smith can do, and you shall lose your bragging red head, my Loki."

Now Loki began to be a little uneasy. He followed Brock back to the smithy in the mountain, where they found Sindri at his forge. Oh, yes! He could beat the poor gifts of which Loki was so proud. But he would not tell what his own three gifts were to be.

First Sindri took a pig's skin and laid it on the fire. Then he went away for a little time; but he set Brock at the bellows and bade him blow – blow – blow the fire until Sindri should return. Now when Sindri was gone, Loki also stole away; for, as usual, he was up to mischief. He had the power of changing his shape and of becoming any creature he chose, which was often very convenient. Thus he turned himself into a huge biting fly. Then he flew back into the smithy where Brock was blow – blow – blowing. Loki buzzed about the dwarf's head, and finally lighted on his hand and stung him, hoping to make him let go the bellows. But no! Brock only cried out, "Oh-ee!" and kept on blowing for dear life. Now soon back came Sindri to the forge and took the pigskin from the fire. Wonder of wonders! It had turned into a hog with golden bristles; a live hog that shone like the sun. Brock was not satisfied, however.

"Well! I don't think much of that," he grumbled.

"Wait a little," said Sindri mysteriously. "Wait and see." Then he went on to make the second gift.

This time he put a lump of gold into the fire. And when he went away, as before, he bade Brock stand at the bellows to blow – blow – blow without stopping. Again, as before, in buzzed Loki the gadfly as soon as the master-smith had gone out. This time he settled on Brock's swarthy neck, and stung him so sorely that the blood came and the dwarf roared till the mountain trembled. Still Brock did not let go the handle of the bellows, but blew and howled – blew and howled with pain till Sindri returned. And this time the dwarf took from the fire a fine gold ring, round as roundness.

"Um! I don't think so much of that," said Brock, again disappointed, for he had expected some wonderful jewel. But Sindri wagged his head wisely.

"Wait a little," he said. "We shall see what we shall see." He heaved a great lump of iron into the fire to make the third gift. But this time when he went away, leaving Brock at the bellows, he charged him to blow – blow – blow without a minute's rest, or everything would be spoiled. For this was to be the best gift of all.

Brock planted himself wide-legged at the forge and blew – blew – blew. But for the third time Loki, winged as a fly, came buzzing into the smithy. This time he fastened viciously below Brock's bushy eyebrow, and stung him so cruelly that the blood trickled down, a red river, into his eyes and the poor dwarf was blinded. With a howl Brock raised his hand to wipe away the blood, and of course in that minute the bellows stood still. Then Loki buzzed away with a sound that seemed like a mocking laugh. At the same moment in rushed Sindri, panting with fright, for he had heard that sound and guessed what it meant.

"What have you done?" he cried. "You have let the bellows rest! You have spoiled everything!"

"Only a little moment, but one little moment," pleaded Brock, in a panic. "It has done no harm, has it?"

Sindri leaned anxiously over the fire, and out of the flames he drew the third gift – an enormous hammer.

"Oh!" said Brock, much disappointed, "only an old iron hammer! I don't think anything of *that*. Look how short the handle is, too."

"That is your fault, brother," returned the smith crossly. "If you had not let the bellows stand still, the handle would have been long enough. Yet as it is – we shall see, we shall see. I think it will at least win for you red Loki's head. Take the three gifts, brother, such as they are, and bear them to Asgard. Let all the gods be judges between you and Loki, which gifts are best, his or yours. But stay – I may as well tell you the secrets of your three treasures, or you will not know how to make them work. Your toy that is not wound up is of no use at all." Which is very true, as we all know. Then he bent over and whispered in Brock's ear. And what he said pleased Brock so much that he jumped straight up into the air and capered like one of Thor's goats.

"What a clever brother you are, to be sure!" he cried.

At that moment Loki, who had ceased to be a gadfly, came in grinning, with his three gifts. "Well, are you ready?" he asked. Then he caught sight of the three gifts which Brock was putting into his sack.

"Ho! A pig, a ring, and a stub-handled hammer!" he shouted. "Is that all you have? Fine gifts, indeed! I was really growing uneasy, but now I see that my head is safe. Let us start for Asgard immediately, where I promise you that I with my three treasures shall be thrice more welcome than you with your stupid pig, your ugly ring, and your half-made hammer."

So together they climbed to Asgard, and there they found the Aesir sitting in the great judgment hall on Ida Plain. There was Father Odin on his high throne, with his two ravens at his head and his two wolves at his feet. There was Queen Frigga by his side; and about them were Balder the beautiful, Frey and Freyia, the fair brother and sister; the mighty Thor, with Sif, his crop-haired wife, and all the rest of the great Aesir who lived in the upper world above the homes of men.

"Brother Aesir," said Loki, bowing politely, for he was a smooth rascal, "we have come each with three gifts, the dwarf and I; and you shall judge which be the most worthy of praise. But if I lose, – I, your brother, – I lose my head to this crooked little dwarf." So he spoke, hoping to put the Aesir on his side from the first. For his head was a very handsome one, and the dwarf was indeed an ill-looking fellow. The gods, however, nodded gravely, and bade the two show what their gifts might be.

Then Loki stepped forward to the foot of Odin's throne. And first he pulled from his great wallet the spear Gungnir, which could not miss aim. This he gave to Odin, the all-wise. And Odin was vastly pleased, as you may imagine, to find himself thenceforth an unequaled marksman. So he smiled upon Loki kindly and said: "Well done, brother."

Next Loki took out the promised hair for Sif, which he handed Thor with a grimace. Now when the golden locks were set upon her head, they grew there like real hair, long and soft and curling – but still real gold. So that Sif was more beautiful than ever before, and more precious, too. You can fancy how pleased Thor was with Loki's gift. He kissed lovely Sif before all the gods and goddesses, and vowed that he forgave Loki for the mischief which he had done in the first place, since he had so nobly made reparation.

Then Loki took out the third gift, all folded up like a paper boat; and it was the ship Skidbladnir, – I am sorry they did not give it a prettier name. This he presented to Frey the peaceful. And you can guess Sindri or not Frey's blue eyes laughed with pleasure at such a gift.

Now when Loki stepped back, all the Aesir clapped their hands and vowed that he had done wondrous well.

"You will have to show us fine things, you dwarf," quoth Father Odin, "to better the gifts of red Loki. Come, what have you in the sack you bear upon your shoulders?"

Then the crooked little Brock hobbled forward, bent almost double under the great load which he carried. "I have what I have," he said.

First, out he pulled the ring Draupnir, round as roundness and shining of gold. This the dwarf gave to Odin, and though it seemed but little, yet it was much. For every ninth night out of this ring, he said, would drop eight other rings of gold, as large and as fair. Then Odin clapped his hands and cried: "Oh, wondrous gift! I like it even better than the magic spear which Loki gave." And all the other Aesir agreed with him.

Then out of the sack came grunting Goldbristle, the hog, all of gold. Brock gave him to Frey, to match the magic ship of Loki. This Goldbristle was so marvelously forged that he could run more swiftly than any horse, on air or water. Moreover, he was a living lantern. For on the darkest night he bristled with light like a million-pointed star, so that one riding on his back would light the air and the sea like a firefly, wherever he went. This idea pleased Frey mightily, for he was the merriest of the gods, and he laughed aloud.

"'Tis a wondrous fine gift," he said. "I like old Goldbristle even better than the compressible boat. For on this lusty steed I can ride about the world when I am tending the crops and the cattle of men and scattering the rain upon them. Master dwarf, I give my vote to you." And all the other Aesir agreed with him.

Then out of the sack Brock drew the third gift. It was the short-handled hammer named Miolnir. And this was the gift which Sindri had made for Thor, the mightiest of the gods; and it was the best gift of all. For with it Thor could burst the hardest metal and shatter the thickest mountain, and nothing could withstand its power. But it never could hurt Thor himself; and no matter how far or how hard it was thrown, it would always fly back into Thor's own hand. Last of all, whenever he so wished, the great hammer would become so small that he could put it in his pocket, quite out of sight. But Brock was sorry that the handle was so short – all owing to his fault, because he had let the bellows rest for that one moment.

When Thor had this gift in his hand, he jumped up with a shout of joy. "'Tis a wondrous fine gift," he cried, "with short handle or with long. And I prize it even more than I prize the golden hair of Sif which Loki gave. For with it I shall fight our enemies, the Frost Giants and the mischievous Trolls and the other monsters – Loki's friends. And all the Aesir will be glad of my gift when they see what deeds I shall do therewith. Now, if I may have my say, I judge that the three gifts made by Sindri the dwarf are the most precious that may be. So Brock has gained the prize of Loki's red head, – a sorry recompense indeed for gifts so masterly." Then Thor sat down. And all the other Aesir shouted that he had spoken well, and that they agreed with him.

So Loki was like to lose his head. He offered to pay instead a huge price, if Brock would let him go. But Brock refused. "The red head of Loki for my gift," he insisted, and the gods nodded that it must be so, since he had earned his wish.

But when Loki saw that the count was all against him, his eyes grew crafty. "Well, take me, then – if you can!" he shouted. And off he shot like an arrow from a bow. For Loki had on magic shoes, with which he could run over sea or land or sky; and the dwarf could never catch him in the world. Then Brock was furious. He stood stamping and chattering, tearing his long beard with rage.

"I am cheated!" he cried. "I have won – but I have lost." Then he turned to Thor, who was playing with his hammer, bursting a mountain or two and splitting a tree here and there. "Mighty Thor," begged the dwarf, "catch me the fellow who has broken his word. I have given you the best gift, – your wonderful hammer. Catch me, then, the boasting red head which I have fairly bought."

Then Thor stopped his game and set out in pursuit of Loki, for he was ever on the side of fairness. No one, however fleet, can escape when Thor follows, for his is the swiftness of a lightning flash. So he soon brought Loki back to Ida Plain, and gave him up a prisoner to the dwarf.

"I have you now, boaster," said Brock fiercely, "and I will cut off your red head in the twinkling of an eye." But just as he was about to do as he said, Loki had another sly idea.

"Hold, sirrah dwarf," he said. "It is true that you have won my head, but not the neck, not an inch of the neck." And all the gods agreed that this was so. Then Brock was puzzled indeed, for how could he cut off Loki's head without an inch of the neck, too? But this he must not do, or he knew the just Aesir would punish him with death. So he was forced to be content with stopping Loki's boasting in another way. He would sew up the bragging lips.

He brought a stout, strong thread and an awl to bore the holes. And in a twinkling he had stitched up the lips of the sly one, firm and fast. So for a time, at least, he put an end to Loki's boasting and his taunts and his lies.

It is a pity that those mischief-making lips were not fastened up forever; for that would have saved much of the trouble and sorrow which came after. But at last, after a long time, Loki got his lips free, and they made great sorrow in Asgard for the gods and on earth for men, as you shall hear.

Now this is the end of the tale which tells of the dwarf's gifts, and especially of Thor's hammer, which was afterwards to be of such service to him and such bane to the enemies of the Aesir. And that also you shall hear before all is done.

Thor's Fishing

ONCE UPON A TIME the Aesir went to take dinner with old Œgir, the king of the ocean. Down under the green waves they went to the coral palace where Œgir lived with his wife, Queen Ran, and his daughters, the Waves. But Œgir was not expecting so large a party to dinner, and he had not mead enough for them all to drink. "I must brew some more mead," he said to himself. But when he came to look for a kettle in which to make the brew, there was none in all the sea large enough for the purpose. At first Œgir did not know what to do; but at last he decided to consult the gods themselves, for he knew how wise and powerful his guests were, and he hoped that they might help him to a kettle.

Now when he told the Aesir his trouble they were much interested, for they were hungry and thirsty, and longed for some of Œgir's good mead. "Where can we find a kettle?" they said to one another. "Who has a kettle huge enough to hold mead for all the Aesir?"

Then Tyr the brave turned to Thor with a grand idea. "My father, the giant Hymir, has such a kettle," he said. "I have seen it often in his great palace near Elivagar, the river of ice. This famous kettle is a mile deep, and surely that is large enough to brew all the mead we may need."

"Surely, surely it is large enough," laughed Œgir. "But how are we to get the kettle, my distinguished guests? Who will go to Giant Land to fetch the kettle a mile deep?"

"That will I," said brave Thor. "I will go to Hymir's dwelling and bring thence the little kettle, if Tyr will go with me to show me the way." So Thor and Tyr set out together for the land of snow and ice, where the giant Hymir lived. They traveled long and they traveled fast, and finally they came to the huge house which had once been Tyr's home, before he went to live with the good folk in Asgard.

Well Tyr knew the way to enter, and it was not long before they found themselves in the hall of Hymir's dwelling, peering about for some sign of the kettle which they had come so far to seek; and sure enough, presently they discovered eight huge kettles hanging in a row from one of the beams in the ceiling. While the two were wondering which kettle might be the one they sought, there came in Tyr's grandmother, – and a terrible grandmother she was. No wonder that Tyr had run away from home when he was very little; for this dreadful creature was a giantess with nine hundred heads, each more ugly than the others, and her temper was as bad as were her looks. She began to roar and bellow; and no one knows what this evil old person would have done to her grandson and his friend had not there come into the hall at this moment another woman, fair and sweet, and glittering with golden ornaments. This was Tyr's good mother, who loved him dearly, and who had mourned his absence during long years.

With a cry of joy she threw herself upon her son's neck, bidding him welcome forty times over. She welcomed Thor also when she found out who he was; but she sent away the wicked old grandmother, that she might not hear, for Thor's name was not dear to the race of giants, to so many of whom he had brought dole and death.

"Why have you come, dear son, after so many years?" she cried. "I know that some great undertaking calls you and this noble fellow to your father's hall. Danger and death wait here for such as you and he; and only some quest with glory for its reward could have brought you to such risks. Tell me your secret, Tyr, and I will not betray it."

Then they told her how that they had come to carry away the giant kettle; and Tyr's mother promised that she would help them all she could. But she warned them that it would be dangerous indeed, for that Hymir had been in a terrible temper for many days, and that the very sight of a stranger made him wild with rage. Hastily she gave them meat and drink, for they were nearly famished after their long journey; and then she looked around to see where she should hide them against Hymir's return, who was now away at the hunt.

"Aha!" she cried. "The very thing! You shall hide in the great kettle itself; and if you escape Hymir's terrible eye, it may hap that you will find a way to make off with your hiding-place, which is what you want." So the kind creature helped them to climb into the great kettle where it hung from one of the rafters in a row with seven others; but this one was the biggest and the strongest of them all.

Hardly had they snuggled down out of sight when Tyr's mother began to tremble. "Hist!" she cried. "I hear him coming. Keep as still as ever you can, O Tyr and Thor!" The floor also began to tremble, and the eight kettles to clatter against one another, as Hymir's giant footsteps approached the house. Outside they could hear the icebergs shaking with a sound like thunder; indeed, the whole earth quivered as if with fear when the terrible giant Hymir strode home from the hunt. He came into the hall puffing and blowing, and immediately the air of the room grew chilly; for his beard was hung with icicles and his face was frosted hard, while his breath was a winter wind, – a freezing blast.

"Ho! wife," he growled, "what news, what news? For I see by the footprints in the snow outside that you have had visitors today."

Then indeed the poor woman trembled; but she tried not to look frightened as she answered, "Yes, you have a guest, O Hymir! – a guest whom you have long wished to see. Your son Tyr has returned to visit his father's hall."

"Humph!" growled Hymir, with a terrible frown. "Whom has he brought here with him, the rascal? There are prints of two persons' feet in the snow. Come, wife, tell me all; for I shall soon find out the truth, whether or no."

"He has brought a friend of his, – a dear friend, O Hymir!" faltered the mother. "Surely, our son's friends are welcome when he brings them to this our home, after so long an absence."

But Hymir howled with rage at the word 'friend.' "Where are they hidden?" he cried. "Friend, indeed! It is one of those bloody fellows from Asgard, I know, – one of those giant-killers whom my good mother taught me to hate with all my might. Let me get at him! Tell me instantly where he is hidden, or I will pull down the hall about your ears!"

Now when the wicked old giant spoke like this, his wife knew that he must be obeyed. Still she tried to put off the fateful moment of the discovery. "They are standing over there behind that pillar," she said. Instantly Hymir glared at the pillar towards which she pointed, and at his frosty glance – snick-snack! – the marble pillar cracked in two, and down crashed the great roof-beam which held the eight kettles. Smash! went the kettles; and there they lay shivered into little pieces at Hymir's feet, – all except one, the largest of them all, and that was the kettle in which Thor and Tyr lay hidden, scarcely daring to breathe lest the giant should guess where they were. Tyr's mother screamed when she saw the big kettle fall with the others: but when she found that this one, alone of them all, lay on its side unbroken, because it was so tough and strong, she held her breath to see what would happen next.

And what happened was this: out stepped Thor and Tyr, and making low bows to Hymir, they stood side by side, smiling and looking as unconcerned as if they really enjoyed all this hubbub; and I dare say that they did indeed, being Tyr the bold and Thor the thunderer, who had been in Giant Land many times ere this.

Hymir gave scarcely a glance at his son, but he eyed Thor with a frown of hatred and suspicion, for he knew that this was one of Father Odin's brave family, though he could not tell which one. However, he thought best to be civil, now that Thor was actually before him. So with gruff politeness he invited the two guests to supper.

Now Thor was a valiant fellow at the table as well as in war, as you remember; and at sight of the good things on the board his eyes sparkled. Three roast oxen there were upon the giant's table, and Thor fell to with a will and finished two of them himself! You should have seen the giant stare.

"Truly, friend, you have a goodly appetite," he said. "You have eaten all the meat that I have in my larder; and if you dine with us tomorrow, I must insist that you catch your own dinner of fish. I cannot undertake to provide food for such an appetite!"

Now this was not hospitable of Hymir, but Thor did not mind: "I like well to fish, good Hymir," he laughed; "and when you fare forth with your boat in the morning, I will go with you and see what I can find for my dinner at the bottom of the sea."

When the morning came, the giant made ready for the fishing, and Thor rose early to go with him.

"Ho, Hymir," exclaimed Thor, "have you bait enough for us both?"

Hymir answered gruffly, "You must dig your own bait when you go fishing with me. I have no time to waste on you, sirrah."

Then Thor looked about to see what he could use for bait; and presently he spied a herd of Hymir's oxen feeding in the meadow. "Aha! just the thing!" he cried; and seizing the hugest ox of all, he trotted down to the shore with it under his arm, as easily as you would carry a handful of clams for bait. When Hymir saw this, he was very angry. He pushed the boat off from shore and began to row away as fast as he could, so that Thor might not have a chance to come aboard. But Thor made one long step and planted himself snugly in the stern of the boat.

"No, no, brother Hymir," he said, laughing. "You invited me to go fishing, and a-fishing I will go; for I have my bait, and my hope is high that great luck I shall see this day." So he took an oar and rowed mightily in the stern, while Hymir the giant rowed mightily at the prow; and no one ever saw boat skip over the water so fast as this one did on the day when these two big fellows went fishing together.

Far and fast they rowed, until they came to a spot where Hymir cried, "Hold! Let us anchor here and fish; this is the place where I have best fortune."

"And what sort of little fish do you catch here, O Hymir?" asked Thor.

"Whales!" answered the giant proudly. "I fish for nothing smaller than whales."

"Pooh!" cried Thor. "Who would fish for such small fry! Whales, indeed; let us row out further, where we can find something really worth catching," and he began to pull even faster than before.

"Stop! stop!" roared the giant. "You do not know what you are doing. These are the haunts of the dreadful Midgard serpent, and it is not safe to fish in these waters."

"Oho! The Midgard serpent!" said Thor, delighted. "That is the very fish I am after. Let us drop in our lines here."

Thor baited his great hook with the whole head of the ox which he had brought, and cast his line, big round as a man's arm, over the side of the boat. Hymir also cast his line, for he did not wish Thor to think him a coward; but his hand trembled as he waited for a bite, and he glanced down into the blue depths with eyes rounded as big as dinner-plates through fear of the horrible creature who lived down below those waves.

"Look! You have a bite!" cried Thor, so suddenly that Hymir started and nearly tumbled out of the boat. Hand over hand he pulled in his line, and lo! he had caught two whales – two great flopping whales – on his one hook! That was a catch indeed.

Hymir smiled proudly, forgetting his fear as he said, "How is that, my friend? Let us see you beat this catch in your morning's fishing."

Lo, just at that moment Thor also had a bite – such a bite! The boat rocked to and fro, and seemed ready to capsize every minute. Then the waves began to roll high and to be lashed into foam for yards and yards about the boat, as if some huge creature were struggling hard below the water.

"I have him!" shouted Thor; "I have the old serpent, the brother of the Fenris wolf! Pull, pull, monster! But you shall not escape me now!"

Sure enough, the Midgard serpent had Thor's hook fixed in his jaw, and struggle as he might, there was no freeing himself from the line; for the harder he pulled the stronger grew Thor. In his Aesir-might Thor waxed so huge and so forceful that his legs went straight through the bottom of the boat and his feet stood on the bottom of the sea. With firm bottom as a brace for his strength, Thor pulled and pulled, and at last up came the head of the Midgard serpent, up to the side of the boat, where it thrust out of the water mountain high, dreadful to behold; his monstrous red eyes were rolling fiercely, his nostrils spouted fire, and from his terrible sharp teeth dripped poison, that sizzled as it fell into the sea. Angrily they glared at each other, Thor and the serpent, while the water streamed into the boat, and the giant turned pale with fear at the danger threatening him on all sides.

Thor seized his hammer, preparing to smite the creature's head; but even as he swung Miolnir high for the fatal blow, Hymir cut the fish-line with his knife, and down into the depths of ocean sank the Midgard serpent amid a whirlpool of eddies. But the hammer had sped from Thor's iron fingers. It crushed the serpent's head as he sank downward to his lair on the sandy bottom; it crushed, but did not kill him, thanks to the giant's treachery. Terrible was the disturbance it caused beneath the waves. It burst the rocks and made the caverns of the ocean shiver into bits. It wrecked the coral groves and tore loose the draperies of sea-weed. The fishes scurried about in every direction, and the sea-monsters wildly sought new places to hide themselves when they found their homes destroyed. The sea itself was stirred to its lowest depths, and the waves ran trembling into one another's arms. The earth, too, shrank and shivered. Hymir, cowering low in the boat, was glad of one thing, which was that the terrible Midgard serpent had vanished out of sight. And that was the last that was ever seen of him, though he still lived, wounded and sore from the shock of Thor's hammer.

Now it was time to return home. Silently and sulkily the giant swam back to land; Thor, bearing the boat upon his shoulders, filled with water and weighted as it was with the great whales which Hymir had caught, waded ashore, and brought his burden to the giant's hall. Here Hymir met him crossly enough, for he was ashamed of the whole morning's work, in which Thor had appeared so much more of a hero than he. Indeed, he was tired of even pretending hospitality towards this unwelcome guest, and was resolved to be rid of him; but first he would put Thor to shame.

"You are a strong fellow," he said, "good at the oar and at the fishing; most wondrously good at the hammer, by which I know that you are Thor. But there is one thing which you cannot do, I warrant, – you cannot break this little cup of mine, hard though you may try."

"That I shall see for myself," answered Thor; and he took the cup in his hand. Now this was a magic cup, and there was but one way of breaking it, but one thing hard enough to shatter its mightiness. Thor threw it with all his force against a stone of the flooring; but instead of breaking the cup, the stone itself was cracked into splinters. Then Thor grew angry, for the giant and all his servants were laughing as if this were the greatest joke ever played.

"Ho, ho! Try again, Thor!" cried Hymir, nearly bursting with delight; for he thought that now he should prove how much mightier he was than the visitor from Asgard. Thor clutched the cup more firmly and hurled it against one of the iron pillars of the hall; but like a rubber ball the magic cup merely bounded back straight into Hymir's hand. At this second failure the giants were full of merriment and danced about, making all manner of fun at the expense of Thor. You can fancy how well Thor the mighty enjoyed this! His brow grew black, and the glance of his eye was terrible. He knew there was some magic in the trick, but he knew not how to meet it. Just then he felt the soft touch of a woman's hand upon his arm, and the voice of Tyr's mother whispered in his ear:

"Cast the cup against Hymir's own forehead, which is the hardest substance in the world." No one except Thor heard the woman say these words, for all the giant folk were doubled up with mirth over their famous joke. But Thor dropped upon one knee, and seizing the cup fiercely, whirled it about his head, then dashed it with all his might straight at Hymir's forehead. Smash! Crash! What had happened? Thor looked eagerly to see. There stood the giant, looking surprised and a little dazed; but his forehead showed not even a scratch, while the strong cup was shivered into little pieces.

"Well done!" exclaimed Hymir hastily, when he had recovered a little from his surprise. But he was mortified at Thor's success, and set about to think up a new task to try his strength. "That was very well," he remarked patronizingly; "now you must perform a harder task. Let us see you carry the mead kettle out of the hall. Do that, my fine fellow, and I shall say you are strong indeed."

The mead kettle! The very thing Thor had come to get! He glanced at Tyr; he shot a look at Tyr's mother; and both of them caught the sparkle, which was very like a wink. To himself Thor muttered, "I must not fail in this! I must not, will not fail!"

"First let me try," cried Tyr; for he wanted to give Thor time for a resting-spell. Twice Tyr the mighty strained at the great kettle, but he could not so much as stir one leg of it from the floor where it rested. He tugged and heaved in vain, growing red in the face, till his mother begged him to give over, for it was quite useless.

Then Thor stepped forth upon the floor. He grasped the rim of the kettle, and stamped his feet through the stone of the flooring as he braced himself to lift. One, two, three! Thor straightened himself, and up swung the giant kettle to his head, while the iron handle clattered about his feet. It was a mighty burden, and Thor staggered as he started for the door; but Tyr was close beside him, and they had covered long leagues of ground on their way home before the astonished giants had recovered sufficiently to follow them. When Thor and Tyr looked back, however, they saw a vast crowd of horrible giants, some of them with a hundred heads, swarming out of the caverns in Hymir's land, howling and prowling upon their track.

"You must stop them, Thor, or they will never let us get away with their precious kettle, – they take such long strides!" cried Tyr. So Thor set down the kettle, and from his pocket drew out Miolnir, his wondrous hammer. Terribly it flashed in the air as he swung it over his head; then forth it flew towards Jotunheim; and before it returned to Thor's hand it had crushed all the heads of those many-headed giants, Hymir's ugly mother and Hymir himself among them. The only one who escaped was the good and beautiful mother of Tyr. And you may be sure she lived happily ever after in the palace which Hymir and his wicked old mother had formerly made so wretched a home for her.

Now Tyr and Thor had the giant kettle which they had gone so far and had met so many dangers to obtain. They took it to Œgir's sea-palace, where the banquet was still going on, and where the Aesir were still waiting patiently for their mead; for time does not go so fast below the quiet waves as on shore. Now that King Œgir had the great kettle, he could brew all the mead they needed. So every one thanked Tyr and congratulated Thor upon the success of their adventure.

"I was sure that Thor would bring the kettle," said fair Sif, smiling upon her brave husband.

"What Thor sets out to do, that he always accomplishes," said Father Odin gravely. And that was praise enough for any one.

Thor's Visit to the Giants

NOWADAYS, since their journey to get the stolen hammer, Thor and Loki were good friends, for Loki seemed to have turned over a new leaf and to be a very decent sort of fellow; but really he was the same sly rascal at heart, only biding his time for mischief. However, in this tale he behaves well enough.

It was a long time since Thor had slain any giants, and he was growing restless for an adventure. "Come, Loki," he said one day, "let us fare forth to Giant Land and see what news there is among the Big Folk."

Loki laughed, saying, "Let us go, Thor. I know I am safe with you;" which was a piece of flattery that happened to be true.

So they mounted the goat chariot as they had done so many times before and rumbled away out of Asgard. All day they rode; and when evening came they stopped at a little house on the edge of a forest, where lived a poor peasant with his wife, his son, and daughter.

"May we rest here for the night, friend?" asked Thor; and noting their poverty, he added, "We bring our own supper, and ask but a bed to sleep in." So the peasant was glad to have them stay. Then Thor, who knew what he was about, killed and cooked his two goats, and invited the family of peasants to sup with him and Loki; but when the meal was ended, he bade them carefully save all the bones and throw them into the goatskins which he had laid beside the hearth. Then Thor and Loki lay down to sleep.

In the morning, very early, before the rest were awake, Thor rose, and taking his hammer, Miolnir, went into the kitchen, where were the remains of his faithful goats. Now the magic hammer was skillful, not only to slay, but to restore, when Thor's hand wielded it. He touched with it the two heaps of skin and bones, and lo! up sprang the goats, alive and well, and as good as new. No, not quite as good as new. What was this? Thor roared with anger, for one of the goats was lame in one of his legs, and limped sorely. "Some one has meddled with the bones!" he cried. "Who has touched the bones that I bade be kept so carefully?"

Thialfi, the peasant's son, had broken one of the thigh-bones in order to get at the sweet marrow, and this Thor soon discovered by the lad's guilty face; then Thor was angry indeed. His knuckles grew white as he clenched the handle of Miolnir, ready to hurl it and destroy the whole unlucky house and family; but the peasant and the other three fell upon their knees, trembling with fear, and begged him to spare them. They offered him all that they owned, – they offered even to become his slaves, – if he would but spare their wretched lives.

They looked so miserable that Thor was sorry for them, and resolved at last to punish them only by taking away Thialfi, the son, and Roskva, the daughter, thenceforth to be his servants. And this was not so bad a bargain for Thor, for Thialfi was the swiftest of foot of any man in the whole world.

So he left the goats behind, and fared forth with his three attendants straight towards the east and Jotunheim. Thialfi carried Thor's wallet with their scanty store of food. They crossed the sea and came at last to a great forest, through which they tramped all day, until once more it was night; and now they must find a place in which all could sleep safely until morning. They wandered about here and there, looking for some sign of a dwelling, and at last they came to a big, queer-shaped house. Very queer indeed it was; for the door at one end was as broad as the house itself! They entered, and lay down to sleep; but at midnight Thor was wakened by a terrible noise. The ground shook under them like an earthquake, and the house trembled as if it would fall to pieces. Thor arose and called to his companions that there was danger about, and that they must be on guard. Groping in the dark, they found a long, narrow chamber on the right, where Loki and the two peasants hid trembling, while Thor guarded the doorway, hammer in hand. All night long the terrible noises continued, and Thor's attendants were frightened almost to death; but early in the morning Thor stole forth to find out what it all meant. And lo! close at hand in the forest lay an enormous giant, sound asleep and snoring loudly. Then Thor understood whence all their night's terror had proceeded, for the giant was so huge that his snoring shook even the trees of the forest, and made the mountains tremble. So much the better! Here at last was a giant for Thor to tackle. He buckled his belt of power more tightly to increase his strength, and laid hold of Miolnir to hurl it at the giant's forehead; but just at that moment the giant waked, rose slowly to his feet, and stood staring mildly at Thor. He did not seem a fierce giant, so Thor did not kill him at once. "Who are you?" asked Thor sturdily.

"I am the giant Skrymir, little fellow," answered the stranger, "and well I know who you are, Thor of Asgard. But what have you been doing with my glove?"

Then the giant stooped and picked up – what do you think? – the queer house in which Thor and his three companions had spent the night! Loki and the two others had run out of their chamber in affright when they felt it lifted; and their chamber was the thumb of the giant's glove. That was a giant indeed, and Thor felt sure that they must be well upon their way to Giant Land.

When Skrymir learned where they were going, he asked if he might not wend with them, and Thor said that he was willing. Now Skrymir untied his wallet and sat down under a tree to eat his breakfast, while Thor and his party chose another place, not far away, for their picnic. When all had finished, the giant said, "Let us put our provisions together in one bag, my friends, and I will carry it for you." This seemed fair enough, for Thor had so little food left that he was not afraid to risk losing it; so he agreed, and Skrymir tied all the provisions in his bag and strode on before them with enormous strides, so fast that even Thialfi could scarcely keep up with him.

The day passed, and late in the evening Skrymir halted under a great oak-tree, saying, "Let us rest here. I must have a nap, and you must have your dinner. Here is the wallet, – open it and help yourselves." Then he lay down on the moss, and was soon snoring lustily.

Thor tried to open the wallet, in vain; he could not loosen a single knot of the huge thongs that fastened it. He strained and tugged, growing angrier and redder after every useless attempt. This was too much; the giant was making him appear absurd before his servants. He seized his hammer, and bracing his feet with all his might, struck Skrymir a blow on his head. Skrymir stirred lazily, yawned, opened one eye, and asked whether a leaf had fallen on his forehead, and whether his companions had dined yet. Thor bit his lip with vexation, but he answered that they were ready for bed; so he and his three followers retired to rest under another oak.

But Thor did not sleep that night. He lay thinking how he had been put to shame, and how Loki had snickered at the sight of Thor's vain struggles with the giant's wallet, and he resolved that it should not happen again. At about midnight, once more he heard the giant's snore resounding like thunder through the forest. Thor arose, clenching Miolnir tight, and stole over to the tree where Skrymir slept; then with all his might he hurled the hammer and struck the giant on the crown of his head, so hard that the hammer sank deep into his skull. At this the giant awoke with a start, exclaiming, "What is that? Did an acorn fall on my head? What are you doing there, Thor?"

Thor stepped back quickly, answering that he had waked up, but that it was only midnight, so they might all sleep some hours longer. "If I can only give him one more blow before morning," he thought, "he will never see daylight again." So he lay watching until Skrymir had fallen asleep once more, which was near daybreak; then Thor arose as before, and going very softly to the giant's side, smote him on the temple so sore that the hammer sank into his skull up to the very handle. "Surely, he is killed now," thought Thor.

But Skrymir only raised himself on his elbow, stroked his chin, and said, "There are birds above me in the tree. Methinks that just now a feather fell upon my head. What, Thor! are you awake? I am afraid you slept but poorly this night. Come, now, it is high time to rise and make ready for the day. You are not far from our giant city, – Utgard we call it. Aha! I have heard you whispering together. You think that I am big; but you will see fellows taller still when you come to Utgard. And now I have a piece of advice to give you. Do not pride yourselves overmuch upon your importance. The followers of Utgard's king think little of such manikins as you, and will not bear any nonsense, I assure you. Be advised; return homeward before it is too late. If you will go on, however, your way lies there to the eastward. Yonder is my path, over the mountains to the north."

So saying, Skrymir hoisted his wallet upon his shoulders, and turning back upon the path that led into the forest, left them staring after him and hoping that they might never see his big bulk again.

Thor and his companions journeyed on until noon, when they saw in the distance a great city, on a lofty plain. As they came nearer, they found the buildings so high that the travelers had to bend back their necks in order to see the tops. "This must be Utgard, the giant city," said Thor. And Utgard indeed it was. At the entrance was a great barred gate, locked so that no one might enter. It was useless to try to force a passage in; even Thor's great strength could not move it on its hinges. But it was a giant gate, and the bars were made to keep out other giants, with no thought of folk so small as these who now were bent upon finding entrance by one way or another. It was not dignified, and noble Thor disliked the idea. Yet it was their only way; so one by one they squeezed and wriggled between the bars, until they stood in a row inside. In front of them was a wonderful great hall with the door wide open. Thor and the three entered, and found themselves in the midst of a company of giants, the very hugest of their kind. At the end of the hall sat the king upon an enormous throne. Thor, who had been in giant companies ere now, went straight up to the throne and greeted the king with civil words. But the giant merely glanced at him with a disagreeable smile, and said:

"It is wearying to ask travelers about their journey. Such little fellows as you four can scarcely have had any adventures worth mentioning. Stay, now! Do I guess aright? Is this manikin Thor of Asgard, or no? Ah, no! I have heard of Thor's might. You cannot really be he, unless you are taller than you seem, and stronger too. Let us see what feats you and your companions can perform to amuse us. No one is allowed here who cannot excel others in some way or another. What can you do best?"

At this word, Loki, who had entered last, spoke up readily: "There is one thing that I can do, – I can eat faster than any man." For Loki was famished with hunger, and thought he saw a way to win a good meal.

Then the king answered, "Truly, that is a noble accomplishment of yours, if you can prove your words true. Let us make the test." So he called forth from among his men Logi, – whose name means "fire," – and bade him match his powers with the stranger.

Now a trough full of meat was set upon the floor, with Loki at one end of it and the giant Logi at the other. Each began to gobble the meat as fast as he could, and it was not a pretty sight to see them. Midway in the trough they met, and at first it would seem as if neither had beaten the other. Loki had indeed done wondrous well in eating the meat from the bones so fast; but Logi, the giant, had in the same time eaten not only meat but bones also, and had swallowed his half of the trough into the bargain. Loki was vanquished at his own game, and retired looking much ashamed and disgusted.

The king then pointed at Thialfi, and asked what that young man could best do. Thialfi answered that of all men he was the swiftest runner, and that he was not afraid to race with any one whom the king might select.

"That is a goodly craft," said the king, smiling; "but you must be a swift runner indeed if you can win a race from my Hugi. Let us go to the racing-ground."

They followed him out to the plain where Hugi, whose name means 'thought,' was ready to race with young Thialfi. In the first run Hugi came in so far ahead that when he reached the goal he turned about and went back to meet Thialfi. "You must do better than that, Thialfi, if you hope to win," said the king, laughing, "though I must allow that no one ever before came here who could run so fast as you."

They ran a second race; and this time when Hugi reached the goal there was a long bow-shot between him and Thialfi.

"You are truly a good runner," exclaimed the king. "I doubt not that no man can race like you; but you cannot win from my giant lad, I think. The last time shall show." Then they ran for the third time, and Thialfi put forth all his strength, speeding like the wind; but all his skill was in vain. Hardly had he reached the middle of the course when he heard the shouts of the giants announcing that Hugi had won the goal. Thialfi, too, was beaten at his own game, and he withdrew, as Loki had done, shamefaced and sulky.

There remained now only Thor to redeem the honor of his party, for Roskva the maiden was useless here. Thor had watched the result of these trials with surprise and anger, though he knew it was no fault of Loki or of Thialfi that they had been worsted by the giants. And Thor was resolved to better even his own former great deeds. The king called to Thor, and asked him what he thought he could best do to prove himself as mighty as the stories told of him. Thor answered that he would undertake to drink more mead than any one of the king's men. At this proposal the king laughed aloud, as if it were a giant joke. He summoned his cup-bearer to fetch his horn of punishment, out of which the giants were wont to drink in turn. And when they returned to the hall, the great vessel was brought to the king.

"When any one empties this horn at one draught, we call him a famous drinker," said the king. "Some of my men empty it in two trials; but no one is so poor a manikin that he cannot empty it in three. Take the horn, Thor, and see what you can do with it."

Now Thor was very thirsty, so he seized the horn eagerly. It did not seem to him so very large, for he had drunk from other mighty vessels ere now. But indeed, it was deep. He raised it to his lips and took a long pull, saying to himself, "There! I have emptied it already, I know." Yet when he set the horn down to see how well he had done, he found that he seemed scarcely to have drained a drop; the horn was brimming as before. The king chuckled.

"Well, you have drunk but little," he said. "I would never have believed that famous Thor would lower the horn so soon. But doubtless you will finish all at a second draught."

Instead of answering, Thor raised the horn once more to his lips, resolved to do better than before. But for some reason the tip of the horn seemed hard to raise, and when he set the vessel down again his heart sank, for he feared that he had drunk even less than at his first trial. Yet he had really done better, for now it was easy to carry the horn without spilling. The king smiled grimly. "How now, Thor!" he cried. "You have left too much for your third trial. I fear you will never be able to empty the little horn in three draughts, as the least of my men can do. Ho, ho! You will not be thought so great a hero here as the folk deem you in Asgard, if you cannot play some other game more skillfully than you do this one."

At this speech Thor grew very angry. He raised the horn to his mouth and drank lustily, as long as he was able. But when he looked into the horn, he found that some drops still remained. He had not been able to empty it in three draughts. Angrily he flung down the horn, and said that he would have no more of it.

"Ah, Master Thor," taunted the king, "it is now plain that you are not so mighty as we thought you. Are you inclined to try some other feats? For indeed, you are easily beaten at this one."

"I will try whatever you like," said Thor; "but your horn is a wondrous one, and among the Aesir such a draught as mine would be called far from little. Come, now, – what game do you next propose, O King?"

The king thought a moment, then answered carelessly, "There is a little game with which my youngsters amuse themselves, though it is so simple as to be almost childish. It is merely the exercise of lifting my cat from the ground. I should never have dared suggest such a feat as this to you, Thor of Asgard, had I not seen that great tasks are beyond your skill. It may be that you will find this hard enough." So he spoke, smiling slyly, and at that moment there came stalking into the hall a monstrous gray cat, with eyes of yellow fire.

"Ho! Is this the creature I am to lift?" queried Thor. And when they said that it was, he seized the cat around its gray, huge body and tugged with all his might to lift it from the floor. Then the wretched cat, lengthening and lengthening, arched its back like the span of a bridge; and though Thor tugged and heaved his best, he could manage to lift but one of its huge feet off the floor. The other three remained as firmly planted as iron pillars.

"Oho, oho!" laughed the king, delighted at this sight. "It is just as I thought it would be. Poor little Thor! My cat is too big for him."

"Little I may seem in this land of monsters," cried Thor wrathfully, "but now let him who dares come hither and try a hug with me."

"Nay, little Thor," said the king, seeking to make him yet more angry, "there is not one of my men who would wrestle with you. Why, they would call it child's play, my little fellow. But, for the joke of it, call in my old foster-mother, Elli. She has wrestled with and worsted many a man who seemed no weaker than you, O Thor. She shall try a fall with you."

Now in came the old crone, Elli, whose very name meant 'age.' She was wrinkled and gray, and her back was bent nearly double with the weight of the years which she carried, but she chuckled when she saw Thor standing with bared arm in the middle of the floor. "Come and be thrown, dearie," she cried in her cracked voice, grinning horribly.

"I will not wrestle with a woman!" exclaimed Thor, eyeing her with pity and disgust, for she was an ugly creature to behold. But the old woman taunted him to his face and the giants clapped their hands, howling that he was "afraid." So there was no way but that Thor must grapple with the hag.

The game began. Thor rushed at the old woman and gripped her tightly in his iron arms, thinking that as soon as she screamed with the pain of his mighty hug, he would give over. But the crone seemed not to mind it at all. Indeed, the more he crushed her old ribs together the firmer and stronger she stood. Now in her turn the witch attempted to trip up Thor's heels, and it was wonderful to see her power and agility. Thor soon began to totter, great Thor, in the hands of a poor old woman! He struggled hard, he braced himself, he turned and twisted. It was no use; the old woman's arms were as strong as knotted oak. In a few moments Thor sank upon one knee, and that was a sign that he was beaten. The king signaled for them to stop. "You need wrestle no more, Thor," he said, with a curl to his lip, "we see what sort of fellow you are. I thought that old Elli would have no difficulty in bringing to his knees him who could not lift my cat. But come, now, night is almost here. We will think no more of contests. You and your companions shall sup with us as welcome guests and bide here till the morrow."

Now as soon as the king had pleased himself in proving how small and weak were these strangers who had come to the giant city, he became very gracious and kind. But you can fancy whether or no Thor and the others had a good appetite for the banquet where all the giants ate so merrily. You can fancy whether or no they were happy when they went to bed after the day of defeats, and you can guess what sweet dreams they had.

The next morning at daybreak the four guests arose and made ready to steal back to Asgard without attracting any more attention. For this adventure alone of all those in which Thor had taken part had been a disgraceful failure. Silently and with bowed heads they were slipping away from the hall when the king himself came to them and begged them to stay.

"You shall not leave Utgard without breakfast," he said kindly, "nor would I have you depart feeling unfriendly to me."

Then he ordered a goodly breakfast for the travelers, with store of choicest dainties for them to eat and drink. When the four had broken fast, he escorted them to the city gate where they were to say farewell. But at the last moment he turned to Thor with a sly, strange smile and asked:

"Tell me now truly, brother Thor; what think you of your visit to the giant city? Do you feel as mighty a fellow as you did before you entered our gates, or are you satisfied that there are folk even sturdier than yourself?"

At this question Thor flushed scarlet, and the lightning flashed angrily in his eye. Briefly enough he answered that he must confess to small pride in his last adventure, for that his visit to the king had been full of shame to the hero of Asgard. "My name will become a joke among your people," quoth he. "You will call me Thor the puny little fellow, which vexes me more than anything; for I have not been wont to blush at my name."

Then the king looked at him frankly, pleased with the humble manner of Thor's speech. "Nay," he said slowly, "hang not your head so shamedly, brave Thor. You have not done so ill as you think. Listen, I have somewhat to tell you, now that you are outside Utgard, – which, if I live, you shall never enter again. Indeed, you should not have entered at all had I guessed what noble strength was really yours, – strength which very nearly brought me and my whole city to destruction."

To these words Thor and his companions listened with open-mouthed astonishment. What could the king mean, they wondered? The giant continued:

"By magic alone were you beaten, Thor. Of magic alone were my triumphs, – not real, but seeming to be so. Do you remember the giant Skrymir whom you found sleeping and snoring in the forest? That was I. I learned your errand and resolved to lower your pride. When you vainly strove to untie my wallet, you did not know that I had fastened it with invisible iron wire, in order that you might be baffled by the knots. Thrice you struck me with your hammer, – ah! what mighty blows were those! The least one would have killed me, had it fallen on my head as you deemed it did. In my hall is a rock with three square hollows in it, one of them deeper than the others. These are the dents of your wondrous hammer, my Thor. For, while you thought I slept, I slipped the rock under the hammer-strokes, and into this hard crust Miolnir bit. Ha, ha! It was a pretty jest."

Now Thor's brow was growing black at this tale of the giant's trickery, but at the same time he held up his head and seemed less ashamed of his weakness, knowing now that it had been no weakness, but lack of guile. He listened frowningly for the rest of the tale. The king went on:

"When you came to my city, still it was magic that worsted your party at every turn. Loki was certainly the hungriest fellow I ever saw, and his deeds at the trencher were marvelous to behold. But the Logi who ate with him was Fire, and easily enough fire can consume your meat, bones, and wood itself. Thialfi, my boy, you are a runner swift as the wind. Never before saw I such a race as yours. But the Hugi who ran with you was Thought, my thought. And who can keep pace with the speed of winged thought? Next, Thor, it was your turn to show your might. Bravely indeed you strove. My heart is sick with envy of your strength and skill. But they availed you naught against my magic. When you drank from the long horn, thinking you had done so ill, in truth you had performed a miracle, – never thought I to behold the like. You guessed not that the end of the horn was out in the ocean, which no one might drain dry. Yet, mighty one, the draughts you swallowed have lowered the tide upon the shore. Henceforth at certain times the sea will ebb; and this is by great Thor's drinking. The cat also which you almost lifted, – it was no cat, but the great Midgard serpent himself who encircles the whole world. He had barely length enough for his head and tail to touch in a circle about the sea. But you raised him so high that he almost touched heaven. How terrified we were when we saw you heave one of his mighty feet from the ground! For who could tell what horror might happen had you raised him bodily. Ah, and your wrestling with old Elli! That was the most marvelous act of all. You had nearly overthrown Age itself; yet there has never lived one, nor will such ever be found, whom Elli, old age, will not cast to earth at last. So you were beaten, Thor, but by a mere trick. Ha, ha! How angry you looked, – I shall never forget! But now we must part, and I think you see that it will be best for both of us that we should not meet again. As I have done once, so can I always protect my city by magic spells. Yes, should you come again to visit us, even better prepared than now, yet you could never do us serious harm. Yet the wear and tear upon the nerves of both of us is something not lightly forgotten."

He ceased, smiling pleasantly, but with a threatening look in his eye. Thor's wrath had been slowly rising during this tedious, grim speech, and he could control it no longer.

"Cheat and trickster!" he cried, "your wiles shall avail you nothing now that I know your true self. You have put me to shame, now my hammer shall shame you beyond all reckoning!" and he raised Miolnir to smite the giant deathfully. But at that moment the king faded before his very eyes. And when he turned to look for the giant city that he might destroy it, – as he had so many giant dwellings, – there was in the place where it had been but a broad, fair plain, with no sign of any palace, wall, or gate. Utgard had vanished. The king had kept one trick of magic for the last.

Then Thor and his three companions wended their way back to Asgard. But they were slower than usual about answering questions concerning their last adventure, their wondrous visit to the giant city. Truth to tell, magic or no magic, Thor and Loki had showed but a poor figure that day. For the first time in all their meeting with Thor the giants had not come off any the worse for the encounter. Perhaps it was a lesson that he sorely needed. I am afraid that he was rather inclined to think well of himself. But then, he had reason, had he not?

The Quest of the Hammer

ONE MORNING Thor the Thunderer awoke with a yawn, and stretching out his knotted arm, felt for his precious hammer, which he kept always under his pillow of clouds. But he started up with a roar of rage, so that all the palace trembled. The hammer was gone!

Now this was a very serious matter, for Thor was the protector of Asgard, and Miolnir, the magic hammer which the dwarf had made, was his mighty weapon, of which the enemies of the Aesir stood so much in dread that they dared not venture near. But if they should learn that Miolnir was gone, who could tell what danger might not threaten the palaces of heaven?

Thor darted his flashing eye into every corner of Cloud Land in search of the hammer. He called his fair wife, Sif of the golden hair, to aid in the search, and his two lovely daughters, Thrude and Lora. They hunted and they hunted; they turned Thrudheim upside down, and set the clouds to rolling wonderfully, as they peeped and pried behind and around and under each billowy mass. But Miolnir was not to be found. Certainly, some one had stolen it.

Thor's yellow beard quivered with rage, and his hair bristled on end like the golden rays of a star, while all his household trembled.

"It is Loki again!" he cried. "I am sure Loki is at the bottom of this mischief!" For since the time when Thor had captured Loki for the dwarf Brock and had given him over to have his bragging lips sewed up, Loki had looked at him with evil eyes; and Thor knew that the red rascal hated him most of all the gods.

But this time Thor was mistaken. It was not Loki who had stolen the hammer, – he was too great a coward for that. And though he meant, before the end, to be revenged upon Thor, he was waiting until a safe chance should come, when Thor himself might stumble into danger, and Loki need only to help the evil by a malicious word or two; and this chance came later, as you shall hear in another tale.

Meanwhile Loki was on his best behavior, trying to appear very kind and obliging; so when Thor came rumbling and roaring up to him, demanding, "What have you done with my hammer, you thief?" Loki looked surprised, but did not lose his temper nor answer rudely.

"Have you indeed missed your hammer, brother Thor?" he said, mumbling, for his mouth was still sore where Brock had sewed the stitches. "That is a pity; for if the giants hear of this, they will be coming to try their might against Asgard."

"Hush!" muttered Thor, grasping him by the shoulder with his iron fingers. "That is what I fear. But look you, Loki: I suspect your hand in the mischief. Come, confess."

Then Loki protested that he had nothing to do with so wicked a deed. "But," he added wheedlingly, "I think I can guess the thief; and because I love you, Thor, I will help you to find him."

"Humph!" growled Thor. "Much love you bear to me! However, you are a wise rascal, the nimblest wit of all the Aesir, and it is better to have you on my side than on the other, when giants are in the game. Tell me, then: who has robbed the Thunder-Lord of his bolt of power?"

Loki drew near and whispered in Thor's ear. "Look, how the storms rage and the winds howl in the world below! Some one is wielding your thunder-hammer all unskillfully. Can you not guess the thief? Who but Thrym, the mighty giant who has ever been your enemy and your imitator, and whose fingers have long itched to grasp the short handle of mighty Miolnir, that the world may name him Thunder-Lord instead of you. But look! What a tempest! The world will be shattered into fragments unless we soon get the hammer back."

Then Thor roared with rage. "I will seek this impudent Thrym!" he cried. "I will crush him into bits, and teach him to meddle with the weapon of the Aesir!"

"Softly, softly," said Loki, smiling maliciously. "He is a shrewd giant, and a mighty. Even you, great Thor, cannot go to him and pluck the hammer from his hand as one would slip the rattle from a baby's pink fist. Nay, you must use craft, Thor; and it is I who will teach you, if you will be patient."

Thor was a brave, blunt fellow, and he hated the ways of Loki, his lies and his deceit. He liked best the way of warriors, – the thundering charge, the flash of weapons, and the heavy blow; but without the hammer he could not fight the giants hand to hand. Loki's advice seemed wise, and he decided to leave the matter to the Red One.

Loki was now all eagerness, for he loved difficulties which would set his wit in play and bring other folk into danger. "Look, now," he said. "We must go to Freyia and borrow her falcon dress. But you must ask; for she loves me so little that she would scarce listen to me."

So first they made their way to Folkvang, the house of maidens, where Freyia dwelt, the loveliest of all in Asgard. She was fairer than fair, and sweeter than sweet, and the tears from her flower-eyes made the dew which blessed the earth-flowers night and morning. Of her Thor borrowed the magic dress of feathers in which Freyia was wont to clothe herself and flit like a great beautiful bird all about the world. She was willing enough to lend it to Thor when he told her that by its aid he hoped to win back the hammer which he had lost; for she well knew the danger threatening herself and all the Aesir until Miolnir should be found.

"Now will I fetch the hammer for you," said Loki. So he put on the falcon plumage, and, spreading his brown wings, flapped away up, up, over the world, down, down, across the great ocean which lies beyond all things that men know. And he came to the dark country where there was no sunshine nor spring, but it was always dreary winter; where mountains were piled up like blocks of ice, and where great caverns yawned hungrily in blackness. And this was Jotunheim, the land of the Frost Giants.

And lo! when Loki came thereto he found Thrym the Giant King sitting outside his palace cave, playing with his dogs and horses. The dogs were as big as elephants, and the horses were as big as houses, but Thrym himself was as huge as a mountain; and Loki trembled, but he tried to seem brave.

"Good-day, Loki," said Thrym, with the terrible voice of which he was so proud, for he fancied it was as loud as Thor's. "How fares it, feathered one, with your little brothers, the Aesir, in Asgard halls? And how dare you venture alone in this guise to Giant Land?"

"It is an ill day in Asgard," sighed Loki, keeping his eye warily upon the giant, "and a stormy one in the world of men. I heard the winds howling and the storms rushing on the earth as I passed by. Some mighty one has stolen the hammer of our Thor. Is it you, Thrym, greatest of all giants, – greater than Thor himself?"

This the crafty one said to flatter Thrym, for Loki well knew the weakness of those who love to be thought greater than they are.

Then Thrym bridled and swelled with pride, and tried to put on the majesty and awe of noble Thor; but he only succeeded in becoming an ugly, puffy monster.

"Well, yes," he admitted. "I have the hammer that belonged to your little Thor; and now how much of a lord is he?"

"Alack!" sighed Loki again, "weak enough he is without his magic weapon. But you, O Thrym, – surely your mightiness needs no such aid. Give me the hammer, that Asgard may no longer be shaken by Thor's grief for his precious toy."

But Thrym was not so easily to be flattered into parting with his stolen treasure. He grinned a dreadful grin, several yards in width, which his teeth barred like jagged boulders across the entrance to a mountain cavern.

"Miolnir the hammer is mine," he said, "and I am Thunder-Lord, mightiest of the mighty. I have hidden it where Thor can never find it, twelve leagues below the sea-caves, where Queen Ran lives with her daughters, the white-capped Waves. But listen, Loki. Go tell the Aesir that I will give back Thor's hammer. I will give it back upon one condition, – that they send Freyia the beautiful to be my wife."

"Freyia the beautiful!" Loki had to stifle a laugh. Fancy the Aesir giving their fairest flower to such an ugly fellow as this! But he only said politely, "Ah, yes; you demand our Freyia in exchange for the little hammer? It is a costly price, great Thrym. But I will be your friend in Asgard. If I have my way, you shall soon see the fairest bride in all the world knocking at your door. Farewell!"

So Loki whizzed back to Asgard on his falcon wings; and as he went he chuckled to think of the evils which were likely to happen because of his words with Thrym. First he gave the message to Thor, – not sparing of Thrym's insolence, to make Thor angry; and then he went to Freyia with the word for her, – not sparing of Thrym's ugliness, to make her shudder. The spiteful fellow!

Now you can imagine the horror that was in Asgard as the Aesir listened to Loki's words. "My hammer!" roared Thor. "The villain confesses that he has stolen my hammer, and boasts that he is Thunder-Lord! Gr-r-r!"

"The ugly giant!" wailed Freyia. "Must I be the bride of that hideous old monster, and live in his gloomy mountain prison all my life?"

"Yes; put on your bridal veil, sweet Freyia," said Loki maliciously, "and come with me to Jotunheim. Hang your famous starry necklace about your neck, and don your bravest robe; for in eight days there will be a wedding, and Thor's hammer is to pay."

Then Freyia fell to weeping. "I cannot go! I will not go!" she cried. "I will not leave the home of gladness and Father Odin's table to dwell in the land of horrors! Thor's hammer is mighty, but mightier the love of the kind Aesir for their little Freyia! Good Odin, dear brother Frey, speak for me! You will not make me go?"

The Aesir looked at her and thought how lonely and bare would Asgard be without her loveliness; for she was fairer than fair, and sweeter than sweet.

"She shall not go!" shouted Frey, putting his arms about his sister's neck.

"No, she shall not go!" cried all the Aesir with one voice.

"But my hammer," insisted Thor. "I must have Miolnir back again."

"And my word to Thrym," said Loki, "that must be made good."

"You are too generous with your words," said Father Odin sternly, for he knew his brother well. "Your word is not a gem of great price, for you have made it cheap."

Then spoke Heimdall, the sleepless watchman who sits on guard at the entrance to the rainbow bridge which leads to Asgard; and Heimdall was the wisest of the Aesir, for he could see into the future, and knew how things would come to pass. Through his golden teeth he spoke, for his teeth were all of gold.

"I have a plan," he said. "Let us dress Thor himself like a bride in Freyia's robes, and send him to Jotunheim to talk with Thrym and to win back his hammer."

But at this word Thor grew very angry. "What! dress me like a girl!" he roared. "I should never hear the last of it! The Aesir will mock me, and call me "maiden"! The giants, and even the puny dwarfs, will have a lasting jest upon me! I will not go! I will fight! I will die, if need be! But dressed as a woman I will not go!"

But Loki answered him with sharp words, for this was a scheme after his own heart. "What, Thor!" he said. "Would you lose your hammer and keep Asgard in danger for so small a whim? Look, now: if you go not, Thrym with his giants will come in a mighty army and drive us from Asgard; then he will indeed make Freyia his bride, and moreover he will have you for his slave under the power of his hammer. How like you this picture, brother of the thunder? Nay, Heimdall's plan is a good one, and I myself will help to carry it out."

Still Thor hesitated; but Freyia came and laid her white hand on his arm, and looked up into his scowling face pleadingly.

"To save me, Thor," she begged. And Thor said he would go.

Then there was great sport among the Aesir, while they dressed Thor like a beautiful maiden. Brunhilde and her sisters, the nine Valkyr, daughters of Odin, had the task in hand. How they laughed as they brushed and curled his yellow hair, and set upon it the wondrous headdress of silk and pearls! They let out seams, and they let down hems, and set on extra pieces, to make it larger, and so they hid his great limbs and knotted arms under Freyia's fairest robe of scarlet; but beneath it all he would wear his shirt of mail and his belt of power that gave him double strength. Freyia herself twisted about his neck her famous necklace of starry jewels, and Queen Frigga, his mother, hung at his girdle a jingling bunch of keys, such as was the custom for the bride to wear at Norse weddings. Last of all, that Thrym might not see Thor's fierce eyes and the yellow beard, that ill became a maiden, they threw over him a long veil of silver white which covered him to the feet. And there he stood, as stately and tall a bride as even a giant might wish to see; but on his hands he wore his iron gloves, and they ached for but one thing, – to grasp the handle of the stolen hammer.

"Ah, what a lovely maid it is!" chuckled Loki; "and how glad will Thrym be to see this Freyia come! Bride Thor, I will go with you as your handmaiden, for I would fain see the fun."

"Come, then," said Thor sulkily, for he was ill pleased, and wore his maiden robes with no good grace. "It is fitting that you go; for I like not these lies and maskings, and I may spoil the mummery without you at my elbow."

There was loud laughter above the clouds when Thor, all veiled and dainty seeming, drove away from Asgard to his wedding, with maid Loki by his side. Thor cracked his whip and chirruped fiercely to his twin goats with golden hoofs, for he wanted to escape the sounds of mirth that echoed from the rainbow bridge, where all the Aesir stood watching. Loki, sitting with his hands meekly folded like a girl, chuckled as he glanced up at Thor's angry face; but he said nothing, for he knew it was not good to joke too far with Thor, even when Miolnir was hidden twelve leagues below the sea in Ran's kingdom.

So off they dashed to Jotunheim, where Thrym was waiting and longing for his beautiful bride. Thor's goats thundered along above the sea and land and people far below, who looked up wondering as the noise rolled overhead. "Hear how the thunder rumbles!" they said. "Thor is on a long journey tonight." And a long journey it was, as the tired goats found before they reached the end.

Thrym heard the sound of their approach, for his ear was eager. "Hola!" he cried. "Some one is coming from Asgard, – only one of Odin's children could make a din so fearful. Hasten, men, and see if they are bringing Freyia to be my wife."

Then the lookout giant stepped down from the top of his mountain, and said that a chariot was bringing two maidens to the door.

"Run, giants, run!" shouted Thrym, in a fever at this news. "My bride is coming! Put silken cushions on the benches for a great banquet, and make the house beautiful for the fairest maid in all space! Bring in all my golden-horned cows and my coal-black oxen, that she may see how rich I am, and heap all my gold and jewels about to dazzle her sweet eyes! She shall find me richest of the rich; and when I have her, – fairest of the fair, – there will be no treasure that I lack, – not one!"

The chariot stopped at the gate, and out stepped the tall bride, hidden from head to foot, and her handmaiden muffled to the chin. "How afraid of catching cold they must be!" whispered the giant ladies, who were peering over one another's shoulders to catch a glimpse of the bride, just as the crowd outside the awning does at a wedding nowadays.

Thrym had sent six splendid servants to escort the maidens: these were the Metal Kings, who served him as lord of them all. There was the Gold King, all in cloth of gold, with fringes of yellow bullion, most glittering to see; and there was the Silver King, almost as gorgeous in a suit of spangled white; and side by side bowed the dark Kings of Iron and Lead, the one mighty in black, the other sullen in blue; and after them were the Copper King, gleaming ruddy and brave, and the Tin King, strutting in his trimmings of gaudy tinsel which looked nearly as well as silver but were more economical. And this fine troop of lackey kings most politely led Thor and Loki into the palace, and gave them of the best, for they never suspected who these seeming maidens really were.

And when evening came there was a wonderful banquet to celebrate the wedding. On a golden throne sat Thrym, uglier than ever in his finery of purple and gold. Beside him was the bride, of whose face no one had yet caught even a glimpse; and at Thrym's other hand stood Loki, the waiting-maid, for he wanted to be near to mend the mistakes which Thor might make.

Now the dishes at the feast were served in a huge way, as befitted the table of giants: great beeves roasted whole, on platters as wide across as a ship's deck; plum-puddings as fat as feather-beds, with plums as big as footballs; and a wedding cake like a snow-capped haymow. The giants ate enormously. But to Thor, because they thought him a dainty maiden, they served small bits of everything on a tiny gold dish. Now Thor's long journey had made him very hungry, and through his veil he whispered to Loki, "I shall starve, Loki! I cannot fare on these nibbles. I must eat a goodly meal as I do at home." And forthwith he helped himself to such morsels as might satisfy his hunger for a little time. You should have seen the giants stare at the meal which the dainty bride devoured!

For first under the silver veil disappeared by pieces a whole roast ox. Then Thor made eight mouthfuls of eight pink salmon, a dish of which he was very fond. And next he looked about and reached for a platter of cakes and sweetmeats that was set aside at one end of the table for the lady guests, and the bride ate them all. You can fancy how the damsels drew down their mouths and looked at one another when they saw their dessert disappear; and they whispered about the table, "Alack! if our future mistress is to sup like this day by day, there will be poor cheer for the rest of us!" And to crown it all, Thor was thirsty, as well he might be; and one after another he raised to his lips and emptied three great barrels of mead, the foamy drink of the giants. Then indeed Thrym was amazed, for Thor's giant appetite had beaten that of the giants themselves.

"Never before saw I a bride so hungry," he cried, "and never before one half so thirsty!"

But Loki, the waiting-maid, whispered to him softly, "The truth is, great Thrym, that my dear mistress was almost starved. For eight days Freyia has eaten nothing at all, so eager was she for Jotunheim."

Then Thrym was delighted, you may be sure. He forgave his hungry bride, and loved her with all his heart. He leaned forward to give her a kiss, raising a corner of her veil; but his hand dropped suddenly, and he started up in terror, for he had caught the angry flash of Thor's eye, which was glaring at him through the bridal veil. Thor was longing for his hammer.

"Why has Freyia so sharp a look?" Thrym cried. "It pierces like lightning and burns like fire."

But again the sly waiting-maid whispered timidly, "Oh, Thrym, be not amazed! The truth is, my poor mistress's eyes are red with wakefulness and bright with longing. For eight nights Freyia has not known a wink of sleep, so eager was she for Jotunheim."

Then again Thrym was doubly delighted, and he longed to call her his very own dear wife. "Bring in the wedding gift!" he cried. "Bring in Thor's hammer, Miolnir, and give it to Freyia, as I promised; for when I have kept my word she will be mine, – all mine!"

Then Thor's big heart laughed under his woman's dress, and his fierce eyes swept eagerly down the hall to meet the servant who was bringing in the hammer on a velvet cushion. Thor's fingers could hardly wait to clutch the stubby handle which they knew so well; but he sat quite still on the throne beside ugly old Thrym, with his hands meekly folded and his head bowed like a bashful bride.

The giant servant drew nearer, nearer, puffing and blowing, strong though he was, beneath the mighty weight. He was about to lay it at Thor's feet (for he thought it so heavy that no maiden could lift it or hold it in her lap), when suddenly Thor's heart swelled, and he gave a most unmaidenly shout of rage and triumph. With one swoop he grasped the hammer in his iron fingers; with the other arm he tore off the veil that hid his terrible face, and trampled it under foot; then he turned to the frightened king, who cowered beside him on the throne.

"Thief!" he cried. "Freyia sends you *this* as a wedding gift!" And he whirled the hammer about his head, then hurled it once, twice, thrice, as it rebounded to his hand; and in the first stroke, as of lightning, Thrym rolled dead from his throne; in the second stroke perished the whole giant household, – these ugly enemies of the Aesir; and in the third stroke the palace itself tumbled together and fell to the ground like a toppling play-house of blocks.

But Loki and Thor stood safely among the ruins, dressed in their tattered maiden robes, a quaint and curious sight; and Loki, full of mischief now as ever, burst out laughing.

"Oh, Thor! if you could see" – he began; but Thor held up his hammer and shook it gently as he said:

"Look now, Loki: it was an excellent joke, and so far you have done well, – after your crafty fashion, which likes me not. But now I have my hammer again, and the joke is done. From you, nor from another, I brook no laughter at my expense. Henceforth we will have no mention of this masquerade, nor of these rags which now I throw away. Do you hear, red laugher?"

And Loki heard, with a look of hate, and stifled his laughter as best he could; for it is not good to laugh at him who holds the hammer.

Not once after that was there mention in Asgard of the time when Thor dressed him as a girl and won his bridal gift from Thrym the giant.

But Miolnir was safe once more in Asgard, and you and I know how it came there; so some one must have told. I wonder if red Loki whispered the tale to some outsider, after all? Perhaps it may be so, for now he knew how best to make Thor angry; and from that day when Thor forbade his laughing, Loki hated him with the mean little hatred of a mean little soul.

Thor's Duel

IN THE DAYS THAT are past a wonderful race of horses pastured in the meadows of heaven, steeds more beautiful and more swift than any which the world knows today. There was Hrîmfaxi, the black, sleek horse who drew the chariot of Night across the sky and scattered the dew from his foaming bit. There was Glad, behind whose flying heels sped the swift chariot of Day. His mane was yellow with gold, and from it beamed light which made the whole world bright. Then there were the two shining horses of the sun, Arvakur the watchful, and Alsvith the rapid; and the nine fierce battle-chargers of the nine Valkyrs, who bore the bodies of fallen heroes from the field of fight to the blessedness of Valhalla. Each of the gods had his own glorious steed, with such pretty names as Gold-mane and Silver-top, Light-foot and Precious-stone; these galloped with their masters over clouds and through the blue air, blowing flame from their nostrils and glinting sparks from their fiery eyes. The Aesir would have been poor indeed without their faithful mounts, and few would be the stories to tell in which these noble creatures do not bear at least a part.

But best of all the horses of heaven was Sleipnir, the eight-legged steed of Father Odin, who because he was so well supplied with sturdy feet could gallop faster over land and sea than any horse which ever lived. Sleipnir was snow-white and beautiful to see, and Odin was very fond and proud of him, you may be sure. He loved to ride forth upon his good horse's back to meet whatever adventure might be upon the way, and sometimes they had wild times together.

One day Odin galloped off from Asgard upon Sleipnir straight towards Jotunheim and the Land of Giants, for it was long since All-Father had been to the cold country, and he wished to see how its mountains and ice-rivers looked. Now as he galloped along a wild road, he met a huge giant standing beside his giant steed.

"Who goes there?" cried the giant gruffly, blocking the way so that Odin could not pass. "You with the golden helmet, who are you, who ride so famously through air and water? For I have been watching you from this mountain-top. Truly, that is a fine horse which you bestride."

"There is no finer horse in all the world," boasted Odin. "Have you not heard of Sleipnir, the pride of Asgard? I will match him against any of your big, clumsy giant horses."

"Ho!" roared the giant angrily, "an excellent horse he is, your little Sleipnir. But I warrant he is no match for my Gullfaxi here. Come, let us try a race; and at its end I shall pay you for your insult to our horses of Jotunheim."

So saying, the giant, whose ugly name was Hrungnir, sprang upon his horse and spurred straight at Odin in the narrow way. Odin turned and galloped back towards Asgard with all his might; for not only must he prove his horse's speed, but he must save himself and Sleipnir from the anger of the giant, who was one of the fiercest and wickedest of all his fierce and wicked race.

How the eight slender legs of Sleipnir twinkled through the blue sky! How his nostrils quivered and shot forth fire and smoke! Like a flash of lightning he darted across the sky, and the giant horse rumbled and thumped along close behind like the thunder following the flash.

"Hi, hi!" yelled the giant. "After them, Gullfaxi! And when we have overtaken the two, we will crush their bones between us!"

"Speed, speed, my Sleipnir!" shouted Odin. "Speed, good horse, or you will never again feed in the dewy pastures of Asgard with the other horses. Speed, speed, and bring us safe within the gates!"

Well Sleipnir understood what his master said, and well he knew the way. Already the rainbow bridge was in sight, with Heimdall the watchman prepared to let them in. His sharp eyes had spied them afar, and had recognized the flash of Sleipnir's white body and of Odin's golden helmet. Gallop and thud! The twelve hoofs were upon the bridge, the giant horse close behind the other. At last Hrungnir knew where he was, and into what danger he was rushing. He pulled at the reins and tried to stop his great beast. But Gullfaxi was tearing along at too terrible a speed. He could not stop. Heimdall threw open the gates of Asgard, and in galloped Sleipnir with his precious burden, safe. Close upon them bolted in Gullfaxi, bearing his giant master, puffing and purple in the face from hard riding and anger. Cling-clang! Heimdall had shut and barred the gates, and there was the giant prisoned in the castle of his enemies.

Now the Aesir were courteous folk, unlike the giants, and they were not anxious to take advantage of a single enemy thus thrown into their power. They invited him to enter Valhalla with them, to rest and sup before the long journey of his return. Thor was not present, so they filled for the giant the great cups which Thor was wont to drain, for they were nearest to the giant size. But you remember that Thor was famous for his power to drink deep. Hrungnir's head was not so steady; Thor's draught was too much for him. He soon lost his wits, of which he had but few; and a witless giant is a most dreadful creature. He raged like a madman, and threatened to pick up Valhalla like a toy house and carry it home with him to Jotunheim. He said he would pull Asgard to pieces and slay all the gods except Freyia the fair and Sif, the golden-haired wife of Thor, whom he would carry off like little dolls for his toy house.

The Aesir knew not what to do, for Thor and his hammer were not there to protect them, and Asgard seemed in danger with this enemy within its very walls. Hrungnir called for more and more mead, which Freyia alone dared to bring and set before him. And the more he drank the fiercer he became. At last the Aesir could bear no longer his insults and his violence. Besides, they feared that there would be no more mead left for their banquets if this unwelcome visitor should keep Freyia pouring out for him Thor's mighty goblets. They bade Heimdall blow his horn and summon Thor; and this Heimdall did in a trice.

Now rumbling and thundering in his chariot of goats came Thor. He dashed into the hall, hammer in hand, and stared in amazement at the unwieldy guest whom he found there.

"A giant feasting in Asgard hall!" he roared. "This is a sight which I never saw before. Who gave the insolent fellow leave to sit in my place? And why does fair Freyia wait upon him as if he were some noble guest at a feast of the high gods? I will slay him at once!" and he raised the hammer to keep his word.

Thor's coming had sobered the giant somewhat, for he knew that this was no enemy to be trifled with. He looked at Thor sulkily and said: "I am Odin's guest. He invited me to this banquet, and therefore I am under his protection."

"You shall be sorry that you accepted the invitation," cried Thor, balancing his hammer and looking very fierce; for Sif had sobbed in his ear how the giant had threatened to carry her away.

Hrungnir now rose to his feet and faced Thor boldly, for the sound of Thor's gruff voice had restored his scattered wits. "I am here alone and without weapons," he said. "You would do ill to slay me now. It would be little like the noble Thor, of whom we hear tales, to do such a thing. The world will count you braver if you let me go and meet me later in single combat, when we shall both be fairly armed."

Thor dropped the hammer to his side. "Your words are true," he said, for he was a just and honorable fellow.

"I was foolish to leave my shield and stone club at home," went on the giant. "If I had my arms with me, we would fight at this moment. But I name you a coward if you slay me now, an unarmed enemy."

"Your words are just," quoth Thor again. "I have never before been challenged by any foe. I will meet you, Hrungnir, at your Stone City, midway between heaven and earth. And there we will fight a duel to see which of us is the better fellow."

Hrungnir departed for Stone City in Jotunheim; and great was the excitement of the other giants when they heard of the duel which one of their number was to fight with Thor, the deadliest enemy of their race.

"We must be sure that Hrungnir wins the victory!" they cried. "It will never do to have Asgard victorious in the first duel that we have fought with her champion. We will make a second hero to aid Hrungnir."

All the giants set to work with a will. They brought great buckets of moist clay, and heaping them up into a huge mound, moulded the mass with their giant hands as a sculptor does his image, until they had made a man of clay, an immense dummy, nine miles high and three miles wide. "Now we must make him live; we must put a heart into him!" they cried. But they could find no heart big enough until they thought of taking that of a mare, and that fitted nicely. A mare's heart is the most cowardly one that beats.

Hrungnir's heart was a three-cornered piece of hard stone. His head also was of stone, and likewise the great shield which he held before him when he stood outside of Stone City waiting for Thor to come to the duel. Over his shoulder he carried his club, and that also was of stone, the kind from which whetstones are made, hard and terrible. By his side stood the huge clay man, Mockuralfi, and they were a dreadful sight to see, these two vast bodies whom Thor must encounter.

But at the very first sight of Thor, who came thundering to the place with swift Thialfi his servant, the timid mare's heart in the man of clay throbbed with fear; he trembled so that his knees knocked together, and his nine miles of height rocked unsteadily.

Thialfi ran up to Hrungnir and began to mock him, saying, "You are careless, giant. I fear you do not know what a mighty enemy has come to fight you. You hold your shield in front of you; but that will serve you nothing. Thor has seen this. He has only to go down into the earth and he can attack you conveniently from beneath your very feet."

At this terrifying news Hrungnir hastened to throw his shield upon the ground and to stand upon it, so that he might be safe from Thor's under-stroke. He grasped his heavy club with both hands and waited. He had not long to wait. There came a blinding flash of lightning and a peal of crashing thunder. Thor had cast his hammer into space. Hrungnir raised his club with both hands and hurled it against the hammer which he saw flying towards him. The two mighty weapons met in the air with an earsplitting shock. Hard as was the stone of the giant's club, it was like glass against the power of Miolnir. The club was dashed into pieces; some fragments fell upon the earth; and these, they say, are the rocks from which whetstones are made unto this day. They are so hard that men use them to sharpen knives and axes and scythes. One splinter of the hard stone struck Thor himself in the forehead, with so fierce a blow that he fell forward upon the ground, and Thialfi feared that he was killed. But Miolnir, not even stopped in its course by meeting the giant's club, sped straight to Hrungnir and crushed his stony skull, so that he fell forward over Thor, and his foot lay on the fallen hero's neck. And that was the end of the giant whose head and heart were of stone.

Meanwhile Thialfi the swift had fought with the man of clay, and had found little trouble in toppling him to earth. For the mare's cowardly heart in his great body gave him little strength to meet Thor's faithful servant; and the trembling limbs of Mockuralfi soon yielded to Thialfi's hearty blows. He fell like an unsteady tower of blocks, and his brittle bulk shivered into a thousand fragments.

Thialfi ran to his master and tried to raise him. The giant's great foot still rested upon his neck, and all Thialfi's strength could not move it away. Swift as the wind he ran for the other Aesir, and when they heard that great Thor, their champion, had fallen and seemed like one dead, they came rushing to the spot in horror and confusion. Together they all attempted to raise Hrungnir's foot from Thor's neck that they might see whether their hero lived or no. But all their efforts were in vain. The foot was not to be lifted by Aesir-might.

At this moment a second hero appeared upon the scene. It was Magni, the son of Thor himself; Magni, who was but three days old, yet already in his babyhood he was almost as big as a giant and had nearly the strength of his father. This wonderful youngster came running to the place where his father lay surrounded by a group of sad-faced and despairing gods. When Magni saw what the matter was, he seized Hrungnir's enormous foot in both his hands, heaved his broad young shoulders, and in a moment Thor's neck was free of the weight which was crushing it.

Best of all, it proved that Thor was not dead, only stunned by the blow of the giant's club and by his fall. He stirred, sat up painfully, and looked around him at the group of eager friends. "Who lifted the weight from my neck?" he asked.

"It was I, father," answered Magni modestly. Thor clasped him in his arms and hugged him tight, beaming with pride and gratitude.

"Truly, you are a fine child!" he cried; "one to make glad your father's heart. Now as a reward for your first great deed you shall have a gift from me. The swift horse of Hrungnir shall be yours, – that same Gullfaxi who was the beginning of all this trouble. You shall ride Gullfaxi; only a giant steed is strong enough to bear the weight of such an infant prodigy as you, my Magni."

Now this word did not wholly please Father Odin, for he thought that a horse so excellent ought to belong to him. He took Thor aside and argued that but for him there would have been no duel, no horse to win. Thor answered simply:

"True, Father Odin, you began this trouble. But I have fought your battle, destroyed your enemy, and suffered great pain for you. Surely, I have won the horse fairly and may give it to whom I choose. My son, who has saved me, deserves a horse as good as any. Yet, as you have proved, even Gullfaxi is scarce a match for your Sleipnir. Verily, Father Odin, you should be content with the best." Odin said no more.

Now Thor went home to his cloud-palace in Thrudvang. And there he was healed of all his hurts except that which the splinter of stone had made in his forehead. For the stone was imbedded so fast that it could not be taken out, and Thor suffered sorely therefor. Sif, his yellow-haired wife, was in despair, knowing not what to do. At last she bethought her of the wise woman, Groa, who had skill in all manner of herbs and witch charms. Sif sent for Groa, who lived all alone and sad because her husband Orvandil had disappeared, she knew not whither. Groa came to Thor and, standing beside his bed while he slept, sang strange songs and gently waved her hands over him. Immediately the stone in his forehead began to loosen, and Thor opened his eyes.

"The stone is loosening, the stone is coming out!" he cried. "How can I reward you, gentle dame? Prithee, what is your name?"

"My name is Groa," answered the woman, weeping, "wife of Orvandil who is lost."

"Now, then, I can reward you, kind Groa!" cried Thor, "for I can bring you tidings of your husband. I met him in the cold country, in Jotunheim, the Land of Giants, which you know I sometimes visit for a bit of good hunting. It was by Elivagar's icy river that I met Orvandil, and there was no way for him to cross. So I put him in an iron basket and myself bore him over the flood. Br-r-r! But that is a cold land! His feet stuck out through the meshes of the basket, and when we reached the other side one of his toes was frozen stiff. So I broke it off and tossed it up into the sky that it might become a star. To prove that what I relate is true, Groa, there is the new star shining over us at this very moment. Look! From this day it shall be known to men as Orvandil's Toe. Do not you weep any longer. After all, the loss of a toe is a little thing; and I promise that your husband shall soon return to you, safe and sound, but for that small token of his wanderings in the land where visitors are not welcome."

At these joyful tidings poor Groa was so overcome that she fainted. And that put an end to the charm which she was weaving to loosen the stone from Thor's forehead. The stone was not yet wholly free, and thenceforth it was in vain to attempt its removal; Thor must always wear the splinter in his forehead. Groa could never forgive herself for the carelessness which had thus made her skill vain to help one to whom she had reason to be so grateful.

Now because of the bit of whetstone in Thor's forehead, folk of olden times were very careful how they used a whetstone; and especially they knew that they must not throw or drop one on the floor. For when they did so, the splinter in Thor's forehead was jarred, and the good Asa suffered great pain.

In the Giant's House

ALTHOUGH THOR HAD SLAIN Thiasse the giant builder, Thrym the thief, Hrungnir, and Hymir, and had rid the world of whole families of wicked giants, there remained many others in Jotunheim to do their evil deeds and to plot mischief against both gods and men; and of these Geirrod was the fiercest and the wickedest. He and his two ugly daughters – Gialp of the red eyes, and Greip of the black teeth – lived in a large palace among the mountains, where Geirrod had his treasures of iron and copper, silver and gold; for, since the death of Thrym, Geirrod was the Lord of the Mines, and all the riches that came out of the earth-caverns belonged to him.

Thrym had been Geirrod's friend, and the tale of Thrym's death through the might of Thor and his hammer had made Geirrod very sad and angry. "If I could but catch Thor, now, without his weapons," he said to his daughters, "what a lesson I would give him! How I would punish him for his deeds against us giants!"

"Oh, what would you do, father?" cried Gialp, twinkling her cruel red eyes, and working her claw fingers as if she would like to fasten them in Thor's golden beard.

"Oh, what would you do, father?" cried Greip, smacking her lips and grinding her black teeth as if she would like a bite out of Thor's stout arm.

"Do to him!" growled Geirrod fiercely. "Do to him! Gr-r-r! I would chew him all up! I would break his bones into little bits! I would smash him into jelly!"

"Oh, good, good! Do it, father, and then give him to us to play with," cried Gialp and Greip, dancing up and down till the hills trembled and all the frightened sheep ran home to their folds thinking that there must be an earthquake; for Gialp was as tall as a pine-tree and many times as thick, while Greip, her little sister, was as large around as a haystack and high as a flagstaff. They both hoped some day to be as huge as their father, whose legs were so long that he could step across the river valleys from one hilltop to another, just as we human folk cross a brook on stepping-stones; and his arms were so stout that he could lift a yoke of oxen in each fist, as if they were red-painted toys.

Geirrod shook his head at his two playful daughters and sighed. "We must catch Master Thor first, my girls, before we do these fine things to him. We must catch him without his mighty hammer, that never fails him, and without his belt, that doubles his strength whenever he puts it on, or even I cannot chew and break and smash him as he deserves; for with these his weapons he is the mightiest creature in the whole world, and I would rather meddle with thunder and lightning than with him. Let us wait, children."

Then Gialp and Greip pouted and sulked like two great babies who cannot have the new plaything which they want; and very ugly they were to see, with tears as big as oranges rolling down their cheeks.

Sooner than they expected they came very near to having their heart's desire fulfilled. And if it had happened as they wished, and if Asgard had lost its goodliest hero, its strongest defense, that would have been red Loki's fault, all Loki's evil planning; for you are now to hear of the wickedest thing that up to this time Loki had ever done. As you know, it was Loki who was Thor's bitterest enemy; and for many months he had been awaiting the chance to repay the Thunder Lord for the dole which Thor had brought upon him at the time of the dwarf's gifts to Asgard.

This is how it came about: Loki had long remembered the fun of skimming as a great bird in Freyia's falcon feathers. He had longed to borrow the wings once again and to fly away over the round world to see what he could see; for he thought that so he could learn many secrets which he was not meant to know, and plan wonderful mischief without being found out. But Freyia would not again loan her feather dress to Loki. She owed him a grudge for naming her as Thrym's bride; and besides, she remembered his treatment of Idun, and she did not trust his oily tongue and fine promises. So Loki saw no way but to borrow the feathers without leave; and this he did one day when Freyia was gone to ride in her chariot drawn by white cats. Loki put on the feather dress, as he had done twice before, – once when he went to Jotunheim to bring back stolen Idunn and her magic apples, once when he went to find out about Thor's hammer.

Away he flew from Asgard as birdlike as you please, chuckling to himself with wicked thoughts. It did not make any particular difference to him where he went. It was such fun to flap and fly, skim and wheel, looking and feeling for all the world like a big brown falcon. He swooped low, thinking, "I wonder what Freyia would say to see me now! Whee-e-e! How angry she would be!" Just then he spied the high wall of a palace on the mountains.

"Oho!" said Loki. "I never saw that place before. It may be a giant's dwelling. I think this must be Jotunheim, from the bigness of things. I must just peep to see." Loki was the most inquisitive of creatures, as wily minded folk are apt to be.

Loki the falcon alighted and hopped to the wall, then giving a flap of his wings he flew up and up to the window ledge, where he perched and peered into the hall. And there within he saw the giant Geirrod with his daughters eating their dinner. They looked so ugly and so greedy, as they sat there gobbling their food in giant mouthfuls, that Loki on the window-sill could not help snickering to himself. Now at that sound Geirrod looked up and saw the big brown bird peeping in at the window.

"Heigha!" cried the giant to one of his servants. "Go you and fetch me the big brown bird up yonder in the window."

Then the servant ran to the wall and tried to climb up to get at Loki; but the window was so high that he could not reach. He jumped and slipped, scrambled and slipped, again and again, while Loki sat just above his clutching fingers, and chuckled so that he nearly fell from his perch. "Te-he! Te-he!" chattered Loki in the falcon tongue. It was such fun to see the fellow grow black in the face with trying to reach him that Loki thought he would wait until the giant's fingers almost touched him, before flying away.

But Loki waited too long. At last, with a quick spring, the giant gained a hold upon the window ledge, and Loki was within reach. When Loki flapped his wings to fly, he found that his feet were tangled in the vine that grew upon the wall. He struggled and twisted with all his might, – but in vain. There he was, caught fast. Then the servant grasped him by the legs, and so brought him to Geirrod, where he sat at table. Now Loki in his feather dress looked exactly like a falcon – except for his eyes. There was no hiding the wise and crafty look of Loki's eyes. As soon as Geirrod looked at him, he suspected that this was no ordinary bird.

"You are no falcon, you!" he cried. "You are spying about my palace in disguise. Speak, and tell me who you are." Loki was afraid to tell, because he knew the giants were angry with him for his part in Thrym's death, – small though his part had really been in that great deed. So he kept his beak closed tight, and refused to speak. The giant stormed and raged and threatened to kill him; but still Loki was silent.

Then Geirrod locked the falcon up in a chest for three long months without food or water, to see how that would suit his bird-ship. You can imagine how hungry and thirsty Loki was at the end of that time, – ready to tell anything he knew, and more also, for the sake of a crumb of bread and a drop of water.

So then Geirrod called through the keyhole, "Well, Sir Falcon, now will you tell me who you are?" And this time Loki piped feebly, "I am Loki of Asgard; give me something to eat!"

"Oho!" quoth the giant fiercely. "You are that Loki who went with Thor to kill my brother Thrym! Oho! Well, you shall die for that, my feathered friend!"

"No, no!" screamed Loki. "Thor is no friend of mine. I love the giants far better! One of them is my wife!" – which was indeed true, as were few of Loki's words.

"Then if Thor is no friend of yours, to save your life will you bring him into my power?" asked Geirrod.

Loki's eyes gleamed wickedly among the feathers. Here all at once was his chance to be free, and to have his revenge upon Thor, his worst enemy. "Ay, that I will!" he cried eagerly. "I will bring Thor into your power."

So Geirrod made him give a solemn promise to do that wrong; and upon this he loosed Loki from the chest and gave him food. Then they formed the wicked plan together, while Gialp and Greip, the giant's ugly daughters, listened and smacked their lips.

Loki was to persuade Thor to come with him to Geirrodsgard. More; he must come without his mighty hammer, and without the iron gloves of power, and without the belt of strength; for so only could the giant have Thor at his mercy.

After their wicked plans were made, Loki bade a friendly farewell to Geirrod and his daughters and flew back to Asgard as quickly as he could. You may be sure he had a sound scolding from Freyia for stealing her feather dress and for keeping it so long. But he told such a pitiful story of being kept prisoner by a cruel giant, and he looked in truth so pale and thin from his long fast, that the gods were fain to pity him and to believe his story, in spite of the many times that he had deceived them. Indeed, most of his tale was true, but he told only half of the truth; for he spoke no word of his promise to the giant. This he kept hidden in his breast.

Now, one day not long after this, Loki invited Thor to go on a journey with him to visit a new friend who, he said, was anxious to know the Thunder Lord. Loki was so pleasant in his manner and seemed so frank in his speech that Thor, whose heart was simple and unsuspicious, never dreamed of any wrong, not even when Loki added, – "And by the bye, my Thor, you must leave behind your hammer, your belt, and your gloves; for it would show little courtesy to wear such weapons in the home of a new friend."

Thor carelessly agreed; for he was pleased with the idea of a new adventure, and with the thought of making a new friend. Besides, on their last journey together, Loki had behaved so well that Thor believed him to have changed his evil ways and to have become his friend. So together they set off in Thor's goat chariot, without weapons of any kind except those which Loki secretly carried. Loki chuckled as they rattled over the clouds, and if Thor had seen the look in his eyes, he would have turned the chariot back to Asgard and to safety, where he had left gentle Sif his wife. But Thor did not notice, and so they rumbled on.

Soon they came to the gate of Giant Land. Thor thought this strange, for he knew they were like to find few friends of his dwelling among the Big Folk. For the first time he began to suspect Loki of some treacherous scheme. However, he said nothing, and pretended to be as gay and careless as before. But he thought of a plan to find out the truth.

Close by the entrance was the cave of Grid, a good giantess, who alone of all her race was a friend of Thor and of the folk in Asgard.

"I will alight here for a moment, Loki," said Thor carelessly. "I long for a draught of water. Hold you the goats tightly by the reins until I return."

So he went into the cave and got his draught of water. But while he was drinking, he questioned good mother Grid to some purpose.

"Who is this friend Geirrod whom I go to see?" he asked her.

"Geirrod your friend! You go to see Geirrod!" she exclaimed. "He is the wickedest giant of us all, and no friend to you. Why do you go, dear Thor?"

"H"m!" muttered Thor. "Red Loki's mischief again!" He told her of the visit that Loki had proposed, and how he had left at home the belt, the gloves, and the hammer which made him stronger than any giant. Then Grid was frightened.

"Go not, go not, Thor!" she begged. "Geirrod will kill you, and those ugly girls, Gialp and Greip, will have the pleasure of crunching your bones. Oh, I know them well, the hussies!"

But Thor declared that he would go, whether or no. "I have promised Loki that I will go," he said, "and go I will; for I always keep my word."

"Then you shall have three little gifts of me," quoth she. "Here is my belt of power – for I also have one like your own." And she buckled about his waist a great belt, at whose touch he felt his strength redoubled. "This is my iron glove," she said, as she put one on his mighty hand, "and with it, as with your own, you can handle lightning and touch unharmed the hottest of red-hot metal. And here, last of all," she added, "is Gridarvoll, my good staff, which you may find useful. Take them, all three; and may Sif see you safe at home again by their aid."

Thor thanked her and went out once more to join Loki, who never suspected what had happened in the cave. For the belt and the glove were hidden under Thor's cloak. And as for the staff, it was quite ordinary looking, as if Thor might have picked it up anywhere along the road.

On they journeyed until they came to the river Vimer, the greatest of all rivers, which roared and tossed in a terrible way between them and the shore which they wanted to reach. It seemed impossible to cross. But Thor drew his belt a little tighter, and planting Grid's staff firmly on the bottom, stepped out into the stream. Loki clung behind to his cloak, frightened out of his wits. But Thor waded on bravely, his strength doubled by Grid's belt, and his steps supported by her magic staff. Higher and higher the waves washed over his knees, his waist, his shoulders, as if they were fierce to drown him. And Thor said:

"Ho there, river Vimer! Do not grow any larger, I pray. It is of no use. The more you crowd upon me, the mightier I grow with my belt and my staff!"

But lo! as he nearly reached the other side, Thor spied some one hiding close down by the bank of the river. It was Gialp of the red eyes, the big elder daughter of Geirrod. She was splashing the water upon Thor, making the great waves that rolled up and threatened to drown him.

"Oho!" cried he. "So it is you who are making the river rise, big little girl. We must see to that;" and seizing a huge boulder, he hurled it at her. It hit her with a thud, for Thor's aim never missed. Giving a scream as loud as a steam-whistle, Gialp limped home as best she could to tell her father, and to prepare a warm reception for the stranger who bore Loki at his back.

When Thor had pulled himself out of the river by some bushes, he soon came to the palace which Loki had first sighted in his falcon dress. And there he found everything most courteously made ready for him. He and Loki were received like dear old friends, with shouts of rejoicing and ringing of bells. Geirrod himself came out to meet them, and would have embraced his new friend Thor; but the Thunder Lord merely seized him by the hand and gave him so hearty a squeeze with the iron glove that the giant howled with pain. Yet he could say nothing, for Thor looked pleased and gentle. And Geirrod said to himself, "Ho, ho, my fine little Thor! I will soon pay you for that handshake, and for many things beside."

All this time Gialp and Greip did not appear, and Loki also had taken himself away, to be out of danger when the hour of Thor's death should come. For he feared that dreadful things might happen before Thor died; and he did not want to be remembered by the big fist of the companion whom he had betrayed. Loki, having kept his promise to the giant, was even now far on the road back to Asgard, where he meant with a sad face to tell the gods that Thor had been slain by a horrible giant; but never to tell them how.

So Thor was all alone when the servants led him to the chamber which Geirrod had made ready for his dear friend. It was a wonderfully fine chamber, to be sure; but the strange thing about it was that among the furnishings there was but one chair, a giant chair, with a drapery all about the legs. Now Thor was very weary with his long journey, and he sat down in the chair to rest. Then, wonderful to tell! – if elevators had been invented in those days, he might have thought he was in one. For instantly the seat of the chair shot up towards the roof, and against this he was in danger of being crushed as Geirrod had longed to see him. But quick as a flash Thor raised the staff which good old Grid had given him, and pushed it against the rafters with all his might to stop his upward journey. It was a tremendous push that he gave. Something cracked; something crashed; the chair fell to the ground as Thor leaped off the seat, and there were two terrible screams.

Then Thor found – what do you think? Why, that Gialp and Greip, the giant's daughters, had hidden under the seat of the chair, and had lifted it up on their backs to crush Thor against the roof! But instead of that, it was Thor who had broken their backs, so that they lay dead upon the floor like limp rag dolls.

Now this little exercise had only given Thor an excellent appetite for supper. So that when word came bidding him to the banquet, he was very glad.

"First," said big Geirrod, grinning horribly, for he did not know what had happened to his daughters, – "first we will see some games, friend Thor."

Then Thor came into the hall, where fires were burning in great chimney places along the walls. "It is here that we play our little games," cried Geirrod. And on the moment, seizing a pair of tongs, he snatched a red-hot wedge of iron from one of the fires and hurled it straight at Thor's head. But Thor was quicker than he. Swift as a flash he caught the flying spark in his iron glove, and calling forth all the might of Grid's belt, he cast the wedge back at the giant. Geirrod dodged behind an iron pillar, but it was in vain. Thor's might was such as no iron could meet. Like a bolt of lightning the wedge passed through the pillar, through Geirrod himself, through the thick wall of the palace, and buried itself deep in the ground, where it lodges to this day, unless some one has dug it up to sell for old iron.

So perished Geirrod and his children, one of the wickedest families of giants that ever lived in Jotunheim. And so Thor escaped from the snares of Loki, who had never done deed worse than this.

When Thor returned home to Asgard, where from Loki's lying tale he found all the gods mourning him as dead, you can fancy what a joyful reception he had. But for Loki, the false-hearted, false-tongued traitor to them all, there was only hatred. He no longer had any friends among the good folk. The wicked giants and the monsters of Utgard were now his only friends, for he had grown to be like them, and even these did not trust him overmuch.

FREYIA AND OTHER GODS

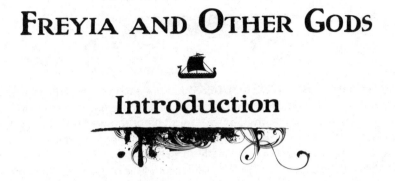

Introduction

FREYIA CAME TO ASGARD from Vanaheim, and before long she was as beloved as if she had been born one of the Aesir. She married well, and brought forth many fine children. She was known particularly for her fine feathered coat, which allowed her – and those she permitted to borrow it – to soar through the air as a hawk. Freyia's story touches on those of many of the other gods, and there are other myths and legends which must be recorded in order to understand how the golden age of Asgard became what it was, how evil entered, and how it eventually fell. There is Niord, who came with Freyia to bring summer, once the seasons had fallen into place. And Tyr, the god of war, who showed bravery which far surpassed any shown by man or god in the heyday of Asgard. And in the stories that follow we meet the elves, and learn why they abandoned their happy existence deep in the bowels of the earth. For every tale leads towards a single inevitable event – Ragnarok, and it hovers at the edge of all, just as it did in those early days of sunlight, when darkness had not yet touched the world of Asgard, and the gods lived a life of splendour....

Freyia and Odur

FREYIA WAS THE NORTHERN GODDESS of beauty and of love, a maiden so fair and graceful that the gods honoured her with the realm of Folkvang and the great hall Sessrymnir, where she would, in eternity, surround herself with all of those who loved her. Like many Viking goddesses, Freyia was fierce and fiery, her cool demeanour masking a passion which lay burning beneath. She was clever, and masterful in battle, and as Valfreyia, she often led the Valkyrs to the battlefields where she would claim many of the slain heroes. She wore a simple, flowing garment, held firmly in place on her torso and arms with the finest shining armour, a helmet and shield.

Slain heroes were taken to Folkvang, where they lived a life such as they had never experienced on earth. Their wives and lovers came to join them and Freyia's reputation spread far and wide among the dead and the living. So luxurious was Folkvang, so exquisite were Freyia's charms that lovers and wives of the slain would often take their own lives in order to meet with their loved ones sooner, and to experience the splendour of her land.

And so it was that Freyia, gold of hair and blue of eyes, came to be a symbol of love and courtship, and through that, the earth – which, of course, represents fecundity and new life. She married Odur who symbolized the sun, and together they had two daughters, Hnoss and Gersemi, beautiful maidens who had inherited their mother's beauty, and their father's charisma and charm. But Odur was a man of wandering eyes, and one who appreciated the inner music of women – and not just that of his wife. He grew tired of her song, and her absorption with their daughters, and he grew restless and reckless. And after many months and then years of growing weary of the smiling face of his lovely wife, he left Freyia and his daughters and set off on travels which would take him to the ends of the earth, and around it.

Freyia sank into a despair that cast a shadow across the earth. Her tears ran across cheeks that no longer bloomed, and as they touched the earth they became golden nuggets, sinking deep into the soil. Even the rocks were softened by her tears which flowed without ceasing as she made her decision. And it was decided by Freyia that she could not live without Odur. As well as being the symbol of the summer sun, Odur represented passion and ardour. Without him, Freyia could no longer find it in her heart to bring love and affection to those around her, and she could not fulfil her duties as goddess of love. It was decided that she should travel to find him, so across the lands she passed, leaving behind her tears which glistened and hardened into the purest gold. She travelled far and wide, and took on disguises as she moved, careful to leave no clue as to her identity in the event that he should hear word of her coming and not wish to see her. She was known as Syr and Skialf, Thrung and Horn, and it was not until she reached the deepest south, where summer clung to the land, that she found Odur.

Her husband lay under the myrtle trees that lined the sunny banks of a stream. Reunited, they lay together there, warm in one another's arms and dusted with the glow of true love. And as the passion drew colour into the cheeks of his wife, Odur knew he had to look no further to find his heart's content. The trees above them cast their scent across this happy couple, endowing them with good fortune. They rose together then, and Odur and Freyia made their way towards their home, and their exquisite daughters. As they walked, the earth rose up to meet them, casting bouquets of fragrant flowers in their path, drawing down the boughs of the flowering trees so they kissed the heads of the lovers. The air was filled with the rosy glow of their love, and everything living joined a chorus of cheers with followed their path. Spring and summer warmed the frozen land which had stood desolate and empty when Odur left.

The loveliest of the new flowers which bloomed were named 'Freyia's hair', and 'Freyia's eyedew' and to this day brides wear myrtle in their hair – a symbol of good fortune and true love.

Ottar and Angantyr

THE NORTHERN PEOPLE were wont to invoke Freyia not only for success in love, prosperity, and increase, but also, at times, for aid and protection. This she vouchsafed to all who served her truly, as appeared in the story of Ottar and Angantyr, two men who, after disputing for some time concerning their rights to a certain piece of property, laid their quarrel before the Thing. That popular assembly decreed that the man who could prove that he had the longest line of noble ancestors should be declared the winner, and a special day was appointed to investigate the genealogy of each claimant.

Ottar, unable to remember the names of more than a few of his progenitors, offered sacrifices to Freyia, entreating her aid. The goddess graciously heard his prayer, and appearing before him, she changed him into a boar, and rode off upon his back to the dwelling of the sorceress Hyndla, a most renowned witch. By threats and entreaties, Freyia compelled the old woman to trace Ottar's genealogy back to Odin, and to name every individual in turn, with a synopsis of his achievements. Then, fearing lest her votary's memory should be unable to retain so many details, Freyia further compelled Hyndla to brew a potion of remembrance, which she gave him to drink.

Thus prepared, Ottar presented himself before the Thing on the appointed day, and glibly reciting his pedigree, he named so many more ancestors than Angantyr could recollect, that he was easily awarded possession of the property he coveted.

Frey

FREY, OR FRO, as he was called in Germany, was the son of Niord and Nerthus, or of Niord and Skadi, and was born in Vanaheim. He therefore belonged to the race of the Vanas, the divinities of water and air, but was warmly welcomed in Asgard when he came thither as hostage with his father. As it was customary among the Northern nations to bestow some valuable gift upon a child when he cut his first tooth, the Aesir gave the infant Frey the beautiful realm of Alfheim or Fairyland, the home of the Light Elves.

Here Frey, the god of the golden sunshine and the warm summer showers, took up his abode, charmed with the society of the elves and fairies, who implicitly obeyed his every order, and at a sign from him flitted to and fro, doing all the good in their power, for they were pre-eminently beneficent spirits.

Frey also received from the gods a marvellous sword (an emblem of the sunbeams), which had the power of fighting successfully, and of its own accord, as soon as it was drawn from its sheath. Frey wielded this principally against the frost giants, whom he hated almost as much as did Thor, and because he carried this glittering weapon, he has sometimes been confounded with the sword-god Tyr or Saxnot.

The dwarfs from Svartalfaheim gave Frey the golden-bristled boar Gullin-bursti (the golden-bristled), a personification of the sun. The radiant bristles of this animal were considered symbolical either of the solar rays, of the golden grain, which at his bidding waved over the harvest fields of Midgard, or of agriculture; for the boar (by tearing up the ground with his sharp tusk) was supposed to have first taught mankind how to plough.

Frey sometimes rode astride of this marvellous boar, whose speed was very great, and at other times harnessed him to his golden chariot, which was said to contain the fruits and flowers which he lavishly scattered abroad over the face of the earth.

Frey was, moreover, the proud possessor not only of the dauntless steed Blodug-hofi, which would dash through fire and water at his command, but also of the magic ship Skidbladnir, a personification of the clouds. This vessel, sailing over land and sea, was always wafted along by favourable winds, and was so elastic that, while it could assume large enough proportions to carry the gods, their steeds, and all their equipments, it could also be folded up like a napkin and thrust into a pocket.

It is related in one of the lays of the Edda that Frey once ventured to ascend Odin's throne Hlidskialf, from which exalted seat his gaze ranged over the wide earth. Looking towards the frozen North, he saw a beautiful young maiden enter the house of the frost giant Gymir, and as she raised her hand to lift the latch her radiant beauty illuminated sea and sky.

A moment later, this lovely creature, whose name was Gerda, and who is considered as a personification of the flashing Northern lights, vanished within her father's house, and Frey pensively wended his way back to Alfheim, his heart oppressed with longing to make this fair maiden his wife. Being deeply in love, he was melancholy and absent-minded in the extreme, and began to behave so strangely that his father, Niord, became greatly alarmed about his health, and bade his favourite servant, Skirnir, discover the cause of this sudden change. After much persuasion, Skirnir finally won from Frey an account of his ascent of Hlidskialf, and of the fair vision he had seen. He confessed his love and also his utter despair, for as Gerda was the daughter of Gymir and Angur-boda, and a relative of the murdered giant Thiassi, he feared she would never view his suit with favour.

Skirnir, however, replied consolingly that he could see no reason why his master should take a despondent view of the case, and he offered to go and woo the maiden in his name, providing Frey would lend him his steed for the journey, and give him his glittering sword for reward.

Overjoyed at the prospect of winning the beautiful Gerda, Frey willingly handed Skirnir the flashing sword, and gave him permission to use his horse. But he quickly relapsed into the state of reverie which had become usual with him since falling in love, and thus he did not notice that Skirnir was still hovering near him, nor did he perceive him cunningly steal the reflection of his face from the surface of the brook near which he was seated, and imprison it in his drinking horn, with intent "to pour it out in Gerda's cup, and by its beauty win the heart of the giantess for the lord" for whom he was about to go a-wooing. Provided with this portrait, with eleven golden apples, and with the magic ring Draupnir, Skirnir now rode off to Jotunheim, to fulfil his embassy. As he came near Gymir's dwelling he heard the loud and persistent howling of his watch-dogs, which were personifications of the wintry winds. A shepherd, guarding his flock in the vicinity, told him, in answer to his inquiry, that it would be impossible to approach the house, on account of the flaming barrier which surrounded it; but Skirnir, knowing that Blodug-hofi would dash through any fire, merely set spurs to his steed, and, riding up unscathed to the giant's door, was soon ushered into the presence of the lovely Gerda.

To induce the fair maiden to lend a favourable ear to his master's proposals, Skirnir showed her the stolen portrait, and proffered the golden apples and magic ring, which, however, she haughtily refused to accept, declaring that her father had gold enough and to spare.

Indignant at her scorn, Skirnir now threatened to decapitate her with his magic sword, but as this did not in the least frighten the maiden, and she calmly defied him, he had recourse to magic arts. Cutting runes in his stick, he told her that unless she yielded ere the spell was ended, she would be condemned either to eternal celibacy, or to marry some aged frost giant whom she could never love.

Terrified into submission by the frightful description of her cheerless future in case she persisted in her refusal, Gerda finally consented to become Frey's wife, and dismissed Skirnir, promising to meet her future spouse on the ninth night, in the land of Buri, the green grove, where she would dispel his sadness and make him happy.

Delighted with his success, Skirnir hurried back to Alfheim, where Frey came eagerly to learn the result of his journey. When he learned that Gerda had consented to become his wife, his face grew radiant with joy; but when Skirnir informed him that he would have to wait nine nights ere he could behold his promised bride, he turned sadly away, declaring the time would appear interminable.

In spite of this loverlike despondency, however, the time of waiting came to an end, and Frey joyfully hastened to the green grove, where, true to her appointment, he found Gerda, and she became his happy wife, and proudly sat upon his throne beside him.

According to some mythologists, Gerda is not a personification of the aurora borealis, but of the earth, which, hard, cold, and unyielding, resists the spring-god's proffers of adornment and fruitfulness (the apples and ring), defies the flashing sunbeams (Frey's sword), and only consents to receive his kiss when it learns that it will else be doomed to perpetual barrenness, or given over entirely into the power of the giants (ice and snow). The nine nights of waiting are typical of the nine winter months, at the end of which the earth becomes the bride of the sun, in the groves where the trees are budding forth into leaf and blossom.

Frey and Gerda, we are told, became the parents of a son called Fiolnir, whose birth consoled Gerda for the loss of her brother Beli. The latter had attacked Frey and had been slain by him, although the sun-god, deprived of his matchless sword, had been obliged to defend himself with a stag horn which he hastily snatched from the wall of his dwelling.

Besides the faithful Skirnir, Frey had two other attendants, a married couple, Beyggvir and Beyla, the personifications of mill refuse and manure, which two ingredients, being used in agriculture for fertilising purposes, were therefore considered Frey's faithful servants, in spite of their unpleasant qualities.

Niord

WHEN THE WAR BETWEEN the Aesir and the Vanir was concluded, and hostages were taken by each side, Niord, with his children, Freyia and Frey, went to live in Asgard. There Niord was made the ruler of the winds and of the sea near the shore, and he was presented with a lush palace on the shores of Asgard, which he called Noatun. Here he took up the role of protecting the Aesir from Aegir, the god of the sea, who had a fiery temper, and who could, at a moment's notice, send waves crashing upon the unprotected shores of Asgard.

Niord was a popular god, and he was as handsome as his children. On his head he wore a circle of shells, and his dress was adorned with fresh, lustrous green seaweed. Niord was the very embodiment of summer, and each spring he was called upon to still the winds and move the clouds so that the sun's bright rays could touch the earth and encourage all to grow.

Niord had been married to Mother Earth, Nerthus, but she had been forced to stay behind when Niord was summoned to become a hostage for the Vanir, so he lived alone in Niord, an arrangement which he did not mind in the least. For from Noatun he could breathe in the fresh salt air, and revel in the flight of the gulls and other seabirds that made their home on the banks. The crashing waves lulled him into a state of serenity, and with the gentle seals, he basked in the sunlight of his new home.

All was well, until Skadi arrived. Skadi had chosen Niord as her husband, because of his clean feet, and he had grudgingly agreed to marry her. There could not have been two more different beings, for Skadi was now goddess of winter, and she dressed in pure white, glittering garments, embroidered with icicles and the fur of the white wolf. Skadi was beautiful, and her skin was like alabaster; her eyes were stormy, and told of a deep passion which burned within her. Niord was happy to take her as his wife, although he longed for the days of solitude that his unmarried days had accorded.

And so it was that Skadi moved her belongings to Noatun, and settled in there. The first night spoke of the nights to come, for from that first instant, Skadi was unable to sleep a wink. The sounds of the waves echoed deep in her head, and the cries of the gulls wakened her every time she drifted into the first ebbs of sleep. So Skadi announced to all that she could not live with Niord in Noatun – he would have to return with her to Thrymheim. Niord was deeply saddened by this arrangement, for the sea was a part of him – food for his soul. He finally agreed to travel with Skadi to Thrymheim, where he would live with her for nine out of every twelve months.

It was many days before Skadi and Niord reached her home, high in the frozen mountains, where frost clung to every surface and the air was filled with the vapour of their breath. The wind howled through the trees, sending showers of ice to the ground below, where it cracked and broke into tiny, glistening shards. The waterfalls roared in the background, sending up spray that glistened in the sunlight. At night the wolves joined the fracas, howling at the icy moon. Niord was quite unable to sleep even one wink.

So an agreement was finally forged between the two – for nine months of the year, Niord would make his home with Skadi in the kingdom of winter. For the other three months they would return to Noatun, where he would invoke summer for everyone in Asgard. This arrangement worked well for many years, but both Niord and Skadi felt saddened by having to vacate their homes for months on end. Finally, despite their affection for one another, it was decided that they should part.

Skadi threw herself into hunting, honing her skills so that she became the finest marksman in the land. She married the historical Odin, and she bore him a son called Saeming. Eventually, she married Uller, the god of winter and the perfect companion for the frigid goddess.

Niord returned to his palace by the sea, and frolicked there with the seals, who basked in the summer sun.

Aegir

BESIDES NIORD AND MIMIR, who were both ocean divinities, the one representing the sea near the coast and the other the primeval ocean whence all things were supposed to have sprung, the Northern races recognised another sea-ruler, called Aegir or Hler, who dwelt either in the cool depths of his liquid realm or had his abode on the Island of Lessoe, in the Cattegat, or Hlesey.

Aegir (the sea), like his brothers Kari (the air) and Loki (fire), is supposed to have belonged to an older dynasty of the gods, for he ranked neither with the Aesir, the Vanas, the giants, dwarfs, or elves, but was considered omnipotent within his realm.

He was supposed to occasion and quiet the great tempests which swept over the deep, and was generally represented as a gaunt old man, with long white beard and hair, and clawlike fingers ever clutching convulsively, as though he longed to have all things within his grasp. Whenever he appeared above the waves, it was only to pursue and overturn vessels, and to greedily drag them to the bottom of the sea, a vocation in which he was thought to take fiendish delight.

Aegir was mated with his sister, the goddess Ran, whose name means 'robber', and who was as cruel, greedy, and insatiable as her husband. Her favourite pastime was to lurk near dangerous rocks, whither she enticed mariners, and there spread her net, her most prized possession, when, having entangled the men in its meshes and broken their vessels on the jagged cliffs, she would calmly draw them down into her cheerless realm.

Ran was considered the goddess of death for all who perished at sea, and the Northern nations fancied that she entertained the drowned in her coral caves, where her couches were spread to receive them, and where the mead flowed freely as in Valhalla. The goddess was further supposed to have a great affection for gold, which was called the 'flame of the sea', and was used to illuminate her halls. This belief originated with the sailors, and sprang from the striking phosphorescent gleam of the waves. To win Ran's good graces, the Northmen were careful to hide some gold about them whenever any special danger threatened them on the sea.

Aegir and Ran had nine beautiful daughters, the Waves, or billow-maidens, whose snowy arms and bosoms, long golden hair, deep-blue eyes, and willowy, sensuous forms were fascinating in the extreme. These maidens delighted in sporting over the surface of their father's vast domain, clad lightly in transparent blue, white, or green veils. They were very moody and capricious, however, varying from playful to sullen and apathetic moods, and at times exciting one another almost to madness, tearing their hair and veils, flinging themselves recklessly upon their hard beds, the rocks, chasing one another with frantic haste, and shrieking aloud with joy or despair. But they seldom came out to play unless their brother, the Wind, were abroad, and according to his mood they were gentle and playful, or rough and boisterous.

The Waves were generally supposed to go about in triplets, and were often said to play around the ships of vikings whom they favoured, smoothing away every obstacle from their course, and helping them to reach speedily their goals.

To the Anglo-Saxons the sea-god Aegir was known by the name of Eagor, and whenever an unusually large wave came thundering towards the shore, the sailors were wont to cry, as the Trent boatmen still do, "Look out, Eagor is coming!" He was also known by the name of Hler (the shelterer) among the Northern nations, and of Gymir (the concealer), because he was always ready to hide things in the depths of his realm, and could be depended upon not to reveal the secrets entrusted to his care. And, because the waters of the sea were frequently said to seethe and hiss, the ocean was often called Aegir's brewing kettle or vat.

The god's two principal servants were Elde and Funfeng, emblems of the phosphorescence of the sea; they were noted for their quickness and they invariably waited upon the guests whom he invited to his banquets in the depths of the sea. Aegir sometimes left his realm to visit the Aesir in Asgard, where he was always royally entertained, and he delighted in Bragi's many tales of the adventures and achievements of the gods. Excited by these narratives, as also by the sparkling mead which accompanied them, the god on one occasion ventured to invite the Aesir to celebrate the harvest feast with him in Hlesey, where he promised to entertain them in his turn.

Surprised at this invitation, one of the gods ventured to remind Aegir that they were accustomed to dainty fare; whereupon the god of the sea declared that as far as eating was concerned they need be in no anxiety, as he was sure that he could cater for the most fastidious appetites; but he confessed that he was not so confident about drink, as his brewing kettle was rather small. Hearing this, Thor immediately volunteered to procure a suitable kettle, and set out with Tyr to obtain it. The two gods journeyed east of the Elivagar in Thor's goat chariot, and leaving this at the house of the peasant Egil, Thialfi's father, they wended their way on foot to the dwelling of the giant Hymir, who was known to own a kettle one mile deep and proportionately wide.

Only the women were at home, however, and Tyr recognised in the elder – an ugly old hag with nine hundred heads – his own grandmother; while the younger, a beautiful young giantess, was, it appeared, his mother, and she received her son and his companion hospitably, and gave them to drink.

After learning their errand, Tyr's mother bade the visitors hide under some huge kettles, which rested upon a beam at the end of the hall, for her husband Hymir was very hasty and often slew his would-be guests with a single baleful glance. The gods quickly followed her advice, and no sooner were they concealed than the old giant Hymir came in. When his wife told him that visitors had come, he frowned so portentously, and flashed such a wrathful look towards their hiding-place, that the rafter split and the kettles fell with a crash, and, except the largest, were all dashed to pieces.

The giant's wife, however, prevailed upon her husband to welcome Tyr and Thor, and he slew three oxen for their refection; but great was his dismay to see the thunder-god eat two of these for his supper. Muttering that he would have to go fishing early the next morning to secure a breakfast for so voracious a guest, the giant retired to rest, and when at dawn the next day he went down to the shore, he was joined by Thor, who said that he had come to help him. The giant bade him secure his own bait, whereupon Thor coolly slew his host's largest ox, Himinbrioter (heaven-breaker), and cutting off its head, he embarked with it and proceeded to row far out to sea. In vain Hymir protested that his usual fishing-ground had been reached, and that they might encounter the terrible Midgard snake were they to venture any farther; Thor persistently rowed on, until he fancied they were directly above this monster.

Baiting his powerful hook with the ox head, Thor angled for Iormungandr, while the giant meantime drew up two whales, which seemed to him to be enough for an early morning meal. He was about to propose to return, therefore, when Thor suddenly felt a jerk, and began pulling as hard as he could, for he knew by the resistance of his prey, and the terrible storm created by its frenzied writhings, that he had hooked the Midgard snake. In his determined efforts to force the snake to rise to the surface, Thor braced his feet so strongly against the bottom of the boat that he went through it and stood on the bed of the sea.

After an indescribable struggle, the monster's terrible venom-breathing head appeared, and Thor, seizing his hammer, was about to annihilate it when the giant, frightened by the proximity of

Iormungandr, and fearing lest the boat should sink and he should become the monster's prey, cut the fishing-line, and thus allowed the snake to drop back like a stone to the bottom of the sea.

Angry with Hymir for his inopportune interference, Thor dealt him a blow with his hammer which knocked him overboard; but Hymir, undismayed, waded ashore, and met the god as he returned to the beach. Hymir then took both whales, his spoil of the sea, upon his back, to carry them to the house; and Thor, wishing also to show his strength, shouldered boat, oars, and fishing tackle, and followed him.

Breakfast being disposed of, Hymir challenged Thor to prove his strength by breaking his beaker; but although the thunder-god threw it with irresistible force against stone pillars and walls, it remained whole and was not even bent. In obedience to a whisper from Tyr's mother, however, Thor suddenly hurled the vessel against the giant's forehead, the only substance tougher than itself, when it fell shattered to the ground. Hymir, having thus tested the might of Thor, told him he could have the kettle which the two gods had come to seek, but Tyr tried to lift it in vain, and Thor could raise it from the floor only after he had drawn his belt of strength to the very last hole.

The wrench with which he finally pulled it up did great damage to the giant's house and his feet broke through the floor. As Tyr and Thor were departing, the latter with the huge pot clapped on his head in place of a hat, Hymir summoned his brother frost giants, and proposed that they should pursue and slay their inveterate foe. Turning round, Thor suddenly became aware of their pursuit, and, hurling Miolnir repeatedly at the giants, he slew them all ere they could overtake him. Tyr and Thor then resumed their journey back to Aegir, carrying the kettle in which he was to brew ale for the harvest feast.

The physical explanation of this myth is, of course, a thunder storm (Thor), in conflict with the raging sea (the Midgard snake), and the breaking up of the polar ice (Hymir's goblet and floor) in the heat of summer.

The gods now arrayed themselves in festive attire and proceeded joyfully to Aegir's feast, and ever after they were wont to celebrate the harvest home in his coral caves.

Aegir, as we have seen, ruled the sea with the help of the treacherous Ran. Both of these divinities were considered cruel by the Northern nations, who had much to suffer from the sea, which, surrounding them on all sides, ran far into the heart of their countries through the numerous fiords, and often swallowed the ships of their vikings, with all their warrior crews.

Besides these principal divinities of the sea, the Northern nations believed in mermen and mermaids, and many stories are related of mermaids who divested themselves for a brief while of swan plumage or seal-garments, which they left upon the beach to be found by mortals who were thus able to compel the fair maidens to remain on land.

There were also malignant marine monsters known as Nicors, from whose name has been derived the proverbial Old Nick. Many of the lesser water divinities had fish tails; the females bore the name of Undines, and the males of Stromkarls, Nixies, Necks, or Neckar. In the middle ages these water spirits were believed sometimes to leave their native streams, to appear at village dances, where they were recognised by the wet hem of their garments. They often sat beside the flowing brook or river, playing on a harp, or sang alluring songs while combing out their long golden or green hair.

The Nixies, Undines, and Stromkarls were particularly gentle and lovable beings, and were very anxious to obtain repeated assurances of their ultimate salvation.

Many stories are told of priests or children meeting them playing by a stream, and taunting them with future damnation, which threat never failed to turn the joyful music into pitiful wails. Often priest or children, discovering their mistake, and touched by the agony of their victims, would hasten back to the stream and assure the green-toothed water sprites of future redemption, when they invariably resumed their happy strains.

Heimdall in Midgard

HEIMDALL WAS CALLED the watchman of the gods, and he was distinguished by his role at the Bifrost bridge, which he had constructed from fire, air and water which glowed as a rainbow in the sky. The Bifrost bridge was also called the Rainbow bridge, and it connected heaven with earth, ending just under the great tree Yggdrasil.

The golden age of Asgard was one of such happiness that there was never any threat to the peace of the land, and so it was that its watchman became bored. Heimdall was easily spotted, so he could not travel far without being recognized and commended for his fine work. He carried over his shoulder a great bugle, Giallarhorn, the blasts of which could summon help from all nine worlds. One fine day, Odin noticed that Heimdall had been hard at work without any respite for many many years. Odin himself would occasionally slip into a disguise in order to go out into the worlds beneath them, and he decided then that Heimdall should have the same opportunity – after all, Asgard was hardly in need of defence when all was quiet.

Heimdall was delighted, for he had been longing to visit Midgard and to get to know the people there. He carefully laid his bugle and his sword to one side, and dressed in the garb of the people of Midgard, he slipped across the bridge and reached a deserted shore. The first people he clapped eyes upon were Edda and Ai, a poor couple who lived on the bare beaches of Midgard, eking a meagre living from the sands. They lived in a tumble-down shack and had little in their possession, but what they did have they offered gladly to Heimdall. Their shack was sparsely furnished, with only a seaweed bed on which to lay, but it was agreed that Heimdall could sleep there with them, and at night he laid himself between the couple and slept well.

After three nights, Heimdall summoned Ai and Edda as they gathered snails and cockles from the seashore. He had put together several pieces of driftwood, and as they watched, he fashioned a pointed stick from one, and cut out a hole in another. The pointed stick was placed inside the hole, and he turned it quickly, so that sparks, and then a slender stream of smoke was produced. And then there was fire. Ai and Edda flew back against the walls of the shack, astonished by this magical feat. It was then that Heimdall took his leave from them.

Ai and Edda's lives were transformed by fire. Their water was heated; the most inedible nuggets from the beach were softened into tender morsels of food. And most of all, they had warmth. Nine months later a second gift appeared to Edda, for she gave birth to a son who she called Thrall. Thrall was an ugly, wretched-looking boy, with a knotted body and a twisted back, but he was kind and he worked hard. When he came of age, he married one like him – a deformed young woman called Serf. Together they had many children, all of whom worked about the house or on the land with the same diligence as their father and mother. These were the ancestors of the thralls.

Heimdall had left the home of Ai and Edda and travelled on. Soon enough he came to a lovely little house occupied by an older couple Amma and Afi. As he arrived, Afi was hard at work, whittling away at beams with which to improve their house. Heimdall set down his belongings and began to work with Afi. Soon they had built together a wonderful loom, which they presented to Amma, who was seated happily by the fire with her spinning wheel. Heimdall ate well that evening, and when the time came for sleep, he was offered a place between them in the only bed. For three nights Heimdall stayed with Afi and Amma, and then he left them. Sure enough, nine months later, and to the astonishment of the elderly couple, Amma gave birth to a son, who they called Karl the Yeoman. Karl was a thick-set, beautiful boy, with sparkling eyes and cheeks of roses. He loved the land and the fresh air was almost food enough for him, he drew so much goodness from it. When he became of age, he married a whirlwind of a woman who saw to it that their household ran as smoothly as a well-oiled rig, and that their children, their oxen and all the other animals on their farm, were fed and comfortable. They grew very successful, and they are the first of the ancestors of the yeoman farmer.

The third visit in Midgard was to a wealthy couple who lived in a fine castle. The man of the household spent many hours honing his hunting bow and spears, and his wife sat prettily by his side, well-dressed and flushed by the heat of the fire in the hearth. They offered him rich and delicious food, and at night he was given a place between them in their luxurious and comfortable bed. Heimdall stayed there for three nights, although he would happily have stayed there forever, after which time he returned to his post at the Bifrost bridge. And so it was, nine months later, that a son was born to that couple in the castle, and they called him Jarl the Earl. His father taught him well the skills of hunting and living off the land, and his mother passed on her refinement and breeding, so that Jarl became known as 'Regal'. When Regal was but a boy, Heimdall returned again to Midgard, and claimed him as his son. Regal remained in Midgard, but his fine pedigree was soon known about the land and he grew to become a great ruler there. He married Erna, who bore him many sons, one of whom was the ancestor of a line of Kings who would rule the land forever.

Heimdall took up his place once more in Asgard, but he was prone to wandering, as all gods are, and there are many more stories of his travels.

Tyr's Sword

TYR, TIU, OR ZIU was the son of Odin, and, according to different mythologists, his mother was Frigga, queen of the gods, or a beautiful giantess whose name is unknown, but who was a personification of the raging sea. He is the god of martial honour, and one of the twelve principal deities of Asgard. Although he appears to have had no special dwelling there, he was always welcome to Vingolf or Valhalla, and occupied one of the twelve thrones in the great council hall of Gladsheim.

As the God of courage and of war, Tyr was frequently invoked by the various nations of the North, who cried to him, as well as to Odin, to obtain victory. That he ranked next to Odin and Thor is proved by his name, Tiu, having been given to one of the days of the week, Tiu's day, which in modern English has become Tuesday. Under the name of Ziu, Tyr was the principal divinity of the Suabians, who originally called their capital, the modern Augsburg, Ziusburg. This people, venerating the god as they did, were wont to worship him under the emblem of a sword, his distinctive attribute, and in his honour held great sword dances, where various figures were performed. Sometimes the participants forming two long lines, crossed their swords, point upward, and challenged the boldest among their number to take a flying leap over them. At other times the warriors joined their sword points closely together in the shape of a rose or wheel, and when this figure was complete invited their chief to stand on the navel thus formed of flat, shining steel blades, and then they bore him upon it through the camp in triumph. The sword point was further considered so sacred that it became customary to register oaths upon it.

A distinctive feature of the worship of this god among the Franks and some other Northern nations was that the priests called Druids or Godi offered up human sacrifices upon his altars, generally cutting the bloody- or spread-eagle upon their victims, that is to say, making a deep incision on either side of the back-bone, turning the ribs thus loosened inside out, and tearing out the viscera through the opening thus made. Of course only prisoners of war were treated thus, and it was considered a point of honour with north European races to endure this torture without a moan. These sacrifices were made upon rude stone altars called dolmens, which can still be seen in Northern Europe. As Tyr was considered the patron god of the sword, it was deemed indispensable to engrave the sign or rune representing him upon the blade of every sword – an observance which the Edda enjoined upon all those who were desirous of obtaining victory.

Tyr was identical with the Saxon god Saxnot (from sax, a sword), and with Er, Heru, or Cheru, the chief divinity of the Cheruski, who also considered him god of the sun, and deemed his shining sword blade an emblem of its rays.

According to an ancient legend, Cheru's sword, which had been fashioned by the same dwarfs, sons of Ivald, who had also made Odin's spear, was held very sacred by his people, to whose care he had entrusted it, declaring that those who possessed it were sure to have the victory over their foes. But although carefully guarded in the temple, where it was hung so that it reflected the first beams of the morning sun, it suddenly and mysteriously disappeared one night. A Vala, druidess, or prophetess, consulted by the priests, revealed that the Norns had decreed that whoever wielded it would conquer the world and come to his death by it; but in spite of all entreaties she refused to tell who had taken it or where it might be found. Some time after this occurrence a tall and dignified stranger came to Cologne, where Vitellius, the Roman prefect, was feasting, and called him away from his beloved dainties. In the presence of the Roman soldiery he gave him the sword, telling him it would bring him glory and renown, and finally hailed him as emperor. The cry was taken up by the assembled legions, and Vitellius, without making any personal effort to secure the honour, found himself elected Emperor of Rome.

The new ruler, however, was so absorbed in indulging his taste for food and drink that he paid but little heed to the divine weapon. One day while leisurely making his way towards Rome he carelessly left it hanging in the antechamber to his pavilion. A German soldier seized this opportunity to substitute in its stead his own rusty blade, and the besotted emperor did not notice the exchange. When he arrived at Rome, he learned that the Eastern legions had named Vespasian emperor, and that he was even then on his way home to claim the throne.

Searching for the sacred weapon to defend his rights, Vitellius now discovered the theft, and, overcome by superstitious fears, did not even attempt to fight. He crawled away into a dark corner of his palace, whence he was ignominiously dragged by the enraged populace to the foot of the Capitoline Hill. There the prophecy was duly fulfilled, for the German soldier, who had joined the opposite faction, coming along at that moment, cut off Vitellius' head with the sacred sword.

The German soldier now changed from one legion to another, and travelled over many lands; but wherever he and his sword were found, victory was assured. After winning great honour and distinction, this man, having grown old, retired from active service to the banks of the Danube, where he secretly buried his treasured weapon, building his hut over its resting-place to guard it as long as he might live. When he lay on his deathbed he was implored to reveal where he had hidden it, but he persistently refused to do so, saying that it would be found by the man who was destined to conquer the world, but that he would not be able to escape the curse. Years passed by. Wave after wave the tide of barbarian invasion swept over that part of the country, and last of all came the terrible Huns under the leadership of Attila, the 'Scourge of God'. As he passed along the river, he saw a peasant mournfully examining his cow's foot, which had been wounded by some sharp instrument hidden in the long grass, and when search was made the point of a buried sword was found sticking out of the soil.

Attila, seeing the beautiful workmanship and the fine state of preservation of this weapon, immediately exclaimed that it was Cheru's sword, and brandishing it above his head he announced that he would conquer the world. Battle after battle was fought by the Huns, who, according to the Saga, were everywhere victorious, until Attila, weary of warfare, settled down in Hungary, taking to wife the beautiful Burgundian princess Ildico, whose father he had slain. This princess, resenting the murder of her kin and wishing to avenge it, took advantage of the king's state of intoxication upon his wedding night to secure possession of the divine sword, with which she slew him in his bed, once more fulfilling the prophecy uttered so many years before.

The magic sword again disappeared for a long time, to be unearthed once more, for the last time, by the Duke of Alva, Charles V.'s general, who shortly after won the victory of Mühlberg (1547). The Franks were wont to celebrate yearly martial games in honour of the sword; but it is said that when the heathen gods were renounced in favour of Christianity, the priests transferred many of their attributes to the saints, and that this sword became the property of the Archangel St. Michael, who has wielded it ever since.

Tyr, whose name was synonymous with bravery and wisdom, was also considered by the ancient Northern people to have the white-armed Valkyrs, Odin's attendants, at his command, and they thought that he it was who designated the warriors whom they should transfer to Valhalla to aid the gods on the last day.

How Tyr Lost His Hand

TYR WAS GENERALLY SPOKEN OF and represented as one-armed, just as Odin was called one-eyed. Various explanations are offered by different authorities; some claim that it was because he could give the victory only to one side; others, because a sword has but one blade. However this may be, the ancients preferred to account for the fact in the following way:

Loki married secretly at Jotunheim the hideous giantess Angur-boda (anguish boding), who bore him three monstrous children – the wolf Fenris, Hel, the parti-coloured goddess of death, and Iormungandr, a terrible serpent. He kept the existence of these monsters secret as long as he could; but they speedily grew so large that they could no longer remain confined in the cave where they had come to light. Odin, from his throne Hlidskialf, soon became aware of their existence, and also of the disquieting rapidity with which they increased in size. Fearful lest the monsters, when they had gained further strength, should invade Asgard and destroy the gods, Allfather determined to get rid of them, and striding off to Jotunheim, he flung Hel into the depths of Niflheim, telling her she could reign over the nine dismal worlds of the dead. He then cast Iormungandr into the sea, where he attained such immense proportions that at last he encircled the earth and could bite his own tail.

None too well pleased that the serpent should attain such fearful dimensions in his new element, Odin resolved to lead Fenris to Asgard, where he hoped, by kindly treatment, to make him gentle and tractable. But the gods one and all shrank in dismay when they saw the wolf, and none dared approach to give him food except Tyr, whom nothing daunted. Seeing that Fenris daily increased in size, strength, voracity, and fierceness, the gods assembled in council to deliberate how they might best dispose of him. They unanimously decided that as it would desecrate their peace-steads to slay him, they would bind him fast so that he could work them no harm.

With that purpose in view, they obtained a strong chain named Laeding, and then playfully proposed to Fenris to bind this about him as a test of his vaunted strength. Confident in his ability to release himself, Fenris patiently allowed them to bind him fast, and when all stood aside, with a mighty effort he stretched himself and easily burst the chain asunder.

Concealing their chagrin, the gods were loud in praise of his strength, but they next produced a much stronger fetter, Droma, which, after some persuasion, the wolf allowed them to fasten around him as before. Again a short, sharp struggle sufficed to burst this bond, and it is proverbial in the North to use the figurative expressions, 'to get loose out of Laeding,' and 'to dash out of Droma,' whenever great difficulties have to be surmounted.

The gods, perceiving now that ordinary bonds, however strong, would never prevail against the Fenris wolf's great strength, bade Skirnir, Frey's servant, go down to Svartalfaheim and bid the dwarfs fashion a bond which nothing could sever.

By magic arts the dark elves manufactured a slender silken rope from such impalpable materials as the sound of a cat's footsteps, a woman's beard, the roots of a mountain, the longings of the bear, the voice of fishes, and the spittle of birds, and when it was finished they gave it to Skirnir, assuring him that no strength would avail to break it, and that the more it was strained the stronger it would become.

Armed with this bond, called Gleipnir, the gods went with Fenris to the Island of Lyngvi, in the middle of Lake Amsvartnir, and again proposed to test his strength. But although Fenris had grown still stronger, he mistrusted the bond which looked so slight. He therefore refused to allow himself to be bound, unless one of the Aesir would consent to put his hand in his mouth, and leave it there, as a pledge of good faith, and that no magic arts were to be used against him.

The gods heard the decision with dismay, and all drew back except Tyr, who, seeing that the others would not venture to comply with this condition, boldly stepped forward and thrust his hand between the monster's jaws. The gods now fastened Gleipnir securely around Fenris's neck and paws, and when they saw that his utmost efforts to free himself were fruitless, they shouted and laughed with glee. Tyr, however, could not share their joy, for the wolf, finding himself captive, bit off the god's hand at the wrist, which since then has been known as the wolf's joint.

Deprived of his right hand, Tyr was now forced to use the maimed arm for his shield, and to wield his sword with his left hand; but such was his dexterity that he slew his enemies as before.

The gods, in spite of the wolf's struggles, drew the end of the fetter Gelgia through the rock Gioll, and fastened it to the boulder Thviti, which was sunk deep in the ground. Opening wide his fearful jaws, Fenris uttered such terrible howls that the gods, to silence him, thrust a sword into his mouth, the hilt resting upon his lower jaw and the point against his palate. The blood then began to pour out in such streams that it formed a great river, called Von. The wolf was destined to remain thus chained fast until the last day, when he would burst his bonds and would be free to avenge his wrongs.

While some mythologists see in this myth an emblem of crime restrained and made innocuous by the power of the law, others see the underground fire, which kept within bounds can injure no one, but which unfettered fills the world with destruction and woe. Just as Odin's second eye is said to rest in Mimir's well, so Tyr's second hand (sword) is found in Fenris's jaws. He has no more use for two weapons than the sky for two suns.

The worship of Tyr is commemorated in sundry places (such as Tübingen, in Germany), which bear more or less modified forms of his name. The name has also been given to the aconite, a plant known in Northern countries as 'Tyr's helm.'

The Norns' Web

THE NORTHERN GODDESSES OF FATE, who were called Norns, were in nowise subject to the other gods, who might neither question nor influence their decrees. They were three sisters, probably descendants of the giant Norvi, from whom sprang Nott (night). As soon as the Golden Age was ended, and sin began to steal even into the heavenly homes of Asgard, the Norns made their appearance under the great ash Yggdrasil, and took up their abode near the Urdar fountain. According to some mythologists, their mission was to warn the gods of future evil, to bid them make good use of the present, and to teach them wholesome lessons from the past.

These three sisters, whose names were Urd, Verdandi, and Skuld, were personifications of the past, present, and future. Their principal occupations were to weave the web of fate, to sprinkle daily the sacred tree with water from the Urdar fountain, and to put fresh clay around its roots, that it might remain fresh and ever green.

Some authorities further state that the Norns kept watch over the golden apples which hung on the branches of the tree of life, experience, and knowledge, allowing none but Idunn to pick the fruit, which was that with which the gods renewed their youth.

The Norns also fed and tenderly cared for two swans which swam over the mirror-like surface of the Urdar fountain, and from this pair of birds all the swans on earth are supposed to be descended. At times, it is said, the Norns clothed themselves with swan plumage to visit the earth, or sported like mermaids along the coast and in various lakes and rivers, appearing to mortals, from time to time, to foretell the future or give them sage advice.

The Norns sometimes wove webs so large that while one of the weavers stood on a high mountain in the extreme east, another waded far out into the western sea. The threads of their woof resembled cords, and varied greatly in hue, according to the nature of the events about to occur, and a black thread, tending from north to south, was invariably considered an omen of death. As these sisters flashed the shuttle to and fro, they chanted a solemn song. They did not seem to weave according to their own wishes, but blindly, as if reluctantly executing the wishes of Orlog, the eternal law of the universe, an older and superior power, who apparently had neither beginning nor end.

Two of the Norns, Urd and Verdandi, were considered to be very beneficent indeed, while the third, it is said, relentlessly undid their work, and often, when nearly finished, tore it angrily to shreds, scattering the remnants to the winds of heaven. As personifications of time, the Norns were represented as sisters of different ages and characters, Urd (Wurd, weird) appearing very old and decrepit, continually looking backward, as if absorbed in contemplating past events and people; Verdandi, the second sister, young, active, and fearless, looked straight before her, while Skuld, the type of the future, was generally represented as closely veiled, with head turned in the direction opposite to where Urd was gazing, and holding a book or scroll which had not yet been opened or unrolled.

These Norns were visited daily by the gods, who loved to consult them; and even Odin himself frequently rode down to the Urdar fountain to bespeak their aid, for they generally answered his questions, maintaining silence only about his own fate and that of his fellow gods.

The Story of Nornagesta

ON ONE OCCASION the three sisters visited Denmark, and entered the dwelling of a nobleman as his first child came into the world. Entering the apartment where the mother lay, the first Norn promised that the child should be handsome and brave, and the second that he should be prosperous and a great scald – predictions which filled the parents' hearts with joy. Meantime news of what was taking place had gone abroad, and the neighbours came thronging the apartment to such a degree that the pressure of the curious crowd caused the third Norn to be pushed rudely from her chair.

Angry at this insult, Skuld proudly rose and declared that her sister's gifts should be of no avail, since she would decree that the child should live only as long as the taper then burning near the bedside. These ominous words filled the mother's heart with terror, and she tremblingly clasped her babe closer to her breast, for the taper was nearly burned out and its extinction could not be very long delayed. The eldest Norn, however, had no intention of seeing her prediction thus set at naught; but as she could not force her sister to retract her words, she quickly seized the taper, put out the light, and giving the smoking stump to the child's mother, bade her carefully treasure it, and never light it again until her son was weary of life.

The boy was named Nornagesta, in honour of the Norns, and grew up to be as beautiful, brave, and talented as any mother could wish. When he was old enough to comprehend the gravity of the trust his mother told him the story of the Norns' visit, and placed in his hands the candle end, which he treasured for many a year, placing it for safe-keeping inside the frame of his harp. When his parents were dead, Nornagesta wandered from place to place, taking part and distinguishing himself in every battle, singing his heroic lays wherever he went. As he was of an enthusiastic and poetic temperament, he did not soon weary of life, and while other heroes grew wrinkled and old, he remained young at heart and vigorous in frame. He therefore witnessed the stirring deeds of the heroic ages, was the boon companion of the ancient warriors, and after living three hundred years, saw the belief in the old heathen gods gradually supplanted by the teachings of Christian missionaries. Finally Nornagesta came to the court of King Olaf Tryggvesson, who, according to his usual custom, converted him almost by force, and compelled him to receive baptism. Then, wishing to convince his people that the time for superstition was past, the king forced the aged scald to produce and light the taper which he had so carefully guarded for more than three centuries.

In spite of his recent conversion, Nornagesta anxiously watched the flame as it flickered, and when, finally, it went out, he sank lifeless to the ground, thus proving that in spite of the baptism just received, he still believed in the prediction of the Norns.

In the middle ages, and even later, the Norns figure in many a story or myth, appearing as fairies or witches, as, for instance, in the tale of 'The Sleeping Beauty,' and Shakespeare's tragedy of *Macbeth*.

Sometimes the Norns bore the name of Vala, or prophetesses, for they had the power of divination – a power which was held in great honour by all the Northern races, who believed that it was restricted to the female sex. The predictions of the Vala were never questioned, and it is said that the Roman general Drusus was so terrified by the appearance of Veleda, one of these prophetesses, who warned him not to cross the Elbe, that he actually beat a retreat. She foretold his approaching death, which indeed happened shortly after through a fall from his steed.

These prophetesses, who were also known as Idises, Dises, or Hagedises, officiated at the forest shrines and in the sacred groves, and always accompanied invading armies. Riding ahead, or in the midst of the host, they would vehemently urge the warriors on to victory, and when the battle was over they would often cut the bloody-eagle upon the bodies of the captives. The blood was collected into great tubs, wherein the Dises plunged their naked arms up to the shoulders, previous to joining in the wild dance with which the ceremony ended.

It is not to be wondered at that these women were greatly feared. Sacrifices were offered to propitiate them, and it was only in later times that they were degraded to the rank of witches, and sent to join the demon host on the Brocken, or Blocksberg, on Valpurgisnacht.

Besides the Norns or Dises, who were also regarded as protective deities, the Northmen ascribed to each human being a guardian spirit named Fylgie, which attended him through life, either in human or brute shape, and was invisible except at the moment of death by all except the initiated few.

The allegorical meaning of the Norns and of their web of fate is too patent to need explanation; still some mythologists have made them demons of the air, and state that their web was the woof of clouds, and that the bands of mists which they strung from rock to tree, and from mountain to mountain, were ruthlessly torn apart by the suddenly rising wind. Some authorities, moreover, declare that Skuld, the third Norn, was at times a Valkyr, and at others personated the goddess of death, the terrible Hel.

Hermod

ANOTHER OF ODIN'S SONS was Hermod, his special attendant, a bright and beautiful young god, who was gifted with great rapidity of motion and was therefore designated as the swift or nimble god.

On account of this important attribute Hermod was usually employed by the gods as messenger, and at a mere sign from Odin he was always ready to speed to any part of creation. As a special mark of favour, Allfather gave him a magnificent corselet and helmet, which he often donned when he prepared to take part in war, and sometimes Odin entrusted to his care the precious spear Gungnir, bidding him cast it over the heads of combatants about to engage in battle, that their ardour might be kindled into murderous fury.

Hermod delighted in battle, and was often called 'the valiant in battle,' and confounded with the god of the universe, Irmin. It is said that he sometimes accompanied the Valkyrs on their ride to earth, and frequently escorted the warriors to Valhalla, wherefore he was considered the leader of the heroic dead.

Hermod's distinctive attribute, besides his corselet and helm, was a wand or staff called Gambantein, the emblem of his office, which he carried with him wherever he went.

Once, oppressed by shadowy fears for the future, and unable to obtain from the Norns satisfactory answers to his questions, Odin bade Hermod don his armour and saddle Sleipnir, which he alone, besides Odin, was allowed to ride, and hasten off to the land of the Finns. This people, who lived in the frozen regions of the pole, besides being able to call up the cold storms which swept down from the North, bringing much ice and snow in their train, were supposed to have great occult powers.

The most noted of these Finnish magicians was Rossthiof (the horse thief) who was wont to entice travellers into his realm by magic arts, that he might rob and slay them; and he had power to predict the future, although he was always very reluctant to do so.

Hermod, 'the swift,' rode rapidly northward, with directions to seek this Finn, and instead of his own wand, he carried Odin's runic staff, which Allfather had given him for the purpose of dispelling any obstacles that Rossthiof might conjure up to hinder his advance. In spite, therefore, of phantom-like monsters and of invisible snares and pitfalls, Hermod was enabled safely to reach the magician's abode, and upon the giant attacking him, he was able to master him with ease, and he bound him hand and foot, declaring that he would not set him free until he promised to reveal all that he wished to know.

Rossthiof, seeing that there was no hope of escape, pledged himself to do as his captor wished, and upon being set at liberty, he began forthwith to mutter incantations, at the mere sound of which the sun hid behind the clouds, the earth trembled and quivered, and the storm winds howled like a pack of hungry wolves.

Pointing to the horizon, the magician bade Hermod look, and the swift god saw in the distance a great stream of blood reddening the ground. While he gazed wonderingly at this stream, a beautiful woman suddenly appeared, and a moment later a little boy stood beside her. To the god's amazement, this child grew with such marvellous rapidity that he soon attained his full growth, and Hermod further noticed that he fiercely brandished a bow and arrows.

Rossthiof now began to explain the omens which his art had conjured up, and he declared that the stream of blood portended the murder of one of Odin's sons, but that if the father of the gods should woo and win Rinda, in the land of the Ruthenes (Russia), she would bear him a son who would attain his full growth in a few hours and would avenge his brother's death.

Hermod listened attentively to the words of Rossthiof and upon his return to Asgard he reported all he had seen and heard to Odin, whose fears were confirmed and who thus definitely ascertained that he was doomed to lose a son by violent death. He consoled himself, however, with the thought that another of his descendants would avenge the crime and thereby obtain the satisfaction which a true Northman ever required.

Vidar

IT IS RELATED THAT ODIN once loved the beautiful giantess Grid, who dwelt in a cave in the desert, and that, wooing her, he prevailed upon her to become his wife. The offspring of this union between Odin (mind) and Grid (matter) was Vidar, a son as strong as he was taciturn, whom the ancients considered a personification of the primaeval forest or of the imperishable forces of Nature.

As the gods, through Heimdall, were intimately connected with the sea, they were also bound by close ties to the forests and Nature in general through Vidar, surnamed 'the silent,' who was destined to survive their destruction and rule over a regenerated earth. This god had his habitation in Landvidi (the wide land), a palace decorated with green boughs and fresh flowers, situated in the midst of an impenetrable primaeval forest where reigned the deep silence and solitude which he loved.

This old Scandinavian conception of the silent Vidar is indeed very grand and poetical, and was inspired by the rugged Northern scenery. "Who has ever wandered through such forests, in a length of many miles, in a boundless expanse, without a path, without a goal, amid their monstrous shadows, their sacred gloom, without being filled with deep reverence for the sublime greatness of Nature above all human agency, without feeling the grandeur of the idea which forms the basis of Vidar's essence?"

Vidar is depicted as tall, well-made, and handsome, clad in armour, girded with a broad-bladed sword, and shod with a great iron or leather shoe. According to some mythologists, he owed this peculiar footgear to his mother Grid, who, knowing that he would be called upon to fight against fire on the last day, designed it as a protection against the fiery element, as her iron gauntlet had shielded Thor in his encounter with Geirrod. But other authorities state that this shoe was made of the leather scraps which Northern cobblers had either given or thrown away. As it was essential that the shoe should be large and strong enough to resist the Fenris wolf's sharp teeth at the last day, it was a matter of religious observance among Northern shoemakers to give away as many odds and ends of leather as possible.

When Vidar joined his peers in Valhalla, they welcomed him gaily, for they knew that his great strength would serve them well in their time of need. After they had lovingly regaled him with the golden mead, Allfather bade him follow to the Urdar fountain, where the Norns were ever busy weaving their web. Questioned by Odin concerning his future and Vidar's destiny, the three sisters answered oracularly; each uttering a sentence:

"Early begun."
"Further spun."
"One day done."

To these their mother, Wyrd, the primitive goddess of fate, added: "With joy once more won." These mysterious answers would have remained totally unintelligible had the goddess not gone on to explain that time progresses, that all must change, but that even if the father fell in the last battle, his son Vidar would be his avenger, and would live to rule over a regenerated world, after having conquered all his enemies.

As Wyrd spoke, the leaves of the world tree fluttered as if agitated by a breeze, the eagle on its topmost bough flapped its wings, and the serpent Nidhug for a moment suspended its work of destruction at the roots of the tree. Grid, joining the father and son, rejoiced with Odin when she heard that their son was destined to survive the older gods and to rule over the new heaven and earth.

Vidar, however, uttered not a word, but slowly wended his way back to his palace Landvidi, in the heart of the primaeval forest, and there, sitting upon his throne, he pondered long about eternity, futurity, and infinity. If he fathomed their secrets he never revealed them, for the ancients averred that he was "as silent as the grave" – a silence which indicated that no man knows what awaits him in the life to come.

Vidar was not only a personification of the imperish-ability of Nature, but he was also a symbol of resurrection and renewal, exhibiting the eternal truth that new shoots and blossoms will spring forth to replace those which have fallen into decay.

The shoe he wore was to be his defence against the wolf Fenris, who, having destroyed Odin, would direct his wrath against him, and open wide his terrible jaws to devour him. But the old Northmen declared that Vidar would brace the foot thus protected against the monster's lower jaw, and, seizing the upper, would struggle with him until he had rent him in twain.

As one shoe only is mentioned in the Vidar myths, some mythologists suppose that he had but one leg, and was the personification of a waterspout, which would rise suddenly on the last day to quench the wild fire personified by the terrible wolf Fenris.

Vali

BILLING, KING OF THE RUTHENES, was sorely dismayed when he heard that a great force was about to invade his kingdom, for he was too old to fight as of yore, and his only child, a daughter named Rinda, although she was of marriageable age, obstinately refused to choose a husband from among her many suitors, and thus give her father the help which he so sadly needed.

While Billing was musing disconsolately in his hall, a stranger suddenly entered his palace. Looking up, the king beheld a middle-aged man wrapped in a wide cloak, with a broad-brimmed hat drawn down over his forehead to conceal the fact that he had but one eye. The stranger courteously enquired the cause of his evident depression, and as there was that in his bearing that compelled confidence, the king told him all, and at the end of the relation he volunteered to command the army of the Ruthenes against their foe.

His services being joyfully accepted, it was not long ere Odin – for it was he – won a signal victory, and, returning in triumph, he asked permission to woo the king's daughter Rinda for his wife. Despite the suitor's advancing years, Billing hoped that his daughter would lend a favourable ear to a wooer who appeared to be very distinguished, and he immediately signified his consent. So Odin, still unknown, presented himself before the princess, but she scornfully rejected his proposal, and rudely boxed his ears when he attempted to kiss her.

Forced to withdraw, Odin nevertheless did not relinquish his purpose to make Rinda his wife, for he knew, thanks to Rossthiof's prophecy, that none but she could bring forth the destined avenger of his murdered son. His next step, therefore, was to assume the form of a smith, in which guise he came back to Billing's hall, and fashioning costly ornaments of silver and gold, he so artfully multiplied these precious trinkets that the king joyfully acquiesced when he inquired whether he might pay his addresses to the princess. The smith, Rosterus as he announced himself, was, however, as unceremoniously dismissed by Rinda as the successful general had been; but although his ear once again tingled with the force of her blow, he was more determined than ever to make her his wife.

The next time Odin presented himself before the capricious damsel, he was disguised as a dashing warrior, for, thought he, a young soldier might perchance touch the maiden's heart; but when he again attempted to kiss her, she pushed him back so suddenly that he stumbled and fell upon one knee.

This third insult so enraged Odin that he drew his magic rune stick out of his breast, pointed it at Rinda, and uttered such a terrible spell that she fell back into the arms of her attendants rigid and apparently lifeless.

When the princess came to life again, her suitor had disappeared, but the king discovered with great dismay that she had entirely lost her senses and was melancholy mad. In vain all the physicians were summoned and all their simples tried; the maiden remained passive and sad, and her distracted father had well-nigh abandoned hope when an old woman, who announced herself as Vecha, or Vak, appeared and offered to undertake the cure of the princess. The seeming old woman, who was Odin in disguise, first prescribed a foot-bath for the patient; but as this did not appear to have any very marked effect, she proposed to try a more drastic treatment.

For this, Vecha declared, the patient must be entrusted to her exclusive care, securely bound so that she could not offer the least resistance. Billing, anxious to save his child, was ready to assent to anything; and having thus gained full power over Rinda, Odin compelled her to wed him, releasing her from bonds and spell only when she had faithfully promised to be his wife.

The prophecy of Rossthiof was now fulfilled, for Rinda duly bore a son named Vali (Ali, Bous, or Beav), a personification of the lengthening days, who grew with such marvellous rapidity that in the course of a single day he attained his full stature. Without waiting even to wash his face or comb his hair, this young god hastened to Asgard, bow and arrow in hand, to avenge the death of Balder upon his murderer, Hodur, the blind god of darkness.

In this myth, Rinda, a personification of the hard-frozen rind of the earth, resists the warm wooing of the sun, Odin, who vainly points out that spring is the time for warlike exploits, and offers the adornments of golden summer. She only yields when, after a shower (the footbath), a thaw sets in. Conquered then by the sun's irresistible might, the earth yields to his embrace, is freed from the spell (ice) which made her hard and cold, and brings forth Vali the nourisher, or Bous the peasant, who emerges from his dark hut when the pleasant days have come. The slaying of Hodur by Vali is therefore emblematical of 'the breaking forth of new light after wintry darkness.'

Vali, who ranked as one of the twelve deities occupying seats in the great hall of Gladsheim, shared with his father the dwelling called Valaskialf, and was destined, even before birth, to survive the last battle and twilight of the gods, and to reign with Vidar over the regenerated earth.

Forseti

SON OF BALDER, god of light, and of Nanna, goddess of immaculate purity, Forseti was the wisest, most eloquent, and most gentle of all the gods. When his presence in Asgard became known, the gods awarded him a seat in the council hall, decreed that he should be patron of justice and righteousness, and gave him as abode the radiant palace Glitnir. This dwelling had a silver roof, supported on pillars of gold, and it shone so brightly that it could be seen from a great distance.

Here, upon an exalted throne, Forseti, the lawgiver, sat day after day, settling the differences of gods and men, patiently listening to both sides of every question, and finally pronouncing sentences so equitable that none ever found fault with his decrees. Such were this god's eloquence and power of persuasion that he always succeeded in touching his hearers' hearts, and never failed to reconcile even the most bitter foes. All who left his presence were thereafter sure to live in peace, for none dared break a vow once made to him, lest they should incur his just anger and be smitten immediately unto death.

As god of justice and eternal law, Forseti was supposed to preside over every judicial assembly; he was invariably appealed to by all who were about to undergo a trial, and it was said that he rarely failed to help the deserving.

In order to facilitate the administration of justice throughout their land it is related that the Frisians commissioned twelve of their wisest men, the Asegeir, or elders, to collect the laws of the various families and tribes composing their nation, and to compile from them a code which should be the basis of uniform laws. The elders, having painstakingly finished their task of collecting this miscellaneous information, embarked upon a small vessel, to seek some secluded spot where they might conduct their deliberations in peace. But no sooner had they pushed away from shore than a tempest arose, which drove their vessel far out to sea, first on this course and then on that, until they entirely lost their bearings. In their distress the twelve jurists called upon Forseti, begging him to help them to reach land once again, and the prayer was scarcely ended when they perceived, to their utter surprise, that the vessel contained a thirteenth passenger.

Seizing the rudder, the newcomer silently brought the vessel round, steering it towards the place where the waves dashed highest, and in an incredibly short space of time they came to an island, where the steersman motioned them to disembark. In awestruck silence the twelve men obeyed; and their surprise was further excited when they saw the stranger fling his battle-axe, and a limpid spring gush forth from the spot on the greensward where it fell. Imitating the stranger, all drank of this water without a word; then they sat down in a circle, marvelling because the newcomer resembled each one of them in some particular, but yet was very different from any one of them in general aspect and mien.

Suddenly the silence was broken, and the stranger began to speak in low tones, which grew firmer and louder as he proceeded to expound a code of laws which combined all the good points of the various existing regulations which the Asegeir had collected. His speech being finished, the speaker vanished as suddenly and mysteriously as he had appeared, and the twelve jurists, recovering power of speech, simultaneously exclaimed that Forseti himself had been among them, and had delivered the code of laws by which the Frisians should henceforth be judged. In commemoration of the god's appearance they declared the island upon which they stood to be holy, and they pronounced a solemn curse upon any who might dare to desecrate its sanctity by quarrel or bloodshed. Accordingly this island, known as Forseti's land or Heligoland (holy land), was greatly respected by all the Northern nations, and even the boldest vikings refrained from raiding its shores, lest they should suffer shipwreck or meet a shameful death in punishment for their crime.

Solemn judicial assemblies were frequently held upon this sacred isle, the jurists always drawing water and drinking it in silence, in memory of Forseti's visit. The waters of his spring were, moreover, considered to be so holy that all who drank of them were held to be sacred, and even the cattle who had tasted of them might not be slain. As Forseti was said to hold his assizes in spring, summer, and autumn, but never in winter, it became customary, in all the Northern countries, to dispense justice in those seasons, the people declaring that it was only when the light shone clearly in the heavens that right could become apparent to all, and that it would be utterly impossible to render an equitable verdict during the dark winter season. Forseti is seldom mentioned except in connection with Balder. He apparently had no share in the closing battle in which all the other gods played such prominent parts.

Uller

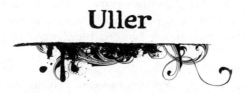

ULLER, THE WINTER-GOD, was the son of Sif, and the stepson of Thor. His father, who is never mentioned in the Northern sagas, must have been one of the dreaded frost giants, for Uller loved the cold and delighted in travelling over the country on his broad snowshoes or glittering skates. This god also delighted in the chase, and pursued his game through the Northern forests, caring but little for ice and snow, against which he was well protected by the thick furs in which he was always clad.

As god of hunting and archery, he is represented with a quiver full of arrows and a huge bow, and as the yew furnishes the best wood for the manufacture of these weapons, it is said to have been his favourite tree. To have a supply of suitable wood ever at hand ready for use, Uller took up his abode at Ydalir, the vale of yews, where it was always very damp.

As winter-god, Uller, or Oller, as he was also called, was considered second only to Odin, whose place he usurped during his absence in the winter months of the year. During this period he exercised full sway over Asgard and Midgard, and even, according to some authorities, took possession of Frigga, Odin's wife, as related in the myth of Vili and Ve. But as Uller was very parsimonious, and never bestowed any gifts upon mankind, they gladly hailed the return of Odin, who drove his supplanter away, forcing him to take refuge either in the frozen North or on the tops of the Alps. Here, if we are to believe the poets, he had built a summer house into which he retreated until, knowing Odin had departed once more, he again dared appear in the valleys.

Uller was also considered god of death, and was supposed to ride in the Wild Hunt, and at times even to lead it. He is specially noted for his rapidity of motion, and as the snowshoes used in Northern regions are sometimes made of bone, and turned up in front like the prow of a ship, it was commonly reported that Uller had spoken magic runes over a piece of bone, changing it into a vessel, which bore him over land or sea at will.

As snowshoes are shaped like a shield, and as the ice with which he yearly enveloped the earth acts as a shield to protect it from harm during the winter, Uller was surnamed the shield-god, and he was specially invoked by all persons about to engage in a duel or in a desperate fight.

In Christian times, his place in popular worship was taken by St. Hubert, the hunter, who, also, was made patron of the first month of the year, which began on November 22, and was dedicated to him as the sun passed through the constellation of Sagittarius, the bowman.

In Anglo-Saxon, Uller was known as Vulder; but in some parts of Germany he was called Holler and considered to be the husband of the fair goddess Holda, whose fields he covered with a thick mantle of snow, to make them more fruitful when the spring came.

By the Scandinavians, Uller was said to have married Skadi, Niord's divorced wife, the female personification of winter and cold, and their tastes were so congenial that they lived in perfect harmony together.

Numerous temples were dedicated to Uller in the North, and on his altars, as well as on those of all the other gods, lay a sacred ring upon which oaths were sworn. This ring was said to have the power of shrinking so violently as to sever the finger of any premeditated perjurer. The people visited Uller's shrine, especially during the months of November and December, to entreat him to send a thick covering of snow over their lands, as earnest of a good harvest; and as he was supposed to send out the glorious flashes of the aurora borealis, which illumine the Northern sky during its long night, he was considered nearly akin to Balder, the personification of light.

According to other authorities, Uller was Balder's special friend, principally because he too spent part of the year in the dismal depths of Niflheim, with Hel, the goddess of death. Uller was supposed to endure a yearly banishment thither, during the summer months, when he was forced to resign his sway over the earth to Odin, the summer god, and there Balder came to join him at Midsummer, the date of his disappearance from Asgard, for then the days began to grow shorter, and the rule of light (Balder) gradually yielded to the ever encroaching power of darkness (Hodur).

GIANTS, DWARFS AND ELVES

Introduction

AS WELL AS MEN AND GODS, the Norse universe was also populated by such creatures as giants, dwarfs and elves. Dwarfs and elves in particular were occasionally interchangeable with each other, with dwarfs being seen as 'black elves' as opposed to the light or white elves, but on the whole throughout the different stories we can trace three different races. The Gods often found themselves in opposition to the giants in particular – and therefore they were represented as paragons of evil to be overcome. However they also played an integral part in the lives of the Gods, for example the dwarfs made many magic items which the Gods come to obtain.

The Giants

AS WE HAVE ALREADY SEEN, the Northern races imagined that the giants were the first creatures who came to life among the icebergs which filled the vast abyss of Ginnunga-gap. These giants were from the very beginning the opponents and rivals of the gods, and as the latter were the personifications of all that is good and lovely, the former were representative of all that was ugly and evil.

When Ymir, the first giant, fell lifeless on the ice, slain by the gods, his progeny were drowned in his blood. One couple only, Bergelmir and his wife, effected their escape to Jotunheim, where they took up their abode and became the parents of all the giant race. In the North the giants were called by various names, each having a particular meaning. Jotun, for instance, meant 'the great eater,' for the giants were noted for their enormous appetites as well as for their uncommon size. They were fond of drinking as well as of eating, wherefore they were also called Thurses, a word which some writers claim had the same meaning as thirst; but others think they owed this name to the high towers ('turseis') which they were supposed to have built. As the giants were antagonistic to the gods, the latter always strove to force them to remain in Jotunheim, which was situated in the cold regions of the Pole. The giants were almost invariably worsted in their encounters with the gods, for they were heavy and slow-witted, and had nothing but stone weapons to oppose to the Aesir's bronze. In spite of this inequality, however, they were sometimes greatly envied by the gods, for they were thoroughly conversant with all knowledge relating to the past. Even Odin was envious of this attribute, and no sooner had he secured it by a draught from Mimir's spring than he hastened to Jotunheim to measure himself against Vafthrudnir, the most learned of the giant brood. But he might never have succeeded in defeating his antagonist in this strange encounter had he not ceased inquiring about the past and propounded a question relating to the future.

Of all the gods Thor was most feared by the Jotuns, for he was continually waging war against the frost and mountain giants, who would fain have bound the earth for ever in their rigid bands, thus preventing men from tilling the soil. In fighting against them, Thor, as we have already seen, generally had recourse to his terrible hammer Miolnir.

According to German legends the uneven surface of the earth was due to the giants, who marred its smoothness by treading upon it while it was still soft and newly created, while streams were formed from the copious tears shed by the giantesses upon seeing the valleys made by their husbands' huge footprints. As such was the Teutonic belief, the people imagined that the giants, who personified the mountains to them, were huge uncouth creatures, who could only move about in the darkness or fog, and were petrified as soon as the first rays of sunlight pierced through the gloom or scattered the clouds.

This belief led them to name one of their principal mountain chains the Riesengebirge (giant mountains). The Scandinavians also shared this belief, and to this day the Icelanders designate their highest mountain peaks by the name of Jokul, a modification of the word 'Jotun.' In Switzerland, where the everlasting snows rest upon the lofty mountain tops, the people still relate old stories of the time when the giants roamed abroad; and when an avalanche came crashing down the mountain side, they say the giants have restlessly shaken off part of the icy burden from their brows and shoulders.

As the giants were also personifications of snow, ice, cold, stone, and subterranean fire, they were said to be descended from the primitive Fornjotnr, whom some authorities identify with Ymir. According to this version of the myth, Fornjotnr had three sons: Hler, the sea; Kari, the air; and Loki, fire. These three divinities, the first gods, formed the oldest trinity, and their respective descendants were the sea giants Mimir, Gymir, and Grendel, the storm giants Thiassi, Thrym, and Beli, and the giants of fire and death, such as the Fenris wolf and Hel.

As all the royal dynasties claimed descent from some mythical being, the Merovingians asserted that their first progenitor was a sea giant, who rose out of the waves in the form of an ox, and surprised the queen while she was walking alone on the seashore, compelling her to become his wife. She gave birth to a son named Meroveus, the founder of the first dynasty of Frankish kings.

Many stories have already been told about the most important giants. They reappear in many of the later myths and fairy-tales, and manifest, after the introduction of Christianity, a peculiar dislike to the sound of church bells and the singing of monks and nuns.

The Scandinavians relate, in this connection, that in the days of Olaf the Saint a giant called Senjemand, dwelt on the Island of Senjen, and he was greatly incensed because a nun on the Island of Grypto daily sang her morning hymn. This giant fell in love with a beautiful maiden called Juterna-jesta, and it was long ere he could find courage to propose to her. When at last he made his halting request, the fair damsel scornfully rejected him, declaring that he was far too old and ugly for her taste.

In his anger at being thus scornfully refused, the giant swore vengeance, and soon after he shot a great flint arrow from his bow at the maiden, who dwelt eighty miles away. Another lover, Torge, also a giant, seeing her peril and wishing to protect her, flung his hat at the speeding arrow. This hat was a thousand feet high and proportionately broad and thick, nevertheless the arrow pierced the headgear, falling short, however, of its aim. Senjemand, seeing that he had failed, and fearing the wrath of Torge, mounted his steed and prepared to ride off as quickly as possible; but the sun, rising just then above the horizon, turned him into stone, together with the arrow and Torge's hat, the huge pile being known as the Torghatten mountain. The people still point to an obelisk which they say is the stone arrow; to a hole in the mountain, 289 feet high and 88 feet wide, which they say is the aperture made by the arrow in its flight through the hat; and to the horseman on Senjen Island, apparently riding a colossal steed and drawing the folds of his wide cavalry cloak closely about him. As for the nun whose singing had so disturbed Senjemand, she was petrified too, and never troubled any one with her psalmody again.

Another legend relates that one of the mountain giants, annoyed by the ringing of church bells more than fifty miles away, once caught up a huge rock, which he hurled at the sacred building. Fortunately it fell short and broke in two. Ever since then, the peasants say that the trolls come on Christmas Eve to raise the largest piece of stone upon golden pillars, and to dance and feast beneath it. A lady, wishing to know whether this tale were true, once sent her groom to the place. The trolls came forward and hospitably offered him a drink from a horn mounted in gold and ornamented with runes. Seizing the horn, the groom flung its contents away and dashed off with it at a mad gallop, closely pursued by the trolls, from whom he escaped only by passing through a stubble field and over running water. Some of their number visited the lady on the morrow to claim this horn, and when she refused to part with it they laid a curse upon her, declaring that her castle would be burned down every time the horn should be removed. The prediction has thrice been fulfilled, and now the family guard the relic with superstitious care. A similar drinking vessel, obtained in much the same fashion by the Oldenburg family, is exhibited in the collection of the King of Denmark.

The giants were not supposed to remain stationary, but were said to move about in the darkness, sometimes transporting masses of earth and sand, which they dropped here and there. The sandhills in northern Germany and Denmark were supposed to have been thus formed.

A North Frisian tradition relates that the giants possessed a colossal ship, called Mannigfual, which constantly cruised about in the Atlantic Ocean. Such was the size of this vessel that the captain was said to patrol the deck on horseback, while the rigging was so extensive and the masts so high that the sailors who went up as youths came down as gray-haired men, having rested and refreshed themselves in rooms fashioned and provisioned for that purpose in the huge blocks and pulleys.

By some mischance it happened that the pilot once directed the immense vessel into the North Sea, and wishing to return to the Atlantic as soon as possible, yet not daring to turn in such a small space, he steered into the English Channel. Imagine the dismay of all on board when they saw the passage growing narrower and narrower the farther they advanced. When they came to the narrowest spot, between Calais and Dover, it seemed barely possible that the vessel, drifting along with the current, could force its way through. The captain, with laudable presence of mind, promptly bade his men soap the sides of the ship, and to lay an extra-thick layer on the starboard, where the rugged cliffs of Dover rose threateningly. These orders were no sooner carried out than the vessel entered the narrow space, and, thanks to the captain's precaution, it slipped safely through. The rocks of Dover scraped off so much soap, however, that ever since they have been particularly white, and the waves dashing against them still have an unusually foamy appearance.

This exciting experience was not the only one through which the Mannigfual passed, for we are told that it once, nobody knows how, penetrated into the Baltic Sea, where, the water not being deep enough to keep the vessel afloat, the captain ordered all the ballast to be thrown overboard. The material thus cast on either side of the vessel into the sea formed the two islands of Bornholm and Christiansoë.

In Thuringia and in the Black Forest the stories of the giants are legion, and one of the favourites with the peasants is that about Ilse, the lovely daughter of the giant of the Ilsenstein. She was so charming that far and wide she was known as the Beautiful Princess Ilse, and was wooed by many knights, of whom she preferred the Lord of Westerburg. But her father did not at all approve of her consorting with a mere mortal, and forbade her to see her lover. Princess Ilse was wilful, however, and in spite of her sire's prohibition she daily visited her lover. The giant, exasperated by her persistency and disobedience, finally stretched out his huge hands and, seizing the rocks, tore a great gap between the height where he dwelt and the castle of Westerburg. Upon this, Princess Ilse, going to the cleft which parted her from her lover, recklessly flung herself over the precipice into the raging flood beneath, and was there changed into a bewitching undine. She dwelt in the limpid waters for many a year, appearing from time to time to exercise her fascinations upon mortals, and even, it is said, captivating the affections of the Emperor Henry, who paid frequent visits to her cascade. Her last appearance, according to popular belief, was at Pentecost, a hundred years ago; and the natives have not yet ceased to look for the beautiful princess, who is said still to haunt the stream and to wave her white arms to entice travellers into the cool spray of the waterfall.

The giants inhabited all the earth before it was given to mankind, and it was only with reluctance that they made way for the human race, and retreated into the waste and barren parts of the country, where they brought up their families in strict seclusion. Such was the ignorance of their offspring, that a young giantess, straying from home, once came to an inhabited valley, where for the first time in her life she saw a farmer ploughing on the hillside. Deeming him a pretty plaything, she caught him up with his team, and thrusting them into her apron, she gleefully carried them home to exhibit to her father. But the giant immediately bade her carry peasant and horses back to the place where she had found them, and when she had done so he sadly explained that the creatures whom she took for mere playthings, would eventually drive the giant folk away, and become masters of the earth.

The Dwarfs

EARLIER WE SAW HOW the black elves, dwarfs, or Svart-alfar, were bred like maggots in the flesh of the slain giant Ymir. The gods, perceiving these tiny, unformed creatures creeping in and out, gave them form and features, and they became known as dark elves, on account of their swarthy complexions. These small beings were so homely, with their dark skin, green eyes, large heads, short legs, and crow's feet, that they were enjoined to hide underground, being commanded never to show themselves during the daytime lest they should be turned into stone. Although less powerful than the gods, they were far more intelligent than men, and as their knowledge was boundless and extended even to the future, gods and men were equally anxious to question them.

The dwarfs were also known as trolls, kobolds, brownies, goblins, pucks, or Huldra folk, according to the country where they dwelt.

These little beings could transport themselves with marvellous celerity from one place to another, and they loved to conceal themselves behind rocks, when they would mischievously repeat the last words of conversations overheard from such hiding-places. Owing to this well-known trick, the echoes were called dwarfs' talk, and people fancied that the reason why the makers of such sounds were never seen was because each dwarf was the proud possessor of a tiny red cap which made the wearer invisible. This cap was called Tarnkappe, and without it the dwarfs dared not appear above the surface of the earth after sunrise for fear of being petrified. When wearing it they were safe from this peril.

Helva, daughter of the Lord of Nesvek, was loved by Esbern Snare, whose suit, however, was rejected by the proud father with the scornful words: "When thou shalt build at Kallundborg a stately church, then will I give thee Helva to wife."

Now Esbern, although of low estate, was proud of heart, even as the lord, and he determined, come what might, to find a way to win his coveted bride. So off he strode to a troll in Ullshoi Hill, and effected a bargain whereby the troll undertook to build a fine church, on completion of which Esbern was to tell the builder's name or forfeit his eyes and heart.

Night and day the troll wrought on, and as the building took shape, sadder grew Esbern Snare. He listened at the crevices of the hill by night; he watched during the day; he wore himself to a shadow by anxious thought; he besought the elves to aid him. All to no purpose. Not a sound did he hear, not a thing did he see, to suggest the name of the builder.

Meantime, rumour was busy, and the fair Helva, hearing of the evil compact, prayed for the soul of the unhappy man.

Time passed until one day the church lacked only one pillar, and worn out by black despair, Esbern sank exhausted upon a bank, whence he heard the troll hammering the last stone in the quarry underground. "Fool that I am," he said bitterly, "I have builded my tomb."

Just then he heard a light footstep, and looking up, he beheld his beloved. "Would that I might die in thy stead," said she, through her tears, and with that Esbern confessed how that for love of her he had imperilled eyes and heart and soul.

Then fast as the troll hammered underground, Helva prayed beside her lover, and the prayers of the maiden prevailed over the spell of the troll, for suddenly Esbern caught the sound of a troll-wife singing to her infant, bidding it be comforted, for that, on the morrow, Father Fine would return bringing a mortal's eyes and heart.

Sure of his victim, the troll hurried to Kallundborg with the last stone. "Too late, Fine!" quoth Esbern, and at the word, the troll vanished with his stone, and it is said that the peasants heard at night the sobbing of a woman underground, and the voice of the troll loud with blame.

The dwarfs, as well as the elves, were ruled by a king, who, in various countries of northern Europe, was known as Andvari, Alberich, Elbegast, Gondemar, Laurin, or Oberon. He dwelt in a magnificent subterranean palace, studded with the gems which his subjects had mined from the bosom of the earth, and, besides untold riches and the Tarnkappe, he owned a magic ring, an invincible sword, and a belt of strength. At his command the little men, who were very clever smiths, would fashion marvellous jewels or weapons, which their ruler would bestow upon favourite mortals.

We have already seen how the dwarfs fashioned Sif's golden hair, the ship Skidbladnir, the point of Odin's spear Gungnir, the ring Draupnir, the golden-bristled boar Gullin-bursti, the hammer Miolnir, and Freyia's golden necklace Brisinga-men. They are also said to have made the magic girdle which Spenser describes in his poem of the 'Faerie Queene,' – a girdle which was said to have the power of revealing whether its wearer were virtuous or a hypocrite.

The dwarfs also manufactured the mythical sword Tyrfing, which could cut through iron and stone, and which they gave to Angantyr. This sword, like Frey's, fought of its own accord, and could not be sheathed, after it was once drawn, until it had tasted blood. Angantyr was so proud of this weapon that he had it buried with him; but his daughter Hervor visited his tomb at midnight, recited magic spells, and forced him to rise from his grave to give her the precious blade. She wielded it bravely, and it eventually became the property of another of the Northern heroes.

Another famous weapon, which according to tradition was forged by the dwarfs in Eastern lands, was the sword Angurvadel which Frithiof received as a portion of his inheritance from his fathers. Its hilt was of hammered gold, and the blade was inscribed with runes which were dull until it was brandished in war, when they flamed red as the comb of the fighting-cock.

The dwarfs were generally kind and helpful; sometimes they kneaded bread, ground flour, brewed beer, performed countless household tasks, and harvested and threshed the grain for the farmers. If ill-treated, however, or turned to ridicule, these little creatures would forsake the house and never come back again. When the old gods ceased to be worshipped in the Northlands, the dwarfs withdrew entirely from the country, and a ferryman related how he had been hired by a mysterious personage to ply his boat back and forth across the river one night, and at every trip his vessel was so heavily laden with invisible passengers that it nearly sank. When his night's work was over, he received a rich reward, and his employer informed him that he had carried the dwarfs across the river, as they were leaving the country for ever in consequence of the unbelief of the people.

According to popular superstition, the dwarfs, in envy of man's taller stature, often tried to improve their race by winning human wives or by stealing unbaptized children, and substituting their own offspring for the human mother to nurse. These dwarf babies were known as changelings, and were recognisable by their puny and wizened forms. To recover possession of her own babe, and to rid herself of the changeling, a woman was obliged either to brew beer in egg-shells or to grease the soles of the child's feet and hold them so near the flames that, attracted by their offspring's distressed cries, the dwarf parents would hasten to claim their own and return the stolen child.

The troll women were said to have the power of changing themselves into Maras or nightmares, and of tormenting any one they pleased; but if the victim succeeded in stopping up the hole through which a Mara made her ingress into his room, she was entirely at his mercy, and he could even force her to wed him if he chose to do so. A wife thus obtained was sure to remain as long as the opening through which she had entered the house was closed, but if the plug were removed, either by accident or design, she immediately effected her escape and never returned.

Naturally, traditions of the little folk abound everywhere throughout the North, and many places are associated with their memory. The well-known Peaks of the Trolls (Trold-Tindterne) in Norway are said to be the scene of a conflict between two bands of trolls, who in the eagerness of combat omitted to note the approach of sunrise, with the result that they were changed into the small points of rock which stand up noticeably upon the crests of the mountain.

Some writers have ventured a conjecture that the dwarfs so often mentioned in the ancient sagas and fairy-tales were real beings, probably the Phoenician miners, who, working the coal, iron, copper, gold, and tin mines of England, Norway, Sweden, etc., took advantage of the simplicity and credulity of the early inhabitants to make them believe that they belonged to a supernatural race and always dwelt underground, in a region which was called Svartalfaheim, or the home of the black elves.

The Elves

BESIDES THE DWARFS there was another numerous class of tiny creatures called Lios-alfar, light or white elves, who inhabited the realms of air between heaven and earth, and were gently governed by the genial god Frey from his palace in Alfheim. They were lovely, beneficent beings, so pure and innocent that, according to some authorities, their name was derived from the same root as the Latin word 'white' (*albus*), which, in a modified form, was given to the snow-covered Alps, and to Albion (England), because of her white chalk cliffs which could be seen afar.

The elves were so small that they could flit about unseen while they tended the flowers, birds, and butterflies; and as they were passionately fond of dancing, they often glided down to earth on a moonbeam, to dance on the green. Holding one another by the hand, they would dance in circles, thereby making the 'fairy rings,' which were to be discerned by the deeper green and greater luxuriance of the grass which their little feet had pressed.

If any mortal stood in the middle of one of these fairy rings he could, according to popular belief in England, see the fairies and enjoy their favour; but the Scandinavians and Teutons vowed that the unhappy man must die. In illustration of this superstition, a story is told of how Sir Olaf, riding off to his wedding, was enticed by the fairies into their ring. On the morrow, instead of a merry marriage, his friends witnessed a triple funeral, for his mother and bride also died when they beheld his lifeless corpse.

These elves, who in England were called fairies or fays, were also enthusiastic musicians, and delighted especially in a certain air known as the elf-dance, which was so irresistible that no one who heard it could refrain from dancing. If a mortal, overhearing the air, ventured to reproduce it, he suddenly found himself incapable of stopping and was forced to play on and on until he died of exhaustion, unless he were deft enough to play the tune backwards, or some one charitably cut the strings of his violin. His hearers, who were forced to dance as long as the tones continued, could only stop when they ceased.

In medieval times, the will-o'-the-wisps were known in the North as elf lights, for these tiny sprites were supposed to mislead travellers; and popular superstition held that the Jack-o'-lanterns were the restless spirits of murderers forced against their will to return to the scene of their crimes. As they nightly walked thither, it is said that they doggedly repeated with every step, "It is right;" but as they returned they sadly reiterated, "It is wrong."

In Scandinavia and Germany sacrifices were offered to the elves to make them propitious. These sacrifices consisted of some small animal, or of a bowl of honey and milk, and were known as Alf-blot. They were quite common until the missionaries taught the people that the elves were mere demons, when they were transferred to the angels, who were long entreated to befriend mortals, and propitiated by the same gifts.

Many of the elves were supposed to live and die with the trees and plants which they tended, but these moss, wood, or tree maidens, while remarkably beautiful when seen in front, were hollow like a trough when viewed from behind. They appear in many of the popular tales, but almost always as benevolent and helpful spirits, for they were anxious to do good to mortals and to cultivate friendly relations with them.

No discussion of the elves is complete without a few words about Oberon. There are stories told far and wide of the fairy king Oberon, and his delicate queen Titiania. Oberon was so exquisitely handsome, that mortals were drawn into his fairy world after just one glance at his elegant profile. In every country across the world, there was a sense of unease on the eve of Midsummer, for this is when the fairies congregate around Oberon and Titiana and dance. Fairy dances are a magical thing, and their music is so compelling that all who hear it find it irresistible. But once a human, or indeed a god, succumbs to the fairy music, and begins to dance, he will be damned to do so until the end of his days, when he will die of an exhaustion like none other.

Oberon was also very powerful, and his tricks above ground became legend throughout many lands. With the passing of the dwarfs, humankind had no help with their work, and the little folk were no longer considered to be a blessed addition to a household. Many believe that Oberon harnessed the powers of Frey when he fell, and used them beneath the earth to set up a kingdom of fairies which was a complex and commanding as Asgard had once been. With his strength, and his overwhelming beauty, he was considered by man to be nothing more than a demon.

In Scandinavia the elves, both light and dark, were worshipped as household divinities, and their images were carved on the doorposts. The Norsemen, who were driven from home by the tyranny of Harald Harfager in 874, took their carved doorposts with them upon their ships. Similar carvings, including images of the gods and heroes, decorated the pillars of their high seats which they also carried away. The exiles showed their trust in their gods by throwing these wooden images overboard when they neared the Icelandic shores and settling where the waves carried the posts, even if the spot scarcely seemed the most desirable. 'Thus they carried with them the religion, the poetry, and the laws of their race, and on this desolate volcanic island they kept these records unchanged for hundreds of years, while other Teutonic nations gradually became affected by their intercourse with Roman and Byzantine Christianity.' These records, carefully collected by Saemund the learned, form the Elder Edda, the most precious relic of ancient Northern literature, without which we should know comparatively little of the religion of our forefathers.

The sagas relate that the first settlements in Greenland and Vinland were made in the same way, – the Norsemen piously landing wherever their household gods drifted ashore.

THE SIGURD SAGA

Introduction

WHILE THE FIRST PART of the *Elder Edda* consists of a collection of alliterative poems describing the creation of the world, the adventures of the gods, their eventual downfall, and gives a complete exposition of the Northern code of ethics, the second part comprises a series of heroic lays describing the exploits of the Volsung family, and especially of their chief representative, Sigurd, the favourite hero of the North.

These lays form the basis of the great Scandinavian epic, the *Volsunga Saga*, and have supplied not only the materials for the *Nibelungenlied*, the German epic, and for countless folk tales, but also for Wagner's celebrated operas, *The Rhinegold*, *Valkyr*, *Siegfried*, and *The Dusk of the Gods*. In England, William Morris has given them the form which they will probably retain in our literature, and it is from his great epic poem that almost all the quotations in this section are taken in preference to extracts from the *Edda*.

The Sword in the Branstock

THE STORY OF THE VOLSUNGS begins with Sigi, a son of Odin, a powerful man, and generally respected, until he killed a man from motives of jealousy, the latter having slain more game when they were out hunting together. In consequence of this crime, Sigi was driven from his own land and declared an outlaw. But it seems that he had not entirely forfeited Odin's favour, for the god now provided him with a well-equipped vessel, together with a number of brave followers, and promised that victory should ever attend him.

Thus aided by Odin, the raids of Sigi became a terror to his foes, and in the end he won the glorious empire of the Huns and for many years reigned as a powerful monarch. But in extreme old age his fortune changed, Odin forsook him, his wife's kindred fell upon him, and he was slain in a treacherous encounter.

His death was soon avenged, however, for Rerir, his son, returning from an expedition upon which he had been absent from the land at the time, put the murderers to death as his first act upon mounting the throne. The rule of Rerir was marked by every sign of prosperity, but his dearest wish, a son to succeed him, remained unfulfilled for many a year. Finally, however, Frigga decided to grant his constant prayer, and to vouchsafe the heir he longed for. She accordingly despatched her swift messenger Gna, or Liod, with a miraculous apple, which she dropped into his lap as he was sitting alone on the hillside. Glancing upward, Rerir recognised the emissary of the goddess, and joyfully hastened home to partake of the apple with his wife. The child who in due time was born under these favourable auspices was a handsome little lad. His parents called him Volsung, and while he was still a mere infant they both died, and the child became ruler of the land.

Years passed and Volsung's wealth and power ever increased. He was the boldest leader, and rallied many brave warriors around him. Full oft did they drink his mead underneath the Branstock, a mighty oak, which, rising in the middle of his hall, pierced the roof and overshadowed the whole house.

Ten stalwart sons were born to Volsung, and one daughter, Signy, came to brighten his home. So lovely was this maiden that when she reached marriageable age many suitors asked for her hand, among whom was Siggeir, King of the Goths, who finally obtained Volsung's consent, although Signy had never seen him.

When the wedding-day came, and the bride beheld her destined husband she shrank in dismay, for his puny form and lowering glances contrasted sadly with her brothers' sturdy frames and open faces. But it was too late to withdraw – the family honour was at stake – and Signy so successfully concealed her dislike that none save her twin brother Sigmund suspected with what reluctance she became Siggeir's wife.

While the wedding feast was in progress, and when the merry-making was at its height, the entrance to the hall was suddenly darkened by the tall form of a one-eyed man, closely enveloped in a mantle of cloudy blue. Without vouchsafing word or glance to any in the assembly, the stranger strode to the Branstock and thrust a glittering sword up to the hilt in its great bole. Then, turning slowly round, he faced the awe-struck and silent assembly, and declared that the weapon would be for the warrior who could pull it out of its oaken sheath, and that it would assure him victory in every battle. The words ended, he then passed out as he had entered, and disappeared, leaving a conviction in the minds of all that Odin, king of the gods, had been in their midst.

Volsung was the first to recover the power of speech, and, waiving his own right first to essay the feat, he invited Siggeir to make the first attempt to draw the divine weapon out of the tree-trunk. The bridegroom anxiously tugged and strained, but the sword remained firmly embedded in the oak and he resumed his seat, with an air of chagrin. Then Volsung tried, with the same result. The weapon was evidently not intended for either of them, and the young Volsung princes were next invited to try their strength.

The nine eldest sons were equally unsuccessful; but when Sigmund, the tenth and youngest, laid his firm young hand upon the hilt, the sword yielded easily to his touch, and he triumphantly drew it out as though it had merely been sheathed in its scabbard.

Nearly all present were gratified at the success of the young prince; but Siggeir's heart was filled with envy, and he coveted possession of the weapon. He offered to purchase it from his young brother-in-law, but Sigmund refused to part with it at any price, declaring that it was clear that the weapon had been intended for him to wear. This refusal so offended Siggeir that he secretly resolved to exterminate the proud Volsungs, and to secure the divine sword at the same time that he indulged his hatred towards his new kinsmen.

Concealing his chagrin, however, he turned to Volsung and cordially invited him to visit his court a month later, together with his sons and kinsmen. The invitation was immediately accepted, and although Signy, suspecting evil, secretly sought her father while her husband slept, and implored him to retract his promise and stay at home, he would not consent to withdraw his plighted word and so exhibit fear.

Siggeir's Treachery

A FEW WEEKS after the return of the bridal couple, therefore, Volsung's well-manned vessels arrived within sight of Siggeir's shores. Signy had been keeping anxious watch, and when she perceived them she hastened down to the beach to implore her kinsmen not to land, warning them that her husband had treacherously planned an ambush, whence they could not escape alive. But Volsung and his sons, whom no peril could daunt, calmly bade her return to her husband's palace, and donning their arms they boldly set foot ashore.

It befell as Signy had said, for on their way to the palace the brave little troop fell into Siggeir's ambush, and, although they fought with heroic courage, they were so borne down by the superior number of their foes that Volsung was slain and all his sons were made captive. The young men were led bound into the presence of the cowardly Siggeir, who had taken no part in the fight, and Sigmund was forced to relinquish his precious sword, after which he and his brothers were condemned to death.

Signy, hearing the cruel sentence, vainly interceded for her brothers: all she could obtain by her prayers and entreaties was that they should be chained to a fallen oak in the forest, to perish of hunger and thirst if the wild beasts should spare them. Then, lest she should visit and succour her brothers, Siggeir confined his wife in the palace, where she was closely guarded night and day.

Every morning early Siggeir himself sent a messenger into the forest to see whether the Volsungs were still living, and every morning the man returned saying a monster had come during the night and had devoured one of the princes, leaving nothing but his bones. At last, when none but Sigmund remained alive, Signy thought of a plan, and she prevailed on one of her servants to carry some honey into the forest and smear it over her brother's face and mouth.

When the wild beast came that night, attracted by the smell of the honey, it licked Sigmund's face, and even thrust its tongue into his mouth. Clinching his teeth upon it, Sigmund, weak and wounded as he was, held on to the animal, and in its frantic struggles his bonds gave way, and he succeeded in slaying the prowling beast who had devoured his brothers. Then he vanished into the forest, where he remained concealed until the king's messenger had come as usual, and until Signy, released from captivity, came speeding to the forest to weep over her kinsmen's remains.

Seeing her intense grief, and knowing that she had not participated in Siggeir's cruelty, Sigmund stole out of his place of concealment and comforted her as best he could. Together they then buried the whitening bones, and Sigmund registered a solemn oath to avenge his family's wrongs. This vow was fully approved by Signy, who, however, bade her brother bide a favourable time, promising to send him aid. Then the brother and sister sadly parted, she to return to her distasteful palace home, and he to a remote part of the forest, where he built a tiny hut and plied the craft of a smith.

Siggeir now took possession of the Volsung kingdom, and during the next few years he proudly watched the growth of his eldest son, whom Signy secretly sent to her brother when he was ten years of age, that Sigmund might train up the child to help him to obtain vengeance if he should prove worthy. Sigmund reluctantly accepted the charge; but as soon as he had tested the boy he found him deficient in physical courage, so he either sent him back to his mother, or, as some versions relate, slew him.

Some time after this Signy's second son was sent into the forest for the same purpose, but Sigmund found him equally lacking in courage. Evidently none but a pure-blooded Volsung would avail for the grim work of revenge, and Signy, realising this, resolved to commit a crime.

Her resolution taken, she summoned a beautiful young witch, and exchanging forms with her, she sought the depths of the dark forest and took shelter in Sigmund's hut. The Volsung did not penetrate his sister's disguise. He deemed her nought but the gypsy she seemed, and being soon won by her coquetry, he made her his wife. Three days later she disappeared from the hut, and, returning to the palace, she resumed her own form, and when she next gave birth to a son, she rejoiced to see in his bold glance and strong frame the promise of a true Volsung hero.

The Story of Sinfiotli

WHEN SINFIOTLI, as the child was called, was ten years of age, she herself made a preliminary test of his courage by sewing his garment to his skin, and then suddenly snatching it off, and as the brave boy did not so much as wince, but laughed aloud, she confidently sent him to the forest hut. Sigmund speedily prepared his usual test, and ere leaving the hut one day he bade Sinfiotli take meal from a certain sack, and knead it and bake some bread. On returning home, Sigmund asked whether his orders had been carried out. The lad replied by showing the bread, and when closely questioned he artlessly confessed that he had been obliged to knead into the loaf a great adder which was hidden in the meal. Pleased to see that the boy, for whom he felt a strange affection, had successfully stood the test which had daunted his brothers, Sigmund bade him refrain from eating of the loaf, for although he was proof against the bite of a reptile, he could not, like his mentor, taste poison unharmed.

Sigmund now began patiently to teach Sinfiotli all that a warrior of the North should know, and the two soon became inseparable companions. One day while ranging the forest together they came to a hut, where they found two men sound asleep. Near by hung two wolf-skins, which suggested immediately that the strangers were werewolves, whom a cruel spell prevented from bearing their natural form save for a short space at a time. Prompted by curiosity, Sigmund and Sinfiotli donned the wolf-skins, and they were soon, in the guise of wolves, rushing through the forest, slaying and devouring all that came in their way.

Such were their wolfish passions that soon they attacked each other, and after a fierce struggle Sinfiotli, the younger and weaker, fell dead. This catastrophe brought Sigmund to his senses, and he hung over his murdered companion in despair.

While thus engaged he saw two weasels come out of the forest and attack each other fiercely until one lay dead. The victor then sprang into the thicket, to return with a leaf, which it laid upon its companion's breast. Then was seen a marvellous thing, for at the touch of the magic herb the dead beast came back to life. A moment later a raven flying overhead dropped a similar leaf at Sigmund's feet, and he, understanding that the gods wished to help him, laid it upon Sinfiotli, who was at once restored to life.

In dire fear lest they might work each other further mischief, Sigmund and Sinfiotli now crept home and patiently waited until the time of their release should come. To their great relief the skins dropped off on the ninth night, and they hastily flung them into the fire, where they were entirely consumed, and the spell was broken for ever.

Sigmund now confided the story of his wrongs to Sinfiotli, who swore that, although Siggeir was his father (for neither he nor Sigmund knew the secret of his birth), he would aid him in his revenge. At nightfall, therefore, he accompanied Sigmund to the king's hall, and they entered unseen, concealing themselves in the cellar, behind the huge vats of beer. Here they were discovered by Signy's two youngest children, who, while playing with golden rings, which rolled into the cellar, came suddenly upon the men in ambush.

They loudly proclaimed their discovery to their father and his guests, but, before Siggeir and his men could take up arms, Signy took both children, and dragging them into the cellar bade her brother slay the little traitors. This Sigmund utterly refused to do, but Sinfiotli struck off their heads ere he turned to fight against the assailants, who were now closing in upon them.

In spite of all efforts Sigmund and his brave young companion soon fell into the hands of the Goths, whereupon Siggeir sentenced them to be buried alive in the same mound, with a stone partition between them so that they could neither see nor touch each other. The prisoners were accordingly confined in their living grave, and their foes were about to place the last stones on the roof, when Signy drew near, bearing a bundle of straw, which she was allowed to throw at Sinfiotli's feet, for the Goths fancied that it contained only a few provisions which would prolong his agony without helping him to escape. When all was still, Sinfiotli undid the sheaf, and great was his joy when he found instead of bread the sword which Odin had given to Sigmund. Knowing that nothing could dull or break the keen edge of this fine weapon, Sinfiotli thrust it through the stone partition, and, aided by Sigmund, he succeeded in cutting an opening, and in the end both effected their escape through the roof.

As soon as they were free, Sigmund and Sinfiotli returned to the king's hall, and piling combustible materials around it, they set fire to the mass. Then stationing themselves on either side of the entrance, they prevented all but the women from passing through. They loudly adjured Signy to escape ere it was too late, but she did not desire to live, and so coming to the entrance for a last embrace she found opportunity to whisper the secret of Sinfiotli's birth, after which she sprang back into the flames and perished with the rest.

The long-planned vengeance for the slaughter of the Volsungs having thus been carried out, Sigmund, feeling that nothing now detained him in the land of the Goths, set sail with Sinfiotli and returned to Hunaland, where he was warmly welcomed to the seat of power under the shade of his ancestral tree, the mighty Branstock. When his authority was fully established, Sigmund married Borghild, a beautiful princess, who bore him two sons, Hamond and Helgi. The latter was visited by the Norns as he lay in his cradle, and they promised him sumptuous entertainment in Valhalla when his earthly career should be ended.

Northern kings generally entrusted their sons' upbringing to a stranger, for they thought that so they would be treated with less indulgence than at home. Accordingly Helgi was fostered by Hagal, and under his care the young prince became so fearless that at the age of fifteen he ventured alone into the hall of Hunding, with whose race his family was at feud. Passing through the hall unmolested and unrecognised, he left an insolent message, which so angered Hunding that he immediately set out in pursuit of the bold young prince, whom he followed to the dwelling of Hagal. Helgi would then have been secured but that meanwhile he had disguised himself as a servant-maid, and was busy grinding corn as if this were his wonted occupation. The invaders marvelled somewhat at the maid's tall stature and brawny arms, nevertheless they departed without suspecting that they had been so near the hero whom they sought.

Having thus cleverly escaped, Helgi joined Sinfiotli, and collecting an army, the two young men marched boldly against the Hundings, with whom they fought a great battle, over which the Valkyrs hovered, waiting to convey the slain to Valhalla. Gudrun, one of the battle-maidens, was so struck by the courage which Helgi displayed, that she openly sought him and promised to be his wife. Only one of the Hunding race, Dag, remained alive, and he was allowed to go free after promising not to endeavour to avenge his kinsmen's death. This promise was not kept, however, and Dag, having obtained possession of Odin's spear Gungnir, treacherously slew Helgi with it. Gudrun, who in the meantime had fulfilled her promise to become his wife, wept many tears at his death, and laid a solemn curse upon his murderer; then, hearing from one of her maids that her slain husband kept calling for her from the depths of the tomb, she fearlessly entered the mound at night and tenderly inquired why he called and why his wounds continued to bleed after death. Helgi answered that he could not rest happy because of her grief, and declared that for every tear she shed a drop of his blood must flow.

To appease the spirit of her beloved husband, Gudrun from that time ceased to weep, but they did not long remain separated; for soon after the spirit of Helgi had ridden over Bifrost and entered Valhalla, to become leader of the Einheriar, he was joined by Gudrun who, as a Valkyr once more, resumed her loving tendance of him. When at Odin's command she left his side for scenes of human strife, it was to seek new recruits for the army which her lord was to lead into battle when Ragnarok, the twilight of the gods, should come.

Sinfiotli, Sigmund's eldest son, also met an early death; for, having slain in a quarrel the brother of Borghild, she determined to poison him. Twice Sinfiotli detected the attempt and told his father that there was poison in his cup. Twice Sigmund, whom no venom could injure, drained the bowl; and when Borghild made a third attempt, he bade Sinfiotli let the wine flow through his beard. Mistaking the meaning of his father's words, Sinfiotli forthwith drained the cup, and fell lifeless to the ground, for the poison was of the most deadly kind.

Speechless with grief, Sigmund tenderly raised his son's body in his arms, and strode out of the hall and down to the shore, where he deposited his precious burden in a skiff which an old one-eyed boatman brought at his call. He would fain have stepped aboard also, but ere he could do so the boatman pushed off and the frail craft was soon lost to sight. The bereaved father then slowly wended his way home, taking comfort from the thought that Odin himself had come to claim the young hero and had rowed away with him 'out into the west.'

The Birth of Sigurd

SIGMUND DEPOSED BORGHILD as his wife and queen in punishment for this crime, and when he was very old he sued for the hand of Hiordis, a fair young princess, daughter of Eglimi, King of the Islands. This young maiden had many suitors, among others King Lygni of Hunding's race, but so great was Sigmund's fame that she gladly accepted him and became his wife. Lygni, the discarded suitor, was so angry at this decision, that he immediately collected a great army and marched against his successful rival, who, though overpowered by superior numbers, fought with the courage of despair.

From the depths of a thicket which commanded the field of battle, Hiordis and her maid anxiously watched the progress of the strife. They saw Sigmund pile the dead around him, for none could stand against him, until at last a tall, one-eyed warrior suddenly appeared, and the press of battle gave way before the terror of his presence.

Without a moment's pause the new champion aimed a fierce blow at Sigmund, which the old hero parried with his sword. The shock shattered the matchless blade, and although the strange assailant vanished as he had come, Sigmund was left defenceless and was soon wounded unto death by his foes.

As the battle was now won, and the Volsung family all slain, Lygni hastened from the battlefield to take possession of the kingdom and force the fair Hiordis to become his wife. As soon as he had gone, however, the beautiful young queen crept from her hiding-place in the thicket, and sought the spot where Sigmund lay all but dead. She caught the stricken hero to her breast in a last passionate embrace, and then listened tearfully while he bade her gather the fragments of his sword and carefully treasure them for their son whom he foretold was soon to be born, and who was destined to avenge his father's death and to be far greater than he.

While Hiordis was mourning over Sigmund's lifeless body, her handmaiden suddenly warned her of the approach of a band of vikings. Retreating into the thicket once more, the two women exchanged garments, after which Hiordis bade the maid walk first and personate the queen, and they went thus to meet the viking Elf (Helfrat or Helferich). Elf received the women graciously, and their story of the battle so excited his admiration for Sigmund that he caused the remains of the slain hero to be reverentially removed to a suitable spot, where they were interred with all due ceremony. He then offered the queen and her maid a safe asylum in his hall, and they gladly accompanied him over the seas.

As he had doubted their relative positions from the first, Elf took the first opportunity after arriving in his kingdom to ask a seemingly idle question in order to ascertain the truth. He asked the pretended queen how she knew the hour had come for rising when the winter days were short and there was no light to announce the coming of morn, and she replied that, as she was in the habit of drinking milk ere she fed the cows, she always awoke thirsty. When the same question was put to the real Hiordis, she answered, with as little reflection, that she knew it was morning because at that hour the golden ring which her father had given her grew cold on her hand.

The suspicions of Elf having thus been confirmed, he offered marriage to the pretended handmaiden, Hiordis, promising to cherish her infant son, a promise which he nobly kept.

When the child was born Elf himself sprinkled him with water – a ceremony which our pagan ancestors scrupulously observed – and bestowed upon him the name of Sigurd. As he grew up he was treated as the king's own son, and his education was entrusted to Regin, the wisest of men, who knew all things, his own fate not even excepted, for it had been revealed to him that he would fall by the hand of a youth.

Under this tutor Sigurd grew daily in wisdom until few could surpass him. He mastered the smith's craft, and the art of carving all manner of runes; he learned languages, music, and eloquence; and, last but not least, he became a doughty warrior whom none could subdue. When he had reached manhood Regin prompted him to ask the king for a war-horse, a request which was immediately granted, and Gripir, the stud-keeper, was bidden to allow him to choose from the royal stables the steed which he most fancied.

On his way to the meadow where the horses were at pasture, Sigurd met a one-eyed stranger, clad in grey and blue, who accosted the young man and bade him drive the horses into the river and select the one which could breast the tide with least difficulty.

Sigurd received the advice gladly, and upon reaching the meadow he drove the horses into the stream which flowed on one side. One of the number, after crossing, raced round the opposite meadow; and, plunging again into the river, returned to his former pasture without showing any signs of fatigue. Sigurd therefore did not hesitate to select this horse, and he gave him the name of Grane or Greyfell. The steed was a descendant of Odin's eight-footed horse Sleipnir, and besides being unusually strong and indefatigable, was as fearless as his master.

One winter day while Regin and his pupil were sitting by the fire, the old man struck his harp, and, after the manner of the Northern scalds, sang or recited in the following tale, the story of his life.

The Treasure of the Dwarf King

HREIDMAR, king of the dwarf folk, was the father of three sons. Fafnir, the eldest, was gifted with a fearless soul and a powerful arm; Otter, the second, with snare and net, and the power of changing his form at will; and Regin, the youngest, with all wisdom and deftness of hand. To please the avaricious Hreidmar, this youngest son fashioned for him a house lined with glittering gold and flashing gems, and this was guarded by Fafnir, whose fierce glances and Aegis helmet none dared encounter.

Now it came to pass that Odin, Hoenir, and Loki once came in human guise, upon one of their wonted expeditions to test the hearts of men, unto the land where Hreidmar dwelt.

As the gods came near to Hreidmar's dwelling, Loki perceived an otter basking in the sun. This was none other than the dwarf king's second son, Otter, who now succumbed to Loki's usual love of destruction. Killing the unfortunate creature he flung its lifeless body over his shoulders, thinking it would furnish a good dish when meal time came.

Loki then hastened after his companions, and entering Hreidmar's house with them, he flung his burden down upon the floor. The moment the dwarf king's glance fell upon the seeming otter, he flew into a towering rage, and ere they could offer effective resistance the gods found themselves lying bound, and they heard Hreidmar declare that never should they recover their liberty until they could satisfy his thirst for gold by giving him of that precious substance enough to cover the skin of the otter inside and out.

As the otter-skin developed the property of stretching itself to a fabulous size, no ordinary treasure could suffice to cover it, and the plight of the gods, therefore, was a very bad one. The case, however, became a little more hopeful when Hreidmar consented to liberate one of their number. The emissary selected was Loki, who lost no time in setting off to the waterfall where the dwarf Andvari dwelt, in order that he might secure the treasure there amassed.

In spite of diligent search, however, Loki could not find the dwarf, until, perceiving a salmon sporting in the foaming waters, it occurred to him that the dwarf might have assumed this shape. Borrowing Ran's net he soon caught the fish, and learned, as he had suspected, that it was Andvari. Finding that there was nothing else for it, the dwarf now reluctantly brought forth his mighty treasure and surrendered it all, including the Helmet of Dread and a hauberk of gold, reserving only a ring which was gifted with miraculous powers, and which, like a magnet, attracted the precious ore. But the greedy Loki, catching sight of it, wrenched it from off the dwarf's finger and departed laughing, while his victim hurled angry curses after him, declaring that the ring would ever prove its possessor's bane and would cause the death of many.

On arriving at Hreidmar's house, Loki found the mighty treasure none too great, for the skin became larger with every object placed upon it, and he was forced to throw in the ring Andvaranaut (Andvari's loom), which he had intended to retain, in order to secure the release of himself and his companions. Andvari's curse of the gold soon began to operate. Fafnir and Regin both coveted a share, while Hriedmar gloated over his treasure night and day, and would not part with an item of it. Fafnir the invincible, seeing at last that he could not otherwise gratify his lust, slew his father, and seized the whole of the treasure, then, when Regin came to claim a share he drove him scornfully away and bade him earn his own living.

Thus exiled, Regin took refuge among men, to whom he taught the arts of sowing and reaping. He showed them how to work metals, sail the seas, tame horses, yoke beasts of burden, build houses, spin, weave, and sew – in short, all the industries of civilised life, which had hitherto been unknown. Years elapsed, and Regin patiently bided his time, hoping that some day he would find a hero strong enough to avenge his wrongs upon Fafnir, whom years of gloating over his treasure had changed into a horrible dragon, the terror of Gnîtaheid (Glittering Heath), where he had taken up his abode.

His story finished, Regin turned suddenly to the attentive Sigurd, saying he knew that the young man could slay the dragon if he wished, and inquiring whether he were ready to aid him to avenge his wrongs.

Sigurd immediately assented, on the condition, however, that the curse should be assumed by Regin, who, also, in order to fitly equip the young man for the coming fight, should forge him a sword, which no blow could break. Twice Regin fashioned a marvellous weapon, but twice Sigurd broke it to pieces on the anvil. Then Sigurd bethought him of the broken fragments of Sigmund's weapon which were treasured by his mother, and going to Hiordis he begged these from her; and either he or Regin forged from them a blade so strong that it divided the great anvil in two without being dinted, and whose temper was such that it neatly severed some wool floating gently upon the stream.

The Fight with the Dragon

SIGURD NOW WENT upon a farewell visit to Gripir, who, knowing the future, foretold every event in his coming career; after which he took leave of his mother, and accompanied by Regin set sail for the land of his fathers, vowing to slay the dragon when he had fulfilled his first duty, which was to avenge the death of Sigmund.

On his way to the land of the Volsungs a most marvellous sight was seen, for there came a man walking on the waters. Sigurd straightway took him on board his dragon ship, and the stranger, who gave his name as Feng or Fiollnir, promised favourable winds. Also he taught Sigurd how to distinguish auspicious omens. In reality the old man was Odin or Hnikar, the wave-stiller, but Sigurd did not suspect his identity.

Sigurd was entirely successful in his descent upon Lygni, whom he slew, together with many of his followers. He then departed from his reconquered kingdom and returned with Regin to slay Fafnir. Together they rode through the mountains, which ever rose higher and higher before them, until they came to a great tract of desert which Regin said was the haunt of Fafnir. Sigurd now rode on alone until he met a one-eyed stranger, who bade him dig trenches in the middle of the track along which the dragon daily dragged his slimy length to the river to quench his thirst, and to lie in wait in one of these until the monster passed over him, when he could thrust his sword straight into its heart.

Sigurd gratefully followed this counsel, and was rewarded with complete success, for as the monster's loathsome folds
rolled overhead, he thrust his sword upward into its left breast, and as he sprang out of the trench the dragon lay gasping in the throes of death.

Regin had prudently remained at a distance until all danger was past, but seeing that his foe was slain, he now came up. He was fearful lest the young hero should claim a reward, so he began to accuse him of having murdered his kin, but, with feigned magnanimity, he declared that instead of requiring life for life, in accordance with the custom of the North, he would consider it sufficient atonement if Sigurd would cut out the monster's heart and roast it for him on a spit.

Sigurd was aware that a true warrior never refused satisfaction of some kind to the kindred of the slain, so he agreed to the seemingly small proposal, and immediately prepared to act as cook, while Regin dozed until the meat was ready. After an interval Sigurd touched the roast to ascertain whether it were tender, but burning his fingers severely, he instinctively thrust them into his mouth to allay the smart. No sooner had Fafnir's blood thus touched his lips than he discovered, to his utter surprise, that he could understand the songs of the birds, many of which were already gathering round the carrion. Listening attentively, he found that they were telling how Regin meditated mischief against him, and how he ought to slay the old man and take the gold, which was his by right of conquest, after which he ought to partake of the heart and blood of the dragon. As this coincided with his own wishes, he slew the evil old man with a thrust of his sword and proceeded to eat and drink as the birds had suggested, reserving a small portion of Fafnir's heart for future consumption. He then wandered off in search of the mighty hoard, and, after donning the Helmet of Dread, the hauberk of gold, and the ring Andvaranaut, and loading Greyfell with as much gold as he could carry, he sprang to the saddle and sat listening eagerly to the birds' songs to know what his future course should be.

The Sleeping Warrior Maiden

SOON HE HEARD of a warrior maiden fast asleep on a mountain and surrounded by a glittering barrier of flames, through which only the bravest of men could pass to arouse her.

This adventure was the very thing for Sigurd, and he set off at once. The way lay through trackless regions, and the journey was long and cheerless, but at length he came to the Hindarfiall in Frankland, a tall mountain whose cloud-wreathed summit seemed circled by fiery flames.

Sigurd rode up the mountain side, and the light grew more and more vivid as he proceeded, until when he had neared the summit a barrier of lurid flames stood before him. The fire burned with a roar which would have daunted the heart of any other, but Sigurd remembered the words of the birds, and without a moment's hesitation he plunged bravely into its very midst.

The threatening flames having now died away, Sigurd pursued his journey over a broad tract of white ashes, directing his course to a great castle, with shield-hung walls. The great gates stood wide open, and Sigurd rode through them unchallenged by warders or men at arms. Proceeding cautiously, for he feared some snare, he at last came to the centre of the courtyard, where he saw a recumbent form cased in armour. Sigurd dismounted from his steed and eagerly removed the helmet, when he started with surprise to behold, instead of a warrior, the face of a most beautiful maiden.

All his efforts to awaken the sleeper were vain, however, until he had removed her armour, and she lay before him in pure-white linen garments, her long hair falling in golden waves around her. Then as the last fastening of her armour gave way, she opened wide her beautiful eyes, which met the rising sun, and first greeting with rapture the glorious spectacle, she turned to her deliverer, and the young hero and the maiden loved each other at first sight.

The maiden now proceeded to tell Sigurd her story. Her name was Brunhild, and according to some authorities she was the daughter of an earthly king whom Odin had raised to the rank of a Valkyr. She had served him faithfully for a long while, but once had ventured to set her own wishes above his, giving to a younger and therefore more attractive opponent the victory which Odin had commanded for another.

In punishment for this act of disobedience, she had been deprived of her office and banished to earth, where Allfather decreed she should wed like any other member of her sex. This sentence filled Brunhild's heart with dismay, for she greatly feared lest it might be her fate to mate with a coward, whom she would despise. To quiet these apprehensions, Odin took her to Hindarfiall or Hindfell, and touching her with the Thorn of Sleep, that she might await in unchanged youth and beauty the coming of her destined husband, he surrounded her with a barrier of flame which none but a hero would venture through.

From the top of Hindarfiall, Brunhild now pointed out to Sigurd her former home, at Lymdale or Hunaland, telling him he would find her there whenever he chose to come and claim her as his wife; and then, while they stood on the lonely mountain top together, Sigurd placed the ring Andvaranaut upon her finger, in token of betrothal, swearing to love her alone as long as life endured.

According to some authorities, the lovers parted after thus plighting their troth; but others say that Sigurd soon sought out and wedded Brunhild, with whom he lived for a while in perfect happiness until forced to leave her and his infant daughter Aslaug. This child, left orphaned at three years of age, was fostered by Brunhild's father, who, driven away from home, concealed her in a cunningly fashioned harp, until reaching a distant land he was murdered by a peasant couple for the sake of the gold they supposed it to contain. Their surprise and disappointment were great indeed when, on breaking the instrument open, they found a beautiful little girl, whom they deemed mute, as she would not speak a word. Time passed, and the child, whom they had trained as a drudge, grew to be a beautiful maiden, and she won the affection of a passing viking, Ragnar Lodbrog, King of the Danes, to whom she told her tale. The viking sailed away to other lands to fulfil the purposes of his voyage, but when a year had passed, during which time he won much glory, he came back and carried away Aslaug as his bride.

In continuation of the story of Sigurd and Brunhild, however, we are told that the young man went to seek adventures in the great world, where he had vowed, as a true hero, to right the wrong and defend the fatherless and oppressed.

The Niblungs

IN THE COURSE of his wanderings, Sigurd came to the land of the Niblungs, the land of continual mist, where Giuki and Grimhild were king and queen. The latter was specially to be feared, as she was well versed in magic lore, and could weave spells and concoct marvellous potions which had power to steep the drinker in temporary forgetfulness and compel him to yield to her will.

The king and queen had three sons, Gunnar, Hogni, and Guttorm, who were brave young men, and one daughter, Gudrun, the gentlest as well as the most beautiful of maidens. All welcomed Sigurd most warmly, and Giuki invited him to tarry awhile. The invitation was very agreeable after his long wanderings, and Sigurd was glad to stay and share the pleasures and occupations of the Niblungs. He accompanied them to war, and so distinguished himself by his valour, that he won the admiration of Grimhild and she resolved to secure him as her daughter's husband. One day, therefore, she brewed one of her magic potions, and when he had partaken of it at the hand of Gudrun, he utterly forgot Brunhild and his plighted troth, and all his love was diverted unto the queen's daughter.

Although there was not wanting a vague fear that he had forgotten some event in the past which should rule his conduct, Sigurd asked for and obtained Gudrun's hand, and their wedding was celebrated amid the rejoicings of the people, who loved the young hero very dearly. Sigurd gave his bride some of Fafnir's heart to eat, and the moment she had tasted it her nature was changed, and she began to grow cold and silent to all except him. To further cement his alliance with the two eldest Giukings (as the sons of Giuki were called) Sigurd entered the 'doom ring' with them, and the three young men cut a sod which was placed upon a shield, beneath which they stood while they bared and slightly cut their right arms, allowing their blood to mingle in the fresh earth. Then, when they had sworn eternal friendship, the sod was replaced.

But although Sigurd loved his wife and felt a true fraternal affection for her brothers, he could not lose his haunting sense of oppression, and was seldom seen to smile as radiantly as of old. Giuki had now died, and his eldest son, Gunnar, ruled in his stead. As the young king was unwedded, Grimhild, his mother, besought him to take a wife, suggesting that none seemed more worthy to become Queen of the Niblungs than Brunhild, who, it was reported, sat in a golden hall surrounded by flames, whence she had declared she would issue only to marry the warrior who would dare brave the fire for her sake.

Gunnar immediately prepared to seek this maiden, and strengthened by one of his mother's magic potions, and encouraged by Sigurd, who accompanied him, he felt confident of success. But when on reaching the summit of the mountain he would have ridden into the fire, his steed drew back affrighted and he could not induce him to advance a step. Seeing that his companion's steed did not show signs of fear, he asked him of Sigurd; but although Greyfell allowed Gunnar to mount, he would not stir because his master was not on his back.

Now as Sigurd carried the Helmet of Dread, and Grimhild had given Gunnar a magic potion in case it should be needed, it was possible for the companions to exchange their forms and features, and seeing that Gunnar could not penetrate the flaming wall Sigurd proposed to assume the appearance of Gunnar and woo the bride for him. The king was greatly disappointed, but as no alternative offered he dismounted, and the necessary exchange was soon effected. Then Sigurd mounted Greyfell in the semblance of his companion, and this time the steed showed not the least hesitation, but leaped into the flames at the first touch on his bridle, and soon brought his rider to the castle, where, in the great hall, sat Brunhild. Neither recognised the other: Sigurd because of the magic spell cast over him by Grimhild; Brunhild because of the altered appearance of her lover.

The maiden shrank in disappointment from the dark-haired intruder, for she had deemed it impossible for any but Sigurd to ride through the flaming circle. But she advanced reluctantly to meet her visitor, and when he declared that he had come to woo her, she permitted him to take a husband's place at her side, for she was bound by solemn injunction to accept as her spouse him who should thus seek her through the flames.

Three days did Sigurd remain with Brunhild, and his bright sword lay bared between him and his bride. This singular behaviour aroused the curiosity of the maiden, wherefore Sigurd told her that the gods had bidden him celebrate his wedding thus.

When the fourth morning dawned, Sigurd drew the ring Andvaranaut from Brunhild's hand, and, replacing it by another, he received her solemn promise that in ten days' time she would appear at the Niblung court to take up her duties as queen and faithful wife.

The promise given, Sigurd again passed out of the palace, through the ashes, and joined Gunnar, with whom, after he had reported the success of his venture, he hastened to exchange forms once more. The warriors then turned their steeds homeward, and only to Gudrun did Sigurd reveal the secret of her brother's wooing, and he gave her the fatal ring, little suspecting the many woes which it was destined to occasion.

True to her promise, Brunhild appeared ten days later, and solemnly blessing the house she was about to enter, she greeted Gunnar kindly, and allowed him to conduct her to the great hall, where sat Sigurd beside Gudrun. The Volsung looked up at that moment and as he encountered Brunhild's reproachful eyes Grimhild's spell was broken and the past came back in a flood of bitter recollection. It was too late, however: both were in honour bound, he to Gudrun and she to Gunnar, whom she passively followed to the high seat, to sit beside him as the scalds entertained the royal couple with the ancient lays of their land.

The days passed, and Brunhild remained apparently indifferent, but her heart was hot with anger, and often did she steal out of her husband's palace to the forest, where she could give vent to her grief in solitude.

Meanwhile, Gunnar perceived the cold indifference of his wife to his protestations of affection, and began to have jealous suspicions, wondering whether Sigurd had honestly told the true story of the wooing, and fearing lest he had taken advantage of his position to win Brunhild's love. Sigurd alone continued the even tenor of his way, striving against none but tyrants and oppressors, and cheering all by his kindly words and smile.

On a day the queens went down together to the Rhine to bathe, and as they were entering the water Gudrun claimed precedence by right of her husband's courage. Brunhild refused to yield what she deemed her right, and a quarrel ensued, in the course of which Gudrun accused her sister-in-law of not having kept her faith, producing the ring Andvaranaut in support of her charge. The sight of the fatal ring in the hand of her rival crushed Brunhild, and she fled homeward, and lay in speechless grief day after day, until all thought she must die. In vain did Gunnar and the members of the royal family seek her in turn and implore her to speak; she would not utter a word until Sigurd came and inquired the cause of her unutterable grief. Then, like a long-pent-up stream, her love and anger burst forth, and she overwhelmed the hero with reproaches, until his heart so swelled with grief for her sorrow that the tight bands of his strong armour gave way.

Words had no power to mend that woeful situation, and Brunhild refused to heed when Sigurd offered to repudiate Gudrun, saying, as she dismissed him, that she would not be faithless to Gunnar. The thought that two living men had called her wife was unendurable to her pride, and the next time her husband sought her presence she implored him to put Sigurd to death, thus increasing his jealousy and suspicion.

He refused to deal violently with Sigurd, however, because of their oath of good fellowship, and so she turned to Hogni for aid. He, too, did not wish to violate his oath, but he induced Guttorm, by means of much persuasion and one of Grimhild's potions, to undertake the dastardly deed.

The Death of Sigurd

ACCORDINGLY, in the dead of night, Guttorm stole into Sigurd's chamber, weapon in hand; but as he bent over the bed he saw Sigurd's bright eyes fixed upon him, and fled precipitately. Later on he returned and the scene was repeated; but towards morning, stealing in for the third time, he found the hero asleep, and traitorously drove his spear through his back.

Although wounded unto death, Sigurd raised himself in bed, and seizing his renowned sword which hung beside him, he flung it with all his remaining strength at the flying murderer, cutting him in two as he reached the door. Then, with a last whispered farewell to the terrified Gudrun, Sigurd sank back and breathed his last.

Sigurd's infant son was slain at the same time, and poor Gudrun mourned over her dead in silent, tearless grief; while Brunhild laughed aloud, thereby incurring the wrath of Gunnar, who repented, too late, that he had not taken measures to avert the dastardly crime.

The grief of the Niblungs found expression in the public funeral celebration which was shortly held. A mighty pyre was erected, to which were brought precious hangings, fresh flowers, and glittering arms, as was the custom for the burial of a prince; and as these sad preparations took shape, Gudrun was the object of tender solicitude from the women, who, fearing lest her heart would break, tried to open the flood-gate of her tears by recounting the bitterest sorrows they had known, one telling of how she too had lost all she held dear. But these attempts to make her weep were utterly vain, until at length they laid her husband's head in her lap, bidding her kiss him as if he were still alive; then her tears began to flow in torrents.

The reaction soon set in for Brunhild also; her resentment was all forgotten when she saw the body of Sigurd laid on the pyre, arrayed as if for battle in burnished armour, with the Helmet of Dread at his head, and accompanied by his steed, which was to be burned with him, together with several of his faithful servants who would not survive his loss. She withdrew to her apartment, and after distributing her possessions among her handmaidens, she donned her richest array, and stabbed herself as she lay stretched upon her bed.

The tidings soon reached Gunnar, who came with all haste to his wife and just in time to receive her dying injunction to lay her beside the hero she loved, with the glittering, unsheathed sword between them, as it had lain when he had wooed her by proxy. When she had breathed her last, these wishes were faithfully executed, and her body was burned with Sigurd's amid the lamentations of all the Niblungs.

In Richard Wagner's story of 'The Ring' Brunhild's end is more picturesque. Mounted on her steed, as when she led the battle-maidens at the command of Odin, she rode into the flames which leaped to heaven from the great funeral pyre, and passed for ever from the sight of men.

The death scene of Sigurd (Siegfried) is far more powerful in the Nibelungenlied. In the Teutonic version his treacherous assailant lures him from a hunting party in the forest to quench his thirst at a brook, where he thrusts him through the back with a spear. His body was thence borne home by the hunters and laid at his wife's feet.

Gudrun, still inconsolable, and loathing the kindred who had treacherously robbed her of all joy in life, fled from her father's house and took refuge with Elf, Sigurd's foster father, who, after the death of Hiordis, had married Thora, the daughter of King Hakon. The two women became great friends, and here Gudrun tarried several years, employing herself in embroidering upon tapestry the great deeds of Sigurd, and watching over her little daughter Swanhild, whose bright eyes reminded her vividly of the husband whom she had lost.

Atli, King of the Huns

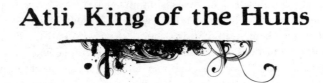

IN THE MEANTIME, Atli, Brunhild's brother, who was now King of the Huns, had sent to Gunnar to demand atonement for his sister's death; and to satisfy his claims Gunnar had promised that when her years of widowhood had been accomplished he would give him Gudrun's hand in marriage. Time passed, and Atli clamoured for the fulfilment of his promise, wherefore the Niblung brothers, with their mother Grimhild, went to seek the long-absent princess, and by the aid of the magic potion administered by Grimhild they succeeded in persuading Gudrun to leave little Swanhild in Denmark and to become Atli's wife in the land of the Huns.

Nevertheless, Gudrun secretly detested her husband, whose avaricious tendencies were extremely repugnant to her; and even the birth of two sons, Erp and Eitel, did not console her for the death of her loved ones and the absence of Swanhild. Her thoughts were continually of the past, and she often spoke of it, little suspecting that her descriptions of the wealth of the Niblungs had excited Atli's greed, and that he was secretly planning some pretext for seizing it.

Atli at last decided to send Knefrud or Wingi, one of his servants, to invite the Niblung princes to visit his court, intending to slay them when he should have them in his power; but Gudrun, fathoming this design, sent a rune message to her brothers, together with the ring Andvaranaut, around which she had twined a wolf's hair. On the way, however, the messenger partly effaced the runes, thus changing their meaning; and when he appeared before the Niblungs, Gunnar accepted the invitation, in spite of Hogni's and Grimhild's warnings, and an ominous dream of Glaumvor, his second wife.

Before departing, however, Gunnar was prevailed upon to bury secretly the great Niblung hoard in the Rhine, and he sank it in a deep hole in the bed of the river, the position of which was known to the royal brothers only, who took a solemn oath never to reveal it.

In martial array the royal band then rode out of the city of the Niblungs, which they were never again to see, and after many adventures they entered the land of the Huns, and arrived at Atli's hall, where, finding that they had been foully entrapped, they slew the traitor Knefrud, and prepared to sell their lives as dearly as possible.

Gudrun hastened to meet them with tender embraces, and, seeing that they must fight, she grasped a weapon and loyally aided them in the terrible massacre which ensued. After the first onslaught, Gunnar kept up the spirits of his followers by playing on his harp, which he laid aside only when the assaults were renewed. Thrice the brave Niblungs resisted the assault of the Huns, until all save Gunnar and Hogni had perished, and the king and his brother, wounded, faint, and weary, fell into the hands of their foes, who cast them, securely bound, into a dungeon to await death.

Atli had prudently abstained from taking any active part in the fight, and he now had his brothers-in-law brought in turn before him, promising them freedom if they would reveal the hiding-place of the golden hoard; but they proudly kept silence, and it was only after much torture that Gunnar spake, saying that he had sworn a solemn oath never to reveal the secret as long as Hogni lived. At the same time he declared that he would believe his brother dead only when his heart was brought to him on a platter.

Urged by greed, Atli gave immediate orders that Hogni's heart should be brought; but his servants, fearing to lay hands on such a grim warrior, slew the cowardly scullion Hialli. The trembling heart of this poor wretch called forth contemptuous words from Gunnar, who declared that such a timorous organ could never have belonged to his fearless brother. Atli again issued angry commands, and this time the unquivering heart of Hogni was produced, whereupon Gunnar, turning to the monarch, solemnly swore that since the secret now rested with him alone it would never be revealed.

Livid with anger, the king bade his servants throw Gunnar, with hands bound, into a den of venomous snakes; but this did not daunt the reckless Niblung, and, his harp having been flung after him in derision, he calmly sat in the pit, harping with his toes, and lulling to sleep all the reptiles save one only. It was said that Atli's mother had taken the form of this snake, and that she it was who now bit him in the side, and silenced his triumphant song for ever.

To celebrate his triumph, Atli now ordered a great feast, commanding Gudrun to be present to wait upon him. At this banquet he ate and drank heartily, little suspecting that his wife had slain both his sons, and had served up their roasted hearts and their blood mixed with wine in cups made of their skulls. After a time the king and his guests became intoxicated, when Gudrun, according to one version of the story, set fire to the palace, and as the drunken men were aroused, too late to escape, she revealed what she had done, and first stabbing her husband, she calmly perished in the flames with the Huns. Another version relates, however, that she murdered Atli with Sigurd's sword, and having placed his body on a ship, which she sent adrift, she cast herself into the sea and was drowned.

According to a third and very different version, Gudrun was not drowned, but was borne by the waves to the land where Jonakur was king. There she became his wife, and the mother of three sons, Sorli, Hamdir, and Erp. She recovered possession, moreover, of her beloved daughter Swanhild, who, in the meantime, had grown into a beautiful maiden of marriageable age.

Swanhild became affianced to Ermenrich, King of Gothland, who sent his son, Randwer, and one of his servants, Sibich, to escort the bride to his kingdom. Sibich was a traitor, and as part of a plan to compass the death of the royal family that he might claim the kingdom, he accused Randwer of having tried to win his young stepmother's affections. This accusation so roused the anger of Ermenrich that he ordered his son to be hanged, and Swanhild to be trampled to death under the feet of wild horses. The beauty of this daughter of Sigurd and Gudrun was such, however, that even the wild steeds could not be induced to harm her until she had been hidden from their sight under a great blanket, when they trod her to death under their cruel hoofs.

Upon learning the fate of her beloved daughter, Gudrun called her three sons to her side, and girding them with armour and weapons against which nothing but stone could prevail, she bade them depart and avenge their murdered sister, after which she died of grief, and was burned on a great pyre.

The three youths, Sorli, Hamdir, and Erp, proceeded to Ermenrich's kingdom, but ere they met their foes, the two eldest, deeming Erp too young to assist them, taunted him with his small size, and finally slew him. Sorli and Hamdir then attacked Ermenrich, cut off his hands and feet, and would have slain him but for a one-eyed stranger who suddenly appeared and bade the bystanders throw stones at the young men. His orders were immediately carried out, and Sorli and Hamdir soon fell slain under the shower of stones, which, as we have seen, alone had power to injure them.

THE STORY OF
FRITHIOF THE BOLD

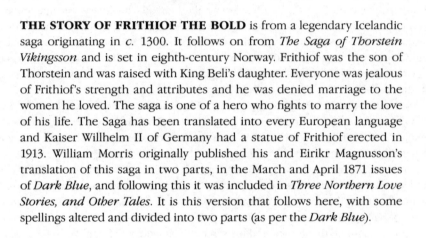

Introduction

THE STORY OF FRITHIOF THE BOLD is from a legendary Icelandic saga originating in *c.* 1300. It follows on from *The Saga of Thorstein Vikingsson* and is set in eighth-century Norway. Frithiof was the son of Thorstein and was raised with King Beli's daughter. Everyone was jealous of Frithiof's strength and attributes and he was denied marriage to the women he loved. The saga is one of a hero who fights to marry the love of his life. The Saga has been translated into every European language and Kaiser Willhelm II of Germany had a statue of Frithiof erected in 1913. William Morris originally published his and Eirikr Magnusson's translation of this saga in two parts, in the March and April 1871 issues of *Dark Blue*, and following this it was included in *Three Northern Love Stories, and Other Tales*. It is this version that follows here, with some spellings altered and divided into two parts (as per the *Dark Blue*).

Part One

Chapter 1
Of King Beli and Thorstein Vikingson and Their Children

THUS BEGINNETH THE TALE, telling how that King Beli ruled over Sogn-land; three children had he, whereof Helgi was his first son, and Halfdan his second, but Ingibjorg his daughter. Ingibjorg was fair of face and wise of mind, and she was ever accounted the foremost of the king's children.

Now a certain strand went west of the firth, and a great stead was thereon, which was called Balder's Meads; a Place of Peace was there, and a great temple, and round about it a great garth of pales: many gods were there, but amidst them all was Balder held of most account. So jealous were the heathen men of this stead, that they would have no hurt done therein to man nor beast, nor might any man have dealings with a woman there.

Sowstrand was the name of that stead whereas the king dwelt; but on the other side the firth was an abode named Foreness, where dwelt a man called Thorstein, the son of Viking; and his stead was over against the king's dwelling.

Thorstein had a son by his wife called Frithiof: he was the tallest and strongest of men, and more furnished of all prowess than any other man, even from his youth up. Frithiof the Bold was he called, and so well beloved was he, that all prayed for good things for him.

Now the king's children were but young when their mother died; but a goodman of Sogn, named Hilding, prayed to have the king's daughter to foster: so there was she reared well and needfully: and she was called Ingibjorg the Fair. Frithiof also was fostered of goodman Hilding, wherefore was he foster-brother to the king's daughter, and they two were peerless among children.

Now King Beli's chattels began to ebb fast away from his hands, for he was grown old.

Thorstein had rule over the third part of the realm, and in him lay the king's greatest strength.

Every third year Thorstein feasted the king at exceeding great cost, and the king feasted Thorstein the two years between.

Helgi, Beli's son, from his youth up turned much to blood-offering: neither were those brethren well-beloved.

Thorstein had a ship called Ellidi, which pulled fifteen oars on either board; it ran up high stem and stern, and was strong-built like an ocean-going ship, and its bulwarks were clamped with iron.

So strong was Frithiof that he pulled the two bow oars of Ellidi; but either oar was thirteen ells long, and two men pulled every oar otherwhere.

Frithiof was deemed peerless amid the young men of that time, and the king's sons envied him, whereas he was more praised than they.

Now King Beli fell sick; and when the sickness lay heavy on him he called his sons to him and said to them: "This sickness will bring me to mine end, therefore will I bid you this, that ye hold fast to those old friends that I have had; for meseems in all things ye fall short of that father and son, Thorstein and Frithiof, yea, both in good counsel and in hardihood. A mound ye shall raise over me."

So with that Beli died.

Thereafter Thorstein fell sick; so he spake to Frithiof: "Kinsman," says he, "I will crave this of thee, that thou bow thy will before the king's sons, for their dignity's sake; yet doth my heart speak goodly things to me concerning thy fortune. Now would I be laid in my mound over against King Beli's mound, down by the sea on this side the firth, whereas it may be easiest for us to cry out each to each of tidings drawing nigh."

A little after this Thorstein departed, and was laid in mound even as he had bidden; but Frithiof took the land and chattels after him. Biorn and Asmund were Frithiof s foster-brethren; they were big and strong men both.

Chapter 2
Frithiof Wooeth Ingibjorg of Those Brethren

SO FRITHIOF BECAME the most famed of men, and the bravest in all things that may try a man.

Biorn, his foster-brother, he held in most account of all, but Asmund served the twain of them.

The ship Ellidi, he gat, the best of good things, of his father's heritage, and another possession therewith – a gold ring; no dearer was in Norway.

So bounteous a man was Frithiof withal, that it was the talk of most, that he was a man of no less honour than those brethren, but it were for the name of king; and for this cause they held Frithiof in hate and enmity, and it was a heavy thing to them that he was called greater than they: furthermore they thought they could see that Ingibjorg, their sister, and Frithiof were of one mind together.

It befell hereon that the kings had to go to a feast to Frithiof s house at Foreness; and there it happened according to wont that he gave to all men beyond that they were worthy of. Now Ingibjorg was there, and she and Frithiof talked long together; and the king's daughter said to him:

"A goodly gold ring hast thou."

"Yea, in good sooth," said he.

Thereafter went those brethren to their own home, and greater grew their enmity of Frithiof.

A little after grew Frithiof heavy of mood, and Biorn, his foster-brother, asked him why he fared so.

He said he had it in his mind to woo Ingibjorg. "For though I be named by a lesser name than those brethren, yet am I not fashioned lesser."

"Even so let us do then," quoth Biorn. So Frithiof fared with certain men unto those brethren; and the kings were sitting on their father's mound when Frithiof greeted them well, and then set forth his wooing, and prayed for their sister Ingibjorg, the daughter of Beli.

The kings said: "Not overwise is this thine asking, whereas thou wouldst have us give her to one who lacketh dignity; wherefore we gainsay thee this utterly."

Said Frithiof: "Then is mine errand soon sped; but in return never will I give help to you henceforward, nay, though ye need it ever so much."

They said they heeded it nought: so Frithiof went home, and was joyous once more.

Chapter 3
Of King Ring and Those Brethren

THERE WAS A KING named Ring, who ruled over Ringrealm, which also was in Norway: a mighty folk-king he was, and a great man, but come by now unto his latter days.

Now he spake to his men: "Lo, I have heard that the sons of King Beli have brought to nought their friendship with Frithiof, who is the noblest of men; wherefore will I send men to these kings, and bid them choose whether they will submit them to me and pay me tribute, or else that I bring war on them: and all things then shall lie ready to my hand to take, for they have neither might nor wisdom to withstand me; yet great fame were it to my old age to overcome them."

After that fared the messengers of King Ring, and found those brethren, Helgi and Halfdan, in Sogn, and spake to them thus: "King Ring sends bidding to you to send him tribute, or else will he war against your realm."

They answered and said that they would not learn in the days of their youth what they would be loth to know in their old age, even how to serve King Ring with shame. "Nay, now shall we draw together all the folk that we may."

Even so they did; but now, when they beheld their force that it was but little, they sent Hilding their fosterer to Frithiof to bid him come help them against King Ring. Now Frithiof sat at the knave-play when Hilding came thither, who spake thus: "Our kings send thee greeting, Frithiof, and would have thy help in battle against King Ring, who cometh against their realm with violence and wrong."

Frithiof answered him nought, but said to Biorn, with whom he was playing: "A bare place in thy board, foster-brother, and nowise mayst thou amend it; nay, for my part I shall beset thy red piece there, and wot whether it be safe."

Then Hilding spake again:

"King Helgi bade me say thus much, Frithiof, that thou shouldst go on this journey with them, or else look for ill at their hands when they at the last come back."

"A double game, foster-brother," said Biorn; "and two ways to meet thy play."

Frithiof said: "Thy play is to fall first on the knave, yet the double game is sure to be."

No other outcome of his errand had Hilding: he went back speedily to the kings, and told them Frithiof's answer.

They asked Hilding what he made out of those words. He said:

"Whereas he spake of the bare place he will have been thinking of the lack in this journey of yours; but when he said he would beset the red piece, that will mean Ingibjorg, your sister; so give ye all the heed ye may to her. But whereas I threatened him with ill from you, Biorn deemed the game a double one; but Frithiof said that the knave must be set on first, speaking thereby of King Ring."

So then the brethren arrayed them for departing; but, ere they went, they let bring Ingibioig and eight women with her to Balder's Meads, saying that Frithiof would not be so mad rash as to go see her thither, since there was none who durst make riot there.

Then fared those brethren south to Jadar, and met King Ring in Sogn-Sound.

Now, herewith was King Ring most of all wroth that the brothers had said that they accounted it a shame to fight with a man so old that he might not get a-horseback unholpen.

Chapter 4
Frithiof Goes to Balder's Meads

STRAIGHTWAY WHENAS the kings were gone away Frithiof took his raiment of state and set the goodly gold ring on his arm; then went the foster-brethren down to the sea and launched Ellidi. Then said Biorn: "Whither away, foster-brother?"

"To Balder's Meads," said Frithiof, "to be glad with Ingibjorg."

Biorn said: "A thing unmeet to do, to make the gods wroth with us."

"Well, it shall be risked this time," said Frithiof; "and withal, more to me is Ingibjorg's grace than Balder's grame."

Therewith they rowed over the firth, and went up to Balder's Meads and to Ingibjorg's bower, and there she sat with eight maidens, and the new comers were eight also.

But when they came there, lo, all the place was hung with cloth of pall and precious webs.

Then Ingibjorg arose and said:

"Why art thou so overbold, Frithiof, that thou art come here without the leave of my brethren to make the gods angry with thee?"

Frithiof says: "Howsoever that may be, I hold thy love of more account than the gods' hate."

Ingibjorg answered: "Welcome art thou here, thou and thy men!"

Then she made place for him to sit beside her, and drank to him in the best of wine; and thus they sat and were merry together.

Then beheld Ingibjorg the goodly ring on his arm, and asked him if that precious thing were his own.

Frithiof said Yea, and she praised the ring much. Then Frithiof said:

"I will give thee the ring if thou wilt promise to give it to no one, but to send it to me when thou no longer shalt have will to keep it: and hereon shall we plight troth each to other."

So with this troth-plighting they exchanged rings.

Frithiof was oft at Balder's Meads a-night time, and every day between whiles would he go thither to be glad with Ingibjorg.

Chapter 5
Those Brethren Come Home Again

NOW TELLS THE TALE of those brethren, that they met King Ring, and he had more folk than they: then went men betwixt them, and sought to make peace, so that no battle should be: thereto King Ring assented on such terms that the brethren should submit them to him, and give him in marriage Ingibjorg their sister, with the third part of all their possessions.

The kings said Yea thereto, for they saw that they had to do with overwhelming might: so the peace was fast bound by oaths, and the wedding was to be at Sogn whenas King Ring should go see his betrothed.

So those brethren fare home with their folk, right ill content with things. But Frithiof, when he deemed that the brethren might be looked for home again, spake to the king's daughter:

"Sweetly and well have ye done to us, neither has goodman Balder been wroth with us; but now as soon as ye wot of the kings' coming home, spread the sheets of your beds abroad on the Hall of the Goddesses, for that is the highest of all the garth, and we may see it from our stead."

The king's daughter said: "Thou dost not after the like of any other: but certes, we welcome dear friends whenas ye come to us."

So Frithiof went home; and the next morning he went out early, and when he came in then he spake and sang:

"Now must I tell
To our good men
That over and done
Are our fair journeys;

No more a-shipboard
Shall we be going,
For there are the sheets
Spread out a-bleaching."

Then they went out, and saw that the Hall of the Goddesses was all thatched with white linen. Biorn spake and said: "Now are the kings come home, and but a little while have we to sit in peace, and good were it, meseems, to gather folk together."

So did they, and men came flocking thither.

Now the brethren soon heard of the ways of Frithiof and Ingibjorg, and of the gathering of men. So King Helgi spake:

"A wondrous thing how Balder will bear what shame soever Frithiof and she will lay on him! Now will I send men to him, and wot what atonement he will offer us, or else will I drive him from the land, for our strength seemeth to me not enough that we should fight with him as now."

So Hilding, their fosterer, bare the king's errand to Frithiof and his friends, and spake in such wise: "This atonement the kings will have of thee, Frithiof, that thou go gather the tribute of the Orkneys, which has not been paid since Beli died, for they need money, whereas they are giving Ingibjorg their sister in marriage, and much of wealth with her."

Frithiof said: "This thing only somewhat urges us to peace, the good will of our kin departed; but no trustiness will those brethren show herein. But this condition I make, that our lands be in good peace while we are away." So this was promised and all bound by oaths.

Then Frithiof arrays him for departing, and is captain of men brave and of good help, eighteen in company.

Now his men asked him if he would not go to King Helgi and make peace with him, and pray himself free from Balder's wrath.

But he answered: "Hereby I swear that I will never pray Helgi for peace."

Then he went aboard Ellidi, and they sailed out along the Sognnrth.

But when Frithiof was gone from home, King Halfdan spake to Helgi his brother: "Better lordship and more had we if Frithiof had payment for his masterful deed: now therefore let us burn his stead, and bring on him and his men such a storm on the sea as shall make an end of them."

Helgi said it was a thing meet to be done.

So then they burned up clean all the stead at Foreness and robbed it of all goods; and after that sent for two witch-wives, Heidi and Hamglom, and gave them money to raise against Frithiof and his men so mighty a storm that they should all be lost at sea. So they sped the witch-song, and went up on the witch-mount with spells and sorcery.

Chapter 6
Frithiof Sails for the Orkneys

SO WHEN FRITHIOF and his men were come out of the Sognfirth there fell on them great wind and storm, and an exceeding heavy sea: but the ship drave on swiftly, for sharp built she was, and the best to breast the sea. So now Frithiof sang:

"Oft let I swim from Sogn
My tarred ship sooty-sided,
When maids sat o'er the mead-horn
Amidst of Balder's Meadows;

> *Now while the storm is wailing*
> *Farewell I bid you maidens,*
> *Still shall ye love us, sweet ones,*
> *Though Ellidi the sea fill."*

Said Biorn: "Thou mightest well find other work to do than singing songs over the maids of Balder's Meadows."

"Of such work shall I not speedily run dry, though," said Frithiof. Then they bore up north to the sounds nigh those isles that are called Solundir, and therewith was the gale at its hardest.

Then sang Frithiof:

> *"Now is the sea a-swelling,*
> *And sweepeth the rack onward;*
> *Spells of old days cast o'er us*
> *Make ocean all unquiet;*
> *No more shall we be striving*
> *Mid storm with wash of billows,*
> *But Solundir shall shelter*
> *Our ship with ice-beat rock-walls."*

So they lay to under the lee of the isles hight Solundir, and were minded to abide there; but straightway thereon the wind fell: then they turned away from under the lee of the islands, and now their voyage seemed hopeful to them, because the wind was fair awhile: but soon it began to freshen again.

Then sang Frithiof:

> *"In days foredone*
> *From Foreness strand*
> *I rowed to meet*
> *Maid Ingibjorg;*
> *But now I sail*
> *Through chilly storm*
> *And wide away*
> *My long-worm driveth."*

And now when they were come far out into the main, once more the sea waxed wondrous troubled, and a storm arose with so great drift of snow, that none might see the stem from the stern; and they shipped seas, so that they must be ever a-baling.

So Frithiof sang:

> *"The salt waves see we nought*
> *As seaward drive we ever*
> *Before the witch-wrought weather,*
> *We well-famed kings'-defenders:*
> *Here are we all a-standing,*
> *With all Solundir hull-down,*

> *Eighteen brave lads a-baling*
> *Black Ellidi to bring home."*

Said Biorn: "Needs must he who fareth far fall in with diverse hap."
"Yea, certes, foster-brother," said Frithiof. And he sang withal:

> *"Helgi it is that helpeth*
> *The white-head billows' waxing;*
> *Cold time unlike the kissing*
> *In the close of Balder's Meadow!*
> *So is the hate of Helgi*
> *To that heart's love she giveth.*
> *O would that here I held her,*
> *Gift high above all giving!"*

"Maybe," said Biorn, "she is looking higher than thou now art: what matter when all is said?"
"Well," says Frithiof, "now is the time to show ourselves to be men of avail, though blither tide it was at Balder's Meadows."
So they turned to in manly wise, for there were the bravest of men come together in the best ship of the Northlands. But Frithiof sang a stave:

> *"So come in the West-sea,*
> *Nought see I the billows,*
> *The sea-water seemeth*
> *As sweeping of wild-fire.*
> *Topple the rollers,*
> *Toss the hills swan-white,*
> *Ellidi wallows*
> *O'er steep of the wave-hills."*

Then they shipped a huge sea, so that all stood a-baling. But Frithiof sang:

> *"With love-moved mouth the maiden*
> *Mepledgeth though I founder.*
> *Ah! bright sheets lay a-bleaching,*
> *East there on brents the swan loves."*

Biorn said: "Art thou of mind belike that the maids of Sogn will weep many tears over thee?"
Said Frithiof: "Surely that was in my mind."
Therewith so great a sea broke over the bows, that the water came in like the in-falling of a river; but it availed them much that the ship was so good, and the crew aboard her so hardy.
Now sang Biorn:

> *"No widow, methinks,*
> *To thee or me drinks;*
> *No ring-bearer fair*
> *Biddeth draw near;*

> *Salt are our eyne*
> *Soaked in the brine;*
> *Strong our arms are no more,*
> *And our eyelids smart sore."*

Quoth Asmund: "Small harm though your arms be tried somewhat, for no pity we had from you when we rubbed our eyes whenas ye must needs rise early a-mornings to go to Balder's Meadows."

"Well," said Frithiof, "why singest thou not, Asmund?"

"Not I," said Asmund; yet sang a ditty straightway:

> *"Sharp work about the sail was*
> *When o'er the ship seas tumbled,*
> *And there was I a-working*
> *Within-board 'gainst eight balers;*
> *Better it was to bower,*
> *Bringing the women breakfast,*
> *Than here to be 'mid billows*
> *Black Ellidi a-baling."*

"Thou accountest thy help of no less worth than it is?" said Frithiof, laughing therewith; "but sure it showeth the thrall's blood in thee that thou wouldst fain be awaiting at table."

Now it blew harder and harder yet, so that to those who were aboard liker to huge peaks and mountains than to waves seemed the sea-breakers that crashed on all sides against the ship.

Then Frithiof sang:

> *"On bolster I sat.*
> *In Balder's Mead erst,*
> *And all songs that I could*
> *To the king's daughter sang;*
> *Now on Ran's bed belike*
> *Must I soon be a-lying,*
> *And another shall be*
> *By Ingibjorg's side."*

Biorn said: "Great fear lieth ahead of us, foster-brother, and now dread hath crept into thy words, which is ill with such a good man as thou."

Says Frithiof: "Neither fear nor fainting is it, though I sing now of those our merry journeys; yet perchance more hath been said of them than need was: but most men would think death surer than life, if they were so bested as we be."

"Yet shall I answer thee somewhat," said Biorn, and sang:

> *"Yet one gain have I gotten*
> *Thou gatst not 'mid thy fortune,*
> *For meet play did I make me*
> *With Ingibjorgs eight maidens;*
> *Red rings we laid together*
> *Aright in Balder's Meadow,*

> *When far off was the warder*
> *Of the wide land of Halfdan."*

"Well," said he, "we must be content with things as they are, foster-brother."

Therewith so great a sea smote them, that the bulwark was broken and both the sheets, and four men were washed overboard and all lost.

Then sang Frithiof:

> *"Both sheets are bursten*
> *Amid the great billows,*
> *Four swains are sunk*
> *In the fathomless sea?"*

"Now, meseems," said Frithiof, "it may well be that some of us will go to the house of Ran, nor shall we deem us well sped if we come not thither in glorious array; wherefore it seems good to me that each man of us here should have somewhat of gold on him."

Then he smote asunder the ring, Ingibjorg's gift, and shared it between all his men, and sang a stave withal:

> *"The red ring here I hew me*
> *Once owned of Halfdan's father,*
> *The wealthy lord of erewhile,*
> *Or the sea waves undo us,*
> *So on the guests shall gold be,*
> *If we have need of guesting;*
> *Meet so for mighty men-folk*
> *Amid Ran's hall to hold them."*

"Not all so sure is it that we come there," said Biorn; "and yet it may well be so."

Now Frithiof and his folk found that the ship had great way on her, and they knew not what lay ahead, for all was mirk on either board, so that none might see the stem or stern from amidships; and therewith was there great drift of spray amid the furious wind, and frost, and snow, and deadly cold.

Now Frithiof went up to the masthead, and when he came down he said to his fellows: "A sight exceeding wondrous have I seen, for a great whale went in a ring about the ship, and I misdoubt me that we come nigh to some land, and that he is keeping the shore against us; for certes King Helgi has dealt with us in no friendly wise, neither will this his messenger be friendly. Moreover I saw two women on the back of the whale, and they it is who will have brought this great storm on us with the worst of spells and witchcraft; but now we shall try which may prevail, my fortune or their devilry, so steer ye at your straightest, and I will smite these evil things with beams."

Therewith he sang a stave:

> *"See I troll women*
> *Twain on the billows,*
> *Even they whom Helgi*
> *Hither hath sent.*
> *Ellidi now*

> *Or ever her way stop*
> *Shall smile the backs*
> *Of these asunder."*

So tells the tale that this wonder went with the good ship Ellidi, that she knew the speech of man.

But Biorn said: "Now may we see the treason of those brethren against us." Therewith he took the tiller, but Frithiof caught up a forked beam, and ran into the prow, and sang a stave:

> *"Ellidi, hail!*
> *Leap high o'er the billows!*
> *Break of the troll wives*
> *Brow or teeth now!*
> *Break cheek or jaw*
> *Of the cursed woman,*
> *One foot or twain*
> *Of the ogress filthy."*

Therewith he drave his fork at one of the skin-changers, and the beak of Ellidi smote the other on the back, and the backs of both were broken; but the whale took the deep, and gat him gone, and they never saw him after.

Then the wind fell, but the ship lay waterlogged; so Frithiof called out to his men, and bade bale out the ship, but Biorn said:

"No need to work now, verily!"

"Be thou not afeard, foster-brother," said Frithiof, "ever was it the wont of good men of old time to be helpful while they might, whatsoever should come after." And therewith he sang a stave:

> *"No need, fairfellows,*
> *To fear the death-day;*
> *Rather be glad,*
> *Good men of mine:*
> *For if dreams wot aught*
> *All nights they say*
> *I yet shall have*
> *My Ingibjorg."*

Then they baled out the ship; and they were now come nigh unto land; but there was yet a flaw of wind in their teeth. So then did Frithiof take the two bow oars again, and rowed full mightily. Therewith the weather brightened, and they saw that they were come out to Effia Sound, and so there they made land.

The crew were exceeding weary; but so stout a man was Frithiof that he bore eight men a-land over the foreshore, but Biorn bore two, and Asmund one. Then sang Frithiof:

> *"Fast bare I up*
> *To the fire-lit house*
> *My men all dazed*
> *With the drift of the storm;*

And the sail moreover
To the sand I carried;
With the might of the sea
Is there no more to do."

Chapter 7
Frithiof at the Orkneys

NOW EARL ANGANTYR was at Effia whenas Frithiof and his folk came a-land there. But his way it was, when he was sitting at the drink, that one of his men should sit at the watch-window, looking weatherward from the drinking hall, and keep watch there. From a great horn drank he ever: and still as one was emptied another was filled for him. And he who held the watch when Frithiof came a-land was called Hallward; and now he saw where Frithiof and his men went, and sang a stave:

"Men see I a-baling
Amid the storm's might;
Six bale on Ellidi
Seven are a-rowing;
Like is he in the stem,
Straining hard at the oars,
To Frithiof the bold,
The brisk in the battle."

So when he had drunk out the horn, he cast it in through the window, and spake to the woman who gave him drink:

"Take up from the floor,
O fair-going woman,
The horn cast adown
Drunk out to the end!
I behold men at sea
Who, storm-beaten, shall need
Help at our hands
Ere the haven they make."

Now the Earl heard what Hallward sang; so he asked for tidings, and Hallward said: "Men are come a-land here, much forewearied, yet brave lads belike: but one of them is so hardy that he beareth the others. ashore."

Then said the Earl, "Go ye, and meet them, and welcome them in seemly wise; if this be Frithiof, the son of Hersir Thorstein, my friend, he is a man famed far and wide for all prowess."

Then there took up the word a man named Atli, a great viking, and he spake: "Now shall that be proven which is told of, that Frithiof hath sworn never to be first in the craving of peace."

There were ten men in company with him, all evil and outrageous, who often wrought berserksgang.

So when they met Frithiof they took to their weapons.

But Atli said:

"Good to turn hither, Frithiof! Clutching ernes should claw; and we no less, Frithiof! Yea, and now may'st thou hold to thy word, and not crave first for peace."

So Frithiof turned to meet them, and sang a stave:

"Nay, nay, in nought
Now shall ye cow us.
Blenching hearts
Isle-abiders!
Alone with you ten
The fight will I try,
Rather than pray
For peace at your hands."

Then came Hallward thereto, and spake: "The Earl wills that ye all be made welcome here: neither shall any set on you."

Frithiof said he would take that with a good heart; howsoever he was ready for either peace or war.

So thereon they went to the Earl, and he made Frithiof and all his men right welcome, and they abode with him, in great honour holden, through the wintertide; and oft would the Earl ask of their voyage: so Biorn sang:

"There baled we, wight fellows,
Washed over and over
On both boards
By billows;
For ten days we baled there,
And eight thereunto."

The Earl said: "Well nigh did the king undo you; it is ill seen of such-like kings as are meet for nought but to overcome men by wizardry. But now I wot," says Angantyr, "of thine errand hither, Frithiof, that thou art sent after the scat: whereto I give thee a speedy answer, that never shall King Helgi get scat of me, but to thee will I give money, even as much as thou wilt; and thou mayest call it scat if thou hast a mind to, or whatso else thou wilt."

So Frithiof said that he would take the money.

Chapter 8
King Ring Weddeth Ingibjorg

NOW SHALL IT BE TOLD of what came to pass in Norway the while Frithiof was away: for those brethren let burn up all the stead at Foreness. Moreover, while the weird sisters were at their spells they tumbled down from off their high witch-mount, and brake both their backs.

That autumn came King Ring north to Sogn to his wedding, and there at a noble feast drank his bridal with Ingibjorg.

"Whence came that goodly ring which thou hast on thine arm?" said King Ring to Ingibjorg.

She said her father had owned it, but he answered and said:

"Nay, for Frithiof s gift it is: so take it off thine arm straightway; for no gold shalt thou lack whenas thou comest to Elfhome."

So she gave the ring to King Helgi's wife, and bade her give it to Frithiof when he came back. Then King Ring wended home with his wife, and loved her with exceeding great love.

Chapter 9
Frithiof Brings the Tribute to the Kings

THE SPRING AFTER these things Frithiof departed from the Orkneys and Earl Angantyr in all good liking; and Hallward went with Frithiof.

But when they came to Norway they heard tell of the burning of Frithiof's stead.

So when he was gotten to Foreness, Frithiof said: "Black is my house waxen now; no friends have been at work here." And he sang withal:

> *"Frank and free,*
> *With my father dead,*
> *In Foreness old*
> *We drank aforetime.*
> *Now my abode*
> *Behold I burned;*
> *For many ill deeds*
> *The kings must I pay."*

Then he sought rede of his men what was to be done; but they bade him look to it: then he said that the scat must first be paid out of hand. So they rowed over the Firth to Sowstrand; and there they heard that the kings were gone to Balder's Meads to sacrifice to the gods; so Frithiof and Biorn went up thither, and bade Hallward and Asmund break up meanwhile all ships, both great and small, that were anigh; and they did so. Then went Frithiof and his fellow to the door at Balder's Meads, and Frithiof would go in. Biorn bade him fare warily, since he must needs go in alone; but Frithiof charged him to abide without, and keep watch; and he sang a stave:

> *"All alone go I*
> *Unto the stead;*
> *No folk I need*
> *For the finding of kings;*
> *But cast ye the fire*
> *O'er the kings' dwellingly*
> *If I come not again*
> *In the cool of the even."*

"Ah," said Biorn, "a goodly singing!"

Then went Frithiof in, and saw but few folk in the Hall of the Goddesses; there were the kings at their blood-offering, sitting a-drinking; a fire was there on the floor, and the wives of the kings sat thereby, a-warming the gods, while others anointed them, and wiped them with napkins.

So Frithiof went up to King Helgi and said: "Have here thy scat!"

And therewith he heaved up the purse wherein was the silver, and drave it on to the face of the king; whereby were two of his teeth knocked out, and he fell down stunned in his high seat; but Halfdan got hold of him, so that he fell not into the fire.

Then sang Frithiof:

"Have here thy scat,
High lord of the warriors!
Heed that and thy teeth,
Lest all tumble about thee!
Lo the silver abideth
At the bight of this bag here,
That Biorn and I
Betwixt us have borne thee."

Now there were but few folk in the chamber, because the drinking was in another place; so Frithiof went out straightway along the floor, and beheld therewith that goodly ring of his on the arm of Helgi's wife as she warmed Balder at the fire; so he took hold of the ring, but it was fast to her arm, and he dragged her by it over the pavement toward the door, and Balder fell from her into the fire; then Halfdan's wife caught hastily at Balder, whereby the god that she was warming fell likewise into the fire, and the fire caught both the gods, for they had been anointed, and ran up thence into the roof, so that the house was all ablaze: but Frithiof got the ring to him ere he came out. So then Biorn asked him what had come of his going in there; but Frithiof held up the ring and sang a stave:

"The heavy purse smote Helgi
Hard 'midst his scoundrel's visage:
Lowly bowed Halfdan's brother,
Fell bundling 'mid the high seat;
There Balder fell a-burning.
But first my bright ring gat I.
Fast from the roaring fire
I dragged the bent crone forward."

Men say that Frithiof cast a firebrand up on to the roof, so that the hall was all ablaze, and therewith sang a stave:

"Down stride we toward the sea-strand,
And strong deeds set a-going,
For now the blue flame bickers
Amidst of Balder's Meadow."

And therewith they went down to the sea.

Chapter 10
Frithiof Made an Outlaw

BUT AS SOON AS King Helgi had come to himself he bade follow after Frithiof speedily, and slay them all, him and his fellows: "A man of forfeit life, who spareth no Place of Peace!"

So they blew the gathering for the kings' men, and when they came out to the hall they saw that it was afire; so King Halfdan went thereto with some of the folk, but King Helgi followed after Frithiof and his men, who were by then gotten a-shipboard and were lying on their oars.

Now King Helgi and his men find that all the ships are scuttled, and they have to turn back to shore, and have lost some men: then waxed King Helgi so wroth that he grew mad, and he bent his bow, and laid an arrow on the string, and drew at Frithiof so mightily that the bow brake asunder in the midst.

But when Frithiof saw that, then he gat him to the two bow oars of Ellidi, and laid so hard on them that they both brake, and with that he sang a stave:

> "Young Ingibjorg
> Kissed I aforetime,
> Kissed Beli's daughter
> In Balder's Meadow.
> So shall the oars
> Of Ellidi
> Break both together
> As Helgi's bow breaks."

Then the land-wind ran down the firth and they hoisted sail and sailed; but Frithiof bade them look to it that they might have no long abiding there. And so withal they sailed out of the Sognfirth, and Frithiof sang:

> "Sail we away from Sogn,
> E'en as we sailed aforetime,
> When flared the fire all over
> The house that was my father's.
> Now is the bale a-burning
> Amidst of Balder's Meadow:
> But wend I as a wild-wolf,
> Well wot I they have sworn it."

"What shall we turn to now, foster-brother?" said Biorn.

"I may not abide here in Norway," said Frithiof: "I will learn the ways of warriors, and sail a-warring."

So they searched the isles and out-skerries the summer long, and gathered thereby riches and renown; but in autumn-tide they made for the Orkneys, and Angantyr gave them good welcome, and they abode there through the winter-tide.

But when Frithiof was gone from Norway the kings held a Thing, whereat was Frithiof made an outlaw throughout their realm: they took his lands to them, moreover, and King Halfdan took up his abode at Foreness, and built up again all Balder's Meadow, though it was long ere the fire was slaked there. This misliked King Helgi most, that the gods were all burned up, and great was the cost or ever Balder's Meadow was built anew fully equal to its first estate.

So King Helgi abode still at Sowstrand.

Part Two

Chapter 11
Frithiof Fareth to See King Ring and Ingibjorg

FRITHIOF WAXED EVER in riches and renown whithersoever he went: evil men he slew, and grimly strong-thieves, but husbandmen and chapmen he let abide in peace; and now was he called anew Frithiof the Bold; he had gotten to him by now a great company well arrayed, and was become exceeding wealthy of chattels.

But when Frithiof had been three winters a-warring he sailed west, and made the Wick; then he said that he would go a-land: "But ye shall fare a-warring without me this winter; for I begin to weary of warfare, and would fain go to the Uplands, and get speech of King Ring: but hither shall ye come to meet me in the summer, and I will be here the first day of summer."

Biorn said: "This counsel is naught wise, though thou must needs rule; rather would I that we fare north to Sogn, and slay both those kings, Helgi and Halfdan."

"It is all naught," said Frithiof; "I must needs go see King Ring and Ingibjorg."

Says Biorn: "Loth am I hereto that thou shouldst risk thyself alone in his hands; for this Ring is a wise man and of great kin, though he be somewhat old."

But Frithiof said he would have his own way: "And thou, Biorn, shalt be captain of our company meanwhile."

So they did as he bade, and Frithiof fared to the Uplands in the autumn, for he desired sore to look upon the love of King Ring and Ingibjorg. But or ever he came there he did on him, over his clothes, a great cloak all shaggy; two staves he had in his hand, and a mask over his face, and he made as if he were exceeding old.

So he met certain herdsmen, and, going heavily, he asked them: "Whence are ye?"

They answered and said: "We are of Streitaland, whereas the king dwelleth."

Quoth the carle: "Is King Ring a mighty king, then?"

They answered: "Thou lookest to us old enough to have cunning to know what manner of man is King Ring in all wise."

The carle said that he had heeded salt-boiling more than the ways of kings; and therewith he goes up to the king's house.

So when the day was well worn he came into the hall, blinking about as a dotard, and took an outward place, pulling his hood over him to hide his visage.

Then spake King Ring to Ingibjorg: "There is come into the hall a man far bigger than other men."

The queen answered: "That is no such great tidings here."

But the king spake to a serving-man who stood before the board, and said: "Go thou, and ask yon cowled man who he is, whence he cometh, and of what kin he is."

So the lad ran down the hall to the new-comer and said: "What art thou called, thou man? Where wert thou last night? Of what kin art thou?"

Said the cowled man: "Quick come thy questions, good fellow! but hast thou skill to understand if I shall tell thee hereof?"

"Yea, certes," said the lad.

"Well," said the cowl-bearer, "Thief is my name, with Wolf was I last night, and in Grief-ham was I reared."

Then ran the lad back to the king, and told him the answer of the new-comer.

"Well told, lad," said the king; "but for that land of Grief-ham, I know it well: it may well be that the man is of no light heart, and yet a wise man shall he be, and of great worth I account him."

Said the queen: "A marvellous fashion of thine, that thou must needs talk so freely with every carle that cometh hither! Yea, what is the worth of him, then?"

"That wottest thou no clearer than I," said the king; "but I see that he thinketh more than he talketh, and is peering all about him."

Therewith the king sent a man after him, and so the cowl-bearer went up before the king, going somewhat bent, and greeted him in a low voice. Then said the king: "What art thou called, thou big man?"

And the cowl-bearer answered and sang:

> "Peace-thief they called me
> On the prow with the Vikings;
> But War-thief whenas
> I set widows a-weeping;
> Spear-thief when I
> Sent forth the barbed shafts;
> Battle-thief when I
> Burst forth on the king;
> Hel-thief when I
> Tossed up the small babies:
> Isle-thief when I
> In the outer isles harried;
> Slaws-thief when I
> Sat aloft over men:
> Yet since have I drifted
> With salt-boiling carls,
> Needy of help
> 'Ere hither I came."

Said the king: "Thou hast gotten thy name of Thief from many a matter, then; but where wert thou last night, and what is thy home?"

The cowl-bearer said: "In Grief-ham I grew up; but heart drave me hither, and home have I nowhere."

The king said: "Maybe indeed that thou hast been nourished in Grief-ham a certain while; yet also maybe that thou wert born in a place of peace. But in the wild-wood must thou have lain last night, for no goodman dwelleth anigh named Wolf; but whereas thou sayest thou hast no home, so is it, that thou belike deemest thy home nought, because of thy heart that drave thee hither."

Then spake Ingibjorg: "Go, Thief, get thee to some other harbour, or in to the guest-hall."

"Nay," said the king, "I am old enow to know how to marshal guests; so do off thy cowl, new-comer, and sit down on my other hand."

"Yea, old, and over old," said the queen, "when thou settest staff-carles by thy side."

"Nay, lord, it beseemeth not," said Thief; "better it were as the queen sayeth. I have been more used to boiling salt than sitting beside lords."

"Do thou my will," said the king, "for I will rule this time."

So Thief cast his cowl from him, and was clad thereunder in a dark blue kirtle; on his arm, moreover, was the goodly gold ring, and a thick silver belt was round about him, with a great purse on it, and therein silver pennies glittering; a sword was girt to his side, and he had a great fur hood on his head, for his eyes were bleared, and his face all wrinkled.

"Ah! now we fare better, say I," quoth the king; "but do thou, queen, give him a goodly mantle, well shapen for him."

"Thou shalt rule, my lord," said the queen; "but in small account do I hold this Thief of thine."

So then he gat a good mantle over him, and sat down in the high-seat beside the king.

The queen waxed red as blood when she saw the goodly ring, yet would she give him never a word; but the king was exceeding blithe with him and said: "A goodly ring hast thou on thine arm there; thou must have boiled salt long enough to get it."

Says he, "That is all the heritage of my father."

"Ah!" says the king, "maybe thou hast more than that; well, few salt-boiling carles are thy peers, I deem, unless eld is deep in mine eyes now."

So Thief was there through the winter amid good entertainment, and well accounted of by all men; he was bounteous of his wealth, and joyous with all men: the queen held but little converse with him; but the king and he were ever blithe together.

Chapter 12
Frithiof Saves the King and Queen on the Ice

THE TALE TELLS that on a time King Ring and the queen, and a great company, would go to a feast. So the king spake to Thief: "Wilt thou fare with us, or abide at home?"

He said he had liefer go; and the king said: "Then am I the more content."

So they went on their ways, and had to cross a certain frozen water. Then said Thief: "I deem this ice untrustworthy; meseemeth ye fare unwarily."

Quoth the king: "It is often shown how heedful in thine heart thou wilt be to us."

So a little after the ice broke in beneath them, and Thief ran thereto, and dragged the wain to him, with all that was therein; and the king and the queen both sat in the same: so Thief drew it all up on to the ice, with the horses that were yoked to the wain.

Then spake King Ring: "Right well drawn, Thief! Frithiof the Bold himself would have drawn no stronger had he been here; doughty followers are such as thou!"

So they came to the feast, and there is nought to tell thereof, and the king went back again with seemly gifts.

Chapter 13
The King Sleeps Before Frithiof

NOW WEARETH AWAY the mid-winter, and when spring cometh, the weather groweth fair, the wood bloometh, the grass groweth, and ships may glide betwixt land and land. So on a day the king says to his folk: "I will that ye come with us for our disport out into the woods, that we may look upon the fairness of the earth."

So did they, and went flock-meal with the king into the woods; but so it befell, that the king and Frithiof were gotten alone together afar from other men, and the king said he was heavy, and would fain sleep. Then said Thief: "Get thee home, then, lord, for it better beseemeth men of high estate to lie at home than abroad."

"Nay," said the king, "so will I not do." And he laid him down therewith, and slept fast, snoring loud. Thief sat close by him, and presently drew his sword from his sheath and cast it far away from him.

A little while after the king woke up, and said: "Was it not so, Frithiof, that a many things came into thy mind e'en now? But well hast thou dealt with them, and great honour shalt thou have of me. Lo, now, I knew thee straightway that first evening thou earnest into our hall: now nowise speedily shalt thou depart from us; and somewhat great abideth thee."

Said Frithiof: "Lord king, thou hast done to me well, and in friendly wise; but yet must I get me gone soon, because my company cometh speedily to meet me, as I have given them charge to do."

So then they rode home from the wood, and the king's folk came flocking to him, and home they fared to the hall and drank joyously; and it was made known to all folk that Frithiof the Bold had been abiding there through the winter-tide.

Chapter 14
King Ring's Gift to Frithiof

EARLY OF A MORNING-TIDE one smote on the door of that hall, wherein slept the king and queen, and many others: then the king asked who it was that called at the hall door; and so he who was without said: "Here am I, Frithiof; and I am arrayed for my departure."

Then was the door opened, and Frithiof came in, and sang a stave:

> *"Have great thanks for the guesting*
> *Thou gavest with all bounty;*
> *Dight fully for wayfaring*
> *Is the feeder of the eagle;*
> *But, Ingidiorg, I mind thee*
> *While yet on earth we tarry;*
> *Live gloriously! I give thee*
> *This gift for many kisses."*

And therewith he cast the goodly ring towards Ingibjorg, and bade her take it.

The king smiled at this stave of his, and said: "Yea, forsooth, she hath more thanks for thy winter quarters than I; yet hath she not been more friendly to thee than I."

Then sent the king his serving-folk to fetch victuals and drink, and saith that they must eat and drink before Frithiof departed. "So arise, queen, and be joyful!" But she said she was loth to fall a-feasting so early.

"Nay, we will eat all together," said King Ring; and they did so.

But when they had drank a while King Ring spake: "I would that thou abide here, Frithiof; for my sons are but children and I am old, and unmeet for the warding of my realm, if any should bring war against it." Frithiof said: "Speedily must I be gone, lord." And he sang:

> *"Oh, live, King Ring,*
> *Both long and hale!*
> *The highest king*
> *Neath heaven's skirt!*
> *Ward well, O king,*
> *Thy wife and land,*
> *For Ingibjorg now*
> *Never more shall I meet."*

Then quoth King Ring:

> *"Fare not away,*
> *O Frithiof, thus,*
> *With downcast heart,*
> *O dearest of chieftains!*
> *For now will I give thee*
> *For all thy good gifts,*
> *Far better things*
> *Than thou wottest thyself."*

And again he sang:

> *"To Frithiof the famous*
> *My fair wife I give,*
> *And all things therewith*
> *That are unto me."*

Then Frithiof took up the word and sang:

> *"Nay, how from thine hands*
> *These gifts may I have,*
> *But if thou hast fared*
> *By the last way of fate."*

The king said: "I would not give thee this, but that I deem it will soon be so, for I sicken now. But of all men I would that thou shouldst have the joy of this; for thou art the crown of all Norway. The name of king will I give thee also; and all this, because Ingibjorg's brethren would begrudge thee any honour; and would be slower in getting thee a wife than I am."

Said Frithiof: "Have all thanks, lord, for thy goodwill beyond that I looked for! But I will have no higher dignity than to be called earl."

Then King Ring gave Frithiof rule over all his realm in due wise, and the name of earl therewith; and Frithiof was to rule it until such time as the sons of King Ring were of age to rule their own realm. So King Ring lay sick a little while, and then died; and great mourning was made for him; then was there a mound cast over him, and much wealth laid therein, according to his bidding.

Thereafter Frithiof made a noble feast, whereunto his folk came; and thereat was drunken at one and the same time the heritage feast after King Ring, and the bridal of Frithiof and Ingibjorg.

After these things Frithiof abode in his realm, and was deemed therein a most noble man; he and Ingibjorg had many children.

Chapter 15
Frithiof King in Sogn

NOW THOSE KINGS OF SOGN, the brethren of Ingibjorg, heard these tidings, how that Frithiof had gotten a king's rule in Ringrealm, and had wedded Ingibjorg their sister. Then says Helgi to Halfdan, his brother, that unheard of it was, and a deed over-bold, that a mere hersir's son should have her to wife: and so thereat they gather together a mighty army, and go their ways therewith to Ringrealm, with the mind to slay Frithiof, and lay all his realm under them.

But when Frithiof was ware of this, he gathered folk, and spake to the queen moreover: "New war is come upon our realm; and now, in whatso wise the dealings go, fain am I that thy ways to me grow no colder."

She said: "In such wise have matters gone that I must needs let thee be the highest."

Now was Biorn come from the east to help Frithiof; so they fared to the fight, and it befell, as ever erst, that Frithiof was the foremost in the peril: King Helgi and he came to handy-blows, and there he slew King Helgi.

Then bade Frithiof raise up the Shield of Peace, and the battle was stayed; and therewith he cried to King Halfdan: "Two choices are in thine hands now, either that thou give up all to my will, or else gettest thou thy bane like thy brother; for now may men see that mine is the better part."

So Halfdan chose to lay himself and his realm under Frithiof's sway; and so now Frithiof became ruler over Sogn-folk, and Halfdan was to be Hersir in Sogn and pay Frithiof tribute, while Frithiof ruled Ringrealm. So Frithiof had the name of King of Sogn-folk from the time that he gave up Ringrealm to the sons of King Ring, and thereafter he won Hordaland also. He and Ingibjorg had two sons, called Gunnthiof and Hunthiof, men of might, both of them.

And so here endeth the story of Frithiof the Bold.

The Story of Gunnlaug the Worm-Tongue and Raven the Skald

Introduction

THE STORY OF GUNNLAUG is an Icelandic saga from the end of the thirteenth century and the first of these sagas to have been published in a scholarly edition. The saga takes place during the early introduction of Christianity and follows two poets as they compete for the love of Helga. This story also displays the court culture of the Viking age. Gift-giving in court had a certain significance as it was a way to gain the support of influential people. Gunnlaug gives the gift of poetry to the leaders of a court, which is significant due to the importance attached to poetry in this era for its potential to enhance legacies. William Morris points out in his preface that it is traditionally thought to have been composed by Ari Þorgilsson (the 'father' of Icelandic history, known as 'Ari the Wise' or 'Ari the Learned'), as the names of people and genealogies within it are accurate enough that it can be seen as a historical tale. Morris and Eirikr Magnusson published a version of their translation of it in 1875 in *Three Northern Love Stories, and Other Tales*, and it is this version that follows here, with some spelling alterations.

Part One

EVEN AS ARI THORGILSON THE LEARNED, the priest, hath told it, who was the man of all Iceland most learned in tales of the land's inhabiting and in lore of time agone.

Chapter 1
Of Thorstein Egilson and His Kin

THERE WAS A MAN called Thorstein, the son of Egil, the son of Skallagrim, the son of Kveldulf the Hersir of Norway. Asgerd was the mother of Thorstein; she was the daughter of Biorn Hold. Thorstein dwelt at Burg in Burg-firth; he was rich of fee, and a great chief, a wise man, meek and of measure in all wise. He was nought of such wondrous growth and strength as his father Egil had been; yet was he a right mighty man, and much beloved of all folk.

Thorstein was goodly to look on, flaxen-haired, and the best-eyed of men; and so say men of lore that many of the kin of the Mere-men, who are come of Egil, have been the goodliest folk; yet, for all that, this kindred have differed much herein, for it is said that some of them have been accounted the most ill-favoured of men: but in that kin have been also many men of great prowess in many wise, such as Kiartan, the son of Olaf Peacock, and Slaying-Bardi, and Skuli, the son of Thorstein. Some have been great bards, too, in that kin, as Biorn, the champion of Hit-dale, priest Einar Skulison, Snorri Sturluson, and many others.

Now, Thorstein had to wife Jofrid, the daughter of Gunnar, the son of Hlifar. This Gunnar was the best skilled in weapons, and the lithest of limb of all bonderfolk who have been in Iceland; the second was Gunnar of Lithend; but Steinthor of Ere was the third. Jofrid was eighteen winters old when Thorstein wedded her; she was a widow, for Thorodd, son of Odd of Tongue, had had her to wife aforetime. Their daughter was Hungerd, who was brought up at Thorstein's at Burg. Jofrid was a very stirring woman; she and Thorstein had many children betwixt them, but few of them come into this tale. Skuli was the eldest of their sons, Kollsvein the second, Egil the third.

Chapter 2
Of Thorstein's Dream

ONE SUMMER, it is said, a ship came from over the main into Gufaros. Bergfinn was he hight who was the master thereof, a Northman of kin, rich in goods, and somewhat stricken in years, and a wise man he was withal.

Now, goodman Thorstein rode to the ship, as it was his wont mostly to rule the market, and this he did now. The Eastmen got housed, but Thorstein took the master to himself, for thither he prayed to go. Bergfinn was of few words throughout the winter, but Thorstein treated him well The Eastman had great joy of dreams.

One day in spring-tide Thorstein asked Bergfinn if he would ride with him up to Hawkfell, where at that time was the Thing-stead of the Burg-firthers; for Thorstein had been told that the walls of his booth had fallen in. The Eastman said he had good will to go, so that day they rode, some three together, from home, and the house-carles of Thorstein withal, till they came up under Hawkfell to a farmstead called Foxholes. There dwelt a man of small wealth called Atli, who was Thorstein's tenant Thorstein bade him come and work with them, and bring with him hoe and spade. This he did, and when they came to the tofts of the booth, they set to work all of them, and did out the walls.

The weather was hot with sunshine that day, and Thorstein and the Eastman grew heavy; and when they had moved out the walls, those two sat down within the tofts, and Thorstein slept, and fared ill in his sleep. The Eastman sat beside him, and let him have his dream fully out, and when he awoke he was much wearied. Then the Eastman asked him what he had dreamt, as he had had such an ill time of it in his sleep.

Thorstein said, "Nay, dreams betoken nought."

But as they rode homeward in the evening, the Eastman asked him again what he had dreamt.

Thorstein said, "If I tell thee the dream, then shalt thou unriddle it to me, as it verily is."

The Eastman said he would risk it.

Then Thorstein said: "This was my dream; for methought I was at home at Burg, standing outside the men's-door, and I looked up at the house-roof, and on the ridge I saw a swan, goodly and fair, and I thought it was mine own, and deemed it good beyond all things. Then I saw a great eagle sweep down from the mountains, and fly thitherward and alight beside the swan, and chuckle over her lovingly; and methouht the swan seemed well content thereat; but I noted that the eagle was black-eyed, and that on him were iron claws: valiant he seemed to me.

"After this I thought I saw another fowl come flying from the south quarter, and he, too, came hither to Burg, and sat down on the house beside the swan, and would fain be fond with her. This also was a mighty eagle.

"But soon I thought that the eagle first-come ruffled up at the coming of the other. Then they fought fiercely and long, and this I saw that both bled, and such was the end of their play, that each tumbled either way down from the house-roof, and there they lay both dead.

"But the swan sat left alone, drooping much, and sad of semblance.

"Then I saw a fowl fly from the west; that was a falcon, and he sat beside the swan and made fondly towards her, and they flew away both together into one and the same quarter, and therewith I awoke.

"But a dream of no mark this is," he says, "and will in all likelihood betoken gales, that they shall meet in the air from those quarters whence I deemed the fowl flew."

The Eastman spake: "I deem it nowise such," saith he.

Thorstein said, "Make of the dream, then, what seemeth likest to thee, and let me hear."

Then said the Eastman: "These birds are like to be fetches of men: but thy wife sickens now, and she will give birth to a woman-child fair and lovely; and dearly thou wilt love her; but high-born men shall woo thy daughter, coming from such quarters as the eagles seemed to fly from, and shall love her with overweening love, and shall fight about her, and both lose their lives thereby. And thereafter a third man, from the quarter whence came the falcon, shall woo her, and to that man shall she be wedded. Now, I have unravelled thy dream, and I think things will befall as I have said."

Thorstein answered: "In evil and unfriendly wise is the dream interpreted, nor do I deem thee fit for the work of unriddling dreams."

Then Eastman said, "Thou shalt find how it will come to pass."

But Thorstein estranged himself from the Eastman thenceforward, and he left that summer, and now he is out of the tale.

Chapter 3
Of the Birth and Fostering of Helga the Fair

THIS SUMMER Thorstein got ready to ride to the Thing, and spake to Jofrid his wife before he went from home. "So is it," he says, "that thou art with child now, but thy child shall be cast forth if thou bear a woman; but nourished if it be a man."

Now, at this time when all the land was heathen, it was somewhat the wont of such men as had little wealth, and were like to have many young children on their hands, to have them cast forth, but an evil deed it was always deemed to be.

And now, when Thorstein had said this, Jofrid answers, "This is a word all unlike thee, such a man as thou art, and surely to a wealthy man like thee it will not seem good that this should be done."

Thorstein answered: "Thou knowest my mind, and that no good will hap if my will be thwarted."

So he rode to the Thing; but while he was gone Jofrid gave birth to a woman-child wondrous fair. The women would fain show her to the mother; she said there was little need thereof, but had her shepherd Thorvard called to her, and spake to him:

"Thou shalt take my horse and saddle it, and bring this child west to Herdholt, to Thorgerd, Egil's daughter, and pray her to nourish it secretly, so that Thorstein may not know thereof. For with such looks of love do I behold this child, that surely I cannot bear to have it cast forth. Here are three marks of silver, have them in reward of thy work; but west there Thorgerd will get thee fare and food over the sea."

Then Thorvard did her bidding; he rode with the child to Herdholt, and gave it into Thorgerd's hands, and she had it nourished at a tenant's of hers who dwelt at Freedmans-stead up in Hvamfirth; but she got fare for Thorvard north in Steingrims-firth, in Shell-creek, and gave him meet outfit for his sea-faring: he went thence abroad, and is now out of the story.

Now when Thorstein came home from the Thing, Jofrid told him that the child had been cast forth according to his word, but that the herdsman had fled away and stolen her horse. Thorstein said she had done well, and got himself another herdsman. So six winters passed, and this matter was nowise wotted of.

Now in those days Thorstein rode to Herdholt, being bidden there as guest of his brother-in-law, Olaf Peacock, the son of Hoskuld, who was then deemed to be the chief highest of worth among all men west there. Good cheer was made Thorstein, as was like to be; and one day at the feast it is said that Thorgerd sat in the high seat talking with her brother Thorstein, while Olaf was talking to other men; but on the bench right over against them sat three little maidens. Then said Thorgerd:

"How dost thou, brother, like the look of these three little maidens sitting straight before us?"

"Right well," he answers, "but one is by far the fairest; she has all the goodliness of Olaf, but the whiteness and the countenance of us, the Mere-men."

Thorgerd answered: "Surely this is true, brother, wherein thou sayest that she has the fairness and countenance of us Mere-folk, but the goodliness of Olaf Peacock she has not got, for she is not his daughter."

"How can that be," says Thorstein, "being thy daughter none the less?"

She answered: "To say sooth, kinsman," quoth she, "this fair maiden is not my daughter, but thine."

And therewith she told him all as it had befallen, and prayed him to forgive her and his own wife that trespass.

Thorstein said: "I cannot blame you two for having done this; most things will fall as they are fated, and well have ye covered over my folly: so look I on this maiden that I deem it great good luck to have so fair a child. But now, what is her name?"

"Helga she is called," says Thorgerd.

"Helga the Fair," says Thorstein. "But now shalt thou make her ready to come home with me."

She did so, and Thorstein was led out with good gifts, and Helga rode with him to his home, and was brought up there with much honour and great love from father and mother and all her kin.

Chapter 4
Of Gunnlaug Worm-Tongue and His Kin

NOW AT THIS TIME there dwelt at Gilsbank, up in White-water-side, Illugi the Black, son of Hallkel, the son of Hrosskel. The mother of Illugi was Thurid Dandle, daughter of Gunnlaug Worm-Tongue.

Illugi was the next greatest chief in Burg-firth after Thorstein Egilson. He was a man of broad lands and hardy of mood, and wont to do well to his friends; he had to wife Ingibjorg, the daughter of Asbiorn Hordson, from Ornolfsdale; the mother of Ingibjorg was Thorgerd, the daughter of Midfirth-Skeggi. The children of Illugi and Ingibjorg were many, but few of them have to do with this story. Hermund was one of their sons, and Gunnlaug another; both were hopeful men, and at this time of ripe growth.

It is told of Gunnlaug that he was quick of growth in his early youth, big, and strong; his hair was light red, and very goodly of fashion; he was dark-eyed, somewhat ugly-nosed, yet of lovesome countenance; thin of flank he was, and broad of shoulder, and the best-wrought of men; his whole mind was very masterful; eager was he from his youth up, and in all wise unsparing and hardy; he was a great skald, but somewhat bitter in his rhyming, and therefore was he called Gunnlaug Worm-Tongue.

Hermund was the best beloved of the two brothers, and had the mien of a great man.

When Gunnlaug was fifteen winters old he prayed his father for goods to fare abroad withal, and said he had will to travel and see the manners of other folk. Master Illugi was slow to take the matter up, and said he was unlike to be deemed good in the out-lands "when I can scarcely shape thee to my own liking at home."

On a morning but a very little afterwards it happened that Illugi came out early, and saw that his storehouse was opened, and that some sacks of wares, six of them, had been brought out into the road, and therewithal too some pack-gear. Now, as he wondered at this, there came up a man leading four horses, and who should it be but his son Gunnlaug. Then said he:

"I it was who brought out the sacks."

Illugi asked him why he had done so. He said that they should make his faring goods.

Illugi said: "In nowise shalt thou thwart my will, nor fare anywhere sooner than I like!" and in again he swung the ware-sacks therewith.

Then Gunnlaug rode thence and came in the evening down to Burg, and goodman Thorstein asked him to bide there, and Gunnlaug was fain of that proffer. He told Thorstein how things had gone betwixt him and his father, and Thorstein offered to let him bide there as long as he liked, and for some seasons Gunnlaug abode there, and learned law-craft of Thorstein, and all men accounted well of him.

Now Gunnlaug and Helga would be always at the chess-playing together, and very soon each found favour with the other, as came to be proven well enough afterwards: they were very nigh of an age.

Helga was so fair, that men of lore say that she was the fairest woman of Iceland, then or since; her hair was so plenteous and long that it could cover her all over, and it was as fair as a band of gold; nor was there any so good to choose as Helga the Fair in all Burgfirth, and far and wide elsewhere.

Now one day, as men sat in the hall at Burg, Gunnlaug spake to Thorstein: "One thing in law there is which thou hast not taught me, and that is how to woo me a wife."

Thorstein said, "That is but a small matter," and therewith taught him how to go about it.

Then said Gunnlaug, "Now shalt thou try if I have understood all: I shall take thee by the hand and make as if I were wooing thy daughter Helga."

"I see no need of that," says Thorstein. Gunnlaug, however, groped then and there after his hand, and seizing it said, "Nay, grant me this though."

"Do as thou wilt, then," said Thorstein; "but be it known to all who are hereby that this shall be as if it had been unspoken, nor shall any guile follow herein."

Then Gunnlaug named for himself witnesses, and betrothed Helga to him, and asked thereafter if it would stand good thus. Thorstein said that it was well; and those who were present were mightily pleased at all this.

Chapter 5
Of Raven and His Kin

THERE WAS A MAN called Onund, who dwelt in the south at Mossfell: he was the wealthiest of men, and had a priesthood south there about the nesses. He was married, and his wife was called Geirny. She was the daughter of Gnup, son of Mold-Gnup, who settled at Grindwick, in the south country. Their sons were Raven, and Thorarin, and Eindridi; they were all hopeful men, but Raven was in all wise the first of them. He was a big man and a strong, the sightliest of men and a good skald; and when he was fully grown he fared between sundry lands, and was well accounted of wherever he came.

Thorod the Sage, the son of Eyvind, then dwelt at Hjalli, south in Olfus, with Skapti his son, who was then the spokesman-at-law in Iceland. The mother of Skapti was Ranveig, daughter of Gnup, the son of Mold-Gnup; and Skapti and the sons of Onund were sisters' sons. Between these kinsmen was much friendship as well as kinship.

At this time Thorfin, the son of Selthorir, dwelt at Red-Mel, and had seven sons, who were all the hopefullest of men; and of them were these – Thorgils, Eyjolf, and Thorir; and they were all the greatest men out there. But these men who have now been named lived all at one and the same time.

Next to this befell those tidings, the best that ever have befallen here in Iceland, that the whole land became Christian, and that all folk cast off the old faith.

Chapter 6
How Helga Was Vowed to Gunnlaug,
and of Gunnlaug's Faring Abroad

GUNNLAUG WORM-TONGUE WAS, as is aforesaid, whiles at Burg with Thorstein, whiles with his father Illugi at Gilsbank, three winters together, and was by now eighteen winters old; and father and son were now much more of a mind.

There was a man called Thorkel the Black; he was a house-carle of Illugi, and near akin to him, and had been brought up in his house. To him fell an heritage north at As, in Water-dale, and he prayed Gunnlaug to go with him thither. This he did, and so they rode, the two together, to As. There they got the fee; it was given up to them by those who had the keeping of it, mostly because of Gunnlaug's furtherance.

But as they rode from the north they guested at Grimstongue, at a rich bonder's who dwelt there; but in the morning a herdsman took Gunnlaug's horse, and it had sweated much by then he got it back. Then Gunnlaug smote the herdsman, and stunned him; but the bonder would in nowise bear this, and claimed boot therefor. Gunnlaug offered to pay him one mark. The bonder thought it too little.

Then Gunnlaug sang:

"Bade I the middling mighty
To have a mark of waves' flame;
Giver of grey seas? glitter,
This gift shalt thou make shift with.
If the elf sun of the waters
From out of purse thou lettest,
O waster of the worm's bedy
Awaits thee sorrow later."

So the peace was made as Gunnlaug bade, and in such wise the two rode south.

Now, a little while after, Gunnlaug asked his father a second time for goods for going abroad.

Illugi says, "Now shalt thou have thy will, for thou hast wrought thyself into something better than thou wert." So Illugi rode hastily from home, and bought for Gunnlaug half a ship which lay in Gufaros, from Audun Festargram – this Audun was he who would not flit abroad the sons of Oswif the Wise, after the slaying of Kiartan Olafson, as is told in the story of the Laxdalemen, which thing though betid later than this. – And when Illugi came home, Gunnlaug thanked him well.

Thorkel the Black betook himself to seafaring with Gunnlaug, and their wares were brought to the ship; but Gunnlaug was at Burg while they made her ready, and found more cheer in talk with Helga than in toiling with chapmen.

Now one day Thorstein asked Gunnlaug if he would ride to his horses with him up to Long-water-dale. Gunnlaug said he would. So they ride both together till they come to the mountain-dairies of Thorstein, called Thorgils-stead. There were stud-horses of Thorstein, four of them together, all red of hue. There was one horse very goodly, but little tried: this horse Thorstein offered to give to Gunnlaug. He said he was in no need of horses, as he was going away from the country; and so they ride to other stud-horses. There was a grey horse with four mares, and he was the best of horses in Burgfirth. This one, too, Thorstein offered to give Gunnlaug, but he said, "I desire these in no wise more than the others; but why dost thou not bid me what I will take?"

"What is that?" said Thorstein.

"Helga the Fair, thy daughter," says Gunnlaug.

"That rede is not to be settled so hastily," said Thorstein; and therewithal got on other talk. And now they ride homewards down along Long-water.

Then said Gunnlaug, "I must needs know what thou wilt answer me about the wooing."

Thorstein answers: "I heed not thy vain talk," says he.

Gunnlaug says, "This is my whole mind, and no vain words."

Thorstein says, "Thou shouldst first know thine own will. Art thou not bound to fare abroad? and yet thou makest as if thou wouldst go marry. Neither art thou an even match for Helga while thou art so unsettled, and therefore this cannot so much as be looked at."

Gunnlaug says, "Where lookest thou for a match for thy daughter, if thou wilt not give her to the son of Illugi the Black; or who are they throughout Burg-firth who are of more note than he?"

Thorstein answered: "I will not play at men-mating," says he, "but if thou wert such a man as he is, thou wouldst not be turned away."

Gunnlaug said, "To whom wilt thou give thy daughter rather than to me?"

Said Thorstein, "Hereabout are many good men to choose from. Thorfin of Red-Mel hath seven sons, and all of them men of good manners."

Gunnlaug answers, "Neither Onund nor Thorfin are men as good as my father. Nay, thou thyself clearly fallest short of him – or what hast thou to set against his strife with Thorgrim the Priest, the son of Kiallak, and his sons, at Thorsness Thing, where he carried all that was in debate?"

Thorstein answers, "I drave away Steinar, the son of Onund Sioni, which was deemed somewhat of a deed."

Gunnlaug says, "Therein thou wast holpen by thy father Egil; and, to end all, it is for few bonders to cast away my alliance."

Said Thorstein, "Carry thy cowing away to the fellows up yonder at the mountains; for down here, on the Meres, it shall avail thee nought."

Now in the evening they come home; but next morning Gunnlaug rode up to Gilsbank, and prayed his father to ride with him a-wooing out to Burg.

Illugi answered, "Thou art an unsettled man, being bound for faring abroad, but makest now as if thou wouldst busy thyself with wife-wooing; and so much do I know, that this is not to Thorstein's mind."

Gunnlaug answers, "I shall go abroad all the same, nor shall I be well pleased but if thou further this."

So after this Illugi rode with eleven men from home down to Burg, and Thorstein greeted him well. Early in the morning Illugi said to Thorstein, "I would speak to thee."

"Let us go, then, to the top of the Burg, and talk together there," says Thorstein; and so they did, and Gunnlaug went with them.

Then said Illugi, "My kinsman Gunnlaug tells me that he has begun a talk with thee on his own behalf, praying that he might woo thy daughter Helga; but now I would fain know what is like to come of this matter. His kin is known to thee, and our possessions; from my hand shall be spared neither land nor rule over men, if such things might perchance further matters."

Thorstein said, "Herein alone Gunnlaug pleases me not, that I find him an unsettled man; but if he were of a mind like thine, little would I hang back."

Illugi said, "It will cut our friendship across if thou gainsayest me and my son an equal match."

Thorstein answers, "For thy words and our friendship then, Helga shall be vowed, but not betrothed, to Gunnlaug, and shall bide for him three winters: but Gunnlaug shall go abroad and shape himself to the ways of good men; but I shall be free from all these matters if he does not then come back, or if his ways are not to my liking."

Thereat they parted; Illugi rode home, but Gunnlaug rode to his ship. But when they had wind at will they sailed for the main, and made the northern part of Norway, and sailed landward along Thrandheim to Nidaros; there they rode in the harbour, and unshipped their goods.

Part Two

Chapter 7
Of Gunnlaug in the East and the West

IN THOSE DAYS Earl Eric, the son of Hakon, and his brother Svein, ruled in Norway. Earl Eric abode as then at Hladir, which was left to him by his father, and a mighty lord he was. Skuli, the son of Thorstein, was with the earl at that time, and was one of his court, and well esteemed.

Now they say that Gunnlaug and Audun Festargram, and seven of them together, went up to Hladir to the earl. Gunnlaug was so clad that he had on a grey kirtle and white long-hose; he had a boil on his foot by the instep, and from this oozed blood and matter as he strode on. In this guise he went before the earl with Audun and the rest of them, and greeted him well. The earl knew Audun, and asked him tidings from Iceland. Audun told him what there was toward. Then the earl asked Gunnlaug who he was, and Gunnlaug told him his name and kin. Then the earl said: "Skuli Thorstein's son, what manner of man is this in Iceland?"

"Lord," says he, "give him good welcome, for he is the son of the best man in Iceland, Illugi the Black of Gilsbank, and my foster-brother withal."

The earl asked, "What ails thy foot, Icelander?"

"A boil, lord," said he.

"And yet thou wentest not halt?"

Gunnlaug answers, "Why go halt while both legs are long alike?"

Then said one of the earl's men, called Thorir: "He swaggereth hugely, this Icelander! It would not be amiss to try him a little."

Gunnlaug looked at him and sang:

> *"A courtman there is*
> *Full evil I wis,*
> *A bad man and black,*
> *Belief let him lack."*

Then would Thorir seize an axe. The earl spake: "Let it be," says he; "to such things men should pay no heed. But now, Icelander, how old a man art thou?"

Gunnlaug answers: "I am eighteen winters old as now," says he.

Then says Earl Eric, "My spell is that thou shalt not live eighteen winters more."

Gunnlaug said, somewhat under his breath: "Pray not against me, but for thyself rather."

The earl asked thereat, "What didst thou say, Icelander?"

Gunnlaug answers, "What I thought well befitting, that thou shouldst bid no prayers against me, but pray well for thyself rather."

"What prayers, then?" says the earl.

"That thou mightest not meet thy death after the manner of Earl Hakon, thy father."

The earl turned red as blood, and bade them take the rascal in haste; but Skuli stepped up to the earl, and said: "Do this for my words, lord, and give this man peace, so that he depart at his swiftest."

The earl answered, "At his swiftest let him be off then, if he will have peace, and never let him come again within mv realm."

Then Skuli went out with Gunnlaug down to the bridges, where there was an England-bound ship ready to put out; therein Skuli got for Gunnlaug a berth, as well as for Thorkel, his kinsman; but Gunnlaug gave his ship into Audun's ward, and so much of his goods as he did not take with him.

Now sail Gunnlaug and his fellows into the English main, and come at autumntide south to London Bridge, where they hauled ashore their ship.

Now at that time King Ethelred, the son of Edgar, ruled over England, and was a good lord; this winter he sat in London. But in those days there was the same tongue in England as in Norway and Denmark; but the tongues changed when William the Bastard won England, for thenceforward French went current there, for he was of French kin.

Gunnlaug went presently to the king, and greeted him well and worthily, The king asked him from what land he came, and Gunnlaug told him all as it was. "But," said he, "I have come to meet thee, lord, for that I have made a song on thee, and I would that it might please thee to hearken to that song." The king said it should be so, and Gunnlaug gave forth the song well and proudly; and this is the burden thereof:

> *"As God are all folk fearing*
> *The free lord King of England,*
> *Kin of all kings and all folk,*
> *To Ethelred the head tow."*

The king thanked him for the song, and gave him as song-reward a scarlet cloak lined with the costliest of furs, and golden-broidered down to the hem; and made him his man; and Gunnlaug was with him all the winter, and was well accounted of.

One day, in the morning early, Gunnlaug met three men in a certain street, and Thororm was the name of their leader; he was big and strong, and right evil to deal with. He said, "Northman, lend me some money."

Gunnlaug answered, "That were ill counselled to lend one's money to unknown men."

He said, "I will pay it thee back on a named day."

"Then shall it be risked," says Gunnlaug; and he lent him the fee withal.

But some time afterwards Gunnlaug met the king, and told him of the money-lending. The king answered, "Now hast thou thriven little, for this is the greatest robber and reiver; deal with him in no wise, but I will give thee money as much as thine was."

Gunnlaug said, "Then do we, your men, do after a sorry sort, if, treading sackless folk under foot, we let such fellows as this deal us out our lot. Nay, that shall never be."

Soon after he met Thororm and claimed the fee of him. He said he was not going to pay it.

Then sang Gunnlaug:

> *"Evil counselled art thou,*
> *Gold from us withholding;*
> *The reddener of the edges,*
> *Pricking on with tricking.*
> *Wot ye what? they called me,*
> *Worm-Tongue, yet a youngling;*
> *Nor for nought so hight I;*
> *Now is time to show it!"*

"Now I will make an offer good in law," says Gunnlaug; "that thou either pay me my money, or else that thou go on holm with me in three nights' space."

Then laughed the viking, and said, "Before thee none have come to that, to call me to holm, despite of all the ruin that many a man has had to take at my hands. Well, I am ready to go."

Thereon they parted for that time.

Gunnlaug told the king what had befallen; and he said, "Now, indeed, have things taken a right hopeless turn; for this man's eyes can dull any weapon. But thou shalt follow my rede; here is a sword I will give thee – with that thou shalt fight, but before the battle show him another."

Gunnlaug thanked the king well therefor.

Now when they were ready for the holm, Thororm asked what sort of a sword it was that he had. Gunnlaug unsheathed it and showed him, but had a loop round the handle of the king's sword, and slipped it over his hand; the bearserk looked on the sword, and said, "I fear not that sword."

But now he dealt a blow on Gunnlaug with his sword, and cut off from him nigh all his shield; Gunnlaug smote in turn with the king's gift; the bearserk stood shieldless before him, thinking he had the same weapon he had shown him, but Gunnlaug smote him his deathblow then and there.

The king thanked him for this work, and he got much fame therefor, both in England and far and wide elsewhere.

In the spring, when ships sailed from land to land, Gunnlaug prayed King Ethelred for leave to sail somewhither; the king asks what he was about then. Gunnlaug said, "I would fulfil what I have given my word to do," and sang this stave withal:

> *"My ways must I be wending*
> *Three kings' walls to see yet,*
> *And earls twain, as I promised*
> *Erewhile to land-sharers.*
> *Neither will I wend me*
> *Back, the worms'-bed lacking,*
> *By war-lord's son, the wealth-free,*
> *For work done gift well given."*

"So be it, then, skald," said the king, and withal he gave him a ring that weighed six ounces; "but," said he, "thou shalt give me thy word to come back next autumn, for I will not let thee go altogether, because of thy great prowess."

Chapter 8
Of Gunnlaug in Ireland

THEREAFTER GUNNLAUG SAILED from England with chapmen north to Dublin. In those days King Sigtrygg Silky-beard, son of King Olaf Kvaran and Queen Kormlada, ruled over Ireland; and he had then borne sway but a little while. Gunnlaug went before the king, and greeted him well and worthily. The king received him as was meet. Then Gunnlaug said, "I have made a song on thee, and I would fain have silence therefor."

The king answered, "No men have before now come forward with songs for me, and surely will I hearken to thine." Then Gunnlaug brought the song, whereof this is the burden:

"Swaru's steed
Doth Sigtrygg feed."

And this is therein also:

"Praise-worth I can
Well measure in man,
And kings, one by one:
Lo here, Kvararis son!
Gruageth the king
Gift of gold ring?
I, singer, know
His wont to bestow.
Let the high king say,
Heard he or this day,
Song drapu-measure
Dearer a treasure?"

The king thanked him for the song, and called his treasurer to him, and said, "How shall the song be rewarded?"

"What hast thou will to give, lord?" says he.

"How will it be rewarded if I give him two ships for it?" said the king.

Then said the treasurer, "This is too much, lord; other kings give in regard of songs good keepsakes, fair swords, or golden rings."

So the king gave him his own raiment of new scarlet, a gold-embroidered kirtle, and a cloak lined with choice furs, and a gold ring which weighed a mark. Gunnlaug thanked him well.

He dwelt a short time here, and then went thence to the Orkneys.

Then was lord in Orkney, Earl Sigurd, the son of Hlodver; he was friendly to Icelanders. Now Gunnlaug greeted the earl well, and said he had a song to bring him. The earl said he would listen thereto, since he was of such great kin in Iceland.

Then Gunnlaug brought the song; it was a shorter lay, and well done. The earl gave him for lay-reward a broad axe, all inlaid with silver, and bade him abide with him.

Gunnlaug thanked him both for his gift and his offer, but said he was bound east for Sweden; and thereafter he went on board ship with chapmen who sailed to Norway.

In the autumn they came east to King's Cliff, Thorkel, his kinsman, being with him all the time. From King's Cliff they got a guide up to West Gothland, and came upon a cheaping-stead, called Skarir: there ruled an earl called Sigurd, a man stricken in years. Gunnlaug went before him, and told him he had made a song on him; the earl gave a willing ear hereto, and Gunnlaug brought the song, which was a shorter lay.

The earl thanked him, and rewarded the song well, and bade him abide there that winter.

Earl Sigurd had a great Yule-feast in the winter, and on Yule-eve came thither men sent from Earl Eric of Norway, twelve of them together, and brought gifts to Earl Sigurd. The earl made them good cheer, and bade them sit by Gunnlaug through the Yule-tide; and there was great mirth at drinks.

Now the Gothlanders said that no earl was greater or of more fame than Earl Sigurd; but the Norwegians thought that Earl Eric was by far the foremost of the two. Hereon would they bandy words, till they both took Gunnlaug to be umpire in the matter.

Then he sang this stave:

"Tell ye, staves of spear-din,
How on sleek-side sea-horse
Oft this earl hath proven
Over-toppling billows;
But Eric, victory's ash-tree,
Oft hath seen in east-seas
More of high blue billows
Before the bows a-roaring."

Both sides were content with his finding, but the Norwegians the best. But after Yule-tide those messengers left with gifts of goodly things, which Earl Sigurd sent to Earl Eric.

Now they told Earl Eric of Gunnlaug's finding: the earl thought that he had shown upright dealing and friendship to him herein, and let out some words, saying that Gunnlaug should have good peace throughout his land. What the earl had said came thereafter to the ears of Gunnlaug.

But now Earl Sigurd gave Gunnlaug a guide east to Tenthland, in Sweden, as he had asked.

Chapter 9
Of the Quarrel Between Gunnlaug and Raven Before the Swedish King

IN THOSE DAYS King Olaf the Swede, son of King Eric the Victorious, and Sigrid the High-counselled, daughter of Skogul Tosti, ruled over Sweden. He was a mighty king and renowned, and full fain of fame.

Gunnlaug came to Upsala towards the time of the Thing of the Swedes in spring-tide; and when he got to see the king, he greeted him. The king took his greeting well, and asked who he was. He said he was an Iceland-man.

Then the king called out: "Raven," says he, "what man is he in Iceland?"

Then one stood up from the lower bench, a big man and a stalwart, and stepped up before the king, and spake: "Lord," says he, "he is of good kin, and himself the most stalwart of men."

"Let him go, then, and sit beside thee," said the king.

Then Gunnlaug said, "I have a song to set forth before thee, king, and I would fain have peace while thou hearkenest thereto."

"Go ye first, and sit ye down," says the king, "for there is no leisure now to sit listening to songs."

So they did as he bade them.

Now Gunnlaug and Raven fell a-talking together, and each told each of his travels. Raven said that he had gone the summer before from Iceland to Norway, and had come east to Sweden in the forepart of winter. They soon got friendly together.

But one day, when the Thing was over, they were both before the king, Gunnlaug and Raven.

Then spake Gunnlaug, "Now, lord, I would that thou shouldst hear the song."

"That I may do now," said the king.

"My song too will I set forth now," says Raven.

"Thou mayst do so," said the king.

Then Gunnlaug said, "I will set forth mine first if thou wilt have it so, king."

"Nay," said Raven, "it behoveth me to be first, lord, for I myself came first to thee."

"Whereto came our fathers forth, so that my father was the little boat towed behind? Whereto, but nowhere?" says Gunnlaug. "And in likewise shall it be with us."

Raven answered, "Let us be courteous enough not to make this a matter of bandying of words. Let the king rule here."

The king said, "Let Gunnlaug set forth his song first, for he will not be at peace till he has his will."

Then Gunnlaug set forth the song which he had made to King Olaf, and when it was at an end the king spake. "Raven," says he, "how is the song done?"

"Right well," he answered; "it is a song full of big words and little beauty; a somewhat rugged song, as is Gunnlaug's own mood."

"Well, Raven, thy song," said the king.

Raven gave it forth, and when it was done the king said, "How is this song made, Gunnlaug?"

"Well it is, lord," he said; "this is a pretty song, as is Raven himself to behold, and delicate of countenance. But why didst thou make a short song on the king, Raven? Didst thou perchance deem him unworthy of a long one?"

Raven answered, "Let us not talk longer on this; matters will be taken up again, though it be later."

And thereat, they parted.

Soon after Raven became a man of King Olaf's, and asked him leave to go away. This the king granted him. And when Raven was ready to go, he spake to Gunnlaug, and said, "Now shall our friendship be ended, for that thou must needs shame me here before great men; but in time to come I shall cast on thee no less shame than thou hadst will to cast on me here."

Gunnlaug answers: "Thy threats grieve me nought. Nowhere are we likely to come where I shall be thought less worthy than thou."

King Olaf gave to Raven good gifts at parting, and thereafter.

Chapter 10
How Raven Came Home to Iceland, and Asked for Helga to Wife

NOW THIS SPRING Raven came from the east to Thrandheim, and fitted out his ship, and sailed in the summer to Iceland. He brought his ship to Leiruvag, below the Heath, and his friends and kinsmen were right fain of him. That winter he was at home with his father, but the summer after he met at the Althing his kinsman, Skapti the law-man.

Then said Raven to him, "Thine aid would I have to go a-wooing to Thorstein Egilson, to bid Helga his daughter."

Skapti answered, "But is she not already vowed to Gunnlaug Worm-Tongue?"

Said Raven, "Is not the appointed time of waiting between them passed by? And far too wanton is he withal, that he should hold or heed it aught."

"Let us then do as thou wouldst," said Skapti.

Thereafter they went with many men to the booth of Thorstein Egilson, and he greeted them well.

Then Skapti spoke: "Raven, my kinsman, is minded to woo thy daughter Helga. Thou knowest well his blood, his wealth, and his good manners, his many mighty kinsmen and friends."

Thorstein said, "She is already the vowed maiden of Gunnlaug, and with him shall I hold all words spoken."

Skapti said, "Are not the three winters worn now that were named between you?"

"Yes," said Thorstein; "but the summer is not yet worn, and he may still come out this summer."

Then Skapti said, "But if he cometh not this summer, what hope may we have of the matter then?"

Thorstein answered, "We are like to come here next summer, and then may we see what may wisely be done, but it will not do to speak hereof longer as at this time."

Thereon they parted. And men rode home from the Althing. But this talk of Raven's wooing of Helga was nought hidden.

That summer Gunnlaug came not out.

The next summer, at the Althing, Skapti and his folk pushed the wooing eagerly, and said that Thorstein was free as to all matters with Gunnlaug.

Thorstein answered, "I have few daughters to see to, and fain am I that they should not be the cause of strife to any man. Now I will first see Illugi the Black." And so he did. .

And when they met, he said to Illugi, "Dost thou not think that I am free from all troth with thy son Gunnlaug?"

Illugi said, "Surely, if thou wiliest it. Little can I say herein, as I do not know clearly what Gunnlaug is about."

Then Thorstein went to Skapti, and a bargain was struck that the wedding should be at Burg, about winter-nights, if Gunnlaug did not come out that summer; but that Thorstein should be free from all troth with Raven if Gunnlaug should come and fetch his bride.

After this men ride home from the Thing, and Gunnlaug's coming was long drawn out. But Helga thought evilly of all these redes.

Chapter 11
Of How Gunnlaug Must Needs Abide Away from Iceland

NOW IT IS TO BE TOLD of Gunnlaug that he went from Sweden the same summer that Raven went to Iceland, and good gifts he had from King Olaf at parting.

King Ethelred welcomed Gunnlaug worthily, and that winter he was with the king, and was held in great honour.

In those days Knut the Great, son of Svein, ruled Denmark, and had new-taken his father's heritage, and he vowed ever to wage war on England, for that his father had won a great realm there before he died west in that same land.

And at that time there was a great army of Danish men west there, whose chief was Heming, the son of Earl Strut-Harald, and brother to Earl Sigvaldi, and he held for King Knut that land that Svein had won.

Now in the spring Gunnlaug asked the king for leave to go away, but he said, "It ill beseems that thou, my man, shouldst go away now, when all bodes such mighty war in the land."

Gunnlaug said, "Thou shalt rule, lord; but give me leave next summer to depart, if the Danes come not."

The king answered, "Then we shall see."

Now this summer went by, and the next winter, but no Danes came; and after midsummer Gunnlaug got his leave to depart from the king, and went thence east to Norway, and found Earl Eric in Thrandheim, at Hladir, and the earl greeted him well, and bade him abide with him. Gunnlaug thanked him for his offer, but said he would first go out to Iceland, to look to his promised maiden.

The earl said, "Now all ships bound for Iceland have sailed."

Then said one of the court, "Here lay, yesterday, Hallfred Troublous-Skald, out tinder Agdaness."

The earl answered, "That may well be; he sailed hence five nights ago."

Then Earl Eric had Gunnlaug rowed put to Hallfred, who greeted him with joy; and forthwith a fair wind bore them from land, and they were right merry.

This was late in the summer: but now Hallfred said to Gunnlaug, "Hast thou heard of how Raven, the son of Onund, is wooing Helga the Fair?"

Gunnlaug said he had heard thereof but dimly. Hallfred tells him all he knew of it, and therewith, too, that it was the talk of many men that Raven was in nowise less brave a man than Gunnlaug. Then Gunnlaug sang this stave:

> *"Light the weather wafteth;*
> *But if this east wind drifted*
> *Week-long, wild upon us*
> *Little were I recking;*
> *More this word I mind of*
> *Me with Raven mated,*
> *Than gain for me the gold-foe*
> *Of days to make me grey-haired."*

Then Hallfred said, "Well, fellow, may'st thou fare better in thy strife with Raven than I did in mine. I brought my ship some winters ago into Leiruvag, and had to pay a half-mark in silver to a house-carle of Raven's, but I held it back from him. So Raven rode at us with sixty men, and cut the moorings of the ship, and she was driven up on the shallows, and we were bound for a wreck. Then I had to give selfdoom to Raven, and a whole mark I had to pay; and that is the tale of my dealings with him."

Then they two talked together alone of Helga the Fair, and Gunnlaug praised her much for her goodliness; and Gunnlaug sang:

> *"He who brand of battle*
> *Beareth over-wary,*
> *Never love shall let him*
> *Hold the linen-folded;*
> *For we when we were younger*
> *In many a way were playing*
> *On the outward nesses*
> *From golden land outstanding."*

"Well sung!" said Hallfred.

Part Three

Chapter 12
Of Gunnlaug's Landing, and How He Found Helga Wedded to Raven

THEY MADE LAND north by Fox-Plain, in Hraunhaven, half a month before winter, and there unshipped their goods. Now there was a man called Thord, a bonder's son of the Plain, there. He fell to wrestling with the chapmen, and they mostly got worsted at his hands.

Then a wrestling was settled between him and Gunnlaug. The night before Thord made vows to Thor for the victory; but the next day, when they met, they fell-to wrestling. Then Gunnlaug tripped both feet from under Thord, and gave him a. great fall; but the foot that Gunnlaug stood on was put out of joint, and Gunnlaug fell together with Thord.

Then said Thord, "Maybe that other things go no better for thee."

"What then?" says Gunnlaug.

"Thy dealings with Raven, if he wed Helga the Fair at winter-nights. I was anigh at the Thing when that was settled last summer."

Gunnlaug answered naught thereto.

Now the foot was swathed, and put into joint again, and it swelled mightily; but he and Hallfred ride twelve in company till they come to Gilsbank, in Burg-firth, the very Saturday night when folk sat at the wedding at Burg. Illugi was fain of his son Gunnlaug and his fellows; but Gunnlaug said he would ride then and there down to Burg. Illugi said it was not wise to do so, and to all but Gunnlaug that seemed good. But Gunnlaug was then unfit to walk, because of his foot, though he would not let that be seen. Therefore there was no faring to Burg.

On the morrow Hallfred rode to Hreda-water, in North-water dale, where Galti, his brother and a brisk man, managed their matters.

Chapter 13
Of the Winter-Wedding at Skaney, and How Gunnlaug Gave the King's Cloak to Helga

TELLS THE TALE of Raven, that he sat at his weddings-feast at Burg, and it was the talk of most men that the bride was but drooping; for true is the saw that saith, "Long we remember what youth gained us," and even so it was with her now.

But this new thing befell at the feast, that Hungerd, the daughter of Thorod and Jofrid, was wooed by a man named Sverting, the son of Hafr-Biorn, the son of Mold-Gnup, and the wedding was to come off that winter after Yule, at Skaney, where dwelt Thorkel, a kinsman of Hungerd, and son of Torn Valbrandsson; and the mother of Torn was Thorodda, the sister of Odd of the Tongue.

Now Raven went home to Mossfell with Helga his wife. When they had been there a little while, one morning early before they rose up, Helga was awake, but Raven slept, and fared ill in his sleep. And when he woke Helga asked him what he had dreamt. Then Raven sang:

"In thine arms, so dreamed I,
Hewn was I, gold island!
Bride, in blood I bled there,
Bed of thine was reddened.
Never more then mightst thou,
Mead-bowl'spourer speedy,
Bind my gashes bloody:
Lind-leek-bough thou likst it."

Helga spake: "Never shall I weep therefor," quoth she; "ye have evilly beguiled me, and Gunnlaug has surely come out." And therewith she wept much.

But, a little after, Gunnlaug's coming was bruited about, and Helga became so hard with Raven, that he could not keep her at home at Mossfell; so that back they had to go to Burg, and Raven got small share of her company.

Now men get ready for the winter-wedding. Thorkel of Skaney bade Illugi the Black and his sons. But when master Illugi got ready, Gunnlaug sat in the hall, and stirred not to go. Illugi went up to him and said, "Why dost thou not get ready, kinsman?"

Gunnlaug answered, "I have no mind to go."

Says Illugi, "Nay, but certes thou shalt go, kinsman," says he; "and cast thou not grief over thee by yearning for one woman. Make as if thou knewest nought of it, for women thou wilt never lack."

Now Gunnlaug did as his father bade him; so they came to the wedding, and Illugi and his sons were set down in the high seat; but Thorstein Egilson, and Raven his son-in-law, and the bridegroom's following, were set in the other high seat, over against Illugi.

The women sat on the dais, and Helga the Fair sat next to the bride. Oft she turned her eyes on Gunnlaug, thereby proving the saw, "Eyes will bewray if maid love man."

Gunnlaug was well arrayed, and had on him that goodly raiment that King Sigtrygg had given him; and now he was thought far above all other men, because of many things, both strength, and goodliness, and growth.

There was little mirth among folk at this wedding. But on the day when all men were making ready to go away the women stood up and got ready to go home. Then went Gunnlaug to talk to Helga, and long they talked together: but Gunnlaug sang:

"Light-heart lived the Worm-Tongue
All day long no longer
In mountain-home, since Helga
Had name of wife of Raven;
Nought foresaw thy father,
Hardener white of fight-thaw,
What my words should come to.
– The maid to gold was wedded."

And again he sang:

"Worst reward I owe them,
Father thine, O wine-may,
And mother, that they made thee
So fair beneath thy maid-gear;

For thou, sweet field of sea-flame,
All joy hast slain within me.
Lo, here, take it, loveliest
E'er made of lord and lady!"

And therewith Gunnlaug gave Helga the cloak, Ethelred's-gift, which was the fairest of things, and she thanked him well for the gift.

Then Gunnlaug went out, and by that time riding-horses had been brought home and saddled, and among them were many very good ones; and they were all tied up in the road. Gunnlaug leaps on to a horse, and rides a hand-gallop along the homefield up to a place where Raven happened to stand just before him; and Raven had to draw out of his way. Then Gunnlaug said:

"No need to slink aback, Raven, for I threaten thee nought as at this time; but thou knowest forsooth, what thou hast earned."

Raven answered and sang:

"God of wound-flamed glitter,
Glorier of fight-goddess,
Must we fall a-fighting
For fairest kirtle-bearer?
Death-staffs many such-like
Fair as she is are there
In south-lands o'er the sea floods.
Sooth saith he who knoweth."

"Maybe there are many such, but they do not seem so to me," said Gunnlaug. Therewith Illugi and Thorstein ran up to them, and would not have them fight. Then Gunnlaug sang:

"The fair-hued golden goddess
For gold to Raven sold they,
(Raven my match as men say)
While the mighty isle-king,
Ethelred, in England
From eastward way delayed me,
Wherefore to gold-waster
Waneth tongue's speech-hunger."

Hereafter both rode home, and all was quiet and tidingless that winter through; but Raven had nought of Helga's fellowship after her meeting with Gunnlaug.

Chapter 14
Of the Holmgang at the Althing

NOW IN SUMMER men ride a very many to the Althing: Illugi the Black and his sons with him, Gunnlaug and Hermund; Thorstein Egilson and Kolsvein his son; Onund, of Mossfell, and his sons all, and Sverting, Hafr-Biorn's son. Skapti yet held the spokesmanship-at-law.

One day at the Thing, as men went thronging to the Hill of Laws, and when the matters of the law were done there, then Gunnlaug craved silence, and said:

"Is Raven, the son of Onund, here?"

He said he was.

Then spake Gunnlaug, "Thou well knowest that thou hast got to wife my avowed bride, and thus hast thou made thyself my foe. Now for this I bid thee to holm here at the Thing, in the holm of the Axe-water, when three nights are gone by."

Raven answers, "This is well bidden, as was to be looked for of thee, and for this I am ready, whenever thou wiliest it."

Now the kin of each deemed this a very ill thing. But, at that time it was lawful for him who thought himself wronged by another to call him to fight on the holm.

So when three nights had gone by they got ready for the holmgang, and Illugi the Black followed his son thither with a great following. But Skapti, the lawman, followed Raven, and his father and other kinsmen of his.

Now before Gunnlaug went upon the holm he sang:

> *"Out to isle ofeel-field*
> *Dight am I to hie me:*
> *Give, O God, thy singer*
> *With glaive to end the striving.*
> *Here shall I the head cleave*
> *Of Helga's love's devourer,*
> *At last my bright sword bringeth*
> *Sundering of head and body."*

Then Raven answered and sang:

> *"Thou, singer, knowest not surely*
> *Which of us twain shall gain it;*
> *With edge for leg-swathe eager,*
> *Here are the wound-scythes bare now.*
> *In whatso-wise we wound us,*
> *The tidings from the Thing here,*
> *And fame of thanes' fair doings,*
> *The fair young maid shall hear it."*

Hermund held shield for his brother, Gunnlaug; but Sverting, Hafr-Biorn's son, was Raven's shield-bearer. Whoso should be wounded was to ransom himself from the holm with three marks of silver.

Now, Raven's part it was to deal the first blow, as he was the challenged man. He hewed at the upper part of Gunnlaug's shield, and the sword brake asunder just beneath the hilt, with so great might he smote; but the point of the sword flew up from the shield and struck Gunnlaug's cheek, whereby he got just grazed; with that their fathers ran in between them, and many other men.

"Now," said Gunnlaug, "I call Raven overcome, as he is weaponless."

"But I say that thou art vanquished, since thou art wounded," said Raven.

Now, Gunnlaug was nigh mad, and very wrathful, and said it was not tried out yet.

Illugi, his father, said they should try no more for that time.

Gunnlaug said, "Beyond all things I desire that I might in such wise meet Raven again, that thou, father, wert not anigh to part us."

And thereat they parted for that time, and all men went back to their booths.

But on the second day after this it was made law in the law-court that, henceforth, all holmgangs should be forbidden; and this was done by the counsel of all the wisest men that were at the Thing; and there, indeed, were all the men of most counsel in all the land. And this was the last holmgang fought in Iceland, this, wherein Gunnlaug and Raven fought.

But this Thing was the third most thronged Thing that has been held in Iceland; the first was after Njal's burning, the second after the Heath-slaughters.

Now, one morning, as the brothers Hermund and Gunnlaug went to Axe-water to wash, on the other side went many women towards the river, and in that company was Helga the Fair. Then said Hermund:

"Dost thou see thy friend Helga there on the other side of the river?"

"Surely, I see her," says Gunnlaug, and withal he sang:

> *"Born was she for men's bickering:*
> *Sore bale hath wrought the war-stemy*
> *And I yearned ever madly*
> *To hold that oak-tree golden.*
> *To me then, me destroyer*
> *Of swan-mead's flame, unneedful*
> *This looking on the dark-eyed,*
> *This golden land's beholding."*

Therewith they crossed the river, and Helga and Gunnlaug spake awhile together, and as the brothers crossed the river eastward back again, Helga stood and gazed long after Gunnlaug.

Then Gunnlaug looked back and sang:

> *"Moon of linen-lapped one,*
> *Leek-sea-bearing goddess,*
> *Hawk-keen out of heaven*
> *Shone all bright upon me;*
> *But that eyelid's moonbeam*
> *Of gold-necklaced goddess*
> *Her hath all undoing*
> *Wrought, and me made nought of."*

Chapter 15
How Gunnlaug and Raven Agreed to Go East to Norway, to Try the Matter Again

NOW AFTER THESE THINGS were gone by men rode home from the Thing, and Gunnlaug dwelt at home at Gilsbank.

On a morning when he awoke all men had risen up, but he alone still lay abed; he lay in a shut-bed behind the seats. Now into the hall came twelve men, all full armed, and who should be there but Raven, Onund's son; Gunnlaug sprang up forthwith, and got to his weapons.

But Raven spake, "Thou art in risk of no hurt this time," quoth he, "but my errand hither is what thou shalt now hear: Thou didst call me to a holmgang last summer at the Althing, and thou didst not deem matters to be fairly tried therein; now I will offer thee this, that we both fare away from Iceland, and go abroad next summer, and go on holm in Norway, for there our kinsmen are not like to stand in our way."

Gunnlaug answered, "Hail to thy words, stoutest of men! this thine offer I take gladly; and here, Raven, mayest thou have cheer as good as thou mayest desire."

"It is well offered," said Raven, "but this time we shall first have to ride away." Thereon they parted.

Now the kinsmen of both sore misliked them of this, but could in no wise undo it, because of the wrath of Gunnlaug and Raven; and, after all, that must betide that drew towards.

Now it is to be said of Raven that he fitted out his ship in Leiruvag; two men are named that went with him, sisters' sons of his father Onund, one hight Grim, the other Olaf, doughty men both. All the kinsmen of Raven thought it great scathe when he went away, but he said he had challenged Gunnlaug to the holmgang because he could have no joy soever of Helga; and he said, withal, that one must fall before the other.

So Raven put to sea, when he had wind at will, and brought his ship to Thrandheim, and was there that winter and heard nought of Gunnlaug that winter through; there lie abode him the summer following: and still another winter was he in Thrandheim, at a place called Lifangr.

Gunnlaug Worm-Tongue took ship with Hallfred Troublous-Skald, in the north at The Plain; they were very late ready for sea.

They sailed into the main when they had a fair wind, and made Orkney a little before the winter. Earl Sigurd Lodverson was still lord over the isles, and Gunnlaug went to him and abode there that winter, and the earl held him of much account.

In the spring the earl would go on warfare, and Gunnlaug made ready to go with him; and that summer they harried wide about the South-isles and Scotland's firths, and had many fights, and Gunnlaug always showed himself the bravest and doughtiest of fellows, and the hardiest of men wherever they came.

Earl Sigurd went back home early in the summer, but Gunnlaug took ship with chapmen, sailing for Norway, and he and Earl Sigurd parted in great friendship.

Gunnlaug fared north to Thrandheim, to Hladir, to see Earl Eric, and dwelt there through the early winter; the earl welcomed him gladly, and made offer to Gunnlaug to stay with him, and Gunnlaug agreed thereto.

The earl had heard already how all had befallen between Gunnlaug and Raven, and he told Gunnlaug that he laid ban on their fighting within his realm; Gunnlaug said the earl should be free to have his will herein.

So Gunnlaug abode there the winter through, ever heavy of mood.

Chapter 16
How the Two Foes Met and Fought at Dingness

BUT ON A DAY in spring Gunnlaug was walking abroad, and his kinsman Thorkel with him; they walked away from the town, till on the meads. before them they saw a ring of men, and in that ring were two men with weapons fencing; but one was named Raven, the other Gunnlaug, while they who stood by said that Icelanders smote light, and were slow to remember their words.

Gunnlaug saw the great mocking hereunder, and much jeering was brought into the play; and withal he went away silent.

So a little while after he said to the earl that he had no mind to bear any longer the jeers and mocks of his courtiers about his dealings with Raven, and therewith he prayed the earl to give him a guide to Lifangr: now before this the earl had been told that Raven had left Lifangr and gone east to Sweden; therefore, he granted Gunnlaug leave to go, and gave him two guides for the journey.

Now Gunnlaug went from Hladir with six men to Lifangr; and, on the morning of the very day whereas Gunnlaug came in in the evening, Raven had left Lifangr with four men. Thence Gunnlaug went to Vera-dale, and came always in the evening to where Raven had been the night before.

So Gunnlaug went on till he came to the uppermost farm in the valley, called Sula, wherefrom had Raven fared in the morning; there he stayed not his journey, but kept on his way through the night.

Then in the morning at sun-rise they saw one another. Raven had got to a place where were two waters, and between them flat meads, and they are called Gleipni's meads: but into one water stretched a little ness called Dingness. There on the ness Raven and his fellows, five together, took their stand. With Raven were his kinsmen, Grim and Olaf.

Now when they met, Gunnlaug said, "It is well that we have found one another."

Raven said that he had nought to quarrel with therein;

"But now," says he, "thou mayest choose as thou wilt, either that we fight alone together, or that we fight all of us man to man."

Gunnlaug said that either way seemed good to him.

Then spake Raven's kinsmen, Grim and Olaf, and said that they would little like to stand by and look on the fight, and in like wise spake Thorkel the Black, the kinsman of Gunnlaug.

Then said Gunnlaug to the earl's guides, "Ye shall sit by and aid neither side, and be here to tell of our meeting;" and so they did.

So they set on, and fought dauntlessly, all of them. Grim and Olaf went both against Gunnlaug alone, and so closed their dealings with him that Gunnlaug slew them both and got no wound. This proves Thord Kolbeinson in a song that he made on Gunnlaug the Wormtongue:

> *"Grim and Olaf great-hearts*
> *In Gondul's din, with thin sword*
> *First did Gunnlaug fell there*
> *Ere at Raven fared he;*
> *Bold, with blood be-drifted*
> *Bane of three the thane was;*
> *War-lord of the wave-horse*
> *Wrought for men folks' slaughter."*

Meanwhile Raven and Thorkel the Black, Gunnlaug's kinsman, fought until Thorkel fell before Raven and lost his life; and so at last all their fellowship fell. Then they two alone fought together with fierce onsets and mighty strokes, which they dealt each the other, falling on furiously without stop or stay.

Gunnlaug had the sword Ethelred's-gift, and that was the best of weapons. At last Gunnlaug dealt a mighty blow at Raven, and cut his leg from under him; but none the more did Raven fall, but swung round up to a tree-stem, whereat he steadied the stump.

Then said Gunnlaug, "Now thou art no more meet for battle, nor will I fight with thee any longer, a maimed man."

Raven answered: "So it is," said he, "that my lot is now all the worser lot, but it were well with me yet, might I but drink somewhat."

Gunnlaug said, "Bewray me not if I bring thee water in my helm."

"I will not bewray thee," said Raven. Then went Gunnlaug to a brook and fetched water in his helm, and brought it to Raven; but Raven stretched forth his left hand to take it, but with his right hand drave his sword into Gunnlaug's head, and that was a mighty great wound.

Then Gunnlaug said, "Evilly hast thou beguiled me, and done traitorously wherein I trusted thee."

Raven answers, "Thou sayest sooth, but this brought me to it, that I begrudged thee to lie in the bosom of Helga the Fair."

Thereat they fought on, recking of nought; but the end of it was that Gunnlaug overcame Raven, and there Raven lost his life..

Then the earl's guides came forward and bound the head-wound of Gunnlaug, and in meanwhile, he sat and sang:

> *"O thou sword-storm stirrer,*
> *Raven, stem of battle*
> *Famous, fared against me*
> *Fiercely in the spear din.*
> *Many a flight of metal*
> *Was borne on me this morning,*
> *By the spear-walls' builder,*
> *Ring-bearer, on hard Dingness."*

After that they buried the dead, and got Gunnlaug on to his horse thereafter, and brought him right down to Lifangr. There he lay three nights, and got all his rights of a priest, and died thereafter, and was buried at the church there.

All men thought it great scathe of both of these men, Gunnlaug and Raven, amid such deeds as they died.

Chapter 17
The News of the Fight Brought to Iceland

NOW THIS SUMMER, before these tidings were brought out hither to Iceland, Illugi the Black, being at home at Gilsbank, dreamed a dream: he thought that Gunnlaug came to him in his sleep, all bloody, and he sang in the dream this stave before him; and Illugi remembered the song when he woke, and sang it before others:

> *"Knew I of the hewing*
> *Of Raven's hilt-finned steel-fish*
> *Byrny-shearing – sword-edge*
> *Sharp clave leg of Raven.*
> *Of warm wounds drank the eagle,*
> *When the war-rod slender,*
> *Cleaver of the corpses,*
> *Clave the head of Gunnlaug."*

This portent befel south at Mossfell, the self-same night, that Onund dreamed how Raven came to him, covered all over with blood, and sang:

> *"Red is the sword, but I now*
> *Am undone by Sword-Odin:*
> *'Gainst shields beyond the sea-flood*
> *The ruin of shields was wielded.*
> *Methinks the blood-fowl blood-stained*
> *In blood o'er men's heads stood there,*
> *The wound-erne yet wound-eager*
> *Trod over wounded bodies?"*

Now the second summer after this, Illugi the Black spoke at the Althing from the Hill of Laws, and said:

"Wherewith wilt thou make atonement to me for my son, whom Raven, thy son, beguiled in his troth?"

Onund answers, "Be it far from me to atone for him, so sorely as their meeting hath wounded me. Yet will I not ask atonement of thee for my son."

"Then shall my wrath come home to some of thy kin," says Illugi. And withal after the Thing was Illugi at most times very sad.

Tells the tale how this autumn Illugi rode from Gilsbank with thirty men, and came to Mossfell early in the morning. Then Onund got into the church with his sons, and took sanctuary; but Illugi caught two of his kin, one called Biorn and the other Thorgrim, and had Biorn slain, but the feet smitten from Thorgrim. And thereafter Illugi rode home, and there was no righting of this for Onund.

Hermund, Illugi's son, had little joy after the death of Gunnlaug his brother, and deemed he was none the more avenged even though this had been wrought.

Now there was a man called Raven, brother's son to Onund of Mossfell; he was a great sea-farer, and had a ship that lay up in Ramfirth: and in the spring Hermund Illugison rode from home alone north over Holt-beacon Heath, even to Ramfirth, and out as far as Board-ere to the ship of the chapmen. The chapmen were then nearly ready for sea; Raven, the ship-master, was on shore, and many men with him; Hermund rode up to him, and thrust him through with his spear, and rode away forthwith: but all Raven's men were bewildered at seeing Hermund.

No atonement came for this slaying, and therewith ended the dealings of Illugi the Black and Onund of Mossfell.

Chapter 18
The Death of Helga the Fair

AS TIME WENT ON, Thorstein Egilson married his daughter Helga to a man called Thorkel, son of Hallkel, who lived west in Hraundale. Helga went to his house with him, but loved him little, for she cannot cease to think of Gunnlaug, though he be dead. Yet was Thorkel a doughty man, and wealthy of goods, and a good skald.

They had children together not a few, one of them was called Thorarin, another Thorstein, and yet more they had.

But Helga's chief joy was to pluck at the threads of that cloak, Gunnlaug's gift, and she would be ever gazing at it.

But on a time there came a great sickness to the house of Thorkel and Helga, and many were bed-ridden for a long time. Helga also fell sick, and yet she could not keep abed.

So one Saturday evening Helga sat in the fire-hall, and leaned her head upon her husband's knees, and had the cloak Gunnlaug's gift sent for; and when the cloak came to her she sat up and plucked at it, and gazed thereon awhile, and then sank back upon her husband's bosom, and was dead. Then Thorkel sang this:

"Dead in mine arms she droopeth,
My dear one, gold-rings bearer,
For God hath changed the life-days
Of this Lady of the linen.
Weary pain hath pined her,
But unto me, the seeker
Of hoard of fishes highway,
Abiding here is wearier."

Helga was buried in the church there, but Thorkel dwelt yet at Hraundale: but a great matter seemed the death of Helga to all, as was to be looked for.

And here endeth the story.

THE STORY OF GRETTIR THE STRONG

Introduction

THIS ICELANDIC SAGA is about Grettir Ásmundarson, and it is believed to be based on a previous account of his life by Sturla Þórðarson. After becoming the longest surviving outlaw in Icelandic history, having spent almost twenty years banished form his homeland, Grettir is about to be returned to society but his enemies defeat him and he dies. During his life he carries out some heroic acts as he defeats foes but he is also blamed for many criminal activities and is the bearer of a large amount of bad luck. William Morris and Eirikr Magnusson first published their translation of this saga in 1869 and it soon received scholarly attention, being compared to other works and Grettir's character being analysed. Morris also visited Grettir's lair in Iceland, an experience which he said changed his view on the story and on the character of Grettir, transforming him into 'an awful and monstrous being'. The original text had chapter titles for Part Two, but not Part One, and though it looks inconsistent we have retained the chapter titles where given.

A life scarce worth the living, a poor fame
Scarce worth the winning, in a wretched land,
Where fear and pain go upon either hand,
As toward the end men fare without an aim
Unto the dull grey dark from whence they came:
Let them alone, the unshadowed sheer rocks stand
Over the twilight graves of that poor band,
Who count so little in the great world's game!

Nay, with the dead I deal not; this man lives,
And that which carried him through good and ill,
Stern against fate while his voice echoed still
From rock to rock, now he lies silent, strives
With wasting time, and through its long lapse gives
Another friend to me, life's void to fill.

William Morris

Part One

THIS FIRST PART tells of the forefathers of Grettir in Norway, and how they fled away before Harald Fairhair, and settled in Iceland; and of their deeds in Iceland before Grettir was born.

Chapter 1

THERE WAS A MAN named Onund, who was the son of Ufeigh Clubfoot, the son of Ivar the Smiter; Onund was brother of Gudbiorg, the mother of Gudbrand Ball, the father of Asta, the mother of King Olaf the Saint. Onund was an Uplander by the kin of his mother; but the kin of his father dwelt chiefly about Rogaland and Hordaland. He was a great viking, and went harrying west over the Sea. Balk of Sotanes, the son of Blaeng, was with him herein, and Orm the Wealthy withal, and Hallvard was the name of the third of them. They had five ships, all well manned, and therewith they harried in the South-isles; and when they came to Barra, they found there a king, called Kiarval, and he, too, had five ships. They gave him battle, and a hard fray there was. The men of Onund were of the eagerest, and on either side many fell; but the end of it was that the king fled with only one ship. So there the men of Onund took both ships and much wealth, and abode there through the winter. For three summers they harried throughout Ireland and Scotland, and thereafter went to Norway.

Chapter 2

IN THOSE DAYS were there great troubles in Norway. Harald the Unshorn, son of Halfdan the Black, was pushing forth for the kingdom. Before that he was King of the Uplands; then he went north through the land, and had many battles there, and ever won the day. Thereafter he harried south in the land, and wheresoever he came, laid all under him; but when he came to Hordaland, swarms of folk came thronging against him; and their captains were Kiotvi the Wealthy, and Thorir Longchin, and those of South Rogaland, and King Sulki. Geirmund Helskin was then in the west over the Sea; nor was he in that battle, though he had a kingdom in Hordaland.

Now that autumn Onund and his fellows came from the west over the Sea; and when Thorir Longchin and King Kiotvi heard thereof, they sent men to meet them, and prayed them for help, and promised them honours. Then they entered into fellowship with Thorir and his men; for they were exceeding fain to try their strength, and said that there would they be whereas the fight was hottest.

Now was the meeting with Harald the King in Rogaland, in that firth which is called Hafrsfirth; and both sides had many men. This was the greatest battle that has ever been fought in Norway, and hereof most Sagas tell; for of those is ever most told, of whom the Sagas are made; and thereto came folk from all the land, and many from other lands and swarms of vikings.

Now Onund laid his ship alongside one board of the ship of Thorir Longchin, about the midst of the fleet, but King Harald laid his on the other board, because Thorir was the greatest bearserk, and the stoutest of men; so the fight was of the fiercest on either side. Then the king cried on his bearserks for an onslaught, and they were called the Wolf-coats, for on them would no steel bite, and when they set on nought might withstand them. Thorir defended him very stoutly, and fell in all hardihood on board his ship; then was it cleared from stem to stern, and cut from the grapplings, and let drift astern betwixt the other ships. Thereafter the king's men laid their ship alongside Onund's, and he was in the forepart thereof and fought manly; then the king's folk said, "Lo, a forward man in the forecastle there, let him have somewhat to mind him how that he was in this battle." Now Onund put one foot out over the bulwark and dealt a blow at a man, and even therewith a spear was aimed at him, and as he put the blow from him he bent backward withal, and one of the king's forecastle men smote at him, and the stroke took his leg below the knee and sheared it off, and forthwith made him unmeet for fight. Then fell the more part of the folk on board his ship; but Onund was brought to the ship of him who is called Thrand; he was the son of Biorn, and brother of Eyvind the Eastman; he was in the fight against King Harald and lay on the other board of Onund's ship.

But now, after these things, the more part of the fleet scattered in flight; Thrand and his men, with the other vikings, got them away each as he might, and sailed west over the Sea; Onund went with him, and Balk and Hallvard Sweeping; Onund was healed, but went with a wooden leg all his life after; therefore as long as he lived was he called Onund Treefoot.

Chapter 3

AT THAT TIME were many great men west over the Sea, such as had fled from their lands in Norway before King Harald, because he had made all those outlaws, who had met him in battle, and taken to him their possessions. So, when Onund was healed of his wounds, he and Thrand went to meet Geirmund Helskin, because he was the most famed of vikings west there over the Sea, and they asked him whether he had any mind to seek after that kingdom which he had in Hordaland, and offered him their fellowship herein; for they deemed they had a sore loss of their lands there, since Onund was both mighty and of great kin.

Geirmund said that so great had grown the strength of King Harald, that he deemed there was little hope that they would win honour in their war with him when men had been worsted, even when all the folk of the land had been drawn together; and yet withal that he was loth to become a king's thrall and pray for that which was his own; that he would find somewhat better to do than that; and now, too, he was no longer young. So Onund and his fellows went back to the South-isles, and there met many of their friends.

There was a man, Ufeigh by name, who was bynamed Grettir; he was the son of Einar, the son of Olvir Bairn-Carle; he was brother to Oleif the Broad, the father of Thormod Shaft; Steinulf was the name of Olvir Bairn-Carle's son, he was the father of Una whom Thorbiorn Salmon-Carle had to wife. Another son of Olvir Bairn-Carle was Steinmod, the father of Konal, who was the father of Aldis of Barra. The son of Konal was Steinmod, the father of Haldora, the wife of Eilif, the son of Ketil the Onehanded. Ufeigh Grettir had to wife Asny, the daughter of Vestar Haengson; and Asmund the Beardless and Asbiorn were the sons of Ufeigh Grettir, but his daughters were these, Aldis, and Asa, and Asvor. Ufeigh had fled away west over the Sea before Harald the king, and so had Thormod Shaft his kinsman, and had with them their kith and kin; and they harried in Scotland, and far and wide west beyond the sea.

Now Thrand and Onund Treefoot made west for Ireland to find Eyvind the Eastman, Thrand's brother, who was Land-ward along the coasts of Ireland; the mother of Eyvind was Hlif, the daughter of Rolf, son of Ingiald, the son of King Frodi; but Thrand's mother was Helga, the daughter of Ondott the Crow; Biorn was the name of the father of Eyvind and Thrand, he was the son of Rolf from Am; he had had to flee from Gothland, for that he had burned in his house Sigfast the son-in-law of King Solver; and thereafter had he gone to Norway, and was the next winter with Grim the hersir, the son of Kolbiorn the Abasher. Now Grim had a mind to murder Biorn for his money, so he fled thence to Ondott the Crow, who dwelt in Hvinisfirth in Agdir; he received Biorn well, and Biorn was with him in the winter, but was in warfare in summer-tide, until Hlif his wife died; and after that Ondott gave Biorn Helga his daughter, and then Biorn left off warring.

Now thereon Eyvind took to him the war-ships of his father, and was become a great chief west over the Sea; he wedded Rafarta, the daughter of Kiarval, King of Ireland; their sons were Helgi the Lean and Snaebiorn.

So when Thrand and Onund came to the South-isles, there they met Ufeigh Grettir and Thormod Shaft, and great friendship grew up betwixt them, for each thought he had gained from hell the last who had been left behind in Norway while the troubles there were at the highest. But Onund was exceeding moody, and when Thrand marked it, he asked what he was brooding over in his mind. Onund answered, and sang this stave:

"What joy since that day can I get
When shield-fire's thunder last I met;
Ah, too soon clutch the claws of ill;
For that axe-edge shall grieve me still.
In eyes of fighting man and thane,
My strength and manhood are but vain,
This is the thing that makes me grow
A joyless man; is it enow?"

Thrand answered that whereso he was, he would still be deemed a brave man, "And now it is meet for thee to settle down and get married, and I would put forth my word and help, if I but knew whereto thou lookest."

Onund said he did in manly wise, but that his good hope for matches of any gain was gone by now.

Thrand answered, "Ufeigh has a daughter who is called Asa, thitherward will we turn if it seem good to thee." Onund showed that he was willing enough hereto; so afterwards they talked the matter over with Ufeigh; he answered well, and said that he knew how that Onund was a man of great kin and rich of chattels; "but his lands," said he, "I put at low worth, nor do I deem him to be a hale man, and withal my daughter is but a child."

Thrand said, that Onund was a brisker man yet than many who were hale of both legs, and so by Thrand's help was this bargain struck; Ufeigh was to give his daughter but chattels for dowry, because those lands that were in Norway neither would lay down any money for.

A little after Thrand wooed the daughter of Thormod Shaft, and both were to sit in troth for three winters.

So thereafter they went a harrying in the summer, but were in Barra in the winter-tide.

Chapter 4

THERE WERE TWO VIKINGS called Vigbiod and Vestmar; they were South-islanders, and lay out both winter and summer; they had thirteen ships, and harried mostly in Ireland, and did many an ill deed there till Eyvind the Eastman took the land-wardship; thereafter they got them gone to the South-isles, and harried there and all about the firths of Scotland: against these went Thrand and Onund, and heard that they had sailed to that island, which is called Bute. Now Onund and his folk came there with five ships; and when the vikings see their ships and know how many they are, they deem they have enough strength gathered there, and take their weapons and lay their ships in the midst betwixt two cliffs, where was a great and deep sound; only on one side could they be set on, and that with but five ships at once. Now Onund was the wisest of men, and bade lay five ships up into the sound, so that he and his might have back way when they would, for there was plenty of sea-room astern. On one board of them too was a certain island, and under the lee thereof he let one ship lie, and his men brought many great stones forth on to the sheer cliffs above, yet might not be seen withal from the ships.

Now the vikings laid their ships boldly enough for the attack, and thought that the others quailed; and Vigbiod asked who they were that were in such jeopardy. Thrand said that he was the brother of Eyvind the Eastman, "and here beside me is Onund Treefoot my fellow."

Then laughed the vikings, and shouted:

"Treefoot, Treefoot, foot of tree,
Trolls take thee and thy company."

"Yea, a sight it is seldom seen of us, that such men should go into battle as have no might over themselves."

Onund said that they could know nought thereof ere it were tried; and withal they laid their ships alongside one of the other, and there began a great fight, and either side did boldly. But when they came to handy blows, Onund gave back toward the cliff, and when the vikings saw this, they deemed he was minded to flee, and made towards his ship, and came as nigh to the cliff as they might. But in that very point of time those came forth on to the edge of the cliff who were appointed so to do, and sent at the vikings so great a flight of stones that they might not withstand it.

Then fell many of the viking-folk, and others were hurt so that they might not bear weapon; and withal they were fain to draw back, and might not, because their ships were even then come into the narrowest of the sound, and they were huddled together both by the ships and the stream; but Onund and his men set on fiercely, whereas Vigbiod was, but Thrand set on Vestmar, and won little thereby; so, when the folk were thinned on Vigbiod's ship, Onund's men and Onund himself got ready to board her: that Vigbiod saw, and cheered on his men without stint: then he turned to meet Onund, and the more part fled before him; but Onund bade his men mark how it went between them; for he was of huge strength. Now they set a log of wood under Onund's knee, so that he stood firmly enow; the viking fought his way forward along the ship till he reached Onund, and he smote at him with his sword, and the stroke took the shield, and sheared off all it met; and then the sword drove into the log that Onund had under his knee, and stuck fast therein; and Vigbiod stooped in drawing it out, and even therewith Onund smote at his shoulder in such wise, that he cut the arm from off him, and then was the viking unmeet for battle.

But when Vestmar knew that his fellow was fallen, he leaped into the furthermost ship and fled with all those who might reach her. Thereafter they ransacked the fallen men; and by then was Vigbiod nigh to his death: Onund went up to him, and sang:

"Yea, seest thou thy wide wounds bleed?
What of shrinking didst thou heed
In the one-foot sling of gold?
What scratch here dost thou behold?

And in e'en such wise as this
Many an axe-breaker there is
Strong of tongue and weak of hand:
Tried thou wert, and might'st not stand."

So there they took much spoil and sailed back to Barra in the autumn.

Chapter 5

THE SUMMER AFTER THIS they made ready to fare west to Ireland. But at that time Balk and Hallvard betook themselves from the lands west over the sea, and went out to Iceland, for from thence came tales of land good to choose. Balk settled land in Ramfirth and dwelt at either Balkstead; Hallvard settled Sweepingsfirth, and Hallwick out to the Stair, and dwelt there.

Now Thrand and Onund met Eyvind the Eastman, and he received his brother well; but when he knew that Onund was come with him, then he waxed wroth, and would fain set on him. Thrand bade him do it not, and said that it was not for him to wage war against Northmen, and least of all such men as fared peaceably. Eyvind said that he fared otherwise before, and had broken the peace of Kiarval the King, and that he should now pay for all. Many words the brothers had over this, till Thrand said at last that one fate should befall both him and Onund; and then Eyvind let himself be appeased.

So they dwelt there long that summer, and went on warfare with Eyvind, who found Onund to be the bravest of men. In the autumn they fared to the South-isles, and Eyvind gave to Thrand to take all the heritage of their father, if Biorn should die before Thrand.

Now were the twain in the South-isles until they wedded their wives, and some winters after withal.

Chapter 6

AND NOW IT CAME TO PASS that Biorn, the father of Thrand, died; and when Grim the hersir hears thereof he went to meet Ondott Crow, and claimed the goods left by Biorn; but Ondott said that Thrand had the heritage after his father; Grim said that Thrand was west over seas, and that Biorn was a Gothlander of kin, and that the king took the heritage of all outland men. Ondott said that he should keep the goods for the hands of Thrand, his daughter's son; and therewith Grim gat him gone, and had nought for his claiming the goods.

Now Thrand had news of his father's death, and straightway got ready to go from the South-isles, and Onund Treefoot with him; but Ufeigh Grettir and Thormod Shaft went out to Iceland with their kith and kin, and came out to the Eres in the south country, and dwelt the first winter with Thorbiorn Salmon-Carle.

Thereafter they settled Gnup-Wards'-rape, Ufeigh, the outward part, between Thwart-river and Kalf-river, and he dwelt at Ufeigh's-stead by Stone-holt; but Thormod settled the eastward part, and abode at Shaft-holt.

The daughters of Thormod were these: Thorvor, mother of Thorod the Godi of Hailti, and Thora, mother of Thorstein, the Godi, the father of Biarni the Sage.

Now it is to be said of Thrand and Onund that they sailed from the lands west over the Sea toward Norway, and had fair wind, and such speed, that no rumour of their voyage was abroad till they came to Ondott Crow.

He gave Thrand good welcome, and told him how Grim the hersir had claimed the heritage left by Biorn. "Meeter it seems to me, kinsman," said he, "that thou take the heritage of thy father and not king's-thralls; good luck has befallen thee, in that none knows of thy coming, but it misdoubts me that Grim will come upon one or other of us if he may; therefore I would that thou shouldst take the inheritance to thee, and get thee gone to other lands."

Thrand said that so he would do, he took to him the chattels and got away from Norway at his speediest; but before he sailed into the sea, he asked Onund Treefoot whether he would not make for Iceland with him; Onund said he would first go see his kin and friends in the south country.

Thrand said, "Then must we part now, but I would that thou shouldst aid my kin, for on them will vengeance fall if I get off clear; but to Iceland shall I go, and I would that thou withal shouldst make that journey."

Onund gave his word to all, and they parted in good love. So Thrand went to Iceland, and Ufeigh and Thormod Shaft received him well. Thrand dwelt at Thrand's-holt, which is west of Steer's-river.

Chapter 7

ONUND WENT SOUTH to Rogaland, and met there many of his kin and friends; he dwelt there in secret at a man's called Kolbein. Now he heard that the king had taken his lands to him and set a man thereover who was called Harek, who was a farmer of the king's; so on a night Onund went to him, and took him in his house; there Harek was led out and cut down, and Onund took all the chattels they found and burnt the homestead; and thereafter he abode in many places that winter.

But that autumn Grim the hersir slew Ondott Crow, because he might not get the heritage-money for the king; and that same night of his slaying, Signy, his wife, brought aboard ship all her chattels, and fared with her sons, Asmund and Asgrim, to Sighvat her father; but a little after sent her sons to Soknadale to Hedin her foster-father; but that seemed good to them but for a little while, and they would fain go back again to their mother; so they departed and came at Yule-tide to Ingiald the Trusty at Hvin; he took them in because of the urgency of Gyda his wife, and they were there the winter through. But in spring came Onund north to Agdir, because he had heard of the slaying of Ondott Crow; but when he found Signy he asked her what help she would have of him.

She said that she would fain have vengeance on Grim the hersir for the slaying of Ondott. Then were the sons of Ondott sent for, and when they met Onund Treefoot, they made up one fellowship together, and had spies abroad on the doings of Grim. Now in the summer was a great ale-drinking held at Grim's, because he had bidden to him Earl Audun; and when Onund and the sons of Ondott knew thereof they went to Grim's homestead and laid fire to the house, for they were come there unawares, and burnt Grim the hersir therein, and nigh thirty men, and many good things they took there withal. Then went Onund to the woods, but the sons of Ondott took a boat of Ingiald's, their foster-father's, and rowed away therein, and lay hid a little way off the homestead. Earl Audun came to the feast, even as had been settled afore, and there "missed friend from stead." Then he gathered men to him, and dwelt there some nights, but nought was heard of Onund and his fellows; and the Earl slept in a loft with two men.

Onund had full tidings from the homestead, and sent after those brothers; and, when they met, Onund asked them whether they would watch the farm or fall on the Earl; but they chose to set on the Earl. So they drove beams at the loft-doors and broke them in; then Asmund caught hold of the two who were with the Earl, and cast them down so hard that they were well-nigh slain; but Asgrim ran at the Earl, and bade him render up weregild for his father, since he had been in the plot and the onslaught with Grim the hersir when Ondott Crow was slain. The Earl said he had no money with him there, and prayed for delay of that payment. Then Asgrim set his spear-point to the Earl's breast and bade him pay there and then; so the Earl took a chain from his neck, and three gold rings, and a cloak of rich web, and gave them up. Asgrim took the goods and gave the Earl a name, and called him Audun Goaty.

But when the bonders and neighbouring folk were ware that war was come among them, they went abroad and would bring help to the Earl, and a hard fight there was, for Onund had many men, and there fell many good bonders and courtmen of the Earl. Now came the brothers, and told how they had fared with the Earl, and Onund said that it was ill that he was not slain, "that would have been somewhat of a revenge on the King for our loss at his hands of fee and friends." They said that this was a greater shame to the Earl; and therewith they went away up to Sorreldale to Eric Alefain, a king's lord, and he took them in for all the winter.

Now at Yule they drank turn and turn about with a man called Hallstein, who was bynamed Horse; Eric gave the first feast, well and truly, and then Hallstein gave his, but thereat was there bickering between them, and Hallstein smote Eric with a deer-horn; Eric gat no revenge therefor, but went home straightway. This sore misliked the sons of Ondott, and a little after Asgrim fared to Hallstein's homestead, and went in alone, and gave him a great wound, but those who were therein sprang up and set on Asgrim. Asgrim defended himself well and got out of their hands in the dark; but they deemed they had slain him.

Onund and Asmund heard thereof and supposed him dead, but deemed they might do nought. Eric counselled them to make for Iceland, and said that would be of no avail to abide there in the land (i.e. in Norway), as soon as the king should bring matters about to his liking. So this they did, and made them ready for Iceland and had each one ship. Hallstein lay wounded, and died before Onund and his folk sailed. Kolbein withal, who is afore mentioned, went abroad with Onund.

Chapter 8

NOW ONUND AND ASMUND sailed into the sea when they were ready, and held company together; then sang Onund this stave:

> *"Meet was I in days agone*
> *For storm, wherein the Sweeping One,*
> *Midst rain of swords, and the darts' breath,*
> *Blew o'er all a gale of death.*
> *Now a maimed, one-footed man*
> *On rollers' steed through waters wan*
> *Out to Iceland must I go;*
> *Ah, the skald is sinking low."*

They had a hard voyage of it and much of baffling gales from the south, and drove north into the main; but they made Iceland, and were by then come to the north off Longness when they found where they were: so little space there was betwixt them that they spake together; and Asmund said that they had best sail to Islefirth, and thereto they both agreed; then they beat up toward the land, and a south-east wind sprang up; but when Onund and his folk laid the ship close to the wind, the yard was sprung; then they took in sail, and therewith were driven off to sea; but Asmund got under the lee of Brakeisle, and there lay till a fair wind brought him into Islefirth; Helgi the Lean gave him all Kraeklings' lithe, and he dwelt at South Glass-river; Asgrim his brother came out some winters later and abode at North Glass-river; he was the father of Ellida-Grim, the father of Asgrim Ellida-Grimson.

Chapter 9

NOW IT IS TO BE TOLD of Onund Treefoot that he drave out to sea for certain days, but at last the wind got round to the north, and they sailed for land: then those knew who had been there before that they had come west off the Skagi; then they sailed into Strand-Bay, and near to the South-Strands, and there rowed toward them six men in a ten-oared boat, who hailed the big ship, and asked who was their captain; Onund named himself, and asked whence they came; they said they were house-carles of Thorvald, from Drangar; Onund asked if all land through the Strands had been settled; they said there was little unsettled in the inner Strands, and none north thereof. Then Onund asked his shipmates, whether they would make for the west country, or take such as they had been told of; they chose to view the land first. So they sailed in up the bay, and brought to in a creek off Arness, then put forth a boat and rowed to land. There dwelt a rich man, Eric Snare, who had taken land betwixt Ingolfs-firth, and Ufoera in Fishless; but when Eric knew that Onund was come there, he bade him take of his hands whatso he would, but said that there was little that had not been settled before. Onund said he would first see what there was, so they went landward south past some firths, till they came to Ufoera; then said Eric, "Here is what there is to look to; all from here is unsettled, and right in to the settlements of Biorn." Now a great mountain went down the eastern side of the firth, and snow had fallen thereon, Onund looked on that mountain, and sang:

> "Brand-whetter's life awry doth go.
> Fair lands and wide full well I know;
> Past house, and field, and fold of man,
> The swift steed of the rollers ran:
> My lands, and kin, I left behind,
> That I this latter day might find,
> Coldback for sunny meads to have;
> Hard fate a bitter bargain drave."

Eric answered, "Many have lost so much in Norway, that it may not be bettered: and I think withal that most lands in the main-settlements are already settled, and therefore I urge thee not to go from hence; but I shall hold to what I spake, that thou mayst have whatso of my lands seems meet to thee." Onund said, that he would take that offer, and so he settled land out from Ufoera over the three creeks, Byrgis Creek, Kolbein's Creek, and Coldback Creek, up to Coldback Cleft. Thereafter Eric gave him all Fishless, and Reekfirth, and all Reekness, out on that side of the firth; but as to drifts there was nought set forth, for they were then so plentiful that every man had of them what he would. Now Onund set up a household at Coldback, and had many men about him; but when his goods began to grow great he had another stead in Reekfirth. Kolbein dwelt at Kolbein's Creek. So Onund abode in peace for certain winters.

Chapter 10

NOW ONUND WAS so brisk a man, that few, even of whole men, could cope with him; and his name withal was well known throughout the land, because of his forefathers. After these things, befell that strife betwixt Ufeigh Grettir and Thorbiorn Earl's-champion, which had such ending, that Ufeigh fell before Thorbiorn in Grettir's-Gill, near Heel. There were many drawn together to the sons of Ufeigh concerning the blood-suit, and Onund Treefoot was sent for, and rode south in the spring, and guested at Hvamm, with Aud the Deeply-wealthy, and she gave him exceeding good welcome, because he had been with her west over the Sea. In those days, Olaf Feilan, her son's son, was a man full grown, and Aud was by then worn with great eld; she bade Onund know that she would have Olaf, her kinsman, married, and was fain that he should woo Aldis of Barra, who was cousin to Asa, whom Onund had to wife. Onund deemed the matter hopeful, and Olaf rode south with him. So when Onund met his friends and kin-in-law they bade him abide with them: then was the suit talked over, and was laid to Kialarnes Thing, for as then the Althing was not yet set up. So the case was settled by umpiredom, and heavy weregild came for the slayings, and Thorbiorn Earl's-champion was outlawed. His son was Solmund, the father of Kari the Singed; father and son dwelt abroad a long time afterwards.

Thrand bade Onund and Olaf to his house, and so did Thormod Shaft, and they backed Olaf's wooing, which was settled with ease, because men knew how mighty a woman Aud was. So the bargain was made, and, so much being done, Onund rode home, and Aud thanked him well for his help to Olaf. That autumn Olaf Feilan wedded Aldis of Barra; and then died Aud the Deeply-wealthy, as is told in the story of the Laxdale men.

Chapter 11

ONUND AND ASA had two sons; the elder was called Thorgeir, the younger Ufeigh Grettir; but Asa soon died. Thereafter Onund got to wife a woman called Thordis, the daughter of Thorgrim, from Gnup in Midfirth, and akin to Midfirth Skeggi. Of her Onund had a son called Thorgrim; he was early a big man, and a strong, wise, and good withal in matters of husbandry. Onund dwelt on at Coldback till he was old, then he died in his bed, and is buried in Treefoot's barrow; he was the briskest and lithest of one-footed men who have ever lived in Iceland.

Now Thorgrim took the lead among the sons of Onund, though others of them were older than he; but when he was twenty-five years old he grew grey-haired, and therefore was he bynamed Greypate; Thordis, his mother, was afterwards wedded north in Willowdale, to Audun Skokul, and their son was Asgeir, of Asgeir's-River. Thorgrim Greypate and his brothers had great possessions in common, nor did they divide the goods between them. Now Eric, who farmed at Arness, as is aforesaid, had to wife Alof, daughter of Ingolf, of Ingolfs-firth; and Flosi was the name of their son, a hopeful man, and of many friends. In those days three brothers came out hither, Ingolf, Ufeigh, and Eyvind, and settled those three firths that are known by their names, and there dwelt afterwards. Olaf was the name of Eyvind's son, he first dwelt at Eyvind's-firth, and after at Drangar, and was a man to hold his own well.

Now there was no strife betwixt these men while their elders were alive; but when Eric died, it seemed to Flosi, that those of Coldback had no lawful title to the lands which Eric had given to Onund; and from this befell much ill-blood betwixt them; but Thorgrim and his kin still held their lands as before, but they might not risk having sports together. Now Thorgeir was head-man of the household of those brothers in Reekfirth, and would ever be rowing out a-fishing, because in those days were the firths full of fish; so those in the Creek made up their plot; a man there was, a house-carle of Flosi in Arness, called Thorfin, him Flosi sent for Thorgeir's head, and he went and hid himself in the boat-stand; that morning, Thorgeir got ready to row out to sea, and two men with him, one called Hamund, the other Brand. Thorgeir went first, and had on his back a leather bottle and drink therein. It was very dark, and as he walked down from the boat-stand Thorfin ran at him, and smote him with an axe betwixt the shoulders, and the axe sank in, and the bottle squeaked, but he let go the axe, for he deemed that there would be little need of binding up, and would save himself as swiftly as might be; and it is to be told of him that he ran off to Arness, and came there before broad day, and told of Thorgeir's slaying, and said that he should have need of Flosi's shelter, and that the only thing to be done was to offer atonement, "for that of all things," said he, "is like to better our strait, great as it has now grown."

Flosi said that he would first hear tidings; "and I am minded to think that thou art afraid after thy big deed."

Now it is to be said of Thorgeir, that he turned from the blow as the axe smote the bottle, nor had he any wound; they made no search for the man because of the dark, so they rowed over the firths to Coldback, and told tidings of what had happed; thereat folk made much mocking, and called Thorgeir, Bottleback, and that was his by-name ever after.

And this was sung withal:

"The brave men of days of old,
Whereof many a tale is told,
Bathed the whiting of the shield,
In wounds' house on battle-field;
But the honour-missing fool,
Both sides of his slaying tool,
Since faint heart his hand made vain.
With but curdled milk must stain."

Chapter 12

IN THOSE DAYS befell such hard times in Iceland, that nought like them has been known there; well-nigh all gettings from the sea, and all drifts, came to an end; and this went on for many seasons. One autumn certain chapmen in a big ship were drifted thither, and were wrecked there in the Creek, and Flosi took to him four or five of them; Stein was the name of their captain; they were housed here and there about the Creek, and were minded to build them a new ship from the wreck; but they were unhandy herein, and the ship was over small stem and stern, but over big amidships.

That spring befell a great storm from the north, which lasted near a week, and after the storm men looked after their drifts. Now there was a man called Thorstein, who dwelt at Reekness; he found a whale driven up on the firthward side of the ness, at a place called Rib-Skerries, and the whale was a big whale.

Thorstein sent forthwith a messenger to Wick to Flosi, and so to the nighest farm-steads. Now Einar was the name of the farmer at Combe, and he was a tenant of those of Coldback, and had the ward of their drifts on that side of the firths; and now withal he was ware of the stranding of the whale: and he took boat and rowed past the firths to Byrgis Creek, whence he sent a man to Coldback; and when Thorgrim and his brothers heard that, they got ready at their swiftest, and were twelve in a ten-oared boat, and Kolbein's sons fared with them, Ivar and Leif, and were six altogether; and all farmers who could bring it about went to the whale.

Now it is to be told of Flosi that he sent to his kin in Ingolfs-firth and Ufeigh's-firth, and for Olaf Eyvindson, who then dwelt at Drangar; and Flosi came first to the whale, with the men of Wick, then they fell to cutting up the whale, and what was cut was forthwith sent ashore; near twenty men were thereat at first, but soon folk came thronging thither.

Therewith came those of Coldback in four boats, and Thorgrim laid claim to the whale and forbade the men of Wick to shear, allot, or carry off aught thereof: Flosi bade him show if Eric had given Onund Treefoot the drift in clear terms, or else he said he should defend himself with arms. Thorgrim thought he and his too few, and would not risk an onset; but therewithal came a boat rowing up the firth, and the rowers therein pulled smartly. Soon they came up, and there was Swan, from Knoll in Biornfirth, and his house-carles; and straightway, when he came, he bade Thorgrim not to let himself be robbed; and great friends they had been heretofore, and now Swan offered his aid. The brothers said they would take it, and therewith set on fiercely; Thorgeir Bottleback first mounted the whale against Flosi's house-carles; there the aforenamed Thorfin was cutting the whale, he was in front nigh the head, and stood in a foot-hold he had cut for himself; then Thorgeir said, "Herewith I bring thee back thy axe," and smote him on the neck, and struck off his head.

Flosi was up on the foreshore when he saw that, and he egged on his men to meet them hardily; now they fought long together, but those of Coldback had the best of it: few men there had weapons except the axes wherewith they were cutting up the whale, and some choppers. So the men of Wick gave back to the foreshores; the Eastmen had weapons, and many a wound they gave; Stein, the captain, smote a foot off Ivar Kolbeinson, but Leif, Ivar's brother, beat to death a fellow of Stein's with a whale-rib; blows were dealt there with whatever could be caught at, and men fell on either side. But now came up Olaf and his men from Drangar in many boats, and gave help to Flosi, and then those of Coldback were borne back overpowered; but they had loaded their boats already, and Swan bade get aboard and thitherward they gave back, and the men of Wick came on after them; and when Swan was come down to the sea, he smote at Stein, the sea-captain, and gave him a great wound, and then leapt aboard his boat; Thorgrim wounded Flosi with a great wound and therewith got away; Olaf cut at Ufeigh Grettir, and wounded him to death; but Thorgeir caught Ufeigh up and leapt aboard with him. Now those of Coldback row east by the firths, and thus they parted; and this was sung of their meeting:

> "At Rib-skerries, I hear folk tell,
> A hard and dreadful fray befell,
> For men unarmed upon that day
> With strips of whale-fat made good play.
> Fierce steel-gods these in turn did meet
> With blubber-slices nowise sweet;
> Certes a wretched thing it is
> To tell of squabbles such as this."

After these things was peace settled between them, and these suits were laid to the Althing; there Thorod the Godi and Midfirth-Skeggi, with many of the south-country folk, aided those of Coldback; Flosi was outlawed, and many of those who had been with him; and his moneys were greatly drained because he chose to pay up all weregild himself. Thorgrim and his folk could not show that they had paid money for the lands and drifts which Flosi claimed. Thorkel Moon was lawman then, and he was bidden to give his decision; he said that to him it seemed law, that something had been paid for those lands, though mayhap not their full worth; "For so did Steinvor the Old to Ingolf, my grandfather, that she had from him all Rosmwhale-ness and gave therefor a spotted cloak, nor has that gift been voided, though certes greater flaws be therein: but here I lay down my rede," said he, "that the land be shared, and that both sides have equal part therein; and henceforth be it made law, that each man have the drifts before his own lands." Now this was done, and the land was so divided that Thorgrim and his folk had to give up Reekfirth and all the lands by the firth-side, but Combe they were to keep still. Ufeigh was atoned with a great sum; Thorfin was unatoned, and boot was given to Thorgeir for the attack on his life; and thereafter were they set at one together. Flosi took ship for Norway with Stein, the ship-master, and sold his lands in the Wick to Geirmund Hiuka-timber, who dwelt there afterwards. Now that ship which the chapmen had made was very broad of beam, so that men called it the Treetub, and by that name is the creek known: but in that keel did Flosi go out, but was driven back to Axefirth, whereof came the tale of Bodmod, and Grimulf, and Gerpir.

Chapter 13

NOW AFTER THIS the brothers Thorgrim and Thorgeir shared their possessions. Thorgrim took the chattels and Thorgeir the land; Thorgrim betook himself to Midfirth and bought land at Biarg by the counsel of Skeggi; he had to wife Thordis, daughter of Asmund of Asmund's-peak, who had settled the Thingere lands: Thorgrim and Thordis had a son who was called Asmund; he was a big man and a strong, wise withal, and the fairest-haired of men, but his head grew grey early, wherefore he was called Asmund the Greyhaired. Thorgrim grew to be a man very busy about his household, and kept all his well to their work. Asmund would do but little work, so the father and son had small fellowship together; and so things fared till Asmund had grown of age; then he asked his father for travelling money; Thorgrim said he should have little enough, but gave him somewhat of huckstering wares.

Then Asmund went abroad, and his goods soon grew great; he sailed to sundry lands, and became the greatest of merchants, and very rich; he was a man well beloved and trusty, and many kinsmen he had in Norway of great birth.

One autumn he guested east in the Wick with a great man who was called Thorstein; he was an Uplander of kin, and had a sister called Ranveig, one to be chosen before all women; her Asmund wooed, and gained her by the help of Thorstein her brother; and there Asmund dwelt a while and was held in good esteem: he had of Ranveig a son hight Thorstein, strong, and the fairest of men, and great of voice; a man tall of growth he was, but somewhat slow in his mien, and therefore was he called Dromund. Now when Thorstein was nigh grown up, his mother fell sick and died, and thereafter Asmund had no joy in Norway; the kin of Thorstein's mother took his goods, and him withal to foster; but Asmund betook himself once more to seafaring, and became a man of great renown. Now he brought his ship into Hunawater, and in those days was Thorkel Krafla chief over the Waterdale folk; and he heard of Asmund's coming out, and rode to the ship and bade Asmund to his house; and he dwelt at Marstead in Waterdale; so Asmund went to be guest there. This Thorkel was the son of Thorgrim the Godi of Cornriver, and was a very wise man.

Now this was after the coming out of Bishop Frederick, and Thorvald Kodran's son, and they dwelt at the Brooks-meet, when these things came to pass: they were the first to preach the law of Christ in the north country; Thorkel let himself be signed with the cross and many men with him, and things enow betid betwixt the bishop and the north-country folk which come not into this tale.

Now at Thorkel's was a woman brought up, Asdis by name, who was the daughter of Bard, the son of Jokul, the son of Ingimund the Old, the son of Thorstein, the son of Ketil the Huge: the mother of Asdis was Aldis the daughter of Ufeigh Grettir, as is aforesaid; Asdis was as yet unwedded, and was deemed the best match among women, both for her kin and her possessions; Asmund was grown weary of seafaring, and was fain to take up his abode in Iceland; so he took up the word, and wooed this woman. Thorkel knew well all his ways, that he was a rich man and of good counsel to hold his wealth; so that came about, that Asmund got Asdis to wife; he became a bosom friend of Thorkel, and a great dealer in matters of farming, cunning in the law, and far-reaching. And now a little after this Thorgrim Greypate died at Biarg, and Asmund took the heritage after him and dwelt there.

Part Two

HERE BEGINS the story of the life of Grettir the Strong.

Chapter 14
Of Grettir as a Child, and His Froward Ways with His Father

ASMUND THE GREYHAIRED kept house at Biarg; great and proud was his household, and many men he had about him, and was a man much beloved. These were the children of him and Asdis. Atli was the eldest son; a man yielding and soft-natured, easy, and meek withal, and all men liked him well: another son they had called Grettir; he was very froward in his childhood; of few words, and rough; worrying both in word and deed. Little fondness he got from his father Asmund, but his mother loved him right well.

Grettir Asmundson was fair to look on, broad-faced, short-faced, red-haired, and much freckled; not of quick growth in his childhood.

Thordis was a daughter of Asmund, whom Glum, the son of Uspak, the son of Kiarlak of Skridinsenni, afterwards had to wife. Ranveig was another daughter of Asmund; she was the wife of Gamli, the son of Thorhal, the son of the Vendlander; they kept house at Meals in Ramfirth; their son was Grim. The son of Glum and Thordis, the daughter of Asmund, was Uspak, who quarrelled with Odd, the son of Ufeigh, as is told in the Bandamanna Saga.

Grettir grew up at Biarg till he was ten years old; then he began to get on a little; but Asmund bade him do some work; Grettir answered that work was not right meet for him, but asked what he should do.

Says Asmund, "Thou shalt watch my home-geese."

Grettir answered and said, "A mean work, a milksop's work."

Asmund said, "Turn it well out of hand, and then matters shall get better between us."

Then Grettir betook himself to watching the home-geese; fifty of them there were, with many goslings; but no long time went by before he found them a troublesome drove, and the goslings slow-paced withal. Thereat he got sore worried, for little did he keep his temper in hand. So some time after this, wayfaring men found the goslings strewn about dead, and the home-geese broken-winged; and this was in autumn. Asmund was mightily vexed hereat, and asked if Grettir had killed the fowl: he sneered mockingly, and answered:

> *"Surely as winter comes, shall I*
> *Twist the goslings' necks awry.*
> *If in like case are the geese,*
> *I have finished each of these."*

"Thou shalt kill them no more," said Asmund.

"Well, *a friend should warn a friend of ill*," said Grettir.

"Another work shall be found for thee then," said Asmund.

"*More one knows the more one tries*," said Grettir; "and what shall I do now?"

Asmund answered, "Thou shalt rub my back at the fire, as I have been wont to have it done."

"Hot for the hand, truly," said Grettir; "but still a milksop's work."

Now Grettir went on with this work for a while; but autumn came on, and Asmund became very fain of heat, and he spurs Grettir on to rub his back briskly. Now, in those times there were wont to be large fire-halls at the homesteads, wherein men sat at long fires in the evenings; boards were set before the men there, and afterwards folk slept out sideways from the fires; there also women worked at the wool in the daytime. Now, one evening, when Grettir had to rub Asmund's back, the old carle said:

"Now thou wilt have to put away thy sloth, thou milk-sop."

Says Grettir, *"Ill is it to goad the foolhardy."*

Asmund answers, "Thou wilt ever be a good-for-nought."

Now Grettir sees where, in one of the seats stood wool-combs: one of these he caught up, and let it go all down Asmund's back. He sprang up, and was mad wroth thereat; and was going to smite Grettir with his staff, but he ran off. Then came the housewife, and asked what was this to-do betwixt them. Then Grettir answered by this ditty:

> *"This jewel-strewer, O ground of gold,*
> *(His counsels I deem over bold),*
> *On both these hands that trouble sow,*
> *(Ah bitter pain) will burn me now;*
> *Therefore with wool-comb's nails unshorn*
> *Somewhat ring-strewer's back is torn:*
> *The hook-clawed bird that wrought his wound:*
> *Lo, now I see it on the ground."*

Hereupon was his mother sore vexed, that he should have taken to a trick like this; she said he would never fail to be the most reckless of men. All this nowise bettered matters between Asmund and Grettir.

Now, some time after this, Asmund had a talk with Grettir, that he should watch his horses. Grettir said this was more to his mind than the back-rubbing.

"Then shalt thou do as I bid thee," said Asmund. "I have a dun mare, which I call Keingala; she is so wise as to shifts of weather, thaws, and the like, that rough weather will never fail to follow, when she will not go out on grazing. At such times thou shalt lock the horses up under cover; but keep them to grazing on the mountain neck yonder, when winter comes on. Now I shall deem it needful that thou turn this work out of hand better than the two I have set thee to already."

Grettir answered, "This is a cold work and a manly, but I deem it ill to trust in the mare, for I know none who has done it yet."

Now Grettir took to the horse-watching, and so the time went on till past Yule-time; then came on much cold weather with snow, that made grazing hard to come at. Now Grettir was ill clad, and as yet little hardened, and he began to be starved by the cold; but Keingala grazed away in the windiest place she could find, let the weather be as rough as it would. Early as she might go to the pasture, never would she go back to stable before nightfall. Now Grettir deemed that he must think of some scurvy trick or other, that Keingala might be paid in full for her way of grazing: so, one morning early, he comes to the horse-stable, opens it, and finds Keingala standing all along before the crib; for, whatever food was given to the horses with her, it was her way to get it all to herself. Grettir got on her back, and had a sharp knife in his hand, and drew it right across Keingala's shoulder, and then all along both sides of the back. Thereat the mare, being both fat and shy, gave a mad bound, and kicked so fiercely, that her hooves clattered against the wall. Grettir fell off; but, getting on his legs, strove to mount her again. Now their struggle is of the sharpest, but the end of it is, that he flays off the whole of the strip along the back to the loins. Thereafter he drove the horses out on grazing; Keingala would bite but at her back, and when noon was barely past, she started off, and ran back to the house. Grettir now locks the stable and goes home. Asmund asked Grettir where the horses were. He said that he had stabled them as he was wont. Asmund said that rough weather was like to be at hand, as the horses would not keep at their grazing in such good weather as now it was.

Grettir said, *"Oft fail in wisdom folk of better trust."*

Now the night goes by, but no rough weather came on. Grettir drove off the horses, but Keingala cannot bear the grazing. This seemed strange to Asmund, as the weather changed in nowise from what it had been theretofore. The third morning Asmund went to the horses, and, coming to Keingala, said:

"I must needs deem these horses to be in sorry case, good as the winter has been, but thy sides will scarce lack flesh, my dun."

"Things boded will happen," said Grettir, *"but so will things unboded."*

Asmund stroked the back of the mare, and, lo, the hide came off beneath his hand; he wondered how this could have happened, and said it was likely to be Grettir's doing. Grettir sneered mockingly, but said nought. Now goodman Asmund went home talking as one mad; he went straight to the fire-hall, and as he came heard the good wife say, "It were good indeed if the horse-keeping of my kinsman had gone off well."

Then Asmund sang this stave:

> *"Grettir has in such wise played,*
> *That Keingala has he flayed,*
> *Whose trustiness would be my boast*
> *(Proudest women talk the most);*
> *So the cunning lad has wrought,*
> *Thinking thereby to do nought*
> *Of my biddings any more.*
> *In thy mind turn these words o'er."*

The housewife answered, "I know not which is least to my mind, that thou shouldst ever be bidding him work, or that he should turn out all his work in one wise."

"That too we will make an end of," said Asmund, "but he shall fare the worse therefor."

Then Grettir said, "Well, let neither make words about it to the other."

So things went on awhile, and Asmund had Keingala killed; and many other scurvy tricks did Grettir in his childhood whereof the story says nought. But he grew great of body, though his strength was not well known, for he was unskilled in wrestling; he would make ditties and rhymes, but was somewhat scurrilous therein. He had no will to lie anight in the fire-hall and was mostly of few words.

Chapter 15
Of the Ball-Play on Midfirth Water

AT THIS TIME there were many growing up to be men in Midfirth; Skald-Torfa dwelt at Torfa's-stead in those days; her son was called Bessi, he was the shapeliest of men and a good skald.

At Meal lived two brothers, Kormak and Thorgils, with them a man called Odd was fostered, and was called the Foundling-skald.

One called Audun was growing up at Audunstead in Willowdale, he was a kind and good man to deal with, and the strongest in those north parts, of all who were of an age with him. Kalf Asgeirson dwelt at Asgeir's-river, and his brother Thorvald with him. Atli also, Grettir's brother, was growing into a ripe man at that time; the gentlest of men he was, and well beloved of all. Now these men settled to have ball-play together on Midfirth Water; thither came the Midfirthers, and Willowdale men, and men from Westhope, and Waterness, and Ramfirth, but those who came from far abode at the play-stead.

Now those who were most even in strength were paired together, and thereat was always the greatest sport in autumn-tide. But when he was fourteen years old Grettir went to the plays, because he was prayed thereto by his brother Atli.

Now were all paired off for the plays, and Grettir was allotted to play against Audun, the aforenamed, who was some winters the eldest of the two; Audun struck the ball over Grettir's head, so that he could not catch it, and it bounded far away along the ice; Grettir got angry thereat, deeming that Audun would outplay him; but he fetches the ball and brings it back, and, when he was within reach of Audun, hurls it right against his forehead, and smites him so that the skin was broken; then Audun struck at Grettir with the bat he held in his hand, but smote him no hard blow, for Grettir ran in under the stroke; and thereat they seized one another with arms clasped, and wrestled. Then all saw that Grettir was stronger than he had been taken to be, for Audun was a man full of strength.

A long tug they had of it, but the end was that Grettir fell, and Audun thrust his knees against his belly and breast, and dealt hardly with him.

Then Atli and Bessi and many others ran up and parted them; but Grettir said there was no need to hold him like a mad dog, "For," said he, "*thralls wreak themselves at once, dastards never.*"

This men suffered not to grow into open strife, for the brothers, Kalf and Thorvald, were fain that all should be at one again, and Audun and Grettir were somewhat akin withal; so the play went on as before, nor did anything else befall to bring about strife.

Chapter 16
Of the Slaying of Skeggi

NOW THORKEL KRAFLA GOT VERY OLD; he had the rule of Waterdale and was a great man. He was bosom friend of Asmund the Greyhaired, as was beseeming for the sake of their kinship; he was wont to ride to Biarg every year and see his kin there, nor did he fail herein the spring following these matters just told. Asmund and Asdis welcomed him most heartily, he was there three nights, and many things did the kinsmen speak of between them. Now Thorkel asked Asmund what his mind foreboded him about his sons, as to what kind of craft they would be likely to take to. Asmund said that he thought Atli would be a great man at farming, foreseeing, and money-making. Thorkel answered, "A useful man and like unto thyself: but what dost thou say of Grettir?"

Asmund said, "Of him I say, that he will be a strong man and an unruly, and, certes, of wrathful mood, and heavy enough he has been to me."

Thorkel answered, "That bodes no good, friend; but how shall we settle about our riding to the Thing next summer?"

Asmund answered, "I am growing heavy for wayfaring, and would fain sit at home."

"Wouldst thou that Atli go in thy stead?" said Thorkel.

"I do not see how I could spare him," says Asmund, "because of the farm-work and ingathering of household stores; but now Grettir will not work, yet he bears about that wit with him that I deem he will know how to keep up the showing forth of the law for me through thy aid."

"Well, thou shall have thy will," said Thorkel, and withal he rode home when he was ready, and Asmund let him go with good gifts.

Some time after this Thorkel made him ready to ride to the Thing, he rode with sixty men, for all went with him who were in his rule: thus he came to Biarg, and therefrom rode Grettir with him.

Now they rode south over the heath that is called Two-days'-ride; but on this mountain the baiting grounds were poor, therefore they rode fast across it down to the settled lands, and when they came down to Fleet-tongue they thought it was time to sleep, so they took the bridles off their horses and let them graze with the saddles on. They lay sleeping till far on in the day, and when they woke, the men went about looking for their horses; but they had gone each his own way, and some of them had been rolling; but Grettir was the last to find his horse.

Now it was the wont in those days that men should carry their own victuals when they rode to the Althing, and most bore meal-bags athwart their saddles; and the saddle was turned under the belly of Grettir's horse, and the meal-bag was gone, so he goes and searches, and finds nought.

Just then he sees a man running fast, Grettir asks who it is who is running there; the man answered that his name was Skeggi, and that he was a house-carle from the Ridge in Waterdale. "I am one of the following of goodman Thorkel," he says, "but, faring heedlessly, I have lost my meal-bag."

Grettir said, "*Odd haps are worst haps*, for I, also, have lost the meal-sack which I owned, and now let us search both together."

This Skeggi liked well, and a while they go thus together; but all of a sudden Skeggi bounded off up along the moors and caught up a meal-sack. Grettir saw him stoop, and asked what he took up there.

"My meal-sack," says Skeggi.

"Who speaks to that besides thyself?" says Grettir; "let me see it, for many a thing has its like."

Skeggi said that no man should take from him what was his own; but Grettir caught at the meal-bag, and now they tug one another along with the meal-sack between them, both trying hard to get the best of it.

"It is to be wondered at," says the house-carle, "that ye Waterdale men should deem, that because other men are not as wealthy as ye, that they should not therefore dare to hold aught of their own in your despite."

Grettir said, that it had nought to do with the worth of men that each should have his own. Skeggi answers, "Too far off is Audun now to throttle thee as at that ball-play."

"Good," said Grettir; "but, howsoever that went, thou at least shall never throttle me."

Then Skeggi got at his axe and hewed at Grettir; when Grettir saw that, he caught the axe-handle with the left hand bladeward of Skeggi's hand, so hard that straightway was the axe loosed from his hold. Then Grettir drave that same axe into his head so that it stood in the brain, and the house-carle fell dead to earth. Then Grettir seized the meal-bag and threw it across his saddle, and thereon rode after his fellows.

Now Thorkel rode ahead of all, for he had no misgiving of such things befalling: but men missed Skeggi from the company, and when Grettir came up they asked him what he knew of Skeggi; then he sang:

"A rock-troll her weight did throw
At Skeggi's throat a while ago:
Over the battle ogress ran
The red blood of the serving-man;
Her deadly iron mouth did gape
Above him, till clean out of shape
She tore his head and let out life:
And certainly I saw their strife."

Then Thorkel's men sprung up and said that surely trolls had not taken the man in broad daylight. Thorkel grew silent, but said presently, "The matter is likely to be quite other than this; methinks Grettir has in all likelihood killed him, or what could befall?"

Then Grettir told all their strife. Thorkel says, "This has come to pass most unluckily, for Skeggi was given to my following, and was, nathless, a man of good kin; but I shall deal thus with the matter: I shall give boot for the man as the doom goes, but the outlawry I may not settle. Now, two things thou hast to choose between, Grettir; whether thou wilt rather go to the Thing and risk the turn of matters, or go back home."

Grettir chose to go to the Thing, and thither he went. But a lawsuit was set on foot by the heirs of the slain man: Thorkel gave handsel, and paid up all fines, but Grettir must needs be outlawed, and keep abroad three winters.

Now when the chiefs rode from the Thing, they baited under Sledgehill before they parted: then Grettir lifted a stone which now lies there in the grass and is called Grettir's-heave; but many men came up to see the stone, and found it a great wonder that so young a man should heave aloft such a huge rock.

Now Grettir rode home to Biarg and tells the tale of his journey; Asmund let out little thereon, but said that he would turn out an unruly man.

Chapter 17
Of Grettir's Voyage Out

THERE WAS A MAN called Haflidi, who dwelt at Reydarfell in Whiteriverside, he was a seafaring man and had a sailing ship, which lay up Whiteriver: there was a man on board his ship, hight Bard, who had a wife with him young and fair. Asmund sent a man to Haflidi, praying him to take Grettir and look after him; Haflidi said that he had heard that the man was ill ruled of mood; yet for the sake of the friendship between him and Asmund he took Grettir to himself, and made ready for sailing abroad.

Asmund would give to his son no faring-goods but victuals for the voyage and a little wadmall. Grettir prayed him for some weapon, but Asmund answered, "Thou hast not been obedient to me, nor do I know how far thou art likely to work with weapons things that may be of any gain; and no weapon shalt thou have of me."

"No deed no reward," says Grettir. Then father and son parted with little love. Many there were who bade Grettir farewell, but few bade him come back.

But his mother brought him on his road, and before they parted she spoke thus, "Thou art not fitted out from home, son, as I fain would thou wert, a man so well born as thou; but, meseems, the greatest shortcoming herein is that thou hast no weapons of any avail, and my mind misgives me that thou wilt perchance need them sorely."

With that she took out from under her cloak a sword well wrought, and a fair thing it was, and then she said, "This sword was owned by Jokul, my father's father, and the earlier Waterdale men, and it gained them many a day; now I give thee the sword, and may it stand thee in good stead."

Grettir thanked her well for this gift, and said he deemed it better than things of more worth; then he went on his way, and Asdis wished him all good hap.

Now Grettir rode south over the heath, and made no stay till he came to the ship. Haflidi gave him a good welcome and asked him for his faring-goods, then Grettir sang:

> *"Rider of wind-driven steed,*
> *Little gat I to my need,*
> *When I left my fair birth-stead,*
> *From the snatchers of worm's bed;*
> *But this man's-bane hanging here,*
> *Gift of woman good of cheer,*
> *Proves the old saw said not ill,*
> *Best to bairn is mother still."*

Haflidi said it was easily seen that she thought the most of him. But now they put to sea when they were ready, and had wind at will; but when they had got out over all shallows they hoisted sail.

Now Grettir made a den for himself under the boat, from whence he would move for nought, neither for baling, nor to do aught at the sail, nor to work at what he was bound to work at in the ship in even shares with the other men, neither would he buy himself off from the work.

Now they sailed south by Reekness and then south from the land; and when they lost land they got much heavy sea; the ship was somewhat leaky, and scarce seaworthy in heavy weather, therefore they had it wet enough. Now Grettir let fly his biting rhymes, whereat the men got sore wroth. One day, when it so happened that the weather was both squally and cold, the men called out to Grettir, and bade him now do manfully, "For," said they, "now our claws grow right cold." Grettir looked up and said:

> *"Good luck, scurvy starvelings, if I should behold*
> *Each finger ye have doubled up with the cold."*

And no work they got out of him, and now it misliked them of their lot as much again as before, and they said that he should pay with his skin for his rhymes and the lawlessness which he did. "Thou art more fain," said they, "of playing with Bard the mate's wife than doing thy duty on board ship, and this is a thing not to be borne at all."

The gale grew greater steadily, and now they stood baling for days and nights together, and all swore to kill Grettir. But when Haflidi heard this, he went up to where Grettir lay, and said, "Methinks the bargain between thee and the chapmen is scarcely fair; first thou dost by them unlawfully, and thereafter thou castest thy rhymes at them; and now they swear that they will throw thee overboard, and this is unseemly work to go on."

"Why should they not be free to do as they will?" says Grettir; "but I well would that one or two of them tarry here behind with me, or ever I go overboard."

Haflidi says, "Such deeds are not to be done, and we shall never thrive if ye rush into such madness; but I shall give thee good rede."

"What is that?" says Grettir.

"They blame thee for singing ill things of them; now, therefore, I would that thou sing some scurvy rhyme to me, for then it might be that they would bear with thee the easier."

"To thee I never sing but good," says Grettir: "I am not going to make thee like these starvelings."

"One may sing so," says Haflidi, "that the lampoon be not so foul when it is searched into, though at first sight it be not over fair."

"I have ever plenty of that skill in me," says Grettir.

Then Haflidi went to the men where they were baling, and said, "Great is your toil, and no wonder that ye have taken ill liking to Grettir."

"But his lampoons we deem worse than all the rest together," they said.

Haflidi said in a loud voice, "He will surely fare ill for it in the end."

But when Grettir heard Haflidi speak blamefully of him, he sang:

> *"Otherwise would matters be,*
> *When this shouting Haflidi*
> *Ate in house at Reydarfell*
> *Curdled milk, and deemed it well;*
> *He who decks the reindeer's side*
> *That 'twixt ness and ness doth glide,*
> *Twice in one day had his fill*
> *Of the feast of dart shower shrill."*

The shipmen thought this foul enough, and said he should not put shame on Skipper Haflidi for nought.

Then said Haflidi, "Grettir is plentifully worthy that ye should do him some shame, but I will not have my honour staked against his ill-will and recklessness; nor is it good for us to wreak vengeance for this forthwith while we have this danger hanging over us; but be ye mindful of it when ye land, if so it seem good to you."

"Well," they said, "why should we not fare even as thou farest? for why should his vile word bite us more than thee?"

And in that mind Haflidi bade them abide; and thence-forward the chapmen made far less noise about Grettir's rhymes than before.

Now a long and a hard voyage they had, and the leak gained on the ship, and men began to be exceeding worn with toil. The young wife of the mate was wont to sew from Grettir's hands, and much would the crew mock him therefor; but Haflidi went up to where Grettir lay and sang:

> *"Grettir, stand up from thy grave,*
> *In the trough of the grey wave*
> *The keel labours, tell my say*
> *Now unto thy merry may;*
> *From thy hands the linen-clad*
> *Fill of sewing now has had,*
> *Till we make the land will she*
> *Deem that labour fitteth thee."*

Then Grettir stood up and sang:

> *"Stand we up, for neath us now*
> *Rides the black ship high enow;*
> *This fair wife will like it ill*

> *If my limbs are laid here still;*
> *Certes, the white trothful one*
> *Will not deem the deed well done,*
> *If the work that I should share*
> *Other folk must ever bear."*

Then he ran aft to where they were baling, and asked what they would he should do; they said he would do mighty little good.

"Well," said he, *"ye may yet be apaid of a man's aid."*

Haflidi bade them not set aside his help, "For it may be he shall deem his hands freed if he offers his aid."

At that time pumping was not used in ships that fared over the main; the manner of baling they used men called tub or cask baling, and a wet work it was and a wearisome; two balers were used, and one went down while the other came up. Now the chapmen bade Grettir have the job of sinking the balers, and said that now it should be tried what he could do; he said that the less it was tried the better it would be. But he goes down and sinks the balers, and now two were got to bale against him; they held out but a little while before they were overcome with weariness, and then four came forward and soon fared in likewise, and, so say some, that eight baled against him before the baling was done and the ship was made dry. Thenceforth the manner of the chapmen's words to Grettir was much changed, for they saw what strength he had to fall back upon; and from that time he was the stoutest and readiest to help, wheresoever need was.

Now they bore off east into the main, and much thick weather they had, and one night unawares they ran suddenly on a rock, so that the nether part of the ship went from under her; then the boat was run down, and women and all the loose goods were brought off: nearby was a little holm whither they brought their matters as they best could in the night; but when it began to dawn they had a talk as to where they were come; then they who had fared between lands before knew the land for Southmere in Norway; there was an island hardby called Haramsey; many folk dwelt there, and therein too was the manor of a lord.

Chapter 18
Of Grettir at Haramsey and His Dealings with Karr the Old

NOW THE LORD who dwelt in the island was called Thorfinn; he was the son of Karr the Old, who had dwelt there long; and Thorfinn was a great chief.

But when day was fully come men saw from the island that the chapmen were brought to great straits. This was made known to Thorfinn, and he quickly bestirred himself, and had a large bark of his launched, rowed by sixteen men, on this bark were nigh thirty men in all; they came up speedily and saved the chapmen's wares; but the ship settled down, and much goods were lost there. Thorfinn brought all men from the ship home to himself, and they abode there a week and dried their wares. Then the chapmen went south into the land, and are now out of the tale.

Grettir was left behind with Thorfinn, and little he stirred, and was at most times mighty short of speech. Thorfinn bade give him meals, but otherwise paid small heed to him; Grettir was loth to follow him, and would not go out with him in the day; this Thorfinn took ill, but had not the heart to have food withheld from him.

Now Thorfinn was fond of stately house-keeping, and was a man of great joyance, and would fain have other men merry too: but Grettir would walk about from house to house, and often went into other farms about the island.

There was a man called Audun who dwelt at Windham; thither Grettir went every day, and he made friends with Audun, and there he was wont to sit till far on in the day. Now one night very late, as Grettir made ready to go home, he saw a great fire burst out on a ness to the north of Audun's farm. Grettir asked what new thing this might be. Audun said that he need be in no haste to know that.

"It would be said," quoth Grettir, "if that were seen in our land, that the flame burned above hid treasure."

The farmer said, "That fire I deem to be ruled over by one into whose matters it avails little to pry."

"Yet fain would I know thereof," said Grettir.

"On that ness," said Audun, "stands a barrow, great and strong, wherein was laid Karr the Old, Thorfinn's father; at first father and son had but one farm in the island; but since Karr died he has so haunted this place that he has swept away all farmers who owned lands here, so that now Thorfinn holds the whole island; but whatsoever man Thorfinn holds his hand over, gets no scathe."

Grettir said that he had told his tale well: "And," says he, "I shall come here tomorrow, and then thou shalt have digging-tools ready."

"Now, I pray thee," says Audun, "to do nought herein, for I know that Thorfinn will cast his hatred on thee therefor."

Grettir said he would risk that.

So the night went by, and Grettir came early on the morrow and the digging-tools were ready; the farmer goes with him to the barrow, and Grettir brake it open, and was rough-handed enough thereat, and did not leave off till he came to the rafters, and by then the day was spent; then he tore away the rafters, and now Audun prayed him hard not to go into the barrow; Grettir bade him guard the rope, "but I shall espy what dwells within here."

Then Grettir entered into the barrow, and right dark it was, and a smell there was therein none of the sweetest. Now he groped about to see how things were below; first he found horse-bones, and then he stumbled against the arm of a high-chair, and in that chair found a man sitting; great treasures of gold and silver were heaped together there, and a small chest was set under the feet of him full of silver; all these riches Grettir carried together to the rope; but as he went out through the barrow he was griped at right strongly; thereon he let go the treasure and rushed against the barrow-dweller, and now they set on one another unsparingly enough.

Everything in their way was kicked out of place, the barrow-wight setting on with hideous eagerness; Grettir gave back before him for a long time, till at last it came to this, that he saw it would not do to hoard his strength any more; now neither spared the other, and they were brought to where the horse-bones were, and thereabout they wrestled long. And now one, now the other, fell on his knee; but the end of the strife was, that the barrow-dweller fell over on his back with huge din. Then ran Audun from the holding of the rope, and deemed Grettir dead. But Grettir drew the sword, 'Jokul's gift,' and drave it at the neck of the barrow-bider so that it took off his head, and Grettir laid it at the thigh of him. Then he went to the rope with the treasure, and lo, Audun was clean gone, so he had to get up the rope by his hands; he had tied a line to the treasure, and therewith he now haled it up.

Grettir had got very stiff with his dealings with Karr, and now he went back to Thorfinn's house with the treasures, whenas all folk had set them down to table. Thorfinn gave Grettir a sharp look when he came into the drinking-hall, and asked him what work he had on hand so needful to do that he might not keep times of meals with other men. Grettir answers, "Many little matters will hap on late eves," and therewith he cast down on the table all the treasure he had taken in the barrow; but one matter there was thereof, on which he must needs keep his eyes; this was a short-sword, so good a weapon, that a better, he said, he had never seen; and this he gave up the last of all. Thorfinn was blithe to see that sword, for it was an heirloom of his house, and had never yet gone out of his kin.

"Whence came these treasures to thine hand?" said Thorfinn.

Grettir sang:

> *"Lessener of the flame of sea,*
> *My strong hope was true to me,*
> *When I deemed that treasure lay*
> *In the barrow; from today*
> *Folk shall know that I was right;*
> *The begetters of the fight*
> *Small joy now shall have therein,*
> *Seeking dragon's-lair to win."*

Thorfinn answered, "Blood will seldom seem blood to thine eyes; no man before thee has had will to break open the barrow; but, because I know that what wealth soever is hid in earth or borne into barrow is wrongly placed, I shall not hold thee blameworthy for thy deed as thou hast brought it all to me; yea, or whence didst thou get the good sword?"

Grettir answered and sang:

> *"Lessener of waves flashing flame,*
> *To my lucky hand this came*
> *In the barrow where that thing*
> *Through the dark fell clattering;*
> *If that helm-fire I should gain,*
> *Made so fair to be the bane*
> *Of the breakers of the bow,*
> *Ne'er from my hand should it go."*

Thorfinn said, "Well hast thou prayed for it, but thou must show some deed of fame before I give thee that sword, for never could I get it of my father while he lived."

Said Grettir, "Who knows to whom most gain will come of it in the end?"

So Thorfinn took the treasures and kept the sword at his bed-head, and the winter wore on toward Yule, so that little else fell out to be told of.

Chapter 19
Of Yule at Haramsey, and How Grettir Dealt with the Bearserks

NOW THE SUMMER before these things Earl Eric Hakonson made ready to go from his land west to England, to see King Knut the Mighty, his brother-in-law, but left behind him in the rule of Norway Hakon, his son, and gave him into the hands of Earl Svein, his brother, for the watching and warding of his realm, for Hakon was a child in years.

But before Earl Eric went away from the land, he called together lords and rich bonders, and many things they spoke on laws and the rule of the land, for Earl Eric was a man good at rule.

Now men thought it an exceeding ill fashion in the land that runagates or bearserks called to holm high-born men for their fee or womankind, in such wise, that whosoever should fall before the other should lie unatoned; hereof many got both shame and loss of goods, and some lost their lives withal; and therefore Earl Eric did away with all holm-gangs and outlawed all bearserks who fared with raids and riots.

In the making of this law, the chief of all, with Earl Eric, was Thorfinn Karrson, from Haramsey, for he was a wise man, and a dear friend of the Earls.

Two brothers are named as being of the worst in these matters, one hight Thorir Paunch, the other Ogmund the Evil; they were of Halogaland kin, bigger and stronger than other men. They wrought the bearserks'-gang and spared nothing in their fury; they would take away the wives of men and hold them for a week or a half-month, and then bring them back to their husbands; they robbed wheresoever they came, or did some other ill deeds. Now Earl Eric made them outlaws through the length and breadth of Norway, and Thorfinn was the eagerest of men in bringing about their outlawry, therefore they deemed that they owed him ill-will enow.

So the Earl went away from the land, as is said in his Saga; but Earl Svein bore sway over Norway. Thorfinn went home to his house, and sat at home till just up to Yule, as is aforesaid; but at Yule he made ready to go to his farm called Slysfirth, which is on the mainland, and thither he had bidden many of his friends. Thorfinn's wife could not go with her husband, for her daughter of ripe years lay ill a-bed, so they both abode at home. Grettir was at home too, and eight house-carles. Now Thorfinn went with thirty freedmen to the Yule-feast, whereat there was the greatest mirth and joyance among men.

Now Yule-eve comes on, and the weather was bright and calm; Grettir was mostly abroad this day, and saw how ships fared north and south along the land, for each one sought the other's home where the Yule drinking was settled to come off. By this time the goodman's daughter was so much better that she could walk about with her mother, and thus the day wore on.

Now Grettir sees how a ship rows up toward the island; it was not right big, but shield-hung it was from stem to stern, and stained all above the sea: these folk rowed smartly, and made for the boat-stands of goodman Thorfinn, and when the keel took land, those who were therein sprang overboard. Grettir cast up the number of the men, and they were twelve altogether; he deemed their guise to be far from peaceful. They took up their ship and bore it up from the sea; thereafter they ran up to the boat-stand, and therein was that big boat of Thorfinn, which was never launched to sea by less than thirty men, but these twelve shot it in one haul down to the shingle of the foreshore; and thereon they took up their own bark and bore it into the boat-stand.

Now Grettir thought that he could see clear enough that they would make themselves at home. But he goes down to meet them, and welcomes them merrily, and asks who they were and what their leader was hight; he to whom these words were spoken answered quickly, and said that his name was Thorir, and that he was called Paunch, and that his brother was Ogmund, and that the others were fellows of theirs.

"I deem," said Thorir, "that thy master Thorfinn has heard tell of us; is he perchance at home?"

Grettir answered, "Lucky men are ye, and hither have come in a good hour, if ye are the men I take you to be; the goodman is gone away with all his home-folk who are freemen, and will not be home again till after Yule; but the mistress is at home, and so is the goodman's daughter; and if I thought that I had some ill-will to pay back, I should have chosen above all things to have come just thus; for here are all matters in plenty whereof ye stand in need both beer, and all other good things."

Thorir held his peace, while Grettir let this tale run on, then he said to Ogmund:

"How far have things come to pass other than as I guessed? and now am I well enough minded to take revenge on Thorfinn for having made us outlaws; and this man is ready enough of tidings, and no need have we to drag the words out of him."

"Words all may use freely," said Grettir, "and I shall give you such cheer as I may; and now come home with me."

They bade him have thanks therefor, and said they would take his offer.

But when they came home to the farm, Grettir took Thorir by the hand and led him into the hall; and now was Grettir mightily full of words. The mistress was in the hall, and had had it decked with hangings, and made all fair and seemly; but when she heard Grettir's talk, she stood still on the floor, and asked whom he welcomed in that earnest wise.

He answered, "Now, mistress, is it right meet to welcome these guests merrily, for here is come goodman Thorir Paunch and the whole twelve of them, and are minded to sit here Yule over, and a right good hap it is, for we were few enough before."

She answered, "Am I to number these among bonders and goodmen, who are the worst of robbers and ill-doers? a large share of my goods had I given that they had not come here as at this time; and ill dost thou reward Thorfinn, for that he took thee a needy man from shipwreck and has held thee through the winter as a free man."

Grettir said, "It would be better to take the wet clothes off these guests than to scold at me; since for that thou mayst have time long enough."

Then said Thorir, "Be not cross-grained, mistress; nought shall thou miss thy husband's being away, for a man shall be got in his place for thee, yea, and for thy daughter a man, and for each of the home-women."

"That is spoken like a man," said Grettir, "nor will they thus have any cause to bewail their lot."

Now all the women rushed forth from the hall smitten with huge dread and weeping; then said Grettir to the bearserks, "Give into my hands what it pleases you to lay aside of weapons and wet clothes, for the folk will not be yielding to us while they are scared."

Thorir said he heeded not how women might squeal; "But," said he, "thee indeed we may set apart from the other home-folk, and methinks we may well make thee our man of trust."

"See to that yourselves," said Grettir, "but certes I do not take to all men alike."

Thereupon they laid aside the more part of their weapons, and thereafter Grettir said:

"Methinks it is a good rede now that ye sit down to table and drink somewhat, for it is right likely that ye are thirsty after the rowing."

They said they were ready enough for that, but knew not where to find out the cellar; Grettir asked if they would that he should see for things and go about for them. The bearserks said they would be right fain of that; so Grettir fetched beer and gave them to drink; they were mightily weary, and drank in huge draughts, and still he let them have the strongest beer that there was, and this went on for a long time, and meanwhile he told them many merry tales. From all this there was din enough to be heard among them, and the home-folk were nowise fain to come to them.

Now Thorir said, "Never yet did I meet a man unknown to me, who would do us such good deeds as this man; now, what reward wilt thou take of us for thy work?"

Grettir answered, "As yet I look to no reward for this; but if we be even such friends when ye go away, as it looks like we shall be, I am minded to join fellowship with you; and though I be of less might than some of you, yet shall I not let any man of big redes."

Hereat they were well pleased, and would settle the fellowship with vows.

Grettir said that this they should not do, "For true is the old saw, *Ale is another man*, nor shall ye settle this in haste any further than as I have said, for on both sides are we men little meet to rule our tempers."

They said that they would not undo what they had said.

Withal the evening wore on till it grew quite dark; then sees Grettir that they were getting very heavy with drink, so he said:

"Do ye not find it time to go to sleep?"

Thorir said, "Time enough forsooth, and sure shall I be to keep to what I have promised the mistress."

Then Grettir went forth from the hall, and cried out loudly:

"Go ye to your beds, women all, for so is goodman Thorir pleased to bid."

They cursed him for this, and to hear them was like hearkening to the noise of many wolves. Now the bearserks came forth from the hall, and Grettir said:

"Let us go out, and I will show you Thorfinn's cloth bower."

They were willing to be led there; so they came to an out-bower exceeding great; a door there was to it, and a strong lock thereon, and the storehouse was very strong withal; there too was a closet good and great, and a shield panelling between the chambers; both chambers stood high, and men went up by steps to them. Now the bearserks got riotous and pushed Grettir about, and he kept tumbling away from them, and when they least thought thereof, he slipped quickly out of the bower, seized the latch, slammed the door to, and put the bolt on. Thorir and his fellows thought at first that the door must have got locked of itself, and paid no heed thereto; they had light with them, for Grettir had showed them many choice things which Thorfinn owned, and these they now noted awhile. Meantime Grettir made all speed home to the farm, and when he came in at the door he called out loudly, and asked where the goodwife was; she held her peace, for she did not dare to answer.

He said, "Here is somewhat of a chance of a good catch; but are there any weapons of avail here?"

She answers, "Weapons there are, but how they may avail thee I know not."

"Let us talk thereof anon," says he, "but now let every man do his best, for later on no better chance shall there be."

The good wife said, "Now God were in garth if our lot might better: over Thorfinn's bed hangs the barbed spear, the big one that was owned by Karr the Old; there, too, is a helmet and a byrni, and the short-sword, the good one; and the arms will not fail if thine heart does well."

Grettir seizes the helmet and spear, girds himself with the short-sword, and rushed out swiftly; and the mistress called upon the house-carles, bidding them follow such a dauntless man, four of them rushed forth and seized their weapons, but the other four durst come nowhere nigh. Now it is to be said of the bearserks that they thought Grettir delayed his coming back strangely; and now they began to doubt if there were not some guile in the matter. They rushed against the door and found it was locked, and now they try the timber walls so that every beam creaked again; at last they brought things so far that they broke down the shield-panelling, got into the passage, and thence out to the steps. Now bearserks'-gang seized them, and they howled like dogs. In that very nick of time Grettir came up and with both hands thrust his spear at the midst of Thorir, as he was about to get down the steps, so that it went through him at once. Now the spear-head was both long and broad, and Ogmund the Evil ran on to Thorir and pushed him on to Grettir's thrust, so that all went up to the barb-ends; then the spear stood out through Thorir's back and into Ogmund's breast, and they both tumbled dead off the spear; then of the others each rushed down the steps as he came forth; Grettir set on each one of them, and in turn hewed with the sword, or thrust with the spear; but they defended themselves with logs that lay on the green, and whatso thing they could lay hands on, therefore the greatest danger it was to deal with them, because of their strength, even though they were weaponless.

Two of the Halogalanders Grettir slew on the green, and then came up the house-carles; they could not come to one mind as to what weapons each should have; now they set on whenever the bearserks gave back, but when they turned about on them, then the house-carles slunk away up to the houses. Six vikings fell there, and of all of them was Grettir the bane. Then the six others got off and came down to the boat-stand, and so into it, and thence they defended themselves with oars. Grettir now got great blows from them, so that at all times he ran the risk of much hurt; but the house-carles went home, and had much to say of their stout onset; the mistress bade them espy what became of Grettir, but that was not to be got out of them. Two more of the bearserks Grettir slew in the boat-stand, but four slipped out by him; and by this, dark night had come on; two of them ran into a corn-barn, at the farm of Windham, which is aforenamed: here they fought for a long time, but at last Grettir killed them both; then was he beyond measure weary and stiff, the night was far gone, and the weather got very cold with the drift of the snow. He was fain to leave the search of the two vikings who were left now, so he walked home to the farm. The mistress had lights lighted in the highest lofts at the windows that they might guide him on his way; and so it was that he found his road home whereas he saw the light.

But when he was come into the door, the mistress went up to him, and bade him welcome.

"Now," she said, "thou hast reaped great glory, and freed me and my house from a shame of which we should never have been healed, but if thou hadst saved us."

Grettir answered, "Methinks I am much the same as I was this evening, when thou didst cast ill words on me."

The mistress answered, "We wotted not that thou wert a man of such prowess as we have now proved thee; now shall all things in the house be at thy will which I may bestow on thee, and which it may be seeming for thee to take; but methinks that Thorfinn will reward thee better still when he comes home."

Grettir answered, "Little of reward will be needed now, but I keep thine offer till the coming of the master; and I have some hope now that ye will sleep in peace as for the bearserks."

Grettir drank little that evening, and lay with his weapons about him through the night. In the morning, when it began to dawn, people were summoned together throughout the island, and a search was set on foot for the bearserks who had escaped the night before; they were found far on in the day under a rock, and were by then dead from cold and wounds; then they were brought unto a tidewashed heap of stones and buried thereunder.

After that folk went home, and the men of that island deemed themselves brought unto fair peace.

Now when Grettir came back to the mistress, he sang this stave:

> *"By the sea's wash have we made*
> *Graves, where twelve spear-groves are laid;*
> *I alone such speedy end,*
> *Unto all these folk did send.*
> *O fair giver forth of gold,*
> *Whereof can great words be told,*
> *'Midst the deeds one man has wrought,*
> *If this deed should come to nought?"*

The good wife said, "Surely thou art like unto very few men who are now living on the earth."

So she set him in the high seat, and all things she did well to him, and now time wore on till Thorfinn's coming home was looked for.

Chapter 20
How Thorfinn Met Grettir at Haramsey Again

AFTER YULE THORFINN made ready for coming home, and he let those folk go with good gifts whom he had bidden to his feast. Now he fares with his following till he comes hard by his boat-stands; they saw a ship lying on the strand, and soon knew it for Thorfinn's bark, the big one. Now Thorfinn had as yet had no news of the vikings, he bade his men hasten landward, "For I fear," said he, "that friends have not been at work here."

Thorfinn was the first to step ashore before his men, and forthwith he went up to the boat-stand; he saw a keel standing there, and knew it for the bearserks' ship. Then he said to his men, "My mind misgives me much that here things have come to pass, even such as I would have given the whole island, yea, every whit of what I have herein, that they might never have happed."

They asked why he spake thus. Then he said, "Here have come the vikings, whom I know to be the worst of all Norway, Thorir Paunch and Ogmund the Evil; in good sooth they will hardly have kept house happily for us, and in an Icelander I have but little trust."

Withal he spoke many things hereabout to his fellows.

Now Grettir was at home, and so brought it about, that folk were slow to go down to the shore; and said he did not care much if the goodman Thorfinn had somewhat of a shake at what he saw before him; but when the mistress asked him leave to go, he said she should have her will as to where she went, but that he himself should stir nowhither. She ran swiftly to meet Thorfinn, and welcomed him cheerily. He was glad thereof, and said, "Praise be to God that I see thee whole and merry, and my daughter in likewise. But how have ye fared since I went from home?"

She answered, "Things have turned out well, but we were near being overtaken by such a shame as we should never have had healing of, if thy winter-guest had not holpen us."

Then Thorfinn spake, "Now shall we sit down, but do thou tell us these tidings."

Then she told all things plainly even as they had come to pass, and praised greatly Grettir's stoutness and great daring; meanwhile Thorfinn held his peace, but when she had made an end of her tale, he said, "How true is the saw, *Long it takes to try a man*. But where is Grettir now?"

The goodwife said, "He is at home in the hall."

Thereupon they went home to the farm.

Thorfinn went up to Grettir and kissed him, and thanked him with many fair words for the great heart which he had shown to him; "And I will say to thee what few say to their friends, that I would thou shouldst be in need of men, that then thou mightest know if I were to thee in a man's stead or not; but for thy good deed I can never reward thee unless thou comest to be in some troublous need; but as to thy abiding with me, that shall ever stand open to thee when thou willest it; and thou shalt be held the first of all my men."

Grettir bade him have much thank therefor. "And," quoth he, "this should I have taken even if thou hadst made me proffer thereof before."

Now Grettir sat there the winter over, and was in the closest friendship with Thorfinn; and for this deed he was now well renowned all over Norway, and there the most, where the bearserks had erst wrought the greatest ill deeds.

This spring Thorfinn asked Grettir what he was about to busy himself with: he said he would go north to Vogar while the fair was. Thorfinn said there was ready for him money as much as he would. Grettir said that he needed no more money at that time than faring-silver: this, Thorfinn said, was full-well due to him, and thereupon went with him to ship.

Now he gave him the short-sword, the good one, which Grettir bore as long as he lived, and the choicest of choice things it was. Withal Thorfinn bade Grettir come to him whenever he might need aid.

But Grettir went north to Vogar, and a many folk were there; many men welcomed him there right heartily who had not seen him before, for the sake of that great deed of prowess which he had done when he saw the vikings; many high-born men prayed him to come and abide with them, but he would fain go back to his friend Thorfinn. Now he took ship in a bark that was owned of a man hight Thorkel, who dwelt in Salft in Halogaland, and was a high-born man. But when Grettir came to Thorkel he welcomed him right heartily, and bade Grettir abide with him that winter, and laid many words thereto.

This offer Grettir took, and was with Thorkel that winter in great joyance and fame.

Chapter 21
Of Grettir and Biorn and the Bear

THERE WAS A MAN, hight Biorn, who was dwelling with Thorkel; he was a man of rash temper, of good birth, and somewhat akin to Thorkel; he was not well loved of men, for he would slander much those who were with Thorkel, and in this wise he sent many away. Grettir and he had little to do together; Biorn thought him of little worth weighed against himself, but Grettir was unyielding, so that things fell athwart between them. Biorn was a mightily boisterous man, and made himself very big; many young men gat into fellowship with him in these things, and would stray abroad by night. Now it befell, that early in winter a savage bear ran abroad from his winter lair, and got so grim that he spared neither man nor beast. Men thought he had been roused by the noise that Biorn and his fellows had made. The brute got so hard to deal with that he tore down the herds of men, and Thorkel had the greatest hurt thereof, for he was the richest man in the neighbourhood.

Now one day Thorkel bade his men to follow him, and search for the lair of the bear. They found it in sheer sea-rocks; there was a high rock and a cave before it down below, but only one track to go up to it: under the cave were scarped rocks, and a heap of stones down by the sea, and sure death it was to all who might fall down there. The bear lay in his lair by day, but went abroad as soon as night fell; no fold could keep sheep safe from him, nor could any dogs be set on him: and all this men thought the heaviest trouble. Biorn, Thorkel's kinsman, said that the greatest part had been done, as the lair had been found. "And now I shall try," said he, "what sort of play we namesakes shall have together." Grettir made as if he knew not what Biorn said on this matter.

Now it happened always when men went to sleep anights that Biorn disappeared: and one night when Biorn went to the lair, he was aware that the beast was there before him, and roaring savagely. Biorn lay down in the track, and had over him his shield, and was going to wait till the beast should stir abroad as his manner was. Now the bear had an inkling of the man, and got somewhat slow to move off. Biorn waxed very sleepy where he lay, and cannot wake up, and just at this time the beast betakes himself from his lair; now he sees where the man lies, and, hooking at him with his claw, he tears from him the shield and throws it down over the rocks. Biorn started up suddenly awake, takes to his legs and runs home, and it was a near thing that the beast gat him not. This his fellows knew, for they had spies about Biorn's ways; in the morning they found the shield, and made the greatest jeering at all this.

At Yule Thorkel went himself, and eight of them altogether, and there was Grettir and Biorn and other followers of Thorkel. Grettir had on a fur-cloak, which he laid aside while they set on the beast. It was awkward for an onslaught there, for thereat could folk come but by spear-thrusts, and all the spear-points the bear turned off him with his teeth. Now Biorn urged them on much to the onset, yet he himself went not so nigh as to run the risk of any hurt. Amid this, when men looked least for it, Biorn suddenly seized Grettir's coat, and cast it into the beast's lair. Now nought they could wreak on him, and had to go back when the day was far spent. But when Grettir was going, he misses his coat, and he could see that the bear has it cast under him. Then he said, "What man of you has wrought the jest of throwing my cloak into the lair?"

Biorn says, "He who is like to dare to own to it."

Grettir answers, "I set no great store on such matters."

Now they went on their way home, and when they had walked awhile, the thong of Grettir's leggings brake. Thorkel bid them wait for him; but Grettir said there was no need of that. Then said Biorn, "Ye need not think that Grettir will run away from his coat; he will have the honour all to himself, and will slay that beast all alone, wherefrom we have gone back all eight of us; thus would he be such as he is said to be: but sluggishly enow has he fared forth today."

"I know not," said Thorkel, "how thou wilt fare in the end, but men of equal prowess I deem you not: lay as few burdens on him as thou mayst, Biorn."

Biorn said, that neither of them should pick and choose words from out his mouth.

Now, when a hill's brow was between them, Grettir went back to the pass, for now there was no striving with others for the onset. He drew the sword, Jokul's gift, but had a loop over the handle of the short-sword, and slipped it up over his hand, and this he did in that he thought he could easier have it at his will if his hand were loose. He went up into the pass forthwith, and when the beast saw a man, it rushed against Grettir exceeding fiercely, and smote at him with that paw which was furthest off from the rock; Grettir hewed against the blow with the sword, and therewith smote the paw above the claws, and took it off; then the beast was fain to smite at Grettir with the paw that was whole, and dropped down therewith on to the docked one, but it was shorter than he wotted of, and withal he tumbled into Grettir's arms. Now he griped at the beast between the ears and held him off, so that he got not at him to bite. And, so Grettir himself says, that herein he deemed he had had the hardest trial of his strength, thus to hold the brute. But now as it struggled fiercely, and the space was narrow, they both tumbled down over the rock; the beast was the heaviest of the two, and came down first upon the stone heap below, Grettir being the uppermost, and the beast was much mangled on its nether side. Now Grettir seized the short-sword and thrust it into the heart of the bear, and that was its bane. Thereafter he went home, taking with him his cloak all tattered, and withal what he had cut from the paw of the bear. Thorkel sat a-drinking when he came into the hall, and much men laughed at the rags of the cloak Grettir had cast over him. Now he threw on to the table what he had chopped off the paw.

Then said Thorkel, "Where is now Biorn my kinsman? never did I see thy irons bite the like of this, Biorn, and my will it is, that thou make Grettir a seemly offer for this shame thou hast wrought on him."

Biorn said that was like to be long about, "and never shall I care whether he likes it well or ill."

Then Grettir sang:

> "Oft that war-god came to hall
> Frighted, when no blood did fall,
> In the dusk; who ever cried
> On the bear last autumn-tide;
> No man saw me sitting there
> Late at eve before the lair;
> Yet the shaggy one today
> From his den I drew away."

"Sure enough," said Biorn, "thou hast fared forth well today, and two tales thou tellest of us twain therefor; and well I know that thou hast had a good hit at me."

Thorkel said, "I would, Grettir, that thou wouldst not avenge thee on Biorn, but for him I will give a full man-gild if thereby ye may be friends."

Biorn said he might well turn his money to better account, than to boot for this; "And, methinks it is wisest that in my dealings with Grettir *one oak should have what from the other it shaves.*"

Grettir said that he should like that very well. But Thorkel said, "Yet I hope, Grettir, that thou wilt do this for my sake, not to do aught against Biorn while ye are with me."

"That shall be," said Grettir.

Biorn said he would walk fearless of Grettir wheresoever they might meet.

Grettir smiled mockingly, but would not take boot for Biorn. So they were here that winter through.

Chapter 22
Of the Slaying of Biorn

IN THE SPRING Grettir went north to Vogar with chapmen. He and Thorkel parted in friendship; but Biorn went west to England, and was the master of Thorkel's ship that went thither. Biorn dwelt thereabout that summer and bought such things for Thorkel as he had given him word to get; but as the autumn wore on he sailed from the west. Grettir was at Vogar till the fleet broke up; then he sailed from the north with some chapmen until they came to a harbour at an island before the mouth of Drontheimfirth, called Gartar, where they pitched their tents. Now when they were housed, a ship came sailing havenward from the south along the land; they soon saw that it was an England farer; she took the strand further out, and her crew went ashore; Grettir and his fellows went to meet them. But when they met, Grettir saw that Biorn was among those men, and spake: "It is well that we have met here; now we may well take up our ancient quarrel, and now I will try which of us twain may do the most."

Biorn said that was an old tale to him, "but if there has been aught of such things between us, I will boot for it, so that thou mayst think thyself well holden thereof."

Then Grettir sang:

"In hard strife I slew the bear,
Thereof many a man doth hear;
Then the cloak I oft had worn,
By the beast to rags was torn;
Thou, O braggart ring-bearer,
Wrought that jest upon me there,
Now thou payest for thy jest,
Not in words am I the best?"

Biorn said, that oft had greater matters than these been atoned for.

Grettir said, "That few had chosen hitherto to strive to trip him up with spite and envy, nor ever had he taken fee for such, and still must matters fare in likewise. Know thou that we shall not both of us go hence whole men if I may have my will, and a coward's name will I lay on thy back, if thou darest not to fight."

Now Biorn saw that it would avail nought to try to talk himself free; so he took his weapons and went aland.

Then they ran one at the other and fought, but not long before Biorn got sore wounded, and presently fell dead to earth. But when Biorn's fellows saw that, they went to their ship, and made off north along the land to meet Thorkel and told him of this hap: he said it had not come to pass ere it might have been looked for.

Soon after this Thorkel went south to Drontheim, and met there Earl Svein. Grettir went south to Mere after the slaying of Biorn, and found his friend Thorfinn, and told him what had befallen. Thorfinn gave him good welcome, and said:

"It is well now that thou art in need of a friend; with me shalt thou abide until these matters have come to an end."

Grettir thanked him for his offer, and said he would take it now.

Earl Svein was dwelling in Drontheim, at Steinker, when he heard of Biorn's slaying; at that time there was with him Hiarandi, the brother of Biorn, and he was the Earl's man; he was exceeding wroth when he heard of the slaying of Biorn, and begged the Earl's aid in the matter, and the Earl gave his word thereto.

Then he sent men to Thorfinn and summoned to him both him and Grettir. Thorfinn and Grettir made ready at once at the Earl's bidding to go north to Drontheim to meet him. Now the Earl held a council on the matter, and bade Hiarandi to be thereat; Hiarandi said he would not bring his brother to purse; "and I shall either fare in a like wise with him, or else wreak vengeance for him." Now when the matter was looked into, the Earl found that Biorn had been guilty towards Grettir in many ways; and Thorfinn offered weregild, such as the Earl deemed might be befitting for Biorn's kin to take; and thereon he had much to say on the freedom which Grettir had wrought for men north there in the land, when he slew the bearserks, as has been aforesaid.

The Earl answered, "With much truth thou sayest this, Thorfinn, that was the greatest land-ridding, and good it seems to us to take weregild because of thy words; and withal Grettir is a man well renowned because of his strength and prowess."

Hiarandi would not take the settlement, and they broke up the meeting. Thorfinn got his kinsman Arnbiorn to go about with Grettir day by day, for he knew that Hiarandi lay in wait for his life.

Chapter 23
The Slaying of Hiarandi

IT HAPPENED ONE DAY that Grettir and Arnbiorn were walking through some streets for their sport, that as they came past a certain court gate, a man bounded forth therefrom with axe borne aloft, and drave it at Grettir with both hands; he was all unawares of this, and walked on slowly; Arnbiorn caught timely sight of the man, and seized Grettir, and thrust him on so hard that he fell on his knee; the axe smote the shoulder-blade, and cut sideways out under the arm-pit, and a great wound it was. Grettir turned about nimbly, and drew the short-sword, and saw that there was Hiarandi. Now the axe stuck fast in the road, and it was slow work for Hiarandi to draw it to him again, and in this very nick of time Grettir hewed at him, and the blow fell on the upper arm, near the shoulder, and cut it off; then the fellows of Hiarandi rushed forth, five of them, and a fight forthwith befell, and speedy change happed there, for Grettir and Arnbiorn slew those who were with Hiarandi, all but one, who got off, and forthwith went to the Earl to tell him these tidings.

The Earl was exceeding wroth when he heard of this, and the second day thereafter he had a Thing summoned. Then they, Thorfinn and Grettir, came both to the Thing. The Earl put forth against Grettir the guilt for these manslaughters; he owned them all, and said he had had to defend his hands.

"Whereof methinks I bear some marks on me," says Grettir, "and surely I had found death if Arnbiorn had not saved me."

The Earl answered that it was ill hap that Grettir was not slain.

"For many a man's bane wilt thou be if thou livest, Grettir."

Then came to the Earl, Bessi, son of Skald-Torfa, a fellow and a friend to Grettir; he and Thorfinn went before the Earl had prayed him respite for Grettir, and offered, that the Earl alone should doom in this matter, but that Grettir might have peace and leave to dwell in the land.

The Earl was slow to come to any settlement, but suffered himself to be led thereto because of their prayers. There respite was granted to Grettir till the next spring; still the Earl would not settle the peace till Gunnar, the brother of Biorn and Hiarandi, was thereat; now Gunnar was a court-owner in Tunsberg.

In the spring, the Earl summoned Grettir and Thorfinn east to Tunsberg, for he would dwell there east while the most sail was thereat. Now they went east thither, and the Earl was before them in the town when they came. Here Grettir found his brother, Thorstein Dromond, who was fain of him and bade him abide with him: Thorstein was a court-owner in the town. Grettir told him all about his matters, and Thorstein gave a good hearing thereto, but bade him beware of Gunnar. And so the spring wore on.

Chapter 24
Of the Slaying of Gunnar, and Grettir's Strife with Earl Svein

NOW GUNNAR WAS IN THE TOWN, and lay in wait for Grettir always and everywhere. It happened on a day that Grettir sat in a booth a-drinking, for he would not throw himself in Gunnar's way. But, when he wotted of it the least, the door was driven at so that it brake asunder, four men all-armed burst in, and there was Gunnar and his fellows.

They set on Grettir; but he caught up his weapons which hung over him, and then drew aback into the corner, whence he defended himself, having before him the shield, but dealing blows with the short-sword, nor did they have speedy luck with him. Now he smote at one of Gunnar's fellows, and more he needed not; then he advanced forth on the floor, and therewith they were driven doorward through the booth, and there fell another man of Gunnar's; then were Gunnar and his fellows fain of flight; one of them got to the door, struck his foot against the threshold and lay there grovelling and was slow in getting to his feet. Gunnar had his shield before him, and gave back before Grettir, but he set on him fiercely and leaped up on the cross-beam by the door. Now the hands of Gunnar and the shield were within the door, but Grettir dealt a blow down amidst Gunnar and the shield and cut off both his hands by the wrist, and he fell aback out of the door; then Grettir dealt him his death-blow.

But in this nick of time got to his feet Gunnar's man, who had lain fallen awhile, and he ran straightway to see the Earl, and to tell him these tidings.

Earl Svein was wondrous wroth at this tale, and forthwith summoned a Thing in the town. But when Thorfinn and Thorstein Dromond knew this, they brought together their kin and friends and came thronging to the Thing. Very cross-grained was the Earl, and it was no easy matter to come to speech with him. Thorfinn went up first before the Earl and said, "For this cause am I come hither, to offer thee peace and honour for these man-slayings that Grettir has wrought; thou alone shall shape and settle all, if the man hath respite of his life."

The Earl answered sore wroth: "Late wilt thou be loth to ask respite for Grettir; but in my mind it is that thou hast no good cause in court; he has now slain three brothers, one at the heels of the other, who were men so brave that they would none bear the other to purse. Now it will not avail thee, Thorfinn, to pray for Grettir, for I will not thus bring wrongs into the land so as to take boot for such unmeasured misdeeds."

Then came forward Bessi, Skald-Torfa's son, and prayed the Earl to take the offered settlement. "Thereto," he said, "I will give up my goods, for Grettir is a man of great kin and a good friend of mine; thou mayst well see, Lord, that it is better to respite one man's life and to have therefor the thanks of many, thyself alone dooming the fines, than to break down thine own honour, and risk whether thou canst seize the man or not."

The Earl answered, "Thou farest well herein, Bessi, and showest at all times that thou art a high-minded man; still I am loth thus to break the laws of the land, giving respite to men of foredoomed lives."

Then stepped forth Thorstein Dromond and greeted the Earl, and made offers on Grettir's behalf, and laid thereto many fair words. The Earl asked for what cause he made offers for this man. Thorstein said that they were brothers. The Earl said that he had not known it before: "Now it is but the part of a man for thee to help him, but because we have made up our mind not to take money for these man-slayings, we shall make all men of equal worth here, and Grettir's life will we have, whatsoever it shall cost and whensoever chance shall serve."

Thereat the Earl sprang up, and would listen in nowise to the offered atonements.

Now Thorfinn and his folk went home to Thorstein's court and made ready. But when the Earl saw this he bade all his men take weapons, and then he went thither with his folk in array. But before he came up Thorfinn and his men ordered themselves for defence before the gate of the court. Foremost stood Thorfinn and Thorstein and Grettir, and then Bessi, and each of them had a large following of men with him.

The Earl bade them to give up Grettir, nor to bring themselves into an evil strait; they made the very same offer as before. The Earl would not hearken thereto. Then Thorfinn and Thorstein said that the Earl should have more ado yet for the getting of Grettir's life, "For one fate shall befall us all, and it will be said thou workest hard for one man's life, if all we have to be laid on earth therefor."

The Earl said he should spare none of them, and now they were at the very point to fight.

Then went to the Earl many men of goodwill, and prayed him not to push matters on to such great evils, and said they would have to pay heavily before all these were slain. The Earl found this rede to be wholesome, and became somewhat softened thereat.

Thereafter they drew up an agreement to which Thorstein and Thorfinn were willing enough, now that Grettir should have respite of his life. The Earl spake: "Know ye," quoth he, "that though I deal by way of mean words with these man-slayings at this time, yet I call this no settlement, but I am loth to fight against my own folk; though I see that ye make little of me in this matter."

Then said Thorfinn, "This is a greater honour for thee, Lord, for that thou alone wilt doom the weregild."

Then the Earl said that Grettir should go in peace, as for him, out to Iceland, when ships fared out, if so they would; they said that they would take this. They paid the Earl fines to his mind, and parted from him with little friendship. Grettir went with Thorfinn; he and his brother Thorstein parted fondly.

Thorfinn got great fame for the aid he had given Grettir against such overwhelming power as he had to deal with: none of the men who had helped Grettir were ever after well loved of the Earl, save Bessi.

So quoth Grettir:

"To our helping came

The great of name;
Thorfinn was there
Born rule to bear;
When all bolts fell
Into locks, and hell
Cried out for my life
In the Tunsberg strife.
The Dromund fair
Of red seas was there,
The stone of the bane
Of steel-gods vain:
From Bylest's kin
My life to win,
Above all men
He laboured then.
Then the king's folk
Would strike no stroke
To win my head;
So great grew dread;
For the leopard came
With byrni's flame,
And on thoughts-burg wall
Should that bright fire fall."

Grettir went back north with Thorfinn, and was with him till he gat him to ship with chapmen who were bound out to Iceland: he gave him many fair gifts of raiment, and a fair-stained saddle and a bridle withal. They parted in friendship, and Thorfinn bade him come to him whensoever he should come back to Norway.

Chapter 25
The Slaying of Thorgils Makson

ASMUND THE GREYHAIRED lived on at Biarg, while Grettir was abroad, and by that time he was thought to be the greatest of bonders in Midfirth. Thorkel Krafla died during those seasons that Grettir was out of Iceland. Thorvald Asgeirson farmed then at the Ridge in Waterdale, and waxed a great chief. He was the father of Dalla whom Isleif had to wife, he who afterwards was bishop at Skalholt.

Asmund had in Thorvald the greatest help in suits and in many other matters. At Asmund's grew up a man, hight Thorgils, called Thorgils Makson, near akin to Asmund. Thorgils was a man of great strength and gained much money by Asmund's foresight.

Asmund bought for Thorgils the land at Brookmeet, and there he farmed. Thorgils was a great store-gatherer, and went a-searching to the Strands every year, and there he gat for himself whales and other gettings; and a stout-hearted man he was.

In those days was at its height the waxing of the foster-brothers, Thorgeir Havarson and Thormod Coalbrowskald; they had a boat and went therein far and wide, and were not thought men of much even-dealing. It chanced one summer that Thorgils Makson found a whale on the common drift-lands, and forthwith he and his folk set about cutting it up.

But when the foster-brothers heard thereof they went thither, and at first their talk had a likely look out. Thorgils offered that they should have the half of the uncut whale; but they would have for themselves all the uncut, or else divide all into halves, both the cut and the uncut. Thorgils flatly refused to give up what was cut of the whale; and thereat things grew hot between them, and forthwithal both sides caught up their weapons and fought. Thorgeir and Thorgils fought long together without either losing or gaining, and both were of the eagerest. Their strife was both fierce and long, but the end of it was, that Thorgils fell dead to earth before Thorgeir; but Thormod and the men of Thorgils fought in another place; Thormod had the best of that strife, and three of Thorgils' men fell before him. After the slaying of Thorgils, his folk went back east to Midfirth, and brought his dead body with them. Men thought that they had the greatest loss in him. But the foster-brothers took all the whale to themselves.

This meeting Thormod tells of in that drapa that he made on Thorgeir dead. Asmund the Greyhaired heard of the slaying of Thorgils his kinsman; he was suitor in the case for Thorgils' slaying, he went and took witnesses to the wounds, and summoned the case before the Althing, for then this seemed to be law, as the case had happened in another quarter. And so time wears on.

Chapter 26
Of Thorstein Kuggson, and the Gathering for the Bloodsuit for the Slaying of Thorgils Makson

THERE WAS A MAN called Thorstein, he was the son of Thorkel Kugg, the son of Thord the Yeller, the son of Olaf Feilan, the son of Thorstein the Red, the son of Aud the Deeply-wealthy. The mother of Thorstein Kuggson was Thurid the daughter of Asgeir Madpate, Asgeir was father's brother of Asmund the Greyhaired.

Thorstein Kuggson was suitor in the case about Thorgils Makson's slaying along with Asmund the Greyhaired, who now sent word to Thorstein that he should come to meet him. Thorstein was a great champion, and the wildest-tempered of men; he went at once to meet his kinsman Asmund, and they talked the blood-suit over together. Thorstein was mightily wroth and said that no atonement should be for this, and said they had strength of kin enough to bring about for the slaying either outlawry or vengeance on men. Asmund said that he would follow him in whatsoever he would have done. They rode north to Thorvald their kinsman to pray his aid, and he quickly gave his word and said yea thereto. So they settled the suit against Thorgeir and Thormod; then Thorstein rode home to his farmstead, he then farmed at Liarskogar in Hvamsveit. Skeggi farmed at Hvam, he also joined in the suit with Thorstein. Skeggi was the son of Thorarinn Fylsenni, the son of Thord the Yeller; the mother of Skeggi was Fridgerd, daughter of Thord of Head.

These had a many men with them at the Thing, and pushed their suit with great eagerness.

Asmund and Thorvald rode from the north with six tens of men, and sat at Liarskogar many nights.

Chapter 27
The Suit for the Slaying of Thorgils Makson

A MAN HIGHT Thorgils abode at Reek-knolls in those days, he was the son of Ari, the son of Mar, the son of Atli the Red, the son of Ulf the Squinter, who settled at Reekness; the mother of Thorgils Arisen was Thorgerd, the daughter of Alf a-Dales; another daughter of Alf was Thorelf, mother of Thorgeir Havarson. There had Thorgeir good kinship to trust in, for Thorgils was the greatest chief in the Westfirthers' quarter. He was a man of such bountifulness, that he gave food to any free-born man as long as he would have it, and therefore there was at all times a throng of people at Reek-knolls; thus had Thorgils much renown of his house-keeping. He was a man withal of good will and foreknowledge. Thorgeir was with Thorgils in winter, but went to the Strands in summer.

After the slaying of Thorgils Makson, Thorgeir went to Reek-knolls and told Thorgils Arisen these tidings; Thorgils said that he was ready to give him harbour with him, "But, methinks," he says, "that they will be heavy in the suit, and I am loth to eke out the troubles. Now I shall send a man to Thorstein and bid weregild for the slaying of Thorgils; but if he will not take atonement I shall not defend the case stiffly."

Thorgeir said he would trust to his foresight. In autumn Thorgils sent a man to Thorstein Kuggson to try settling the case, but he was cross-grained to deal with as to the taking money for the blood-suit of Thorgils Makson; but about the other man-slayings, he said he would do as wise men should urge him. Now when Thorgils heard this, he called Thorgeir to him for a talk, and asked him what kind of aid he now deemed meetest for him; Thorgeir said that it was most to his mind to go abroad if he should be outlawed. Thorgils said that should be tried. A ship lay up Northriver in Burgfirth; in that keel Thorgils secretly paid faring for the foster-brothers, and thus the winter passed. Thorgils heard that Asmund and Thorstein drew together many men to the Althing, and sat in Liarskogar. He drew out the time of riding from home, for he would that Asmund and Thorstein should have ridden by before him to the south, when he came from the west; and so it fell out. Thorgils rode south, and with him rode the foster-brothers. In this ride Thorgeir killed Bundle-Torfi of Marswell, and Skuf withal, and Biarni in Dog-dale; thus says Thormod in Thorgeir's-Drapa:

> "Mighty strife the warrior made,
> When to earth was Makson laid,
> Well the sword-shower wrought he there,
> Flesh the ravens got to tear;
> Then when Skuf and Biarni fell,
> He was there the tale to tell;
> Sea-steed's rider took his way
> Through the thickest of the fray."

Thorgils settled the peace for the slaying of Skuf and Biarni then and there in the Dale, and delayed no longer than his will was before; Thorgeir went to ship, but Thorgils to the Althing, and came not thither until men were going to the courts.

Then Asmund the Greyhaired challenged the defence for the blood-suit on the slaying of Thorgils Makson. Thorgils went to the court and offered weregild for the slaying, if thereby Thorgeir might become free of guilt; he put forth for defence in the suit whether they had not free catch on all common foreshores. The lawman was asked if this was a lawful defence. Skapti was the lawman, and backed Asmund for the sake of their kinship. He said this was law if they were equal men, but said that bonders had a right to take before batchelors. Asmund said that Thorgils had offered an even sharing to the foster-brothers in so much of the whale as was uncut when they came thereto; and therewith that way of defence was closed against them. Now Thorstein and his kin followed up the suit with much eagerness, and nought was good to them but that Thorgeir should be made guilty.

Thorgils saw that one of two things was to be done, either to set on with many men, not knowing what might be gained thereby, or to suffer them to go on as they would; and, whereas Thorgeir had been got on board ship, Thorgils let the suit go on unheeded.

Thorgeir was outlawed, but for Thormod was taken weregild, and he to be quit. By this blood-suit Thorstein and Asmund were deemed to have waxed much. And now men ride home from the Thing.

Some men would hold talk that Thorgils had lightly backed the case, but he heeded their talk little, and let any one say thereon what he would.

But when Thorgeir heard of this outlawry, he said:

"Fain am I that those who have made me an outlaw should have full pay for this, ere all be over."

There was a man called Gaut Sleitason, who was akin to Thorgils Makson. Gaut had made ready to go in this same ship wherein Thorgeir was to sail. He bristled up against Thorgeir, and showed mighty ill-will against him and went about scowling; when the chapmen found this out, they thought it far from safe that both should sail in one ship. Thorgeir said he heeded not how much soever Gaut would bend his brows on him; still it was agreed that Gaut should take himself off from the ship, whereupon he went north into the upper settlements, and that time nought happed between him and Thorgeir, but out of this sprang up between them ill blood, as matters showed after.

Chapter 28
Grettir Comes out to Iceland Again

THIS SUMMER Grettir Asmundson came out to Skagafirth: he was in those days so famed a man for strength and prowess, that none was deemed his like among young men. He rode home to Biarg forthwith, and Asmund welcomed him meetly. At that time Atli managed the farming matters, and well things befell betwixt the brothers.

But now Grettir waxed so overbearing, that he deemed that nought was too much for him to do. At that time had many men grown into full manhood who were young in the days when Grettir was wont to play with them on Midfirth-water before he went abroad; one of these was Audun, who then dwelt at Audunstead, in Willowdale; he was the son of Asgeir, the son of Audun, the son of Asgeir Madpate; of all men he was the strongest north there; but he was thought to be the gentlest of neighbours. Now it came into Grettir's mind that he had had the worst of Audun in that ball-play whereof is told before; and now he would fain try which of the twain had ripened the most since then. For this cause Grettir took his way from home, and fared unto Audunstead. This was in early mowing tide; Grettir was well dight, and rode in a fair-stained saddle of very excellent workmanship, which Thorfinn had given him; a good horse he had withal, and all weapons of the best. Grettir came early in the day to Audunstead, and knocked at the door. Few folk were within; Grettir asked if Audun was at home. Men said that he had gone to fetch victuals from the hill-dairy. Then Grettir took the bridle off his horse; the field was unmowed, and the horse went whereas the grass was the highest. Grettir went into the hall, sat down on the seat-beam, and thereon fell asleep. Soon after Audun came home, and sees a horse grazing in the field with a fair-stained saddle on; Audun was bringing victuals on two horses, and carried curds on one of them, in drawn-up hides, tied round about: this fashion men called curd-bags. Audun took the loads off the horses and carried the curd-bags in his arms into the house.

Now it was dark before his eyes, and Grettir stretched his foot from out the beam so that Audun fell flat down head-foremost on to the curd-bag, whereby the bonds of the bag brake; Audun leaped up and asked who was that rascal in the way. Grettir named himself.

Then said Audun, "Rashly hast thou done herein; what is thine errand then?"

Grettir said, "I will fight with thee."

"First I will see about my victuals," said Audun.

"That thou mayst well do," said Grettir, "if thou canst not charge other folk therewith."

Then Audun stooped down and caught up the curd-bag and dashed it against Grettir's bosom, and bade him first take what was sent him; and therewith was Grettir all smothered in the curds; and a greater shame he deemed that than if Audun had given him a great wound.

Now thereon they rushed at one another and wrestled fiercely; Grettir set on with great eagerness, but Audun gave back before him. Yet he feels that Grettir has outgrown him in strength. Now all things in their way were kicked out of place, and they were borne on wrestling to and fro throughout all the hall; neither spared his might, but still Grettir was the toughest of the twain, and at last Audun fell, having torn all weapons from Grettir.

Now they grapple hard with one another, and huge cracking was all around them. Withal a great din was heard coming through the earth underneath the farmstead, and Grettir heard some one ride up to the houses, get off his horse, and stride in with great strides; he sees a man come up, of goodly growth, in a red kirtle and with a helmet on his head. He took his way into the hall, for he had heard clamorous doings there as they were struggling together; he asked what was in the hall.

Grettir named himself, "But who asks thereof?" quoth he.

"Bardi am I hight," said the new comer.

"Art thou Bardi, the son of Gudmund, from Asbiornsness?"

"That very man am I," said Bardi; "but what art thou doing?"

Grettir said, "We, Audun and I, are playing here in sport."

"I know not as to the sport thereof," said Bardi, "nor are ye even men either; thou art full of unfairness and overbearing, and he is easy and good to deal with; so let him stand up forthwith."

Grettir said, *"Many a man stretches round the door to the lock*; and meseems it lies more in thy way to avenge thy brother Hall than to meddle in the dealings betwixt me and Audun."

"At all times I hear this," said Bardi, "nor know I if that will be avenged, but none the less I will that thou let Audun be at peace, for he is a quiet man."

Grettir did so at Bardi's bidding, nathless, little did it please him. Bardi asked for what cause they strove.

Grettir sang:

"Prithee, Audun, who can tell,
But that now thy throat shall swell;
That from rough hands thou shalt gain
By our strife a certain pain.
E'en such wrong as I have done,
I of yore from Audun won,
When the young, fell-creeping lad
At his hands a choking had."

Bardi said that certes it was a matter to be borne with, if he had had to avenge himself.

"Now I will settle matters between you," quoth Bardi; "I will that ye part, leaving things as they are, that thereby there may be an end of all between you."

This they let hold good, but Grettir took ill liking to Bardi and his brothers.

Now they all rode off, and when they were somewhat on their way, Grettir spake:

"I have heard that thou hast will to go to Burgfirth this summer, and I now offer to go south with thee; and methinks that herein I do for thee more than thou art worthy of."

Hereat was Bardi glad, and speedily said yea thereto, and bade him have thanks for this; and thereupon they parted. But a little after Bardi came back and said:

"I will have it known that thou goest not unless my foster-father Thorarin will have it so, for he shall have all the rule of the faring."

"Well mightest thou, methinks, have full freedom as to thine own redes," said Grettir, "and my faring I will not have laid under the choice of other folk; and I shall mislike it if thou easiest me aside from thy fellowship."

Now either went their way, and Bardi said he should let Grettir know for sure if Thorarin would that he should fare with him, but that otherwise he might sit quiet at home. Grettir rode home to Biarg, but Bardi to his own house.

Chapter 29
Of the Horse-fight at Longfit

THAT SUMMER WAS SETTLED to be a great horse-fight at Longfit, below Reeks. Thither came many men. Atli of Biarg had a good horse, a black-maned roan of Keingala's kin, and father and son had great love for that horse. The brothers, Kormak and Thorgils of Meal, had a brown horse, trusty in fight. These were to fight their horse against Atli of Biarg. And many other good horses were there.

Odd, the Foundling-skald, of Kormak's kin, was to follow the horse of his kinsman through the day. Odd was then growing a big man, and bragged much of himself, and was untameable and reckless. Grettir asked of Atli his brother, who should follow his horse.

"I am not so clear about that," said he.

"Wilt thou that I stand by it?" said Grettir.

"Be thou then very peaceable, kinsman," said Atli, "for here have we to deal with overbearing men."

"Well, let them pay for their own insolence," said Grettir, "if they know not how to hold it back."

Now are the horses led out, but all stood forth on the river-bank tied together. There was a deep hollow in the river down below the bank. The horses bit well at each other, and the greatest sport it was.

Odd drave on his horse with all his might, but Grettir held back, and seized the tail with one hand, and the staff wherewith he goaded the horse he held in the other. Odd stood far before his horse, nor was it so sure that he did not goad Atli's horse from his hold. Grettir made as if he saw it not. Now the horses bore forth towards the river. Then Odd drave his staff at Grettir, and smote the shoulder-blade, for that Grettir turned the shoulder towards him: that was so mighty a stroke, that the flesh shrank from under it, but Grettir was little scratched.

Now in that nick of time the horses reared up high, and Grettir ran under his horse's hocks, and thrust his staff so hard at the side of Odd that three ribs brake in him, but he was hurled out into deep water, together with his horse and all the horses that were tied together. Then men swam out to him and dragged him out of the river; then was a great hooting made thereat; Kormak's folk ran to their weapons, as did the men of Biarg in another place. But when the Ramfirthers and the men of Waterness saw that, they went betwixt them, and they were parted and went home, but both sides had ill-will one with the other, though they sat peacefully at home for a while.

Atli was sparing of speech over this, but Grettir was right unsparing, and said that they would meet another time if his will came to pass.

Chapter 30
Of Thorbiorn Oxmain and Thorbiorn Tardy, and of Grettir's Meeting with Kormak on Ramfirth-neck

THORBIORN WAS THE NAME of a man who dwelt at Thorodstead in Ramfirth; he was the son of Arnor Hay-nose, the son of Thorod, who had settled Ramfirth on that side out as far as Bank was on the other.

Thorbiorn was the strongest of all men; he was called Oxmain. Thorod was the name of his brother, he was called Drapa-Stump; their mother was Gerd, daughter of Bodvar, from Bodvars-knolls. Thorbiorn was a great and hardy warrior, and had many men with him; he was noted as being worse at getting servants than other men, and barely gave he wages to any man, nor was he thought a good man to deal with. There was a kinsman of his hight Thorbiorn, and bynamed Tardy; he was a sailor, and the namesakes were partners. He was ever at Thorodstead, and was thought to better Thorbiorn but little. He was a fault-finding fellow, and went about jeering at most men.

There was a man hight Thorir, the son of Thorkel of Boardere. He farmed first at Meals in Ramfirth; his daughter was Helga, whom Sleita-Helgi had to wife, but after the man-slaying in Fairslope Thorir set up for himself his abode south in Hawkdale, and farmed at the Pass, and sold the land at Meals to Thorhall, son of Gamli the Vendlander. His son was Gamli, who had to wife Ranveig, daughter of Asmund the Greyhaired, and Grettir's sister. They dwelt at that time at Meals, and had good hap. Thorir of the Pass had two sons, one hight Gunnar, the other Thorgeir; they were both hopeful men, and had then taken the farm after their father, yet were for ever with Thorbiorn Oxmain, and were growing exceeding unruly.

The summer after that just told, Kormak and Thorgils and Narfi their kinsman rode south to Northriverdale, on some errand of theirs. Odd the Foundling-skald fared also with them, and by then was gotten healed of the stiffness he gained at the horse-fight. But while they were south of the heath, Grettir fared from Biarg, and with him two house-carles of Atli's. They rode over to Bowerfell, and thence over the mountain neck to Ramfirth, and came to Meals in the evening.

They were there three nights; Ranveig and Gamli welcomed Grettir well, and bade him abide with them, but he had will to ride home.

Then Grettir heard that Kormak and his fellows were come from the south, and had guested at Tongue through the night. Grettir got ready early to leave Meals; Gamli offered him men to go with him. Now Grim was the name of Gamli's brother; he was of all men the swiftest; he rode with Grettir with another man; they were five in all. Thus they rode on till they came to Ramfirth-neck, west of Bowerfell. There stands a huge stone that is called Grettir's heave; for he tried long that day to lift that stone, and thus they delayed till Kormak and his fellows were come. Grettir rode to meet them, and both sides jumped off their horses. Grettir said it was more like free men now to deal blows of the biggest, than to fight with staves like wandering churles. Then Kormak bade them take the challenge in manly wise, and do their best. Thereafter they ran at one another and fought. Grettir went before his men, and bade them take heed, that none came at his back. Thus they fought a while, and men were wounded on both sides.

Now Thorbiorn Oxmain had ridden that day over the neck to Bowerfell, and when he rode back he saw their meeting. There were with him then Thorbiorn the Tardy, and Gunnar and Thorgeir, Thorir's sons, and Thorod Drapa-Stump. Now when they came thereto, Thorbiorn called on his men to go between them. But the others were by then so eager that they could do nought. Grettir broke forth fiercely, and before him were the sons of Thorir, and they both fell as he thrust them from him; they waxed exceeding furious thereat, insomuch that

Gunnar dealt a death-blow at a house-carle of Atli; and when Thorbiorn saw that, he bade them part, saying withal that he would aid which side soever should pay heed to his words. By then were fallen two house-carles of Kormak, but Grettir saw, that it would hardly do if Thorbiorn should bring aid to them against him, wherefore now he gave up the battle, and all were wounded who had been at that meeting. But much it misliked Grettir that they had been parted.

Thereafter either side rode home, nor did they settle peace after these slayings. Thorbiorn the Tardy made much mocking at all this, therefore things began to worsen betwixt the men of Biarg and Thorbiorn Oxmain, so that therefrom fell much ill-will as came to be known after. No boot was bidden to Atli for his house-carle, but he made as if he knew it not. Grettir sat at home at Biarg until Twainmonth. Nor is it said in story that he and Kormak met ever again after these things betid.

Chapter 31
How Grettir Met Bardi, the Son of Gudmund, as He Came Back from the Heath-slayings

BARDI, THE SON OF GUDMUND, and his brothers, rode home to Asbiornsness after their parting with Grettir.

They were the sons of Gudmund, the son of Solmund. The mother of Solmund was Thorlaug, the daughter of Saemund, the South-Island man, the foster-brother of Ingimund the Old, and Bardi was a very noble man.

Now soon he rode to find Thorarin the Wise, his foster-father. He welcomed Bardi well, and asked what gain he had got of followers and aid, for they had before taken counsel over Bardi's journey. Bardi answered that he had got the aid of that man to his fellow, whose aid he deemed better than that of any other twain. Thorarin got silent thereat, and then said:

"That man will be Grettir Asmundson."

"*Sooth is the sage's guess*," said Bardi; "that is the very man, foster-father."

Thorarin answered, "True it is, that Grettir is much before any other man of those who are to choose in our land, and late will he be won with weapons, if he be hale, yet it misdoubts me how far he will bring thee luck; but of thy following all must not be luckless, and enough ye will do, though he fare not with thee: nowise shall he go if I may have my will."

"This I could not have deemed, foster-father," said he, "that thou wouldst grudge me the aid of the bravest of men, if my need should be hard. A man cannot foresee all things when he is driven on as methinks I am."

"Thou wilt do well," said Thorarin; "though thou abidest by my foresight."

Now thus must things be, even as Thorarin would, that no word more was sent to Grettir, but Bardi fared south to Burgfirth, and then befell the Heath-slayings.

Grettir was at Biarg when he heard that Bardi had ridden south; he started up in anger for that no word had been sent to him, and said that not thus should they part. He had news of them when they were looked for coming from the south, and thereat he rode down to Thorey's-peak, for the waylaying of Bardi's folk as they came back from the south: he fared from the homestead up on to the hill-side, and abode there. That same day rode Bardi and his men north over Twodaysway, from the Heath-slayings; they were six in all, and every man sore wounded; and when they came forth by the homestead, then said Bardi:

"A man there is up on the hill-side; a big man, armed. What man do ye take him to be?"

They said that they wotted not who he was.

Bardi said, "Methinks there," quoth he, "is Grettir Asmundson; and if so it is, there will he meet us. I deem that it has misliked him that he fared not with us, but methinks we are not in good case, if he be bent on doing us harm. I now shall send after men to Thorey's-peak, and stake nought on the chance of his ill-will."

They said this was a good rede, and so was it done.

Thereafter Bardi and his folk rode on their way. Grettir saw where they fared, and went in the way before them, and when they met, either greeted other.

Grettir asked for tidings, but Bardi told them fearlessly, even as they were. Grettir asked what men were in that journey with him. Bardi said that there were his brothers, and Eyulf his brother-in-law.

"Thou hast now cleared thyself from all blame," said Grettir; "but now is it best that we try between us who is of most might here."

Said Bardi, "Too nigh to my garth have deeds of hard need been, than that I should fight with thee without a cause, and well methinks have I thrust these from me."

"Thou growest soft, methinks, Bardi," said Grettir, "since thou durst not fight with me."

"Call that what thou wilt," said Bardi; "but in some other stead would I that thou wreak thine high-handedness than here on me; and that is like enough, for now does thy rashness pass all bounds."

Grettir thought ill of his spaedom, and now doubted within himself whether he should set on one or other of them; but it seemed rash to him, as they were six and he one: and in that nick of time came up the men from Thorey's-peak to the aid of Bardi and his folk; then Grettir drew off from them, and turned aside to his horse. But Bardi and his fellows went on their way, nor were there farewells between them at parting.

No further dealings between Bardi and Grettir are told of after these things betid.

Now so has Grettir said that he deemed himself well matched to fight with most men, though they were three together, but he would have no mind to flee before four, without trying it; but against more would he fight only if he must needs defend his hand, as is said in this stave:

> *"My life trust I 'gainst three*
> *Skilled in Mist's mystery;*
> *Whatso in Hilda's weather*
> *Shall bring the swords together;*
> *If over four they are*
> *My wayfaring that bar*
> *No gale of swords will I*
> *Wake with them willingly."*

After his parting with Bardi, Grettir fared to Biarg, and very ill he it thought that he might nowhere try his strength, and searched all about if anywhere might be somewhat wherewith he might contend.

Chapter 32
Of the Haunting at Thorhall-stead; and How Thorhall Took a Shepherd by the Rede of Skapti the Lawman, and of What Befell Thereafter

THERE WAS A MAN HIGHT Thorhall, who dwelt at Thorhall-stead, in Shady-vale, which runs up from Waterdale. Thorhall was the son of Grim, son of Thorhall, the son of Fridmund, who settled Shady-vale. Thorhall had a wife hight Gudrun. Grim was their son, and Thurid their daughter; they were well-nigh grown up.

Thorhall was a rich man, but mostly in cattle, so that no man had so much of live-stock as he. He was no chief, but an honest bonder he was. Much was that place haunted, and hardly could he get a shepherd that he deemed should serve his turn. He sought counsel of many men as to what he might do therewith, but none gave him a rede that might serve him. Thorhall rode each summer to the Thing, and good horses he had. But one summer at the Althing, Thorhall went to the booth of Skapti Thorodson the Lawman. Skapti was the wisest of men, and wholesome were his redes when folk prayed him for them. But he and his father differed thus much, that Thorod was foretelling, and yet was called under-handed of some folk; but Skapti showed forth to every man what he deemed would avail most, if it were not departed from, therefore was he called 'Father-betterer.'

Now Thorhall went into Skapti's booth, and Skapti greeted him well, for he knew that he was a man rich in cattle, and he asked him what were the tidings.

Thorhall answered, "A wholesome counsel would I have from thee."

"Little am I meet for that," said Skapti; "but what dost thou stand in need of?"

Thorhall said, "So is the matter grown to be, that but a little while do my shepherds avail me; for ever will they get badly hurt; but others will not serve to the end, and now no one will take the job when he knows what bides in the way."

Skapti answered, "Some evil things shall be there then, since men are more unwilling to watch thy sheep than those of other men. Now, therefore, as thou hast sought rede of me, I shall get thee a shepherd who is hight Glam, a Swede, from Sylgsdale, who came out last summer, a big man and a strong, though he is not much to the mind of most folk."

Thorhall said he heeded that little if he watched the sheep well.

Skapti said that little would be the look out for others, if he could not watch them, despite his strength and daring.

Then Thorhall went out from him, and this was towards the breaking up of the Thing. Thorhall missed two dun horses, and fared himself to seek for them; wherefore folk deem that he was no great man. He went up to Sledgehill, and south along the fell which is called Armansfell; then he saw how a man fared down from Godi's-wood, and bore faggots on a horse. Soon they met together, and Thorhall asked him of his name. He said that he was called Glam. This man was great of growth, uncouth to look on; his eyes were grey and glaring, and his hair was wolf-grey.

Thorhall stared at him somewhat when he saw this man, till he saw that this was he to whom he had been sent.

"What work hast thou best will to do?" said Thorhall.

Glam said, "That he was of good mind to watch sheep in winter."

"Wilt thou watch my sheep?" said Thorhall. "Skapti has given thee to my will."

"So only shall my service avail thee, if I go of my own will, for I am evil of mood if matters mislike me," quoth Glam.

"I fear no hurt thereof," said Thorhall, "and I will that thou fare to my house."

"That may I do," said Glam, "perchance there are some troubles there?"

"Folk deem the place haunted," said Thorhall.

"Such bugs will not scare me," quoth Glam; "life seems to me less irksome thereby."

"It must needs seem so," said Thorhall, "and truly it is better that a mannikin be not there."

Thereafter they struck bargain together, and Glam is to come at winter nights: then they parted, and Thorhall found his horses even where he had just been searching. Thorhall rode home, and thanked Skapti for his good deed.

Summer slipped away, and Thorhall heard nought of his shepherd, nor did any man know aught about him; but at the appointed time he came to Thorhall-stead. The bonder greeted him well, but none of the other folk could abide him, and the good wife least of all.

Now he took to the sheep-watching, and little trouble it seemed to give him; he was big-voiced and husky, and all the beasts would run together when he whooped. There was a church at Thorhall-stead, but nowise would Glam come therein; he was a loather of church-song, and godless, foul-tempered, and surly, and no man might abide him.

Now passed the time till it came to Yule-eve; then Glam got up and straightway called for his meat. The good wife said:

"No Christian man is wont to eat meat this day, be-. cause that on the morrow is the first day of Yule," says she, "wherefore must men first fast today."

He answers, "Many follies have ye, whereof I see no good come, nor know I that men fare better now than when they paid no heed to such things; and methinks the ways of men were better when they were called heathens; and now will I have my meat, and none of this fooling."

Then said the housewife, "I know for sure that thou shall fare ill today, if thou takest up this evil turn."

Glam bade her bring food straightway, and said that she should fare the worse else. She durst do but as he would, and so when he was full, he went out, growling and grumbling.

Now the weather was such, that mirk was over all, and the snow-flakes drave down, and great din there was, and still all grew much the worse, as the day slipped away.

Men heard the shepherd through the early morning, but less of him as the day wore; then it took to snowing, and by evening there was a great storm; then men went to church, and thus time drew on to nightfall; and Glam came not home; then folk held talk, as to whether search should not be made for him, but, because of the snow-storm and pitch darkness, that came to nought.

Now he came not home on the night of Yule-eve; and thus men abide till after the time of worship; but further on in the day men fared out to the search, and found the sheep scattered wide about in fens, beaten down by the storm, or strayed up into the mountains. Thereafter they came on a great beaten place high up in the valley, and they thought it was as if strong wrestling had gone on there; for that all about the stones had been uptorn and the earth withal; now they looked closely and saw where Glam lay a little way therefrom; he was dead, and as blue as hell, and as great as a neat.

Huge loathing took them, at the sight of him, and they shuddered in their souls at him, yet they strove to bring him to church, but could get him only as far as a certain gil-edge a little way below.

Then they fared home to the farm, and told the bonder what had happed. He asked what was like to have been Glam's bane. They said they had tracked steps as great as if a cask-bottom had been stamped down, from there where the beaten place was, up to beneath sheer rocks which were high up the valley, and there along went great stains of blood. Now men drew from this, that the evil wight which had been there before had killed Glam, but had got such wounds as had been full enough for him, for of him none has since been ware.

The second day of Yule men went afresh to try to bring Glam to church; drag horses were put to him, but could move him nowhere where they had to go on even ground and not down hill; then folk had to go away therefrom leaving things done so far.

The third day the priest fared with them, and they sought all day, but found not Glam. The priest would go no more on such search, but the herdsman was found whenso the priest was not in their company. Then they let alone striving to bring him to church, and buried him there whereto he had been brought.

A little time after men were ware that Glam lay not quiet. Folk got great hurt therefrom, so that many fell into swoons when they saw him, but others lost their wits thereby. But just after Yule men thought they saw him home at the farm. Folk became exceeding afeard thereat, and many fled there and then. Next Glam took to riding the house-roofs at night, so that he went nigh to breaking them in. Now he walked well-nigh night and day. Hardly durst men fare up into the dale, though they had errands enough there. And much scathe the men of the country-side deemed all this.

Chapter 33
Of the Doings of Glam at Thorhall-Stead

IN THE SPRING Thorhall got serving-men, and set up house at his farm; then the hauntings began to go off while the sun was at its height; and so things went on to midsummer. That summer a ship came out to Hunawater, wherein was a man named Thorgaut. He was an outlander of kin, big and stout, and two men's strength he had. He was unhired and single, and would fain do some work, for he was moneyless. Now Thorhall rode to the ship, and asked Thorgaut if he would work for him. Thorgaut said that might be, and moreover that he was not nice about work.

"Be sure in thy mind," said Thorhall, "that mannikins are of small avail there because of the hauntings that have been going on there for one while now; for I will not draw thee on by wiles."

Thorgaut answers, "I deem not myself given up, though I should see some wraithlings; matters will not be light when I am scared, nor will I give up my service for that."

Now they come speedily to a bargain, and Thorgaut is to watch the sheep when winter comes. So the summer wore on, and Thorgaut betook himself to the shepherding at winter nights, and all liked him well. But ever came Glam home and rode the house-roofs; this Thorgaut deemed sport enough, and quoth he:

"The thrall must come nigher to scare me."

Thorhall bade him keep silence over that. "Better will it be that ye have no trial together."

Thorgaut said, "Surely all might is shaken out of you, nor shall I drop down betwixt morn and eve at such talk."

Now so things go through the winter till Yule-tide. On Yule eve the shepherd would fare out to his sheep. Then said the good wife:

"Need is it that things go not the old way."

He answered, "Have no fear thereof, goodwife; something worth telling of will betide if I come not back."

And thereafter he went to his sheep; and the weather was somewhat cold, and there was much snow. Thorgaut was wont to come home when twilight had set in, and now he came not at that time. Folk went to church as they were wont. Men now thought things looked not unlike what they did before; the bonder would have search made for the shepherd, but the church-goers begged off, and said that they would not give themselves into the hands of trolls by night; so the bonder durst not go, and the search came to nought.

Yule-day, when men were full, they fared out and searched for the shepherd; they first went to Glam's cairn, because men thought that from his deeds came the loss of the herdsman. But when they came nigh to the cairn, there they saw great tidings, for there they found the shepherd, and his neck was broken, and every bone in him smashed. Then they brought him to church, and no harm came to men from Thorgaut afterwards.

But Glam began afresh to wax mighty; and such deeds he wrought, that all men fled away from Thorhall-stead, except the good man and his goodwife. Now the same neatherd had long been there, and Thorhall would not let him go, because of his good will and safe ward; he was well on in years, and was very loth to fare away, for he saw that all things the bonder had went to nought from not being watched.

Now after midwinter one morning the housewife fared to the byre to milk the cows after the wonted time; by then was it broad daylight, for none other than the neatherd would trust themselves out before day; but he went out at dawn. She heard great cracking in the byre, with bellowing and roaring; she ran back crying out, and said she knew not what uncouth things were going on in the byre.

The bonder went out and came to the cows, which were goring one another; so he thought it not good to go in there, but went in to the hay-barn. There he saw where lay the neatherd, and had his head in one boose and his feet in the other; and he lay cast on his back. The bonder went up to him, and felt him all over with his hand, and finds soon that he was dead, and the spine of him broken asunder; it had been broken over the raised stone-edge of a boose.

Now the goodman thought there was no abiding there longer; so he fled away from the farm with all that he might take away; but all such live stock as was left behind Glam killed, and then he fared all over the valley and destroyed farms up from Tongue. But Thorhall was with his friends the rest of the winter.

No man might fare up the dale with horse or hound, because straightway it was slain. But when spring came, and the sun-light was the greatest, somewhat the hauntings abated; and now would Thorhall go back to his own land; he had no easy task in getting servants, nathless he set up house again at Thorhall-stead; but all went the same way as before; for when autumn came, the hauntings began to wax again; the bonder's daughter was most set on, and fared so that she died thereof. Many redes were sought, but nought could be done; men thought it like that all Waterdale would be laid waste if nought were found to better this.

Chapter 34
Grettir Hears of the Hauntings

NOW WE TAKE UP THE STORY where Grettir Asmundson sat at Biarg through the autumn after they parted, he and Slaying-Bardi at Thoreys-peak; and when the time of winter-nights had well-nigh come, Grettir rode from home north over the neck to Willowdale, and guested at Audunstead; he and Audun made a full peace, and Grettir gave Audun a good axe, and they talked of friendship between them. Audun dwelt long at Audunstead, and was a man of many and hopeful kin; his son was Egil, who married Ulfheid, daughter of Eyulf Gudmundson, and their son was Eyulf, who was slain at the Althing, he was the father of Orm, who was the chaplain of Bishop Thorlak.

Grettir rode north to Waterdale, and came to see his kin at Tongue. In those days dwelt there Jokull, the son of Bard, the mother's brother of Grettir: Jokull was a big man and a strong, and the most violent of men; he was a seafaring man, very wild, and yet a man of great account.

He greeted Grettir well, and he was there three nights. There were so many words about Glam's hauntings, that nought was so much spoken of as of that. Grettir asked closely about all things that had happed. Jokull said that thereof was told no more than the very truth; "And, perchance, thou art wishful to go there, kinsman?"

Grettir said that so it was.

Jokull bade him do it not, "Because it is a great risk for thy good luck, and thy kinsmen have much to hazard where thou art," said he, "for of young men we think there is none such as thou; but *from ill cometh ill* whereas Glam is; and far better it is to deal with men than with such evil wights."

Grettir said, "That he had a mind to go to Thorhall-stead and see how things went there."

Said Jokull, "Now I see it is of no avail to let thee; but so it is, as men say, *Good luck and goodliness are twain.*"

"*Woe is before one's own door when it is inside one's neighbour's*; think how it may fare with thyself ere things are ended," said Grettir.

Jokull answered, "Maybe we may both see somewhat of things to come, but neither may help aught herein."

They parted thereafter, and neither thought well of the other's foretelling.

Chapter 35
Grettir Goes to Thorhall-Stead, and Has to Do with Glam

GRETTIR RODE TO THORHALL-STEAD, and the bonder gave him good welcome; he asked whither Grettir was minded to fare, but Grettir said he would be there that night if the bonder would have it so.

Thorhall said that he thanked him therefor, "But few have thought it a treat to guest here for any time; thou must needs have heard what is going on here, and I fain would that thou shouldest have no trouble from me: but though thou shouldest come off whole thyself, that know I for sure, that thou wilt lose thy horse, for none keeps his horse whole who comes here."

Grettir said that horses were to be had in plenty whatsoever might hap to this. Then Thorhall was glad that Grettir was to be there, and gave him a hearty welcome.

Now Grettir's horse was locked up in a strong house, and they went to sleep; and so the night slipped by, and Glam came not home.

Then said Thorhall, "Things have gone well at thy coming, for every night is Glam wont to ride the house-roofs, or break open doors, as thou mayest well see."

Grettir said, "Then shall one of two things be, either he shall not hold himself back for long, or the hauntings will abate for more than one night; I will bide here another night and see how things fare."

Thereafter they went to Grettir's horse, and nought had been tried against it; then all seemed to the bonder to go one way.

Now is Grettir there another night, and neither came the thrall home; that the farmer deemed very hopeful; withal he fared to see after Grettir's horse. When the farmer came there, he found the house broken into, but the horse was dragged out to the door, and every bone in him broken to pieces. Thorhall told Grettir what had happed there, and bade him save himself, "For sure is thy death if thou abidest Glam."

Grettir answered, "I must not have less for my horse than a sight of the thrall."

The bonder said it was no boon to see him, for he was unlike any shape of man; "but good methinks is every hour that thou art here."

Now the day goes by, and when men should go to sleep Grettir would not put off his clothes, but lay down on the seat over against the bonder's lock-bed. He had a drugget cloak over him, and wrapped one skirt of it under his feet, and twined the other under his head, and looked out through the head-opening; a seat-beam was before the seat, a very strong one, and against this he set his feet. The door-fittings were all broken from the outer door, but a wrecked door was now bound thereby, and all was fitted up in the wretchedest wise. The panelling which had been before the seat athwart the hall, was all broken away both above and below the cross-beam; all beds had been torn out of place, and an uncouth place it was.

Light burned in the hall through the night; and when the third part of the night was passed, Grettir heard huge din without, and then one went up upon the houses and rode the hall, and drave his heels against the thatch so that every rafter cracked again.

That went on long, and then he came down from the house and went to the door; and as the door opened, Grettir saw that the thrall stretched in his head, which seemed to him monstrously big, and wondrous thick cut.

Glam fared slowly when he came into the door and stretched himself high up under the roof, and turned looking along the hall, and laid his arms on the tie-beam, and glared inwards over the place. The farmer would not let himself be heard, for he deemed he had had enough in hearing himself what had gone on outside. Grettir lay quiet, and moved no whit; then Glam saw that some bundle lay on the seat, and therewith he stalked up the hall and griped at the wrapper wondrous hard; but Grettir set his foot against the beam, and moved in no wise; Glam pulled again much harder, but still the wrapper moved not at all; the third time he pulled with both hands so hard, that he drew Grettir upright from the seat; and now they tore the wrapper asunder between them.

Glam gazed at the rag he held in his hand, and wondered much who might pull so hard against him; and therewithal Grettir ran under his hands and gripped him round the middle, and bent back his spine as hard as he might, and his mind it was that Glam should shrink thereat; but the thrall lay so hard on Grettir's arms, that he shrank all aback because of Glam's strength.

Then Grettir bore back before him into sundry seats; but the seat-beams were driven out of place, and all was broken that was before them. Glam was fain to get out, but Grettir set his feet against all things that he might; nathless Glam got him dragged from out the hall; there had they a wondrous hard wrestling, because the thrall had a mind to bring him out of the house; but Grettir saw that ill as it was to deal with Glam within doors, yet worse would it be without; therefore he struggled with all his might and main against going out-a-doors.

Now Glam gathered up his strength and knit Grettir towards him when they came to the outer door; but when Grettir saw that he might not set his feet against that, all of a sudden in one rush he drave his hardest against the thrall's breast, and spurned both feet against the half-sunken stone that stood in the threshold of the door; for this the thrall was not ready, for he had been tugging to draw Grettir to him, therefore he reeled aback and spun out against the door, so that his shoulders caught the upper door-case, and the roof burst asunder, both rafters and frozen thatch, and therewith he fell open-armed aback out of the house, and Grettir over him.

Bright moonlight was there without, and the drift was broken, now drawn over the moon, now driven from off her; and, even as Glam fell, a cloud was driven from the moon, and Glam glared up against her. And Grettir himself says that by that sight only was he dismayed amidst all that he ever saw.

Then his soul sank within him so, from all these things both from weariness, and because he had seen Glam turn his eyes so horribly, that he might not draw the short-sword, and lay well-nigh 'twixt home and hell.

But herein was there more fiendish craft in Glam than in most other ghosts, that he spake now in this wise:

"Exceeding eagerly hast thou wrought to meet me, Grettir, but no wonder will it be deemed, though thou gettest no good hap of me; and this must I tell thee, that thou now hast got half the strength and manhood, which was thy lot if thou hadst not met me: now I may not take from thee the strength which thou hast got before this; but that may I rule, that thou shalt never be mightier than now thou art; and nathless art thou mighty enow, and that shall many an one learn. Hitherto hast thou earned fame by thy deeds, but henceforth will wrongs and man-slayings fall on thee, and the most part of thy doings will turn to thy woe and ill-hap; an outlaw shalt thou be made, and ever shall it be thy lot to dwell alone abroad; therefore this weird I lay on thee, ever in those days to see these eyes with thine eyes, and thou wilt find it hard to be alone – and that shall drag thee unto death."

Now when the thrall had thus said, the astonishment fell from Grettir that had lain on him, and therewith he drew the short-sword and hewed the head from Glam, and laid it at his thigh.

Then came the farmer out; he had clad himself while Glam had his spell going, but he durst come nowhere nigh till Glam had fallen.

Thorhall praised God therefor, and thanked Grettir well for that he had won this unclean spirit. Then they set to work and burned Glam to cold coals, thereafter they gathered his ashes into the skin of a beast, and dug it down whereas sheep-pastures were fewest, or the ways of men. They walked home thereafter, and by then it had got far on towards day; Grettir laid him down, for he was very stiff: but Thorhall sent to the nearest farm for men, and both showed them and told them how all things had fared.

All men who heard thereof deemed this a deed of great worth, and in those days it was said by all that none in all the land was like to Grettir Asmundson for great heart and prowess.

Thorhall saw off Grettir handsomely, and gave him a good horse and seemly clothes, for those were all torn to pieces that he had worn before; so they parted in friendly wise. Grettir rode thence to the Ridge in Waterdale, and Thorvald received him well, and asked closely about the struggle with Glam. Grettir told him all, and said thereto that he had never had such a trial of strength, so long was their struggle.

Thorvald bade him keep quiet, "Then all will go well with thee, else wilt thou be a man of many troubles."

Grettir said that his temper had been nowise bettered by this, that he was worse to quiet than before, and that he deemed all trouble worse than it was; but that herein he found the greatest change, in that he was become so fearsome a man in the dark, that he durst go nowhither alone after nightfall, for then he seemed to see all kinds of horrors.

And that has fallen since into a proverb, that Glam lends eyes, or gives Glamsight to those who see things nowise as they are.

But Grettir rode home to Biarg when he had done his errands, and sat at home through the winter.

Chapter 36
Of Thorbiorn Oxmain's Autumn-feast, and the Mocks of Thorbiorn Tardy

THORBIORN OXMAIN held a great autumn feast, and many men came thither to him, and that was while Grettir fared north to Waterdale in the autumn; Thorbiorn the Tardy was there at the feast, and many things were spoken of there. There the Ramfirthers asked of those dealings of Grettir on the neck the summer before.

Thorbiorn Oxmain told the story right fairly as towards Grettir, and said that Kormak would have got the worst of it, if none had come there to part them.

Then spake Thorbiorn the Tardy, "Both these things are true," said he: "I saw Grettir win no great honour, and I deem withal that fear shot through his heart when we came thereto, and right blithe was he to part, nor did I see him seek for vengeance when Atli's house-carle was slain; therefore do I deem that there is no heart in him if he is not holpen enow."

And thereat Thorbiorn went on gabbling at his most; but many put in a word, and said that this was worthless fooling, and that Grettir would not leave things thus, if he heard that talk.

Nought else befell worth telling of at the feast, and men went home; but much ill-will there was betwixt them that winter, though neither set on other; nor were there other tidings through the winter.

Chapter 37
Olaf the Saint, King in Norway; the Slaying of Thorbiorn
Tardy; Grettir Goes to Norway

EARLY THE SPRING AFTER came out a ship from Norway; and that was before the Thing; these folk knew many things to tell, and first that there was change of rulers in Norway, for Olaf Haraldson was come to be king, and Earl Svein had fled the country in the spring after the fight at Ness. Many noteworthy matters were told of King Olaf, and this withal, that he received such men in the best of ways who were of prowess in any deeds, and that he made such his men.

Thereat were many young men glad, and listed to go abroad, and when Grettir heard the tidings he became much minded to sail out; for he, like others, hoped for honour at the king's hands.

A ship lay in Goose-ere in Eyjafirth, therein Grettir got him a berth and made ready for the voyage, nor had he yet much of faring-goods.

Now Asmund was growing very feeble with eld, and was well-nigh bedridden; he and Asdis had a young son who was called Illugi, and was the hopefullest of men; and, by this time, Atli tended all farming and money-keeping, and this was deemed to better matters, because he was a peaceable and foreseeing man.

Now Grettir went shipward, but in that same ship had Thorbiorn the Tardy taken passage, before folk knew that Grettir would sail therein. Now men would hinder Thorbiorn from sailing in the same ship with Grettir, but Thorbiorn said that he would go for all that. He gat him ready for the voyage out, and was somewhat late thereat, nor did he come to the north to Goose-ere before the ship was ready for sea; and before Thorbiorn fared from the west, Asmund the Greyhaired fell sick and was bedridden.

Now Thorbiorn the Tardy came late one day down to the sand; men were getting ready to go to table, and were washing their hands outside the booths; but when Thorbiorn rode up the lane betwixt the booths, he was greeted, and asked for tidings. He made as if there was nought to tell, "Save that I deem that Asmund, the champion of Biarg, is now dead."

Many men said that there where he went, departed a worthy goodman from the world.

"But what brought it about?" said they.

He answered, "Little went to the death of that champion, for in the chamber smoke was he smothered like a dog; nor is there loss therein, for he was grown a dotard."

"Thou speakest marvellously of such a man," said they, "nor would Grettir like thy words well, if he heard them."

"That must I bear," said Thorbiorn, "and higher must Grettir bear the sword than he did last summer at Ramfirth-neck, if I am to tremble at him."

Now Grettir heard full well what Thorbiorn said, and paid no heed thereto while he let his tale run on; but when he had made an end, then spake Grettir:

"That fate I foretell for thee, Tardy," said he, "that thou wilt not die in chamber smoke, yet may be withal thou wilt not die of eld; but it is strangely done to speak scorn of sackless men."

Thorbiorn said, "I have no will to hold in about these things, and methinks thou didst not bear thyself so briskly when we got thee off that time when the men of Meals beat thee like a neat's head."

Then sang Grettir:

"Day by day full over long,
Arrow-dealer, grows thy tongue;
Such a man there is, that thou
Mayst be paid for all words now;

Many a man, who has been fain,
Wound-worm's tower with hands to gain,
With less deeds his death has bought,
Than thou, Tardy-one, hast wrought."

Said Thorbiorn, "About as feign do I deem myself as before, despite thy squealing."

Grettir answered, "Heretofore my spaedom has not been long-lived, and so shall things go still; now beware if thou wilt, hereafter will no out-look be left."

Therewith Grettir hewed at Thorbiorn, but he swung up his hand, with the mind to ward the stroke from him, but that stroke came on his arm about the wrist, and withal the short-sword drave into his neck so that the head was smitten off.

Then said the chapmen that he was a man of mighty strokes, and that such should king's men be; and no scathe they deemed it though Thorbiorn were slain, in that he had been both quarrelsome and spiteful.

A little after they sailed into the sea, and came in late summer to Norway, south at Hordaland, and then they heard that King Olaf was north at Drontheim; then Grettir took ship in a trading keel to go north therefrom, because he would fain see the king.

Chapter 38
Of Thorir of Garth and His Sons; and How Grettir Fetched Fire for His Shipmates

THERE WAS A MAN named Thorir, who lived at Garth, in Maindale, he was the son of Skeggi, the son of Botulf. Skeggi had settled Well-wharf up to Well-ness; he had to wife Helga, daughter of Thorkel, of Fishbrook; Thorir, his son, was a great chief, and a seafaring man. He had two sons, one called Thorgeir and one Skeggi, they were both hopeful men, and fully grown in those days. Thorir had been in Norway that summer, when King Olaf came east from England, and got into great friendship with the king, and with Bishop Sigurd as well; and this is a token thereof, that Thorir had had a large ship built in the wood, and prayed Bishop Sigurd to hallow it, and so he did. Thereafter Thorir fared out to Iceland and caused the ship to be broken up, when he grew weary of sailing, but the beaks of the ship, he had set up over his outer door, and they were there long afterwards, and were so full of weather wisdom, that the one whistled before a south wind, and the other before a north wind.

But when Thorir knew that King Olaf had got the sole rule over all Norway, he deemed that he had some friendship there to fall back on; then he sent his sons to Norway to meet the king, and was minded that they should become his men. They came there south, late in autumn, and got to themselves a row-barge, and fared north along the land, with the mind to go and meet the king.

They came to a haven south of Stead, and lay there some nights, and kept themselves in good case as to meat and drink, and were not much abroad when the weather was foul.

Now it is to be told that Grettir and his fellows fared north along the land, and often had hard weather, because it was then the beginning of winter; and when they bore down north on Stead, they had much foul weather, with snow and frost, and with exceeding trouble they make land one evening all much worn with wet; so they lay to by a certain dyke, and could thus save their money and goods; the chapmen were hard put to it for the cold, because they could not light any fire, though thereon they deemed well-nigh their life and health lay.

Thus they lay that evening in evil plight; but as the night wore on they saw that a great fire sprang up in the midst of the sound over against there whereas they had come. But when Grettir's shipmates saw the fire, they said one to the other that he would be a happy man who might get it, and they doubted whether they should unmoor the ship, but to all of them there seemed danger in that. Then they had a long talk over it, whether any man was of might enow to fetch that fire.

Grettir gave little heed thereto, but said, that such men had been as would not have feared the task. The chapmen said that they were not bettered by what had been, if now there was nought to take to.

"Perchance thou deemest thyself man enough thereto, Grettir," said they, "since thou art called the man of most prowess among the men of Iceland, and thou wottest well enough what our need is."

Grettir answered, "It seems to me no great deed to fetch the fire, but I wot not if ye will reward it according to the prayer of him who does it."

They said, "Why deemest thou us such shameful men as that we should reward that deed but with good?"

Quoth he, "I may try this if so be that ye think much lies on it, but my mind bids me hope to get nought of good thereby."

They said that that should never be, and bade all hail to his words; and thereafter Grettir made ready for swimming, and cast his clothes from off him; of clothes he had on but a cape and sail-cloth breeches; he girt up the cape and tied a bast-rope strongly round his middle, and had with him a cask; then he leaped overboard; he stretched across the sound, and got aland.

There he saw a house stand, and heard therefrom the talk of men, and much clatter, and therewith he turned toward that house.

Now is it to be said of those that were there before, that here were come the sons of Thorir, as is aforesaid; they had lain there many nights, and bided there the falling of the gale, that they might have wind at will to go north, beyond Stead. They had set them down a-drinking, and were twelve men in all; their ship rode in the main haven, and they were at a house of refuge for such men to guest in, as went along the coast.

Much straw had been borne into the house, and there was a great fire on the floor; Grettir burst into the house, and wotted not who was there before; his cape was all over ice when he came aland, and he himself was wondrous great to behold, even as a troll; now those first comers were exceeding amazed at him, and deemed he must be some evil wight; they smote at him with all things they might lay hold of, and mighty din went on around them; but Grettir put off all blows strongly with his arms, then some smote him with fire-brands, and the fire burst off over all the house, and therewith he got off with the fire and fared back again to his fellows.

They mightily praised his journey and the prowess of it, and said that his like would never be. And now the night wore, and they deemed themselves happy in that they had got the fire.

The next morning the weather was fair; the chapmen woke early and got them ready to depart, and they talked together that now they should meet those who had had the rule of that fire, and wot who they were.

Now they unmoored their ship, and crossed over the sound; there they found no hall, but saw a great heap of ashes, and found therein many bones of men; then they deemed that this house of refuge had been utterly burned up, with all those men who had been therein.

Thereat they asked if Grettir had brought about that ill-hap, and said that it was the greatest misdeed.

Grettir said, that now had come to pass even as he had misdoubted, that they should reward him ill for the fetching of the fire, and that it was ill to help unmanly men.

Grettir got such hurt of this, that the chapmen said, wheresoever they came, that Grettir had burned those men. The news soon got abroad that in that house were lost the aforenamed sons of Thorir of Garth, and their fellows; then they drave Grettir from their ship and would not have him with them; and now he became so ill looked on that scarce any one would do good to him.

Now he deemed that matters were utterly hopeless, but before all things would go to meet the king, and so made north to Drontheim. The king was there before him, and knew all or ever Grettir came there, who had been much slandered to the king. And Grettir was some days in the town before he could get to meet the king.

Chapter 39
How Grettir Would Fain Bear Iron Before the King

NOW ON A DAY WHEN the king sat in council, Grettir went before the king and greeted him well. The king looked at him and said, "Art thou Grettir the Strong?"

He answered, "So have I been called, and for that cause am I come to thee, that I hope from thee deliverance from the evil tale that is laid on me, though I deem that I nowise wrought that deed."

King Olaf said, "Thou art great enough, but I know not what luck thou mayest bear about to cast off this matter from thee; but it is like, indeed, that thou didst not willingly burn the men."

Grettir said he was fain to put from him this slander, if the king thought he might do so; the king bade him tell truthfully, how it had gone betwixt him and those men: Grettir told him all, even as has been said before, and this withal, that they were all alive when he came out with the fire:

"And now I will offer to free myself in such wise as ye may deem will stand good in law therefor."

Olaf the king said, "We will grant thee to bear iron for this matter if thy luck will have it so."

Grettir liked this exceeding well; and now took to fasting for the iron; and so the time wore on till the day came whereas the trial should come off; then went the king to the church, and the bishop and much folk, for many were eager to have a sight of Grettir, so much as had been told of him.

Then was Grettir led to the church, and when he came thither, many of those who were there before gazed at him and said one to the other, that he was little like to most folk, because of his strength and greatness of growth.

Now, as Grettir went up the church-floor, there started up a lad of ripe growth, wondrous wild of look, and he said to Grettir:

"Marvellous is now the custom in this land, as men are called Christians therein, that ill-doers, and folk riotous, and thieves shall go their ways in peace and become free by trials; yea, and what would the evil man do but save his life while he might? So here now is a misdoer, proven clearly a man of misdeeds, and has burnt sackless men withal, and yet shall he, too, have a trial to free him; ah, a mighty ill custom!"

Therewith he went up to Grettir and pointed finger, and wagged head at him, and called him mermaid's son, and many other ill names.

Grettir grew wroth beyond measure hereat, and could not keep himself in; he lifted up his fist, and smote the lad under the ear, so that forthwith he fell down stunned, but some say that he was slain there and then. None seemed to know whence that lad came or what became of him, but men are mostly minded to think, that it was some unclean spirit, sent thither for Grettir's hurt.

Now a great clamour rose in the church, and it was told the king, "He who should bear the iron is smiting all about him;" then King Olaf went down the church, and saw what was going on, and spake:

"A most unlucky man art thou," said he, "that now the trial should not be, as ready as all things were thereto, nor will it be easy to deal with thine ill-luck."

Grettir answered, "I was minded that I should have gained more honour from thee, Lord, for the sake of my kin, than now seems like to be;" and he told withal how men were faring to King Olaf, as was said afore, "and now I am fain," said he, "that thou wouldest take me to thee; thou hast here many men with thee, who will not be deemed more like men-at-arms than I?"

"That see I well," said the king, "that few men are like unto thee for strength and stoutness of heart, but thou art far too luckless a man to abide with us: now shall thou go in peace for me, wheresoever thou wilt, the winter long, but next summer go thou out to Iceland, for there will it be thy fate to leave thy bones."

Grettir answered, "First would I put from me this affair of the burning, if I might, for I did not the deed willingly."

"It is most like," said the king; "but yet, because the trial is now come to nought for thy heedlessness' sake, thou will not get this charge cast from thee more than now it is, *For ill-heed still to ill doth lead*, and if ever man has been cursed, of all men must thou have been."

So Grettir dwelt a while in the town thereafter, but dealt no more with the king than has been told.

Then he fared into the south country, and was minded east for Tunsberg, to find Thorstein Dromond, his brother, and there is nought told of his travels till he came east to Jadar.

Chapter 40
Of Grettir and Snoekoll

AT YULE CAME GRETTIR to a bonder who was called Einar, he was a rich man, and was married and had one daughter of marriageable age, who was called Gyrid; she was a fair woman, and was deemed a right good match; Einar bade Grettir abide with him through Yule, and that proffer he took.

Then was it the wont far and wide in Norway that woodmen and misdoers would break out of the woods and challenge men for their women, or they took away men's goods with violence, whereas they had not much help of men.

Now it so befell here, that one day in Yule there came to Einar the bonder many ill-doers together, and he was called Snoekoll who was the head of them, and a great bearserk he was. He challenged goodman Einar to give up his daughter, or to defend her, if he thought himself man enough thereto; but the bonder was then past his youth, and was no man for fighting; he deemed he had a great trouble on his hands, and asked Grettir, in a whisper, what rede he would give thereto: "Since thou art called a famous man." Grettir bade him say yea to those things alone, which he thought of no shame to him.

The bearserk sat on his horse, and had a helm on his head, but the cheek-pieces were not made fast; he had an iron-rimmed shield before him, and went on in the most monstrous wise.

Now he said to the bonder, "Make one or other choice speedily, or what counsel is that big churl giving thee who stands there before thee; is it not so that he will play with me?"

Grettir said, "We are about equal herein, the bonder and I, for neither of us is skilled in arms."

Snoekoll said, "Ye will both of you be somewhat afraid to deal with me, if I grow wroth."

"That is known when it is tried," said Grettir.

Now the bearserk saw that there was some edging out of the matter going on, and he began to roar aloud, and bit the rim of his shield, and thrust it up into his mouth, and gaped over the corner of the shield, and went on very madly. Grettir took a sweep along over the field, and when he came alongside of the bearserk's horse, sent up his foot under the tail of the shield so hard, that the shield went up into the mouth of him, and his throat was riven asunder, and his jaws fell down on his breast. Then he wrought so that, all in one rush, he caught hold of the helmet with his left hand, and swept the viking off his horse; and with the other hand drew the short-sword that he was girt withal, and drave it at his neck, so that off the head flew. But when Snoekoll's fellows saw that, they fled, each his own way, and Grettir had no mind to follow, for he saw there was no heart in them.

The bonder thanked him well for his work and many other men too; and that deed was deemed to have been wrought both swiftly and hardily.

Grettir was there through Yule, and the farmer saw him off handsomely: then he went east to Tunsberg, and met his brother Thorstein; he received Grettir fondly, and asked of his travels and how he won the bearserk. Then Grettir sang a stave:

> *"There the shield that men doth save*
> *Mighty spurn with foot I gave.*
> *Snoekoll's throat it smote aright,*
> *The fierce follower of the fight,*
> *And by mighty dint of it*
> *Were the tofts of tooth-hedge split;*
> *The strong spear-walk's iron rim,*
> *Tore adown the jaws of him."*

Thorstein said, "Deft wouldst thou be at many things, kinsman, if mishaps went not therewith." Grettir answered, *"Deeds done will be told of."*

Chapter 41
Of Thorstein Dromond's Arms, and What He Deemed They Might Do

NOW GRETTIR WAS WITH THORSTEIN for the rest of the winter and on into the spring; and it befell one morning, as those brothers, Thorstein and Grettir, lay in their sleeping-loft, that Grettir had laid his arms outside the bed-clothes; and Thorstein was awake and saw it. Now Grettir woke up a little after, and then spake Thorstein:

"I have seen thine arms, kinsman," said he, "and I deem it nowise wonderful, though thy strokes fall heavy on many, for no man's arms have I seen like thine."

"Thou mayst know well enough," said Grettir, "that I should not have brought such things to pass as I have wrought, if I were not well knit."

"Better should I deem it," said Thorstein, "if they were slenderer and somewhat luckier withal." Grettir said, "True it is, as folk say, *No man makes himself;* but let me see thine arms," said he.

Thorstein did so; he was the longest and gauntest of men; and Grettir laughed, and said:

"No need to look at that longer; hooked together are the ribs in thee; nor, methinks, have I ever seen such tongs as thou bearest about, and I deem thee to be scarce of a woman's strength."

"That may be," said Thorstein; "yet shall thou know that these same thin arms shall avenge thee, else shall thou never be avenged; who may know what shall be, when all is over and done?"

No more is told of their talk together; the spring wore on, and Grettir took ship in the summer. The brothers parted in friendship, and saw each other never after.

Chapter 42
Of the Death of Asmund the Grey Haired

NOW MUST THE TALE be taken up where it was left before, for Thorbiorn Oxmain heard how Thorbiorn Tardy was slain, as aforesaid, and broke out into great wrath, and said it would please him well that *now this and now that should have strokes in his garth.*

Asmund the Greyhaired lay long sick that summer, and when he thought his ailings drew closer on him, he called to him his kin, and said that it was his will, that Atli should have charge of all his goods after his day.

"But my mind misgives me," said Asmund, "that thou mayst scarce sit quiet because of the iniquity of men, and I would that all ye of my kin should help him to the uttermost but of Grettir nought can I say, for methinks overmuch on a whirling wheel his life turns; and though he be a mighty man, yet I fear me that he will have to heed his own troubles more than the helping of his kin: but Illugi, though he be young, yet shall he become a man of prowess, if he keep himself whole."

So, when Asmund had settled matters about his sons as he would, his sickness lay hard on him, and in a little while he died, and was laid in earth at Biarg; for there had he let make a church; but his death his neighbours deemed a great loss.

Now Atli became a mighty bonder, and had many with him, and was a great gatherer of household-stuff. When the summer was far gone, he went out to Snowfellness to get him stockfish. He drave many horses, and rode from home to Meals in Ramfirth to Gamli his brother-in-law; and on this journey rode with him Grim Thorhallson, Gamli's brother, and another man withal. They rode west to Hawkdale Pass, and so on, as the road lay west to Ness: there they bought much stockfish, and loaded seven horses therewith, and turned homeward when they were ready.

Chapter 43
The Onset on Atli at the Pass and the Slaying of Gunnar and Thorgeir

THORBIORN OXMAIN HEARD that Atli and Grim were on a journey from home, and there were with him the sons of Thorir from the Pass, Gunnar and Thorgeir. Now Thorbiorn envied Atli for his many friendships, and therefore he egged on the two brothers, the sons of Thorir, to way-lay Atli as he came back from the outer ness. Then they rode home to the Pass, and abode there till Atli and his fellows went by with their train; but when they came as far as the homestead at the Pass, their riding was seen, and those brothers brake out swiftly with their house-carles and rode after them; but when Atli and his folk saw their faring, Atli bade them take the loads from the horses, "for perchance they will give me atonement for my house-carle, whom Gunnar slew last summer. Let us not begin the work, but defend ourselves if they be first to raise strife with us."

Now the brothers came up and leaped off their horses. Atli welcomed them, and asked for tidings: "Perchance, Gunnar, thou wilt give me some atonement for my house-carle."

Gunnar answered, "Something else is your due, men of Biarg, than that I should lay down aught good therefor; yea, atonement is due withal for the slaying of Thorbiorn, whom Grettir slew."

"It is not for me to answer thereto," said Atli; "nor art thou a suitor in that case."

Gunnar said he would stand in that stead none-the-less. "Come, let us set on them, and make much of it, that Grettir is not nigh them now."

Then they ran at Atli, eight of them altogether, but Atli and his folk were six.

Atli went before his men, and drew the sword, Jokul's gift, which Grettir had given him.

Then said Thorgeir, "Many like ways have those who deem themselves good; high aloft did Grettir bear his short-sword last summer on the Ramfirth-neck."

Atli answered, "Yea, he is more wont to deal in great deeds than I."

Thereafter they fought; Gunnar set on Atli exceeding fiercely, and was of the maddest; and when they had fought awhile, Atli said:

"No fame there is in thus killing workmen each for the other; more seeming it is that we ourselves play together, for never have I fought with weapons till now."

Gunnar would not have it so, but Atli bade his house-carles look to the burdens; "But I will see what these will do herein."

Then he went forward so mightily that Gunnar and his folk shrank back before him, and he slew two of the men of those brothers, and thereafter turned to meet Gunnar, and smote at him, so that the shield was cleft asunder almost below the handle, and the stroke fell on his leg below the knee, and then he smote at him again, and that was his bane.

Now is it to be told of Grim Thorhallson that he went against Thorgeir, and they strove together long, for each was a hardy man. Thorgeir saw the fall of his brother Gunnar, and was fain to draw off. Grim ran after him, and followed him till Thorgeir stumbled, and fell face foremost; then Grim smote at him with an axe betwixt the shoulders, so that it stood deep sunken therein.

Then they gave peace to three of their followers who were left; and thereafter they bound up their wounds, and laid the burdens on the horses, and then fared home, and made these man-slayings known.

Atli sat at home with many men through the winter. Thorbiorn Oxmain took these doings exceedingly ill, but could do naught therein because Atli was a man well befriended. Grim was with him through the winter, and Gamli, his brother-in-law; and there was Glum, son of Uspak, another kinsman-in-law of his, who at that time dwelt at Ere in Bitra. They had many men dwelling at Biarg, and great mirth was thereat through the winter.

Chapter 44
The Suit for the Slaying of the Sons of Thorir of the Pass

THORBIORN OXMAIN TOOK on himself the suit for the slaying of the sons of Thorir of the Pass. He made ready a suit against Grim and Atli, but they set forth for their defence onset and attack, to make those brothers fall unatoned. The suit was brought to the Hunawater Thing, and men came thronging to both sides. Atli had good help because he was exceeding strong of kin.

Now the friends of both stood forth and talked of peace, and all said that Atli's ways were good, a peaceful man, but stout in danger none-the-less.

Now Thorbiorn deemed that by nought would his honour be served better than by taking the peace offered. Atli laid down before-hand that he would have neither district outlawry nor banishment.

Then were men chosen for the judges. Thorvald, son of Asgeir, on Atli's side, and on Thorbiorn's, Solvi the Proud, who was the son of Asbrand, the son of Thorbrand, the son of Harald Ring, who had settled all Waterness from the Foreland up to Bond-maids River on the west, but on the east all up to Cross-river, and there right across to Berg-ridge, and all on that side of the Bergs down to the sea: this Solvi was a man of great stateliness and a wise man, therefore Thorbiorn chose him to be judge on his behoof.

Now they set forth their judgment, that half-fines should be paid for the sons of Thorir, but half fell away because of the onslaught and attack, and attempt on Atli's life, the slaying of Atli's house-carle, who was slain on Ramfirth-neck, and the slaying of those twain who fell with the sons of

Thorir were set off one against the other. Grim Thorhallson should leave dwelling in the district, but Atli alone should pay the money atonement.

This peace pleased Atli much, but Thorbiorn misliked it, but they parted appeased, as far as words went; howsoever it fell from Thorbiorn that their dealings would not be made an end of yet, if things went as he would.

But Atli rode home from the Thing, and thanked Thorvald well for his aid. Grim Thorhallson went south to Burgfirth, and dwelt at Gilsbank, and was a great bonder.

Chapter 45
Of the Slaying of Atli Asmundson

THERE WAS A MAN with Thorbiorn Oxmain who was called Ali; he was a house-carle, a somewhat lazy and unruly man.

Thorbiorn bade him work better, or he would beat him. Ali said he had no list thereto, and was beyond measure worrying. Thorbiorn would not abide it, and drave him under him, and handled him hardly. Then Ali went off from his service, and fared over the Neck to Midfirth, and made no stay till he came to Biarg. Atli was at home, and asked whither he went. He said that he sought service.

"Art thou not Thorbiorn's workman?" said Atli.

"That did not go off so pleasantly," said Ali; "I was not there long, and evil I deemed it while I was there, and we parted, so that I deemed his song about my throat nowise sweet; and I will go to dwell there no more, whatso else may hap to me; and true it is that much unlike ye are in the luck ye have with servants, and now I would fain work with thee if I might have the choice."

Atli answered, "Enough I have of workmen, though I reach not out to Thorbiorn's hands for such men as he has hired, and methinks there is no gain in thee, so go back to him."

Ali said, "Thither I go not of my own free-will."

And now he dwells there awhile; but one morning he went out to work with Atli's house-carles, and worked so that his hands were everywhere, and thus he went on till far into summer. Atli said nought to him, but bade give him meat, for he liked his working well.

Now Thorbiorn hears that Ali is at Biarg; then he rode to Biarg with two men, and called out Atli to talk with him. Atli went out and welcomed him.

Thorbiorn said, "Still wilt thou take up afresh ill-will against me, and trouble me, Atli. Why hast thou taken my workman? Wrongfully is this done."

Atli answered, "It is not proven to me that he is thy workman, nor will I withhold him from thee, if thou showest proofs thereof, yet am I loth to drag him out of my house."

"Thou must have thy will now," said Thorbiorn; "but I claim the man, and forbid him to work here; and I will come again another time, and I know not if we shall then part better friends than now."

Atli said, "I shall abide at home, and take what may come to hand."

Then Thorbiorn rode home; but when the workmen come home in the evening, Atli tells all the talk betwixt him and Thorbiorn, and bids Ali go his way, and said he should not abide there longer.

Ali answered, "True is the old saw, *over-praised and first to fail*. I deemed not that thou wouldst drive me away after I had toiled here all the summer enough to break my heart, and I hoped that thou wouldst stand up for me somehow; but this is the way of you, though ye look as if good might be hoped from you. I shall be beaten here before thine eyes if thou givest me not some defence or help."

Atli altered his mind at this talk of his, and had no heart now to drive him away from him.

Now the time wore, till men began hay-harvest, and one day, somewhat before midsummer, Thorbiorn Oxmain rode to Biarg, he was so attired that he had a helm on his head, and was girt with a sword, and had a spear in his hand. A barbed spear it was, and the barbs were broad.

It was wet abroad that day. Atli had sent his house-carles to the mowing, but some of them were north at Horn a-fishing. Atli was at home, and few other men.

Thorbiorn came there about high-noon; alone he was, and rode up to the outer door; the door was locked, and no men were abroad. Thorbiorn smote on the door, and then drew aback behind the houses, so that none might see him from the door. The home-folk heard that the door was knocked at, and a woman went out. Thorbiorn had an inkling of the woman, and would not let himself be seen, for he had a mind to do something else.

Now the woman went into the chamber, and Atli asked who was come there. She said, "I have seen nought stirring abroad." And even as they spake Thorbiorn let drive a great stroke on the door.

Then said Atli, "This one would see me, and he must have some errand with me, whatever may be the gain thereof to me."

Then he went forth and out of the door, and saw no one without. Exceeding wet it was, therefore he went not out, but laid a hand on either door-post, and so peered about him.

In that point of time Thorbiorn swung round before the door, and thrust the spear with both hands amidst of Atli, so that it pierced him through.

Then said Atli, when he got the thrust, *"Broad spears are about now,"* says he, and fell forward over the threshold.

Then came out women who had been in the chamber, and saw that Atli was dead. By then was Thorbiorn on horseback, and he gave out the slaying as having been done by his hand, and thereafter rode home.

The goodwife Asdis sent for her men, and Atli's corpse was laid out, and he was buried beside his father. Great mourning folk made for his death, for he had been a wise man, and of many friends.

No weregild came for the slaying of Atli, nor did any claim atonement for him, because Grettir had the blood-suit to take up if he should come out; so these matters stood still for that summer. Thorbiorn was little thanked for that deed of his; but he sat at peace in his homestead.

Chapter 46
Grettir Outlawed at the Thing at the Suit of Thorir of Garth

THIS SUMMER, whereof the tale was telling e'en now, a ship came out to Goose-ere before the Thing. Then was the news told of Grettir's travels, and therewithal men spake of that house-burning; and at that story was Thorir of Garth mad wroth, and deemed that there whereas Grettir was he had to look for vengeance for his sons. He rode with many men and set forth at the Thing the case for the burning, but men deemed they knew nought to say therein, while there was none to answer.

Thorir said that he would have nought, but that Grettir should be made an outlaw throughout the land for such misdeeds.

Then answered Skapti the Lawman, "Surely an ill deed it is, if things are as is said; but a tale is half told if one man tells it, for most folk are readiest to bring their stories to the worser side when there are two ways of telling them; now, therefore, I shall not give my word that Grettir be made guilty for this that has been done."

Now Thorir was a man of might in his district and a great chief, and well befriended of many great men; and he pushed on matters so hard that nought could avail to acquit Grettir; and so this Thorir made Grettir an outlaw throughout all the land, and was ever thenceforth the heaviest of all his foes, as things would oft show.

Now he put a price on his head, as was wont to be done with other wood-folk, and thereafter rode home.

Many men got saying that this was done rather by the high hand than according to law; but so it stood as it was done; and now nought else happed to tell of till past midsummer.

Chapter 47
Grettir Comes out to Iceland Again

WHEN SUMMER was far spent came Grettir Asmundson out to Whiteriver in Burgfirth; folk went down to the ship from thereabout, and these tidings came all at once to Grettir; the first, that his father was dead, the second, that his brother was slain, the third, that he himself was made an outlaw throughout all the land. Then sang Grettir this stave:

"Heavy tidings thick and fast
On the singer now are cast;
My father dead, my brother dead,
A price set upon my head;
Yet, O grove of Hedin's maid,
May these things one day be paid;
Yea upon another morn
Others may be more forlorn."

So men say that Grettir changed nowise at these tidings, but was even as merry as before.

Now he abode with the ship awhile, because he could get no horse to his mind. But there was a man called Svein, who dwelt at Bank up from Thingness, he was a good bonder and a merry man, and often sang such songs as were gamesome to hear; he had a mare black to behold, the swiftest of all horses, and her Svein called Saddle-fair.

Now Grettir went one night away from the wolds, but he would not that the chapmen should be ware of his ways; he got a black cape, and threw it over his clothes, and so was disguised; he went up past Thingness, and so up to Bank, and by then it was daylight. He saw a black horse in the homefield and went up to it, and laid bridle on it, leapt on the back of it, and rode up along Whiteriver, and below Bye up to Flokedale-river, and then up the tracks above Kalfness; the workmen at Bank got up now and told the bonder of the man who had got on his mare; he got up and laughed, and sang:

"One that helm-fire well can wield
Rode off from my well-fenced field,
Helm-stalk stole away from me
Saddle-fair, the swift to see;
Certes, more great deeds this Frey
Yet shall do in such-like way
As this was done; I deem him then
Most overbold and rash of men."

Then he took horse and rode after him; Grettir rode on till he came up to the homestead at Kropp; there he met a man called Hall, who said that he was going down to the ship at the Wolds; Grettir sang a stave:

"In broad-peopled lands say thou
> *That thou sawest even now*
> *Unto Kropp-farm's gate anigh,*
> *Saddle-fair and Elm-stalk high;*
> *That thou sawest stiff on steed*
> *(Get thee gone at greatest speed),*
> *One who loveth game and play*
> *Clad in cape of black today."*

Then they part, and Hall went down the track and all the way down to Kalfness, before Svein met him; they greeted one another hastily, then sang Svein:

> *"Sawest thou him who did me harm*
> *On my horse by yonder farm?*
> *Even such an one was he,*
> *Sluggish yet a thief to see;*
> *From the neighbours presently*
> *Doom of thief shall he abye*
> *And a blue skin shall he wear,*
> *If his back I come anear."*

"That thou mayst yet do," said Hall, "I saw that man who said that he rode on Saddle-fair, and bade me tell it over the peopled lands and settlements; great of growth he was, and was clad in a black cape."

"He deems he has something to fall back on," said the bonder, "but I shall ride after him and find out who he is."

Now Grettir came to Deildar-Tongue, and there was a woman without the door; Grettir went up to talk to her, and sang this stave:

> *"Say to guard of deep-sea's flame*
> *That here worm-land's haunter came;*
> *Well-born goddess of red gold,*
> *Thus let gamesome rhyme be told.*
> *"Giver forth of Odin's mead*
> *Of thy black mare have I need;*
> *For to Gilsbank will I ride,*
> *Meed of my rash words to bide."*

The woman learned this song, and thereafter Grettir rode on his way; Svein came there a little after, and she was not yet gone in, and as he came he sang this:

> *"What foreteller of spear-shower*
> *E'en within this nigh-passed hour,*
> *Swift through the rough weather rode*
> *Past the gate of this abode?*
> *He, the hound-eyed reckless one,*
> *By all good deeds left alone,*

Surely long upon this day
From my hands will flee away."

Then she told him what she had been bidden to; he thought over the ditty, and said, "It is not unlike that he will be no man to play with; natheless, I will find him out."

Now he rode along the peopled lands, and each man ever saw the other's riding; and the weather was both squally and wet.

Grettir came to Gilsbank that day, and when Grim Thorhallson knew thereof, he welcomed him with great joy, and bade him abide with him. This Grettir agreed to; then he let loose Saddle-fair, and told Grim how she had been come by. Therewith came Svein, and leapt from his horse, and saw his own mare, and sang this withal:

"Who rode on my mare away?
What is that which thou wilt pay?
Who a greater theft has seen?
What does the cowl-covered mean?"

Grettir by then had doft his wet clothes, and he heard the stave, and answered:

"I did ride thy mare to Grim
(Thou art feeble weighed with him),
Little will I pay to thee,
Yet good fellows let us be."

"Well, so be it then," said the farmer, "and the ride is well paid for."

Then each sang his own songs, and Grettir said he had no fault to find, though he failed to hold his own; the bonder was there that night, and the twain of them together, and great game they made of this: and they called all this Saddle-fair's lays. Next morning the bonder rode home, and he and Grettir parted good friends.

Now Grim told Grettir of many things from the north and Midfirth, that had befallen while he was abroad, and this withal, that Atli was unatoned, and how that Thorbiorn Oxmain waxed so great, and was so high-handed, that it was not sure that goodwife Asdis might abide at Biarg if matters still went so.

Grettir abode but few nights with Grim, for he was fain that no news should go before him north over the Heaths. Grim bade him come thither if he should have any need of safeguard.

"Yet shall I shun being made guilty in law for the harbouring of thee."

Grettir said he did well. "But it is more like that later on I may need thy good deed more."

Now Grettir rode north over Twodaysway, and so to Biarg, and came there in the dead of night, when all folk were asleep save his mother. He went in by the back of the house and through a door that was there, for the ways of the house were well known to him, and came to the hall, and got to his mother's bed, and groped about before him.

She asked who was there, and Grettir told her; then she sat up and kissed him, and sighed withal, heavily, and spake, "Be welcome; son," she said, "but my joyance in my sons is slipping from me; for he is slain who was of most avail, and thou art made an outlaw and a guilty man, and the third is so young; that he may do nought for me."

"An old saw it is," said Grettir, "*Even so shall bale be bettered, by biding greater bale*; but there are more things to be thought of by men than money atonements alone, and most like it is that

Atli will be avenged; but as to things that may fall to me, many must even take their lot at my hand in dealing with me, and like it as they may."

She said that was not unlike. And now Grettir was there a while with the knowledge of few folk; and he had news of the doings of the folk of the country-side; and men knew not that Grettir was come into Midfirth: but he heard that Thorbiorn Oxmain was at home with few men; and that was after the homefield hay-harvest.

Chapter 48
The Slaying of Thorbiorn Oxmain

ON A FAIR DAY Grettir rode west over the Necks to Thorodstead, and came there about noon, and knocked at the door; women came out and welcomed him, but knew him not; he asked for Thorbiorn, but they said he was gone to the meadow to bind hay, and with him his son of sixteen winters, who was called Arnor; for Thorbiorn was a very busy man, and well-nigh never idle.

So when Grettir knew this, he bade them well betide, and went his way on the road toward Reeks, there a marsh stretches down from the hill-side, and on it was much grass to mow, and much hay had Thorbiorn made there, and now it was fully dry, and he was minded to bind it up for home, he and the lad with him, but a woman did the raking.

Now Grettir rode from below up into the field, but the father and son were higher up, and had bound one load, and were now at another; Thorbiorn had set his shield and sword against the load, and the lad had a hand-axe beside him.

Now Thorbiorn saw a man coming, and said to the lad, "Yonder is a man riding toward us, let us leave binding the hay, and know what he will with us."

So did they, and Grettir leapt off his horse; he had a helm on his head, and was girt with the short-sword, and bore a great spear in his hand, a spear without barbs, and the socket inlaid with silver. Now he sat down and knocked out the socket-nail, because he would not that Thorbiorn should cast the spear back.

Then said Thorbiorn, "He is a big man, and no man in field know I, if that is not Grettir Asmundson, and he must needs think he has enough against us; so let us meet him sharply, and let him see no signs of failing in us. We shall deal cunningly; for I will go against him in front, and take thou heed how matters go betwixt us, for I will trust myself against any man if I have one alone to meet; but do thou go behind him, and drive the axe at him with both hands atwixt his shoulders; thou needest not fear that he will do thee hurt, as his back will be turned to thee."

Neither Thorbiorn nor his son had a helm.

Now Grettir got into the mead, and when he came within spear-throw of them, he cast his spear at Thorbiorn, but the head was looser on the shaft than he deemed it would be, and it swerved in its flight, and fell down from the shaft to the earth: then Thorbiorn took his shield, and put it before him, but drew his sword and went against Grettir when he knew him; then Grettir drew his short-sword, and turned about somewhat, so that he saw how the lad stood at his back, wherefore he kept himself free to move here or there, till he saw that the lad was come within reach of him, and therewith he raised the short-sword high aloft, and sent it back against Arnor's head so mightily that the skull was shattered, and that was his bane. Then Thorbiorn ran against Grettir and smote at him, but he thrust forth his buckler with his left hand, and put the blow from him, and smote with the short-sword withal, and cleft the shield of Thorbiorn, and the short-sword smote so hard into his head that it went even unto the brain, and he fell dead to earth beneath that stroke, nor did Grettir give him any other wound.

Then he sought for his spear-head, and found it not; so he went to his horse and rode out to Reeks, and there told of the slayings. Withal the woman who was in the meadow saw the slayings, and ran home full of fear, and said that Thorbiorn was slain, and his son both; this took those of the house utterly unawares, for they knew nought of Grettir's travelling. So were men sent for to the next homestead, and soon came many folk, and brought the bodies to church. Thorod Drapa-Stump took up the blood-suit for these slayings and had folk a-field forthwith.

But Grettir rode home to Biarg, and found his mother, and told her what had happed; and she was glad thereat, and said that now he got to be like unto the Waterdale kin. "Yet will this be the root and stem of thine outlawry, and I know for sooth that thou mayest not abide here long because of the kin of Thorbiorn; but now may they know that thou mayest be angered."

Grettir sang this stave thereupon:

"Giant's friend fell dead to earth
On the grass of Wetherfirth,
No fierce fighting would avail,
Oxmain in the Odin's gale.
So, and in no other wise,
Has been paid a fitting price
For that Atli, who of yore,
Lay dead-slain anigh his door."

Goodwife Asdis said that was true; "But I know not what rede thou art minded to take?"

Grettir said that he would seek help of his friends and kin in the west; "But on thee shall no trouble fall for my sake," said he.

So he made ready to go, and mother and son parted in love; but first he went to Meals in Ramfirth, and told Gamli his brother-in-law all, even as it had happed, concerning the slaying of Thorbiorn.

Gamli told him he must needs depart from Ramfirth while Thorbiorn's kin had their folk about; "But our aid in the suit for Atli's slaying we shall yield thee as we may."

So thereafter Grettir rode west over Laxdale-heath, and stayed not till he came to Liarskogar to Thorstein Kuggson, where he dwelt long that autumn.

Chapter 49
The Gathering to Avenge Thorbiorn Oxmain

THOROD DRAPA-STUMP sought tidings of this who might have slain Thorbiorn and his son, and when he came to Reeks, it was told him that Grettir had been there and given out the slayings as from his hand. Now, Thorod deemed he saw how things had come to pass; so he went to Biarg, and there found many folk, but he asked if Grettir were there.

The goodwife said he had ridden away, and that she would not slip him into hiding-places if he were there.

"Now ye will be well pleased that matters have so been wrought; nor was the slaying of Atli over-avenged, though this was paid for it. Ye asked not then what grief of heart I had; and now, too, it is well that things are even so."

Therewith they rode home, and found it not easy to do aught therein.

Now that spear-head which Grettir lost was not found till within the memory of men living now; it was found in the latter days of Sturla Thordson the lawman, and in that marsh where Thorbiorn fell, which is now called Spear-mead; and that sign men have to show that Thorbiorn was slain there, though in some places it is said that he was slain on Midfit.

Thorod and his kin heard that Grettir abode at Liarskogar; then they gathered men, and were minded to go thither; but when Gamli of Meals was ware thereof, he made Thorstein and Grettir sure of the farings of the Ramfirthers; and when Thorstein knew it, he sent Grettir in to Tongue to Snorri Godi, for then there was no strife between them, and Thorstein gave that counsel to Grettir that he should pray Snorri the Godi for his watch and ward; but if he would not grant it, he made Grettir go west to Reek-knolls to Thorgils Arisen, "and he will take thee to him through this winter, and keep within the Westfirths till these matters are settled."

Grettir said he would take good heed to his counsels; then he rode into Tongue, and found Snorri the Godi, and talked with him, and prayed him to take him in.

Snorri answered, "I grow an old man now, and loth am I to harbour outlawed men if no need drive me thereto. What has come to pass that the elder put thee off from him?"

Grettir said that Thorstein had often done well to him; "But more shall I need than him alone, if things are to go well."

Said Snorri, "My good word I shall put in for thee if that may avail thee aught, but in some other place than with me must thou seek a dwelling."

With these words they parted, and Grettir turned west to Reekness; the Ramfirthers with their band got as far as Samstead, and there they heard that Grettir had departed from Liarskogar, and thereat they went back home.

Chapter 50
Grettir and the Foster-brothers at Reek-Knolls

NOW GRETTIR CAME to Reek-knolls about winter-nights, and prayed Thorgils for winter abode; Thorgils said, that for him as for other free men meat was ready; "but the fare of guests here is nowise choice." Grettir said he was not nice about that.

"There is yet another thing here for thy trouble," said Thorgils: "Men are minded to harbour here, who are deemed somewhat hard to keep quiet, even as those foster-brothers, Thorgeir and Thormod; I wot not how meet it may be for you to be together; but their dwelling shall ever be here if they will it so: now mayst thou abide here if thou wilt, but I will not have it that either of you make strife with the other."

Grettir said he would not be the first to raise strife with any man, and so much the less as the bonder's will was such.

A little after came those foster-brothers home; things went not merrily betwixt Thorgeir and Grettir, but Thormod bore himself well. Goodman Thorgils said to the foster-brothers even as he had said to Grettir; and of such worth they held him, that neither cast an untoward word at the other although their minds went nowise the same way: and so wore the early winter.

Now men say that Thorgils owned those isles, which are called Olaf's-isles, and lie out in the firth a sea-mile and a half off Reekness; there had bonder Thorgils a good ox that he might not fetch home in the autumn; and he was ever saying that he would fain have him against Yule. Now, one day those foster-brothers got ready to seek the ox, if a third man could be gotten to their aid: Grettir offered to go with them, and they were well pleased thereat; they went, the three of them, in a ten-oared boat: the weather was cold, and the wind shifting from the north, and the craft lay up on Whaleshead-holm.

Now they sail out, and somewhat the wind got up, but they came to the isle and got hold of the ox; then asked Grettir which they would do, bear the ox aboard or keep hold of the craft, because the surf at the isle was great; then they bade him hold the boat; so he stood amidships on that side which looked from shore, and the sea took him up to the shoulder-blades, yet he held her so that she moved nowise: but Thorgeir took the ox behind and Thormod before, and so hove it down to the boat; then they sat down to row, and Thormod rowed in the bows, Thorgeir amidships, and Grettir aft, and therewith they made out into the open bay; but when they came off Goat-rock, a squall caught them, then said Thorgeir, "The stern is fain to lag behind."

Then said Grettir, "The stern will not be left if the rowing afore be good."

Thereat Thorgeir fell to rowing so hard that both the tholes were broken: then said he, "Row on, Grettir, while I mend the thole-pins."

Then Grettir pulled mightily while Thorgeir did his mending, but when Thorgeir took to rowing again, the oars had got so worn that Grettir shook them asunder on the gunwale.

"Better," quoth Thormod, "to row less and break nought."

Then Grettir caught up two unshapen oar beams that lay in the boat and bored large holes in the gunwales, and rowed withal so mightily that every beam creaked, but whereas the craft was good, and the men somewhat of the brisker sort, they reached Whaleshead-holm.

Then Grettir asked whether they would rather go home with the ox or haul up the boat; they chose to haul up the boat, and hauled it up with all the sea that was in it, and all the ice, for it was much covered with icicles: but Grettir led home the ox, and exceeding stiff in tow he was, and very fat, and he grew very weary, and when they came up below Titling-stead could go no more.

The foster-brothers went up to the house, for neither would help the other in his allotted work; Thorgils asked after Grettir, but they told him where they had parted; then he sent men to meet him, and when they came down to Cave-knolls they saw how there came towards them a man with a neat on his back, and lo, there was Grettir come, bearing the ox: then all men wondered at his great might.

Now Thorgeir got very envious of Grettir's strength, and one day somewhat after Yule, Grettir went alone to bathe; Thorgeir knew thereof, and said to Thormod, "Let us go on now, and try how Grettir will start if I set on him as he comes from his bathing."

"That is not my mind," said Thormod, "and no good wilt thou get from him."

"I will go though," says Thorgeir; and therewith he went down to the slope, and bore aloft an axe.

By then was Grettir walking up from the bath, and when they met, Thorgeir said; "Is it true, Grettir," says he, "that thou hast said so much as that thou wouldst never run before one man?"

"That I know not for sure," said Grettir, "yet but a little way have I run before thee."

Thorgeir raised aloft the axe, but therewith Grettir ran in under Thorgeir and gave him an exceeding great fall: then said Thorgeir to Thormod, "Wilt thou stand by and see this fiend drive me down under him?"

Thormod caught hold of Grettir's feet, and was minded to pull him from off Thorgeir, but could do nought thereat: he was girt with a short-sword and was going to draw it, when goodman Thorgils came up and bade them be quiet and have nought to do with Grettir.

So did they and turned it all to game, and no more is told of their dealings; and men thought Thorgils had great luck in that he kept such reckless men in good peace.

But when spring came they all went away; Grettir went round to Codfirth, and he was asked, how he liked the fare of the winter abode at Reek-knolls; he answered, "There have I ever been as fain as might be of my meals when I got at them."

Thereafter he went west over the heaths.

Chapter 51
Of the Suit for the Slaying of Thorbiorn Oxmain, and How Thorir of Garth Would Not that Grettir Should Be Made Sackless

THORGILS ARISON RODE to the Thing with many men; and thither came all the great men of the land. Now Thorgils and Skapti the Lawman soon met, and fell to talking.

Then said Skapti, "Is it true, Thorgils, that thou hast harboured those three men through the winter who are deemed to be the wildest of all men; yea, and all of them outlawed withal, and yet hast kept them so quiet, that no one of them has done hurt to the other?"

Thorgils said it was true enough.

Skapti said that great might over men it showed forth in him; "But how goes it, thinkest thou, with the temper of each of them; and which of them thinkest thou the bravest man?"

Thorgils said, "I deem they are all of them full stout of heart; but two of them I deem know what fear is, and yet in unlike ways; for Thormod is a great believer and fears God much; but Grettir is so fearsome in the dark, that he dares go nowhither after dusk has set in, if he may do after his own mind. But my kinsman Thorgeir I deem knows not how to fear."

"Yea, so it is with their minds as thou sayest," said Skapti; and with that they left talking.

Now, at this Althing Thorod Drapa-Stump brought forward a suit for the slaying of Thorbiorn Oxmain, which he had not brought to a hearing at the Hunawater Thing, because of the kin of Atli, and he deemed that here his case would be less like to be thrown over. The kinsmen of Atli sought counsel of Skapti about the case; and he said he saw in it a lawful defence, so that full atonement would be forthcoming therefor. Then were these matters laid unto umpiredom, and most men were minded that the slayings of Atli and Thorbiorn should be set one against the other.

But when Skapti knew that, he went to the judges, and asked whence they had that? They said that they deemed the slain men were bonders of equal worth.

Then Skapti asked, which was the first, the outlawry of Grettir or the slaying of Atli? So, when that was reckoned up, there was a week's space betwixt Grettir's outlawry at the Althing and the slaying of Atli, which befell just after it.

Then said Skapti, "Thereof my mind misgave me, that ye had made an oversight in setting on foot the suit in that ye made him a suitor, who was outlawed already, and could neither defend nor prosecute his own case. Now I say that Grettir has nought to do with the case of the slaying, but let him take up the blood-suit, who is nighest of kin by law."

Then said Thorod Drapa-Stump, "And who shall answer for the slaying of Thorbiorn my brother?"

"See ye to that for yourselves," said Skapti; "but the kin of Grettir will never pour out fee for him or his works, if no peace is to be bought for him."

Now when Thorvald Asgeirson was aware that Grettir was set aside from following the blood-suit, he and his sought concerning who was the next of kin; and that turned out to be Skeggi, son of Gamli of Meals, and Uspak, son of Glum of Ere in Bitra; they were both of them exceeding zealous and pushing.

Now must Thorod give atonement for Atli's slaying, and two hundreds in silver he had to pay.

Then spake Snorri the Godi, "Will ye now, Ramfirthers," says he, "that this money-fine should fall away, and that Grettir be made sackless withal, for in my mind it is that as a guilty man he will be sorely felt?"

Grettir's kin took up his word well, and said that they heeded the fee nought if he might have peace and freedom. Thorod said that he saw Grettir's lot would be full of heavy trouble, and made as if he would take the offer, for his part. Then Snorri bade them first know if Thorir of Garth would give his leave to Grettir being made free; but when Thorir heard thereof he turned away exceeding wroth, and said that Grettir should never either get out of his outlawry or be brought out of it: "And the more to bring that about," said he, "a greater price shall be put on his head than on the head of any outlaw or wood-man yet."

So, when he took the thing so ill, the freeing of Grettir came to nought, and Gamli and his fellows took the money to them, and kept it in their ward; but Thorod Drapa-Stump had no atonement for his brother Thorbiorn.

Now Thorir and Thorod set each of them on Grettir's head three marks of silver, and that folk deemed a new thing, for never had any greater price been laid down to such an end before than three marks in all.

Snorri said it was unwisely done to make a sport of keeping a man in outlawry who might work so much ill, and that many a man would have to pay for it.

But now men part and ride home from the Thing.

Chapter 52
How Grettir Was Taken by the Icefirth Carles

WHEN GRETTIR CAME OVER Codfirth-heath down into Longdale, he swept up unsparingly the goods of the petty bonders, and had of every man what he would; from some he took weapons, from some clothes; and these folk gave up in very unlike ways; but as soon as he was gone, all said they gave them unwillingly.

In those days dwelt in Waterfirth Vermund the Slender, the brother of Slaying-Styr; he had to wife Thorbiorg, the daughter of Olaf Peacock, son of Hoskuld. She was called Thorbiorg the Big; but at the time that Grettir was in Longdale had Vermund ridden to the Thing.

Now Grettir went over the neck to Bathstead. There dwelt a man called Helgi, who was the biggest of bonders thereabout: from there had Grettir a good horse, which the bonder owned, and thence he went to Giorvidale, where farmed a man named Thorkel. He was well stored with victuals, yet a mannikin withal: therefrom took Grettir what he would, nor durst Thorkel blame him or withhold aught from him.

Thence went Grettir to Ere, and out along the side of the firth, and had from every farm victuals and clothes, and dealt hardly with many; so that most men deemed him a heavy trouble to live under.

Now he fared fearlessly withal, and took no keep of himself, and so went on till he came to Waterfirth-dale, and went to the mountain-dairy, and there he dwelt a many nights, and lay in the woods there, and took no heed to himself; but when the herdsmen knew that, they went to the farm, and said that to that stead was a fiend come whom they deemed nowise easy to deal with; then the farmers gathered together, and were thirty men in all: they lurked in the wood, so that Grettir was unaware of them, and let a shepherd spy on Grettir till they might get at him, yet they wotted not clearly who the man was.

Now so it befell that on a day as Grettir lay sleeping, the bonders came upon him, and when they saw him they took counsel how they should take him at the least cost of life, and settled so that ten men should leap on him, while some laid bonds on his feet; and this they did, and threw themselves on him, but Grettir broke forth so mightily that they fell from off him, and he got to his knees, yet thereby they might cast the bonds over him, and round about his feet; then Grettir spurned two of them so hard about the ears that they lay stunned on the earth. Now one after the other rushed at him, and he struggled hard and long, yet had they might to overcome him at the last, and so bound him.

Thereafter they talked over what they should do with him, and they bade Helgi of Bathstead take him and keep him in ward till Vermund came home from the Thing. He answered:

"Other things I deem more helpful to me than to let my house-carles sit over him, for my lands are hard to work, nor shall he ever come across me."

Then they bade Thorkel of Giorvidale take and keep him, and said that he was a man who had enow.

But Thorkel spake against it, and said that for nought would he do that: "Whereas I live alone in my house with my Carline, far from other men; nor shall ye lay that box on me," said he.

"Then, Thoralf of Ere," said they, "do thou take Grettir and do well to him till after the Thing; or else bring him on to the next farm, and be answerable that he get not loose, but deliver him bound as now thou hast him."

He answers, "Nay, I will not take Grettir, for I have neither victuals nor money to keep him withal, nor has he been taken on my land, and I deem it more trouble than honour to take him, or to have aught to do with him, nor shall he ever come into my house."

Thereafter they tried it with every bonder, but one and all spake against it; and after this talk have merry men made that lay which is hight Grettir's-faring, and added many words of good game thereto for the sport of men.

So when they had talked it over long, they said, with one assent, that they would not make ill hap of their good-hap; so they went about and straightway reared up a gallows there in the wood, with the mind to hang Grettir, and made great clatter thereover.

Even therewith they see six folk riding down below in the dale, and one in coloured clothes, and they guessed that there would goodwife Thorbiorg be going from Waterfirth; and so it was, and she was going to the mountain-dairy. Now she was a very stirring woman, and exceeding wise; she had the ruling of the neighbourhood, and settled all matters, when Vermund was from home. Now she turned to where the men were gathered, and was helped off her horse, and the bonders gave her good welcome.

Then said she, "What have ye here? or who is the big-necked one who sits in bonds yonder?"

Grettir named himself, and greeted her.

She spake again, "What drove thee to this, Grettir," says she, "that thou must needs do riotously among my Thing-men?"

"I may not look to everything; I must needs be somewhere," said he.

"Great ill luck it is," says she, "that these milksops should take thee in such wise that none should fall before thee. What are ye minded to do with him?"

The bonders told her that they were going to tie him up to the gallows for his lawlessness.

She answers, "Maybe Grettir is guilty enough therefor, but it is too great a deed for you, Icefirthers, to take his life, for he is a famous man, and of mighty kin, albeit he is no lucky man; but now what wilt thou do for thy life, Grettir, if I give it thee?"

He answered, "What sayest thou thereto?"

She said, "Thou shalt make oath to work no evil riots here in Icefirth, and take no revenge on whomsoever has been at the taking of thee."

Grettir said that she should have her will, and so he was loosed; and he says of himself that at that time of all times did he most rule his temper, when he smote them not as they made themselves great before him.

Now Thorbiorg bade him go home with her, and gave him a horse for his riding; so he went to Waterfirth and abode there till Vermund came home, and the housewife did well to him, and for this deed was she much renowned far and wide in the district.

But Vermund took this ill at his coming home, and asked what made Grettir there? Then Thorbiorg told him how all had gone betwixt Grettir and the Icefirthers.

"What reward was due to him," said Vermund, "that thou gavest him his life?"

"Many grounds there were thereto," said Thorbiorg; "and this, first of all, that thou wilt be deemed a greater chief than before in that thou hast a wife who has dared to do such a deed; and then withal surely would Hrefna his kinswoman say that I should not let men slay him; and, thirdly, he is a man of the greatest prowess in many wise."

"A wise wife thou art withal," said Vermund, "and have thou thanks therefor."

Then he said to Grettir, "Stout as thou art, but little was to be paid for thee, when thou must needs be taken of mannikins; but so ever it fares with men riotous."

Then Grettir sang this stave:

"Ill luck-to me
That I should be
On sea-roof-firth
Borne unto earth;
Ill luck enow
To lie alow,
This head of mine
Griped fast by swine."

"What were they minded to do to thee," said Vermund, "when they took thee there?"
Quoth Grettir:

"There many men
Bade give me then
E'en Sigar's meed
For lovesome deed;
Till found me there
That willow fair,
Whose leaves are praise,
Her stems good days."

Vermund asked, "Would they have hanged thee then, if they alone had had to meddle with matters?"
Said Grettir:

"Yea, to the snare
That dangled there
My head must I
Soon bring anigh;
But Thorbiorg came
The brightest dame,
And from that need
The singer freed."

Then said Vermund, "Did she bid thee to her?"

Grettir answered:

> *"Sif's lord's good aid,*
> *My saviour, bade*
> *To take my way*
> *With her that day;*
> *So did it fall;*
> *And therewithal*
> *A horse she gave;*
> *Good peace I have."*

"Mighty will thy life be and troublous," said Vermund; "but now thou hast learned to beware of thy foes; but I have no will to harbour thee, and gain therefor the ill-will of many rich men; but best is it for thee to seek thy kinsmen, though few men will be willing to take thee in if they may do aught else; nor to most men art thou an easy fellow withal."

Now Grettir was in Waterfirth a certain space, and then fared thence to the Westfirths, and sought shelter of many great men; but something ever came to pass whereby none of them would harbour him.

Chapter 53
Grettir with Thorstein Kuggson

WHEN THE AUTUMN was somewhat spent, Grettir turned back by the south, and made no stay till he came to Liarskogar to Thorstein Kuggson, his kinsman, and there had he good welcome, for Thorstein bade him abide there through the winter, and that bidding he agreed to. Thorstein was a busy man and a good smith, and kept men close to their work; but Grettir had little mind to work, wherefore their tempers went but little together.

Thorstein had let make a church at his homestead; and a bridge he had made out from his house, wrought with great craft; for in the outside bridge, under the beams that held it up, were rings wrought all about, and din-bells, so that one might hear over to Scarf-stead, half a sea-mile off, if aught went over the bridge, because of the shaking of the rings. Thorstein had much to do over this work, for he was a great worker of iron; but Grettir went fiercely at the iron-smiting, yet was in many minds thereover; but he was quiet through the winter, so that nought befell worthy telling. But when the Ramfirthers knew that Grettir was with Thorstein, they had their band afoot as soon as spring came. So when Thorstein knew that, he bade Grettir seek some other shelter than his house, "For I see thou wilt not work, and men who will do nought are not meet men for me."

"Where wouldst thou have me go, then?" said Grettir.

Thorstein bade him fare to the south country, and find his kin, "But come to me if they avail thee not."

Now so Grettir wrought that he went south to Burgfirth, to Grim Thorhallson, and dwelt there till over the Thing. Then Grim sent him on to Skapti the Lawman at Hjalli, and he went south by the lower heaths and stayed not till he came to Thorhall, son of Asgrim, son of Ellida-grim, and went little in the peopled lands. Thorhall knew Grettir because of his father and mother, and, indeed, by then was the name of Grettir well renowned through all the land because of his great deeds.

Thorhall was a wise man, and he did well to Grettir, but would not let him abide there long.

Chapter 54
Grettir Meets Hallmund on the Keel

NOW GRETTIR FARED from Tongue up to Hawkdale, and thence north upon the Keel, and kept about there long that summer; nor was there trust of him that he would not take men's goods from them, as they went from or to the north over the Keel, because he was hard put to it to get wares.

Now on a day, when as Grettir would keep about the north at Doveness-path, he saw a man riding from the north over the Keel; he was huge to behold on horseback, and had a good horse, and an embossed bridle well wrought; another horse he had in tow and bags thereon; this man had withal a slouched hat on his head, nor could his face be clearly seen.

Now Grettir looked hard at the horse and the goods thereon, and went to meet the man, and greeting him asked his name, but he said he was called Air. "I wot well what thou art called," said he, "for thou shalt be Grettir the Strong, the son of Asmund. Whither art thou bound?"

"As to the place I have not named it yet," said Grettir; "but as to my errand, it is to know if thou wilt lay down some of the goods thou farest with."

Said Air, "Why should I give thee mine own, or what wilt thou give me therefor?"

Grettir answers, "Hast thou not heard that I take, and give no money again? and yet it seems to most men that I get what I will."

Said Air, "Give such choice as this to those who deem it good, but not thus will I give up what I have; let each of us go his own way."

And therewithal he rode forth past Grettir and spurred his horse.

"Nay, we part not so hastily," said Grettir, and laid hold of the reins of Air's horse in front of his hands, and held on with both hands.

Said Air, "Go thy ways, nought thou hast of me if I may hold mine own."

"That will now be proven," said Grettir.

Now Air stretched his hands down the head-gear and laid hold of the reins betwixt Grettir's hands and the snaffle-rings and dragged at them so hard that Grettir's hands were drawn down along the reins, till Air dragged all the bridle from him.

Grettir looked into the hollow of his hands, and saw that this man must have strength in claws rather than not, and he looked after him, and said, "Whither art thou minded to fare?"

Air answered and sang:

> *"To the Kettle's side*
> *Now will I ride,*
> *Where the waters fall*
> *From the great ice-wall;*
> *If thou hast mind*
> *There mayest thou find*
> *With little stone*
> *Fist's land alone."*

Grettir said, "It is of no avail to seek after thine abode if thou tellest of it no clearer than this."

Then Air spake and sang:

> *"I would not hide*
> *Where I abide,*

> *If thou art fain*
> *To see me again;*
> *From that lone weald,*
> *Over Burgfirth field,*
> *That ye men name*
> *Balljokul, I came."*

Thereat they parted, and Grettir sees that he has no strength against this man; and therewithal he sang a stave:

> *"Too far on this luckless day,*
> *Atli, good at weapon-play,*
> *Brisk Illugi were from me;*
> *Such-like oft I shall not be*
> *As I was, when I must stand*
> *With the reins drawn through my hand*
> *By the unflinching losel Air.*
> *Maids weep when they know I fear."*

Thereafter Grettir went to the south from the Keel; and rode to Hjalli and found Skapti, and prayed for watch and ward from him.

Skapti said, "It is told me that thou farest somewhat lawlessly, and layest hand on other men's goods; and this beseems thee ill, great of kin as thou art. Now all would make a better tale, if thou didst not rob and reive; but whereas I have to bear the name of lawman in the land, folk would not abide that I should take outlawed men to me, and break the laws thereby. I will that thou seek some place wherein thou wilt not have need to take men's goods from them." Grettir said he would do even so, yet withal that he might scarcely be alone because he so feared the dark.

Skapti said that of that one thing then, which he deemed the best, he might not avail himself; "But put not such trust in any as to fare as thou didst in the Westfirths; it has been many a man's bane that he has been too trustful."

Grettir thanked him for his wholesome redes, and so turned back to Burgfirth in the autumn, and found Grim Thorhallson, his friend, and told him of Skapti's counsels; so Grim bade him fare north to Fishwater lakes on Ernewaterheath; and thus did he.

Chapter 55
Of Grettir on Ernewaterheath, and His Dealings with Grim There

GRETTIR WENT UP TO Ernewaterheath and made there a hut for himself (whereof are yet signs left) and dwelt there, for now was he fain to do anything rather than rob and reive; he got him nets and a boat and caught fish for his food; exceeding dreary he deemed it in the mountains, because he was so fearsome of the dark.

But when other outlaws heard this, that Grettir was come down there, many of them had a mind to see him, because they thought there was much avail of him. There was a man called Grim, a Northlander, who was an outlaw; with him the Northlanders made a bargain that he should slay Grettir, and promised him freedom and gifts of money, if he should bring it to pass; so he went to meet Grettir, and prayed him to take him in.

Grettir answers, "I see not how thou art the more holpen for being with me, and troublous to heed are ye wood-folk; but ill I deem it to be alone, if other choice there were; but I will that such an one only be with me as shall do whatso work may befall."

Grim said he was of no other mind, and prayed hard that he might dwell there; then Grettir let himself be talked round, and took him in; and he was there on into the winter, and watched Grettir, but deemed it no little matter to set on him. Grettir misdoubted him, and had his weapons by his side night and day, nor durst Grim attack him while he was awake.

But one morning whenas Grim came in from fishing, he went into the hut and stamped with his foot, and would know whether Grettir slept, but he started in nowise, but lay still; and the short-sword hung up over Grettir's head.

Now Grim thought that no better chance would happen, so he made a great noise, that Grettir might chide him, therefore, if he were awake, but that befell not. Now he thought that Grettir must surely be asleep, so he went stealthily up to the bed and reached out for the short-sword, and took it down, and unsheathed it. But even therewith Grettir sprang up on to the floor, and caught the short-sword just as the other raised it aloft, and laid the other hand on Grim betwixt the shoulders, and cast him down with such a fall, that he was well-nigh stunned; "Ah, such hast thou shown thyself," said he, "though thou wouldest give me good hope of thee." Then he had a true story from him, and thereafter slew him.

And now Grettir deemed he saw what it was to take in wood-folk, and so the winter wore; and nothing Grettir thought to be of more trouble than his dread of the dark.

Chapter 56
Of Grettir and Thorir Redbeard

NOW THORIR OF GARTH heard where Grettir had set himself down, and was fain to set afoot some plot whereby he might be slain. There was a man called Thorir Redbeard; he was the biggest of men, and a great man-slayer, and therefore was he made outlaw throughout the land. Thorir of Garth sent word to him, and when they met he bade him go on an errand of his, and slay Grettir the Strong. Redbeard said that was no easy task, and that Grettir was a wise man and a wary.

Thorir bade him make up his mind to this; "A manly task it is for so brisk a fellow as thou; but I shall bring thee out of thine outlawry, and therewithal give thee money enough."

So by that counsel Redbeard abode, and Thorir told him how he should go about the winning of Grettir. So thereafter he went round the land by the east, for thus he deemed his faring would be the less misdoubted; so he came to Ernewaterheath when Grettir had been there a winter. But when he met Grettir, he prayed for winter dwelling at his hands.

Grettir answered, "I cannot suffer you often to play the like play with me that he did who came here last autumn, who bepraised me cunningly, and when he had been here a little while lay in wait for my life; now, therefore, I have no mind to run the risk any more of the taking in of wood-folk."

Thorir answered, "My mind goes fully with thine in that thou deemest ill of outlawed men: and thou wilt have heard tell of me as of a man-slayer and a misdoer, but not as of a doer of such foul deeds as to betray my master. Now, *ill it is ill to be*, for many deem others to do after their own ways; nor should I have been minded to come hither, if I might have had a choice of better things; withal I deem we shall not easily be won while we stand together; thou mightest risk trying at first how thou likest me, and let me go my ways whenso thou markest ill faith in me."

Grettir answered, "Once more then will I risk it, even with thee; but wot thou well, that if I misdoubt me of thee, that will be thy bane."

Thorir bade him do even so, and thereafter Grettir received him, and found this, that he must have the strength of twain, what work soever he took in hand: he was ready for anything that Grettir might set him to, and Grettir need turn to nothing, nor had he found his life so good since he had been outlawed, yet was he ever so wary of himself that Thorir never got a chance against him.

Thorir Redbeard was with Grettir on the heath for two winters, and now he began to loathe his life on the heath, and falls to thinking what deed he shall do that Grettir will not see through; so one night in spring a great storm arose while they were asleep; Grettir awoke therewith, and asked where was their boat. Thorir sprang up, and ran down to the boat, and brake it all to pieces, and threw the broken pieces about here and there, so that it seemed as though the storm had driven them along. Then he went into the hut, and called out aloud:

"Good things have not befallen us, my friend," said he; "for our boat is all broken to pieces, and the nets lie a long way out in the water."

"Go and bring them in then," said Grettir, "for methinks it is with thy goodwill that the boat is broken."

Thorir answered, "Among manly deeds swimming is the least handy to me, but most other deeds, I think, I may do against men who are not marvellous; thou mayest wot well enough that I was minded that thou shouldst not have to work while I abode here, and this I would not bid if it were in me to do it."

Then Grettir arose and took his weapons, and went to the water-side. Now the land was so wrought there that a ness ran into the water, and a great creek was on the other side, and the water was deep right up to the shore.

Now Grettir spake: "Swim off to the nets, and let me see how skilled a man thou art."

"I told thee before," said Thorir, "that I might not swim; and now I know not what is gone with thy manliness and daring."

"Well, the nets I may get in," said Grettir, "but betray thou me not, since I trust in thee."

Said Thorir, "Deem me not to be so shamed and worthless."

"Thou wilt thyself prove thyself, what thou art," said Grettir, and therewith he put off his clothes and weapons, and swam off for the nets. He swept them up together, and brought them to land, and cast them on to the bank; but when he was minded to come aland, then Thorir caught up the short-sword and drew it hastily, and ran therewith swiftly on Grettir, and smote at him as he set foot on the bank; but Grettir fell on his back down into the water, and sank like a stone; and Thorir stood gazing out on to the water, to keep him off from the shore if he came up again; but Grettir dived and groped along the bottom as near as he might to the bank, so that Thorir might not see him till he came into the creek at his back, and got aland; and Thorir heeded him not, and felt nought till Grettir heaved him up over his head, and cast him down so hard that the short-sword flew out of his hand; then Grettir got hold of it and had no words with him, but smote off his head straightway, and this was the end of his life.

But after this would Grettir never take outlaws to him, yet hardly might he bear to be alone.

Chapter 57
How Thorir of Garth Set on Grettir on Ernewaterheath

AT THE ALTHING Thorir of Garth heard of the slaying of Thorir Redbeard, and now he thought he saw that he had no light task to deal with; but such rede he took that he rode west over the lower heathlands from the Thing with well-nigh eighty men, and was minded to go and take Grettir's life: but when Grim Thorhallson knew thereof he sent Grettir word and bade him beware of himself, so Grettir ever took heed to the goings of men. But one day he saw many men riding who took the way to his abode; so he ran into a rift in the rocks, nor would he flee because he had not seen all the strength of those folk.

Then up came Thorir and all his men, and bade them smite Grettir's head from his body, and said that the ill-doer's life would be had cheaply now.

Grettir answered, *"Though the spoon has taken it up, yet the mouth has had no sup.* From afar have ye come, and marks of the game shall some have ere we part."

Then Thorir egged on his men busily to set on him; but the pass was narrow, and he could defend it well from one side; yet hereat he marvelled, that howsoever they went round to the back of him, yet no hurt he got thereby; some fell of Thorir's company, and some were wounded, but nothing might they do.

Then said Thorir, "Oft have I heard that Grettir is a man of marvel before all others for prowess and good heart, but never knew I that he was so wise a wizard as now I behold him; for half as many again fall at his back as fall before him; lo, now we have to do with trolls and no men."

So he bid them turn away and they did so. Grettir marvelled how that might be, for withal he was utterly foredone.

Thorir and his men turn away and ride toward the north country, and men deemed their journey to be of the shame fullest; eighteen men had they left there and many were wounded withal.

Now Grettir went up into the pass, and found there one great of growth, who sat leaning against the rock and was sore wounded. Grettir asked him of his name, and he said he was hight Hallmund.

"And this I will tell thee to know me by, that thou didst deem me to have a good hold of the reins that summer when we met on the Keel; now, methinks, I have paid thee back therefor."

"Yea, in sooth," said Grettir, "I deem that thou hast shown great manliness toward me; whenso I may, I will reward thee."

Hallmund said, "But now I will that thou come to my abode, for thou must e'en think time drags heavily here on the heaths."

Grettir said he was fain thereof; and now they fare both together south under Balljokul, and there had Hallmund a huge cave, and a daughter great of growth and of high mind; there they did well to Grettir, and the woman healed the wounds of both of them, and Grettir dwelt long there that summer, and a lay he made on Hallmund, wherein is this:

> *"Wide and high doth Hallmund stride*
> *In the hollow mountain side."*

And this stave also is therein:

> *"At Ernewater, one by one,*
> *Stole the swords forth in the sun,*
> *Eager for the road of death*
> *Swept athwart by sharp spears' breath;*
> *Many a dead Wellwharfer's lands*
> *That day gave to other hands.*
> *Hallmund, dweller in the cave,*
> *Grettir's life that day did save."*

Men say that Grettir slew six men in that meeting, but Hallmund twelve.

Now as the summer wore Grettir yearned for the peopled country, to see his friends and kin; Hallmund bade him visit him when he came to the south country again, and Grettir promised him so to do; then he went west to Burgfirth, and thence to the Broadfirth Dales, and sought counsel of Thorstein Kuggson as to where he should now seek for protection, but Thorstein said that his foes were now so many that few would harbour him; "But thou mightest fare south to the Marshes and see what fate abides thee there."

So in the autumn Grettir went south to the Marshes.

Chapter 58
Grettir in Fairwoodfell

IN THOSE DAYS DWELT at Holm Biorn the Hitdale-Champion, who was the son of Arngeir, the son of Berse the Godless, the son of Balk, who settled Ramfirth as is aforesaid; Biorn was a great chief and a hardy man, and would ever harbour outlawed men.

Now Grettir came to Holm, and Biorn gave him good cheer, for there had been friendship between the earlier kin of both of them; so Grettir asked if he would give him harbourage; but Biorn said that he had got to himself so many feuds through all the land that men would shun harbouring him so long as to be made outlaws therefor: "But some gain will I be to thee, if thou lettest those men dwell in peace who are under my ward, whatsoever thou dost by other men in the country-side."

Grettir said yea thereto. Then said Biorn, "Well, I have thought over it, and in that mountain, which stretches forth outside of Hitriver, is a stead good for defence, and a good hiding-place withal, if it be cunningly dealt with; for there is a hollow through the mountain, that is seen from the way below; for the highway lies beneath it, but above is a slip of sand and stones so exceeding steep, that few men may come up there if one hardy man stand on his defence above in the lair. Now this seems to me the best rede for thee, and the one thing worth talking of for thine abode, because, withal, it is easy to go thence and get goods from the Marshes, and right away to the sea."

Grettir said that he would trust in his foresight if he would give him any help. Then he went up to Fairwoodfell and made his abode there; he hung grey wadmal before the hole in the mountain, and from the way below it was like to behold as if one saw through. Now he was wont to ride for things needful through the country-side, and men deemed a woful guest had come among them whereas he went.

Thord Kolbeinson dwelt at Hitness in those days, and a good skald he was; at that time was there great enmity betwixt him and Biorn; and Biorn was but half loth, though Grettir wrought some ill on Thord's men or his goods.

Grettir was ever with Biorn, and they tried their skill in many sports, and it is shown in the story of Biorn that they were deemed equal in prowess, but it is the mind of most that Grettir was the strongest man ever known in the land, since Orm the son of Storolf, and Thoralf the son of Skolm, left off their trials of strength. Grettir and Biorn swam in one spell all down Hitriver, from the lake right away to the sea: they brought those stepping-stones into the river that have never since been washed away either by floods, or the drift of ice, or glacier slips.

So Grettir abode in Fairwoodfell for one winter, in such wise, that none set on him, though many lost their goods at his hands and could do nought therefor, for a good place for defence he had, and was ever good friend to those nighest to him.

Chapter 59
Gisli's Meeting with Grettir

THERE WAS A MAN hight Gisli, the son of that Thorstein whom Snorri Godi had slain. Gisli was a big man and strong, a man showy in weapons and clothes, who made much of himself, and was somewhat of a self-praiser; he was a seafaring man, and came one summer out to Whiteriver, whenas Grettir had been a winter on the fell. Thord, son of Kolbein, rode to his ship, and Gisli gave him good welcome, and bade him take of his wares whatso he would; thereto Thord agreed, and then they fell to talk one with the other, and Gisli said:

"Is that true which is told me, that ye have no counsel that avails to rid you of a certain outlaw who is doing you great ill?"

Thord said, "We have not tried aught on him yet, but to many he seems a man hard to deal with, and that has been proven on many a man."

"It is like, methinks, that you should find Biorn a heavy trouble, if ye may not drive away this man: luckless it is for you withal, that I shall be too far off this winter to better matters for you."

"Thou wilt be better pleased to deal with him by hearsay."

"Nay, no need to tell me of Grettir," said Gisli; "I have borne harder brunts when I was in warfare along with King Knut the Mighty, and west over the Sea, and I was ever thought to hold my own; and if I should have a chance at him I would trust myself and my weapons well enough."

Thord said he would not work for nought if he prevailed against Grettir; "For there is more put upon his head than on the head of any other of wood-folk; six marks of silver it was; but last summer Thorir of Garth laid thereto yet three marks; and men deem he will have enough to do therefor whose lot it is to win it."

"All things soever will men do for money," says Gisli, "and we chapmen not the least; but now shall we keep this talk hushed up, for mayhap he will be the warier," says he, "if he come to know that I am with you against him: now I am minded to abide this winter at Snowfellsness at Wave-ridge. Is his lair on my way at all? for he will not foresee this, nor shall I draw together many men against him."

Thord liked the plot well, he rode home therewith and held his peace about this; but now things went according to the saw, *a listening ear in the holt is anear*; men had been by at the talk betwixt Thord and Gisli, who were friends to Biorn of Hitdale, and they told him all from end to end; so when Biorn and Grettir met, Biorn showed forth the whole matter to him, and said that now he might prove how he could meet a foe.

"It would not be bad sport," said he, "if thou wert to handle him roughly, but to slay him not, if thou mightest do otherwise."

Grettir smiled thereat, but spake little.

Now at the folding time in the autumn Grettir went down to Flysia-wharf and got sheep for himself; he had laid hold on four wethers; but the bonders became ware of his ways and went after him; and these two things befell at the same time, that he got up under the fell-side, and that they came upon him, and would drive the sheep from him, yet bare they no weapon against him; they were six altogether, and stood thick in his path. Now the sheep troubled him and he waxed wroth, and caught up two of those men, and cast them down over the hill-side, so that they lay stunned; and when the others saw that, they came on less eagerly; then Grettir took up the sheep and locked them together by the horns, and threw them over his shoulders, two on each side, and went up into his lair.

So the bonders turned back, and deemed they had got but ill from him, and their lot misliked them now worse than before.

Now Gisli abode at his ship through the autumn till it was rolled ashore. Many things made him abide there, so he was ready late, and rode away but a little before winter-nights. Then he went from the south, and guested under Raun on the south side of Hitriver. In the morning, before he rode thence, he began a talk with his fellows:

"Now shall we ride in coloured clothes today, and let the outlaw see that we are not like other wayfarers who are drifted about here day by day."

So this they did, and they were three in all: but when they came west over the river, he spake again to them:

"Here in these bents, I am told, lurks the outlaw, and no easy way is there up to him; but may it not perchance seem good to him to come and meet us and behold our array?"

They said that it was ever his wont so to do. Now that morning Grettir had risen early in his lair; the weather was cold and frosty, and snow had fallen, but not much of it. He saw how three men rode from the south over Hitriver, and their state raiment glittered and their inlaid shields. Then it came into his mind who these should be, and he deems it would be good for him to get some rag of their array; and he was right wishful withal to meet such braggarts: so he catches up his weapons and runs down the slip-side. And when Gisli heard the clatter of the stones, he spake thus:

"There goes a man down the hill-side, and somewhat big he is, and he is coming to meet us: now, therefore, let us go against him briskly, for here is good getting come to hand."

His fellows said that this one would scarce run into their very hands, if he knew not his might; "And good it is that *he bewail who brought the woe.*"

So they leapt off their horses, and therewith Grettir came up to them, and laid hands on a clothes-bag that Gisli had tied to his saddle behind him, and said:

"This will I have, for oft I lowt for little things."

Gisli answers, "Nay, it shall not be; dost thou know with whom thou hast to do?"

Says Grettir, "I am not very clear about that; nor will I have much respect for persons, since I am lowly now, and ask for little."

"Mayhap thou thinkest it little," says he, "but I had rather pay down thirty hundreds; but robbery and wrong are ever uppermost in thy mind methinks; so on him, good fellows, and let see what he may do."

So did they, and Grettir gave back before them to a stone which stands by the way and is called Grettir's-Heave, and thence defended himself; and Gisli egged on his fellows eagerly; but Grettir saw now that he was no such a hardy heart as he had made believe, for he was ever behind his fellows' backs; and withal he grew aweary of this fulling business, and swept round the short-sword, and smote one of Gisli's fellows to the death, and leaped down from the stone, and set on so fiercely, that Gisli shrank aback before him all along the hill-side: there Gisli's other fellow was slain, and then Grettir spake:

"Little is it seen in thee that thou hast done well wide in the world, and in ill wise dost thou part from thy fellows."

Gisli answers, *"Hottest is the fire that lies on oneself – with hell's-man are dealings ill."*

Then they gave and took but a little, before Gisli cast away his weapons, and took to his heels out along the mountain. Grettir gave him time to cast off whatso he would, and every time Gisli saw a chance for it he threw off somewhat of his clothes; and Grettir never followed him so close but that there was still some space betwixt them. Gisli ran right past that mountain and then across Coldriver-dale, and then through Aslaug's-lithe and above by Kolbeinstead, and then out into Burgh-lava; and by then was he in shirt and breech alone, and was now exceeding weary. Grettir still followed after him, and there was ever a stone's throw between them; and now he pulled up a great bush. But Gisli made no stay till he came out at Haf-firth-river, and it was swollen with ice and ill to ford; Gisli made straightway for the river, but Grettir ran in on him and seized him, and then the strength of either was soon known: Grettir drave him down under him, and said:

"Art thou that Gisli who would fain meet Grettir Asmundson?"

Gisli answers, "I have found him now, in good sooth, nor do I know in what wise we shall part: keep that which thou hast got, and let me go free."

Grettir said, "Nay, thou art scarce deft enow to learn what I have to teach thee, so needs must I give thee somewhat to remember it by."

Therewith he pulls the shirt up over his head and let the twigs go all down his back, and along both sides of him, and Gisli strove all he might to wriggle away from him; but Grettir flogged him through and through, and then let him go; and Gisli thought he would learn no more of Grettir and have such another flogging withal; nor did he ever again earn the like skin-rubbing.

But when he got his legs under him again, he ran off unto a great pool in the river, and swam it, and came by night to a farm called Horseholt, and utterly foredone he was by then. There he lay a week with his body all swollen, and then fared to his abode.

Grettir turned back, and took up the things Gisli had cast down, and brought them to his place, nor from that time forth gat Gisli aught thereof.

Many men thought Gisli had his due herein for the noise and swagger he had made about himself; and Grettir sang this about their dealings together:

> *"In fighting ring where steed meets steed,*
> *The sluggish brute of mongrel breed,*
> *Certes will shrink back nothing less*
> *Before the stallion's dauntlessness,*
> *Than Gisli before me today;*
> *As, casting shame and clothes away,*
> *And sweating o'er the marsh with fear,*
> *He helped the wind from mouth and rear."*

The next spring Gisli got ready to go to his ship, and bade men above all things beware of carrying aught of his goods south along the mountain, and said that the very fiend dwelt there.

Gisli rode south along the sea all the way to his ship, and never met Grettir again; and now he is out of the story.

But things grew worse between Thord Kolbeinson and Grettir, and Thord set on foot many a plot to get Grettir driven away or slain.

Chapter 60
Of the Fight at Hitriver

WHEN GRETTIR HAD BEEN two winters at Fairwoodfell, and the third was now come, he fared south to the Marshes, to the farm called Brook-bow, and had thence six wethers against the will of him who owned them. Then he went to Acres and took away two neat for slaughtering, and many sheep, and then went up south of Hitriver.

But when the bonders were ware of his ways, they sent word to Thord at Hitness, and bade him take in hand the slaying of Grettir; but he hung back, yet for the prayers of men got his son Arnor, who was afterwards called Earls' Skald, to go with them, and bade them withal to take heed that Grettir escaped not.

Then were men sent throughout all the country-side. There was a man called Biarni, who dwelt at Jorvi in Flysia-wharf, and he gathered men together from without Hitriver; and their purpose was that a band should be on either bank of the river.

Now Grettir had two men with him; a man called Eyolf, the son of the bonder at Fairwood, and a stout man; and another he had besides.

First came up Thorarin of Acres and Thorfinn of Brook-bow, and there were nigh twenty men in their company. Then was Grettir fain to make westward across the river, but therewith came up on the west side thereof Arnor and Biarni. A narrow ness ran into the water on the side whereas Grettir stood; so he drave the beasts into the furthermost parts of the ness, when he saw the men coming up, for never would he give up what he had once laid his hands on.

Now the Marsh-men straightway made ready for an onslaught, and made themselves very big; Grettir bade his fellows take heed that none came at his back; and not many men could come on at once.

Now a hard fight there was betwixt them, Grettir smote with the short-sword with both hands, and no easy matter it was to get at him; some of the Marsh-men fell, and some were wounded; those on the other side of the river were slow in coming up, because the ford was not very near, nor did the fight go on long before they fell off; Thorarin of Acres was a very old man, so that he was not at this onslaught. But when this fight was over, then came up Thrand, son of Thorarin, and Thorgils Ingialdson, the brother's son of Thorarin, and Finnbogi, son of Thorgeir Thorhaddson of Hitdale, and Steinulf Thorleifson from Lavadale; these egged on their men eagerly to set on, and yet another fierce onslaught they made. Now Grettir saw that he must either flee or spare himself nought; and now he went forth so fiercely that none might withstand him; because they were so many that he saw not how he might escape, but that he did his best before he fell; he was fain withal that the life of such an one as he deemed of some worth might be paid for his life; so he ran at Steinulf of Lavadale, and smote him on the head and clave him down to the shoulders, and straightway with another blow smote Thorgils Ingialdson in the midst and well-nigh cut him asunder; then would Thrand run forth to revenge his kinsman, but Grettir smote him on the right thigh, so that the blow took off all the muscle, and straightway was he unmeet for fight; and thereafter withal a great wound Grettir gave to Finnbogi.

Then Thorarin cried out and bade them fall back, "For the longer ye fight the worse ye will get of him, and he picks out men even as he willeth from your company."

So did they, and turned away; and there had ten men fallen, and five were wounded to death, or crippled, but most of those who had been at that meeting had some hurt or other; Grettir was marvellously wearied and yet but a little wounded.

And now the Marsh-men made off with great loss of men, for many stout fellows had fallen there.

But those on the other side of the river fared slowly, and came not up till the meeting was all done; and when they saw how ill their men had fared, then Arnor would not risk himself, and much rebuke he got therefor from his father and many others; and men are minded to think that he was no man of prowess.

Now that place where they fought is called Grettir's-point today.

Chapter 61
How Grettir Left Fairwoodfell, and of His Abiding in Thorir's-Dale

BUT GRETTIR AND HIS MEN took horse and rode up to the fell, for they were all wounded, and when they came to Fairwood there was Eyolf left; the farmer's daughter was out of doors, and asked for tidings; Grettir told all as clearly as might be, and sang a stave withal:

"O thou warder of horn's wave:

> *Not on this side of the grave*
> *Will Steinulf's head be whole again;*
> *Many more there gat their bane;*
> *Little hope of Thorgils now*
> *After that bone-breaking blow:*
> *Eight Gold-scatterers more they say,*
> *Dead along the river lay."*

Thereafter Grettir went to his lair and sat there through the winter; but when he and Biorn met, Biorn said to him, that he deemed that much had been done; "and no peace thou wilt have here in the long run: now hast thou slain both kin and friends of mine, yet shall I not cast aside what I have promised thee whiles thou art here."

Grettir said he must needs defend his hands and life, "but ill it is if thou mislikest it."

Biorn said that things must needs be as they were. A little after came men to Biorn who had lost kinsmen at Grettir's hands, and bade him not to suffer that riotous man to abide there longer in their despite; and Biorn said that it should be as they would as soon as the winter was over.

Now Thrand, the son of Thorarin of Acres, was healed; a stout man he was, and had to wife Steinun, daughter of Rut of Combeness; Thorlcif of Lavadale, the father of Steinulf, was a very mighty man, and from him are come the men of Lavadale.

Now nought more is told of the dealings of Grettir with the Marsh-men while he was on the mountain; Biorn still kept up his friendship with him, though his friends grew somewhat the fewer for that he let Grettir abide there, because men took it ill that their kin should fall unatoned.

At the time of the Thing, Grettir departed from the Marsh-country, and went to Burgfirth and found Grim Thorhallson, and sought counsel of him, as to what to do now. Grim said he had no strength to keep him, therefore fared Grettir to find Hallmund his friend, and dwelt there that summer till it wore to its latter end.

In the autumn Grettir went to Goatland, and waited there till bright weather came on; then he went up to Goatland Jokul, and made for the south-east, and had with him a kettle, and tools to strike fire withal. But men deem that he went there by the counsel of Hallmund, for far and wide was the land known of him.

So Grettir went on till he found a dale in the jokul, long and somewhat narrow, locked up by jokuls all about, in such wise that they overhung the dale. He came down somehow, and then he saw fair hill-sides grass-grown and set with bushes. Hot springs there were therein, and it seemed to him that it was by reason of earth-fires that the ice-cliffs did not close up over the vale.

A little river ran along down the dale, with level shores on either side thereof. There the sun came but seldom; but he deemed he might scarcely tell over the sheep that were in that valley, so many they were; and far better and fatter than any he had ever seen.

Now Grettir abode there, and made himself a hut of such wood as he could come by. He took of the sheep for his meat, and there was more on one of them than on two elsewhere: one ewe there was, brown with a polled head, with her lamb, that he deemed the greatest beauty for her goodly growth. He was fain to take the lamb, and so he did, and thereafter slaughtered it: three stone of suet there was in it, but the whole carcase was even better. But when Brownhead missed her lamb, she went up on Grettir's hut every night, and bleated in suchwise that he might not sleep anight, so that it misliked him above all things that he had slaughtered the lamb, because of her troubling.

But every evening at twilight he heard some one hoot up in the valley, and then all the sheep ran together to one fold every evening.

So Grettir says, that a half-troll ruled over the valley, a giant hight Thorir, and in trust of his keeping did Grettir abide there; by him did Grettir name the valley, calling it Thorir's-dale. He said withal that Thorir had daughters, with whom he himself had good game, and that they took it well, for not many were the new-comers thereto; but when fasting time was, Grettir made this change therein, that fat and livers should be eaten in Lent.

Now nought happed to be told of through the winter. At last Grettir found it so dreary there, that he might abide there no longer: then he gat him gone from the valley, and went south across the jokul, and came from the north, right against the midst of Shieldbroadfell.

He raised up a flat stone and bored a hole therein, and said that whoso put his eye to the hole in that stone should straightway behold the gulf of the pass that leads from Thorir's-vale.

So he fared south through the land, and thence to the Eastfirths; and in this journey he was that summer long, and the winter, and met all the great men there, but somewhat ever thrust him aside that nowhere got he harbouring or abode; then he went back by the north, and dwelt at sundry places.

Chapter 62
Of the Death of Hallmund, Grettir's Friend

A LITTLE AFTER Grettir had gone from Ernewaterheath, there came a man thither, Grim by name, the son of the widow at Kropp. He had slain the son of Eid Skeggison of the Ridge, and had been outlawed therefor; he abode whereas Grettir had dwelt afore, and got much fish from the water. Hallmund took it ill that he had come in Grettir's stead, and was minded that he should have little good hap how much fish soever he caught.

So it chanced on a day that Grim had caught a hundred fish, and he bore them to his hut and hung them up outside, but the next morning when he came thereto they were all gone; that he deemed marvellous, and went to the water; and now he caught two hundred fish, went home and stored them up; and all went the same way, for they were all gone in the morning; and now he thought it hard to trace all to one spring. But the third day he caught three hundred fish, brought them home and watched over them from his shed, looking out through a hole in the door to see if aught might come anigh. Thus wore the night somewhat, and when the third part of the night was gone by, he heard one going along outside with heavy footfalls; and when he was ware thereof, he took an axe that he had, the sharpest of weapons, for he was fain to know what this one was about; and he saw that the new-comer had a great basket on his back. Now he set it down, and peered about, and saw no man abroad; he gropes about to the fishes, and deems he has got a good handful, and into the basket he scoops them one and all; then is the basket full, but the fishes were so big that Grim thought that no horse might bear more. Now he takes them up and puts himself under the load, and at that very point of time, when he was about to stand upright, Grim ran out, and with both hands smote at his neck, so that the axe sank into the shoulder; thereat he turned off sharp, and set off running with the basket south over the mountain.

Grim turned off after him, and was fain to know if he had got enough. They went south all the way to Balljokul, and there this man went into a cave; a bright fire burnt in the cave, and thereby sat a woman, great of growth, but shapely withal. Grim heard how she welcomed her father, and called him Hallmund. He cast down his burden heavily, and groaned aloud; she asked him why he was all covered with blood, but he answered and sang:

"Now know I aright:

> *That in man's might,*
> *And in man's bliss,*

No trust there is;
On the day of bale
Shall all things fail;
Courage is o'er,
Luck mocks no more."

She asked him closely of their dealings, but he told her all even as it had befallen.

"Now shall thou hearken," said he, "for I shall tell of my deeds and sing a song thereon, and thou shall cut it on a staff as I give it out."

So she did, and he sung Hallmund's song withal, wherein is this:

"When I drew adown
The bridle brown
Grettir's hard hold,
Men deemed me bold;
Long while looked then
The brave of men
In his hollow hands,
The harm of lands.

"Then came the day
Of Thorir's play
On Ernelakeheath,
When we from death
Our life must gain;
Alone we twain
With eighty men
Must needs play then.

"Good craft enow
Did Grettir show
On many a shield
In that same field;
Natheless I hear
That my marks were
The deepest still;
The worst to fill.

"Those who were fain
His back to gain
Lost head and hand,
Till of the band,
From the Well-wharf-side,
Must there abide
Eighteen behind
That none can find.

"With the giant's kin
Have I oft raised din;
To the rock folk
Have I dealt out stroke;
Ill things could tell
That I smote full well;
The half-trolls know
My baneful blow.

"Small gain in me
Did the elf-folk see,
Or the evil wights
Who ride anights."

Many other deeds of his did Hallmund sing in that song, for he had fared through all the land.

Then spake his daughter, "A man of no slippery hand was that; nor was it unlike that this should hap, for in evil wise didst thou begin with him: and now what man will avenge thee?"

Hallmund answered, "It is not so sure to know how that may be; but, methinks, I know that Grettir would avenge me if he might come thereto; but no easy matter will it be to go against the luck of this man, for much greatness lies stored up for him."

Thereafter so much did Hallmund's might wane as the song wore, that well-nigh at one while it befell that the song was done and Hallmund dead; then she grew very sad and wept right sore. Then came Grim forth and bade her be of better cheer, *"For all must fare when they are fetched. This has been brought about by his own deed, for I could scarce look on while he robbed me."*

She said he had much to say for it, *"For ill deed gains ill hap."*

Now as they talked she grew of better cheer, and Grim abode many nights in the cave, and got the song by heart, and things went smoothly betwixt them. Grim abode at Ernewaterheath all the winter after Hallmund's death, and thereafter came Thorkel Eyulfson to meet him on the Heath, and they fought together; but such was the end of their play that Grim might have his will of Thorkel's life, and slew him not. So Thorkel took him to him, and got him sent abroad and gave him many goods; and therein either was deemed to have done well to the other. Grim betook himself to seafaring, and a great tale is told of him.

Chapter 63
How Grettir Beguiled Thorir of Garth When He Was Nigh Taking Him

NOW THE STORY is to be taken up where Grettir came from the firths of the east-country; and now he fared with hidden-head for that he would not meet Thorir, and lay out that summer on Madderdale-heath and in sundry places, and at whiles he was at Reek-heath.

Thorir heard that Grettir was at Reek-heath, so he gathered men and rode to the heath, and was well minded that Grettir should not escape this time.

Now Grettir was scarce aware of them before they were on him; he was just by a mountain-dairy that stood back a little from the wayside, and another man there was with him, and when he saw their band, speedy counsel must he take; so he bade that they should fell the horses and drag them into the dairy shed, and so it was done.

Then Thorir rode north over the heath by the dairy, and *missed friend from stead*, for he found nought, and so turned back withal. But when his band had ridden away west, then said Grettir, "They will not deem their journey good if we be not found; so now shall thou watch our horses while I go meet them, a fair play would be shown them if they knew me not."

His fellow strove to let him herein, yet he went none-the-less, and did on him other attire, with a slouched hat over his face and a staff in his hand, then he went in the way before them. They greeted him and asked if he had seen any men riding over the heath.

"Those men that ye seek have I seen; but little was wanting e'ennow but that ye found them, for there they were, on the south of yon bogs to the left."

Now when they heard that, off they galloped out on to the bogs, but so great a mire was there that nohow could they get on, and had to drag their horses out, and were wallowing there the more part of the day; and they gave to the devil withal the wandering churl who had so befooled them.

But Grettir turned back speedily to meet his fellow, and when they met he sang this stave:

"Now make I no battle-field
With the searching stems of shield.
Rife with danger is my day,
And alone I go my way:
Nor shall I go meet, this tide,
Odin's storm, but rather bide
Whatso fate I next may have;
Scarce, then, shall thou deem me brave.

"Thence where Thorir's company
Thronging ride, I needs must flee;
If with them I raised the din,
Little thereby should I win;
Brave men's clashing swords I shun,
Woods must hide the hunted one;
For through all things, good and ill,
Unto life shall I hold still."

Now they ride at their swiftest west over the heath and forth by the homestead at Garth, before ever Thorir came from the wilderness with his band; and when they drew nigh to the homestead a man fell in with them who knew them not.

Then saw they how a woman, young and grand of attire, stood without, so Grettir asked who that woman would be. The new-comer said that she was Thorir's daughter. Then Grettir sang this stave:

"O wise sun of golden stall,
When thy sire comes back to hall,
Thou mayst tell him without sin
This, though little lies therein,
That thou saw'st me ride hereby,
With but two in company,
Past the door of Skeggi's son,
Nigh his hearth, O glittering one."

Hereby the new-comer thought he knew who this would be, and he rode to peopled parts and told how Grettir had ridden by.

So when Thorir came home, many deemed that Grettir had done the bed well over their heads. But Thorir set spies on Grettir's ways, whereso he might be. Grettir fell on such rede that he sent his fellow to the west country with his horses; but he went up to the mountains and was in disguised attire, and fared about north there in the early winter, so that he was not known.

But all men deemed that Thorir had got a worse part than before in their dealings together.

Chapter 64
Of the Ill Haps at Sand-Heaps, and How Guest Came to the Goodwife There

THERE WAS A PRIEST called Stein, who dwelt at Isledale-river, in Bard-dale; he was good at husbandry and rich in beasts; his son was Kiartan, a brisk man and a well grown. Thorstein the White was the name of him who dwelt at Sand-heaps, south of Isledale-river; his wife was called Steinvor, a young woman and merry-hearted, and children they had, who were young in those days. But that place men deemed much haunted by the goings of trolls.

Now it befell two winters before Grettir came into the north country that Steinvor the goodwife of Sand-heaps fared at Yule-tide to the stead of Isledale-river according to her wont, but the goodman abode at home. Men lay down to sleep in the evening, but in the night they heard a huge crashing about the bonder's bed; none durst arise and see thereto, for very few folk were there. In the morning the goodwife came home, but the goodman was gone, and none knew what had become of him.

Now the next year wears through its seasons, but the winter after the goodwife would fain go to worship, and bade her house-carle abide behind at home; thereto was he loth, but said nathless that she must rule; so all went the same way and the house-carle vanished; and marvellous men deemed it; but folk saw certain stains of blood about the outer door; therefore they deemed it sure that an evil wight had taken them both.

Now that was heard of wide through the country-side, and Grettir withal was told thereof; so he took his way to Bard-dale, and came to Sand-heaps at Yule-eve, and made stay there, and called himself Guest. The goodwife saw that he was marvellous great of growth, but the home-folk were exceeding afeard of him; he prayed for guesting there; the mistress said that there was meat ready for him, "but as to thy safety see to that thyself."

He said that so he should do: "Here will I abide, but thou shalt go to worship if thou wilt."

She answered, "Meseems thou art a brave man if thou durst abide at home here."

"*For one thing alone will I not be known*," said he.

She said, "I have no will to abide at home, but I may not cross the river."

"I will go with thee," says Guest.

Then she made her ready for worship, and her little daughter with her. It thawed fast abroad, and the river was in flood, and therein was the drift of ice great: then said the goodwife:

"No way across is there either for man or horse."

"Nay, there will be fords there," said Guest, "be not afeard."

"Carry over the little maiden first," said the goodwife; "she is the lightest."

"I am loth to make two journeys of it," said Guest, "I will bear thee in my arms."

She crossed herself, and said, "This will not serve; what wilt thou do with the maiden?"

"A rede I see for that," said he, and therewith caught them both up, and laid the little one in her mother's lap, and set both of them thus on his left arm, but had his right free; and so he took the ford withal, nor durst they cry out, so afeard were they.

Now the river took him up to his breast forthwith, and a great ice-floe drave against him, but he put forth the hand that was free and thrust it from him; then it grew so deep, that the stream broke on his shoulder; but he waded through it stoutly, till he came to the further shore, and there cast them aland: then he turned back, and it was twilight already by then he came home to Sand-heaps, and called for his meat.

So when he was fulfilled, he bade the home-folk go into the chamber; then he took boards and loose timber, and dragged it athwart the chamber, and made a great bar, so that none of the home-folk might come thereover: none durst say aught against him, nor would any of them make the least sound. The entrance to the hall was through the side wall by the gable, and dais was there within; there Guest lay down, but did not put off his clothes, and light burned in the chamber over against the door: and thus Guest lay till far on in the night.

The goodwife came to Isledale-river at church-time, and men marvelled how she had crossed the river; and she said she knew not whether a man or a troll had brought her over.

The priest said he was surely a man, though a match for few; "But let us hold our peace hereon," he said; "maybe he is chosen for the bettering of thy troubles." So the goodwife was there through the night.

Chapter 65
Of Guest and the Troll-wife

NOW IT IS TO BE TOLD of Guest, that when it drew towards midnight, he heard great din without, and thereafter into the hall came a huge troll-wife, with a trough in one hand and a chopper wondrous great in the other; she peered about when she came in, and saw where Guest lay, and ran at him; but he sprang up to meet her, and they fell a-wrestling terribly, and struggled together for long in the hall. She was the stronger, but he gave back with craft, and all that was before them was broken, yea, the cross-panelling withal of the chamber. She dragged him out through the door, and so into the outer doorway, and then he betook himself to struggling hard against her. She was fain to drag him from the house, but might not until they had broken away all the fittings of the outer door, and borne them out on their shoulders: then she laboured away with him down towards the river, and right down to the deep gulfs.

By then was Guest exceeding weary, yet must he either gather his might together, or be cast by her into the gulf. All night did they contend in such wise; never, he deemed, had he fought with such a horror for her strength's sake; she held him to her so hard that he might turn his arms to no account save to keep fast hold on the middle of the witch.

But now when they came on to the gulf of the river, he gives the hag a swing round, and therewith got his right hand free, and swiftly seized the short-sword that he was girt withal, and smote the troll therewith on the shoulder, and struck off her arm; and therewithal was he free, but she fell into the gulf and was carried down the force.

Then was Guest both stiff and weary, and lay there long on the rocks, then he went home, as it began to grow light, and lay down in bed, and all swollen and blue he was.

But when the goodwife came from church, she thought her house had been somewhat roughly handled: so she went to Guest and asked what had happed that all was broken and down-trodden. He told her all as it had befallen: she deemed these things imported much, and asked him what man he was in good sooth. So he told her the truth, and prayed that the priest might be fetched, for that he would fain see him: and so it was done.

But when Stein the priest came to Sand-heaps, he knew forthwith, that thither was come Grettir Asmundson, under the name of Guest.

So the priest asked what he deemed had become of those men who had vanished; and Grettir said that he thought they would have gone into the gulf: the priest said that he might not trow that, if no signs could be seen thereof: then said Grettir that later on that should be known more thoroughly. So the priest went home.

Grettir lay many nights a-bed, and the mistress did well to him, and so Yule-tide wore.

Now Grettir's story is that the troll-wife cast herself into the gulf when she got her wound; but the men of Bard-dale say that day dawned on her, while they wrestled, and that she burst, when he cut the arm from her; and that there she stands yet on the cliff, a rock in the likeness of a woman.

Now the dale-dwellers kept Grettir in hiding there; but in the winter after Yule, Grettir fared to Isledale-river, and when he met the priest, he said, "Well, priest, I see that thou hadst little faith in my tale; now will I, that thou go with me to the river, and see what likelihood there is of that tale being true."

So the priest did; and when they came to the force-side, they saw a cave up under the cliff; a sheer rock that cliff was, so great that in no place might man come up thereby, and well-nigh fifty fathoms was it down to the water. Now they had a rope with them, but the priest said:

"A risk beyond all measure, I deem it to go down here."

"Nay," said Grettir, "it is to be done, truly, but men of the greatest prowess are meetest therefor: now will I know what is in the force, but thou shall watch the rope."

The priest bade him follow his own rede, and drave a peg down into the sward on the cliff, and heaped stones up over it, and sat thereby.

Chapter 66
Of the Dweller in the Cave Under the Force

NOW IT IS TO BE TOLD of Grettir that he set a stone in a bight of the rope and let it sink down into the water.

"In what wise hast thou mind to go?" said the priest.

"I will not go bound into the force," said Grettir; "such things doth my heart forebode."

With that he got ready for his journey, and was lightly clad, and girt with the short-sword, and had no weapon more.

Then he leapt off the cliff into the force; the priest saw the soles of his feet, and knew not afterwards what was become of him. But Grettir dived under the force, and hard work it was, because the whirlpool was strong, and he had to dive down to the bottom, before he might come up under the force. But thereby was a rock jutting out, and thereon he gat; a great cave was under the force, and the river fell over it from the sheer rocks. He went up into the cave, and there was a great fire flaming from amidst of brands; and there he saw a giant sitting withal, marvellously great and dreadful to look on. But when Grettir came anigh, the giant leapt up and caught up a glaive and smote at the new-comer, for with that glaive might a man both cut and thrust; a wooden shaft it had, and that fashion of weapon men called then, heft-sax. Grettir hewed back against him with the short-sword, and smote the shaft so that he struck it asunder; then was the giant fain to stretch aback for a sword that hung up there in the cave; but therewithal Grettir smote him afore into the breast, and smote off well-nigh all the breast bone and the belly, so that the bowels tumbled out of him and fell into the river, and were driven down along the stream; and as the priest sat by the rope, he saw certain fibres all covered with blood swept down the swirls of the stream; then he grew unsteady in his place, and thought for sure that Grettir was dead, so he ran from the holding of the rope, and gat him home. Thither he came in the evening and said, as one who knew it well, that Grettir was dead, and that great scathe was it of such a man.

Now of Grettir must it be told that he let little space go betwixt his blows or ever the giant was dead; then he went up the cave, and kindled a light and espied the cave. The story tells not how much he got therein, but men deem that it must have been something great. But there he abode on into the night; and he found there the bones of two men, and bore them together in a bag; then he made off from the cave and swam to the rope and shook it, and thought that the priest would be there yet; but when he knew that the priest had gone home, then must he draw himself up by strength of hand, and thus he came up out on to the cliff.

Then he fared home to Isledale-river, and brought into the church porch the bag with the bones, and therewithal a rune-staff whereon this song was marvellous well cut:

> *"There into gloomy gulf I passed,*
> *O'er which from the rock's throat is cast*
> *The swirling rush of waters wan,*
> *To meet the sword-player feared of man.*
> *By giant's hall the strong stream pressed*
> *Cold hands against the singer's breast;*
> *Huge weight upon him there did hurl*
> *The swallower of the changing whirl."*

And this other one withal:

> *"The dreadful dweller of the cave*
> *Great strokes and many 'gainst me drave;*
> *Full hard he had to strive for it,*
> *But toiling long he wan no whit;*
> *For from its mighty shaft of tree*
> *The heft-sax smote I speedily;*
> *And dulled the flashing war-flame fair*
> *In the black breast that met me there."*

Herein was it said how that Grettir had brought those bones from the cave; but when the priest came to the church in the morning he found the staff and that which went with it, but Grettir was gone home to Sand-heaps.

Chapter 67
Grettir Driven from Sand-Heaps to the West

BUT WHEN THE PRIEST met Grettir he asked him closely about what had happed; so he told him all the tale of his doings, and said withal that the priest had been unfaithful to him in the matter of the rope-holding; and the priest must needs say that so it was.

Now men deemed they could see that these evil wights had wrought the loss of the men there in the dale; nor had folk hurt ever after from aught haunting the valley, and Grettir was thought to have done great deeds for the cleansing of the land. So the priest laid those bones in earth in the churchyard.

But Grettir abode at Sand-heaps the winter long, and was hidden there from all the world.

But when Thorir of Garth heard certain rumours of Grettir being in Bard-dale, he sent men for his head; then men gave him counsel to get him gone therefrom, so he took his way to the west.

Now when he came to Maddervales to Gudmund the Rich, he prayed Gudmund for watch and ward; but Gudmund said he might not well keep him. "But that only is good for thee," said he, "to set thee down there, whereas thou shouldst have no fear of thy life."

Grettir said he wotted not where such a place might be.

Gudmund said, "An isle there lies in Skagafirth called Drangey; so good a place for defence it is, that no man may come thereon unless ladders be set thereto. If thou mightest get there, I know for sure that no man who might come against thee, could have good hope while thou wert on the top thereof, of overcoming thee, either by weapons or craft, if so be thou shouldst watch the ladders well."

"That shall be tried," said Grettir, "but so fearsome of the dark am I grown, that not even for the keeping of my life may I be alone."

Gudmund said, "Well, that may be; but trust no man whatsoever so much as not to trust thyself better; for many men are hard to see through."

Grettir thanked him for his wholesome redes, and then fared away from Maddervales, nor made stay before he came to Biarg; there his mother and Illugi his brother welcomed him joyfully, and he abode there certain nights.

There he heard of the slaying of Thorstein Kuggson, which had befallen the autumn before Grettir went to Bard-dale; and he deemed therewithal that felling went on fast enough.

Then Grettir rode south to Holtbeacon-heath, and was minded to avenge Hallmund if he might meet Grim; but when he came to Northriverdale, he heard that Grim had been gone two winters ago, as is aforesaid; but Grettir had heard so late of these tidings because he had gone about disguised those two winters, and the third winter he had been in Thorirs-dale, and had seen no man who might tell him any news. Then he betook himself to the Broadfirth-dales, and dwelt in Eastriverdale, and lay in wait for folk who fared over Steep-brent; and once more he swept away with the strong hand the goods of the small bonders. This was about the height of summer-tide.

Now when the summer was well worn, Steinvor of Sand-heaps bore a man-child, who was named Skeggi; he was first fathered on Kiartan, the son of Stein, the priest of Isle-dale-river. Skeggi was unlike unto his kin because of his strength and growth, but when he was fifteen winters old he was the strongest man in the north-country, and was then known as Grettir's son; men deemed he would be a marvel among men, but he died when he was seventeen years of age, and no tale there is of him.

Chapter 68
How Thorod, the Son of Snorri Godi, Went Against Grettir

AFTER THE SLAYING of Thorstein Kuggson, Snorri Godi would have little to do with his son Thorod, or with Sam, the son of Bork the Fat; it is not said what they had done therefor, unless it might be that they had had no will to do some great deed that Snorri set them to; but withal Snorri drave his son Thorod away, and said he should not come back till he had slain some wood-dweller; and so must matters stand.

So Thorod went over to the Dales; and at that time dwelt at Broadlair-stead in Sokkolfsdale a widow called Geirlaug; a herdsman she kept, who had been outlawed for some onslaught; and he was a growing lad. Now Thorod Snorrison heard thereof, and rode in to Broadlair-stead, and asked where was the herdsman; the goodwife said that he was with the sheep.

"What wilt thou have to do with him?"

"His life will I have," says Thorod, "because he is an outlaw, and a wood-wight."

She answers, "No glory is it for such a great warrior as thou deemest thyself, to slay a mannikin like that; I will show thee a greater deed, if thine heart is so great that thou must needs try thyself."

"Well, and what deed?" says he.

She answers, "Up in the fell here, lies Grettir Asmundson; play thou with him, for such a game is more meet for thee."

Thorod took her talk well; "So shall it be," says he, and therewith he smote his horse with his spurs, and rode along the valley; and when he came to the hill below Eastriver, he saw where was a dun horse, with his saddle on, and thereby a big man armed, so he turned thence to meet him.

Grettir greeted him, and asked who he was. Thorod named himself, and said:

"Why askest thou not of my errand rather than of my name?"

"Why, because," said Grettir, "it is like to be such as is of little weight: art thou son to Snorri Godi?"

"Yea, yea," says Thorod; "but now shall we try which of us may do the most."

"A matter easy to be known," says Grettir; "hast thou not heard that I have ever been a treasure-hill that most men grope in with little luck?"

"Yea, I know it," said Thorod; "yet must somewhat be risked."

And now he drew his sword therewith and set on Grettir eagerly; but Grettir warded himself with his shield, but bore no weapon against Thorod; and so things went awhile, nor was Grettir wounded.

At last he said, "Let us leave this play, for thou wilt not have victory in our strife."

But Thorod went on dealing blows at his maddest. Now Grettir got aweary of dealing with him, and caught him and set him down by his side, and said:

"I may do with thee even as I will, nor do I fear that thou wilt ever be my bane; but the grey old carle, thy father, Snorri, I fear in good sooth, and his counsels that have brought most men to their knees: and for thee, thou shouldst turn thy mind to such things alone as thou mayst get done, nor is it child's play to fight with me."

But when Thorod saw that he might bring nought to pass, he grew somewhat appeased, and therewithal they parted. Thorod rode home to Tongue and told his father of his dealings with Grettir. Snorri Godi smiled thereat, and said:

"*Many a man lies hid within himself*, and far unlike were your doings; for thou must needs rush at him to slay him, and he might have done with thee even as he would. Yet wisely has Grettir done herein, that he slew thee not; for I should scarce have had a mind to let thee lie unavenged; but now indeed shall I give him aid, if I have aught to do with any of his matters."

It was well seen of Snorri, that he deemed Grettir had done well to Thorod, and he ever after gave his good word for Grettir.

Chapter 69
How Grettir Took Leave of His Mother at Biarg, and Fared with Illugi his Brother to Drangey

GRETTIR RODE NORTH to Biarg a little after he parted with Thorod, and lay hid there yet awhile; then so great grew his fear in the dark, that he durst go nowhere as soon as dusk set in. His mother bade him abide there, but said withal, that she saw that it would scarce avail him aught, since he had so many cases against him throughout all the land. Grettir said that she should never have trouble brought on her for his sake.

"But I shall no longer do so much for the keeping of my life," says he, "as to be alone."

Now Illugi his brother was by that time about fifteen winters old, and the goodliest to look on of all men; and he overheard their talk together. Grettir was telling his mother what rede

Gudmund the Rich had given him, and now that he should try, if he had a chance, to get out to Drangey, but he said withal, that he might not abide there, unless he might get some trusty man to be with him. Then said Illugi:

"I will go with thee, brother, though I know not that I shall be of any help to thee, unless it be that I shall be ever true to thee, nor run from thee whiles thou standest up; and moreover I shall know more surely how thou farest if I am still in thy fellowship."

Grettir answered, "Such a man thou art, that I am gladder in thee than in any other; and if it cross not my mother's mind, fain were I that thou shouldst fare with me."

Then said Asdis, "Now can I see that it has come to this, that two troubles lie before us: for meseems I may ill spare Illugi, yet I know that so hard is thy lot, Grettir, that thou must in somewise find rede therefor: and howsoever it grieves me, O my sons, to see you both turn your backs on me, yet thus much will I do, if Grettir might thereby be somewhat more holpen than heretofore."

Hereat was Illugi glad, for that he deemed it good to go with Grettir.

So she gave them much of her chattels, and they made them ready for their journey. Asdis led them from out the garth, and before they parted she spake thus:

"Ah, my sons twain, there ye depart from me, and one death ye shall have together; for no man may flee from that which is wrought for him: on no day now shall I see either of you once again; let one fate be over you both, then; for I know not what weal ye go to get for yourselves in Drangey, but there shall ye both lay your bones, and many will begrudge you that abiding place. Keep ye heedfully from wiles, yet none the less there shall ye be bitten of the edge of the sword, for marvellously have my dreams gone: be well ware of sorcery, for *little can cope with the cunning of eld*."

And when she had thus spoken she wept right sore.

Then said Grettir, "Weep not, mother, for if we be set on with weapons, it shall be said of thee, that thou hast had sons, and not daughters: live on, well and hale."

Therewithal they parted. They fared north through the country side and saw their kin; and thus they lingered out the autumn into winter; then they turned toward Skagafirth and went north through Waterpass and thence to Reekpass, and down Saemunds-lithe and so unto Longholt, and came to Dinby late in the day.

Grettir had cast his hood back on to his shoulders, for in that wise he went ever abroad whether the day were better or worse. So they went thence, and when they had gone but a little way, there met them a man, big-headed, tall, and gaunt, and ill clad; he greeted them, and either asked other for their names; they said who they were, but he called himself Thorbiorn: he was a land-louper, a man too lazy to work, and a great swaggerer, and much game and fooling was made with him by some folk: he thrust himself into their company, and told them much from the upper country about the folk there. Grettir had great game and merriment of him; so he asked if they had no need of a man who should work for them, "for I would fain fare with you," says he; and withal he got so much from their talk that they suffered him to follow them.

Much snow there was that day, and it was cold; but whereas that man swaggered exceedingly, and was the greatest of tomfools, he had a by-name, and was called Noise.

"Great wonder had those of Dinby when thou wentest by e'en now unhooded, in the foul weather," said Noise, "as to whether thou wouldst have as little fear of men as of the cold: there were two bonders' sons, both men of great strength, and the shepherd called them forth to go to the sheep-watching with him, and scarcely could they clothe themselves for the cold."

Grettir said, "I saw within doors there a young man who pulled on his mittens, and another going betwixt byre and midden, and of neither of them should I be afeared."

Thereafter they went down to Sorbness, and were there through the night; then they fared out along the strand to a farm called Reeks, where dwelt a man, Thorwald by name, a good bonder. Him Grettir prayed for watch and ward, and told him how he was minded to get out to Drangey: the bonder said that those of Skagafirth would think him no god-send, and excused himself therewithal.

Then Grettir took a purse his mother had given to him, and gave it to the bonder; his brows lightened over the money, and he got three house-carles of his to bring them out in the night time by the light of the moon. It is but a little way from Reeks out to the island, one sea-mile only. So when they came to the isle, Grettir deemed it good to behold, because it was grass-grown, and rose up sheer from the sea, so that no man might come up thereon save there where the ladders were let down, and if the uppermost ladder were drawn up, it was no man's deed to get upon the island. There also were the cliffs full of fowl in the summer-tide, and there were eighty sheep upon the island which the bonders owned, and they were mostly rams and ewes which they had mind to slaughter.

There Grettir set himself down in peace; and by then had he been fifteen or sixteen winters in outlawry, as Sturla Thordson has said.

Chapter 70
Of the Bonders Who Owned Drangey Between Them

IN THE DAYS WHEN Grettir came to Drangey, these were chief men of the country side of Skagafirth. Hialti dwelt at Hof in Hialtidale, he was the son of Thord, the son of Hialti, the son of Thord the Scalp: Hialti was a great chief, a right noble man, and much befriended. Thorbiorn Angle was the name of his brother, a big man and a strong, hardy and wild withal. Thord, the father of these twain, had married again in his old age, and that wife was not the mother of the brothers; and she did ill to her step-children, but served Thorbiorn the worst, for that he was hard to deal with and reckless. And on a day Thorbiorn Angle sat playing at tables, and his stepmother passed by and saw that he was playing at the knave-game, and the fashion of the game was the large tail-game. Now she deemed him thriftless, and cast some word at him, but he gave an evil answer; so she caught up one of the men, and drave the tail thereof into Thorbiorn's cheek-bone wherefrom it glanced into his eye, so that it hung out on his cheek. He sprang up, caught hold of her, and handled her roughly, insomuch that she took to her bed, and died thereof afterwards, and folk say that she was then big with child.

Thereafter Thorbiorn became of all men the most riotous; he took his heritage, and dwelt at first in Woodwick.

Haldor the son of Thorgeir, who was the son of Head-Thord, dwelt at Hof on Head-strand, he had to wife Thordis, the daughter of Thord Hialtison, and sister to those brothers Hialti and Thorbiorn Angle. Haldor was a great bonder, and rich in goods.

Biorn was the name of a man who dwelt at Meadness in the Fleets; he was a friend to Haldor of Hof. These men held to each other in all cases.

Tongue-Stein dwelt at Stonestead; he was the son of Biorn, the son of Ufeigh Thinbeard, son of that Crow-Hreidar to whom Eric of God-dales gave the tongue of land down from Hall-marsh. Stein was a man of great renown.

One named Eric was the son of Holmgang-Starri, the son of Eric of God-dales, the son of Hroald, the son of Geirmund Thick-beard; Eric dwelt at Hof in God-dales.

Now all these were men of great account.

Two brothers there were who dwelt at a place called Broad-river in Flat-lithe, and they were both called Thord; they were wondrous strong, and yet withal peaceable men both of them.

All these men had share in Drangey, and it is said that no less than twenty in all had some part in the island, nor would any sell his share to another; but the sons of Thord, Hialti and Thorbiorn Angle, had the largest share, because they were the richest men.

Chapter 71
How Those of Skagafirth Found Grettir on Drangey

NOW TIME WEARS ON towards the winter solstice; then the bonders get ready to go fetch the fat beasts for slaughter from the island; so they manned a great barge, and every owner had one to go in his stead, and some two.

But when these came anigh the island they saw men going about there; they deemed that strange, but guessed that men had been shipwrecked, and got aland there: so they row up to where the ladders were, when lo, the first-comers drew up the ladders.

Then the bonders deemed that things were taking a strange turn, and hailed those men and asked them who they were: Grettir named himself and his fellows withal: but the bonders asked who had brought him there.

Grettir answered, "He who owned the keel and had the hands, and who was more my friend than yours."

The bonders answered and said, "Let us now get our sheep, but come thou aland with us, keeping freely whatso of our sheep thou hast slaughtered."

"A good offer," said Grettir, "but this time let each keep what he has got; and I tell you, once for all, that hence I go not, till I am dragged away dead; for it is not my way to let that go loose which I have once laid hand on."

Thereat the bonders held their peace, and deemed that a woeful guest had come to Drangey; then they gave him choice of many things, both moneys and fair words, but Grettir said nay to one and all, and they gat them gone with things in such a stead, and were ill content with their fate; and told the men of the country-side what a wolf had got on to the island.

This took them all unawares, but they could think of nought to do herein; plentifully they talked over it that winter, but could see no rede whereby to get Grettir from the island.

Chapter 72
Of the Sports at Heron-ness Thing

NOW THE DAYS wore till such time as men went to the Heron-ness Thing in spring-tide, and many came thronging there from that part of the country, wherefrom men had to go to that Thing for their suits. Men sat there long time both over the suits and over sports, for there were many blithe men in that country-side. But when Grettir heard that all men fared to the Thing, he made a plot with his friends; for he was in goodwill with those who dwelt nighest to him, and for them he spared nought that he could get. But now he said that he would go aland, and gather victuals, but that Illugi and Noise should stay behind. Illugi thought this ill counselled, but let things go as Grettir would.

So Grettir bade them watch the ladders well, for that all things lay thereon; and thereafter he went to the mainland, and got what he deemed needful: he hid himself from men whereso he came, nor did any one know that he was on the land. Withal he heard concerning the Thing, that there was much sport there, and was fain to go thither; so he did on old gear and evil, and thus came to the Thing, whenas men went from the courts home to their booths. Then fell certain young men to talking how that the day was fair and good, and that it were well, belike, for the young men to betake them to wrestling and merrymaking. Folk said it was well counselled; and so men went and sat them down out from the booths.

Now the sons of Thord, Hialti and Thorbiorn Angle, were the chief men in this sport; Thorbiorn Angle was boisterous beyond measure, and drove men hard and fast to the place of the sports, and every man must needs go whereas his will was; and he would take this man and that by the hands and drag him forth unto the playing-ground.

Now first those wrestled who were weakest, and then each man in his turn, and therewith the game and glee waxed great; but when most men had wrestled but those who were the strongest, the bonders fell to talking as to who would be like to lay hand to either of the Thords, who have been aforenamed; but there was no man ready for that. Then the Thords went up to sundry men, and put themselves forward for wrestling, but *the nigher the call the further the man*. Then Thorbiorn Angle looks about, and sees where a man sits, great of growth, and his face hidden somewhat. Thorbiorn laid hold of him, and tugged hard at him, but he sat quiet and moved no whit. Then said Thorbiorn:

"No one has kept his place before me today like thou hast; what man art thou?"

He answers, "Guest am I hight."

Said Thorbiorn, "Belike thou wilt do somewhat for our merriment; a wished-for guest wilt thou be."

He answered, "About and about, methinks, will things change speedily; nor shall I cast myself into play with you here, where all is unknown to me."

Then many men said he were worthy of good at their hands, if he, an unknown man, gave sport to the people. Then he asked what they would of him; so they prayed him to wrestle with some one.

He said he had left wrestling, "though time agone it was somewhat of a sport to me."

So, when he did not deny them utterly, they prayed him thereto yet the more.

He said, "Well, if ye are so fain that I be dragged about here, ye must do so much therefor, as to handsel me peace, here at the Thing, and until such time as I come back to my home."

Then they all sprang up and said that so they would do indeed; but Hafr was the name of him who urged most that peace should be given to the man. This Hafr was the son of Thorarin, the son of Hafr, the son of Thord Knob, who had settled land up from the Weir in the Fleets to Tongue-river, and who dwelt at Knobstead; and a wordy man was Hafr.

So now he gave forth the handselling grandly with open mouth, and this is the beginning thereof.

Chapter 73
The Handselling of Peace

SAYS HE, "HEREWITH I establish peace betwixt all men, but most of all betwixt all men and this same Guest who sits here, and so is named; that is to say, all men of rule, and goodly bonders, and all men young, and fit to bear arms, and all other men of the country-side of Heron-ness Thing, whencesoever any may have come here, of men named or unnamed. Let us handsel safety and full peace to that unknown new-comer, yclept Guest by name, for game, wrestling, and all glee, for abiding here, and going home, whether he has need to fare over water, or over land, or over ferry; safety shall he have, in all steads named and unnamed, even so long as needs be for his coming home whole, under faith holden. This peace I establish on behoof of us, and of our kin, friends, and men of affinity, women even as men, bondswomen, even as bondsmen, swains and men of estate. Let him be a shamed peace-breaker, who breaks the peace, or spills the troth settled; turned away and driven forth from God, and good men of the kingdom of

Heaven, and all Holy ones. A man not to be borne of any man, but cast out from all, as wide as wolves stray, or Christian men make for Churches, or heathen in God's-houses do sacrifice, or fire burns, or earth brings forth, or a child, new-come to speech, calls mother, or mother bears son, or the sons of men kindle fire, or ships sweep on, or shields glitter, or the sun shines, or the snow falls, or a Finn sweeps on skates, or a fir-tree waxes, or a falcon flies the spring-long day with a fair wind under either wing, or the Heavens dwindle far away, or the world is built, or the wind turns waters seaward, or carles sow corn. Let him shun churches, and Christian folk, and heathen men, houses and caves, and every home but the home of Hell. Now shall we be at peace and of one mind each with the other, and of goodwill, whether we meet on fell or foreshore, ship or snow-shoes, earth or ice-mount, sea or swift steed, even as each found his friend on water, or his brother on broad ways; in just such peace one with other, as father with son, or son with father in all dealings together. Now we lay hands together, each and all of us, to hold well this say of peace, and all words spoken in our settled troth: As witness God and good men, and all those who hear my words, and nigh this stead chance to stand."

Chapter 74
Of Grettir's Wrestling: and How Thorbiorn Angle Now Bought the More Part of Drangey

THEN MANY FELL to saying that many and great words had been spoken hereon; but now Guest said:

"Good is thy say and well hast thou spoken it; if ye spill not things hereafter, I shall not withhold that which I have to show forth."

So he cast off his hood, and therewith all his outer clothes.

Then they gazed one on the other, and awe spread over their faces, for they deemed they knew surely that this was Grettir Asmundson, for that he was unlike other men for his growth and prowess' sake: and all stood silent, but Hafr deemed he had made himself a fool. Now the men of the country-side fell into twos and twos together, and one upbraided the other, but him the most of all, who had given forth the words of peace.

Then said Grettir; "Make clear to me what ye have in your minds, because for no long time will I sit thus unclad; it is more your matter than mine, whether ye will hold the peace, or hold it not."

They answered few words and then sat down: and now the sons of Thord, and Halldor their brother-in-law, talked the matter over together; and some would hold the peace, and some not; so as they elbowed one another, and laid their heads together. Grettir sang a stave:

> "I, well known to men, have been
> On this morn both hid and seen;
> Double face my fortune wears,
> Evil now, now good it bears;
> Doubtful play-board have I shown
> Unto these men, who have grown
> Doubtful of their given word;
> Hafr's big noise goes overboard."

Then said Tongue-stein, "Thinkest thou that, Grettir? Knowest thou then what the chiefs will make their minds up to? but true it is thou art a man above all others for thy great heart's sake: yea, but dost thou not see how they rub their noses one against the other?"

 329

Then Grettir sang a stave:

> *"Raisers-up of roof of war,*
> *Nose to nose in counsel are;*
> *Wakeners of the shield-rain sit*
> *Wagging beard to talk of it:*
> *Scatterers of the serpent's bed*
> *Round about lay head to head.*
> *For belike they heard my name;*
> *And must balance peace and shame."*

Then spake Hialti the son of Thord; "So shall it not be," says he; "we shall hold to our peace and troth given, though we have been beguiled, for I will not that men should have such a deed to follow after, if we depart from that peace, that we ourselves have settled and handselled: Grettir shall go whither he will, and have peace until such time as he comes back from this journey; and then and not till then shall this word of truce be void, whatsoever may befall betwixt us meanwhile."

All thanked him therefor, and deemed that he had done as a great chief, such blood-guilt as there was on the other side: but the speech of Thorbiorn Angle was little and low thereupon.

Now men said that both the Thords should lay hand to Grettir, and he bade them have it as they would: so one of the brothers stood forth; and Grettir stood up stiff before him, and he ran at Grettir at his briskest, but Grettir moved no whit from his place: then Grettir stretched out his hand down Thord's back, over the head of him, and caught hold of him by the breeches, and tripped up his feet, and cast him backward over his head in such wise that he fell on his shoulder, and a mighty fall was that.

Then men said that both those brothers should go against Grettir at once; and thus was it done, and great swinging and pulling about there was, now one side, now the other getting the best of it, though one or other of the brothers Grettir ever had under him; but each in turn must fall on his knee, or have some slip one of the other; and so hard they griped each at each, that they were all blue and bruised.

All men thought this the best of sport, and when they had made an end of it, thanked them for the wrestling; and it was the deeming of those who sat thereby, that the two brothers together were no stronger than Grettir alone, though each of them had the strength of two men of the strongest: so evenly matched they were withal, that neither might get the better of the other if they tried it between them.

Grettir abode no long time at the Thing; the bonders bade him give up the island, but he said nay to this, nor might they do aught herein.

So Grettir fared back to Drangey, and Illugi was as fain of him as might be; and there they abode peacefully, and Grettir told them the story of his doings and his journeys; and thus the summer wore away.

All men deemed that those of Skagafirth had shown great manliness herein, that they held to their peace given; and folk may well mark how trusty men were in those days, whereas Grettir had done such deeds against them.

Now the less rich men of the bonders spake together, that there was little gain to them in holding small shares in Drangey; so they offered to sell their part to the sons of Thord; Hialti said that he would not deal with them herein, for the bonders made it part of the bargain, that he who bought of them should either slay Grettir or get him away. But Thorbiorn Angle said, that he would not spare to take the lead of an onset against Grettir if they would give him wealth therefor. So his brother Hialti gave up to him his share in the island, for that he was the hardest man, and the least befriended of the twain; and in likewise too did other bonders; so Thorbiorn Angle got the more part of the island for little worth, but bound himself withal to get Grettir away.

Chapter 75
Thorbiorn Angle Goes to Drangey to Speak with Grettir

WHENAS SUMMER WAS FAR SPENT, Thorbiorn Angle went with a well-manned barge out to Drangey, and Grettir and his fellows stood forth on the cliff's edge; so there they talked together. Thorbiorn prayed Grettir to do so much for his word, as to depart from the island; Grettir said there was no hope of such an end.

Then said Thorbiorn, "Belike I may give thee meet aid if thou dost this, for now have many bonders given up to me their shares in the island."

Grettir answered, "Now hast thou shown forth that which brings me to settle in my mind that I will never go hence, whereas thou sayest that thou now hast the more part of the island; and good is it that we twain alone share the kale: for in sooth, hard I found it to have all the men of Skagafirth against me; but now let neither spare the other, for not such are we twain, as are like to be smothered in the friendship of men; and thou mayst leave coming hither, for on my side is all over and done."

"*All things bide their day*," said Thorbiorn, "and an ill day thou bidest."

"I am content to risk it," said Grettir; and in such wise they parted, and Thorbiorn went home.

Chapter 76
How Noise Let the Fire out on Drangey, and How Grettir Must Needs Go Aland for More

SO THE TALE TELLS, that by then they had been two winters on Drangey, they had slaughtered well-nigh all the sheep that were there, but one ram, as men say, they let live; he was piebald of belly and head, and exceeding big-horned; great game they had of him, for he was so wise that he would stand waiting without, and run after them whereso they went; and he would come home to the hut anights and rub his horns against the door.

Now they deemed it good to abide on the island, for food was plenty, because of the fowl and their eggs; but firewood was right hard to come by; and ever Grettir would let the thrall go watch for drift, and logs were often drifted there, and he would bear them to the fire; but no need had the brothers to do any work beyond climbing into the cliffs when it liked them. But the thrall took to loathing his work, and got more grumbling and heedless than he was wont heretofore: his part it was to watch the fire night by night, and Grettir gave him good warning thereon, for no boat they had with them.

Now so it befell that on a certain night their fire went out; Grettir was wroth thereat, and said it was but his due if Noise were beaten for that deed; but the thrall said that his life was an evil life, if he must lie there in outlawry, and be shaken and beaten withal if aught went amiss.

Grettir asked Illugi what rede there was for the matter, but he said he could see none, but that they should abide there till some keel should be brought thither: Grettir said it was but blindness to hope for that. "Rather will I risk whether I may not come aland."

"Much my mind misgives me thereof," said Illugi, "for we are all lost if thou comest to any ill."

"I shall not be swallowed up swimming," said Grettir; "but henceforward I shall trust the thrall the worse for this, so much as lies hereon."

Now the shortest way to the mainland from the island, was a sea-mile long.

Chapter 77
Grettir at the Home-stead of Reeks

NOW GRETTIR GOT ALL READY for swimming, and had on a cowl of market-wadmal, and his breeches girt about him, and he got his fingers webbed together, and the weather was fair. So he went from the island late in the day, and desperate Illugi deemed his journey. Grettir made out into the bay, and the stream was with him, and a calm was over all. He swam on fast, and came aland at Reekness by then the sun had set: he went up to the homestead at Reeks, and into a bath that night, and then went into the chamber; it was very warm there, for there had been a fire therein that evening, and the heat was not yet out of the place; but he was exceeding weary, and there fell into a deep sleep, and so lay till far on into the next day.

Now as the morning wore the home folk arose, and two women came into the chamber, a handmaid and the goodman's daughter. Grettir was asleep, and the bed-clothes had been cast off him on to the floor; so they saw that a man lay there, and knew him.

Then said the handmaiden: "So may I thrive, sister! here is Grettir Asmundson lying bare, and I call him right well ribbed about the chest, but few might think he would be so small of growth below; and so then that does not go along with other kinds of bigness."

The goodman's daughter answered: "Why wilt thou have everything on thy tongue's end? Thou art a measure-less fool; be still."

"Dear sister, how can I be still about it?" says the handmaid. "I would not have believed it, though one had told me."

And now she would whiles run up to him and look, and whiles run back again to the goodman's daughter, screaming and laughing; but Grettir heard what she said, and as she ran in over the floor by him he caught hold of her, and sang this stave:

> "Stay a little, foolish one!
> When the shield-shower is all done,
> With the conquered carles and lords,
> Men bide not to measure swords:
> Many a man had there been glad,
> Lesser war-gear to have had.
> With a heart more void of fear;
> Such I am not, sweet and dear."

Therewithal he swept her up into the bed, but the bonder's daughter ran out of the place; then sang Grettir this other stave:

> "Sweet amender of the seam,
> Weak and worn thou dost me deem:
> O light-handed dear delight,
> Certes thou must say aright.
> Weak I am, and certainly
> Long in white arms must I lie:

Hast thou heart to leave me then,
Fair-limbed gladdener of great men?"

The handmaid shrieked out, but in such wise did they part that she laid no blame on Grettir when all was over.

A little after, Grettir arose, and went to Thorvald the goodman, and told him of his trouble, and prayed bring him out; so did he, and lent him a boat, and brought him out, and Grettir thanked him well for his manliness.

But when it was heard that Grettir had swam a sea-mile, all deemed his prowess both on sea and land to be marvellous.

Those of Skagafirth had many words to say against Thorbiorn Angle, in that he drave not Grettir away from Drangey, and said they would take back each his own share; but he said he found the task no easy one, and prayed them be good to him, and abide awhile.

Chapter 78
Of Haring at Drangey, and the End of Him

THAT SAME SUMMER a ship came to the Gangpass-mouth, and therein was a man called Haering – a young man he was, and so lithe that there was no cliff that he might not climb. He went to dwell with Thorbiorn Angle, and was there on into the autumn; and he was ever urging Thorbiorn to go to Drangey, saying that he would fain see whether the cliffs were so high that none might come up them. Thorbiorn said that he should not work for nought if he got up into the island, and slew Grettir, or gave him some wound; and withal he made it worth coveting to Haering. So they fared to Drangey, and set the eastman ashore in a certain place, and he was to set on them unawares if he might come up on to the island, but they laid their keel by the ladders, and fell to talking with Grettir; and Thorbiorn asked him if he were minded now to leave the place; but he said that to nought was his mind so made up as to stay there.

"A great game hast thou played with us," said Thorbiorn; "but thou seemest not much afeard for thyself."

Thus a long while they gave and took in words, and came nowise together hereon.

But of Haering it is to be told that he climbed the cliffs, going on the right hand and the left, and got up by such a road as no man has gone by before or since; but when he came to the top of the cliff, he saw where the brothers stood, with their backs turned toward him, and thought in a little space to win both goods and great fame; nor were they at all aware of his ways, for they deemed that no man might come up, but there whereas the ladders were. Grettir was talking with Thorbiorn, nor lacked there words of the biggest on either side; but withal Illugi chanced to look aside, and saw a man drawing anigh them.

Then he said, "Here comes a man at us, with axe raised aloft, and in right warlike wise he seems to fare."

"Turn thou to meet him," says Grettir, "but I will watch the ladders."

So Illugi turned to meet Haering, and when the eastman saw him, he turned and fled here and there over the island. Illugi chased him while the island lasted, but when he came forth on to the cliff's edge Haering leapt down thence, and every bone in him was broken, and so ended his life; but the place where he was lost has been called Haering's-leap ever since.

Illugi came back, and Grettir asked how he had parted from this one who had doomed them to die.

"He would have nought to do," says Illugi, "with my seeing after his affairs, but must needs break his neck over the rock; so let the bonders pray for him as one dead."

So when Angle heard that, he bade his folk make off. "Twice have I fared to meet Grettir, but no third time will I go, if I am nought the wiser first; and now belike they may sit in Drangey as for me; but in my mind it is, that Grettir will abide here but a lesser time than heretofore."

With that they went home, and men deemed this journey of theirs worser than the first, and Grettir abode that winter in Drangey, nor in that season did he and Thorbiorn meet again.

In those days died Skapti Thorodson the Lawman, and great scathe was that to Grettir, for he had promised to busy himself about his acquittal as soon as he had been twenty winters in outlawry, and this year, of which the tale was told e'en now, was the nineteenth year thereof.

In the spring died Snorri the Godi, and many matters befell in that season that come not into this story.

Chapter 79
Of the Talk at the Thing About Grettir's Outlawry

THAT SUMMER, at the Althing, the kin of Grettir spake many things concerning his outlawry, and some deemed he had outworn the years thereof, if he had come at all into the twentieth year; but they who had blood-suits against him would not have it so, and said, that he had done many an outlaw's deed since he was first outlawed, and deemed his time ought to last longer therefor.

At that time was a new lawman made, Stein, the son of Thorgest, the son of Stein the Far-sailing, the son of Thorir Autumn-mirk; the mother of Stein was Arnora, the daughter of Thord the Yeller; and Stein was a wise man.

Now was he prayed for the word of decision; and he bade them search and see whether this were the twentieth summer since Grettir was made an outlaw, and thus it seemed to be.

But then stood forth Thorir of Garth, and brought all into dispute again, for he found that Grettir had been one winter out here a sackless man, amidst the times of his outlawry, and then nineteen were the winters of his outlawry found to be. Then said the lawman that no one should be longer in outlawry than twenty winters in all, though he had done outlaw's deeds in that time.

"But before that, I declare no man sackless."

Now because of this was the acquittal delayed for this time, but it was thought a sure thing that he would be made sackless the next summer. But that misliked the Skagafirthers exceeding ill, if Grettir were to come out of his outlawry, and they bade Thorbiorn Angle do one of two things, either give back the island or slay Grettir; but he deemed well that he had a work on his hands, for he saw no rede for the winning of Grettir, and yet was he fain to hold the island; and so all manner of craft he sought for the overcoming of Grettir, if he might prevail either by guile or hardihood, or in any wise soever.

Chapter 80
Thorbiorn Angle Goes with His Foster-mother out to Drangey

THORBIORN ANGLE had a foster-mother, Thurid by name, exceeding old, and meet for little, as folk deemed, very cunning she had been in many and great matters of lore, when she was young, and men were yet heathen; but men thought of her as of one, who had lost all that. But now, though Christ's law were established in the land, yet abode still many sparks of heathendom. It had been law in the land, that men were not forbidden to sacrifice secretly, or deal with other lore of eld, but it was lesser outlawry if such doings oozed out. Now in such wise it fared with many, that *hand for wont did yearn*, and things grew handiest by time that had been learned in youth.

So now, whenas Thorbiorn Angle was empty of all plots, he sought for help there, whereas most folk deemed it most unlike that help was – at the hands of his foster-mother, in sooth, and asked, what counsel was in her therefor.

She answered, "Now belike matters have come to this, even as the saw says – *To the goat-house for wool*: but what could I do less than this, to think myself before folk of the country-side, but be a man of nought, whenso anything came to be tried? nor see I how I may fare worse than thou, though I may scarce rise from my bed. But if thou art to have my rede, then shall I have my will as to how and what things are done."

He gave his assent thereto, and said that she had long been of wholesome counsel to him.

Now the time wore on to Twainmonth of summer; and one fair-weather day the carline spake to Angle:

"Now is the weather calm and bright, and I will now that thou fare to Drangey and pick a quarrel with Grettir; I shall go with thee, and watch how heedful he may be of his words; and if I see them, I shall have some sure token as to how far they are befriended of fortune, and then shall I speak over them such words as seem good to me."

Angle answered, "Loth am I to be faring to Drangey, for ever am I of worser mind when I depart thence than when I come thereto."

Then said the carline, "Nought will I do for thee if thou sufferest me to rule in no wise."

"Nay, so shall it not be, foster-mother," said he; "but so much have I said, as that I would so come thither the third time that somewhat should be made of the matter betwixt us."

"The chance of that must be taken," said the carline "and many a heavy labour must thou have, or ever Grettir be laid to earth; and oft will it be doubtful to thee what fortune thine shall be, and heavy troubles wilt thou get therefrom when that is done; yet art thou so bounden here-under, that to somewhat must thou make up thy mind."

Thereafter Thorbiorn Angle let put forth a ten-oared boat, and he went thereon with eleven men, and the carline was in their company.

So they fell to rowing as the weather went, out to Drangey; and when the brothers saw that, they stood forth at the ladders, and they began to talk the matter over yet once more; and Thorbiorn said, that he was come yet again, to talk anew of their leaving the island, and that he would deal lightly with his loss of money and Grettir's dwelling there, if so be they might part without harm. But Grettir said that he had no words to make atwixt and atween of his going thence.

"Oft have I so said," says he, "and no need there is for thee to talk to me thereon; ye must even do as ye will, but here will I abide, whatso may come to hand."

Now Thorbiorn deemed, that this time also his errand was come to nought, and he said:

"Yea, I deemed I knew with what men of hell I had to do; and most like it is that a day or two will pass away ere I come hither again."

"I account that not in the number of my griefs, though thou never comest back," said Grettir.

Now the carline lay in the stern, with clothes heaped up about and over her, and with that she moved, and said:

"Brave will these men be, and luckless withal; far hast thou outdone them in manliness; thou biddest them choice of many goodly things, but they say nay to all, and few things lead surer to ill, than not to know how to take good. Now this I cast over thee, Grettir, that thou be left of all health, wealth, and good-hap, all good heed and wisdom: yea, and that the more, the longer thou livest; good hope I have, Grettir, that thy days of gladness shall be fewer here in time to come than in the time gone by."

Now when Grettir heard these words, he was astonied withal, and said, "What fiend is there in the boat with them?"

Illugi answers, "I deem that it will be the carline, Thorbiorn's foster-mother."

"Curses on the witch-wight!" says Grettir, "nought worse could have been looked for; at no words have I shuddered like as I shuddered at those words she spake; and well I wot that from her, and her foul cunning, some evil will be brought on us; yet shall she have some token to mind her that she has sought us here."

Therewithal he caught up a marvellous great stone, and cast it down on to the boat, and it smote that clothes-heap; and a longer stone-throw was that than Thorbiorn deemed any man might make; but therewithal a great shriek arose, for the stone had smitten the carline's thigh, and broken it.

Then said Illugi, "I would thou hadst not done that!"

"Blame me not therefor," said Grettir, "I fear me the stroke has been too little, for certes not overmuch weregild were paid for the twain of us, though the price should be one carline's life."

"Must she alone be paid?" said Illugi, "little enough then will be laid down for us twain."

Now Thorbiorn got him gone homeward, with no greetings at parting. But he said to the carline:

"Now have matters gone as I thought, that a journey of little glory thou shouldst make to the island; thou hast got maimed, and honour is no nigher to us than before, yea, we must have bootless shame on bootless shame."

She answered, "This will be the springing of ill-hap to them; and I deem that henceforth they are on the wane; neither do I fear if I live, but that I shall have revenge for this deed they have thus done me."

"Stiff is thine heart, meseems, foster-mother," said Thorbiorn. With that they came home, but the carline was laid in her bed, and abode there nigh a month; by then was the hurt thigh-bone grown together again, and she began to be afoot once more.

Great laughter men made at that journey of Thorbiorn and the carline, and deemed he had been often enow out-played in his dealings with Grettir: first, at the Spring-Thing in the peace handselling; next, when Haering was lost, and now again, this third time, when the carline's thigh-bone was broken, and no stroke had been played against these from his part. But great shame and grief had Thorbiorn Angle from all these words.

Chapter 81
Of the Carline's Evil Gift to Grettir

NOW WORE AWAY the time of autumn till it wanted but three weeks of winter; then the carline bade bear her to the sea-shore. Thorbiorn asked what she would there.

"Little is my errand, yet maybe," she says, "it is a foreboding of greater tidings."

Now was it done as she bade, and when she came down to the strand, she went limping along by the sea, as if she were led thereto, unto a place where lay before her an uprooted tree, as big as a man might bear on his shoulder. She looked at the tree and bade them turn it over before her eyes, and on one side it was as if singed and rubbed; so there whereas it was rubbed she let cut a little flat space; and then she took her knife and cut runes on the root, and made them red with her blood, and sang witch-words over them; then she went backwards and widdershins round about the tree, and cast over it many a strong spell; thereafter she let thrust the tree forth into the sea, and spake in such wise over it, that it should drive out to Drangey, and that Grettir should have all hurt therefrom that might be. Thereafter she went back home to Woodwick; and Thorbiorn said that he knew not if that would come to aught; but the carline answered that he should wot better anon.

Now the wind blew landward up the firth, yet the carline's root went in the teeth of the wind, and belike it sailed swifter than might have been looked for of it. Grettir abode in Drangey with his fellows as is aforesaid, and in good case they were; but the day after the carline had wrought her witch-craft on the tree the brothers went down below the cliffs searching for firewood, so when they came to the west of the island, there they found that tree drifted ashore.

Then said Illugi, "A big log of firewood, kinsman, let us bear it home."

Grettir kicked it with his foot and said, "An evil tree from evil sent; other firewood than this shall we have."

Therewithal he cast it out into the sea, and bade Illugi beware of bearing it home, "For it is sent us for our ill-hap." And therewith they went unto their abode, and said nought about it to the thrall. But the next day they found the tree again, and it was nigher to the ladders than heretofore; Grettir drave it out to sea, and said that it should never be borne home.

Now the days wore on into summer, and a gale came on with much wet, and the brothers were loth to be abroad, and bade Noise go search for firewood.

He took it ill, and said he was ill served in that he had to drudge and labour abroad in all the foulest weather; but withal he went down to the beach before the ladders and found the carline's tree there, and deemed things had gone well because of it; so he took it up and bore it to the hut, and cast it down thereby with a mighty thump.

Grettir heard it and said, "Noise has got something, so I shall go out and see what it is."

Therewithal he took up a wood-axe, and went out, and straightway Noise said:

"Split it up in as good wise as I have brought it home, then."

Grettir grew short of temper with the thrall, and smote the axe with both hands at the log, nor heeded what tree it was; but as soon as ever the axe touched the wood, it turned flatlings and glanced off therefrom into Grettir's right leg above the knee, in such wise that it stood in the bone, and a great wound was that. Then he looked at the tree and said:

"Now has evil heart prevailed, nor will this hap go alone, since that same tree has now come back to us that I have cast out to sea on these two days. But for thee, Noise, two slips hast thou had, first, when thou must needs let the fire be slaked, and now this bearing home of that tree of ill-hap; but if a third thou hast, thy bane will it be, and the bane of us all."

With that came Illugi and bound up Grettir's hurt, and it bled little, and Grettir slept well that night; and so three nights slipped by in such wise that no pain came of the wound, and when they loosed the swathings, the lips of the wound were come together so that it was well-nigh grown over again. Then said Illugi:

"Belike thou wilt have no long hurt of this wound."

"Well were it then," said Grettir, "but marvellously has this befallen, whatso may come of it; and my mind misgives me of the way things will take."

Chapter 82
Grettir Sings of His Great Deeds

NOW THEY LAY them down that evening, but at midnight Grettir began to tumble about exceedingly. Illugi asked why he was so unquiet. Grettir said that his leg had taken to paining him, "And methinks it is like that some change of hue there be therein."

Then they kindled a light, and when the swathings were undone, the leg showed all swollen and coal-blue, and the wound had broken open, and was far more evil of aspect than at first; much pain there went therewith so that he might not abide at rest in any wise, and never came sleep on his eyes.

Then spake Grettir, "Let us make up our minds to it, that this sickness which I have gotten is not done for nought, for it is of sorcery, and the carline is minded to avenge her of that stone."

Illugi said, "Yea, I told thee that thou wouldst get no good from that hag."

"*All will come to one end*," said Grettir, and sang this song withal:

> "*Doubtful played the foredoomed fate*
> *Round the sword in that debate,*
> *When the bearserks' outlawed crew,*
> *In the days of yore I slew.*
> *Screamed the worm of clashing lands*
> *When Hiarandi dropped his hands*
> *Biorn and Gunnar cast away,*
> *Hope of dwelling in the day.*

> "*Home again then travelled I;*
> *The broad-boarded ship must lie,*
> *Under Door-holm, as I went,*
> *Still with weapon play content,*
> *Through the land; and there the thane*
> *Called me to the iron rain,*
> *Bade me make the spear-storm rise,*
> *Torfi Vebrandson the wise.*

> "*To such plight the Skald was brought,*
> *Wounder of the walls of thought,*
> *Howsoever many men*
> *Stood, all armed, about us then,*
> *That his hand that knew the oar,*
> *Grip of sword might touch no more;*
> *Yet to me the wound who gave*
> *Did he give a horse to have.*

> "*Thorbiorn Arnor's son, men said:*
> *Of no great deed was afraid,*
> *Folk spake of him far and wide;*
> *He forbade me to abide*
> *Longer on the lovely earth;*
> *Yet his heart was little worth,*
> *Not more safe alone was I,*
> *Than when armed he drew anigh.*

> "*From the sword's edge and the spears*
> *From my many waylayers,*

While might was, and my good day,
Often did I snatch away;
Now a hag, whose life outworn
Wicked craft and ill hath borne,
Meet for death lives long enow,
Grettir's might to overthrow."

"Now must we take good heed to ourselves," said Grettir, "for Thorbiorn Angle must be minded that this hap shall not go alone; and I will, Noise, that thou watch the ladders every day from this time forth, but pull them up in the evening, and see thou do it well and truly, even as though much lay thereon, but if thou bewrayest us, short will be thy road to ill."

So Noise promised great things concerning this. Now the weather grew harder, and a north-east wind came on with great cold: every night Grettir asked if the ladders were drawn up.

Then said Noise, "Yea, certainly! men are above all things to be looked for now. Can any man have such a mind to take thy life, that he will do so much as to slay himself therefor? for this gale is far other than fair; lo now, methinks thy so great bravery and hardihood has come utterly to an end, if thou must needs think that all things soever will be thy bane."

"Worse wilt thou bear thyself than either of us," said Grettir, "when the need is on us; but now go watch the ladders, whatsoever will thou hast thereto."

So every morning they drave him out, and ill he bore it.

But Grettir's hurt waxed in such wise that all the leg swelled up, and the thigh began to gather matter both above and below, and the lips of the wound were all turned out, so that Grettir's death was looked for.

Illugi sat over him night and day, and took heed to nought else, and by then it was the second week since Grettir hurt himself.

Chapter 83
How Thorbiorn Angle Gathered Force and Set Sail for Drangey

THORBIORN ANGLE SAT this while at home at Woodwick, and was ill-content in that he might not win Grettir; but when a certain space had passed since the carline had put the sorcery into the root, she comes to talk with Thorbiorn, and asks if he were not minded to go see Grettir. He answers, that to nought was his mind so made up as that he would not go; "perchance thou wilt go meet him, foster-mother," says Thorbiorn.

"Nay, I shall not go meet-him," says the carline; "but I have sent my greeting to him, and some hope I have that it has come home to him; and good it seems to me that thou go speedily to meet him, or else shalt thou never have such good hap as to overcome him."

Thorbiorn answered: "So many shameful journeys have I made thither, that there I go not ever again; moreover that alone is full enough to stay me, that such foul weather it is, that it is safe to go nowhither, whatso the need may be."

She answered: "Ill counselled thou art, not to see how to overcome herein. Now yet once again will I lay down a rede for this; go thou first and get thee strength of men, and ride to Hof to Halldor thy brother-in-law, and take counsel of him. But if I may rule in some way how Grettir's health goes, how shall it be said that it is past hope that I may also deal with the gale that has been veering about this while?"

Thorbiorn deemed it might well be that the carline saw further than he had thought she might, and straightway sent up into the country-side for men; but speedy answer there came that none of those who had given up their shares would do aught to ease his task, and they said that Thorbiorn should have to himself both the owning of the island and the onset on Grettir. But Tongue-Stein gave him two of his followers, and Hialti, his brother, sent him three men, and Eric of God-dales one, and from his own homestead he had six. So the twelve of them ride from Woodwick out to Hof. Halldor bade them abide there, and asked their errand; then Thorbiorn told it as clearly as might be. Halldor asked whose rede this might be, and Thorbiorn said that his foster-mother urged him much thereto.

"That will bear no good," said Halldor, "because she is cunning in sorcery, and such-like things are now forbidden."

"I may not look closely into all these matters before-hand," said Thorbiorn, "but in somewise or other shall this thing have an end if I may have my will. Now, how shall I go about it, so that I may come to the island?"

"Meseems," says Halldor, "that thou trustest in somewhat, though I wot not how good that may be. But now if thou wilt go forward with it, go thou out to Meadness in the Fleets to Biorn my friend; a good keel he has, so tell him of my word, that I would he should lend you the craft, and thence ye may sail out to Drangey. But the end of your journey I see not, if Grettir is sound and hale: yea, and be thou sure that if ye win him not in manly wise, he leaves enough of folk behind to take up the blood-suit after him. And slay not Illugi if ye may do otherwise. But methinks I see that all is not according to Christ's law in these redes."

Then Halldor gave them six men withal for their journey; one was called Karr, another Thorleif, and a third Brand, but the rest are not named.

So they fared thence, eighteen in company, out to the Fleets, and came to Meadness and gave Biorn Halldor's message, he said that it was but due for Halldor's sake, but that he owed nought to Thorbiorn; withal it seemed to him that they went on a mad journey, and he let them from it all he might.

They said they might not turn back, and so went down to the sea, and put forth the craft, and all its gear was in the boat-stand hard by; so they made them ready for sailing, and foul enow the weather seemed to all who stood on land. But they hoisted sail, and the craft shot swiftly far into the firth, but when they came out into the main part thereof into deep water, the wind abated in such wise that they deemed it blew none too hard.

So in the evening at dusk they came to Drangey.

Chapter 84
The Slaying of Grettir Asmundson

NOW IT IS TO BE TOLD, that Grettir was so sick, that he might not stand on his feet, but Illugi sat beside him, and Noise was to keep watch and ward; and many words he had against that, and said that they would still think that life was falling from them, though nought had happed to bring it about; so he went out from their abode right unwillingly, and when he came to the ladders he spake to himself and said that now he would not draw them up; withal he grew exceeding sleepy, and lay down and slept all day long, and right on till Thorbiorn came to the island.

So now they see that the ladders are not drawn up; then spake Thorbiorn, "Now are things changed from what the wont was, in that there are none afoot, and their ladder stands in its place withal; maybe more things will betide in this our journey than we had thought of in the beginning: but now let us hasten to the hut, and let no man lack courage; for, wot this well, that if these men are hale, each one of us must needs do his best."

Then they went up on to the island, and looked round about, and saw where a man lay a little space off the landing-place, and snored hard and fast. Therewith Thorbiorn knew Noise, and went up to him and drave the hilt of his sword against the ear of him, and bade him, "Wake up, beast! certes in evil stead is he who trusts his life to thy faith and troth."

Noise looked up thereat and said, "Ah! Now are they minded to go on according to their wont; do ye, may-happen, think my freedom too great, though I lie out here in the cold?"

"Art thou witless," said Angle, "that thou seest not that thy foes are come upon thee, and will slay you all?"

Then Noise answered nought, but yelled out all he might, when he knew the men who they were.

"Do one thing or other," says Angle, "either hold thy peace forthwith, and tell us of your abode, or else be slain of us."

Thereat was Noise as silent as if he had been thrust under water; but Thorbiorn said, "Are they at their hut, those brothers? Why are they not afoot?"

"Scarce might that be," said Noise, "for Grettir is sick and come nigh to his death, and Illugi sits over him."

Then Angle asked how it was with their health, and what things had befallen. So Noise told him in what wise Grettir's hurt had come about.

Then Angle laughed and said, "Yea, sooth is the old saw, *Old friends are the last to sever*; and this withal, *Ill if a thrall is thine only friend*, whereso thou art, Noise; for shamefully hast thou bewrayed thy master, albeit he was nought good."

Then many laid evil things to his charge for his ill faith, and beat him till he was well-nigh past booting for, and let him lie there; but they went up to the hut and smote mightily on the door.

"Pied-belly is knocking hard at the door, brother," says Illugi.

"Yea, yea, hard, and over hard," says Grettir; and therewithal the door brake asunder.

Then sprang Illugi to his weapons and guarded the door, in such wise that there was no getting in for them. Long time they set on him there, and could bring nought against him save spear-thrusts, and still Illugi smote all the spear-heads from the shafts. But when they saw that they might thus bring nought to pass, they leapt up on to the roof of the hut, and tore off the thatch; then Grettir got to his feet and caught up a spear, and thrust out betwixt the rafters; but before that stroke was Karr, a home-man of Halldor of Hof, and forthwithal it pierced him through.

Then spoke Angle, and bade men fare warily and guard themselves well, "for we may prevail against them if we follow wary redes."

So they tore away the thatch from the ends of the ridge-beam, and bore on the beam till it brake asunder.

Now Grettir might not rise from his knee, but he caught up the short-sword, Karr's-loom, and even therewith down leapt those men in betwixt the walls, and a hard fray befell betwixt them. Grettir smote with the short-sword at Vikar, one of the followers of Hialti Thordson, and caught him on the left shoulder, even as he leapt in betwixt the walls, and cleft him athwart the shoulder down unto the right side, so that the man fell asunder, and the body so smitten atwain tumbled over on to Grettir, and for that cause he might not heave aloft the short-sword as speedily as he would, and therewith Thorbiorn Angle thrust him betwixt the shoulders, and great was that wound he gave.

Then cried Grettir, "*Bare is the back of the brotherless*." And Illugi threw his shield over Grettir, and warded him in so stout a wise that all men praised his defence.

Then said Grettir to Angle, "Who then showed thee the way here to the island?"

Said Angle, "The Lord Christ showed it us."

"Nay," said Grettir, "but I guess that the accursed hag, thy foster-mother, showed it thee, for in her redes must thou needs have trusted."

"All shall be one to thee now," said Angle, "in whomsoever I have put my trust."

Then they set on them fiercely, and Illugi made defence for both in most manly wise; but Grettir was utterly unmeet for fight, both for his wounds' sake and for his sickness. So Angle bade bear down Illugi with shields, "For never have I met his like, amongst men of such age."

Now thus they did, besetting him with beams and weapons till he might ward himself no longer; and then they laid hands on him, and so held him fast. But he had given some wound or other to the more part of those who had been at the onset, and had slain outright three of Angle's fellows.

Thereafter they went up to Grettir, but he was fallen forward on to his face, and no defence there was of him, for that he was already come to death's door by reason of the hurt in his leg, for all the thigh was one sore, even up to the small guts; but there they gave him many a wound, yet little or nought he bled.

So when they thought he was dead, Angle laid hold of the short-sword, and said that he had carried it long enough; but Grettir's fingers yet kept fast hold of the grip thereof, nor could the short-sword be loosened; many went up and tried at it, but could get nothing done therewith; eight of them were about it before the end, but none the more might bring it to pass.

Then said Angle, "Why should we spare this wood-man here? lay his hand on the block."

So when that was done they smote off his hand at the wrist, and the fingers straightened, and were loosed from the handle. Then Angle took the short-sword in both hands and smote at Grettir's head, and a right great stroke that was, so that the short-sword might not abide it, and a shard was broken from the midst of the edge thereof; and when men saw that, they asked why he must needs spoil a fair thing in such wise.

But Angle answered, "More easy is it to know that weapon now if it should be asked for."

They said it needed not such a deed since the man was dead already.

"Ah! but yet more shall be done," said Angle, and hewed therewith twice or thrice at Grettir's neck, or ever the head came off; and then he spake:

"Now know I for sure that Grettir is dead."

In such wise Grettir lost his life, the bravest man of all who have dwelt in Iceland; he lacked but one winter of forty-five years whenas he was slain; but he was fourteen winters old when he slew Skeggi, his first man-slaying; and from thenceforth all things turned to his fame, till the time when he dealt with Glam, the Thrall; and in those days was he of twenty winters-; but when he fell into outlawry, he was twenty-five years old; but in outlawry was he nigh nineteen winters, and full oft was he the while in great trials of men; and such as his life was, and his needs, he held well to his faith and troth, and most haps did he foresee, though he might do nought to meet them.

Chapter 85
How Thorbiorn Angle Claimed Grettir's Head-money

"A GREAT CHAMPION have we laid to earth here," said Thorbiorn; "now shall we bring the head aland with us, for I will not lose the money which has been laid thereon; nor may they then feign that they know not if I have slain Grettir."

They bade him do his will, but had few words to say hereon, for to all the deed seemed a deed of little prowess.

Then Angle fell to speaking with Illugi:

"Great scathe it is of such a brave man as thou art, that thou hast fallen to such folly, as to betake thee to ill deeds with this outlaw here, and must needs lie slain and unatoned therefore."

Illugi answered, "Then first when the Althing is over this summer, wilt thou know who are outlaws; but neither thou nor the carline, thy foster-mother, will judge in this matter, because that your sorcery and craft of old days have slain Grettir, though thou didst, indeed, bear steel against him, as he lay at death's door, and wrought that so great coward's deed there, over and above thy sorcery."

Then said Angle, "In manly wise speakest thou, but not thus will it be; and I will show thee that I think great scathe in thy death, for thy life will I give thee if thou wilt swear an oath for us here, to avenge thyself on none of those who have been in this journey."

Illugi said, "That might I have deemed a thing to talk about, if Grettir had been suffered to defend himself, and ye had won him with manliness and hardihood; but now nowise is it to be thought, that I will do so much for the keeping of my life, as to become base, even as thou art: and here I tell thee, once for all, that no one of men shall be of less gain to thee than I, if I live; for long will it be or ever I forget how ye have prevailed against Grettir. – Yea, much rather do I choose to die."

Then Thorbiorn Angle held talk with his fellows, whether they should let Illugi live or not; they said that, whereas he had ruled the journey, so should he rule the deeds; so Angle said that he knew not how to have that man hanging over his head, who would neither give troth, nor promise aught.

But when Illugi knew that they were fully minded to slay him, he laughed, and spake thus:

"Yea, now have your counsels sped, even as my heart would."

So at the dawning of the day they brought him to the eastern end of the island, and there slaughtered him; but all men praised his great heart, and deemed him unlike to any of his age.

They laid both the brothers in cairn on the island there; and thereafter took Grettir's head, and bore it away with them, and whatso goods there were in weapons or clothes; but the good short-sword Angle would not put into the things to be shared, and he bare it himself long afterwards. Noise they took with them, and he bore himself as ill as might be.

At nightfall the gale abated, and they rowed aland in the morning. Angle took land at the handiest place, and sent the craft out to Biorn; but by then they were come hard by Oyce-land, Noise began to bear himself so ill, that they were loth to fare any longer with him, so there they slew him, and long and loud he greeted or ever he was cut down.

Thorbiorn Angle went home to Woodwick, and deemed he had done in manly wise in this journey; but Grettir's head they laid in salt in the out-bower at Woodwick, which was called therefrom Grettir's-bower; and there it lay the winter long. But Angle was exceeding ill thought of for this work of his, as soon as folk knew that Grettir had been overcome by sorcery.

Thorbiorn Angle sat quiet till past Yule; then he rode to meet Thorir of Garth, and told him of these slayings; and this withal, that he deemed that money his due which had been put on Grettir's head. Thorir said that he might not hide that he had brought about Grettir's outlawry:

"Yea, and oft have I dealt hardly with him, yet so much for the taking of his life I would not have done, as to make me a misdoer, a man of evil craft, even as thou hast done; and the less shall I lay down that money for thee, in that I deem thee surely to be a man of forfeit life because of thy sorcery and wizard-craft."

Thorbiorn Angle answers, "Meseems thou art urged hereto more by closefistedness and a poor mind, than by any heed of how Grettir was won."

Thorir said that a short way they might make of it, in that they should abide the Althing, and take whatso the Lawman might deem most rightful: and in such wise they parted that there was no little ill-will betwixt Thorir and Thorbiorn Angle.

Chapter 86
How Thorbiorn Angle Brought Grettir's Head to Biarg

THE KIN OF GRETTIR and Illugi were exceeding ill-content when they heard of these slayings, and they so looked on matters as deeming that Angle had wrought a shameful deed in slaying a man at death's door; and that, besides that, he had become guilty of sorcery. They sought the counsel of the wisest men, and everywhere was Angle's work ill spoken of. As for him, he rode to Midfirth, when it lacked four weeks of summer; and when his ways were heard of, Asdis gathered men to her, and there came many of her friends: Gamli and Glum, her brothers-in-law, and their sons, Skeggi, who was called the Short-handed, and Uspak, who is aforesaid. Asdis was so well befriended, that all the Midfirthers came to aid her; yea, even those who were aforetime foes to Grettir; and the first man there was Thorod Drapa-Stump, and the more part of the Ramfirthers.

Now Angle came to Biarg with twenty men, and had Grettir's head with him; but not all those had come yet who had promised aid to Asdis; so Angle and his folk went into the chamber with the head, and set it down on the floor; the goodwife was there in the chamber, and many men with her; nor did it come to greetings on either side; but Angle sang this stave:

"A greedy head I bring with me
Up from the borders of the sea;
Now may the needle-pliers weep,
The red-haired outlaw lies asleep;
Gold-bearer, cast adown thine eyes,
And see how on the pavement lies,
The peace-destroying head brought low,
That but for salt had gone ere now."

The goodwife sat silent when he gave forth the stave, and thereafter she sang:

"O thou poor wretch, as sheep that flee
To treacherous ice when wolves they see,
So in the waves would ye have drowned
Your shame and fear, had ye but found
That steel-god hale upon the isle:
Now heavy shame, woe worth the while!
Hangs over the north country-side,
Nor I my loathing care to hide."

Then many said that it was nought wonderful, though she had brave sons, so brave as she herself was, amid such grief of heart as was brought on her.

Uspak was without, and held talk with such of Angle's folk as had not gone in, and asked concerning the slayings; and all men praised Illugi's defence; and they told withal how fast Grettir had held the short-sword after he was dead, and marvellous that seemed to men.

Amidst these things were seen many men riding from the west, and thither were coming many friends of the goodwife, with Gamli and Skeggi west from Meals.

Now Angle had been minded to take out execution after Illugi, for he and his men claimed all his goods; but when that crowd of men came up, Angle saw that he might do nought therein, but Gamli and Uspak were of the eagerest, and were fain to set on Angle; but those who were wisest bade them take the rede of Thorwald their kinsman, and the other chief men, and said that worse would be deemed of Angle's case the more wise men sat in judgment over it; then such truce there was that Angle rode away, having Grettir's head with him, because he was minded to bear it to the Althing.

So he rode home, and thought matters looked heavy enough, because well-nigh all the chief men of the land were either akin to Grettir and Illugi, or tied to them and theirs by marriage: that summer, moreover, Skeggi the Short-handed took to wife the daughter of Thorod Drapa-Stump, and therewithal Thorod joined Grettir's kin in these matters.

Chapter 87
Affairs at the Althing

NOW MEN RODE to the Althing, and Angle's helpers were fewer than he had looked for, because that his case was spoken ill of far and wide.

Then asked Halldor whether they were to carry Grettir's head with them to the Althing.

Angle said that he would bear it with him.

"Ill-counselled is that," said Halldor; "for many enough will thy foes be, though thou doest nought to jog the memories of folk, or wake up their grief."

By then were they come on their way, and were minded to ride south over the Sand; so Angle let take the head, and bury it in a hillock of sand, which is called Grettir's Hillock.

Thronged was the Althing, and Angle put forth his case, and praised his own deeds mightily, in that he had slain the greatest outlaw in all the land, and claimed the money as his, which had been put on Grettir's head. But Thorir had the same answer for him as was told afore.

Then was the Lawman prayed for a decision, and he said that he would fain hear if any charges came against this, whereby Angle should forfeit his blood-money, or else he said he must have whatsoever had been put on Grettir's head.

Then Thorvald Asgeirson called on Skeggi the Short-handed to put forth his case, and he summoned Thorbiorn Angle with a first summons for the witch-craft and sorcery, whereby Grettir must have got his bane, and then with another summons withal, for that they had borne weapons against a half-dead man, and hereon he claimed an award of outlawry.

Now folk drew much together on this side and on that, but few they were that gave aid to Thorbiorn; and things turned out otherwise than he had looked for, because Thorvald, and Isleif, his son-in-law, deemed it a deed worthy of death to bring men to their end by evil sorcery; but through the words of wise men these cases had such end, that Thorbiorn should sail away that same summer, and never come back to Iceland while any such were alive, as had the blood-suit for Grettir and Illugi.

And then, moreover, was it made law that all workers of olden craft should be made outlaws.

So when Angle saw what his lot would be, he gat him gone from the Thing, because it might well hap that Grettir's kin would set on him; nor did he get aught of the fee that was put on

Grettir's head, for that Stein the Lawman would not that it should be paid for a deed of shame. None of those men of Thorbiorn's company who had fallen in Drangey were atoned, for they were to be made equal to the slaying of Illugi, but their kin were exceeding ill content therewith.

So men rode home from the Thing, and all blood-suits that men had against Grettir fell away.

Skeggi, the son of Gamli, who was son-in-law of Thorod Drapa-Stump, and sister's son of Grettir, went north to Skagafirth at the instance of Thorvald Asgeirson, and Isleif his son-in-law, who was afterwards Bishop of Skalholt, and by the consent of all the people got to him a keel, and went to Drangey to seek the corpses of the brothers, Grettir and Illugi; and he brought them back to Reeks, in Reek-strand, and buried them there at the church; and it is for a token that Grettir lies there, that in the days of the Sturlungs, when the church of the Reeks was moved, Grettir's bones were dug up, nor were they deemed so wondrous great, great enough though they were. The bones of Illugi were buried afterwards north of the church, but Grettir's head at home in the church at Biarg.

Goodwife Asdis abode at home at Biarg, and so well beloved she was, that no trouble was ever brought against her, no, not even while Grettir was in outlawry.

Skeggi the Short-handed took the household at Biarg after Asdis, and a mighty man he was; his son was Gamli, the father of Skeggi of Scarf-stead, and Asdis the mother of Odd the Monk. Many men are come from him.

Chapter 88
Thorbiorn Angle Goes to Norway, and Thence to Micklegarth

THORNBIORN ANGLE TOOK SHIP at Goose-ere, with whatso of his goods he might take with him; but Hialti his brother took to him his lands, and Angle gave him Drangey withal. Hialti became a great chief in aftertimes, but he has nought more to do with this tale.

So Angle fared out to Norway; he yet made much of himself, for he deemed he had wrought a great deed in the slaying of Grettir, and so thought many others, who knew not how all had come to pass, for many knew how renowned a man Grettir had been; withal Angle told just so much of their dealings together as might do him honour, and let such of the tale lie quiet as was of lesser glory.

Now this tale came in the autumn-tide east to Tunsberg, and when Thorstein Dromund heard of the slayings he grew all silent, because it was told him that Angle was a mighty man and a hardy; and he called to mind the words which he had spoken when he and Grettir talked together, long time agone, concerning the fashion of their arms.

So Thorstein put out spies on Angle's goings; they were both in Norway through the winter, but Thorbiorn was in the north-country, and Thorstein in Tunsberg, nor had either seen other; yet was Angle ware that Grettir had a brother in Norway, and thought it hard to keep guard of himself in an unknown land, wherefore he sought counsel as to where he should betake himself. Now in those days many Northmen went out to Micklegarth, and took war-pay there; so Thorbiorn deemed it would be good to go thither and get to him thereby both fee and fame, nor to abide in the North-lands because of the kin of Grettir. So he made ready to go from Norway, and get him gone from out the land, and made no stay till he came to Micklegarth, and there took war-hire.

Chapter 89
How the Short-Sword Was the Easier Known When Sought for by Reason of the Notch in the Blade

THORSTEIN DROMUND was a mighty man, and of the greatest account; and now he heard that Thorbiorn Angle had got him gone from the land out to Micklegarth; speedy were his doings thereon, he gave over his lands into his kinsmen's hands, and betook himself to journeying and to search for Angle; and ever he followed after whereas Angle had gone afore, nor was Angle ware of his goings.

So Thorstein Dromund came out to Micklegarth a little after Angle, and was fain above all things to slay him, but neither knew the other. Now had they will to be taken into the company of the Varangians, and the matter went well as soon as the Varangians knew that they were Northmen; and in those days was Michael Katalak king over Micklegarth.

Thorstein Dromund watched for Angle, if in some wise he might know him, but won not the game because of the many people there; and ever would he lie awake, ill-content with his lot, and thinking how great was his loss.

Now hereupon it befell that the Varangians were to go on certain warfare, and free the land from harrying; and their manner and law it was before they went from home to hold a weapon-show, and so it was now done; and when the weapon-show was established, then were all Varangians to come there, and those withal who were minded to fall into their company, and they were to show forth their weapons.

Thither came both Thorstein and Angle; but Thorbiorn Angle showed forth his weapons first; and he had the short-sword, Grettir's-loom; but when he showed it many praised it and said that it was an exceeding good weapon, but that it was a great blemish, that notch in the edge thereof; and asked him withal what had brought that to pass.

Angle said it was a thing worthy to be told of, "For this is the next thing to be said," says he, "that out in Iceland I slew that champion who was called Grettir the Strong, and who was the greatest warrior and the stoutest-hearted of all men of that land, for him could no man vanquish till I came forth for that end; and whereas I had the good hap to win him, I took his life; though indeed he had my strength many times over; then I drave this short-sword into his head, and thereby was a shard broken from out its edge."

So those who stood nigh said, that he must have been hard of head then, and each showed the short-sword to the other; but hereby Thorstein deemed he knew now who this man was, and he prayed withal to see the short-sword even as the others; then Angle gave it up with good will, for all were praising his bravery and that daring onset, and even in such wise did he think this one would do; and in no wise did he misdoubt him that Thorstein was there, or that the man was akin to Grettir.

Then Dromund took the short-sword, and raised it aloft, and hewed at Angle and smote him on the head, and so great was the stroke that it stayed but at the jaw-teeth, and Thorbiorn Angle fell to earth dead and dishonoured.

Thereat all men became hushed; but the Chancellor of the town seized Thorstein straightway, and asked for what cause he did such an ill-deed there at the hallowed Thing.

Thorstein said that he was the brother of Grettir the Strong, and that withal he had never been able to bring vengeance to pass till then; so thereupon many put in their word, and said that the strong man must needs have been of great might and nobleness, in that Thorstein had fared so far forth into the world to avenge him: the rulers of the city deemed that like enough; but whereas there was none there to bear witness in aught to Thorstein's word, that law of theirs prevailed, that whosoever slew a man should lose nought but his life.

So then speedy doom and hard enow did Thorstein get; for in a dark chamber of a dungeon should he be cast and there abide his death, if none redeemed him therefrom with money. But when Thorstein came into the dungeon, there was a man there already, who had come to death's door from misery; and both foul and cold was that abode; Thorstein spake to that man and said:

"How deemest thou of thy life?"

He answered, "As of a right evil life, for of nought can I be holpen, nor have I kinsmen to redeem me."

Thorstein said, "Nought is of less avail in such matters than lack of good rede; let us be merry then, and do somewhat that will be glee and game to us."

The man said that he might have no glee of aught.

"Nay, then, but let us try it," said Thorstein. And therewithal he fell to singing; and he was a man of such goodly voice that scarcely might his like be found therefor, nor did he now spare himself.

Now the highway was but a little way from the dungeon, and Thorstein sang so loud and clear that the walls resounded therewith, and great game this seemed to him who had been half-dead erst; and in such wise did Thorstein keep it going till the evening.

Chapter 90
How the Lady Spes Redeemed Thorstein from the Dungeon

THERE WAS A GREAT LADY of a castle in that town called Spes, exceeding rich and of great kin; Sigurd was the name of her husband, a rich man too, but of lesser kin than she was, and for money had she been wedded to him; no great love there was betwixt them, for she thought she had been wedded far beneath her; high-minded she was and a very stirring woman.

Now so it befell, that, as Thorstein made him merry that night, Spes walked in the street hard by the dungeon, and heard thence so fair a voice, that she said she had never yet heard its like. She went with many folk, and so now she bade them go learn who had that noble voice. So they called out and asked who lay there in such evil plight; and Thorstein named himself.

Then said Spes, "Art thou a man as much skilled in other matters as in singing?"

He said there was but little to show for that.

"What ill-deed hast thou done," said she, "that thou must needs be tormented here to the death?"

He said that he had slain a man, and avenged his brother thereby, "But I could not show that by witnesses," said Thorstein, "and therefore have I been cast into ward here, unless some man should redeem me, nor do I hope therefor, for no man have I here akin to me."

"Great loss of thee if thou art slain! and that brother of thine whom thou didst avenge, was he a man so famed, then?"

He said that he was more mighty than he by the half; and so she asked what token there was thereof. Then sang Thorstein this stave:

> "Field of rings, eight men, who raise
> Din of sword in clattering ways,
> Strove the good short-sword in vain
> From the strong dead hand to gain;
> So they ever strained and strove,
> Till at last it did behove,
> The feared quickener of the fight,
> From the glorious man to smite."

"Great prowess such a thing shows of the man," said those who understood the stave; and when she knew thereof, she spake thus:

"Wilt thou take thy life from me, if such a choice is given thee?"

"That will I," said Thorstein, "if this fellow of mine, who sits hereby, is redeemed along with me; or else will we both abide here together."

She answers, "More of a prize do I deem thee than him."

"Howsoever that may be," said Thorstein, "we shall go away in company both of us together, or else shall neither go."

Then she went there, whereas were the Varangians, and prayed for freedom for Thorstein, and offered money to that end; and to this were they right willing; and so she brought about by her mighty friendships and her wealth that they were both set free. But as soon as Thorstein came out of the dungeon he went to see goodwife Spes, and she took him to her and kept him privily; but whiles was he with the Varangians in warfare, and in all onsets showed himself the stoutest of hearts.

Chapter 91
Of the Doings of Thorstein and the Lady Spes

IN THOSE DAYS was Harald Sigurdson at Micklegarth, and Thorstein fell into friendship with him. Of much account was Thorstein held, for Spes let him lack no money; and greatly they turned their hearts one to the other, Thorstein and Spes; and many folk beside her deemed great things of his prowess.

Now her money was much squandered, because she ever gave herself to the getting of great friends; and her husband deemed that he could see that she was much changed, both in temper and many other of her ways, but most of all in the spending of money; both gold and good things he missed, which were gone from her keeping.

So on a time Sigurd her husband talks with her, and says that she has taken to strange ways. "Thou givest no heed to our goods," says he, "but squanderest them in many wise; and, moreover, it is even as if I saw thee ever in a dream, nor ever wilt thou be there whereas I am; and I know for sure that something must bring this about."

She answered, "I told thee, and my kinsfolk told thee, whenas we came together, that I would have my full will and freedom over all such things as it was beseeming for me to bestow, and for that cause I spare not thy goods. Hast thou perchance aught to say to me concerning other matters which may be to my shame?"

He answers, "Somewhat do I misdoubt me that thou holdest some man or other whom thou deemest better than I be."

"I wot not," says she, "what ground there may be thereto; but meseems thou mayest speak with little truth; and yet, none-the-less, we two alone shall not speak on this matter if thou layest this slander on me."

So he let the talk drop for that time; she and Thorstein went on in the same way, nor were they wary of the words of evil folk, for she ever trusted in her many and wise friends. Oft they sat talking together and making merry; and on an evening as they sat in a certain loft, wherein were goodly things of hers, she bade Thorstein sing somewhat, for she thought the goodman was sitting at the drink, as his wont was, so she bolted the door. But, when he had sung a certain while, the door was driven at, and one called from outside to open; and there was come the husband with many of his folk.

The goodwife had unlocked a great chest to show Thorstein her dainty things; so when she knew who was there, she would not unlock the door, but speaks to Thorstein, "Quick is my rede, jump into the chest and keep silent."

So he did, and she shot the bolt of the chest and sat thereon herself; and even therewith in came the husband into the loft, for he and his had broken open the door thereof.

Then said the lady, "Why do ye fare with all this uproar? are your foes after you then?"

The goodman answered, "Now it is well that thou thyself givest proof of thyself what thou art; where is the man who trolled out that song so well e'en now? I wot thou deemest him of far fairer voice than I be."

She said: "Not altogether a fool is he who can be silent; but so it fares not with thee: thou deemest thyself cunning, and art minded to bind thy lie on my back. Well, then, let proof be made thereof! If there be truth in thy words, take the man; he will scarce have leapt out through the walls or the roof."

So he searched through the place, and found him not, and she said, "Why dost thou not take him then, since thou deemest the thing so sure?"

He was silent, nor knew in sooth amid what wiles he was come; then he asked his fellows if they had not heard him even as he had. But whereas they saw that the mistress misliked the matter, their witness came to nought, for they said that oft folk heard not things as they were in very sooth. So the husband went out, and deemed he knew that sooth well enough, though they had not found the man; and now for a long time he left spying on his wife and her ways.

Another time, long after, Thorstein and Spes sat in a certain cloth-bower, and therein were clothes, both cut and uncut, which the wedded folk owned; there she showed to Thorstein many kinds of cloth, and they unfolded them; but when they were least ware of it the husband came on them with many men, and brake into the loft; but while they were about that she heaped up clothes over Thorstein, and leaned against the clothes-stack when they came into the chamber.

"Wilt thou still deny," said the goodman, "that there was a man with thee, when such men there are as saw you both?"

She bade them not to go on so madly. "This time ye will not fail, belike; but let me be at peace, and worry me not."

So they searched through the place and found nought, and at last gave it up.

Then the goodwife answered and said, "It is ever good to give better proof than the guesses of certain folk; nor was it to be looked for that ye should find that which was not. Wilt thou now confess thy folly, husband, and free me from this slander?"

He said, "The less will I free thee from it in that I trow thou art in very sooth guilty of that which I have laid to thy charge; and thou wilt have to put forth all thy might in this case, if thou art to get this thrust from thee."

She said that that was in nowise against her mind, and therewithal they parted.

Thereafter was Thorstein ever with the Varangians, and men say that he sought counsel of Harald Sigurdson, and their mind it is that Thorstein and Spes would not have taken to those redes but for the trust they had in him and his wisdom.

Now as time wore on, goodman Sigurd gave out that he would fare from home on certain errands of his own. The goodwife nowise let him herein; and when he was gone, Thorstein came to Spes, and the twain were ever together. Now such was the fashion of her castle that it was built forth over the sea, and there were certain chambers therein whereunder the sea flowed; in such a chamber Thorstein and Spes ever sat; and a little trap-door there was in the floor of it, whereof none knew but those twain, and it might be opened if there were hasty need thereof.

Now it is to be told of the husband that he went nowhither, save into hiding, that he might spy the ways of the housewife; so it befell that, one night as they sat alone in the sea-loft and were glad together, the husband came on them unawares with a crowd of folk, for he had brought certain men to a window of the chamber, and bade them see if things were not even according to his word: and all said that he spake but the sooth, and that so belike he had done aforetime.

So they ran into the loft, but when Spes heard the crash, she said to Thorstein:

"Needs must thou go down hereby, whatsoever be the cost, but give me some token if thou comest safe from the place."

He said yea thereto, and plunged down through the floor, and the housewife spurned her foot at the lid, and it fell back again into its place, and no new work was to be seen on the floor.

Now the husband and his men came into the loft, and went about searching, and found nought, as was likely; the loft was empty, so that there was nought therein save the floor and the cross-benches, and there sat the goodwife, and played with the gold on her fingers; she heeded them little, and made as if there was nought to do.

All this the goodman thought the strangest of all, and asked his folk if they had not seen the man, and they said that they had in good sooth seen him.

Then said the goodwife, "Hereto shall things come as is said; *thrice of yore have all things happed*, and in likewise hast thou fared, Sigurd," says she, "for three times hadst thou undone my peace, meseems, and are ye any wiser than in the beginning?"

"This time I was not alone in my tale," said the goodman; "and now to make an end, shall thou go through the freeing by law, for in nowise will I have this shame unbooted."

"Meseems," says the goodwife, "thou biddest me what I would bid of thee, for good above all things I deem it to free myself from this slander, which has spread so wide and high, that it would be great dishonour if I thrust it not from off me."

"In likewise," said the goodman, "shalt thou prove that thou hast not given away or taken to thyself my goods."

She answers, "At that time when I free myself shall I in one wise thrust off from me all charges that thou hast to bring against me; but take thou heed whereto all shall come; I will at once free myself from all words that have been spoken here on this charge that thou now makest."

The goodman was well content therewith, and got him gone with his men.

Now it is to be told of Thorstein that he swam forth from under the chamber, and went aland where he would, and took a burning log, and held it up in such wise that it might be seen from the goodwife's castle, and she was abroad for long that evening, and right into the night, for that she would fain know if Thorstein had come aland; and so when she saw the fire, she deemed that she knew that Thorstein had taken land, for even such a token had they agreed on betwixt them.

The next morning Spes bade her husband speak of their matters to the bishop, and thereto was he fully ready. Now they come before the bishop, and the goodman put forward all the aforesaid charges against her.

The bishop asked if she had been known for such an one aforetime, but none said that they had heard thereof. Then he asked with what likelihood he brought those things against her. So the goodman brought forward men who had seen her sit in a locked room with a man beside her, and they twain alone: and therewith the goodman said that he misdoubted him of that man beguiling her.

The bishop said that she might well free herself lawfully from this charge if so she would. She said that it liked her well so to do, "and good hope I have," said Spes, "that I shall have great plenty of women to purge me by oath in this case."

Now was an oath set forward in words for her, and a day settled whereon the case should come about; and thereafter she went home, and was glad at heart, and Thorstein and Spes met, and settled fully what they should do.

Chapter 92
Of the Oath that Spes Made Before the Bishop

NOW THAT DAY PAST, and time wore on to the day when Spes should make oath, and she bade thereto all her friends and kin, and arrayed herself in the best attire she had, and many noble ladies went with her.

Wet was the weather about that time, and the ways were miry, and a certain slough there was to go over or ever they might come to the church; and whenas Spes and her company came forth anigh this slough, a great crowd was there before them, and a multitude of poor folk who prayed them of alms, for this was in the common highway, and all who knew her deemed it was their part to welcome her, and prayed for good things for her as for one who had oft holpen them well.

A certain staff-propped carle there was amidst those poor folk, great of growth and long-bearded. Now the women made stay at the slough, because that the great people deemed the passage across over miry, and therewith when that staff-carle saw the goodwife, that she was better arrayed than the other women, he spake to her on this wise:

"Good mistress," said he, "be so lowly as to suffer me to bear thee over this slough, for it is the bounden duty of us staff-carles to serve thee all we may."

"What then," says she, "wilt thou bear me well, when thou mayst not bear thyself?"

"Yet would it show forth thy lowliness," says he, "nor may I offer better than I have withal; and in all things wilt thou fare the better, if thou hast no pride against poor folk."

"Wot thou well, then," says she, "that if thou bearest me not well it shall be for a beating to thee, or some other shame greater yet."

"Well, I would fain risk it," said he; and therewithal he got on to his feet and stood in the slough. She made as if she were sore afeard of his carrying her, yet nathless she went on, borne on his back; and he staggered along exceeding slowly, going on two crutches, and when he got midmost of the slough he began to reel from side to side. She bade him gather up his strength.

"Never shalt thou have made a worse journey than this if thou easiest me down here."

Then the poor wretch staggers on, and gathers up all his courage and strength, and gets close to the dry land, but stumbles withal, and falls head-foremost in such wise, that he cast her on to the bank, but fell into the ditch up to his armpits, and therewithal as he lay there caught at the goodwife, and gat no firm hold of her clothes, but set his miry hand on her knee right up to the bare thigh.

She sprang up and cursed him, and said that ever would evil come from wretched gangrel churles: "and thy full due it were to be beaten, if I thought it not a shame, because of thy misery."

Then said he, "Meted in unlike ways is man's bliss; me-thought I had done well to thee, and I looked for an alms at thy hands, and lo, in place thereof, I get but threats and ill-usage and no good again withal;" and he made as if he were exceeding angry.

Many deemed that he looked right poor and wretched, but she said that he was the wiliest of old churles; but whereas many prayed for him, she took her purse to her, and therein was many a penny of gold; then she shook down the money and said:

"Take thou this, carle; nowise good were it, if thou hadst not full pay for the hard words thou hadst of me; now have I parted with thee, even according to thy worth."

Then he picked up the gold, and thanked her for her good deed. Spes went to the church, and a great crowd was there before her. Sigurd pushed the case forward eagerly, and bade her free herself from those charges he had brought against her.

She said, "I heed not thy charges; what man dost thou say thou hast seen in my chamber with me? Lo now oft it befalls that some worthy man will be with me, and that do I deem void of any shame; but hereby will I swear that to no man have I given gold, and of no man have I had fleshly defilement save of my husband, and that wretched staff-carle who laid his miry hand on my thigh when I was borne over the slough this same day."

Now many deemed that this was a full oath, and that no shame it was to her, though the carle had laid hand on her unwittingly; but she said that all things must be told even as they were.

Thereafter she swore the oath in such form as is said afore, and many said thereon that she showed the old saw to be true, *swear loud and say little.* But for her, she said that wise men would think that this was not done by guile.

Then her kin fell to saying that great shame and grief it was for high-born women to have such lying charges brought against them bootless, whereas it was a crime worthy of death if it were openly known of any woman that she had done whoredoms against her husband. Therewithal Spes prayed the bishop to make out a divorce betwixt her and her husband Sigurd, because she said she might nowise bear his slanderous lying charges. Her kinsfolk pushed the matter forward for her, and so brought it about by their urgency that they were divorced, and Sigurd got little of the goods, and was driven away from the land withal, for here matters went as is oft shown that they will, and *the lower must lowt*; nor could he bring aught about to avail him, though he had but said the very sooth.

Now Spes took to her all their money, and was deemed the greatest of stirring women; but when folk looked into her oath, it seemed to them that there was some guile in it, and were of a mind that wise men must have taught her that way of swearing; and men dug out this withal, that the staff-carle who had carried her was even Thorstein Dromund. Yet for all that Sigurd got no righting of the matter.

Chapter 93
Thorstein and Spes Come out to Norway

THORSTEIN DROMUND WAS with the Varangians while the talk ran highest about these matters; so famed did he become that it was deemed that scarce had any man of the like prowess come thither; the greatest honours he gat from Harald Sigurdson, for he was of his kin; and after his counsels did Thorstein do, as men are minded to think.

But a little after Sigurd was driven from the land, Thorstein fell to wooing Spes to wife, and she took it meetly, but went to her kinsmen for rede; then they held meetings thereon, and were of one accord that she herself must rule the matter; then was the bargain struck, and good was their wedded life, and they were rich in money, and all men deemed Thorstein to be a man of exceeding good luck, since he had delivered himself from all his troubles.

The twain were together for two winters in Micklegarth, and then Thorstein said to his goodwife that he would fain go back to see his possessions in Norway. She said he should have his will, so they sold the lands they had there, and gat them great wealth of chattels, and then betook them from that land, with a fair company, and went all the way till they came to Norway. Thorstein's kin welcomed them both right heartily, and soon saw that Spes was bountiful and high-minded, and she speedily became exceeding well befriended. Some children they had between them, and they abode on their lands, and were well content with their life.

In those days was Magnus the Good king over Norway. Thorstein soon went to meet him, and had good welcome of him, for he had grown famous for the avenging of Grettir the Strong (for men scarce know of its happening that any other Icelander, save Grettir Asmundson, was avenged in Micklegarth); and folk say that Thorstein became a man of King Magnus, and for nine winters after he had come to Norway he abode in peace, and folk of the greatest honour were they deemed, he and his wife.

Then came home from Micklegarth king Harald Sigurdson, and King Magnus gave him half Norway, and they were both kings therein for a while; but after the death of King Magnus many of those who had been his friends were ill-content, for all men loved him; but folk might not abide the temper of King Harald, for that he was hard and was wont to punish men heavily.

But Thorstein Dromund was fallen into eld, though he was still the halest of men; and now was the slaying of Grettir Asmundson sixteen winters agone.

Chapter 94
Thorstein Dromund and Spes Leave Norway Again

AT THAT TIME many urged Thorstein to go meet King Harald, and become his man; but he took not kindly to it.

Then Spes spake, "I will, Thorstein," says she, "that thou go not to meet Harald the king, for to another king have we much more to pay, and need there is that we turn our minds to that; for now we both grow old and our youth is long departed, and far more have we followed after worldly devices, than the teaching of Christ, or the ways of justice and uprightness; now wot I well that this debt can be paid for us neither by our kindred or our goods, and I will that we ourselves should pay it: now will I therefore that we change our way of life and fare away from this land and unto the abode of the Pope, because I well believe that so only may my case be made easy to me."

Thorstein said, "As well known to me as to thee are the things thou talkest of; and it is meet that thou have thy will herein, since thou didst ever give me my will, in a matter of far less hope; and in all things will we do as thou biddest."

This took men utterly unawares; Thorstein was by then sixty-seven years of age, yet hale in all wise.

So now he bid to him all his kindred and folk allied to him, and laid before them the things he had determined on. Wise men gave good words thereto, though they deemed of their departing as of the greatest loss.

But Thorstein said that there was nought sure about his coming back: "Now do I give thanks to all of you," says he, "for the heed ye paid to my goods when I was last away from the land; now I will offer you, and pray you to take to you my children's havings, and my children, and bring them up according to the manliness that is in you; for I am fallen so far into eld that there is little to say as to whether I may return or not, though I may live; but ye shall in such wise look after all that I leave behind me here, even as if I should never come back to Norway."

Then men answered, that good redes would be plenteous if the housewife should abide behind to look after his affairs; but she said:

"For that cause did I come hither from the out-lands, and from Micklegarth, with Thorstein, leaving behind both kin and goods, for that I was fain that one fate might be over us both; now have I thought it good to be here; but I have no will to abide long in Norway or the North-lands if he goes away; ever has there been great love betwixt us withal, and nought has happed to divide us; now therefore will we depart together, for to both of us is known the truth about many things that befell since we first met."

So, when they had settled their affairs in this wise, Thorstein bade chosen folk divide his goods into halves; and his kin took the half which his children were to own, and they were brought up by their father's kin, and were in aftertimes the mightiest of men, and great kin in the Wick has come from them. But Thorstein and Spes divided their share of the goods, and some they gave to churches for their souls' health, and some they took with them. Then they betook themselves Romeward, and many folk prayed well for them.

Chapter 95
How Thorstein Dromund and Spes Fared to Rome and Died There

NOW THEY WENT their ways till they came to Rome-town; and so when they came before him, who was appointed to hear the shrifts of men, they told him well and truly all things even as they had happed, and with what cunning and craft they had joined together in wedlock; therewithal they gave themselves up with great humility to such penance for the amending of their lives as he should lay on them; but because that they themselves had turned their minds to the atoning of their faults, without any urging or anger from the rulers of the church, they were eased of all fines as much as might be, but were bidden gently that they should now and henceforth concern themselves reasonably for their souls' health, and from this time forward live in chastity, since they had gotten them release from all their guilt; and herewith they were deemed to have fared well and wisely.

Then said Spes, "Now, meseems, our matters have gone well and are come to an end, and no unlucky life have we had together; yet maybe fools will do after the pattern of our former life; now therefore let us make such an end to all, that good men also may follow after us and do the like: so let us go bargain with those who are deft in stone-craft; that they make for each of us a cell of stone, that we may thereby atone for what we have done against God."

So Thorstein laid down money for the making of a stone cell for each of them, and for such-like other things as they might need, and might not be without for the keeping of their lives; and then, when the stone work was done, and the time was meet therefor and all things were ready, they departed their worldly fellowship of their own free will, that they might the more enjoy a holy fellowship in another world. And there they abode both in their stone cells, and lived as long as God would have it, and so ended their lives. And most men say that Thorstein Dromund and Spes his wife may be deemed to be folk of the greatest good luck, all things being accounted of; but neither his children or any of his issue have come to Iceland for a tale to be made of them.

Now Sturla the Lawman says so much as that he deems no outlawed man ever to have been so mighty as Grettir the Strong; and thereto he puts forth three reasons:

And first in that he was the wisest of them all; for the longest in outlawry he was of any man, and was never won whiles he was hale.

And again, in that he was the strongest in all the land among men of a like age; and more fitted to lay ghosts and do away with hauntings than any other.

And thirdly, in that he was avenged out in Micklegarth, even as no other man of Iceland has been; and this withal, that Thorstein Dromund, who avenged him, was so lucky a man in his last days.

So here ends the story of Grettir Asmundson, our fellow-countryman. Thank have they who listened thereto; but thank little enow to him who scribbled out the tale.

Good people, here the work hath end:
May all folk to the good god wend!

Laxdaela Saga

Introduction

WRITTEN IN THE THIRTEENTH CENTURY this saga is set in Iceland and Norway from the late ninth to the early eleventh century and is one of the most famous from Iceland of the Middle Ages. The story focuses on a love triangle between Gudrun Osvifrsdottir, Kjartan Olafsson and Bolli Porleiksson which had been an unusual theme for literature up until then. Although the author of this tale is unknown, it is often thought to be a woman due to its romantic theme and more 'feminine' nature. The tale follows several generations from two families which are descended from Norwegian chiefs. This Icelandic saga continues to be an influential piece of Scandinavian literature and has been likened by some to Shakespeare's *Romeo and Juliet*.

Part One

Chapter 1
Of Ketill Flatnose and His Descendants, 9th Century AD

KETILL FLATNOSE was the name of a man. He was the son of Bjorn the Ungartered. Ketill was a mighty and high-born chieftain (hersir) in Norway. He abode in Raumsdale, within the folkland of the Raumsdale people, which lies between Southmere and Northmere.

Ketill Flatnose had for wife Yngvild, daughter of Ketill Wether, who was a man of exceeding great worth. They had five children; one was named Bjorn the Eastman, and another Helgi Bjolan. Thorunn the Horned was the name of one of Ketill's daughters, who was the wife of Helgi the Lean, son of Eyvind Eastman, and Rafarta, daughter of Kjarval, the Irish king.

Unn 'the Deep-minded' was another of Ketill's daughters, and was the wife of Olaf the White, son of Ingjald, who was son of Frodi the Valiant, who was slain by the Svertlings.

Jorunn, 'Men's Wit-breaker,' was the name of yet another of Ketill's daughters. She was the mother of Ketill the Finn, who settled on land at Kirkby. His son was Asbjorn, father of Thorstein, father of Surt, the father of Sighat the Speaker-at-Law.

Chapter 2
Ketill and His Sons Prepare to Leave Norway

IN THE LATTER DAYS of Ketill arose the power of King Harald the Fairhaired, in such a way that no folkland king or other great men could thrive in the land unless he alone ruled what title should be theirs. When Ketill heard that King Harald was minded to put to him the same choice as to other men of might – namely, not only to put up with his kinsmen being left unatoned, but to be made himself a hireling to boot – he calls together a meeting of his kinsmen, and began his speech in this wise:

"You all know what dealings there have been between me and King Harald, the which there is no need of setting forth; for a greater need besets us, to wit, to take counsel as to the troubles that now are in store for us. I have true news of King Harald's enmity towards us, and to me it seems that we may abide no trust from that quarter. It seems to me that there are two choices left us, either to fly the land or to be slaughtered each in his own seat. Now, as for me, my will is rather to abide the same death that my kinsmen suffer, but I would not lead you by my wilfulness into so great a trouble, for I know the temper of my kinsmen and friends, that ye would not desert me, even though it would be some trial of manhood to follow me."

Bjorn, the son of Ketill, answered: "I will make known my wishes at once. I will follow the example of noble men, and fly this land. For I deem myself no greater a man by abiding at home the thralls of King Harald, that they may chase me away from my own possessions, or that else I may have to come by utter death at their hands."

At this there was made a good cheer, and they all thought it was spoken bravely. This counsel then was settled, that they should leave the country, for the sons of Ketill urged it much, and no one spoke against it. Bjorn and Helgi wished to go to Iceland, for they said they had heard many pleasing news thereof. They had been told that there was good land to be had there, and no need to pay money for it; they said there was plenty of whale and salmon and other fishing all the year round there.

But Ketill said, "Into that fishing place I shall never come in my old age."

So Ketill then told his mind, saying his desire was rather to go west over the sea, for there was a chance of getting a good livelihood. He knew lands there wide about, for there he had harried far and wide.

Chapter 3
Ketill's Sons Go to Iceland

AFTER THAT KETILL MADE a great feast, and at it he married his daughter Thorunn the Horned to Helgi the Lean, as has been said before. After that Ketill arrayed his journey west over the sea. Unn, his daughter, and many others of his relations went with him.

That same summer Ketill's sons went to Iceland with Helgi, their brother-in-law. Bjorn, Ketill's son, brought his ship to the west coast of Iceland, to Broadfirth, and sailed up the firth along the southern shore, till he came to where a bay cuts into the land, and a high mountain stood on the ness on the inner side of the bay, but an island lay a little way off the land. Bjorn said that they should stay there for a while. Bjorn then went on land with a few men, and wandered along the coast, and but a narrow strip of land was there between fell and foreshore. This spot he thought suitable for habitation. Bjorn found the pillars of his temple washed up in a certain creek, and he thought that showed where he ought to build his house. Afterwards Bjorn took for himself all the land between Staff-river and Lavafirth, and abode in the place that ever after was called Bjornhaven.

He was called Bjorn the Eastman. His wife, Gjaflaug, was the daughter of Kjallak the Old. Their sons were Ottar and Kjallak, whose son was Thorgrim, the father of Fight-Styr and Vemund, but the daughter of Kjallak was named Helga, who was the wife of Vestar of Eyr, son of Thorolf "Bladder-skull," who settled Eyr. Their son was Thorlak, father of Steinthor of Eyr.

Helgi Bjolan brought his ship to the south of the land, and took all Keelness, between Kollafirth and Whalefirth, and lived at Esjuberg to old age.

Helgi the Lean brought his ship to the north of the land, and took Islefirth, all along between Mastness and Rowanness, and lived at Kristness. From Helgi and Thornunn all the Islefirthers are sprung.

Chapter 4
Ketill Goes to Scotland, AD 890

KETILL FLATNOSE BROUGHT his ship to Scotland, and was well received by the great men there; for he was a renowned man, and of high birth. They offered him there such station as he would like to take, and Ketill and his company of kinsfolk settled down there – all except Thorstein, his daughter's son, who forthwith betook himself to warring, and harried Scotland far and wide, and was always victorious. Later on he made peace with the Scotch, and got for his own one-half of Scotland. He had for wife Thurid, daughter of Eyvind, and sister of Helgi the Lean. The Scotch did not keep the peace long, but treacherously murdered him. Ari, Thorgil's son, the Wise, writing of his death, says that he fell in Caithness.

Unn the Deep-minded was in Caithness when her son Thorstein fell. When she heard that Thorstein was dead, and her father had breathed his last, she deemed she would have no prospering in store there. So she had a ship built secretly in a wood, and when it was ready built she arrayed it, and had great wealth withal; and she took with her all her kinsfolk who were left alive; and men deem that scarce may an example be found that any one, a woman only, has ever got out of such a state of war with so much wealth and so great a following. From this it may be seen how peerless among women she was.

Unn had with her many men of great worth and high birth. A man named Koll was one of the worthiest amongst her followers, chiefly owing to his descent, he being by title a "Hersir." There was also in the journey with Unn a man named Hord, and he too was also a man of high birth and of great worth.

When she was ready, Unn took her ship to the Orkneys; there she stayed a little while, and there she married off Gro, the daughter of Thorstein the Red. She was the mother of Greilad, who married Earl Thorfinn, the son of Earl Turf-Einar, son of Rognvald Mere-Earl. Their son was Hlodvir, the father of Earl Sigurd, the father of Earl Thorfinn, and from them come all the kin of the Orkney Earls. After that Unn steered her ship to the Faroe Isles, and stayed there for some time. There she married off another daughter of Thorstein, named Olof, and from her sprung the noblest race of that land, who are called the Gate-Beards.

Chapter 5
Unn goes to Iceland, AD 895

UNN NOW GOT READY to go away from the Faroe Isles, and made it known to her shipmates that she was going to Iceland. She had with her Olaf 'Feilan,' the son of Thorstein, and those of his sisters who were unmarried. After that she put to sea, and, the weather being favourable, she came with her ship to the south of Iceland to Pumice-Course (Vikrarskeid). There they had their ship broken into splinters, but all the men and goods were saved.

After that she went to find Helgi, her brother, followed by twenty men; and when she came there he went out to meet her, and bade her come stay with him with ten of her folk. She answered in anger, and said she had not known that he was such a churl; and she went away, being minded to find Bjorn, her brother in Broadfirth, and when he heard she was coming, he went to meet her with many followers, and greeted her warmly, and invited her and all her followers to stay with him, for he knew his sister's high-mindedness. She liked that right well, and thanked him for his lordly behaviour. She stayed there all the winter, and was entertained in the grandest manner, for there was no lack of means, and money was not spared.

In the spring she went across Broadfirth, and came to a certain ness, where they ate their mid-day meal, and since that it has been called Daymealness, from whence Middlefell-strand stretches (eastward). Then she steered her ship up Hvammsfirth and came to a certain ness, and stayed there a little while. There Unn lost her comb, so it was afterwards called Combness.

Then she went about all the Broadfirth-Dales, and took to her lands as wide as she wanted. After that Unn steered her ship to the head of the bay, and there her high-seat pillars were washed ashore, and then she deemed it was easy to know where she was to take up her abode.

She had a house built there: it was afterwards called Hvamm, and she lived there.

The same spring as Unn set up household at Hvamm, Koll married Thorgerd, daughter of Thorstein the Red. Unn gave, at her own cost, the bridal-feast, and let Thorgerd have for her dowry all Salmonriver-Dale; and Koll set up a household there on the south side of the Salmon-river.

Koll was a man of the greatest mettle: their son was named Hoskuld.

Chapter 6
Unn Divides Her Land

AFTER THAT UNN GAVE to more men parts of her land-take. To Hord she gave all Hord-Dale as far as Skramuhlaups River. He lived at Hordabolstad (Hord-Lair-Stead), and was a man of the greatest mark, and blessed with noble offspring. His son was Asbjorn the Wealthy, who lived in Ornolfsdale, at Asbjornstead, and had to wife Thorbjorg, daughter of Midfirth-Skeggi. Their daughter was Ingibjorg, who married Illugi the Black, and their sons were Hermund and Gunnlaug Worm-Tongue. They are called the Gilsbecking-race.

Unn spoke to her men and said: "Now you shall be rewarded for all your work, for now I do not lack means with which to pay each one of you for your toil and good-will. You all know that I have given the man named Erp, son of Earl Meldun, his freedom, for far away was it from my wish that so high-born a man should bear the name of thrall."

Afterwards Unn gave him the lands of Sheepfell, between Tongue River and Mid River. His children were Orm and Asgeir, Gunbjorn, and Halldis, whom Alf o' Dales had for wife.

To Sokkolf Unn gave Sokkolfsdale, where he abode to old age.

Hundi was the name of one of her freedmen. He was of Scottish kin. To him she gave Hundidale.

Osk was the name of the fourth daughter of Thorstein the Red. She was the mother of Thorstein Swart, the Wise, who found the 'Summer eeke.'

Thorhild was the name of a fifth daughter of Thorstein. She was the mother of Alf o' Dales, and many great men trace back their line of descent to him. His daughter was Thorgerd, wife of Ari Marson of Reekness, the son of Atli, the son of Ulf the Squinter and Bjorg, Eyvond's daughter, the sister of Helgi the Lean. From them come all the Reeknessings.

Vigdis was the name of the sixth daughter of Thorstein the Red. From her come the men of Headland of Islefirth.

Chapter 7
Of the Wedding of Olaf 'Feilan,' AD 920

OLAF 'FEILAN' was the youngest of Thorstein's children. He was a tall man and strong, goodly to look at, and a man of the greatest mettle. Unn loved him above all men, and made it known to people that she was minded to settle on Olaf all her belongings at Hvamm after her day.

Unn now became very weary with old age, and she called Olaf 'Feilan' to her and said: "It is on my mind, kinsman, that you should settle down and marry."

Olaf took this well, and said he would lean on her foresight in that matter.

Unn said: "It is chiefly in my mind that your wedding-feast should be held at the end of the summer, for that is the easiest time to get in all the means needed, for to me it seems a near guess that our friends will come hither in great numbers, and I have made up my mind that this shall be the last bridal feast arrayed by me."

Olaf answered: "That is well spoken; but such a woman alone I mean to take to wife who shall rob thee neither of wealth nor rule (over thine own)."

That same summer Olaf 'Feilan' married Alfdis. Their wedding was at Hvamm. Unn spent much money on this feast, for she let be bidden thereto men of high degree wide about from other parts. She invited Bjorn and Helgi 'Bjolan,' her brothers, and they came with many followers. There came Koll o' Dales, her kinsman-in-law, and Hord of Hord-Dale, and many other great men. The wedding feast was very crowded; yet there did not come nearly so many as Unn had asked, because the Islefirth people had such a long way to come.

Old age fell now fast upon Unn, so that she did not get up till mid-day, and went early to bed. No one did she allow to come to her for advice between the time she went to sleep at night and the time she was aroused, and she was very angry if any one asked how it fared with her strength.

On this day Unn slept somewhat late; yet she was on foot when the guests came, and went to meet them and greeted her kinsfolk and friends with great courtesy, and said they had shown their affection to her in "coming hither from so far, and I specially name for this Bjorn and Helgi, but I wish to thank you all who are here assembled."

After that Unn went into the hall and a great company with her, and when all seats were taken in the hall, every one was much struck by the lordliness of the feast.

Then Unn said: "Bjorn and Helgi, my brothers, and all my other kindred and friends, I call witnesses to this, that this dwelling with all its belongings that you now see before you, I give into the hands of my kinsman, Olaf, to own and to manage."

After that Unn stood up and said she would go to the bower where she was wont to sleep, but bade every one have for pastime whatever was most to his mind, and that ale should be the cheer of the common folk. So the tale goes, that Unn was a woman both tall and portly. She walked at a quick step out along the hall, and people could not help saying to each other how stately the lady was yet.

They feasted that evening till they thought it time to go to bed. But the day after Olaf went to the sleeping bower of Unn, his grandmother, and when he came into the chamber there was Unn sitting up against her pillow, and she was dead. Olaf went into the hall after that and told these tidings. Every one thought it a wonderful thing, how Unn had upheld her dignity to the day of her death.

So they now drank together Olaf's wedding and Unn's funeral honours, and the last day of the feast Unn was carried to the howe (burial mound) that was made for her. She was laid in a ship in the cairn, and much treasure with her, and after that the cairn was closed up.

Then Olaf 'Feilan' took over the household of Hvamm and all charge of the wealth there, by the advice of his kinsmen who were there. When the feast came to an end Olaf gave lordly gifts to the men most held in honour before they went away.

Olaf became a mighty man and a great chieftain. He lived at Hvamm to old age.

The children of Olaf and Alfdis were Thord Yeller, who married Hrodny, daughter of Midfirth Skeggi; and their sons were, Eyjolf the Grey, Thorarin Fylsenni, and Thorkell Kuggi. One daughter of Olaf Feilan was Thora, whom Thorstein Cod-biter, son of Thorolf Most-Beard, had for wife; their sons were Bork the Stout, and Thorgrim, father of Snori the Priest. Helga was another daughter of Olaf; she was the wife of Gunnar Hlifarson; their daughter was Jofrid, whom Thorodd, son of Tongue-Odd, had for wife, and afterwards Thorstein, Egil's son. Thorunn was the name of yet one of his daughters. She was the wife of Herstein, son of Thorkell Blund-Ketill's son. Thordis was the name of a third daughter of Olaf: she was the wife of Thorarin, the Speaker-at-Law, brother of Ragi.

At that time, when Olaf was living at Hvamm, Koll o' Dales, his brother-in-law, fell ill and died. Hoskuld, the son of Koll, was young at the time of his father's death: he was fulfilled of wits before the tale of his years. Hoskuld was a hopeful man, and well made of body. He took over his father's goods and household. The homestead where Koll lived was named after him, being afterwards called Hoskuldstead. Hoskuld was soon in his householding blessed with friends, for that many supports stood thereunder, both kinsmen and friends whom Koll had gathered round him.

Thorgerd, Thorstein's daughter, the mother of Hoskuld, was still a young woman and most goodly; she did not care for Iceland after the death of Koll. She told Hoskuld her son that she wished to go abroad, and take with her that share of goods which fell to her lot. Hoskuld said he took it much to heart that they should part, but he would not go against her in this any more than in anything else. After that Hoskuld bought the half-part in a ship that was standing beached off Daymealness, on behalf of his mother. Thorgerd betook herself on board there, taking with her a great deal of goods. After that Thorgerd put to sea and had a very good voyage, and arrived in Norway. Thorgerd had much kindred and many noble kinsmen there. They greeted her warmly, and gave her the choice of whatever she liked to take at their hands. Thorgerd was pleased at this, and said it was her wish to settle down in that land. She had not been a widow long before a man came forward to woo her. His name was Herjolf; he was a 'landed man' as to title, rich, and of much account. Herjolf was a tall and strong man, but he was not fair of feature; yet the most high-mettled of men, and was of all men the best skilled at arms.

Now as they sat taking counsel on this matter, it was Thorgerd's place to reply to it herself, as she was a widow; and, with the advice of her relations, she said she would not refuse the offer. So Thorgerd married Herjolf, and went with him to his home, and they loved each other dearly. Thorgerd soon showed by her ways that she was a woman of the greatest mettle, and Herjolf's manner of life was deemed much better and more highly to be honoured now that he had got such an one as she was for his wife.

Chapter 8
The Birth of Hrut and Thorgerd's Second Widowhood, AD 923

HERJOLF AND THORGERD had not long been together before they had a son. The boy was sprinkled with water, and was given the name of Hrut. He was at an early age both big and strong as he grew up; and as to growth of body, he was goodlier than any man, tall and broad-shouldered, slender of waist, with fine limbs and well-made hands and feet. Hrut was of all men the fairest of feature, and like what Thorstein, his mother's father, had been, or like Ketill Flatnose. And all things taken together, he was a man of the greatest mettle.

Herjolf now fell ill and died, and men deemed that a great loss. After that Thorgerd wished to go to Iceland to visit Hoskuld her son, for she still loved him best of all men, and Hrut was left behind well placed with his relations. Thorgerd arrayed her journey to Iceland, and went to find Hoskuld in his home in Salmonriver-Dale. He received his mother with honour. She was possessed of great wealth, and remained with Hoskuld to the day of her death.

A few winters after Thorgerd came to Iceland she fell sick and died. Hoskuld took to himself all her money, but Hrut his brother owned one-half thereof.

Chapter 9
Hoskuld's Marriage, AD 935

AT THIS TIME Norway was ruled by Hakon, Athelstan's fosterling. Hoskuld was one of his bodyguard, and stayed each year, turn and turn about, at Hakon's court, or at his own home, and was a very renowned man both in Norway and in Iceland. Bjorn was the name of a man who lived at Bjornfirth, where he had taken land, the firth being named after him. This firth cuts into the land north from Steingrim's firth, and a neck of land runs out between them.

Bjorn was a man of high birth, with a great deal of money: Ljufa was the name of his wife. Their daughter was Jorunn: she was a most beautiful woman, and very proud and extremely clever, and so was thought the best match in all the firths of the West.

Of this woman Hoskuld had heard, and he had heard besides that Bjorn was the wealthiest yeoman throughout all the Strands. Hoskuld rode from home with ten men, and went to Bjorn's house at Bjornfirth. He was well received, for to Bjorn his ways were well known. Then Hoskuld made his proposal, and Bjorn said he was pleased, for his daughter could not be better married, yet turned the matter over to her decision. And when the proposal was set before Jorunn, she answered in this way: "From all the reports I have heard of you, Hoskuld, I cannot but answer your proposal well, for I think that the woman would be well cared for who should marry you; yet my father must have most to say in this matter, and I will agree in this with his wishes."

And the long and short of it was, that Jorunn was promised to Hoskuld with much money, and the wedding was to be at Hoskuldstead. Hoskuld now went away with matters thus settled, and home to his abode, and stays now at home until this wedding feast was to be held. Bjorn came from the north for the wedding with a brave company of followers. Hoskuld had also asked many guests, both friends and relations, and the feast was of the grandest. Now, when the feast was over each one returned to his home in good friendship and with seemly gifts.

Jorunn Bjorn's daughter sits behind at Hoskuldstead, and takes over the care of the household with Hoskuld. It was very soon seen that she was wise and well up in things, and of manifold knowledge, though rather high-tempered at most times. Hoskuld and she loved each other well, though in their daily ways they made no show thereof.

Hoskuld became a great chieftain; he was mighty and pushing, and had no lack of money, and was thought to be nowise less of his ways than his father, Koll.

Hoskuld and Jorunn had not been married long before they came to have children. A son of theirs was named Thorliek. He was the eldest of their children. Bard was another son of theirs. One of their daughters was called Hallgerd, afterwards surnamed 'Long-Breeks.' Another daughter was called Thurid. All their children were most hopeful.

Thorliek was a very tall man, strong and handsome, though silent and rough; and men thought that such was the turn of his temper, as that he would be no man of fair dealings, and Hoskuld often would say, that he would take very much after the race of the men of the Strands.

Bard, Hoskuld's son, was most manly to look at, and of goodly strength, and from his appearance it was easy to see that he would take more after his father's people. Bard was of quiet ways while he was growing up, and a man lucky in friends, and Hoskuld loved him best of all his children.

The house of Hoskuld now stood in great honour and renown. About this time Hoskuld gave his sister Groa in marriage to Velief the Old, and their son was 'Holmgang'-Bersi.

Chapter 10
Of Viga Hrapp

HRAPP WAS THE NAME of a man who lived in Salmon-river-Dale, on the north bank of the river on the opposite side to Hoskuldstead, at the place that was called later on Hrappstead, where there is now waste land.

Hrapp was the son of Sumarlid, and was called Fight-Hrapp. He was Scotch on his father's side, and his mother's kin came from Sodor, where he was brought up. He was a very big, strong man, and one not willing to give in even in face of some odds; and for the reason that was most overbearing, and would never make good what he had misdone, he had had to fly from West-over-the-sea, and had bought the land on which he afterwards lived.

His wife was named Vigdis, and was Hallstein's daughter; and their son was named Sumarlid. Her brother was named Thorstein Surt; he lived at Thorsness, as has been written before. Sumarlid was brought up there, and was a most promising young man.

Thorstein had been married, but by this time his wife was dead. He had two daughters, one named Gudrid, and the other Osk. Thorkell trefill married Gudrid, and they lived in Svignaskard.

He was a great chieftain, and a sage of wits; he was the son of Raudabjorn. Osk, Thorstein's daughter, was given in marriage to a man of Broadfirth named Thorarin. He was a valiant man, and very popular, and lived with Thorstein, his father-in-law, who was sunk in age and much in need of their care.

Hrapp was disliked by most people, being overbearing to his neighbours; and at times he would hint to them that theirs would be a heavy lot as neighbours, if they held any other man for better than himself. All the goodmen took one counsel, and went to Hoskuld and told him their trouble. Hoskuld bade them tell him if Hrapp did any one any harm, "For he shall not plunder me of men or money."

Chapter 11
About Thord Goddi and Thorbjorn Skrjup

THORD GODDI WAS THE NAME of a man who lived in Salmon-river-Dale on the northern side of the river, and his house was Vigdis called Goddistead. He was a very wealthy man; he had no children, and had bought the land he lived on. He was a neighbour of Hrapp's, and was very often badly treated by him. Hoskuld looked after him, so that he kept his dwelling in peace. Vigdis was the name of his wife. She was daughter of Ingjald, son of Olaf Feilan, and brother's daughter of Thord Yeller, and sister's daughter of Thorolf Rednose of Sheepfell. This Thorolf was a great hero, and in a very good position, and his kinsmen often went to him for protection. Vigdis had married more for money than high station.

Thord had a thrall who had come to Iceland with him, named Asgaut. He was a big man, and shapely of body; and though he was called a thrall, yet few could be found his equal amongst those called freemen, and he knew well how to serve his master. Thord had many other thralls, though this one is the only one mentioned here.

Thorbjorn was the name of a man. He lived in Salmon-river-Dale, next to Thord, up valley away from his homestead, and was called Skrjup. He was very rich in chattels, mostly in gold and silver. He was an huge man and of great strength. No squanderer of money on common folk was he. Hoskuld, Dalakoll's son, deemed it a drawback to his state that his house was worse built than he wished it should be; so he bought a ship from a Shetland man. The ship lay up in the mouth of the river Blanda. That ship he gets ready, and makes it known that he is going abroad, leaving Jorunn to take care of house and children.

They now put out to sea, and all went well with them; and they hove somewhat southwardly into Norway, making Hordaland, where the market-town called Biorgvin was afterwards built. Hoskuld put up his ship, and had there great strength of kinsmen, though here they be not named.

Hakon, the king, had then his seat in the Wick. Hoskuld did not go to the king, as his kinsfolk welcomed him with open arms. That winter all was quiet (in Norway).

Chapter 12
Hoskuld Buys a Slave Woman

THERE WERE TIDINGS at the beginning of the summer that the king went with his fleet eastward to a tryst in Brenn-isles, to settle peace for his land, even as the law laid down should be done every third summer. This meeting was held between rulers with a view to settling such matters as kings had to adjudge – matters of international policy between Norway, Sweden, and Denmark. It was deemed a pleasure trip to go to this meeting, for thither came men from well-nigh all such lands as we know of.

Hoskuld ran out his ship, being desirous also to go to the meeting; moreover, he had not been to see the king all the winter through. There was also a fair to be made for.

At the meeting there were great crowds of people, and much amusement to be got – drinking, and games, and all sorts of entertainment. Nought, however, of great interest happened there. Hoskuld met many of his kinsfolk there who were come from Denmark.

Now, one day as Hoskuld went out to disport himself with some other men, he saw a stately tent far away from the other booths. Hoskuld went thither, and into the tent, and there sat a man before him in costly raiment, and a Russian hat on his head. Hoskuld asked him his name.

He said he was called Gilli: "But many call to mind the man if they hear my nickname – I am called Gilli the Russian."

Hoskuld said he had often heard talk of him, and that he held him to be the richest of men that had ever belonged to the guild of merchants. Still Hoskuld spoke: "You must have things to sell such as we should wish to buy."

Gilli asked what he and his companions wished to buy.

Hoskuld said he should like to buy some bonds-woman, "if you have one to sell."

Gilli answers: "There, you mean to give me trouble by this, in asking for things you don't expect me to have in stock; but it is not sure that follows."

Hoskuld then saw that right across the booth there was drawn a curtain; and Gilli then lifted the curtain, and Hoskuld saw that there were twelve women seated behind the curtain. So Gilli said that Hoskuld should come on and have a look, if he would care to buy any of these women. Hoskuld did so. They sat all together across the booth. Hoskuld looks carefully at these women. He saw a woman sitting out by the skirt of the tent, and she was very ill-clad. Hoskuld thought, as far as he could see, this woman was fair to look upon.

Then said Hoskuld, "What is the price of that woman if I should wish to buy her?"

Gilli replied, "Three silver pieces is what you must weigh me out for her."

"It seems to me," said Hoskuld, "that you charge very highly for this bonds-woman, for that is the price of three (such)."

Then Gilli said, "You speak truly, that I value her worth more than the others. Choose any of the other eleven, and pay one mark of silver for her, this one being left in my possession."

Hoskuld said, "I must first see how much silver there is in the purse I have on my belt," and he asked Gilli to take the scales while he searched the purse.

Gilli then said, "On my side there shall be no guile in this matter; for, as to the ways of this woman, there is a great drawback which I wish, Hoskuld, that you know before we strike this bargain."

Hoskuld asked what it was.

Gilli replied, "The woman is dumb. I have tried in many ways to get her to talk, but have never got a word out of her, and I feel quite sure that this woman knows not how to speak."

Then, said Hoskuld, "Bring out the scales, and let us see how much the purse I have got here may weigh."

Gilli did so, and now they weigh the silver, and there were just three marks weighed. Then said Hoskuld, "Now the matter stands so that we can close our bargain. You take the money for yourself, and I will take the woman. I take it that you have behaved honestly in this affair, for, to be sure, you had no mind to deceive me herein."

Hoskuld then went home to his booth. That same night Hoskuld went into bed with her.

The next morning when men got dressed, spake Hoskuld, "The clothes Gilli the Rich gave you do not appear to be very grand, though it is true that to him it is more of a task to dress twelve women than it is to me to dress only one."

After that Hoskuld opened a chest, and took out some fine women's clothes and gave them to her; and it was the saying of every one that she looked very well when she was dressed. But when the rulers had there talked matters over according as the law provided, this meeting was broken up. Then Hoskuld went to see King Hakon, and greeted him worthily, according to custom. The king cast a side glance at him, and said, "We should have taken well your greeting, Hoskuld, even if you had saluted us sooner; but so shall it be even now."

Chapter 13
Hoskuld Returns to Iceland, AD 948

AFTER THAT THE KING received Hoskuld most graciously, and bade him come on board his own ship, and "be with us so long as you care to remain in Norway."

Hoskuld answered: "Thank you for your offer; but now, this summer, I have much to be busy about, and that is mostly the reason I was so long before I came to see you, for I wanted to get for myself house-timber."

The king bade him bring his ship in to the Wick, and Hoskuld tarried with the king for a while. The king got house-timber for him, and had his ship laden for him. Then the king said to Hoskuld, "You shall not be delayed here longer than you like, though we shall find it difficult to find a man to take your place."

After that the king saw Hoskuld off to his ship, and said: "I have found you an honourable man, and now my mind misgives me that you are sailing for the last time from Norway, whilst I am lord over that land." The king drew a gold ring off his arm that weighed a mark, and gave it to Hoskuld; and he gave him for another gift a sword on which there was half a mark of gold. Hoskuld thanked the king for his gifts, and for all the honour he had done him. After that Hoskuld went on board his ship, and put to sea. They had a fair wind, and hove in to the south of Iceland; and after that sailed west by Reekness, and so by Snowfellness in to Broadfirth. Hoskuld landed at Salmon-river-Mouth. He had the cargo taken out of his ship, which he took into the river and beached, having a shed built for it. A ruin is to be seen now where he built the shed. There he set up his booths, and that place is called Booths'-Dale.

After that Hoskuld had the timber taken home, which was very easy, as it was not far off. Hoskuld rode home after that with a few men, and was warmly greeted, as was to be looked for. He found that all his belongings had been kept well since he left.

Jorunn asked, "What woman that was who journeyed with him?"

Hoskuld answered, "You will think I am giving you a mocking answer when I tell you that I do not know her name."

Jorunn said, "One of two things there must be: either the talk is a lie that has come to my ears, or you must have spoken to her so much as to have asked her her name."

Hoskuld said he could not gainsay that, and so told her the truth, and bade that the woman should be kindly treated, and said it was his wish she should stay in service with them.

Jorunn said, "I am not going to wrangle with the mistress you have brought out of Norway, should she find living near me no pleasure; least of all should I think of it if she is both deaf and dumb."

Hoskuld slept with his wife every night after he came home, and had very little to say to the mistress. Every one clearly saw that there was something betokening high birth in the way she bore herself, and that she was no fool.

Towards the end of the winter Hoskuld's mistress gave birth to a male child. Hoskuld was called, and was shown the child, and he thought, as others did, that he had never seen a goodlier or a more noble-looking child. Hoskuld was asked what the boy should be called. He said it should be named Olaf, for Olaf Feilan had died a little time before, who was his mother's brother.

Olaf was far before other children, and Hoskuld bestowed great love on the boy.

The next summer Jorunn said, "That the woman must do some work or other, or else go away."

Hoskuld said she should wait on him and his wife, and take care of her boy besides. When the boy was two years old he had got full speech, and ran about like children of four years old.

Early one morning, as Hoskuld had gone out to look about his manor, the weather being fine, and the sun, as yet little risen in the sky, shining brightly, it happened that he heard some voices of people talking; so he went down to where a little brook ran past the home-field slope, and he saw two people there whom he recognised as his son Olaf and his mother, and he discovered she was not speechless, for she was talking a great deal to the boy. Then Hoskuld went to her and asked her her name, and said it was useless for her to hide it any longer. She said so it should be, and they sat down on the brink of the field.

Then she said, "If you want to know my name, I am called Melkorka."

Hoskuld bade her tell him more of her kindred. She answered, "Myr Kjartan is the name of my father, and he is a king in Ireland; and I was taken a prisoner of war from there when I was fifteen winters old."

Hoskuld said she had kept silence far too long about so noble a descent. After that Hoskuld went on, and told Jorunn what he had just found out during his walk. Jorunn said that she "could not tell if this were true," and said she had no fondness for any manner of wizards; and so the matter dropped. Jorunn was no kinder to her than before, but Hoskuld had somewhat more to say to her.

A little while after this, when Jorunn was going to bed, Melkorka was undressing her, and put her shoes on the floor, when Jorunn took the stockings and smote her with them about the head. Melkorka got angry, and struck Jorunn on the nose with her fist, so that the blood flowed. Hoskuld came in and parted them. After that he let Melkorka go away, and got a dwelling ready for her up in Salmon-river-Dale, at the place that was afterwards called Melkorkastad, which is now waste land on the south of the Salmon river. Melkorka now set up household there, and Hoskuld had everything brought there that she needed; and Olaf, their son, went with her.

It was soon seen that Olaf, as he grew up, was far superior to other men, both on account of his beauty and courtesy.

Chapter 14
The Murder of Hall, Ingjald's Brother

INGJALD WAS THE NAME of a man. He lived in Sheepisles, that lie out in Broadfirth. He was called Sheepisles' Priest. He was rich, and a mighty man of his hand. Hall was the name of his brother. He was big, and had the makings of a man in him; he was, however, a man of small means, and looked upon by most people as an unprofitable sort of man. The brothers did not usually agree very well together. Ingjald thought Hall did not shape himself after the fashion of doughty men, and Hall thought Ingjald was but little minded to lend furtherance to his affairs.

There is a fishing place in Broadfirth called Bjorn isles. These islands lie many together, and were profitable in many ways. At that time men went there a great deal for the fishing, and at all seasons there were a great many men there. Wise men set great store by people in outlying fishing-stations living peacefully together, and said that it would be unlucky for the fishing if there was any quarrelling; and most men gave good heed to this.

It is told how one summer Hall, the brother of Ingjald, the Sheepisles' Priest, came to Bjorn isles for fishing. He took ship as one of the crew with a man called Thorolf. He was a Broadfirth man, and was well-nigh a penniless vagrant, and yet a brisk sort of a man. Hall was there for some time, and palmed himself off as being much above other men. It happened one evening when they were come to land, Hall and Thorolf, and began to divide the catch, that Hall wished both to choose and to divide, for he thought himself the greater man of the two. Thorolf would not give in, and there were some high words, and sharp things were said on both sides, as each stuck to his own way of thinking. So Hall seized up a chopper that lay by him, and was about to heave it at Thorolf's head, but men leapt between them and stopped Hall; but he was of the maddest, and yet unable to have his way as at this time. The catch of fish remained undivided. Thorolf betook himself away that evening, and Hall took possession of the catch that belonged to them both, for then the odds of might carried the day. Hall now got another man in Thorolf's place in the boat, and went on fishing as before.

Thorolf was ill-contented with his lot, for he felt he had come to shame in their dealings together; yet he remained in the islands with the determination to set straight the humble plight to which he had been made to bow against his will. Hall, in the meantime, did not fear any danger, and thought that no one would dare to try to get even with him in his own country.

So one fair-weather day it happened that Hall rowed out, and there were three of them together in the boat. The fish bit well through the day, and as they rowed home in the evening they were very merry. Thorolf kept spying about Hall's doings during the day, and is standing in the landing-place when Hall came to land. Hall rowed in the forehold of the boat, and leapt overboard, intending to steady the boat; and as he jumped to land Thorolf happens to be standing near, and forthwith hews at him, and the blow caught him on his neck against the shoulder, and off flew his head. Thorolf fled away after that, and Hall's followers were all in a flurried bustle about him.

The story of Hall's murder was told all over the islands, and every one thought it was indeed great news; for the man was of high birth, although he had had little good luck.

Thorolf now fled from the islands, for he knew no man there who would shelter him after such a deed, and he had no kinsmen he could expect help from; while in the neighbourhood were men from whom it might be surely looked for that they would beset his life, being moreover men of much power, such as was Ingjald, the Sheepisles' Priest, the brother of Hall. Thorolf got himself ferried across to the mainland. He went with great secrecy. Nothing is told of his journey, until one evening he came to Goddistead. Vigdis, the wife of Thord Goddi, was some sort of relation to Thorolf, and on that account he turned towards that house. Thorolf had also heard before how matters stood there, and how Vigdis was endowed with a good deal more courage than Thord, her husband.

And forthwith the same evening that Thorolf came to Goddistead he went to Vigdis to tell her his trouble, and to beg her help.

Vigdis answered his pleading in this way: "I do not deny our relationship, and in this way alone I can look upon the deed you have done, that I deem you in no way the worser man for it. Yet this I see, that those who shelter you will thereby have at stake their lives and means, seeing what great men they are who will be taking up the blood-suit. And Thord," she said, "my husband, is not much of a warrior; but the counsels of us women are mostly guided by little foresight if anything is wanted. Yet I am loath to keep aloof from you altogether, seeing that, though I am but a woman, you have set your heart on finding some shelter here."

After that Vigdis led him to an outhouse, and told him to wait for her there, and put a lock on the door. Then she went to Thord, and said, "A man has come here as a guest, named Thorolf. He is some sort of relation of mine, and I think he will need to dwell here some long time if you will allow it."

Thord said he could not away with men coming to put up at his house, but bade him rest there over the next day if he had no trouble on hand, but otherwise he should be off at his swiftest.

Vigdis answered, "I have offered him already to stay on, and I cannot take back my word, though he be not in even friendship with all men."

After that she told Thord of the slaying of Hall, and that Thorolf who was come there was the man who had killed him. Thord was very cross-grained at this, and said he well knew how that Ingjald would take a great deal of money from him for the sheltering that had been given him already, seeing that doors here have been locked after this man.

Vigdis answered, "Ingjald shall take none of your money for giving one night's shelter to Thorolf, and he shall remain here all this winter through."

Thord said, "In this manner you can checkmate me most thoroughly, but it is against my wish that a man of such evil luck should stay here."

Still Thorolf stayed there all the winter.

Ingjald, who had to take up the blood-suit for his brother, heard this, and so arrayed him for a journey into the Dales at the end of the winter, and ran out a ferry of his whereon they went twelve together. They sailed from the west with a sharp north-west wind, and landed in Salmon-river-Mouth in the evening. They put up their ferry-boat, and came to Goddistead in the evening, arriving there not unawares, and were cheerfully welcomed.

Ingjald took Thord aside for a talk with him, and told him his errand, and said he had heard of Thorolf, the slayer of his brother, being there. Thord said there was no truth in that. Ingjald bade him not to deny it. "Let us rather come to a bargain together: you give up the man, and put me to no toil in the matter of getting at him. I have three marks of silver that you shall have, and I will overlook the offences you have brought on your hands for the shelter given to Thorolf."

Thord thought the money fair, and had now a promise of acquittal of the offences for which he had hitherto most dreaded and for which he would have to abide sore loss of money. So he said, "I shall no doubt hear people speak ill of me for this, none the less this will have to be our bargain." They slept until it wore towards the latter end of the night, when it lacked an hour of day.

Chapter 15
Thorolf's Escape with Asgaut the Thrall

INGJALD AND HIS MEN got up and dressed.

Vigdis asked Thord what his talk with Ingjald had been about the evening before. Thord said they had talked about many things, amongst others how the place was to be ransacked, and how they should be clear of the case if Thorolf was not found there. "So I let Asgaut, my thrall, take the man away."

Vigdis said she had no fondness for lies, and said she should be very loath to have Ingjald sniffing about her house, but bade him, however, do as he liked. After that Ingjald ransacked the place, and did not hit upon the man there. At that moment Asgaut came back, and Vigdis asked him where he had parted with Thorolf.

Asgaut replied, "I took him to our sheephouses as Thord told me to."

Vigdis replied, "Can anything be more exactly in Ingjald's way as he returns to his ship? Nor shall any risk be run, lest they should have made this plan up between them last night. I wish you to go at once, and take him away as soon as possible. You shall take him to Sheepfell to Thorolf;

and if you do as I tell you, you shall get something for it. I will give you your freedom and money, that you may go where you will."

Asgaut agreed to this, and went to the sheephouse to find Thorolf, and bade him get ready to go at once. At this time Ingjald rode out of Goddistead, for he was now anxious to get his money's worth. As he was come down from the farmstead (into the plain) he saw two men coming to meet him; they were Thorolf and Asgaut. This was early in the morning, and there was yet but little daylight. Asgaut and Thorolf now found themselves in a hole, for Ingjald was on one side of them and the Salmon River on the other. The river was terribly swollen, and there were great masses of ice on either bank, while in the middle it had burst open, and it was an ill-looking river to try to ford.

Thorolf said to Asgaut, "It seems to me we have two choices before us. One is to remain here and fight as well as valour and manhood will serve us, and yet the thing most likely is that Ingjald and his men will take our lives without delay; and the other is to tackle the river, and yet that, I think, is still a somewhat dangerous one."

Asgaut said that Thorolf should have his way, and he would not desert him, "whatever plan you are minded to follow in this matter."

Thorolf said, "We will make for the river, then," and so they did, and arrayed themselves as light as possible. After this they got over the main ice, and plunged into the water. And because the men were brave, and Fate had ordained them longer lives, they got across the river and upon the ice on the other side.

Directly after they had got across, Ingjald with his followers came to the spot opposite to them on the other side of the river.

Ingjald spoke out, and said to his companions, "What plan shall we follow now? Shall we tackle the river or not?"

They said he should choose, and they would rely on his foresight, though they thought the river looked impassable. Ingjald said that so it was, and "we will turn away from the river;" and when Thorolf and Asgaut saw that Ingjald had made up his mind not to cross the river, they first wring their clothes and then make ready to go on. They went on all that day, and came in the evening to Sheepfell. They were well received there, for it was an open house for all guests; and forthwith that same evening Asgaut went to see Thorolf Rednose, and told him all the matters concerning their errand, "how Vigdis, his kinswoman, had sent him this man to keep in safety." Asgaut also told him all that had happened between Ingjald and Thord Goddi; therewithal he took forth the tokens Vigdis had sent.

Thorolf replied thus, "I cannot doubt these tokens. I shall indeed take this man in at her request. I think, too, that Vigdis has dealt most bravely with this matter and it is a great pity that such a woman should have so feeble a husband. And you, Asgaut, shall dwell here as long as you like."

Asgaut said he would tarry there for no length of time. Thorolf now takes unto him his namesake, and made him one of his followers; and Asgaut and they parted good friends, and he went on his homeward journey.

And now to tell of Ingjald. He turned back to Goddistead when he and Thorolf parted. By that time men had come there from the nearest farmsteads at the summons of Vigdis, and no fewer than twenty men had gathered there already. But when Ingjald and his men came to the place, he called Thord to him, "You have dealt in a most cowardly way with me, Thord," says he, "for I take it to be the truth that you have got the man off."

Thord said this had not happened with his knowledge; and now all the plotting that had been between Ingjald and Thord came out. Ingjald now claimed to have back his money that he had given to Thord.

Vigdis was standing near during this talk, and said it had fared with them as was meet, and prayed Thord by no means to hold back this money, "For you, Thord," she said, "have got this money in a most cowardly way."

Thord said she must needs have her will herein. After that Vigdis went inside, and to a chest that belonged to Thord, and found at the bottom a large purse. She took out the purse, and went outside with it up to where Ingjald was, and bade him take the money. Ingjald's brow cleared at that, and he stretched out his hand to take the purse. Vigdis raised the purse, and struck him on the nose with it, so that forthwith blood fell on the earth. Therewith she overwhelmed him with mocking words, ending by telling him that henceforth he should never have the money, and bidding him go his way.

Ingjald saw that his best choice was to be off, and the sooner the better, which indeed he did, nor stopped in his journey until he got home, and was mightily ill at ease over his travel.

Chapter 16
Thord Becomes Olaf's Foster Father, AD 950

ABOUT THIS TIME Asgaut came home. Vigdis greeted him, and asked him what sort of reception they had had at Sheepfell. He gave a good account of it, and told her the words wherewith Thorolf had spoken out his mind. She was very pleased at that. "And you, Asgaut," she said, "have done your part well and faithfully, and you shall now know speedily what wages you have worked for. I give you your freedom, so that from this day forth you shall bear the title of a freeman. Therewith you shall take the money that Thord took as the price for the head of Thorolf, my kinsman, and now that money will be better bestowed."

Asgaut thanked her for her gift with fair words.

The next summer Asgaut took a berth in Day-Meal-Ness, and the ship put to sea, and they came in for heavy gales, but not a long sea-voyage, and made Norway. After that Asgaut went to Denmark and settled there, and was thought a valiant and true man. And herewith comes to an end the tale of him.

But after the plot Thord Goddi had made up with Ingjald, the Sheepisles priest, when they made up their minds to compass the death of Thorolf, Vigdis' kinsman, she returned that deed with hatred, and divorced herself from Thord Goddi, and went to her kinsfolk and told them the tale. Thord Yeller was not pleased at this; yet matters went off quietly.

Vigdis did not take away with her from Goddistead any more goods than her own heirlooms. The men of Hvamm let it out that they meant to have for themselves one-half of the wealth that Thord was possessed of. And on hearing this he becomes exceeding faint-hearted, and rides forthwith to see Hoskuld to tell him of his troubles.

Hoskuld said, "Times have been that you have been terror-struck, through not having with such overwhelming odds to deal."

Then Thord offered Hoskuld money for his help, and said he would not look at the matter with a niggard's eye. Hoskuld said, "This is clear, that you will not by peaceful consent allow any man to have the enjoyment of your wealth."

Answers Thord, "No, not quite that though; for I fain would that you should take over all my goods. That being settled, I will ask to foster your son Olaf, and leave him all my wealth after my days are done; for I have no heir here in this land, and I think my means would be better bestowed then, than that the kinsmen of Vigdis should grab it."

To this Hoskuld agreed, and had it bound by witnesses. This Melkorka took heavily, deeming the fostering too low. Hoskuld said she ought not to think that, "for Thord is an old man, and childless, and I wish Olaf to have all his money after his day, but you can always go to see him at any time you like."

Thereupon Thord took Olaf to him, seven years old, and loved him very dearly.

Hearing this, the men who had on hand the case against Thord Goddi thought that now it would be even more difficult than before to lay claim to the money. Hoskuld sent some handsome presents to Thord Yeller, and bade him not be angry over this, seeing that in law they had no claim on Thord's money, inasmuch as Vigdis had brought no true charges against Thord, or any such as justified desertion by her. "Moreover, Thord was no worse a man for casting about for counsel to rid himself of a man that had been thrust upon his means, and was as beset with guilt as a juniper bush is with prickles."

But when these words came to Thord from Hoskuld, and with them large gifts of money, then Thord allowed himself to be pacified, and said he thought the money was well placed that Hoskuld looked after, and took the gifts; and all was quiet after that, but their friendship was rather less warm than formerly.

Olaf grew up with Thord, and became a great man and strong. He was so handsome that his equal was not to be found, and when he was twelve years old he rode to the Thing meeting, and men in other countrysides looked upon it as a great errand to go, and to wonder at the splendid way he was made. In keeping herewith was the manner of Olaf's war-gear and raiment, and therefore he was easily distinguished from all other men.

Thord got on much better after Olaf came to live with him.

Hoskuld gave Olaf a nickname, and called him Peacock, and the name stuck to him.

Chapter 17
About Viga Hrapp's Ghost, AD 950

THE TALE IS TOLD of Hrapp that he became most violent in his behaviour, and did his neighbours such harm that they could hardly hold their own against him. But from the time that Olaf grew up Hrapp got no hold of Thord. Hrapp had the same temper, but his powers waned, in that old age was fast coming upon him, so that he had to lie in bed. Hrapp called Vigdis, his wife, to him, and said, "I have never been of ailing health in life," said he, "and it is therefore most likely that this illness will put an end to our life together. Now, when I am dead, I wish my grave to be dug in the doorway of my fire hall, and that I be put: thereinto, standing there in the doorway; then I shall be able to keep a more searching eye on my dwelling."

After that Hrapp died, and all was done as he said, for Vigdis did not dare do otherwise. And as evil as he had been to deal with in his life, just so he was by a great deal more when he was dead, for he walked again a great deal after he was dead. People said that he killed most of his servants in his ghostly appearances. He caused a great deal of trouble to those who lived near, and the house of Hrappstead became deserted. Vigdis, Hrapp's wife, betook herself west to Thorstein Swart, her brother. He took her and her goods in.

And now things went as before, in that men went to find Hoskuld, and told him all the troubles that Hrapp was doing to them, and asked him to do something to put an end to this. Hoskuld said this should be done, and he went with some men to Hrappstead, and has Hrapp dug up, and taken away to a place near to which cattle were least likely to roam or men to go about. After that Hrapp's walkings-again abated somewhat.

Sumarlid, Hrapp's son, inherited all Hrapp's wealth, which was both great and goodly. Sumarlid set up household at Hrappstead the next spring; but after he Thorstein Swart leaves home had kept house there for a little time he was seized of frenzy, and died shortly afterwards.

Now it was the turn of his mother, Vigdis, to take there alone all this wealth; but as she would not go to the estate of Hrappstead, Thorstein Swart took all the wealth to himself to take care of. Thorstein was by then rather old, though still one of the most healthy and hearty of men.

Chapter 18
Of the Drowning of Thorstein Swart

AT THAT TIME there rose to honour among men in Thorness, the kinsmen of Thorstein, named Bork the Stout and his brother, Thorgrim. It was soon found out how these brothers would fain be the greatest men there, and were most highly accounted of. And when Thorstein found that out, he would not elbow them aside, and so made it known to people that he wished to change his abode, and take his household to Hrappstead, in Salmon-river-Dale.

Thorstein Swart got ready to start after the spring Thing, but his cattle were driven round along the shore. Thorstein got on board a ferry-boat, and took twelve men with him; and Thorarin, his brother-in-law, and Osk, Thorstein's daughter, and Hild, her daughter, who was three years old, went with them too. Thorstein fell in with a high south-westerly gale, and they sailed up towards the roosts, and into that roost which is called Coal-chest-Roost, which is the biggest of the currents in Broadfirth. They made little way sailing, chiefly because the tide was ebbing, and the wind was not favourable, the weather being squally, with high wind when the squalls broke over, but with little wind between whiles. Thorstein steered, and had the braces of the sail round his shoulders, because the boat was blocked up with goods, chiefly piled-up chests, and the cargo was heaped up very high; but land was near about, while on the boat there was but little way, because of the raging current against them. Then they sailed on to a hidden rock, but were not wrecked.

Thorstein bade them let down the sail as quickly as possible, and take punt poles to push off the ship. This shift was tried to no avail, because on either board the sea was so deep that the poles struck no bottom; so they were obliged to wait for the incoming tide, and now the water ebbs away under the ship.

Throughout the day they saw a seal in the current larger by much than any others, and through the day it would be swimming round about the ship, with flappers none of the shortest, and to all of them it seemed that in him there were human eyes. Thorstein bade them shoot the seal, and they tried, but it came to nought.

Now the tide rose; and just as the ship was getting afloat there broke upon them a violent squall, and the boat heeled over, and every one on board the boat was drowned, save one man, named Gudmund, who drifted ashore with some timber. The place where he was washed up was afterwards called Gudmund's Isles.

Gudrid, whom Thorkell Trefill had for wife, was entitled to the inheritance left by Thorstein, her father.

These tidings spread far and near of the drowning of Thorstein Swart, and the men who were lost there.

Thorkell sent straightway for the man Gudmund, who had been washed ashore, and when he came and met Thorkell, he (Thorkell) struck a bargain with him, to the end that he should tell the story of the loss of lives even as he (Thorkell) was going to dictate it to him. Gudmund agreed. Thorkell now asked him to tell the story of this mishap in the hearing of a good many people.

Then Gudmund spake on this wise: "Thorstein was drowned first, and then his son-in-law, Thorarin" – so that then it was the turn of Hild to come in for the money, as she was the daughter of Thorarin. Then he said the maiden was drowned, because the next in inheritance to her was

Osk, her mother, and she lost her life the last of them, so that all the money thus came to Thorkell Trefill, in that his wife Gudrid must take inheritance after her sister.

Now this tale is spread abroad by Thorkell and his men; but Gudmund ere this had told the tale in somewhat another way. Now the kinsmen of Thorarin misdoubted this tale somewhat, and said they would not believe it unproved, and claimed one-half of the heritage against Thorkell; but Thorkell maintained it belonged to him alone, and bade that ordeal should be taken on the matter, according to their custom.

This was the ordeal at that time, that men had had to pass under "earth-chain," which was a slip of sward cut loose from the soil, but both ends thereof were left adhering to the earth, and the man who should go through with the ordeal should walk thereunder.

Thorkell Trefill now had some misgivings himself as to whether the deaths of the people had indeed taken place as he and Gudmund had said the second time. Heathen men deemed that on them rested no less responsibility when ceremonies of this kind had to be gone through than Christian men do when ordeals are decreed. He who passed under "earth-chain" cleared himself if the sward-slip did not fall down upon him. Thorkell made an arrangement with two men that they should feign quarrelling over something or another, and be close to the spot when the ordeal was being gone through with, and touch the sward-slip so unmistakably that all men might see that it was they who knocked it down.

After this comes forward he who was to go through with the ordeal, and at the nick of time when he had got under the 'earth-chain,' these men who had been put up to it fall on each other with weapons, meeting close to the arch of the sward-slip, and lie there fallen, and down tumbles the 'earth-chain', as was likely enough. Then men rush up between them and part them, which was easy enough, for they fought with no mind to do any harm. Thorkell Trefill then asked people as to what they thought about the ordeal, and all his men now said that it would have turned out all right if no one had spoilt it.

Then Thorkell took all the chattels to himself, but the land at Hrapstead was left to lie fallow.

Chapter 19
Hrut Comes to Iceland

NOW OF HOSKULD it is to be told that his state is one of great honour, and that he is a great chieftain. He had in his keep a great deal of Hrut in Norway money that belonged to his (half) brother, Hrut, Herjolf's son. Many men would have it that Hoskuld's means would be heavily cut into if he should be made to pay to the full the heritage of his (Hrut's) mother.

Hrut was of the bodyguard of King Harald, Gunnhild's son, and was much honoured by him, chiefly for the reason that he approved himself the best man in all deeds of manly trials, while, on the other hand, Gunnhild, the Queen, loved him so much that she held there was not his equal within the guard, either in talking or in anything else. Even when men were compared, and noblemen therein were pointed to, all men easily saw that Gunnhild thought that at the bottom there must be sheer thoughtlessness, or else envy, if any man was said to be Hrut's equal.

Now, inasmuch as Hrut had in Iceland much money to look after, and many noble kinsfolk to go and see, he desired to go there, and now arrays his journey for Iceland. The king gave him a ship at parting and said he had proved a brave man and true.

Gunnhild saw Hrut off to his ship, and said, "Not in a hushed voice shall this be spoken, that I have proved you to be a most noble man, in that you have prowess equal to the best man here in this land, but are in wits a long way before them".

Then she gave him a gold ring and bade him farewell. Whereupon she drew her mantle over her head and went swiftly home.

Hrut went on board his ship, and put to sea. He had a good breeze, and came to Broadfirth. He sailed up the bay, up to the island, and, steering in through Broadsound, he landed at Combness, where he put his gangways to land.

The news of the coming of this ship spread about, as also that Hrut, Herjolf's son, was the captain. Hoskuld gave no good cheer to these tidings, and did not go to meet Hrut.

Hrut put up his ship, and made her snug. He built himself a dwelling, which since has been called Combness. Then he rode to see Hoskuld, to get his share of his mother's inheritance. Hoskuld said he had no money to pay him, and said his mother had not gone without means out of Iceland when she met with Herjolf. Hrut liked this very ill, but rode away, and there the matter rested. All Hrut's kinsfolk, excepting Hoskuld, did honour to Hrut. Hrut now lived three winters at Combness, and was always demanding the money from Hoskuld at the Thing meetings and other law gatherings, and he spoke well on the matter. And most men held that Hrut had right on his side. Hoskuld said that Thorgerd had not married Herjolf by his counsel, and that he was her lawful guardian, and there the matter dropped.

That same autumn Hoskuld went to a feast at Thord Goddi's, and hearing that, Hrut rode with twelve men to Hoskuldstead and took away twenty oxen, leaving as many behind. Then he sent some men to Hoskuld, telling them where he might search for the cattle. Hoskuld's house-carles sprang forthwith up, and seized their weapons, and words were sent to the nearest neighbours for help, so that they were a party of fifteen together, and they rode each one as fast as they possibly could. Hrut and his followers did not see the pursuit till they were a little way from the enclosure at Combness. And forthwith he and his men jumped off their horses, and tied them up, and went forward unto a certain sandhill. Hrut said that there they would make a stand, and added that though the money claim against Hoskuld sped slowly, never should that be said that he had run away before his thralls.

Hrut's followers said that they had odds to deal with. Hrut said he would never heed that; said they should fare all the worse the more they were in number.

The men of Salmon-river-Dale now jumped off their horses, and got ready to fight. Hrut bade his men not trouble themselves about the odds, and goes for them at a rush. Hrut had a helmet on his head, a drawn sword in one hand and a shield in the other. He was of all men the most skilled at arms. Hrut was then so wild that few could keep up with him. Both sides fought briskly for a while; but the men of Salmon-river-Dale very soon found that in Hrut they had to deal with one for whom they were no match, for now he slew two men at every onslaught. After that the men of Salmon-river-Dale begged for peace. Hrut replied that they should surely have peace. All the house-carles of Hoskuld who were yet alive were wounded, and four were killed.

Hrut then went home, being somewhat wounded himself; but his followers only slightly or not at all, for he had been the foremost in the fight. The place has since been called Fight-Dale where they fought. After that Hrut had the cattle killed.

Now it must be told how Hoskuld got men together in a hurry when he heard of the robbery and rode home. Much at the same time as he arrived his house-carles came home too, and told how their journey had gone anything but smoothly. Hoskuld was wild with wrath at this, and said he meant to take at Hrut's hand no robbery or loss of lives again, and gathered to him men all that day.

Then Jorunn, his wife, went and talked to him, and asked him what he had made his mind up to.

He said, "It is but little I have made up my mind to, but I fain would that men should oftener talk of something else than the slaying of my house-carles".

Jorunn answered, "You are after a fearful deed if you mean to kill such a man as your brother, seeing that some men will have it that it would not have been without cause if Hrut had seized these goods even before this; and now he has shown that, taking after the race he comes from, he means no longer to be an outcast, kept from what is his own. Now, surely he cannot have made up his mind to try his strength with you till he knew that he might hope for some backing-up from the more powerful among men; for, indeed, I am told that messages have been passing in quiet between Hrut and Thord Yeller. And to me, at least, such matters seem worthy of heed being paid to them. No doubt Thord will be glad to back up matters of this kind, seeing how clear are the bearings of the case. Moreover you know, Hoskuld, that since the quarrel between Thord Goddi and Vigdis, there has not been the same fond friendship between you and Thord Yeller as before, although by means of gifts you staved off the enmity of him and his kinsmen in the beginning. I also think, Hoskuld," she said, "that in that matter, much to the trial of their temper, they feel they have come off worst at the hands of yourself and your son, Olaf. Now this seems to me the wiser counsel: to make your brother an honourable offer, for there a hard grip from greedy wolf may be looked for. I am sure that Hrut will take that matter in good part, for I am told he is a wise man, and he will see that that would be an honour to both of you."

Hoskuld quieted down greatly at Jorunn's speech, and thought this was likely to be true. Then men went between them who were friends of both sides, bearing words of peace from Hoskuld to Hrut. Hrut received them well, and said he would indeed make friends with Hoskuld, and added that he had long been ready for their coming to terms as behoved kinsmen, if but Hoskuld had been willing to grant him his right. Hrut also said he was ready to do honour to Hoskuld for what he on his side had misdone.

So now these matters were shaped and settled between the brothers, who now take to living together in good brotherhood from this time forth.

Hrut now looks after his homestead, and became mighty man of his ways. He did not mix himself up in general things, but in whatever matter he took a part he would have his own way. Hrut now moved his dwelling, and abode to old age at a place which now is called Hrutstead. He made a temple in his home-field, of which the remains are still to be seen. It is called Trolls' walk now, and there is the high road.

Hrut married a woman named Unn, daughter of Mord Fiddle. Unn left him, and thence sprang the quarrels between the men of Salmon-river-Dale and the men of Fleetlithe.

Hrut's second wife was named Thorbjorg. She was Armod's daughter. Hrut married a third wife, but her we do not name. Hrut had sixteen sons and ten daughters by these two wives. And men say that one summer Hrut rode to the Thing meeting, and fourteen of his sons were with him. Of this mention is made, because it was thought a sign of greatness and might. All his sons were right goodly men.

Chapter 20
Melkorka's Marriage and Olaf the Peacock's Journey, AD 955

HOSKULD NOW REMAINED quietly at home, and began now to sink into old age, and his sons were now all grown up.

Thorliek sets up household of his own at a place called Combness, and Hoskuld handed over to him his portion. After that he married a woman named Gjaflaug, daughter of Arnbjorn, son of Sleitu Bjorn, and Thordaug, the daughter of Thord of Headland. It was a noble match, Gjaflaug being a very beautiful and high-minded woman. Thorliek was not an easy man to get on with, but was most warlike. There was not much friendship between the kinsmen Hrut and Thorliek. Bard Hoskuld's son stayed at home with his father, looked after the household affairs no less than Hoskuld himself.

The daughters of Hoskuld do not have much to do with this story, yet men are known who are descended from them.

Olaf, Hoskuld's son, was now grown up, and was the handsomest of all men that people ever set eyes on. He arrayed himself always well, both as to clothes and weapons. Melkorka, Olaf's mother, lived at Melkorkastead, as has been told before. Hoskuld looked less after Melkorka's household ways than he used to do, saying that that matter concerned Olaf, her son. Olaf said he would give her such help as he had to offer her. Melkorka thought Hoskuld had done shamefully by her, and makes up her mind to do something to him at which he should not be over pleased.

Thorbjorn Skrjup had chiefly had on hand the care of Melkorka's household affairs. He had made her an offer of marriage, after she had been an householder for but a little while, but Melkorka refused him flatly.

There was a ship up by Board-Ere in Ramfirth, and Orn was the name of the captain. He was one of the bodyguard of King Harald, Gunnhild's son.

Melkorka spoke to Olaf, her son, and said that she wished he should journey abroad to find his noble relations, "For I have told the truth that Myrkjartan is really my father, and he is king of the Irish and it would be easy for you betake you on board the ship that is now at Board-Ere."

Olaf said, "I have spoken about it to my father, but he seemed to want to have but little to do with it; and as to the manner of my foster-father's money affairs, it so happens that his wealth is more in land or cattle than in stores of islandic market goods."

Melkorka said, "I cannot bear your being called the son of a slave-woman any longer; and if it stands in the way of the journey, that you think you have not enough money, then I would rather go to the length even of marrying Thorbjorn, if then you should be more willing than before to betake yourself to the journey. For I think he will be willing to hand out to you as much wares as you think you may need, if I give my consent to his marrying me. Above all I look to this, that then Hoskuld will like two things mightily ill when he comes to hear of them, namely, that you have gone out of the land, and that I am married."

Olaf bade his mother follow her own counsel. After that Olaf talked to Thorbjorn as to how he wished to borrow wares of him, and a great deal thereof.

Thorbjorn answered, "I will do it on one condition, and that is that I shall marry Melkorka for them; it seems to me, you will be as welcome to my money as to that which you have in your keep."

Olaf said that this should then be settled; whereupon they talked between them of such matters as seemed needful, but all these things they agreed should be kept quiet.

Hoskuld wished Olaf to ride with him to the Thing. Olaf said he could not do that on account of household affairs, as he also wanted to fence off a grazing paddock for lambs by Salmon River. Hoskuld was very pleased that he should busy himself with the homestead.

Then Hoskuld rode to the Thing; but at Lambstead a wedding feast was arrayed, and Olaf settled the agreement alone. Olaf took out of the undivided estate thirty hundred ells' worth of wares, and should pay no money for them. Bard, Hoskuld's son, was at the wedding, and was a party with them to all these doings. When the feast was ended Olaf rode off to the ship, and found Orn the captain, and took berth with him.

Before Olaf and Melkorka parted she gave him a great gold finger-ring, and said, "This gift my father gave me for a teething gift, and I know he will recognise it when he sees it." She also put into his hands a knife and a belt, and bade him give them to her nurse: "I am sure she will not doubt these tokens." And still further Melkorka spake, "I have fitted you out from home as best I know how, and taught you to speak Irish, so that it will make no difference to you where you are brought to shore in Ireland."

After that they parted. There arose forthwith a fair wind, when Olaf got on board, and they sailed straightway out to sea.

Chapter 21
Olaf the Peacock Goes to Ireland, AD 955

NOW HOSKULD CAME BACK from the Thing and heard these tidings, and was very much displeased. But seeing that his near akin were concerned in the matter, he quieted down and let things alone.

Olaf and his companions had a good voyage, and came to Norway. Orn urges Olaf to go to the court of King Harald, who, he said, bestowed goodly honour on men of no better breeding than Olaf was. Olaf said he thought he would take that counsel. Olaf and Orn now went to the court, and were well received. The king at once recognised Olaf for the sake of his kindred, and forthwith bade him stay with him.

Gunnhild paid great heed to Olaf when she knew he was Hrut's brother's son; but some men would have it, that she took pleasure in talking to Olaf without his needing other people's aid to introduce him.

As the winter wore on, Olaf grew sadder of mood. Orn asked him what was the matter of his sorrow?

Olaf answered, "I have on hand a journey to go west over the sea; and I set much store by it and that you should lend me your help, so that it may be undertaken in the course of next summer."

Orn bade Olaf not set his heart on going, and said he did not know of any ships going west over the sea. Gunnhild joined in their talk, and said, "Now I hear you talk together in a manner that has not happened before, in that each of you wants to have his own way!"

Olaf greeted Gunnhild well, without letting drop their talk. After that Orn went away, but Gunnhild and Olaf kept conversing together. Olaf told her of his wish, and how much store he set by carrying it out, saying he knew for certain that Myrkjartan, the king, was his mother's father.

Then Gunnhild said, "I will lend you help for this voyage, so that you may go on it as richly furnished as you please."

Olaf thanked her for her promise. Then Gunnhild had a ship prepared and a crew got together, and bade Olaf say how many men he would have to go west over the sea with him. Olaf fixed the number at sixty; but said that it was a matter of much concern to him, that such a company should be more like warriors than merchants. She said that so it should be; and Orn is the only man mentioned by name in company with Olaf on this journey. The company were well fitted out.

King Harald and Gunnhild led Olaf to his ship, and they said they wished to bestow on him their good-luck over and above other friendship they had bestowed on him already. King Harald said that was an easy matter; for they must say that no goodlier a man had in their days come out of Iceland. Then Harald the king asked how old a man he was.

Olaf answered, "I am now eighteen winters."

The king replied, "Of exceeding worth, indeed, are such men as you are, for as yet you have left the age of child but a short way behind; and be sure to come and see us when you come back again."

Then the king and Gunnhild bade Olaf farewell. Then Olaf and his men got on board, and sailed out to sea. They came in for unfavourable weather through the summer, had fogs plentiful, and little wind, and what there was was unfavourable; and wide about the main they drifted, and on most on board fell 'sea-bewilderment.' But at last the fog lifted over-head; and the wind rose, and they put up sail. Then they began to discuss in which direction Ireland was to be sought; and they did not agree on that. Orn said one thing, and most of the men went against him, and said that Orn was all bewildered: they should rule who were the greater in number. Then Olaf was asked to decide. He said, "I think we should follow the counsel of the wisest; for the counsels of foolish men I think will be of all the worse service for us in the greater number they gather together."

And now they deemed the matter settled, since Olaf spake in this manner; and Orn took the steering from that time. They sailed for days and nights, but always with very little wind. One night the watchmen leapt up, and bade every one wake at once, and said they saw land so near that they had almost struck on it. The sail was up, but there was but little wind. Every one got up, and Orn bade them clear away from the land, if they could.

Olaf said, "That is not the way out of our plight, for I see reefs all about astern; so let down the sail at once, and we will take our counsel when there is daylight, and we know what land this is."

Then they cast anchors, and they caught bottom at once. There was much talk during the night as to where they could be come to; and when daylight was up they recognised that it was Ireland.

Orn said, "I don't think we have come to a good place, for this is far away from the harbours or market-towns, whose strangers enjoy peace; and we are now left high and dry, like sticklebacks, and near enough, I think, I come to the laws of the Irish in saying that they will lay claim to the goods we have on board as their lawful prize, for as flotsam they put down ships even when sea has ebbed out shorter from the stern (than here)."

Olaf said no harm would happen, "But I have seen that today there is a gathering of men up inland; so the Irish think, no doubt, the arrival of this ship a great thing. During the ebb-tide today I noticed that there was a dip, and that out of the dip the sea fell without emptying it out; and if our ship has not been damaged, we can put out our boat and tow the ship into it."

There was a bottom of loam where they had been riding at anchor, so that not a plank of the ship was damaged. So Olaf and his men tow their boat to the dip, cast anchor there.

Now, as day drew on, crowds drifted down to the shore. At last two men rowed a boat out to the ship. They asked what men they were who had charge of that ship, and Olaf answered, speaking in Irish, to their inquiries. When the Irish knew they were Norwegians they pleaded their law, and bade them give up their goods; and if they did so, they would do them no harm till the king had sat in judgment on their case.

Olaf said the law only held good when merchants had no interpreter with them. "But I can say with truth these are peaceful men, and we will not give ourselves up untried."

The Irish then raised a great war-cry, and waded out into the sea, and wished to drag the ship, with them on board, to the shore, the water being no deeper than reaching up to their armpits, or to the belts of the tallest. But the pool was so deep where the ship was floating that they could not touch the bottom. Olaf bade the crew fetch out their weapons, and range in line of battle from stem to stern on the ship; and so thick they stood, that shield overlapped shield all round the ship, and a spear-point stood out at the lower end of every shield.

Olaf walked fore to the prow, and was thus arrayed: he had a coat of mail, and a gold-reddened helmet on his head; girt with a sword with gold-inlaid hilt, and in his hand a barbed spear chased and well engraved. A red shield he had before him, on which was drawn a lion in gold.

When the Irish saw this array fear shot through their hearts, and they thought it would not be so easy a matter as they had thought to master the booty. So now the Irish break their journey, and run all together to a village near. Then there arose great murmur in the crowd, as they deemed that, sure enough, this must be a warship, and that they must expect many others; so they sent speedily word to the king, which was easy, as he was at that time a short way off, feasting. Straightway he rides with a company of men to where the ship was. Between the land and the place where the ship lay afloat the space was no greater than that one might well hear men talking together. Now Olaf stood forth in the same arrayal whereof is written before, and men marvelled much how noble was the appearance of the man who was the captain of the ship. But when the shipmates of Olaf see how a large company of knights rides towards them, looking a company of the bravest, they grow hushed, for they deemed here were great odds to deal with. But when Olaf heard the murmur which went round among his followers, he bade them take heart, "For now our affairs are in a fair way; the Irish are now greeting Myrkjartan, their king."

Then they rode together so near to the ship, that each could hear what the other said. The king asked who was the master of the ship. Olaf told his name, and asked who was the valiant-looking knight with whom he then was talking.

He answered, "I am called Myrkjartan."

Olaf asked, "Are you then a king of the Irish?"

He said he was. Then the king asked Olaf for news commonly talked of, and Olaf gave good answers as to all news he was asked about. Then the king asked whence they had put to sea, and whose men they were. And still the king asked, more searchingly than before, about Olaf's kindred, for the king found that this man was of haughty bearing, and would not answer any further than the king asked.

Olaf said, "Let it be known to you that we ran our ship afloat from the coast of Norway, and these are of the bodyguard of King Harald, the son of Gunnhild, who are here on board. And as for my race, I have, sire, to tell you this, that my father lives in Iceland, and is named Hoskuld, a man of high birth; but of my mother's kindred, I think you must have seen many more than I have. For my mother is called Melkorka, and it has been told me as a truth that she is your daughter, king. Now, this has driven me upon this long journey, and to me it is a matter most weighty what answer you give in my case."

The king then grew silent, and had a converse with his men. The wise men asked the king what might be the real truth of the story that this man was telling. The king answered, "This is clearly seen in this Olaf, that he is high-born man, whether he be a kinsman of mine or not, as well as this, that of all men he speaks the best of Irish."

After that the king stood up, and said, "Now I will give answer to your speech, in so far as we grant to you and all your shipmates peace; but on the kinship you claim with us, we must talk more before I give answer to that."

After that they put out their gangways to the shore, and Olaf and his followers went on land from the ship; and the Irish now marvel much how warrior-like these men are. Olaf greeted the king well, taking off his helmet and bowing to the king, who welcomes Olaf with all fondness. Thereupon they fall to talking together, Olaf pleading his case again in a speech long and frank; and at the end of his speech he said he had a ring on his hand that Melkorka had given him at parting in Iceland, saying "that you, king, gave it her as a tooth gift."

The king took and looked at the ring, and his face grew wondrous red to look at; and then the king said, "True enough are the tokens, and become by no means less notable thereby that you have so many of your mother's family features, and that even by them you might be easily recognised; and because of these things I will in sooth acknowledge your kinship, Olaf, by the witnessing of these men that here are near and hear my speech. And this shall also follow that I will ask you to my court, with all your suite, but the honour of you all will depend thereon of what worth as a man I find you to be when I try you more."

After that the king orders riding-horses to be given to them, and appoints men to look after their ship, and to guard the goods belonging to them. The King now rode to Dublin, and men thought this great tidings, that with the king should be journeying the son of his daughter, who had been carried off in war long ago when she was only fifteen winters old.

But most startled of all at these tidings was the foster-mother of Melkorka, who was then bed-ridden, both from heavy sickness and old age; yet she walked with no staff even to support her, to meet Olaf.

The king said to Olaf, "Here is come Melkorka's foster-mother, and she will wish to hear all the tidings you can tell about Melkorka's life."

Olaf took her with open arms, and set the old woman on his knee, and said her foster-daughter was well settled and in a good position in Iceland. Then Olaf put in her hands the knife and the belt, and the old woman recognised the gifts, and wept for joy, and said it was easy to see that Melkorka's son was one of high mettle, and no wonder, seeing what stock he comes of. The old woman was strong and well, and in good spirits all that winter.

The king was seldom at rest, for at that time the lands in the west were at all times raided by war-bands. The king drove from his land that winter both Vikings and raiders. Olaf was with his suite in the king's ship, and those who came against them thought his was indeed a grim company to deal with. The king talked over with Olaf and his followers all matters needing counsel, for Olaf proved himself to the king both wise and eager-minded in all deeds of prowess. But towards the latter end of the winter the king summoned a Thing, and great numbers came. The king stood up and spoke.

He began his speech thus: "You all know that last autumn there came hither a man who is the son of my daughter, and high-born also on his father's side; and it seems to me that Olaf is a man of such prowess and courage that here such men are not to be found. Now I offer him my kingdom after my day is done, for Olaf is much more suitable for a ruler than my own sons."

Olaf thanked him for this offer with many graceful and fair words, and said he would not run the risk as to how his sons might behave when Myrkjartan was no more; said it was better to gain swift honour than lasting shame; and added that he wished to go to Norway when ships could safely journey from land to land, and that his mother would have little delight in life if he did not return to her. The king bade Olaf do as he thought best. Then the Thing was broken up.

When Olaf's ship was ready, the king saw him off on board; and gave him a spear chased with gold, and a gold-bedecked sword, and much money besides. Olaf begged that he might take Melkorka's *Olaf comes to Norway again* foster-mother with him; but the king said there was no necessity for that, so she did not go. Then Olaf got on board his ship, and he and the king parted with the greatest friendship. Then Olaf sailed out to sea. They had a good voyage, and made land in Norway; and Olaf's journey became very famous. They set up their ship; and Olaf got horses for himself, and went, together with his followers, to find King Harald.

Chapter 22
Olaf the Peacock Comes Home to Iceland, AD 957

OLAF HOSKULDSON THEN WENT to the court of King Harald. The king gave him a good welcome, but Gunnhild a much better. With many fair words they begged him to stay with them, and Olaf agreed to it, and both he and Orn entered the king's court. King Harald and Gunnhild set so great a store by Olaf that no foreigner had ever been held in such honour by them. Olaf gave to the king and Gunnhild many rare gifts, which he had got west in Ireland. King Harald gave Olaf at Yule a set of clothes made out of scarlet stuff.

So now Olaf stayed there quietly all the winter. In the spring, as it was wearing on, Olaf and the king had a conversation together, and Olaf begged the king's leave to go to Iceland in the summer, "For I have noble kinsfolk there I want to go and see."

The king answered, "It would be more to my mind that you should settle down with us, and take whatever position in our service you like best yourself." Olaf thanked the king for all the honour he was offering him, but said he wished very much to go to Iceland, if that was not against the king's will. The king answered, "Nothing shall be done in this in an unfriendly manner to you, Olaf. You shall go out to Iceland in the summer, for I see you have set your heart on it; but neither trouble nor toil shall you have over your preparations, for I will see after all that," and thereupon they part talking.

King Harald had a ship launched in the spring; it was a merchant ship, both great and good. This ship the king ordered to be laden with wood, and fitted out with full rigging. When the ship was ready the king had Olaf called to him, and said, "This ship shall be your own, Olaf, for I should not like you to start from Norway this summer as a passenger in any one else's ship."

Olaf thanked the king in fair words for his generosity. After that Olaf got ready for his journey; and when he was ready and a fair wind arose, Olaf sailed out to sea, and King Harald and he parted with the greatest affection. That summer Olaf had a good voyage. He brought his ship into Ramfirth, to Board-Ere.

The arrival of the ship was soon heard of, and also who the captain was. Hoskuld heard of the arrival of Olaf, his son, and was very much pleased, and rode forthwith north to Hrutafjord with some men, and there was a joyful meeting between the father and son. Hoskuld invited Olaf to come to him, and Olaf said he would agree to that; so he set up his ship, but his goods were brought (on horseback) Melkorka receives Olaf from the north. And when this business was over Olaf himself rode with twelve men home to Hoskuldstead, and Hoskuld greeted his son joyfully, and his brothers also received him fondly, as well as all his kinsfolk; but between Olaf and Bard was love the fondest.

Olaf became very renowned for this journey; and now was proclaimed the descent of Olaf, that he was the daughter's son of Myrkjartan, king of Ireland. The news of this spread over the land, as well as of the honour that mighty men, whom he had gone to see, had bestowed on him.

Melkorka came soon to see Olaf, her son, and Olaf greeted her with great joy. She asked about many things in Ireland, first of her father and then of her other relations. Olaf replied to everything she asked. Then she asked if her foster-mother still lived. Olaf said she was still alive. Melkorka asked why he had not tried to give her the pleasure of bringing her over to Iceland.

Olaf replied, "They would not allow me to bring your foster-mother out of Ireland, mother."

"That may be so," she replied, and it could be seen that this she took much to heart.

Melkorka and Thorbjorn had one son, who was named Lambi. He was a tall man and strong, like his father in looks as well as in temper.

When Olaf had been in Iceland a month, and spring came on, father and son took counsel together.

"I will, Olaf," said Hoskuld, "that a match should be sought for you, and that then you should take over the house of your foster-father at Goddistead, where still there are great means stored up, and that then you should look after the affairs of that household under my guidance."

Olaf answered, "Little have I set my mind on that sort of thing hitherto; besides, I do not know where that woman lives whom to marry would mean any great good luck to me. You must know I shall look high for a wife. But I see clearly that you would not have broached this matter till you had made up your mind as to where it was to end."

Hoskuld said, "You guess that right. There is a man named Egil. He is Skallagrim's son. He lives at Borg, in Borgarfjord. This Egil has a daughter who is called Thorgerd, and she is the woman I have made up my mind to woo on your behalf, for she is the very best match in all Borgarfjord, and even if one went further afield. Moreover, it is to be looked for, that an alliance with the Mere-men would mean more power to you."

Olaf answered, "Herein I shall trust to your foresight, for if this match were to come off it would be altogether to my liking. But this you must bear in mind, father, that should this matter be set forth, and not come off, I should take it very ill."

Hoskuld answered, "I think I shall venture to bring the matter about."

Olaf bade him do as he liked. Now time wears on towards Olaf's proposal the Thing. Hoskuld prepares his journey from home with a crowded company, and Olaf, his son, also accompanies him on the journey. They set up their booth. A great many people were there. Egil Skallagrim's son was at the Thing. Every one who saw Olaf remarked what a handsome man he was, and how noble his bearing, well arrayed as he was as to weapons and clothes.

Chapter 23
The Marriage of Olaf Peacock and Thorgerd, the Daughter of Egil, AD 959

IT IS TOLD HOW one day the father and son, Hoskuld and Olaf, went forth from their booth to find Egil. Egil greeted them well, for he and Hoskuld knew each other very well by word of mouth. Hoskuld now broaches the wooing on behalf of Olaf, and asks for the hand of Thorgerd. She was also at the Thing.

Egil took the matter well, and said he had always heard both father and son well spoken of, "and I also know, Hoskuld," said Egil, "that you are a high-born man and of great worth, and Olaf is much renowned on account of his journey, and it is no wonder that such men should look high for a match, for he lacks neither family nor good looks; but yet this must be talked over with Thorgerd, for it is no man's task to get Thorgerd for wife against her will."

Hoskuld said, "I wish, Egil, that you would talk this over with your daughter."

Egil said that that should be done. Egil now went away to find his daughter, and they talked together. Egil said, "There is here a man Thorgerd's refusal named Olaf, who is Hoskuld's son, and he is now one of the most renowned of men. Hoskuld, his father, has broached a wooing on behalf of Olaf, and has sued for your hand; and I have left that matter mostly for you to deal with. Now I want to know your answer. But it seems to me that it behoves you to give a good answer to such a matter, for this match is a noble one."

Thorgerd answered, "I have often heard you say that you love me best of all your children, but now it seems to me you make that a falsehood if you wish me to marry the son of a bonds-woman, however goodly and great a dandy he may be."

Egil said, "In this matter you are not so well up, as in others. Have you not heard that he is the son of the daughter of Myrkjartan, king of Ireland? So that he is much higher born on his mother's side than on his father's, which, however, would be quite good enough for us."

Thorgerd would not see this; and so they dropped the talk, each being somewhat of a different mind.

The next day Egil went to Hoskuld's booth. Hoskuld gave him a good welcome, and so they fell a-talking together. Hoskuld asked how this wooing matter had sped. Egil held out but little hope, and told him all that had come to pass. Hoskuld said it looked like a closed matter, "Yet I think you have behaved well."

Olaf did not hear this talk of theirs. After that Egil went away. Olaf now asks, "How speeds the wooing?"

Hoskuld said, "It pointed to slow speed on her side."

Olaf said, "It is now as I told you, Olaf proposes himself father, that I should take it very ill if in answer (to the wooing) I should have to take shaming words, seeing that the broaching of the wooing gives undue right to the wooed. And now I shall have my way so far, that this shall not drop here. For true is the saw, that 'others' errands eat the wolves'; and now I shall go straightway to Egil's booth."

Hoskuld bade him have his own way. Olaf now dressed himself in this way, that he had on the scarlet clothes King Harald had given him, and a golden helmet on his head, and the gold-adorned sword in his hand that King Myrkjartan had given him. Then Hoskuld and Olaf went to Egil's booth. Hoskuld went first, and Olaf followed close on his heels. Egil greeted him well, and Hoskuld sat down by him, but Olaf stood up and looked about him. He saw a woman sitting on the dais in the booth, she was goodly and had the looks of one of high degree, and very well dressed. He thought to himself this must be Thorgerd, Egil's daughter. Olaf went up to the dais and sat down by her. Thorgerd greeted the man, and asked who he was.

Olaf told his own and his father's name, and "You must think it very bold that the son of a slave should dare to sit down by you and presume to talk to you!"

She said, "You cannot but mean that you must be thinking you have done deeds of greater daring than that of talking to women."

Then they began to talk together, and they talked all day. But nobody heard their conversation. And before they parted Egil and Hoskuld were called to them; and the matter of Olaf's wooing was now talked over again, and Thorgerd came round to her father's wish. Now the affair was all easily settled and the betrothal took place. The honour was conceded to the Salmon-river-Dale men that the bride should be brought home to them, for by law the bride-groom should have gone to the bride's home to be married. The wedding was to take place at Hoskuldstead when seven weeks summer had passed.

After that Egil and Hoskuld separated. The father and son rode home to Hoskuldstead, and all was quiet the rest of the summer.

After that things were got ready for the wedding at Hoskuldstead, and nothing was spared, for means were plentiful. The guests came at the time settled, and the Burgfirthmen mustered in a great company. Egil was there, and Thorstein, his son. The bride was in the journey too, and with her a chosen company out of all the countryside. Hoskuld had also a great company awaiting them. The feast was a brave one, and the guests were seen off with good gifts on leaving. Olaf gave to Egil the sword, Myrkjartan's gift, and Egil's brow brightened greatly at the gift. Nothing in the way of tidings befell, and every one went home.

Chapter 24
The Building of Herdholt, AD 960

OLAF AND THORGERD LIVED at Hoskuldstead and loved each other very dearly; it was easily seen by every one that she was a woman of very high mettle, though she meddled little with every-day things, but whatever Thorgerd put her hand to must be carried through as she wished. Olaf and Thorgerd spent that winter turn and turn about at Hoskuldstead, or with Olaf's foster-father. In the spring Olaf took over the household business at Goddistead.

The following summer Thord fell ill, and the illness ended in his death. Olaf had a cairn raised over him on the ness that runs out into the Salmon-river and is called Drafn-ness, with a wall round which is called Howes-garth.

After that liegemen crowded to Olaf and he became a great chieftain. Hoskuld was not envious of this, for he always wished that Olaf should be consulted in all great matters. The place Olaf owned was the stateliest in Salmon-river-Dale.

There were two brothers with Olaf, both named An. One was called An the White and the other An the Black. They had a third brother who was named Beiner the Strong. These were Olaf's smiths, and very valiant men.

Thorgerd and Olaf had a daughter who was named Thurid.

The land that Hrapp had owned all lay waste, as has been told before. Olaf thought that it lay well and set before his father his wishes on the matter; how they should send down to Trefill with this errand, that Olaf wished to buy the land and other things thereto belonging at Hrappstead. It was soon arranged and the bargain settled, for Trefill saw that better was one crow in the hand than two in the wood. The bargain arranged was that Olaf should give three marks of silver for the land; yet that was not fair price, for the lands were wide and fair and very rich in useful produce, such as good salmon fishing and seal catching.

There were wide woods too, a little further up than Hoskuldstead, north of the Salmon-river, in which was a space cleared, and it was well-nigh a matter of certainty that the flocks of Olaf would gather together there whether the weather was hard or mild. One autumn it befell that on that same hill Olaf had built a dwelling of the timber that was cut out of the forest, though some he got together from drift-wood strands. This was a very lofty dwelling. The buildings stood empty through the winter. The next spring Olaf went thither and first gathered together all his flocks which had grown to be a great multitude; for, indeed, no man was richer in live stock in all Broadfirth. Olaf now sent word to his father that he should be standing out of doors and have a look at his train as he was moving to his new home, and should give him his good wishes. Hoskuld said so it should be.

Olaf now arranged how it should be done. He ordered that all the shiest of his cattle should be driven first and then the milking live stock, then came the dry cattle, and the pack horses came in the last place; and men were ranged with the animals to keep them from straying out of straight line. When the van of the train had got to the new homestead, Olaf was just riding out of Goddistead and there was nowhere a gap breaking the line.

Hoskuld stood outside his door together with those of his household. Then Hoskuld spake, bidding Olaf his son welcome and abide all honour to this new dwelling of his, "And somehow my mind forebodes me that this will follow, that for a long time his name will be remembered."

Jorunn his wife said, "Wealth enough the slave's son has got for his name to be long remembered."

At the moment that the house-carles had unloaded the pack horses Olaf rode into the place. Then he said, "Now you shall have your curiosity satisfied with regard to what you have been talking about all the winter, as to what this place shall be called; it shall be called Herdholt."

Every one thought this a very happy name, in view of what used to happen there. Olaf now sets up his household at Herdholt, and a stately one it soon became, and nothing was lacking there.

And now the honour of Olaf greatly increased, there being many causes to bring it about: Olaf was the most beloved of men, for whatever he had to do with affairs of men, he did so that all were well contented with their lot. His father backed him up very much towards being a widely honoured man, and Olaf gained much in power from his alliance with the Mere-men. Olaf was considered the noblest of all Hoskuld's sons.

The first winter that Olaf kept house at Herdholt, he had many servants and workmen, and work was divided amongst the house-carles; one looked after the dry cattle and another after the cows. The fold was out in the wood, some way from the homestead.

One evening the man who looked after the dry cattle came to Olaf and asked him to make some other man look after the neat and "set apart for me some other work."

Olaf answered, "I wish you to go on with this same work of yours."

The man said he would sooner go away.

"Then you think there is something wrong," said Olaf. "I will go this evening with you when you do up the cattle, and if I think there is any excuse for you in this I will say nothing about it, but otherwise you will find that your lot will take some turn for the worse."

Olaf took his gold-set spear, the king's gift, in his hand, and left home, and with him the house-carle. There was some snow on the ground. They came to the fold, which was open, and Olaf bade the house-carle go in. "I will drive up the cattle and you tie them up as they come in."

The house-carle went to the fold-door. And all unawares Olaf finds him leaping into his open arms. Olaf asked why he went on so terrified?

He replied, "Hrapp stands in the doorway of the fold, and felt after me, but I have had my fill of wrestling with him."

Olaf went to the fold door and struck at him with his spear. Hrapp took the socket of the spear in both hands and wrenched it aside, so that forthwith the spear shaft broke. Olaf was about to run at Hrapp but he disappeared there where he stood, and there they parted, Olaf having the shaft and Hrapp the spear-head. After that Olaf and the house-carle tied up the cattle and went home. Olaf saw the house-carle was not to blame for his grumbling.

The next morning Olaf went to where Hrapp was buried and had him dug up. Hrapp was found undecayed, and there Olaf also found his spear-head. After that he had a pyre made and had Hrapp burnt on it, and his ashes were flung out to sea. After that no one had any more trouble with Hrapp's ghost.

Chapter 25
About Hoskuld's Sons

NOW HOSKULD'S SONS shall be told about. Thorliek, Hoskuld's son, had Of Thorliek Hoskuldson been a great seafarer, and taken service with men in lordly station when he was on his merchant voyages before he settled down as a householder, and a man of mark he was thought to be. He had also been on Viking raids, and given good account of himself by reason of his courage. Bard, Hoskuld's son, had also been a seafarer, and was well accounted of wherever he went, for he was the best of brave men and true, and a man of moderation in all things. Bard married a Broadfirth woman, named Astrid, who came of a good stock. Bard's son was named Thorarin, and his daughter Gudney, who married Hall, the son of Fight Styr, and from them are descended many great families.

Hrut, Herjolf's son, gave a thrall of his, named Hrolf, his freedom, and with it a certain amount of money, and a dwelling-place where his land joined with Hoskuld's. And it lay so near the landmark that Hrut's people had made a mistake in the matter, and settled the freedman down on the land belonging to Hoskuld. He soon gained there much wealth. Hoskuld took it very much to heart that Hrut should have placed his freedman right up against his ear, and bade the freedman pay him money for the lands he lived on "for it is mine own."

The freedman went to Hrut and told him all they had spoken together. Hrut bade him give no heed, and pay no money to Hoskuld. "For I do not know," he said, "to which of us the land belonged."

So the freedman went home, and goes on with his household just as before. A little later, Thorliek, Hoskuld's son, went at the advice of his father to the dwelling of the freedman and took him and killed him, and Thorliek claimed as his and his father's own all the money the freedman had made.

Hrut heard this, and he and his sons liked it very ill. They were most of them grown up, and the band of kinsmen was deemed a most forbidding one to grapple with. Hrut fell back on the law as to how this ought to turn out, and when the matter was searched into by lawyers, Hrut and his son stood at but little advantage, for it was held a matter of great weight that Hrut had set the freedman down without leave on Hoskuld's land, where he had made money, Thorliek having slain the man within his and his father's own lands. Hrut took his lot very much to heart; but things remained quiet.

After that Thorliek had a homestead built on the boundary of Hrut and Hoskuld's lands, and it was called Combness. There Thorliek lived for a while, as has been told before. Thorliek begat a son of his wife. The boy was sprinkled with water and called Bolli. He was at an early age a very promising man.

Chapter 26
The Death of Hoskuld, AD 985

HOSKULD, KOLL O' DALES' SON, fell ill in his old age, and he sent for his sons and other kinsfolk, and when they were come Hoskuld spoke to the brothers Bard and Thorliek, and said, "I have taken some sickness, and as I have not been much in the way of falling ill before, I think this may bring me to death; and now, as you know, you are both begotten in wedlock, and are entitled to all inheritance left by me. But there is a third son of mine, one who is not born in wedlock, and I will ask you brothers to allow him, Olaf to wit, to be adopted, so that he take of my means one-third with you."

Bard answered first, and said that he would do as his father wished, "for I look for honour from Olaf in every way, the more so the wealthier he becomes."

Then Thorliek said, "It is far from my wish that Olaf be adopted; he has plenty of money already; and you, father, have for a long time given him a great deal, and for a very long time dealt unevenly with us. I will not freely give up the honour to which I am born."

Hoskuld said, "Surely you will not rob me of the law that allows me to give twelve ounces to my son, seeing how high-born Olaf is on his mother's side."

To this Thorliek now agreed. Then Hoskuld took the gold ring, Hakon's gift, that weighed a mark, and the sword, King's gift whereon was half a mark of gold, and gave them to Olaf, his son, and therewith his good luck and that of the family, saying he did not speak in this way because he did not know well enough that the luck had already come to him. Olaf took his gifts, and said he would risk how Thorliek would like it. Thorliek liked it very ill, and thought that Hoskuld had behaved in a very underhand way to him.

Olaf said, "I shall not give up the gifts, Thorliek, for you agreed to the gift in the face of witnesses; and I shall run the risk to keep it."

Bard said he would obey his father's wishes.

After that Hoskuld died, and his death was very much grieved for, in the first place by his sons, and next by all his relations and friends. His sons had a worthy cairn made for him; but little money was put into it with him.

And when this was over, the brothers began to talk over the matter of preparing an "arvale" (burial feast) after their father, for at that time such was the custom. Olaf said, "It seems to me that we should not be in a hurry about preparing this feast, if it is to be as noble as we should think right; now the autumn is very far worn, and the ingathering of means for it is no longer easy; most people who have to come a long way would find that a hard matter in the autumn days; so that it is certain that many would not come of the men we most should like to see. So I will now make the offer, next summer at the Thing, to bid men to the feast, and I will bear one-third of the cost of the wassail."

The brothers agreed to that, and Olaf now went home. Thorliek and Bard now share the goods between them. Bard had the estate and lands, which was what most men held to, as he was the most popular; but Thorliek got for his share more of the chattels. Olaf and Bard got on well together, but Olaf and Thorliek rather snappishly.

Now the next winter passed, and summer comes, and time wears on towards the Thing. The sons of Hoskuld got ready to go to the Thing. It was soon seen clearly enough how Olaf took the lead of the brothers. When they got to the Thing they set up three booths, and make themselves comfortable in a handsome manner.

Chapter 27
The Funeral Feast for Hoskuld

IT IS TOLD HOW ONE DAY when people went to the law rock Olaf stood up and asked for a hearing, and told them first of the death of his father, "and there are now here many men, kinsmen and friends of his. It is the will of my brothers that I ask you to a funeral feast in memory of Hoskuld our father. All you chieftains, for most of the mightier men are such, as were bound by alliances to him, I let it be known that no one of the greater men shall go away giftless. And herewith I bid all the farmers and any who will accept – rich or poor – to a half month's feast at Hoskuldstead ten weeks before the winter."

And when Olaf finished his speech good cheer was made thereto, and his bidding was looked upon as a right lordly one. And when Olaf came home to the booth he told his brothers what he had settled to do. The brothers were not much pleased, and thought that this was going in for far too much state. After the Thing the brothers rode home and the summer now wears on. Then the brothers got ready for the feast, and Olaf put forward unstintedly his third part, and the feast was furnished with the best of provisions. Great stores were laid in for this feast, for it was expected many folk would come. And when the time came it is said that most of the chief men came that were asked. There were so many that most men say that there could not be far short of nine hundred (1080). This is the most crowded burial feast that has been in Iceland, second to that which the sons of Hialti gave at the funeral of their father, at which time there were 1440 guests.

But this feast was of the bravest in every way, and the brothers got great honour therefrom, Olaf being at the head of the affair throughout. Olaf took even share with his brothers in the gifts; and gifts were bestowed on all the chiefs.

When most of the men had gone away Olaf went to have a talk with Thorliek his brother, and said, "So it is, kinsman, as you know, that no love has been lost between us; now I would beg for a better understanding in our brotherhood. I know you did not like when I took the heirlooms my father gave me on his dying day. Now if you think yourself wronged in this, I will do as much for gaining back your whole good-will as to give fostering to your son. For it is said that ever he is the lesser man who fosters another's child."

Thorliek took this in good part, and said, as was true, that this was honourably offered. And now Olaf took home Bolli, the son of Thorliek, who at this time was three winters old. They parted now with the utmost affection, and Bolli went home to Herdholt with Olaf. Thorgerd received him well, and Bolli grew up there and was loved no less than their own children.

Chapter 28
The Birth of Kjartan, Olaf's Son, AD 978

OLAF AND THORGERD had a son, and the boy was sprinkled with water and a name was given him, Olaf letting him be called Kjartan after Myrkjartan his mother's father. Bolli and Kjartan were much of an age.

Olaf and Thorgerd had still more children; three sons were called Steinthor and Halldor and Helgi, and Hoskuld was the name of the youngest of Olaf's sons. The daughters of Olaf and his wife were named Bergthora, Thorgerd, and Thorbjorg. All their children were of goodly promise as they grew up.

At that time Holmgang Bersi lived in Saurby at an abode called Tongue. He comes to see Olaf and asked for Halldor his son to foster. Olaf agreed to this and Halldor went home with him, being then one winter old.

That summer Bersi fell ill, and lay in bed for a great part of the summer. It is told how one day, when all the men were out haymaking at Tongue and only they two, Bersi and Halldor, were left in the house, Halldor lay in his cradle and the cradle fell over under the boy and he fell out of it on to the floor, and Bersi could not get to him. Then Bersi said this ditty:

"Here we both lie
In helpless plight, Halldor and I,
Have no power left us;
Old age afflicts me,
Youth afflicts you,
You will get better
But I shall get worse."

Later on people came in and picked Halldor up off the floor, and Bersi got better. Halldor was brought up there, and was a tall man and doughty looking.

Kjartan, Olaf's son, grew up at home at Herdholt. He was of all men the goodliest of those who have been born in Iceland. He was striking of countenance and fair of feature, he had the finest eyes of any man, and was light of hue. He had a great deal of hair as fair as silk, falling in curls; he was a big man, and strong, taking after his mother's father Egil, or his uncle Thorolf. Kjartan was better proportioned than any man, so that all wondered who saw him. He was better skilled at arms than most men; he was a deft craftsman, and the best swimmer of all men. In all deeds of strength he was far before others, more gentle than any other man, and so engaging that every child loved him; he was light of heart, and free with his money. Olaf loved Kjartan best of all his children.

Bolli, his foster-brother, was a great man, he came next to Kjartan in all deeds of strength and prowess; he was strong, and fair of face and courteous, and most warrior-like, and a great dandy. The foster-brothers were very fond of each other.

Olaf now remained quietly in his home, and for a good many years.

Chapter 29
Olaf's Second Journey to Norway, AD 975

IT IS TOLD HOW one spring Olaf broke the news to Thorgerd that he wished to go out voyaging – "And I wish you to look after our household and children."

Thorgerd said she did not much care about doing that; but Olaf said he would have his way. He bought a ship that stood up in the West, at Vadill. Olaf started during the summer, and brought his ship to Hordaland.

There, a short way inland, lived a man whose name was Giermund Roar, a mighty man and wealthy, and a great Viking; he was an evil man to deal with, but had now settled down in quiet at home, and was of the bodyguard of Earl Hakon.

The mighty Giermund went down to his ship and soon recognised Olaf, for he had heard him spoken of before. Giermund bade Olaf come and stay with him, with as many of his men as he liked to bring. Olaf accepted his invitation, and went there with seven men. The crew of Olaf went into lodgings about Hordaland. Giermund entertained Olaf well. His house was a lofty one, and there were many men there, and plenty of amusement all the winter.

And towards the end of the winter Olaf told Giermund the reason of his voyage, which was that he wished to get for himself some house-timber, and said he set great store by obtaining timber of a choice kind.

Giermund said, "Earl Hakon has the best of woods, and I know quite well if you went to see him you would be made welcome to them, for the Earl receives well, men who are not half so well-bred as you, Olaf, when they go to see him."

In the spring Olaf got ready to go and find Hakon Earl; and the Earl gave him exceeding good welcome, and bade Olaf stay with him as long as he liked. Olaf told the Earl the reason of his journey, "And I beg this of you, sir, that you give us permission to cut wood for house-building from your forests."

The Earl answered, "You are welcome to load your ship with timber, and I will give it you. For I think it no every-day occurrence when such men as you come from Iceland to visit me."

At parting the Earl gave him a gold-inlaid axe, and the best of keepsakes it was; and therewith they parted in the greatest friendship.

Giermund in the meantime set stewards over his estates secretly, and made up his mind to go to Iceland in the summer in Olaf's ship. He kept this secret from every one. Olaf knew nothing about it till Giermund brought his money to Olaf's ship, and very great wealth it was.

Olaf said, "You should not have gone in my ship if I had known of this before-hand, for I think there are those in Iceland for whom it would be better never to have seen you. But since you have come with so much goods, I cannot drive you out like a straying cur."

Giermund said, "I shall not return for all your high words, for I mean to be your passenger."

Olaf and his got on board, and put out to sea. They had a good voyage and made Broadfirth, and they put out their gangways and landed at Salmon-river-Mouth. Olaf had the wood taken out of his ship, and the ship put up in the shed his father had made. Olaf then asked Giermund to come and stay with him.

That summer Olaf had a fire-hall built at Herdholt, a greater and better than had ever been seen before. Noble legends were painted on its wainscoting and in the roof, and this was so well done that the hall was thought even more beautiful when the hangings were not up.

Giermund did not meddle with every-day matters, but was uncouth to most people. He was usually dressed in this way – he wore a scarlet kirtle below and a grey cloak outside, and a bearskin cap on his head, and a sword in his hand. This was a great weapon and good, with a hilt of walrus tooth, with no silver on it; the brand was sharp, and no rust would stay thereon. This sword he called Footbiter, and he never let it out of his hands.

Giermund had not been there long before he fell in love with Thured, Olaf's daughter, and proposed to Olaf for her hand; but he gave him a straight refusal. Then Giermund gave some money to Thorgerd with a view to gaining the match. She took the money, for it was offered unstintedly. Then Thorgerd broached the matter to Olaf, and said she thought their daughter could not be better married, "for he is a very brave man, wealthy and high-mettled."

Then Olaf answered, "I will not go against you in this any more than in other things, though I would sooner marry Thured to some one else."

Thorgerd went away and thought her business had sped well, and now told Giermund the upshot of it. He thanked her for her help and her determination, and Giermund broached the wooing a second time to Olaf, and now won the day easily. After that Giermund and Thured were betrothed, and the wedding was to be held at the end of the winter at Herdholt. The wedding feast was a very crowded one, for the new hall was finished.

Ulf Uggason was of the bidden guests, and he had made a poem on Olaf Hoskuldson and of the legends that were painted round the hall, and he gave it forth at the feast. This poem is called the 'House Song,' and is well made. Olaf rewarded him well for the poem.

Olaf gave great gifts to all the chief men who came. Olaf was considered to have gained in renown by this feast.

Chapter 30
About Giermund and Thured, AD 978

GIERMUND AND THURED did not get on very well together, and little love was lost between them on either side. When Giermund had stayed with Olaf three winters he wished to go away, and gave out that Thured and his daughter Groa should remain behind. This little maid was by then a year old, and Giermund would not leave behind any money for them.

This the mother and daughter liked very ill, and told Olaf so.

Olaf said, "What is the matter now, Thorgerd? is the Eastman now not so bounteous as he was that autumn when he asked for the alliance?"

They could get Olaf to do nothing, for he was an easygoing man, and said the girl should remain until she wished to go, or knew how in some way to shift for herself.

At parting Olaf gave Giermund the merchant ship all fitted out. Giermund thanked him well therefor, and said it was a noble gift. Then he got on board his ship, and sailed out of the Salmon-river-Mouth by a north-east breeze, which dropped as they came out to the islands. He now lies by Oxe-isle half a month without a fair wind rising for a start.

At that time Olaf had to leave home to look after his foreshore drifts. Then Thured, his daughter, called to his house-carles, and bade them come with her. She had the maid Groa with her, and they were a party of ten together. She lets run out into the water a ferry-boat that belonged to Olaf, and Thured bade them sail and row down along Hvamfirth, and when they came out to the islands she bade them put out the cock-boat that was in the ferry. Thured got into the boat with two men, and bade the others take care of the ship she left behind until she returned.

She took the little maid in her arms, and bade the men row across the current until they should reach the ship (of Giermund). She took a gimlet out of the boat's locker, and gave it to one of her companions, and bade him go to the cockle-boat belonging to the merchant ship and bore a hole in it so as to disable it if they needed it in a hurry. Then she had herself put ashore with the little maid still in her arms. This was at the hour of sunrise. She went across the gangway into the ship, where all men were asleep. She went to the hammock where Giermund slept. His sword Footbiter hung on a peg pole. Thured now sets the little maid in the hammock, and snatched off Footbiter and took it with her. Then she left the ship and rejoined her companions.

Now the little maid began to cry, and with that Giermund woke up and recognised the child, and thought he knew who must be at the bottom of this. He springs up wanting to seize his sword, and misses it, as was to be expected, and then went to the gunwale, and saw that they were rowing away from the ship. Giermund called to his men, and bade them leap into the cockle-boat and row after them. They did so, but when they got a little way they found how the coal-blue sea poured into them, so they went back to the ship.

Then Giermund called Thured and bade her come back and give him his sword Footbiter, "and take your little maid, and with her as much money as you like."

Thured answered, "Would you rather than not have the sword back?"

Giermund answered, "I would give a great deal of money before I should care to let my sword go."

Thured answered, "Then you shall never have it again, for you have in many ways behaved cowardly towards me, and here we shall part for good."

Then Giermund said, "Little luck will you get with the sword." Thured said she would take the risk of that.

"Then I lay thereon this spell," said Giermund, "That this sword shall do to death the man in your family in who would be the greatest loss, and in a manner most ill-fated."

After that Thured went home to Herdholt. Olaf had then come home, and showed his displeasure at her deed, yet all was quiet.

Thured gave Bolli, her cousin, the sword Footbiter, for she loved him in no way less than her brothers. Bolli bore that sword for a long time after.

After this Giermund got a favourable wind, and sailed out to sea, and came to Norway in the autumn. They sailed one night on to some hidden rocks before Stade, and then Giermund and all his crew perished. And that is the end of all there is to tell about Giermund.

Chapter 31
Thured's Second Marriage, AD 980

OLAF HOSKULDSON now stayed at home in much honour, as has been told before.

There was a man named Gudmund, who was the son of Solmund, and lived at Asbjornness north in Willowdale. He wooed Thured, and got her and a great deal of wealth with her. Thured was a wise woman, high-tempered and most stirring. Their sons were called Hall and Bard and Stein and Steingrim. Gudrun and Olof were their daughters.

Thorbjorg, Olaf's daughter, was of women the most beautiful and stout of build. She was called Thorbjorg the Stout, and was married west in Waterfirth to Asgier, the son of Knott. He was a noble man. Their son was Kjartan, father of Thorvald, the father of Thord, the father of Snorri, the father of Thorvald, from whom is sprung the Waterfirth race.

Afterwards, Vermund, the son of Thorgrim, had Thorbjorg for wife. Their daughter was Thorfinna, whom Thorstein Kuggason had for wife.

Bergthora, Olaf's daughter, was married west in Deepfirth to Thorhall the Priest. Their son was Kjartan, father of Smith-Sturla, the foster son of Thord Gilson.

Olaf Peacock had many costly cattle. He had one very good ox named Harri; it was dapple-grey of coat, and bigger than any other of his cattle. It had four horns, two great and fair ones, the third stood straight up, and a fourth stood out of its forehead, stretching down below its eyes. It was with this that he opened the ice in winter to get water. He scraped snow away to get at pasture like a horse.

One very hard winter he went from Herdholt into the Broadfirth-Dales to a place that is now called Harristead. There he roamed through the winter with sixteen other cattle, and got grazing for them all. In the spring he returned to the home pastures, to the place now called Harris'-Lair in Herdholt land.

When Harri was eighteen winters old his ice-breaking horn fell off, and that same autumn Olaf had him killed. The next night Olaf dreamed that a woman came to him, and she was great and wrathful to look at.

She spoke and said, "Are you asleep?"

He said he was awake.

The woman said, "You are asleep, though it comes to the same thing as if you were awake. You have had my son slain, and let him come to my hand in a shapeless plight, and for this deed you shall see your son, blood-stained all over through my doing, and him I shall choose thereto whom I know you would like to lose least of all."

After that she disappeared, and Olaf woke up and still thought he saw the features of the woman. Olaf took the dream very much to heart, and told it to his friends, but no one could read it to his liking. He thought those spoke best about this matter who said that what had appeared to him was only a dream or fancy.

Part Two

Chapter 32
Of Osvif Helgeson

OSVIF WAS THE NAME of a man. He was the son of Helgi, who was the son of Ottar, the son of Bjorn the Eastman, who was the son of Ketill Flatnose, the son of Bjorn Buna. The mother of Osvif was named Nidbiorg. Her mother was Kadlin, the daughter of Ganging-Hrolf, the son of Ox-Thorir, who was a most renowned "Hersir" (war-lord) east in Wick. Why he was so called, was that he owned three islands with eighty oxen on each. He gave one island and its oxen to Hakon the King, and his gift was much talked about. Osvif was a great sage. He lived at Laugar in Salingsdale. The homestead of Laugar stands on the northern side of Salingsdale-river, over against Tongue. The name of his wife was Thordis, daughter of Thjodolf the Low. Ospak was the name of one of their sons. Another was named Helgi, and a third Vandrad, and a fourth Jorrad, and a fifth Thorolf. They were all doughty men for fighting.

Gudrun was the name of their daughter. She was the goodliest of women who grew up in Iceland, both as to looks and wits. Gudrun was such a woman of state that at that time whatever other women wore in the way of finery of dress was looked upon as children's gewgaws beside hers. She was the most cunning and the fairest spoken of all women, and an open-handed woman withal.

There was a woman living with Osvif who was named Thorhalla, and was called the Chatterer. She was some sort of relation to Osvif. She had two sons, one named Odd and the other Stein. They were muscular men, and in a great measure the hardest toilers for Osvif's household. They were talkative like their mother, but ill liked by people; yet were upheld greatly by the sons of Osvif.

At Tongue there lived a man named Thorarin, son of Thorir Saeling (the Voluptuous). He was a well-off yeoman, a big man and strong. He had very good land, but less of live stock. Osvif wished to buy some of his land from him, for he had lack of land but a multitude of live stock. So this then came about that Osvif bought of the land of Thorarin all the tract from Gnupaskard along both sides of the valley to Stack-gill, and very good and fattening land it was. He had on it an out-dairy. Osvif had at all times a great many servants, and his way of living was most noble.

West in Saurby is a place called Hol, there lived three kinsmen-in-law – Thorkell the Whelp and Knut, who were brothers, they were very well-born men, and their brother-in-law, who shared their household with them, who was named Thord. He was, after his mother, called Ingun's-son. The father of Thord was Glum Gierison.

Thord was a handsome and valiant man, well knit, and a great man of law-suits. Thord had for wife the sister of Thorkell and Knut, who was called Aud, neither a goodly nor a bucksome woman. Thord loved her little, as he had chiefly married her for her money, for there a great wealth was stored together, and the household flourished from the time that Thord came to have hand in it with them.

Chapter 33
Of Gest Oddleifson and Gudrun's Dreams

GEST ODDLEIFSON lived west at Bardastrand, at Hagi. He was a great chieftain and a sage; was fore-seeing in many things and in good friendship with all the great men, and many came to him for counsel. He rode every summer to the Thing, and always would put up at Hol.

One time it so happened once more that Gest rode to the Thing and was a guest at Hol. He got ready to leave early in the morning, for the journey was a long one and he meant to get to Thickshaw in the evening to Armod, his brother-in-law's, who had for wife Thorunn, a sister of Gest's. Their sons were Ornolf and Haldor.

Gest rode all that day from Saurby and came to the Saelingsdale spring, and tarried there for a while. Gudrun came to the spring and greeted her relative, Gest, warmly. Gest gave her a good welcome, and they began to talk together, both being wise and of ready speech.

And as the day was wearing on, Gudrun said, "I wish, cousin, you would ride home with us with all your followers, for it is the wish of my father, though he gave me the honour of bearing the message, and told me to say that he would wish you to come and stay with us every time you rode to or from the west."

Gest received the message well, and thought it a very manly offer, but said he must ride on now as he had purposed.

Gudrun said, "I have dreamt many dreams this winter; but four of the dreams do trouble my mind much, and no man has been able to explain them as I like, and yet I ask not for any favourable interpretation of them."

Gest said, "Tell me your dreams, it may be that I can make something of them."

Gudrun said, "I thought I stood out of doors by a certain brook, and I had a crooked coif on my head, and I thought it misfitted me, and I wished to alter the coif, and many people told me I should not do so, but I did not listen to them, and I tore the hood from my head, and cast it into the brook, and that was the end of that dream."

Then Gudrun said again, "This is the next dream. I thought I stood near some water, and I thought there was a silver ring on my arm. I thought it was my own, and that it fitted me exceeding well. I thought it was a most precious thing, and long I wished to keep it. But when I was least aware of it, the ring slipped off my arm and into the water, and nothing more did I see of it afterwards. I felt this loss much more than it was likely I should ever feel the loss of a mere keepsake. Then I awoke."

Gest answered this alone: "No lesser a dream is that one."

Gudrun still spoke: "This is the third dream, I thought I had a gold ring on my hand, which I thought belonged to me, and I thought my loss was now made good again. And the thought entered my mind that I would keep this ring longer than the first; but it did not seem to me that this keepsake suited me better than the former at anything like the rate that gold is more precious than silver. Then I thought I fell, and tried to steady myself with my hand, but then the gold ring struck on a certain stone and broke in two, and the two pieces bled. What I had to bear after this felt more like grief than regret for a loss. And it struck me now that there must have been some flaw in the ring, and when I looked at the pieces I thought I saw sundry more flaws in them; yet I had a feeling that if I had taken better care of it, it might still have been whole; and this dream was no longer."

Gest said, "The dreams are not waning."

Then said Gudrun, "This is my fourth dream. I thought I had a helm of gold upon my head, set with many precious stones. And I thought this precious thing belonged to me, but what I chiefly found fault with was that it was rather too heavy, and I could scarcely bear it, so that I carried my head on one side; yet I did not blame the helm for this, nor had I any mind to part with it. Yet the helm tumbled from my head out into Hvammfirth, and after that I awoke. Now I have told you all my dreams."

Gest answered, "I clearly see what these dreams betoken; but you will find my unravelling savouring much of sameness, for I must read them all nearly in the same way. You will have four husbands, and it misdoubts me when you are married to the first it will be no love match. Inasmuch as you thought you had a great coif on your head and thought it ill-fitting, that shows you will love him but little. And whereas you took it off your head and cast it into the water, that shows that you will leave him. For that, men say, is 'cast on to the sea,' when a man loses what is his own, and gets nothing in return for it."

And still Gest spake: "Your second dream was that you thought you had a silver ring on your arm, and that shows you will marry a nobleman whom you will love much, but enjoy him for but a short time, and I should not wonder if you lose him by drowning. That is all I have to tell of that dream.

"And in the third dream you thought you had a gold ring on your hand; that shows you will have a third husband; he will not excel the former at the rate that you deemed this metal more rare and precious than silver; but my mind forebodes me that by that time a change of faith will have come about, and your husband will have taken the faith which we are minded to think is the more exalted. And whereas you thought the ring broke in two through some misheed of yours, and blood came from the two pieces, that shows that this husband of yours will be slain, and then you will think you see for the first time clearly all the flaws of that match."

Still Gest went on to say: "This is your fourth dream, that you thought you had a helm on your head, of gold set with precious stones, and that it was a heavy one for you to bear. This shows you will have a fourth husband who will be the greatest nobleman (of the four), and will bear somewhat a helm of awe over you. And whereas you thought it tumbled out into Hvammfirth, it shows that that same firth will be in his way on the last day of his life. And now I go no further with this dream."

Gudrun sat with her cheeks blood red whilst the dreams were unravelled, but said not a word till Gest came to the end of his speech. Then said Gudrun, "You would have fairer prophecies in this matter if my delivery of it into your hands had warranted; have my thanks all the same for unravelling the dreams. But it is a fearful thing to think of, if all this is to come to pass as you say."

Gudrun then begged Gest would stay there the day out, and said that he and Osvif would have many wise things to say between them. He answered, "I must ride on now as I have made up my mind. But bring your father my greeting and tell him also these my words, that the day will come when there will be a shorter distance between Osvif's and my dwellings, and then we may talk at ease, if then we are allowed to converse together."

Then Gudrun went home and Gest rode away. Gest met a servant of Olaf's by the home-field fence, who invited Gest to Herdholt, at the bidding of Olaf. Gest said he would go and see Olaf during the day, but would stay (the night) at Thickshaw.

The servant returned home and told Olaf so. Olaf had his horse brought and rode with several men out to meet Gest. He and Gest met up at Lea-river. Olaf greeted him well and asked him in with all his followers. Gest thanked him for the invitation, and said he would ride up to the homestead and have a look and see how he was housed, but he must stay with Armod. Gest tarried but a little while, yet he saw over the homestead and admired it and said, "No money has been spared for this place."

Olaf rode away with Gest to the Salmon-river. The foster-brothers had been swimming there during the day, and at this sport the sons of Olaf mostly took the lead. There were many other young men from the other houses swimming too. Kjartan and Bolli leapt out of the water as the company rode down and were nearly dressed when Olaf and Gest came up to them. Gest looked at these young men for a while, and told Olaf where Kjartan was sitting as well as Bolli, and then Gest pointed his spear shaft to each one of Olaf's sons and named by name all of them that were there. But there were many other handsome young men there who had just left off swimming and sat on the river-bank with Kjartan and Bolli. Gest said he did not discover the family features of Olaf in any of these young men.

Then said Olaf: "Never is there too much said about your wits, Gest, knowing, as you do, men you have never seen before. Now I wish you to tell me which of those young men will be the mightiest man."

Gest replied, "That will fall out much in keeping with your own love, for Kjartan will be the most highly accounted of so long as he lives."

Then Gest smote his horse and rode away. A little while after Thord the Low rode up to his side, and said, "What has now come to pass, father, that you are shedding tears?"

Gest answered, "It is needless to tell it, yet I am loath to keep silence on matters that will happen in your own days. To me it will not come unawares if Bolli one day should *have* at his feet the head of Kjartan slain, and should by the deed bring about his own death, and this is an ill thing to know of such sterling men."

Then they rode on to the Thing, and it was an uneventful meeting.

Chapter 34
Gudrun's First Marriage, AD 989

THORVALD WAS THE NAME of a man, son of Haldor Garpdale's Priest. He lived at Garpsdale in Gilsfirth, a wealthy man, but not much of a hero. At the Thing he wooed Gudrun, Osvif's daughter, when she was fifteen years old. The matter was not taken up in a very adverse manner, yet Osvif said that against the match it would tell, that he and Gudrun were not of equal standing. Thorvald spoke gently, and said he was wooing a wife, not money. After that Gudrun was betrothed to Thorvald, and Osvif settled alone the marriage contract, whereby it was provided that Gudrun should alone manage their money affairs straightway when they came into one bed, and be entitled to one-half thereof as her own, whether their married life were long or short. He should also buy her jewels, so that no woman of equal wealth should have better to show. Yet he should retain his farm-stock unimpaired by such purchases.

And now men ride home from the Thing. Gudrun was not asked about it, and took it much to heart; yet things went on quietly.

The wedding was at Garpsdale, in Twinmonth (latter part of August to the latter part of September). Gudrun loved Thorvald but little, and was extravagant in buying finery. There was no jewel so costly in all the West-firths that Gudrun did not deem it fitting that it should be hers, and rewarded Thorvald with anger if he did not buy it for her, however dear it might be.

Thord, Ingun's son, made himself very friendly with Thorvald and Gudrun, and stayed with them for long times together, and there was much talk of the love of Thord and Gudrun for each other.

Once upon a time Gudrun bade Thorvald buy a gift for her, and Thorvald said she showed no moderation in her demands, and gave her a box on the ear.

Then said Gudrun, "Now you have given me that which we women set great store by having to perfection – a fine colour in the cheeks – and thereby have also taught me how to leave off importuning you."

That same evening Thord came there. Gudrun told him about the shameful mishandling, and asked him how she should repay it.

Thord smiled, and said: "I know a very good counsel for this: make him a shirt with such a large neck-hole that you may have a good excuse for separating from him, because he has a low neck like a woman."

Gudrun said nothing against this, and they dropped their talk. That same spring Gudrun separated herself from Thorvald, and she went home to Laugar. After that the money was divided between Gudrun and Thorvald, and she had half of all the wealth, which now was even greater than before (her marriage). They had lived two winters together.

That same spring Ingun sold her land in Crookfirth, the estate which was afterwards called Ingunstead, and went west to Skalmness. Glum Gierison had formerly had her for wife, as has been before written.

At that time Hallstein the Priest lived at Hallsteinness, on the west side of Codfirth. He was a mighty man, but middling well off as regards friends.

Chapter 35
Gudrun's Second Marriage, AD 991

KOTKELL WAS THE NAME OF A MAN who had only come to Iceland a short time before, Grima was the name of his wife. Their sons were Hallbjorn Whetstone-eye, and Stigandi. These people were natives of Sodor. They were all wizards and the greatest of enchanters. Hallstein Godi took them in and settled them down at Urdir in Skalm-firth, and their dwelling there was none of the best liked.

That summer Gest went to the Thing and went in a ship to Saurby as he was wont. He stayed as guest at Hol in Saurby. The brothers-in-law found him in horses as was their former wont. Thord Ingunson was amongst the followers of Gest on this journey and came to Laugar in Salingsdale. Gudrun Osvif's daughter rode to the Thing, and Thord Ingunson rode with her.

It happened one day as they were riding over Blueshaw-heath, the weather being fine, that Gudrun said, "Is it true, Thord, that your wife Aud always goes about in breeches with gores in the seat, winding swathings round her legs almost to her feet?"

Thord said, "He had not noticed that."

"Well, then, there must be but little in the tale," said Gudrun, "if you have not found it out, but for what then is she called Breeches Aud?"

Thord said, "I think she has been called so for but a short time."

Gudrun answered, "What is of more moment to her is that she bear the name for a long time hereafter."

After that people arrived at the Thing and no tidings befell there. Thord spent much time in Gest's booth and always talked to Gudrun.

One day Thord Ingunson asked Gudrun what the penalty was for a woman who went about always in breeches like men. Gudrun replied, "She deserves the same penalty as a man who is dressed in a shirt with so low a neck that his naked breast be seen – separation in either case."

Then Thord said, "Would you advise me to proclaim my separation from Aud here at the Thing or in the country by the counsel of many men? For I have to deal with high-tempered men who will count themselves as ill-treated in this affair."

Gudrun answered after a while, "For evening waits the idler's suit."

Then Thord sprang up and went to the law rock and named to him witnesses, declared his separation from Aud, and gave as his reason that she made for herself gored breeches like a man. Aud's brothers disliked this very much, but things kept quiet. Then Thord rode away from the Thing with the sons of Osvif. When Aud heard these tidings, she said, "Good! Well, that I know that I am left thus single."

Then Thord rode, to divide the money, west into Saurby and twelve men with him, and it all went off easily, for Thord made no difficulties as to how the money was divided. Thord drove from the west unto Laugar a great deal of livestock. After that he wooed Gudrun and that matter was easily settled; Osvif and Gudrun said nothing against it. The wedding was to take place in the tenth week of the summer, and that was a right noble feast.

Thord and Gudrun lived happily together.

What alone withheld Thorkell Whelp and Knut from setting afoot a lawsuit against Thord Ingunson was, that they got no backing up to that end.

The next summer the men of Hol had an out-dairy business in Hvammdale, and Aud stayed at the dairy. The men of Laugar had their out-dairy in Lambdale, which cuts westward into the mountains off Salingsdale. Aud asked the man who looked after the sheep how often he met the shepherd from Laugar. He said nearly always as was likely since there was only a neck of land between the two dairies.

Then said Aud, "You shall meet the shepherd from Laugar today, and you can tell me who there are staying at the winter-dwelling or who at the dairy, and speak in a friendly way of Thord as it behoves you to do."

The boy promised to do as she told him. And in the evening when the shepherd came home Aud asked what tidings he brought.

The shepherd answered, "I have heard tidings which you will think good, that now there is a broad bedroom-floor between the beds of Thord and Gudrun, for she is at the dairy and he is swinging at the rear of the hall, he and Osvif being two together alone at the winter-dwelling."

"You have espied well," said she, "and see to have saddled two horses at the time when people are going to bed." The shepherd did as she bade him. A little before sunset Aud mounted, and was now indeed in breeches.

The shepherd rode the other horse and could hardly keep up with her, so hard did she push on riding. She rode south over Salingsdale-heath and never stopped before she got to the home-field fence at Laugar. Then she dismounted, and bade the shepherd look after the horses whilst she went to the house. Aud went to the door and found it open, and she went into the fire-hall to the locked-bed in the wall. Thord lay asleep, the door had fallen to, but the bolt was not on, so she walked into the bedroom. Thord lay asleep on his back. Then Aud woke Thord, and he turned on his side when he saw a man had come in. Then she drew a sword and thrust it at Thord and gave him great wounds, the sword striking his right arm and wounding him on both nipples. So hard did she follow up the stroke that the sword stuck in the bolster.

Then Aud went away and to her horse and leapt on to its back, and thereupon rode home.

Thord tried to spring up when he got the blow, but could not, because of his loss of blood. Then Osvif awoke and asked what had happened, and Thord told that he had been wounded somewhat. Osvif asked if he knew who had done the deed on him, and got up and bound up his wounds. Thord said he was minded to think that Aud had done it. Osvif offered to ride after her, and said she must have gone on this errand with few men, and her penalty was ready-made for her. Thord said that should not be done at all, for she had only done what she ought to have done.

Aud got home at sunrise, and her brothers asked her where she had been to. Aud said she had been to Laugar, and told them what tidings had befallen in her journey. They were pleased at this, and said that too little was likely to have been done by her.

Thord lay wounded a long time. His chest wound healed well, but his arm grew no better for work than before (*i.e.* when it first was wounded).

All was now quiet that winter. But in the following spring Ingun, Thord's mother, came west from Skalmness. Thord greeted her warmly: she said she wished to place herself under his protection, and said that Kotkell and his wife and sons were giving her much trouble by stealing her goods, and through witchcraft, but had a strong support in Hallstein the Priest.

Thord took this matter up swiftly, and said he should have the right of these thieves no matter how it might displease Hallstein. He got speedily ready for the journey with ten men, and Ingun went west with him. He got a ferry-boat out of Tjaldness. Then they went to Skalmness. Thord had put on board ship all the chattels his mother owned there, and the cattle were to be driven round the heads of the firths. There were twelve of them altogether in the boat, with Ingun and another woman.

Thord and ten men went to Kotkell's place. The sons of Kotkell were not at home. He then summoned Kotkell and Grima and their sons for theft and witchcraft, and claimed outlawry as award. He laid the case to the Althing, and then returned to his ship.

Hallbjorn and Stigandi came home when Thord had got out but a little way from land, and Kotkell told his sons what had happened there. The brothers were furious at that, and said that hitherto people had taken care not to show them in so barefaced a manner such open enmity. Then Kotkell had a great spell-working scaffold made, and they all went up on to it, and they sang hard twisted songs that were enchantments. And presently a great tempest arose.

Thord, Ingun's son, and his companions, continued out at sea as he was, soon knew that the storm was raised against him. Now the ship is driven west beyond Skalmness, and Thord showed great courage with seamanship. The men who were on land saw how he threw overboard all that made up the boat's lading, saving the men; and the people who were on land expected Thord would come to shore, for they had passed the place that was the rockiest; but next there arose a breaker on a rock a little way from the shore that no man had ever known to break sea before, and smote the ship so that forthwith up turned keel uppermost.

There Thord and all his followers were drowned, and the ship was broken to pieces, and the keel was washed up at a place now called Keelisle. Thord's shield was washed up on an island that has since been called Shieldisle. Thord's body and the bodies of his followers were all washed ashore, and a great howe was raised over their corpses at the place now called Howesness.

Chapter 36
About Kotkell and Grima

THESE TIDINGS SPREAD far and wide, and were very ill-spoken of; they were accounted of as men of doomed lives, who wrought such witchcraft as that which Kotkell and his had now shown.

Gudrun took the death of Thord sorely to heart, for she was now a woman not hale, and coming close to her time. After that Gudrun gave birth to a boy, who was sprinkled with water and called Thord.

At that time Snorri the Priest lived at Holyfell; he was a kinsman and a friend of Osvif's, and Gudrun and her people trusted him very much.

Snorri went thither (to Laugar), being asked to a feast there. Then Gudrun told her trouble to Snorri, and he said he would back up their case when it seemed good to him, but offered to

Gudrun to foster her child to comfort her. This Gudrun agreed to, and said she would rely on his foresight. This Thord was surnamed the Cat, and was father of the poet Stúf.

After that Gest Oddleifson went to see Hallstein, and gave him choice of two things, either that he should send away these wizards or he said that he would kill them, "and yet it comes too late." Hallstein made his choice at once, and bade them rather be off, and put up nowhere west of Daleheath, adding that it was more justly they ought to be slain.

After that Kotkell and his went away with no other goods than four stud-horses. The stallion was black; he was both great and fair and very strong, and tried in horse-fighting. Nothing is told of their journey till they came to Combeness, to Thorliek, Hoskuld's son. He asked to buy the horses from them, for he said that they were exceeding fine beasts.

Kotkell replied, "I'll give you the choice. Take you the horses and give me some place to dwell in here in your neighbourhood."

Thorliek said, "Will the horses not be rather dear, then, for I have heard tell you are thought rather guilty in this countryside?"

Kotkell answers, "In this you are hinting at the men of Laugar."

Thorliek said that was true.

Then Kotkell said, "Matters point quite another way, as concerning our guilt towards Gudrun and her brothers, than you have been told; people have overwhelmed us with slander for no cause at all. Take the horses, nor let these matters stand in the way. Such tales alone are told of you, moreover, as would show that we shall not be easily tripped up by the folk of this countryside, if we have your help to fall back upon."

Thorliek now changed his mind in this matter, for the horses seemed fair to him, and Kotkell pleaded his case cunningly; so Thorliek took the horses, and gave them a dwelling at Ludolfstead in Salmon-river-Dale, and stocked them with farming beasts.

This the men of Laugar heard, and the sons of Osvif wished to fall forthwith on Kotkell and his sons; but Osvif said, "Let us take now the counsel of Priest Snorri, and leave this business to others, for short time will pass before the neighbours of Kotkell will have brand new cases against him and his, and Thorliek, as is most fitting, will abide the greatest hurt from them. In a short while many will become his enemies from whom heretofore he has only had good will. But I shall not stop you from doing whatever hurt you please to Kotkell and his, if other men do not come forward to drive them out of the countryside or to take their lives, by the time that three winters have worn away."

Gudrun and her brothers said it should be as he said.

Kotkell and his did not do much in working for their livelihood, but that winter they were in no need to buy hay or food; but an unbefriended neighbourhood was theirs, though men did not see their way to disturbing their dwelling because of Thorliek.

Chapter 37
About Hrut and Eldgrim, AD 995

ONE SUMMER AT THE THING, as Thorliek was sitting in his booth, a very big man walked into the booth. He greeted Thorliek, who took well the greeting of this man and asked his name and whence he was. He said he was called Eldgrim, and lived in Burgfirth at a place called Eldgrimstead – but that abode lies in the valley which cuts westward into the mountains between Mull and Pigtongue, and is now called Grimsdale.

Thorliek said, "I have heard you spoken of as being no small man."

Eldgrim said, "My errand here is that I want to buy from you the stud-horses, those valuable ones that Kotkell gave you last summer."

Thorliek answered, "The horses are not for sale."

Eldgrim said, "I will offer you equally many stud-horses for them and some other things thrown in, and many would say that I offer you twice as much as the horses are worth."

Thorliek said, "I am no haggler, but these horses you will never have, not even though you offer three times their worth."

Eldgrim said, "I take it to be no lie that you are proud and self-willed, and I should, indeed, like to see you getting a somewhat less handsome price for them than I have now offered you, and that you should have to let the horses go none the less."

Thorliek got angered at these words, and said, "You need, Eldgrim, to come to closer quarters if you mean to frighten out me the horses."

Eldgrim said, "You think it unlikely that you will be beaten by me, but this summer I shall go and see the horses, and we will see which of us will own them after that."

Thorliek said, "Do as you like, but bring up no odds against me."

Then they dropped their talk. The man who heard this said that for this sort of dealing together here were two just fitting matches for each other. After that people went home from the Thing, and nothing happened to tell tidings of.

It happened one morning early that a man looked out at Hrutstead at goodman Hrut's, Herjolf's son's, and when he came in Hrut asked what news he brought. He said he had no other tidings to tell save that he saw a man riding from beyond Vadlar towards where Thorliek's horses were, and that the man got off his horse and took the horses.

Hrut asked where the horses were then, and the house-carle replied, "Oh, they have stuck well to their pasture, for they stood as usual in your meadows down below the fence-wall."

Hrut replied, "Verily, Thorliek, my kinsman, is not particular as to where he grazes his beasts; and I still think it more likely that it is not by his order that the horses are driven away."

Then Hrut sprang up in his shirt and linen breeches, and cast over him a grey cloak and took in his hand his gold inlaid halberd that King Harald had given him. He went out quickly and saw where a man was riding after horses down below the wall. Hrut went to meet him, and saw that it was Eldgrim driving the horses. Hrut greeted him, and Eldgrim returned his greeting, but rather slowly. Hrut asked him why he was driving the horses.

Eldgrim replied, "I will not hide it from you, though I know what kinship there is between you and Thorliek; but I tell you I have come after these horses, meaning that he shall never have them again. I have also kept what I promised him at the Thing, that I have not gone after the horses with any great company."

Hrut said, "That is no deed of fame to you to take away the horses while Thorliek lies in his bed and sleeps; you would keep best what you agreed upon if you go and meet himself before you drive the horses out of the countryside."

Eldgrim said, "Go and warn Thorliek if you wish, for you may see I have prepared myself in such a manner as that I should like it well if we were to meet together, I and Thorliek," and therewith he brandished the barbed spear he had in his hand. He had also a helmet on his head, and a sword girded on his side, and a shield on his flank, and had on a chain coat.

Hrut said, "I think I must seek for something else than to go to Combeness for I am heavy of foot; but I mean not to allow Thorliek to be robbed if I have means thereto, no matter how little love there may go with our kinship."

Eldgrim said, "And do you mean to take the horses away from me?"

Hrut said, "I will give you other stud-horses if you will let these alone, though they may not be quite so good as these are."

Eldgrim said, "You speak most kindly, Hrut, but since I have got hold of Thorliek's horses you will not pluck them out of my hands either by bribes or threats."

Hrut replied, "Then I think you are making for both of us the choice that answers the worst."

Eldgrim now wanted to part, and gave the whip to his horse, and when Hrut saw that, he raised up his halberd and struck Eldgrim through the back between the shoulders so that the coat of mail was torn open and the halberd flew out through the chest, and Eldgrim fell dead off his horse, as was only natural. After that Hrut covered up his body at the place called Eldgrim's-holt south of Combeness.

Then Hrut rode over to Combeness and told Thorliek the tidings. Thorliek burst into a rage, and thought a great shame had been done him by this deed, while Hrut thought he had shown him great friendship thereby. Thorliek said that not only had he done this for an evil purpose, but that, moreover, no good would come in return for it. Hrut said that Thorliek must do what pleased him, and so they parted in no loving kindness.

Hrut was eighty years old when he killed Eldgrim, and he was considered by that deed to have added much to his fame.

Thorliek thought that Hrut was none the worthier of any good from him for being more renowned for this deed, for he held it was perfectly clear he would have himself have got the better of Eldgrim if they had had a trial of arms between them, seeing how little was needed to trip Eldgrim up. Thorliek now went to see his tenants Kotkell and Grima, and bade them do something to the shame of Hrut. They took this up gladly, and said they were quite ready to do so. Thorliek now went home.

A little later they, Kotkell and Grima and their sons, started on a journey from home, and that was by night. They went to Hrut's dwelling, and made great incantations there, and when the spell-working began, those within were at a loss to make out what could be the reason of it; but sweet indeed was that singing they heard. Hrut alone knew what these goings-on meant, and bade no man look out that night, "and let every one who may keep awake, and no harm will come to us if that counsel is followed."

But all the people fell asleep. Hrut watched longest, and at last he too slept.

Kari was the name of a son of Hrut, and he was then twelve winters old. He was the most promising of all Hrut's sons, and Hrut loved him much. Kari hardly slept at all, for to him the play was made; he did not sleep very soundly, and at last he got up and looked out, and walked in the direction of the enchantment, and fell down dead at once.

Hrut awoke in the morning, as also did his household, and missed his son, who was found dead a short way from the door. This Hrut felt as the greatest bereavement, and had a cairn raised over Kari.

Then he rode to Olaf Hoskuldson and told him the tidings of what had happened there. Olaf was madly wroth at this, and said it showed great lack of forethought that they had allowed such scoundrels as Kotkell and his family to live so near to him, and said that Thorliek had shaped for himself an evil lot by dealing as he had done with Hrut, but added that more must have been done than Thorliek had ever could have wished. Olaf said too that forthwith Kotkell and his wife and sons must be slain, "late though it is now."

Olaf and Hrut set out with fifteen men. But when Kotkell and his family saw the company of men riding up to their dwelling, they took to their heels up to the mountain. There Hallbjorn Whetstone-eye was caught and a bag was drawn over his head, and while some men were left to guard him others went in pursuit of Kotkell, Grima, and Stigandi up on the mountain. Kotkell and Grima were laid hands on on the neck of land between Hawkdale and Salmon-river-Dale, and were stoned to death and a heap of stones thrown up over them, and the remains are still to be seen, being called Scratch-beacon.

Stigandi took to his heels south over the neck towards Hawkdale, and there got out of their sight.

Hrut and his sons went down to the sea with Hallbjorn, and put out a boat and rowed out from land with him, and they took the bag off his head and tied a stone round his neck. Hallbjorn set gloating glances on the land, and the manner of his look was nowise of the goodliest.

Then Hallbjorn said, "It was no day of bliss when we, kinsfolk, came to this Combeness and met with Thorliek. And this spell I utter," says he, "that Thorliek shall from henceforth have but few happy days, and that all who fill his place have a troublous life there."

And this spell, men deem, has taken great effect.

After that they drowned him, and rowed back to land.

A little while afterwards Hrut went to find Olaf his kinsman, and told him that he would not leave matters with Thorliek as they stood, and bade him furnish him with men to go and make a house-raid on Thorliek.

Olaf replied, "It is not right that you two kinsmen should be laying hands on each other; on Thorliek's behalf this has turned out a matter of most evil luck. I would sooner try and bring about peace between you, and you have often waited well and long for your good turn."

Hrut said, "It is no good casting about for this; the sores between us two will never heal up; and I should like that from henceforth we should not both live in Salmon-river-Dale."

Olaf replied, "It will not be easy for you to go further against Thorliek than I am willing to allow; but if you do it, it is not unlikely that dale and hill will meet."

Hrut thought he now saw things stuck hard and fast before him; so he went home mightily ill pleased; but all was quiet or was called so. And for that year men kept quiet at home.

Chapter 38
The Death of Stigandi; Thorliek Leaves Iceland

NOW, TO TELL OF STIGANDI, he became an outlaw and an evil to deal with.

Thord was the name of a man who lived at Hundidale; he was a rich man, but had no manly greatness. A startling thing happened that summer in Hundidale, in that the milking stock did not yield much milk, but a woman looked after the beast there. At last people found out that she grew wealthy in precious things, and that she would disappear long and often, and no one knew where she was. Thord brought pressure to bear on her for confession, and when she got frightened she said a man was wont to come and meet her, "a big one," she said, "and in my eyes very handsome."

Thord then asked how soon the man would come again to meet her, and she said she thought it would be soon.

After that Thord went to see Olaf, and told him that Stigandi must be about, not far away from there, and bade him bestir himself with his men and catch him. Olaf got ready at once and came to Hundidale, and the bonds-woman was fetched for Olaf to have talk of her. Olaf asked her where the lair of Stigandi was. She said she did not know. Olaf offered to pay her money if she would bring Stigandi within reach of him and his men; and on this they came to a bargain together.

The next day she went out to herd her cattle, and Stigandi comes that day to meet her. She greeted him well, and offers to look through (the hair of) his head. He laid his head down on her knee, and soon went to sleep. Then she slunk away from under his head, and went to meet Olaf and his men, and told them what had happened.

Then they went towards Stigandi, and took counsel between them as to how it should not fare with him as his brother, that he should cast his glance on many things from which evil would befall them. They take now a bag, and draw it over his head. Stigandi woke at that, and made no struggle, for now there were many men to one. The sack had a slit in it, and Stigandi could see out through it the slope on the other side; there the lay of the land was fair, and it was covered with thick grass. But suddenly something like a whirlwind came on, and turned the sward topsy-turvy, so that the grass never grew there again. It is now called Brenna.

Then they stoned Stigandi to death, and there he was buried under a heap of stones. Olaf kept his word to the bonds-woman, and gave her her freedom, and she went home to Herdholt.

Hallbjorn Whetstone-eye was washed up by the surf a short time after he was drowned. It was called Knorstone where he was put in the earth, and his ghost walked about there a great deal.

There was a man named Thorkell Skull who lived at Thickshaw on his father's inheritance. He was a man of very dauntless heart and mighty of muscle. One evening a cow was missing at Thickshaw, and Thorkell and his house-carle went to look for it. It was after sunset, but was bright moonlight. Thorkell said they must separate in their search, and when Thorkell was alone he thought he saw the cow on a hill-rise in front of him, but when he came up to it he saw it was Whetstone-eye and no cow. They fell upon each in mighty strength. Hallbjorn kept on the defensive, and when Thorkell least expected it he crept down into the earth out of his hands. After that Thorkell went home. The house-carle had come home already, and had found the cow. No more harm befell ever again from Hallbjorn.

Thorbjorn Skrjup was dead by then, and so was Melkorka, and they both lie in a cairn in Salmon-river-Dale. Lambi, their son, kept house there after them. He was very warrior-like, and had a great deal of money. Lambi was more thought of by people than his father had been, chiefly because of his mother's relations; and between him and Olaf there was fond brotherhood.

Now the winter next after the killing of Kotkell passed away. In the spring the brothers Olaf and Thorliek met, and Olaf asked if Thorliek was minded to keep on his house. Thorliek said he was.

Olaf said, "Yet I would beg you, kinsman, to change your way of life, and go abroad; you will be thought an honourable man whereever you come; but as to Hrut, our kinsman, I know he feels how your dealings with him come home to him. And it is little to my mind that the risk of your sitting so near to each other should be run any longer. For Hrut has a strong run of luck to fall back upon, and his sons are but reckless bravos. On account of my kinship I feel I should be placed in a difficulty if you, my kinsman, should come to quarrel in full enmity."

Thorliek replied, "I am not afraid of not being able to hold myself straight in the face of Hrut and his sons, and that is no reason why I should depart the country. But if you, brother, set much store by it, and feel yourself in a difficult position in this matter, then, for your words I will do this; for then I was best contented with my lot in life when I lived abroad. And I know you will not treat my son Bolli any the worse for my being nowhere near; for of all men I love him the best."

Olaf said, "You have, indeed, taken an honourable course in this matter, if you do after my prayer; but as touching Bolli, I am minded to do to him henceforth as I have done hitherto, and to be to him and hold him no worse than my own sons."

After that the brothers parted in great affection. Thorliek now sold his land, and spent his money on his journey abroad. He bought a ship that stood up in Daymealness; and when he was full ready he stepped on board ship with his wife and household. That ship made a good voyage, and they made Norway in the autumn. Thence he went south to Denmark, as he did not feel at home in Norway, his kinsmen and friends there being either dead or driven out of the land. After that Thorliek went to Gautland. It is said by most men that Thorliek had little to do with old age; yet he was held a man of great worth throughout life. And there we close the story of Thorliek.

Chapter 39
Of Kjartan's Friendship for Bolli

AT THAT TIME, as concerning the strife between Hrut and Thorliek, it was ever the greatest gossip throughout the Broadfirth-Dales how that Hrut had had to abide a heavy lot at the hands of Kotkell and his sons. Then Osvif spoke to Gudrun and her brothers, and bade them call to mind whether they thought now it would have been the best counsel aforetime then and there to have plunged into the danger of dealing with such 'hell-men' (terrible people) as Kotkell and his were.

Then said Gudrun, "He is not counsel-bereft, father, who has the help of thy counsel."

Olaf now abode at his manor in much honour, and all his sons are at home there, as was Bolli, their kinsman and foster-brother. Kjartan was foremost of all the sons of Olaf. Kjartan and Bolli loved each other the most, and Kjartan went nowhere that Bolli did not follow.

Often Kjartan would go to the Saelingdale-spring, and mostly it happened that Gudrun was at the spring too. Kjartan liked talking to Gudrun, for she was both a woman of wits and clever of speech. It was the talk of all folk that of all men who were growing up at the time Kjartan was the most even match for Gudrun.

Between Olaf and Osvif there was also great friendship, and often they would invite one another, and not the less frequently so when fondness was growing up between the young folk.

One day when Olaf was talking to Kjartan, he said: "I do not know why it is that I always take it to heart when you go to Laugar and talk to Gudrun. It is not because I do not consider Gudrun the foremost of all other women, for she is the one among womenkind whom I look upon as a thoroughly suitable match for you. But it is my foreboding, though I will not prophesy it, that we, my kinsmen and I, and the men of Laugar will not bring altogether good luck to bear on our dealings together."

Kjartan said he would do nothing against his father's will where he could help himself, but he hoped things would turn out better than he made a guess to.

Kjartan holds to his usual ways as to his visits (to Laugar), and Bolli always went with him, and so the next seasons passed.

Chapter 40
Kjartan and Bolli Voyage to Norway, AD 996

ASGEIR WAS THE NAME OF A MAN, he was called Eider-drake. He lived at Asgeir's-river, in Willowdale; he was the son of Audun Skokul; he was the first of his kinsmen who came to Iceland; he took to himself Willowdale. Another son of Audun was named Thorgrim Hoaryhead; he was the father of Asmund, the father of Gretter.

Asgeir Eider-drake had five children; one of his sons was called Audun, father of Asgeir, father of Audun, father of Egil, who had for wife Ulfeid, the daughter of Eyjolf the Lame; their son was Eyjolf, who was slain at the All Thing. Another of Asgeir's sons was named Thorvald; his daughter was Wala, whom Bishop Isleef had for wife; their son was Gizor, the bishop. A third son of Asgeir was named Kalf. All Asgeir's sons were hopeful men. Kalf Asgeirson was at that time out travelling, and was accounted of as the worthiest of men. One of Asgeir's daughters was named Thured; she married Thorkell Kuggi, the son of Thord Yeller; their son was Thorstein. Another of Asgeir's daughters was named Hrefna; she was the fairest woman in those northern countrysides and very winsome.

Asgeir was a very mighty man.

It is told how one time Kjartan Olafson went on a journey south to Burgfirth. Nothing is told of his journey before he got to Burg. There at that time lived Thorstein, Egil's son, his mother's brother. Bolli was with him, for the foster-brothers loved each other so dearly that neither thought he could enjoy himself if they were not together. Thorstein received Kjartan with loving kindness, and said he should be glad for his staying there a long rather than a short time. So Kjartan stayed awhile at Burg.

That summer there was a ship standing up in Steam-river-Mouth, and this ship belonged to Kalf Asgeirson, who had been staying through the winter with Thorstein, Egil's son. Kjartan told Thorstein in secret that his chief errand to the south then was, that he wished to buy the half of Kalf's ship, "for I have set my mind on going abroad," and he asked Thorstein what sort of a man he thought Kalf was.

Thorstein said he thought he was a good man and true. "I can easily understand," said Thorstein, "that you wish to see other men's ways of life, and your journey will be remarkable in one way or another, and your kinsfolk will be very anxious as to how the journey may speed for you."

Kjartan said it would speed well enough. After that Kjartan bought a half share in Kalf's ship, and they made up half-shares partnership between them; Kjartan was to come on board when ten weeks of summer had passed. Kjartan was seen off with gifts on leaving Burg, and he and Bolli then rode home.

When Olaf heard of this arrangement he said he thought Kjartan had made up his mind rather suddenly, but added that he would not foreclose the matter.

A little later Kjartan rode to Laugar to tell Gudrun of his proposed journey abroad.

Gudrun said, "You have decided this very suddenly, Kjartan," and she let fall sundry words about this, from which Kjartan got to understand that Gudrun was displeased with it.

Kjartan said, "Do not let this displease you. I will do something else that shall please you."

Gudrun said, "Be then a man of your word, for I shall speedily let you know what I want."

Kjartan bade her do so.

Gudrun said, "Then, I wish to go out with you this summer; if that comes off, you would have made amends to me for this hasty resolve, for I do not care for Iceland."

Kjartan said, "That cannot be, your brothers are unsettled yet, and your father is old, and they would be bereft of all care if you went out of the land; so you wait for me three winters."

Gudrun said she would promise nothing as to that matter, and each was at variance with the other, and therewith they parted. Kjartan rode home.

Olaf rode to the Thing that summer, and Kjartan rode with his father from the west out of Herdholt, and they parted at North-river-Dale. From thence Kjartan rode to his ship, and his kinsman Bolli went along with him. There were ten Icelanders altogether who went with Kjartan on this journey, and none would part with him for the sake of the love they bore him. So with this following Kjartan went to the ship, and Kalf Asgeirson greeted them warmly. Kjartan and Bolli took a great many goods with them abroad.

They now got ready to start, and when the wind blew they sailed out along Burgfirth with a light and good breeze, and then out to sea. They had a good journey, and got to Norway to the northwards and came into Thrandhome, and fell in with men there and asked for tidings.

They were told that change of lords over the land had befallen, in that Earl Hakon had fallen and King Olaf Tryggvason had come in, and all Norway had fallen under his power. King Olaf was ordering a change of faith in Norway, and the people took to it most unequally.

Kjartan and his companions took their craft up to Nidaross. At that time many Icelanders had come to Norway who were men of high degree. There lay beside the landing-stage three ships, all owned by Icelanders.

One of the ships belonged to Brand the Bounteous, son of Vermund Thorgrimson. And another ship belonged to Hallfred the Trouble-Bard. The third ship belonged to two brothers, one named Bjarni, and the other Thorhall; they were sons of Broad-river-Skeggi, out of Fleetlithe in the east. All these men had wanted to go west to Iceland that summer, but the king had forbidden all these ships to sail because the Icelanders would not take the new faith that he was preaching.

All the Icelanders greeted Kjartan warmly, but especially Brand, as they had known each other already before. The Icelanders now took counsel together and came to an agreement among themselves that they would refuse this faith that the king preached, and all the men previously named bound themselves together to do this.

Kjartan and his companions brought their ship up to the landing-stage and unloaded it and disposed of their goods.

King Olaf was then in the town. He heard of the coming of the ship and that men of great account were on board.

It happened one fair-weather day in the autumn that the men went out of the town to swim in the river Nid. Kjartan and his friends saw this. Then Kjartan said to his companions that they should also go and disport themselves that day. They did so.

There was one man who was by much the best at this sport. Kjartan asked Bolli if he felt willing to try swimming against the townsman.

Bolli answered, "I don't think I am a match for him."

"I cannot think where your courage can now have got to," said Kjartan, "so I shall go and try."

Bolli replied, "That you may do if you like."

Kjartan then plunges into the river and up to this man who was the best swimmer and drags him forthwith under and keeps him down for awhile, and then lets him go up again. And when they had been up for a long while, this man suddenly clutches Kjartan and drags him under; and they keep down for such a time as Kjartan thought quite long enough, when up they come a second time. Not a word had either to say to the other. The third time they went down together, and now they keep under for much the longest time, and Kjartan now misdoubted him how this play would end, and thought he had never before found himself in such a tight place; but at last they come up and strike out for the bank.

Then said the townsman, "Who is this man?"

Kjartan told him his name.

The townsman said, "You are very deft at swimming. Are you as good at other deeds of prowess as at this?"

Kjartan answered rather coldly, "It was said when I was in Iceland that the others kept pace with this one. But now this one is not worth much."

The townsman replied, "It makes some odds with whom you have had to do. But why do you not ask me anything?"

Kjartan replied, "I do not want to know your name."

The townsman answered, "You are not only a stalwart man, but you bear yourself very proudly as well, but none the less you shall know my name, and with whom you have been having a swimming match. Here is Olaf the king, the son of Tryggvi."

Kjartan answered nothing, but turned away forthwith without his cloak. He had on a kirtle of red scarlet. The king was then well-nigh dressed; he called to Kjartan and bade him not go away so soon. Kjartan turned back, but rather slowly. The king then took a very good cloak off his shoulders and gave it to Kjartan, saying he should not go back cloakless to his companions. Kjartan thanked the king for the gift, and went to his own men and showed them the cloak.

His men were nowise pleased as this, for they thought Kjartan had got too much into the king's power; but matters went on quietly.

The weather set in very hard that autumn, and there was a great deal of frost, the season being cold. The heathen men said it was not to be wondered at that the weather should be so bad; "it is all because of the newfangled ways of the king and this new faith that the gods are angry."

The Icelanders kept all together in the town during the winter, and Kjartan took mostly the lead among them. On the weather taking a turn for the better, many people came to the town at the summons of King Olaf. Many people had become Christians in Thrandhome, yet there were a great many more who withstood the king. One day the king had a meeting out at Eyrar, and preached the new faith to men – a long harangue and telling. The people of Thrandhome had a whole host of men, and in turn offered battle to the king. The king said they must know that he had had greater things to cope with than fighting there with churls out of Thrandhome. Then the good men lost heart and gave the whole case into the king's power, and many people were baptized then and there. After that, the meeting came to an end.

That same evening the king sent men to the lodgings of the Icelanders, and bade them get sure knowledge of what they were saying. They did so. They heard much noise within. Then Kjartan began to speak, and said to Bolli, "How far are you willing, kinsman, to take this new faith the king preaches?"

"I certainly am not willing thereto," said Bolli, "for their faith seems to me to be most feeble."

Kjartan said, "Did ye not think the king was holding out threats against those who should be unwilling to submit to his will?"

Bolli answered, "It certainly seemed to me that he spoke out very clearly that they would have to take exceeding hard treatment at his hands."

"I will be forced under no one's thumb," said Kjartan, "while I have power to stand up and wield my weapons. I think it most unmanly, too, to be taken like a lamb in a fold or a fox in a trap. I think that is a better thing to choose, if a man must die in any case, to do first some such deed as shall be held aloft for a long time afterwards."

Bolli said, "What will you do?"

"I will not hide it from you," Kjartan replied; "I will burn the king in his hall."

"There is nothing cowardly in that," said Bolli; "but this is not likely to come to pass, as far as I can see. The king, I take it, is one of great good luck and his guardian spirit mighty, and, besides, he has a faithful guard watching both day and night."

Kjartan said that what most men failed in was daring, however valiant they might otherwise be. Bolli said it was not so certain who would have to be taunted for want of courage in the end. But here many men joined in, saying this was but an idle talk. Now when the king's spies had overheard this, they went away and told the king all that had been said.

The next morning the king wished to hold a meeting, and summoned all the Icelanders to it; and when the meeting was opened the king stood up and thanked men for coming, all those who were his friends and had taken the new faith. Then he called to him for a parley the Icelanders. The king asked them if they would be baptized, but they gave little reply to that. The king said they were making for themselves the choice that would answer the worst. "But, by the way, who of you thought it the best thing to do to burn me in my hall?"

Then Kjartan answered, "You no doubt think that he who did say it would not have the pluck to confess it; but here you can see him."

"I can indeed see you," said the king, "man of no small counsels, but it is not fated for you to stand over my head, done to death by you; and you have done quite enough that you should be prevented making a vow to burn more kings in their houses yet, for the reason of being taught better things than you know and because I do not know whether your heart was in your speech, and that you have bravely acknowledged it, I will not take your life. It may also be that you follow the faith the better the more outspoken you are against it; and I can also see this, that on the day you let yourself be baptized of your own free will, several ships' crews will on that day also take the faith. And I think it likely to happen that your relations and friends will give much heed to what you speak to them when you return to Iceland. And it is in my mind that you, Kjartan, will have a better faith when you return from Norway than you had when you came hither. Go now in peace and safety wheresoever you like from the meeting. For the time being you shall not be tormented into Christianity, for God says that He wills that no one shall come to Him unwillingly."

Good cheer was made at the king's speech, though mostly from the Christian men; but the heathen left it to Kjartan to answer as he liked.

Kjartan said, "We thank you, king, that you grant safe peace unto us, and the way whereby you may most surely draw us to take the faith is, on the one hand, to forgive us great offences, and on the other to speak in this kindly manner on all matters, in spite of your this day having us and all our concerns in your power even as it pleases you. Now, as for myself, I shall receive the faith in Norway on that understanding alone that I shall give some little worship to Thor the next winter when I get back to Iceland."

Then the king said and smiled, "It may be seen from the mien of Kjartan that he puts more trust in his own weapons and strength than in Thor and Odin."

Then the meeting was broken up.

After a while many men egged the king on to force Kjartan and his followers to receive the faith, and thought it unwise to have so many heathen men near about him. The king answered wrathfully, and said he thought there were many Christians who were not nearly so well-behaved as was Kjartan or his company either, "and for such one would have long to wait."

The king caused many profitable things to be done that winter; he had a church built and the market-town greatly enlarged. This church was finished at Christmas.

Then Kjartan said they should go so near the church that they might see the ceremonies of this faith the Christians followed; and many fell in, saying that would be right good pastime. Kjartan with his following and Bolli went to the church; in that train was also Hallfred and many other Icelanders. The king preached the faith before the people, and spoke both long and tellingly, and the Christians made good cheer at his speech.

And when Kjartan and his company went back to their chambers, a great deal of talk arose as to how they had liked the looks of the king at this time, which Christians accounted of as the next greatest festival. "For the king said, so that we might hear, that this night was born the Lord, in whom we are now to believe, if we do as the king bids us."

Kjartan says: "So greatly was I taken with the looks of the king when I saw him for the first time, that I knew at once that he was a man of the highest excellence, and that feeling has kept steadfast ever since, when I have seen him at folk-meetings, and that but by much the best, however, I liked the looks of him today; and I cannot help thinking that the turn of our concerns hangs altogether on our believing Him to be the true God in whom the king bids us to believe, and the king cannot by any means be more eager in wishing that I take this faith than I am to let myself be baptized. The only thing that puts off my going straightway to see the king now is that the day is far spent, and the king, I take it, is now at table; but that day will be delayed, on which we, companions, will let ourselves all be baptized."

Bolli took to this kindly, and bade Kjartan alone look to their affairs.

The king had heard of the talk between Kjartan and his people before the tables were cleared away, for he had his spies in every chamber of the heathens. The king was very glad at this, and said, "In Kjartan has come true the saw: 'High tides best for happy signs.'"

And the first thing the next morning early, when the king went to church, Kjartan met him in the street with a great company of men. Kjartan greeted the king with great cheerfulness, and said he had a pressing errand with him. The king took his greeting well, and said he had had a thoroughly clear news as to what his errand must be, "and that matter will be easily settled by you."

Kjartan begged they should not delay fetching the water, and said that a great deal would be needed. The king answered and smiled. "Yes, Kjartan," says he, "on this matter I do not think your eager-mindedness would part us, not even if you put the price higher still."

After that Kjartan and Bolli were baptized and all their crew, and a multitude of other men as well. This was on the second day of Yule before Holy Service. After that the king invited Kjartan to his Yule feast with Bolli his kinsman. It is the tale of most men that Kjartan on the day he laid aside his white baptismal-robes became a liegeman of the king's, he and Bolli both.

Hallfred was not baptized that day, for he made it a point that the king himself should be his godfather, so the king put it off till the next day.

Kjartan and Bolli stayed with Olaf the king the rest of the winter. The king held Kjartan before all other men for the sake of his race and manly prowess, and it is by all people said that Kjartan was so winsome that he had not a single enemy within the court. Every one said that there had never before come from Iceland such a man as Kjartan.

Bolli was also one of the most stalwart of men, and was held in high esteem by all good men.

The winter now passes away, and, as spring came on, men got ready for their journeys, each as he had a mind to.

Chapter 41
Bolli Returns to Iceland, AD 999

KALF ASGEIRSON WENT to see Kjartan and asks what he was minded to do that summer. Kjartan said, "I have been thinking chiefly that we had better take our ship to England, where there is a good market for Christian men. But first I will go and see the king before I settle this, for he did not seem pleased at my going on this journey when we talked about it in the spring."

Then Kalf went away and Kjartan went to speak to the king, greeting him courteously. The king received him most kindly, and asked what he and his companion (Kalf) had been talking about. Kjartan told what they had mostly in mind to do, but said that his errand to the king was to beg leave to go on this journey.

"As to that matter, I will give you your choice, Kjartan. Either you will go to Iceland this summer, and bring men to Christianity by force or by expedients; but if you think this too difficult a journey, I will not let you go away on any account, for you are much better suited to serve noble men than to turn here into a chapman."

Kjartan chose rather to stay with the king than to go to Iceland and preach the faith to them there, and said he could not be contending by force against his own kindred. "Moreover, it would be more likely that my father and other chiefs, who are near kinsmen of mine, would go against thy will with all the less stubbornness the better beholden I am under your power."

The king said, "This is chosen both wisely and as beseems a great man."

The king gave Kjartan a whole set of new clothes, all cut out of scarlet cloth, and they suited him well; for people said that King Olaf and Kjartan were of an even height when they went under measure.

King Olaf sent the court priest, named Thangbrand, to Iceland. He brought his ship to Swanfirth, and stayed with Side-Hall all the winter at Wash-river, and set forth the faith to people both with fair words and harsh punishments. Thangbrand slew two men who went most against him. Hall received the faith in the spring, and was baptized on the Saturday before Easter, with all his household; then Gizor the White let himself be baptized, so did Hjalti Skeggjason and many other chiefs, though there were many more who spoke against it; and then dealings between heathen men and Christians became scarcely free of danger.

Sundry chiefs even took counsel together to slay Thangbrand, as well as such men who should stand up for him. Because of this turmoil Thangbrand ran away to Norway, and came to meet King Olaf, and told him the tidings of what had befallen in his journey, and said he thought Christianity would never thrive in Iceland. The king was very wroth at this, and said that many Icelanders would rue the day unless they came round to him.

That summer Hjalti Skeggjason was made an outlaw at the Thing for blaspheming the gods. Runolf Ulfson, who lived in Dale, under Isles'-fells, the greatest of chieftains, upheld the lawsuit against him. That summer Gizor left Iceland and Hjalti with him, and they came to Norway, and went forthwith to find King Olaf. The king gave them a good welcome, and said they had taken a wise counsel; he bade them stay with him, and that offer they took with thanks.

Sverling, son of Runolf of Dale, had been in Norway that winter, and was bound for Iceland in the summer. His ship was floating beside the landing stage all ready, only waiting for a wind. The king forbade him to go away, and said that no ships should go to Iceland that summer. Sverling went to the king and pleaded his case, and begged leave to go, and said it mattered a great deal to him, that they should not have to unship their cargo again. The king spake, and then he was wroth: "It is well for the son of a sacrificer to be where he likes it worst."

So Sverling went no whither.

That winter nothing to tell of befell. The next summer the king sent Gizor and Hjalti Skeggjason to Iceland to preach the faith anew, and kept four men back as hostages Kjartan Olafson, Halldor, the son of Gudmund the Mighty, Kolbein, son of Thord the priest of Frey, and Sverling, son of Runolf of Dale.

Bolli made up his mind to journey with Gizor and Hjalti, and went to Kjartan, his kinsman, and said, "I am now ready to depart; I should wait for you through the next winter, if next summer you were more free to go away than you are now. But I cannot help thinking that the king will on no account let you go free. I also take it to be the truth that you yourself call to mind but few of the things that afford pastime in Iceland when you sit talking to Ingibjorg, the king's sister."

She was at the court of King Olaf, and the most beautiful of all the women who were at that time in the land.

Kjartan said, "Do not say such things, but bear my greeting to both my kinsfolk and friends."

Chapter 42
Bolli Makes Love to Gudrun, AD 1000

AFTER THAT Kjartan and Bolli parted, and Gizor and Hjalti sailed from Norway and had a good journey, and came to the Westmen's Isles at the time the Althing was sitting, and went from thence to the mainland, and had there meetings and parleys with their kinsmen. Thereupon they went to the Althing and preached the faith to the people in an harangue both long and telling, and then all men in Iceland received the faith. Bolli rode from the Thing to Herdholt in fellowship with his uncle Olaf, who received him with much loving-kindness.

Bolli rode to Laugar to disport himself after he had been at home for a short time, and a good welcome he had there. Gudrun asked very carefully about his journey and then about Kjartan. Bolli answered right readily all Gudrun asked, and said there were no tidings to tell of his journey. "But as to what concerns Kjartan there are, in truth, the most excellent news to be told of his ways of life, for he is in the king's bodyguard, and is there taken before every other man; but I should not wonder if he did not care to have much to do with this country for the next few winters to come."

Gudrun then asked if there was any other reason for it than the friendship between Kjartan and the king. Bolli then tells what sort of way people were talking about the friendship of Kjartan with Ingibjorg the king's sister, and said he could not help thinking the king would sooner marry Ingibjorg to Kjartan than let him go away if the choice lay between the two things.

Gudrun said these were good tidings, "but Kjartan would be fairly matched only if he got a good wife."

Then she let the talk drop all of a sudden and went away and was very red in the face; but other people doubted if she really thought these tidings as good as she gave out she thought they were.

Bolli remained at home in Herdholt all that summer, and had gained much honour from his journey; all his kinsfolk and acquaintances set great store by his valiant bearing; he had, moreover, brought home with him a great deal of wealth. He would often go over to Laugar and while away time talking to Gudrun.

One day Bolli asked Gudrun what she would answer if he were to ask her in marriage.

Gudrun replied at once, "No need for you to bespeak such a thing, Bolli, for I cannot marry any man whilst I know Kjartan to be still alive."

Bolli answered, "I think then you will have to abide husbandless for sundry winters if you are to wait for Kjartan; he might have chosen to give me some message concerning the matter if he set his heart at all greatly on it."

Sundry words they gave and took, each at variance with the other. Then Bolli rode home.

Chapter 43
Kjartan Comes Back to Iceland, AD 1001

A LITTLE AFTER THIS Bolli talked to his uncle Olaf, and said, "It has come to this, uncle, that I have it in mind to settle down and marry, for I am now grown up to man's estate. In this matter I should like to have the assistance of your words and your backing-up, for most of the men hereabouts are such as will set much store by your words."

Olaf replied, "Such is the case with most women, I am minded to think, that they would be fully well matched in you for a husband. And I take it you have not broached this matter without first having made up your mind as to where you mean to come down."

Bolli said, "I shall not go beyond this countryside to woo myself a wife whilst there is such an goodly match so near at hand. My will is to woo Gudrun, Osvif's daughter, for she is now the most renowned of women."

Olaf answered, "Ah, that is just a matter with which I will have nothing to do. To you it is in no way less well known, Bolli, than to me, what talk there was of the love between Kjartan and Gudrun; but if you have set your heart very much on this, I will put no hindrance in the way if you and Osvif settle the matter between you. But have you said anything to Gudrun about it?"

Bolli said that he had once hinted at it, but that she had not given much heed to it, "but I think, however, that Osvif will have most to say in the matter."

Olaf said Bolli could go about the business as it pleased himself. Not very long after Bolli rode from home with Olaf's sons, Halldor and Steinthor; there were twelve of them together. They rode to Laugar, and Osvif and his sons gave them a good welcome. Bolli said he wished to speak to Osvif, and he set forth his wooing, and asked for the hand of Gudrun, his daughter.

Osvif answered in this wise, "As you know, Bolli, Gudrun is a widow, and has herself to answer for her, but, as for myself, I shall urge this on."

Osvif now went to see Gudrun, and told her that Bolli Thorliekson had come there, "and has asked you in marriage; it is for you now to give the answer to this matter. And herein I may speedily make known my own will, which is, that Bolli will not be turned away if my counsel shall avail."

Gudrun answered, "You make a swift work of looking into this matter; Bolli himself once bespoke it before me, and I rather warded it off, and the same is still uppermost in my mind."

Osvif said, "Many a man will tell you that this is spoken more in overweening pride than in wise forethought if you refuse such a man as is Bolli. But as long as I am alive, I shall look out for you, my children, in all affairs which I know better how to see through things than you do."

And as Osvif took such a strong view of the matter, Gudrun, as far as she was concerned, would not give an utter refusal, yet was most unwilling on all points. The sons of Osvif's urged the matter on eagerly, seeing what great avail an alliance with Bolli would be to them; so the long and short of the matter was that the betrothal took place then and there, and the wedding was to be held at the time of the winter nights.

Thereupon Bolli rode home and told this settlement to Olaf, who did not hide his displeasure thereat.

Bolli stayed on at home till he was to go to the wedding. He asked his uncle to it, but Olaf accepted it nowise quickly, though, at last, he yielded to the prayers of Bolli. It was a noble feast this at Laugar.

Bolli stayed there the winter after. There was not much love between Gudrun and Bolli so far as she was concerned.

When the summer came, and ships began to go and come between Iceland and Norway, the tidings spread to Norway that Iceland was all Christian. King Olaf was very glad at that, and gave leave to go to Iceland unto all those men whom he had kept as hostages, and to fare whenever they liked.

Kjartan answered, for he took the lead of all those who had been hostages, "Have great thanks, Lord King, and this will be the choice we take, to go and see Iceland this summer."

Then King Olaf said, "I must not take back my word, Kjartan, yet my order pointed rather to other men than to yourself, for in my view you, Kjartan, have been more of a friend than a hostage through your stay here. My wish would be, that you should not set your heart on going to Iceland though you have noble relations there; for, I take it, you could choose for yourself such a station in life in Norway, the like of which would not be found in Iceland."

Then Kjartan answered, "May our Lord reward you, sire, for all the honours you have bestowed on me since I came into your power, but I am still in hopes that you will give leave to me, no less than to the others you have kept back for a while."

The king said so it should be, but avowed that it would be hard for him to get in his place any untitled man such as Kjartan was.

That winter Kalf Asgeirson had been in Norway and had brought, the autumn before, west-away from England, the ship and merchandise he and Kjartan had owned. And when Kjartan had got leave for his journey to Iceland Kalf and he set themselves to get the ship ready.

And when the ship was all ready Kjartan went to see Ingibjorg, the king's sister. She gave him a cheery welcome, and made room for him to sit beside her, and they fell a-talking together, and Kjartan tells Ingibjorg that he has arranged his journey to Iceland.

Then Ingibjorg said, "I am minded to think, Kjartan, that you have done this of your own wilfulness rather than because you have been urged by men to go away from Norway and to Iceland."

But thenceforth words between them were drowned in silence.

Amidst this Ingibjorg turns to a "mead-cask" that stood near her, and takes out of it a white coif inwoven with gold and gives it to Kjartan, saying, that it was far too good for Gudrun Osvif's daughter to fold it round her head, yet "you will give her the coif as a bridal gift, for I wish the wives of the Icelanders to see as much as that she with whom you have had your talks in Norway comes of no thrall's blood." It was in a pocket of costly stuff, and was altogether a most precious thing. "Now I shall not go to see you off," said Ingibjorg. "Fare you well, and hail!"

After that Kjartan stood up and embraced Ingibjorg, and people told it as a true story that they took it sorely to heart being parted.

And now Kjartan went away and unto the king, and told the king he now was ready for his journey. Then the king led Kjartan to his ship and many men with him, and when they came to where the ship was floating with one of its gangways to land, the king said, "Here is a sword, Kjartan, that you shall take from me at our parting; let this weapon be always with you, for my mind tells me you will never be a 'weapon-bitten' man if you bear this sword."

It was a most noble keepsake, and much ornamented. Kjartan thanked the king with fair words for all the honour and advancement he had bestowed on him while he had been in Norway.

Then the king spoke, "This I will bid you, Kjartan, that you keep your faith well."

After that they parted, the king and Kjartan in dear friendship, and Kjartan stepped on board his ship. The king looked after him and said, "Great is the worth of Kjartan and his kindred, but to cope with their fate is not an easy matter."

Chapter 44
Kjartan Comes Home, AD 1001

NOW KJARTAN AND KALF set sail for the main. They had a good wind, and were only a short time out at sea. They hove into White-river, in Burgfirth.

The tidings spread far and wide of the coming of Kjartan. When Olaf, his father, and his other kinsfolk heard of it they were greatly rejoiced. Olaf rode at once from the west out of the Dales and south to Burgfirth, and there was a very joyful meeting between father and son. Olaf asked Kjartan to go and stay with him, with as many of his men as he liked to bring. Kjartan took that well, and said that there only of all places in Iceland he meant to abide. Olaf now rides home to Herdholt, and Kjartan remained with his ship during the summer. He now heard of the marriage of Gudrun, but did not trouble himself at all over it; but that had heretofore been a matter of anxiety to many.

Gudmund, Solmund's son, Kjartan's brother-in-law, and Thurid, his sister, came to his ship, and Kjartan gave them a cheery welcome. Asgeir Eider-drake came to the ship too to meet his son Kalf, and journeying with him was Hrefna his daughter, the fairest of women.

Kjartan bade his sister Thurid have such of his wares as she liked, and the same Kalf said to Hrefna. Kalf now unlocked a great chest and bade them go and have a look at it.

That day a gale sprang up, and Kjartan and Kalf had to go out to moor their ship, and when that was done they went home to the booths. Kalf was the first to enter the booth, where Thurid and Hrefna had turned out most of the things in the chest. Just then Hrefna snatched up the coif and unfolded it, and they had much to say as to how precious a thing it was. Then Hrefna said she would coif herself with it, and Thurid said she had better, and Hrefna did so.

When Kalf saw that he gave her to understand that she had done amiss, and bade her take it off at her swiftest. "For that is the one thing that we, Kjartan and I, do not own in common."

And as he said this Kjartan came into the booth. He had heard their talk, and fell in at once and told them there was nothing amiss. So Hrefna sat still with the head-dress on. Kjartan looked at her heedfully and said, "I think the coif becomes you very well, Hrefna," says he, "and I think it fits the best that both together, coif and maiden, be mine."

Then Hrefna answered, "Most people take it that you are in no hurry to marry, and also that the woman you woo, you will be sure to get for wife."

Kjartan said it would not matter much whom he married, but he would not stand being kept long a waiting wooer by any woman. "Now I see that this gear suits you well, and it suits well that you become my wife."

Hrefna now took off the head-dress and gave it to Kjartan, who put it away in a safe place.

Gudmund and Thurid asked Kjartan to come north to them for a friendly stay some time that winter, and Kjartan promised the journey.

Kalf Asgeirson betook himself north with his father. Kjartan and he now divided their partnership, and that went off altogether in good-nature and friendship.

Kjartan also rode from his ship westward to the Dales, and they were twelve of them together. Kjartan now came home to Herdholt, and was joyfully received by everybody. Kjartan had his goods taken to the west from the ship during the autumn. The twelve men who rode with Kjartan stayed at Herdholt all the winter.

Olaf and Osvif kept to the same wont of asking each other to their house, which was that each should go to the other every other autumn. That autumn the wassail was to be at Laugar, and Olaf and all the Herdholtings were to go thither.

Gudrun now spoke to Bolli, and said she did not think he had told her the truth in all things about the coming back of Kjartan. Bolli said he had told the truth about it as best he knew it. Gudrun spoke little on this matter, but it could be easily seen that she was very displeased, and most people would have it that she still was pining for Kjartan, although she tried to hide it.

Now time glides on till the autumn feast was to be held at Laugar. Olaf got ready and bade Kjartan come with him. Kjartan said he would stay at home and look after the household. Olaf bade him not to show that he was angry with his kinsmen. "Call this to mind, Kjartan, that you have loved no man so much as your foster-brother Bolli, and it is my wish that you should come, for things will soon settle themselves between you, kinsmen, if you meet each other."

Kjartan did as his father bade him. He took the scarlet clothes that King Olaf had given him at parting, and dressed himself gaily; he girded his sword, the king's gift, on; and he had a gilt helm on his head, and on his side a red shield with the Holy Cross painted on it in gold; he had in his hand a spear, with the socket inlaid with gold. All his men were gaily dressed. There were in all between twenty and thirty men of them. They now rode out of Herdholt and went on till they came to Laugar. There were a great many men gathered together already.

Chapter 45
Kjartan Marries Hrefna, AD 1002

BOLLI, TOGETHER WITH the sons of Osvif, went out to meet Olaf and his company, and gave them a cheery welcome. Bolli went to Kjartan and kissed him, and Kjartan took his greeting. After that they were seen into the house, Bolli was of the merriest towards them, and Olaf responded to that most heartily, but Kjartan was rather silent.

The feast went off well.

Now Bolli had some stud-horses which were looked upon as the best of their kind. The stallion was great and goodly, and had never failed at fight; it was light of coat, with red ears and forelock. Three mares went with it, of the same hue as the stallion. These horses Bolli wished to give to Kjartan, but Kjartan said he was not a horsey man, and could not take the gift. Olaf bade him take the horses, "for these are most noble gifts." Kjartan gave a flat refusal.

They parted after this nowise blithely, and the Herdholtings went home, and all was quiet.

Kjartan was rather gloomy all the winter, and people could have but little talk of him. Olaf thought this a great misfortune.

That winter after Yule Kjartan got ready to leave home, and there were twelve of them together, bound for the countrysides of the north. They now rode on their way till they came to Asbjornness, north in Willowdale, and there Kjartan was greeted with the greatest blitheness and cheerfulness. The housing there was of the noblest.

Hall, the son of Gudmund, was about twenty winters old, and took much after the kindred of the men of Salmon-river-Dale; and it is all men's say, there was no more valiant-looking a man in all the north land.

Hall greeted Kjartan, his uncle, with the greatest blitheness. Sports are now at once started at Asbjornness, and men were gathered together from far and near throughout the countrysides, and people came from the west from Midfirth and from Waterness and Waterdale all the way and from out of Longdale, and there was a great gathering together. It was the talk of all folk how strikingly Kjartan showed above other men.

Now the sports were set going, and Hall took the lead. He asked Kjartan to join in the play, "and I wish, kinsman, you would show your courtesy in this."

Kjartan said, "I have been training for sports but little of late, for there were other things to do with King Olaf, but I will not refuse you this for once."

So Kjartan now got ready to play, and the strongest men there were chosen out to go against him. The game went on all day long, but no man had either strength or litheness of limb to cope with Kjartan.

And in the evening when the games were ended, Hall stood up and said, "It is the wish and offer of my father concerning those men who have come from the farthest hither, that they all stay here over night and take up the pastime again tomorrow."

At this message there was made a good cheer, and the offer deemed worthy of a great man.

Kalf Asgeirson was there, and he and Kjartan were dearly fond of each other. His sister Hrefna was there also, and was dressed most showily. There were over a hundred [*i.e.* over 120] men in the house that night.

And the next day sides were divided for the games again. Kjartan sat by and looked on at the sports. Thurid, his sister, went to talk to him, and said, "It is told me, brother, that you have been rather silent all the winter, and men say it must be because you are pining after Gudrun, and set forth as a proof thereof that no fondness now is shown between you and Bolli, such as through all time there had been between you. Do now the good and befitting thing, and don't allow yourself to take this to heart, and grudge not your kinsman a good wife. To me it seems your best counsel to marry, as you bespoke it last summer, although the match be not altogether even for you, where Hrefna is, for such a match you cannot find within this land. Asgeir, her father, is a noble and a high-born man, and he does not lack wealth wherewith to make this match fairer still; moreover, another daughter of his is married to a mighty man. You have also told me yourself that Kalf Asgeirson is the doughtiest of men, and their way of life is of the stateliest. It is my wish that you go and talk to Hrefna, and I ween you will find that there great wits and goodliness go together."

Kjartan took this matter up well, and said she had ably pleaded the case. After this Kjartan and Hrefna are brought together that they may have their talk by themselves, and they talked together all day.

In the evening Thurid asked Kjartan how he liked the manner in which Hrefna turned her speech. He was well pleased about it, and said he thought the woman was in all ways one of the noblest as far as he could see.

The next morning men were sent to Asgeir to ask him to Asbjornness. And now they had a parley between them on this affair, and Kjartan wooed Hrefna, Asgeir's daughter. Asgeir took up the matter with a good will, for he was a wise man, and saw what an honourable offer was made to them. Kalf, too, urged the matter on very much, saying, "I will not let anything be spared (towards the dowry)."

Hrefna, in her turn, did not make unwilling answers, but bade her father follow his own counsel. So now the match was covenanted and settled before witnesses.

Kjartan would hear of nothing but that the wedding should be held at Herdholt, and Asgeir and Kalf had nothing to say against it. The wedding was then settled to take place at Herdholt when five weeks of summer had passed. After that Kjartan rode home with great gifts. Olaf was delighted at these tidings, for Kjartan was much merrier than before he left home.

Kjartan kept fast through Lent, following therein the example of no man in this land; and it is said he was the first man who ever kept fast in this land. Men thought it so wonderful a thing that Kjartan could live so long without meat, that people came over long ways to see him. In a like manner Kjartan's other ways went beyond those of other men.

Now Easter passed, and after that Kjartan and Olaf made ready a great feast. At the appointed time Asgeir and Kalf came from the north as well as Gudmund and Hall, and altogether there were sixty men. Olaf and Kjartan had already many men gathered together there. It was a most brave feast, and for a whole week the feasting went on.

Kjartan made Hrefna a bridal gift of the rich head-dress, and a most famous gift was that; for no one was there so knowing or so rich as ever to have seen or possessed such a treasure, for it is the saying of thoughtful men that eight ounces of gold were woven into the coif.

Kjartan was so merry at the feast that he entertained every one with his talk, telling of his journey. Men did marvel much how great were the matters that entered into that tale; for he had served the noblest of lords – King Olaf Tryggvason.

And when the feast was ended Kjartan gave Gudmund and Hall good gifts, as he did to all the other great men. The father and son gained great renown from this feast.

Kjartan and Hrefna loved each other very dearly.

Chapter 46
Feast at Herdholt and the Loss of Kjartan's Sword, AD 1002

OLAF AND OSVIF were still friends, though there was some deal of ill-will between the younger people.

That summer Olaf had his feast half a month before winter. And Osvif was also making ready a feast, to be held at 'Winter-nights,' and they each asked the other to their homes, with as many men as each deemed most honourable to himself. It was Osvif's turn to go first to the feast at Olaf's, and he came to Herdholt at the time appointed. In his company were Bolli and Gudrun and the sons of Osvif.

In the morning one of the women on going down the hall was talking how the ladies would be shown to their seats. And just as Gudrun had come right against the bedroom wherein

Kjartan was wont to rest, and where even then he was dressing and slipping on a red kirtle of scarlet, he called out to the woman who had been speaking about the seating of the women, for no one else was quicker in giving the answer, "Hrefna shall sit in the high seat and be most honoured in all things so long as I am alive."

But before this Gudrun had always had the high seat at Herdholt and everywhere else. Gudrun heard this, and looked at Kjartan and flushed up, but said nothing.

The next day Gudrun was talking to Hrefna, and said she ought to coif herself with the head-dress, and show people the most costly treasure that had ever come to Iceland. Kjartan was near, but not quite close, and heard what Gudrun said, and he was quicker to answer than Hrefna. "She shall not coif herself with the headgear at this feast, for I set more store by Hrefna owning the greatest of treasures than by the guests having it to feast thereon their eyes at this time."

The feast at Olaf's was to last a week.

The next day Gudrun spoke on the sly to Hrefna, and asked her to show her the head-dress, and Hrefna said she would. The next day they went to the out-bower where the precious things were kept, and Hrefna opened a chest and took out the pocket of costly stuff, and took from thence the coif and showed it to Gudrun. She unfolded the coif and looked at it a while, but said no word of praise or blame. After that Hrefna put it back, and they went to their places, and after that all was joy and amusement.

And the day the guests should ride away Kjartan busied himself much about matters in hand, getting change of horses for those who had come from afar, and speeding each one on his journey as he needed. Kjartan had not his sword "King's-gift" with him while he was taken up with these matters, yet was he seldom wont to let it go out of his hand. After this he went to his room where the sword had been, and found it now gone. He then went and told his father of the loss.

Olaf said, "We must go about this most gently. I will get men to spy into each batch of them as they ride away," and he did so.

An the White had to ride with Osvif's company, and to keep an eye upon men turning aside, or baiting. They rode up past Lea-shaws, and past the homesteads which are called Shaws, and stopped at one of the homesteads at Shaws, and got off their horses. Thorolf, son of Osvif, went out from the homestead with a few other men. They went out of sight amongst the brushwood, whilst the others tarried at the Shaws' homestead.

An followed him all the way unto Salmon-river, where it flows out of Saelingsdale, and said he would turn back there. Thorolf said it would have done no harm though he had gone nowhere at all.

The night before a little snow had fallen so that footprints could be traced. An rode back to the brushwood, and followed the footprints of Thorolf to a certain ditch or bog. He groped down with his hand, and grasped the hilt of a sword. An wished to have witnesses with him to this, and rode for Thorarin in Saelingsdale Tongue, and he went with An to take up the sword. After that An brought the sword back to Kjartan. Kjartan wrapt it in a cloth, and laid it in a chest. The place was afterwards called Sword-ditch, where An and Thorarin had found the 'King's-gift.'

This was all kept quiet. The scabbard was never found again. Kjartan always treasured the sword less hereafter than heretofore.

This affair Kjartan took much to heart, and would not let the matter rest there.

Olaf said, "Do not let it pain you; true, they have done a nowise pretty trick, but you have got no harm from it. We shall not let people have this to laugh at, that we make a quarrel about such a thing, these being but friends and kinsmen on the other side."

And through these reasonings of Olaf, Kjartan let matters rest in quiet.

After that Olaf got ready to go to the feast at Laugar at 'winter nights,' and told Kjartan he must go too. Kjartan was very unwilling thereto, but promised to go at the bidding of his father.

Hrefna was also to go, but she wished to leave her coif behind. "Goodwife," Thorgerd said, "whenever will you take out such a peerless keepsake if it is to lie down in chests when you go to feasts?"

Hrefna said, "Many folk say that it is not unlikely that I may come to places where I have fewer people to envy me than at Laugar."

Thorgerd said, "I have no great belief in people who let such things fly here from house to house."

And because Thorgerd urged it eagerly Hrefna took the coif, and Kjartan did not forbid it when he saw how the will of his mother went.

After that they betake themselves to the journey and came to Laugar in the evening, and had a goodly welcome there.

Thorgerd and Hrefna handed out their clothes to be taken care of. But in the morning when the women should dress themselves Hrefna looked for the coif and it was gone from where she had put it away. It was looked for far and near, and could not be found. Gudrun said it was most likely the coif had been left behind at home, or that she had packed it so carelessly that it had fallen out on the way.

Hrefna now told Kjartan that the coif was lost. He answered and said it was no easy matter to try to make them take care of things, and bade her now leave matters quiet; and told his father what game was up.

Olaf said, "My will is still as before, that you leave alone and let pass by this trouble and I will probe this matter to the bottom in quiet; for I would do anything that you and Bolli should not fall out. Best to bind up a whole flesh, kinsman," says he.

Kjartan said, "I know well, father, that you wish the best for everybody in this affair; yet I know not whether I can put up with being thus overborne by these folk of Laugar."

The day that men were to ride away from the feast Kjartan raised his voice and said, "I call on you, Cousin Bolli, to show yourself more willing henceforth than hitherto to do to us as behoves a good man and true. I shall not set this matter forth in a whisper, for within the knowledge of many people it is that a loss has befallen here of a thing which we think has slipped into your own keep. This harvest, when we gave a feast at Herdholt, my sword was taken; it came back to me, but not the scabbard. Now again there has been lost here a keepsake which men will esteem a thing of price. Come what may, I will have them both back."

Bolli answered, "What you put down to me, Kjartan, is not my fault, and I should have looked for anything else from you sooner than that you would charge me with theft." Kjartan says, "I must think that the people who have been putting their heads together in this affair are so near to you that it ought to be in your power to make things good if you but would. You affront us far beyond necessity, and long we have kept peaceful in face on your enmity. But now it must be made known that matters will not rest as they are now."

Then Gudrun answered his speech and said, "Now you rake up a fire which it would be better should not smoke. Now, let it be granted, as you say, that there be some people here who have put their heads together with a view to the coif disappearing. I can only think that they have gone and taken what was their own. Think what you like of what has become of the head-dress, but I cannot say I dislike it though it should be bestowed in such a way as that Hrefna should have little chance to improve her apparel with it henceforth."

After that they parted heavy of heart, and the Herdholtings rode home. That was the end of the feasts, yet everything was to all appearances quiet. Nothing was ever heard of the head-dress. But many people held the truth to be that Thorolf had burnt it in fire by the order of Gudrun, his sister.

Early that winter Asgeir Eider-drake died. His sons inherited his estate and chattels.

Chapter 47
Kjartan Goes to Laugar, and of the Bargain for Tongue, AD 1003

AFTER YULE THAT WINTER Kjartan got men together, and they mustered sixty men altogether. Kjartan did not tell his father the reason of his journey, and Olaf asked but little about it. Kjartan took with him tents and stores, and rode on his way until he came to Laugar. He bade his men get off their horses, and said that some should look after the horses and some put up the tents.

At that time it was the custom that outhouses were outside, and not so very far away from the dwelling-house, and so it was at Laugar. Kjartan had all the doors of the house taken, and forbade all the inmates to go outside, and for three nights he made them do their errands within the house. After that Kjartan rode home to Herdholt, and each of his followers rode to his own home. Olaf was very ill-pleased with this raid, but Thorgerd said there was no reason for blame, for the men of Laugar had deserved this, yea, and a still greater shame.

Then Hrefna said, "Did you have any talk with any one at Laugar, Kjartan?"

He answered, "There was but little chance of that," and said he and Bolli had exchanged only a few words.

Then Hrefna smiled and said, "It was told me as truth that you and Gudrun had some talk together, and I have likewise heard how she was arrayed, that she had coifed herself with the head-dress, and it suited her exceeding well."

Kjartan answered, and coloured up, and it was easy to see he was angry with her for making a mockery of this. "Nothing of what you say, Hrefna, passed before my eyes, and there was no need for Gudrun to coif herself with the head-dress to look statelier than all other women."

Thereat Hrefna dropped the talk.

The men of Laugar bore this exceedingly ill, and thought it by much a greater and worse disgrace than if Kjartan had even killed a man or two of them. The sons of Osvif were the wildest over this matter, but Bolli quieted them rather. Gudrun was the fewest-spoken on the matter, yet men gathered from her words that it was uncertain whether any one took it as sorely to heart as she did.

Full enmity now grows up between the men of Laugar and the Herdholtings.

As the winter wore on Hrefna gave birth to a child, a boy, and he was named Asgier.

Thorarin, the goodman of Tongue, let it be known that he wished to sell the land of Tongue. The reason was that he was drained of money, and that he thought ill-will was swelling too much between the people of the countryside, he himself being a friend of either side. Bolli thought he would like to buy the land and settle down on it, for the men of Laugar had little land and much cattle. Bolli and Gudrun rode to Tongue at the advice of Osvif; they thought it a very handy chance to be able to secure this land so near to themselves, and Osvif bade them not to let a small matter stand in the way of a covenant. Then they (Bolli and Gudrun) bespoke the purchase with Thorarin, and came to terms as to what the price should be, and also as to the kind wherein it should be paid, and the bargain was settled with Thorarin. But the buying was not done in the presence of witnesses, for there were not so many men there at the time as were lawfully necessary. Bolli and Gudrun rode home after that.

But when Kjartan Olafson hears of these tidings he rides off with twelve men, and came to Tongue early one day. Thorarin greeted him well, and asked him to stay there. Kjartan said he must ride back again in the morning, but would tarry there for some time. Thorarin asked his errand, and Kjartan said, "My errand here is to speak about a certain sale of land that you and Bolli have agreed upon, for it is very much against my wishes if you sell this land to Bolli and Gudrun."

Thorarin said that to do otherwise would be unbecoming to him, "For the price that Bolli has offered for the land is liberal, and is to be paid up speedily."

Kjartan said, "You shall come in for no loss even if Bolli does not buy your land; for I will buy it at the same price, and it will not be of much avail to you to speak against what I have made up my mind to have done. Indeed it will soon be found out that I shall want to have the most to say within this countryside, being more ready, however, to do the will of others than that of the men of Laugar."

Thorarin answered, "Mighty to me will be the master's word in this matter, but it would be most to my mind that this bargain should be left alone as I and Bolli have settled it."

Kjartan said, "I do not call that a sale of land which is not bound by witnesses. Now you do one of two things, either sell me the lands on the same terms as you agreed upon with the others, or live on your land yourself."

Thorarin chooses to sell him the land, and witnesses were forthwith taken to the sale, and after the purchase Kjartan rode home.

That same evening this was told at Laugar. Then Gudrun said, "It seems to me, Bolli, that Kjartan has given you two choices somewhat harder than those he gave Thorarin – that you must either leave the countryside with little honour, or show yourself at some meeting with him a good deal less slow than you have been heretofore."

Bolli did not answer, but went forthwith away from this talk.

All was quiet now throughout what was left of Lent.

The third day after Easter Kjartan rode from home with one other man, on the beach, for a follower. They came to Tongue in the day. Kjartan wished Thorarin to ride with them to Saurby to gather in debts due to him, for Kjartan had much money-at-call in these parts. But Thorarin had ridden to another place. Kjartan stopped there awhile, and waited for him.

That same day Thorhalla the Chatterbox was come there. She asked Kjartan where he was minded to go. He said he was going west to Saurby.

She asked, "Which road will you take?"

Kjartan replied, "I am going by Saelingsdale to the west, and by Swinedale from the west."

She asked how long he would be.

Kjartan answered, "Most likely I shall be riding from the west next Thursday (the fifth day of the week)."

"Would you do an errand for me?" said Thorhalla. "I have a kinsman west at Whitedale and Saurby; he has promised me half a mark's worth of homespun, and I would like you to claim it for me, and bring it with you from the west."

Kjartan promised to do this.

After this Thorarin came home, and betook himself to the journey with them. They rode westward over Saelingsdale heath, and came to Hol in the evening to the brothers and sister there. There Kjartan got the best of welcomes, for between him and them there was the greatest friendship.

Thorhalla the Chatterbox came home to Laugar that evening. The sons of Osvif asked her who she had met during the day. She said she had met Kjartan Olafson. They asked where he was going. She answered, telling them all she knew about it, "And never has he looked braver than now, and it is not wonderful at all that such men should look upon everything as low beside themselves;" and Thorhalla still went on, "and it was clear to me that Kjartan liked to talk of nothing so well as of his land bargain with Thorarin."

Gudrun spoke, "Kjartan may well do things as boldly as it pleases him, for it is proven that for whatever insult he may pay others, there is none who dares even to shoot a shaft at him."

Present at this talk of Gudrun and Thorhalla were both Bolli and the sons of Osvif. Ospak and his brothers said but little, but what there was, rather stinging for Kjartan, as was always their way. Bolli behaved as if he did not hear, as he always did when Kjartan was spoken ill of, for his wont was either to hold his peace, or to gainsay them.

Chapter 48
The Men of Laugar and Gudrun Plan an Ambush for Kjartan, AD 1003

KJARTAN SPENT THE FOURTH day after Easter at Hol, and there was the greatest merriment and gaiety.

The night after An was very ill at ease in his sleep, so they waked him. They asked him what he had dreamt.

He answered, "A woman came to me most evil-looking and pulled me forth unto the bedside. She had in one hand a short sword, and in the other a trough; she drove the sword into my breast and cut open all the belly, and took out all my inwards and put brushwood in their place. After that she went outside."

Kjartan and the others laughed very much at this dream, and said he should be called An 'brushwood belly,' and they caught hold of him and said they wished to feel if he had the brushwood in his stomach.

Then Aud said, "There is no need to mock so much at this; and my counsel is that Kjartan do one of two things: either tarry here longer, or, if he will ride away, then let him ride with more followers hence than hither he did."

Kjartan said, "You may hold An 'brushwood belly' a man very sage as he sits and talks to you all day, since you think that whatever he dreams must be a very vision, but go I must, as I have already made up my mind to, in spite of this dream."

Kjartan got ready to go on the fifth day in Easter week; and at the advice of Aud, so did Thorkell Whelp and Knut his brother. They rode on the way with Kjartan a band of twelve together.

Kjartan came to Whitedale and fetched the homespun for Thorhalla Chatterbox as he had said he would. After that he rode south through Swinedale.

It is told how at Laugar in Saelingsdale Gudrun was early afoot directly after sunrise. She went to where her brothers were sleeping. She roused Ospak and he woke up at once, and then too the other brothers. And when Ospak saw that there was his sister, he asked her what she wanted that she was up so early. Gudrun said she wanted to know what they would be doing that day. Ospak said he would keep at rest, "for there is little work to do."

Gudrun said, "You would have the right sort of temper if you were the daughters of some peasant, letting neither good nor bad be done by you. Why, after all the disgrace and shame that Kjartan has done to you, you none the less lie quietly sleeping, though he rides past this place with but one other man. Such men indeed are richly endowed with the memory of swine. I think it is past hoping that you will ever have courage enough to go and seek out Kjartan in his home, if you dare not meet him now that he rides with but one other man or two; but here you sit at home and bear yourselves as if you were hopeful men; yea, in sooth there are too many of you."

Ospak said she did not mince matters and it was hard to gainsay her, and he sprang up forthwith and dressed, as did also each of the brothers one after the other. Then they got ready to lay an ambush for Kjartan.

Then Gudrun called on Bolli to bestir him with them. Bolli said it behoved him not for the sake of his kinship with Kjartan, set forth how lovingly Olaf had brought him up.

Gudrun answered, "Therein you speak the truth, but you will not have the good luck always to do what pleases all men, and if you cut yourself out of this journey, our married life must be at an end."

And through Gudrun's harping on the matter Bolli's mind swelled at all the enmity and guilts that lay at the door of Kjartan, and speedily he donned his weapons, and they grew a band of nine together. There were the five sons of Osvif – Ospak, Helgi, Vandrad, Torrad, and Thorolf. Bolli was the sixth and Gudlaug, the son of Osvif's sister, the hopefullest of men, the seventh. There were also Odd and Stein, sons of Thorhalla Chatterbox.

They rode to Swinedale and took up their stand beside the gill which is called Goat-gill. They bound up their horses and sat down. Bolli was silent all day, and lay up on the top of the gill bank.

Now when Kjartan and his followers were come south past Narrowsound, where the dale begins to widen out, Kjartan said that Thorkell and the others had better turn back. Thorkell said they would ride to the end of the dale. Then when they came south past the out-dairies called Northdairies Kjartan spake to the brothers and bade them not to ride any farther. "Thorolf the thief," he said, "shall not have that matter to laugh at that I dare not ride on my way with few men."

Thorkell Whelp said, "We will yield to you in not following you any farther; but we should rue it indeed not to be near if you should stand in need of men today."

Then Kjartan said, "Never will Bolli, my kinsman, join hands with plotters against my life. But if the sons of Osvif lie in wait for me, there is no knowing which side will live to tell the tale, even though I may have some odds to deal with."

Thereupon the brothers rode back to the west.

Chapter 49
The Death of Kjartan

NOW KJARTAN RODE SOUTH through the dale, he and they three together, himself, An the Black, and Thorarin.

Thorkell was the name of a man who lived at Goat-peaks in Swinedale, where now there is waste land. He had been seeing after his horses that day, and a shepherd of his with him. They saw the two parties, the men of Laugar in ambush and Kjartan and his where they were riding down the dale three together. Then the shepherd said they had better turn to meet Kjartan and his; it would be, quoth he, a great good hap to them if they could stave off so great a trouble as now both sides were steering into.

Thorkell said, "Hold your tongue at once. Do you think, fool as you are, you will ever give life to a man to whom fate has ordained death? And, truth to tell, I would spare neither of them from having now as evil dealings together as they like. It seems to me a better plan for us to get to a place where we stand in danger of nothing, and from where we can have a good look at their meeting, so as to have some fun over their play. For all men make a marvel thereof, how Kjartan is of all men the best skilled at arms. I think he will want it now, for we two know how overwhelming the odds are."

And so it had to be as Thorkell wished.

Kjartan and his followers now rode on to Goat-gill.

On the other hand the sons of Osvif misdoubt them why Bolli should have sought out a place for himself from where he might well be seen by men riding from the west. So they now put their heads together, and, being of one mind that Bolli was playing them false, they go for him up unto the brink and took to wrestling and horse-playing with him, and took him by the feet and dragged him down over the brink.

But Kjartan and his followers came up apace as they were riding fast, and when they came to the south side of the gill they saw the ambush and knew the men. Kjartan at once sprung off his horse and turned upon the sons of Osvif. There stood near by a great stone, against which Kjartan ordered they should wait the onset (he and his). Before they met Kjartan flung his spear, and it struck through Thorolf's shield above the handle, so that therewith the shield was pressed against him, the spear piercing the shield and the arm above the elbow, where it sundered the main muscle, Thorolf dropping the shield, and his arm being of no avail to him through the day.

Thereupon Kjartan drew his sword, but he held not the 'King's-gift.' The sons of Thorhalla went at Thorarin, for that was the task allotted to them. That outset was a hard one, for Thorarin was mightily strong, and it was hard to tell which would outlast the other.

Osvif's sons and Gudlaug set on Kjartan, they being five together, and Kjartan and An but two. An warded himself valiantly, and would ever be going in front of Kjartan. Bolli stood aloof with Footbiter. Kjartan smote hard, but his sword was of little avail (and bent so), he often had to straighten it under his foot. In this attack both the sons of Osvif and An were wounded, but Kjartan had no wound as yet. Kjartan fought so swiftly and dauntlessly that Osvif's sons recoiled and turned to where An was. At that moment An fell, having fought for some time, with his inwards coming out. In this attack Kjartan cut off one leg of Gudlaug above the knee, and that hurt was enough to cause death.

Then the four sons of Osvif made an onset on Kjartan, but he warded himself so bravely that in no way did he give them the chance of any advantage.

Then spake Kjartan, "Kinsman Bolli, why did you leave home if you meant quietly to stand by? Now the choice lies before you, to help one side or the other, and try now how Footbiter will do."

Bolli made as if he did not hear. And when Ospak saw that they would no how bear Kjartan over, he egged on Bolli in every way, and said he surely would not wish that shame to follow after him, to have promised them his aid in this fight and not to grant it now. "Why, heavy enough in dealings with us was Kjartan then, when by none so big a deed as this we had offended him; but if Kjartan is now to get away from us, then for you, Bolli, as even for us, the way to exceeding hardships will be equally short."

Then Bolli drew Footbiter, and now turned upon Kjartan.

Then Kjartan said to Bolli, "Surely thou art minded now, my kinsman, to do a dastard's deed; but oh, my kinsman, I am much more fain to take my death from you than to cause the same to you myself."

Then Kjartan flung away his weapons and would defend himself no longer; yet he was but slightly wounded, though very tired with fighting.

Bolli gave no answer to Kjartan's words, but all the same he dealt him his death-wound. And straightway Bolli sat down under the shoulders of him, and Kjartan breathed his last in the lap of Bolli. Bolli rued at once his deed, and declared the manslaughter due to his hand. Bolli sent the sons of Osvif into the countryside, but he stayed behind together with Thorarin by the dead bodies. And when the sons of Osvif came to Laugar they told the tidings. Gudrun gave out her pleasure thereat, and then the arm of Thorolf was bound up; it healed slowly, and was never after any use to him.

The body of Kjartan was brought home to Tongue, but Bolli rode home to Laugar. Gudrun went to meet him, and asked what time of day it was. Bolli said it was near noontide.

Then spake Gudrun, "Harm spurs on to hard deeds (work); I have spun yarn for twelve ells of homespun, and you have killed Kjartan."

Bolli replied, "That unhappy deed might well go late from my mind even if you did not remind me of it."

Gudrun said "Such things I do not count among mishaps. It seemed to me you stood in higher station during the year Kjartan was in Norway than now, when he trod you under foot when he came back to Iceland. But I count that last which to me is dearest, that Hrefna will not go laughing to her bed tonight."

Then Bolli said and right wroth he was, "I think it is quite uncertain that she will turn paler at these tidings than you do; and I have my doubts as to whether you would not have been less startled if I had been lying behind on the field of battle, and Kjartan had told the tidings."

Gudrun saw that Bolli was wroth, and spake, "Do not upbraid me with such things, for I am very grateful to you for your deed; for now I think I know that you will not do anything against my mind."

After that Osvif's sons went and hid in an underground chamber, which had been made for them in secret, but Thorhalla's sons were sent west to Holy-Fell to tell Snorri Godi the Priest these tidings, and therewith the message that they bade him send them speedily all availing strength against Olaf and those men to whom it came to follow up the blood-suit after Kjartan.

At Saelingsdale Tongue it happened, the night after the day on which the fight befell, that An sat up, he who they had all thought was dead. Those who waked the bodies were very much afraid, and thought this a wondrous marvel. Then An spake to them, "I beg you, in God's name, not to be afraid of me, for I have had both my life and my wits all unto the hour when on me fell the heaviness of a swoon. Then I dreamed of the same woman as before, and methought she now took the brushwood out of my belly and put my own inwards in instead, and the change seemed good to me."

Then the wounds that An had were bound up and he became a hale man, and was ever afterwards called An Brushwood-belly.

But now when Olaf Hoskuld's son heard these tidings he took the slaying of Kjartan most sorely to heart, though he bore it like a brave man. His sons wanted to set on Bolli forthwith and kill him.

Olaf said, "Far be it from me, for my son is none the more atoned to me though Bolli be slain; moreover, I loved Kjartan before all men, but as to Bolli, I could not bear any harm befalling him. But I see a more befitting business for you to do. Go ye and meet the sons of Thorhalla, who are now sent to Holy-Fell with the errand of summoning up a band against us. I shall be well pleased for you to put them to any penalty you like."

Then Olaf's sons swiftly turn to journeying, and went on board a ferry-boat that Olaf owned, being seven of them together, and rowed out down Hvamsfirth, pushing on their journey at their lustiest. They had but little wind, but fair what there was, and they rowed with the sail until they came under Scoreisle, where they tarried for some while and asked about the journeyings of men thereabouts. A little while after they saw a ship coming from the west across the firth, and soon they saw who the men were, for there were the sons of Thorhalla, and Halldor and his followers boarded them straightway. They met with no resistance, for the sons of Olaf leapt forthwith on board their ships and set upon them. Stein and his brother were laid hands on and beheaded overboard.

The sons of Olaf now turn back, and their journey was deemed to have sped most briskly.

Chapter 50
The End of Hrefna; The Peace Settled, AD 1003

OLAF WENT TO MEET Kjartan's body. He sent men south to Burg to tell Thorstein Egilson these tidings, and also that he would have his help for the blood-suit; and if any great men should band themselves together against him with the sons of Osvif, he said he wanted to have the whole matter in his own hands.

The same message he sent north to Willowdale, to Gudmund, his son-in-law, and to the sons of Asgeir; with the further information that he had charged as guilty of the slaying of Kjartan all the men who had taken part in the ambush, except Ospak, son of Osvif, for he was already under outlawry because of a woman who was called Aldis, the daughter of Holmganga-Ljot of Ingjaldsand. Their son was Ulf, who later became a marshal to King Harold Sigurdsson, and had for wife Jorunn, the daughter of Thorberg. Their son was Jon, father of Erlend the Laggard, the father of Archbishop Egstein.

Olaf had proclaimed that the blood-suit should be taken into court at Thorness Thing.

He had Kjartan's body brought home, and a tent was rigged over it, for there was as yet no church built in the Dales. But when Olaf heard that Thorstein had bestirred him swiftly and raised up a band of great many men, and that the Willowdale men had done likewise, he had men gathered together throughout all the Dales, and a great multitude they were. The whole of this band Olaf sent to Laugar, with this order: "It is my will that you guard Bolli if he stand in need thereof, and do it no less faithfully than if you were following me; for my mind misgives me that the men from beyond this countryside, whom, coming soon, we shall be having on our hands, will deem that they have somewhat of a loss to make up with Bolli."

And when he had put the matter in order in this manner, Thorstein, with his following, and also the Willowdale men, came on, all wild with rage. Hall Gudmund's son and Kalf Asgeirson egged them on most to go and force Bolli to let search be made for the sons of Osvif till they should be found, for they could be gone nowhere out of the countryside. But because Olaf set himself so much against their making a raid on Laugar, messages of peace were borne between the two parties, and Bolli was most willing, and bade Olaf settle all terms on his behalf, and Osvif said it was not in his power to speak against this, for no help had come to him from Snorri the Priest.

A peace meeting, therefore, took place at Lea-Shaws, and the whole case was laid freely in Olaf's hand. For the slaughter of Kjartan there were to come such fines and penalties as Olaf liked. Then the peace meeting came to an end. Bolli, by the counsel of Olaf, did not go to this meeting. The award should be made known at Thorness Thing.

Now the Mere-men and Willowdale men rode to Herdholt. Thorstein Kuggison begged for Asgeir, son of Kjartan, to foster, as a comfort to Hrefna.

Hrefna went north with her brothers, and was much weighed down with grief, nevertheless she bore her sorrow with dignity, and was easy of speech with every man. Hrefna took no other husband after Kjartan. She lived but a little while after coming to the north; and the tale goes that she died of a broken heart.

Chapter 51
Osvif's Sons Are Banished

KJARTAN'S BODY LAY in state for a week in Herdholt. Thorstein Egilson had had a church built at Burg. He took the body of Kjartan home with him, and Kjartan was buried at Burg. The church was newly consecrated, and as yet hung in white.

Now time wore on towards the Thorness Thing, and the award was given against Osvif's sons, who were all banished the country. Money was given to pay the cost of their going into exile, but they were forbidden to come back to Iceland so long as any of Olaf's sons, or Asgeir, Kjartan's son, should be alive. For Gudlaug, the son of Osvif's sister, no weregild (atonement) should be paid, because of his having set out against, and laid ambush for, Kjartan, neither should Thorolf have any compensation for the wounds he had got.

Olaf would not let Bolli be prosecuted, and bade him ransom himself with a money fine. This Halldor and Stein, and all the sons of Olaf, liked mightily ill, and said it would go hard with Bolli if he was allowed to stay in the same countryside as themselves. Olaf saw that would work well enough as long as he was on his legs.

There was a ship in Bjornhaven which belonged to Audun Cable-hound. He was at the Thing, and said, "As matters stand, the guilt of these men will be no less in Norway, so long as any of Kjartan's friends are alive."

Then Osvif said, "You, Cable-hound, will be no soothsayer in this matter, for my sons will be highly accounted of among men of high degree, whilst you, Cable-hound, will pass, this summer, into the power of trolls."

Audun Cable-hound went out a voyage that summer and the ship was wrecked amongst the Faroe Isles and every man's child on board perished, and Osvif's prophecy was thought to have come thoroughly home.

The sons of Osvif went abroad that summer, and none ever came back again. In such a manner the blood-suit came to an end that Olaf was held to have shown himself all the greater a man, because where it was due, in the case of the sons of Osvif, to wit, he drove matters home to the very bone, but spared Bolli for the sake of their kinship. Olaf thanked men well for the help they had afforded him.

By Olaf's counsel Bolli bought the land at Tongue.

It is told that Olaf lived three winters after Kjartan was slain. After he was dead his sons shared the inheritance he left behind. Halldor took over the manor of Herdholt. Thorgerd, their mother, lived with Halldor; she was most hatefully-minded towards Bolli, and thought the reward he paid for his fostering a bitter one.

Chapter 52
The Killing of Thorkell of Goat's Peak

IN THE SPRING Bolli and Gudrun set up householding at Saelingsdale-Tongue, and it soon became a stately one. Bolli and Gudrun begat a son. To that boy a name was given, and he was called Thorleik; he was early a very fine lad, and a right nimble one.

Halldor Olafson lived at Herdholt, as has before been written, and he was in most matters at the head of his brothers.

The spring that Kjartan was slain Thorgerd Egil's daughter placed a lad, as kin to her, with Thorkell of Goat-Peaks, and the lad herded sheep there through the summer. Like other people he was much grieved over Kjartan's death. He could never speak of Kjartan if Thorkell was near, for he always spoke ill of him, and said he had been a "white" man and of no heart; he often mimicked how Kjartan had taken his death-wound. The lad took this very ill, and went to Herdholt and told Halldor and Thorgerd and begged them to take him in. Thorgerd bade him remain in his service till the winter.

The lad said he had no strength to bear being there any longer. "And you would not ask this of me if you knew what heart-burn I suffer from all this."

Then Thorgerd's heart turned at the tale of his grief, and she said that as far as she was concerned, she would make a place for him there.

Halldor said, "Give no heed to this lad, he is not worth taking in earnest."

Then Thorgerd answered, "The lad is of little account," says she, "but Thorkell has behaved evilly in every way in this matter, for he knew of the ambush the men of Laugar laid for Kjartan, and would not warn him, but made fun and sport of their dealings together, and has since said many unfriendly things about the matter; but it seems a matter far beyond you brothers ever to seek revenge where odds are against you, now that you cannot pay out for their doings such scoundrels as Thorkell is."

Halldor answered little to that, but bade Thorgerd do what she liked about the lad's service. A few days after Halldor rode from home, he and sundry other men together. He went to Goat-Peaks, and surrounded Thorkell's house. Thorkell was led out and slain, and he met his death with the utmost cowardice. Halldor allowed no plunder, and they went home when this was done. Thorgerd was well pleased over this deed, and thought this reminder better than none.

That summer all was quiet, so to speak, and yet there was the greatest ill-will between the sons of Olaf and Bolli. The brothers bore themselves in the most unyielding manner towards Bolli, while he gave in to his kinsmen in all matters as long as he did not lower himself in any way by so doing, for he was a very proud man. Bolli had many followers and lived richly, for there was no lack of money.

Steinthor, Olaf's son, lived in Danastead in Salmon-river-Dale. He had for wife Thurid, Asgeir's daughter, who had before been married to Thorkell Kuggi. Their son was Steinthor, who was called 'Stone-grig.'

Chapter 53
Thorgerd's Egging, AD 1007

THE NEXT WINTER after the death of Olaf Hoskuldson, Thorgerd, Egil's daughter, sent word to her son Steinthor that he should come and meet her. When the mother and son met she told him she wished to go up west to Saurby, and see her friend Aud. She told Halldor to come too. They were five together, and Halldor followed his mother. They went on till they came to a place in front of the homestead of Saelingsdale Tongue.

Then Thorgerd turned her horse towards the house and asked, "What is this place called?"

Halldor answered, "You ask this, mother, not because you don't know it. This place is called Tongue."

"Who lives here?" said she.

He answered, "You know that, mother."

Thorgerd said and snorted, "I know that well enough," she said. "Here lives Bolli, the slayer of your brother, and marvellously unlike your noble kindred you turn out in that you will not avenge such a brother as Kjartan was; never would Egil, your mother's father, have behaved in such a manner; and a piteous thing it is to have dolts for sons; indeed, I think it would have suited you better if you had been your father's daughter and had married. For here, Halldor, it comes to the old saw: "No stock without a duffer," and this is the ill-luck of Olaf I see most clearly, how he blundered in begetting his sons. This I would bring home to you, Halldor," says she, "because you look upon yourself as being the foremost among your brothers. Now we will turn back again, for all my errand here was to put you in mind of this, lest you should have forgotten it already."

Then Halldor answered, "We shall not put it down as your fault, mother, if this should slip out of our minds."

By way of answer Halldor had few words to say about this, but his heart swelled with wrath towards Bolli.

The winter now passed and summer came, and time glided on towards the Thing. Halldor and his brothers made it known that they will ride to the Thing. They rode with a great company, and set up the booth Olaf had owned. The Thing was quiet, and no tidings to tell of it.

There were at the Thing from the north the Willowdale men, the sons of Gudmund Solmundson. Bardi Gudmundson was then eighteen winters old; he was a great and strong man. The sons of Olaf asked Bardi, their nephew, to go home with them, and added many pressing words to the invitation. Hall, the son of Gudmund, was not in Iceland then. Bardi took up their bidding gladly, for there was much love between those kinsmen. Bardi rode west from the Thing with the sons of Olaf. They came home to Herdholt, and Bardi tarried the rest of the summer time.

Chapter 54
Halldor Prepares to Avenge Kjartan

NOW HALLDOR TOLD BARDI in secret that the brothers had made up their minds to set on Bolli, for they could no longer withstand the taunts of their mother. "And we will not conceal from you, kinsman Bardi, that what mostly lay behind the invitation to you was this, that we wished to have your help and fellowship."

Then Bardi answered, "That will be a matter ill spoken of, to break the peace on one's own kinsmen, and on the other hand it seems to me nowise an easy thing to set on Bolli. He has many men about him and is himself the best of fighters, and is not at a loss for wise counsel with Gudrun and Osvif at his side. Taking all these matters together they seem to me nowise easy to overcome."

Halldor said, "There are things we stand more in need of than to make the most of the difficulties of this affair. Nor have I broached it till I knew that it must come to pass, that we make earnest of wreaking revenge on Bolli. And I hope, kinsman, you will not withdraw from doing this journey with us."

Bardi answered, "I know you do not think it likely that I will draw back, neither do I desire to do so if I see that I cannot get you to give it up yourselves."

"There you do your share in the matter honourably," said Halldor, "as was to be looked for from you."

Bardi said they must set about it with care. Halldor said he had heard that Bolli had sent his house-carles from home, some north to Ramfirth to meet a ship and some out to Middlefell strand. "It is also told me that Bolli is staying at the out-dairy in Saelingsdale with no more than the house-carles who are doing the haymaking. And it seems to me we shall never have a better chance of seeking a meeting with Bolli than now."

So this then Halldor and Bardi settled between them.

There was a man named Thorstein the Black, a wise man and wealthy; he lived at Hundidale in the Broadfirth-Dales; he had long been a friend of Olaf Peacock's. A sister of Thorstein was called Solveig; she was married to a man who was named Helgi, who was son of Hardbein. Helgi was a very tall and strong man, and a great sailor; he had lately come to Iceland, and was staying with his brother-in-law Thorstein.

Halldor sent word to Thorstein the Black and Helgi his brother-in-law, and when they were come to Herdholt Halldor told them what he was about, and how he meant to carry it out, and asked them to join in the journey with him.

Thorstein showed an utter dislike of this undertaking, saying, "It is the most heinous thing that you kinsmen should go on killing each other off like that; and now there are but few men left in your family equal to Bolli."

But though Thorstein spoke in this wise it went for nought.

Halldor sent word to Lambi, his father's brother, and when he came and met Halldor he told him what he was about, and Lambi urged hard that this should be carried out. Goodwife Thorgerd also egged them on eagerly to make an earnest of their journey, and said she should never look upon Kjartan as avenged until Bolli paid for him with his life.

After this they got ready for the journey. In this raid there were the four sons of Olaf and the fifth was Bardi. There were the sons of Olaf, Halldor, Steinthor, Helgi, and Hoskuld, but Bardi was Gudmund's son. Lambi was the sixth, the seventh was Thorstein, and the eighth Helgi, his brother-in-law, the ninth An Brushwood-belly.

Thorgerd betook herself also to the raid with them; but they set themselves against it, and said that such were no journeys for women. She said she would go indeed, "For so much I know of you, my sons, that whetting is what you want."

They said she must have her own way.

Chapter 55
The Death of Bolli

AFTER THAT they rode away from home out of Herdholt, the nine of them together, Thorgerd making the tenth. They rode up along the foreshore and so to Lea-shaws during the early part of the night. They did not stop before they got to Saelingsdale in the early morning tide.

There was a thick wood in the valley at that time. Bolli was there in the out-dairy, as Halldor had heard. The dairy stood near the river at the place now called Bolli's-tofts. Above the dairy there is a large hill-rise stretching all the way down to Stack-gill. Between the mountain slope above and the hill-rise there is a wide meadow called Barni; it was there Bolli's house-carles were working.

Halldor and his companions rode across Ran-meads unto Oxgrove, and thence above Hammer-Meadow, which was right against the dairy. They knew there were many men at the dairy, so they got off their horses with a view to biding the time when the men should leave the dairy for their work.

Bolli's shepherd went early that morning after the flocks up into the mountain side, and from there he saw the men in the wood as well as the horses tied up, and misdoubted that those who went on the sly in this manner would be no men of peace. So forthwith he makes for the dairy by the straightest cut in order to tell Bolli that men were come there.

Halldor was a man of keen sight. He saw how that a man was running down the mountain side and making for the dairy. He said to his companions that "That must surely be Bolli's shepherd, and he must have seen our coming; so we must go and meet him, and let him take no news to the dairy."

They did as he bade them. An Brushwood-belly went the fastest of them and overtook the man, picked him up, and flung him down. Such was that fall that the lad's back-bone was broken.

After that they rode to the dairy. Now the dairy was divided into two parts, the sleeping-room and the byre.

Bolli had been early afoot in the morning ordering the men to their work, and had lain down again to sleep when the house-carles went away. In the dairy therefore there were left the two, Gudrun and Bolli. They awoke with the din when they got off their horses, and they also heard them talking as to who should first go on to the dairy to set on Bolli.

Bolli knew the voice of Halldor, as well as that of sundry more of his followers. Bolli spoke to Gudrun, and bade her leave the dairy and go away, and said that their meeting would not be such as would afford her much pastime. Gudrun said she thought such things alone would befall there worthy of tidings as she might be allowed to look upon, and held that she would be of no hurt to Bolli by taking her stand near to him. Bolli said that in this matter he would have his way, and so it was that Gudrun went out of the dairy; she went down over the brink to a brook that ran there, and began to wash some linen.

Bolli was now alone in the dairy; he took his weapon, set his helm on his head, held a shield before him, and had his sword, Footbiter, in his hand: he had no mail coat.

Halldor and his followers were talking to each other outside as to how they should set to work, for no one was very eager to go into the dairy.

Then said An Brushwood-belly, "There are men here in this train nearer in kinship to Kjartan than I am, but not one there will be in whose mind abides more steadfastly than in mine the event when Kjartan lost his life. When I was being brought more dead than alive home to Tongue, and Kjartan lay slain, my one thought was that I would gladly do Bolli some harm whenever I should get the chance. So I shall be the first to go into the dairy."

Then Thorstein the Black answered, "Most valiantly is that spoken; but it would be wiser not to plunge headlong beyond heed, so let us go warily now, for Bolli will not be standing quiet when he is beset; and however underhanded he may be where he is, you may make up your mind for a brisk defence on his part, strong and skilled at arms as he is. He also has a sword that for a weapon is a trusty one."

Then An went into the dairy hard and swift, and held his shield over his head, turning forward the narrower part of it. Bolli dealt him a blow with Footbiter, and cut off the tail-end of the shield, and clove An through the head down to the shoulder, and forthwith he gat his death.

Then Lambi went in; he held his shield before him, and a drawn sword in his hand. In the nick of time Bolli pulled Footbiter out of the wound, whereat his shield veered aside so as to lay him open to attack. So Lambi made a thrust at him in the thigh, and a great wound that was. Bolli hewed in return, and struck Lambi's shoulder, and the sword flew down along the side of him, and he was rendered forthwith unfit to fight, and never after that time for the rest of his life was his arm any more use to him.

At this brunt Helgi, the son of Hardbien, rushed in with a spear, the head of which was an ell long, and the shaft bound with iron. When Bolli saw that he cast away his sword, and took his shield in both hands, and went towards the dairy door to meet Helgi. Helgi thrust at Bolli with the spear right through the shield and through him. Now Bolli leaned up against the dairy wall, and the men rushed into the dairy, Halldor and his brothers, to wit, and Thorgerd went into the dairy as well.

Then spoke Bolli, "Now it is safe, brothers, to come nearer than hitherto you have done," and said he weened that defence now would be but short.

Thorgerd answered his speech, and said there was no need to shrink from dealing unflinchingly with Bolli, and bade them "walk between head and trunk." Bolli stood still against the dairy wall, and held tight to him his kirtle lest his inside should come out. Then Steinthor Olafson leapt at Bolli, and hewed at his neck with a large axe just above his shoulders, and forthwith his head flew off.

Thorgerd bade him "hale enjoy hands," and said that Gudrun would have now a while a red hair to trim for Bolli.

After that they went out of the dairy.

Gudrun now came up from the brook, and spoke to Halldor, and asked for tidings of what had befallen in their dealings with Bolli. They told her all that had happened. Gudrun was dressed in a kirtle of 'rám'-stuff, and a tight-fitting woven bodice, a high bent coif on her head, and she had tied a scarf round her with dark-blue stripes, and fringed at the ends.

Helgi Hardbienson went up to Gudrun, and caught hold of the scarf end, and wiped the blood off the spear with it, the same spear with which he had thrust Bolli through.

Gudrun glanced at him and smiled slightly.

Then Halldor said, "That was blackguardly and gruesomely done."

Helgi bade him not be angry about it, "For I am minded to think that under this scarf end abides undoer of my life."

Then they took their horses and rode away. Gudrun went along with them talking with them for a while, and then she turned back.

Chapter 56
Bolli Bollison Is Born, AD 1008

THE FOLLOWERS OF Halldor now fell a-talking how that Gudrun must think but little of the slaying of Bolli, since she had seen them off chatting and talked to them altogether as if they had done nothing that she might take to heart.

Then Halldor answered, "That is not my feeling, that Gudrun thinks little of Bolli's death; I think the reason of her seeing us off with a chat was far rather, that she wanted to gain a thorough knowledge as to who the men were who had partaken in this journey. Nor is it too much said of Gudrun that in all mettle of mind and heart she is far above other women. Indeed, it is only what might be looked for that Gudrun should take sorely to heart the death of Bolli, for, truth to tell, in such men as was Bolli there is the greatest loss, though we kinsmen, bore not about the good luck to live in peace together."

After that they rode home to Herdholt.

These tidings spread quickly far and wide and were thought startling, and at Bolli's death there was the greatest grief.

Gudrun sent straightway men to Snorri the Priest, for Osvif and she thought that all their trust was where Snorri was. Snorri started quickly at the bidding of Gudrun and came to Tongue with sixty men, and a great ease to Gudrun's heart his coming was. He offered her to try to bring about a peaceful settlement, but Gudrun was but little minded on behalf of Thorleik to agree to taking money for the slaughter of Bolli.

"It seems to me, Snorri, that the best help you can afford me," she said, "is to exchange dwellings with me, so that I be not next-door neighbour to the Herdholtings."

At that time Snorri had great quarrels with the dwellers at Eyr, but said he would do this for the sake of his friendship with Gudrun. "Yet, Gudrun, you will have to stay on this year at Tongue."

Snorri then made ready to go away, and Gudrun gave him honourable gifts. And now Snorri rides away, and things went pretty quietly on that year.

The next winter after the killing of Bolli Gudrun gave birth to a child; it was a male, and he was named Bolli. He was at an early age both big and goodly, and Gudrun loved him very much.

Now as the winter passed by and the spring came the bargain took place which had been bespoken in that Snorri and Gudrun changed lands. Snorri went to Tongue and lived there for the rest of his life, and Gudrun went to Holyfell, she and Osvif, and there they set up a stately house. There Thorleik and Bolli, the sons of Gudrun, grew up. Thorleik was four years old at the time when Bolli his father was slain.

Part Three

Chapter 57
About Thorgils Hallason, AD 1018

THERE WAS A MAN NAMED Thorgils Hallason; he was known by his mother's name, as she lived longer than his father, whose name was Snorri, son of Alf o' Dales. Halla, Thorgil's mother, was daughter of Gest Oddliefson. Thorgils lived in Horddale at a place called Tongue. Thorgils was a man great and goodly of body, the greatest swaggerer, and was spoken of as one of no fairness in dealings with men. Between him and Snorri the Priest there was often little love lost, for Snorri found Thorgils both meddlesome and flaunting of demeanour.

Thorgils would get up many errands on which to go west into the countryside, and always came to Holyfell offering Gudrun to look after her affairs, but she only took the matter quietly and made but little of it all.

Thorgils asked for her son Thorleik to go home with him, and he stayed for the most part at Tongue and learnt law from Thorgils, for he was a man most skilled in law-craft.

At that time Thorkell Eyjolfson was busy in trading journeys; he was a most renowned man, and of high birth, and withal a great friend of Snorri the Priest. He would always be staying with Thorstein Kuggison, his kinsman, when he was out here (in Iceland).

Now, one time when Thorkell had a ship standing up in Vadil, on Bardistrand, it befell, in Burgfirth, that the son of Eid of Ridge was killed by the sons of Helga from Kropp. Grim was the name of the man who had done the manslaughter, and that of his brother was Nial, who was drowned in White-river; a little later on Grim was outlawed to the woods because of the manslaughter, and he lay out in the mountains whilst he was under the award of outlawry. He was a great man and strong. Eid was then very old when this happened, so the case was not followed up. People blamed Thorkell very much that he did not see matters righted.

The next spring when Thorkell had got his ship ready he went south across Broadfirth-country, and got a horse there and rode alone, not stopping in his journey till he got as far as Ridge, to Eid, his kinsman. Eid took him in joyfully. Thorkell told him his errand, how that he would go and find Grim, and asked Eid if he knew at all where his lair was.

Eid answered, "I am nowise eager for this; it seems to me you have much to risk as to how the journey may speed, seeing that you will have to deal with a man of Hel's strength, such as Grim. But if you will go, then start with many men, so that you may have it all your own way."

"That to me is no prowess," said Thorkell, "to draw together a great company against one man. But what I wish is, that you would lend me the sword Skofnung, for then I ween I shall be able to overcome a mere runagate, be he never so mighty a man of his hands."

"You must have your way in this," said Eid, "but it will not come to me unawares, if, some day, you should come to rue this wilfulness. But inasmuch as you will have it that you are doing this for my sake, what you ask for shall not be withheld, for I think Skofnung well bestowed if you bear it. But the nature of the sword is such that the sun must not shine upon its hilt, nor must it be drawn if a woman should be near. If a man be wounded by the sword the hurt may not be healed, unless the healing-stone that goes with the sword be rubbed thereon."

Thorkell said he would pay careful heed to this, and takes over the sword, asking Eid to point out to him the way to where Grim might have his lair. Eid said he was most minded to think that Grim had his lair north on Twodays-Heath by the Fishwaters. Then Thorkell rode northward upon the heath the way which Eid did point out to him, and when he had got a long way onward over the heath he saw near some great water a hut, and makes his way for it.

Chapter 53
Thorkell and Grim, and Their Voyage Abroad

THORKELL NOW COMES to the hut, he sees where a man is sitting by the water at the mouth of a brook, where he was line-fishing, and had a cloak over his head.

Thorkell leapt off his horse and tied it up under the wall of the hut. Then he walks down to the water to where the man was sitting. Grim saw the shadow of a man cast on the water, and springs up at once. By then Thorkell had got very nearly close up to him, and strikes at him. The blow caught him on his arm just above the wolf-joint (the wrist), but that was not a great wound. Grim sprang forthwith upon Thorkell, and they seized each other wrestling-wise, and speedily the odds of strength told, and Thorkell fell and Grim on the top of him.

Then Grim asked who this man might be. Thorkell said that did not at all matter to him.

Grim said, "Now things have befallen otherwise than you must have thought they would, for now your life will be in my power."

Thorkell said he would not pray for peace for himself, "for lucklessly I have taken this in hand."

Grim said he had had enough mishaps for him to give this one the slip, "for to you some other fate is ordained than that of dying at this our meeting, and I shall give you your life, while you repay me in whatever kind you please."

Now they both stand up and walk home to the hut. Thorkell sees that Grim was growing faint from loss of blood, so he took Skofnung's-stone and rubbed it on, and ties it to the arm of Grim, and it took forthwith all smarting pain and swelling out of the wound.

They stayed there that night. In the morning Thorkell got ready to go away, and asked if Grim would go with him. He said that sure enough that was his will. Thorkell turns straightway westward without going to meet Eid, nor halted he till he came to Saelingsdale Tongue.

Snorri the Priest welcomes him with great blitheness. Thorkell told him that his journey had sped lucklessly. Snorri said it had turned out well, "for Grim looks to me a man endowed with good luck, and my will is that you make matters up with him handsomely. But now, my friend, I would like to counsel you to leave off trade-journeyings, and to settle down and marry, and become a chief as befits your high birth."

Thorkell answered, "Often your counsels have stood me in good stead," and he asked if Snorri had bethought him of the woman he should woo. Snorri answers, "You must woo the woman who is the best match for you, and that woman is Gudrun, Osvif's daughter."

Thorkell said it was true that a marriage with her would be an honourable one. "But," says he, "I think her fierce heart and reckless-mindedness weigh heavily, for she will want to have her husband, Bolli, avenged. Besides, it is said that on this matter there is some understanding between her and Thorgils Hallason, and it may be that this will not be altogether to his liking. Otherwise, Gudrun pleases me well."

Snorri said, "I will undertake to see that no harm shall come to you from Thorgils; but as to the revenge for Bolli, I am rather in hopes that concerning that matter some change will have befallen before these seasons (this year) are out."

Thorkell answered, "It may be that these be no empty words you are speaking now. But as to the revenge of Bolli, that does not seem to me more likely to happen now than it did a while ago, unless into that strife some of the greater men may be drawn."

Snorri said, "I should be well pleased to see you go abroad once more this summer, to let us see then what happens." Thorkell said so it should be, and they parted, leaving matters where they now stood. Thorkell went west over Broadfirth-country to his ship. He took Grim with him abroad. They had a good summer-voyage, and came to the south of Norway.

Then Thorkell said to Grim, "You know how the case stands, and what things happened to bring about our acquaintance, so I need say nothing about that matter; but I would fain that it should turn out better than at one time it seemed likely it would. I have found you a valiant man, and for that reason I will so part from you, as if I had never borne you any grudge. I will give you as much merchandise as you need in order to be able to join the guild of good merchants. But do not settle down here in the north of this land, for many of Eid's kinsmen are about on trading journeys who bear you heavy ill-will."

Grim thanked him for these words, and said he could never have thought of asking for as much as he offered. At parting Thorkell gave to Grim a goodly deal of merchandise, and many men said that this deed bore the stamp of a great man.

After that Grim went east in the Wick, settled there, and was looked upon as a mighty man of his ways; and therewith comes to an end what there is to be told about Grim.

Thorkell was in Norway through the winter, and was thought a man of much account; he was exceeding wealthy in chattels.

Now this matter must be left for a while, and the story must be taken up out in Iceland, so let us hear what matters befell there for tidings to be told of whilst Thorkell was abroad.

Chapter 59
Gudrun Demands Revenge for Bolli, AD 1019

IN "TWINMONTH" that summer Gudrun, Osvif's daughter, went from home up into the Dales. She rode to Thickshaw; and at this time Thorleik was sometimes at Thickshaw with the sons of Armod Halldor and Ornolf, and sometimes Tongue with Thorgils.

The same night Gudrun sent a man to Snorri Godi saying that she wished to meet him without fail the next day. Snorri got ready at once and rode with one other man until he came to Hawkdale-river; on the northern side of that river stands a crag by the river called Head, within the land of Lea-Shaw. At this spot Gudrun had bespoken that she and Snorri should meet.

They both came there at one and the same time. With Gudrun there was only one man, and he was Bolli, son of Bolli; he was now twelve years old, but fulfilled of strength and wits was he, so much so, that many were they who were no whit more powerful at the time of ripe manhood; and now he carried Footbiter.

Snorri and Gudrun now fell to talking together; but Bolli and Snorri's follower sat on the crag and watched people travelling up and down the countryside. When Snorri and Gudrun had asked each other for news, Snorri inquired on what errand he was called, and what had come to pass lately that she sent him word so hurriedly.

Gudrun said, "Truth to tell, to me is ever fresh the event which I am about to bring up, and yet it befell twelve years ago; for it is about the revenge of Bolli I wish to speak, and it ought not to take you unawares. I have called it to your mind from time to time. I must also bring this home to you that to this end you have promised me some help if I but waited patiently, but now I think it past hope that you will give any heed to our case. I have now waited as long as my temper would hold out, and I must have whole-hearted counsel from you as to where this revenge is to be brought home."

Snorri asked what she chiefly had in her mind's eye.

Gudrun said, "It is my wish that all Olaf's sons should not go scatheless."

Snorri said he must forbid any onset on the men who were not only of the greatest account in the countryside, but also closely akin to those who stand nearest to back up the revenge; and it is high time already that these family feuds come to an end.

Gudrun said, "Then Lambi shall be set upon and slain; for then he, who is the most eager of them for evil, would be put out of the way."

Snorri said, "Lambi is guilty enough that he should be slain; but I do not think Bolli any the more revenged for that; for when at length peace should come to be settled, no such disparity between them would be acknowledged as ought to be due to Bolli when the manslaughters of both should come up for award."

Gudrun spoke, "It may be that we shall not get our right out of the men of Salmon-river-Dale, but some one shall pay dear for it, whatever dale he may dwell in. So we shall turn upon Thorstein the Black, for no one has taken a worse share in these matters than he."

Snorri spake, "Thorstein's guilt against you is the same as that of the other men who joined in the raid against Bolli, but did not wound him. But you leave such men to sit by in quiet on whom it seems to me revenge wrought would be revenge indeed, and who, moreover, did take the life of Bolli, such as was Helgi Hardbienson."

Gudrun said, "That is true, but I cannot be sure that, in that case, all these men against whom I have been stirring up enmity will sit quietly by doing nothing."

Snorri said, "I see a good way to hinder that. Lambi and Thorstein shall join the train of your sons, and that is a fitting ransom for those fellows, Lambi and Thorstein; but if they will not do this, then I shall not plead for them to be let off, whatever penalty you may be pleased to put upon them."

Gudrun spake: "How shall we set about getting these men that you have named to go on this journey?"

Snorri spake: "That is the business of them who are to be at the head of the journey."

Gudrun spake: "In this we must have your foresight as to who shall rule the journey and be the leader."

Then Snorri smiled and said, "You have chosen your own men for it."

Gudrun replied, "You are speaking of Thorgils."

Snorri said so it was.

Gudrun spake: "I have talked the matter over already with Thorgils, but now it is as good as all over, for he gave me the one choice, which I would not even look at. He did not back out of undertaking to avenge Bolli, if he could have me in marriage in return; but that is past all hope, so I cannot ask him to go this journey."

Snorri spoke: "On this I will give you a counsel, for I do not begrudge Thorgils this journey. You shall promise marriage to him, yet you shall do it in language of this double meaning, that of men in this land you will marry none other but Thorgils, and that shall be holden to, for Thorkell Eyjolfson is not, for the time being, in this land, but it is he whom I have in my mind's eye for this marriage."

Gudrun spake: "He will see through this trick."

Snorri answered, "Indeed he will not see through it, for Thorgils is better known for foolhardiness than wits. Make the covenant with but few men for witnesses, and let Halldor, his foster-brother, be there, but not Ornolf, for he has more wits, and lay the blame on me if this will not work out."

After that they parted their talk and each bade the other farewell, Snorri riding home, and Gudrun unto Thickshaw.

The next morning Gudrun rode from Thickshaw and her sons with her, and when they ride west along Shawstrand they see that men are riding after them. They ride on quickly and catch them up swiftly, and lo, there was Thorgils Hallason. They greeted each other well, and now ride on in the day all together, out to Holyfell.

Chapter 60
The Egging of Gudrun

A FEW NIGHTS AFTER Gudrun had come home she called her sons to her to have a talk with them in her orchard; and when they were come there they saw how there were lying out some linen clothes, a shirt and linen breeches, and they were much stained with blood.

Then spake Gudrun: "These same clothes you see here cry to you for your father's revenge. I will not say many words on this matter, for it is past hope that you will heed an egging-on by words alone if you bring not home to your minds such hints and reminders as these."

The brothers were much startled as this, and at what Gudrun had to say; but yet this way they made answer that they had been too young to seek for revenge without a leader; they knew not, they felt, how to frame a counsel for themselves or others either. "But we might well bear in mind what we have lost."

Gudrun said, "They would be likely to give more thought to horse-fights or sports."

After that they went away. The next night the brothers could not sleep. Thorgils got aware of this, and asked them what was the matter. They told him all the talk they had had with their mother, and this withal that they could no longer bear their grief or their mother's taunts.

"We will seek revenge," said Bolli, "now that we brothers have come to so ripe an age that men will be much after us if we do not take the matter in hand."

The next day Gudrun and Thorgils had a talk together, and Gudrun started speaking in this wise: "I am given to think, Thorgils, that my sons brook it ill to sit thus quietly on any longer without seeking revenge for their father's death. But what mostly has delayed the matter hitherto is that up to now I deemed Thorleik and Bolli too young to be busy in taking men's lives. But need enough there has been to call this to mind a good long time before this."

Thorgils answered, "There is no use in your talking this matter over with me, because you have given a flat denial to 'walking with me' (marrying me). But I am in just the same frame of mind as I have been before, when we have had talks about this matter. If I can marry you, I shall not think twice about killing either or both of the two who had most to do with the murder of Bolli."

Gudrun spoke: "I am given to think that to Thorleik no man seems as well fitted as you to be the leader if anything is to be done in the way of deeds of hardihood. Nor is it a matter to be hidden from you that the lads are minded to go for Helgi Hardbienson the 'Bareserk,' who sits at home in his house in Skorridale misdoubting himself of nothing."

Thorgils spake: "I never care whether he is called Helgi or by any other name, for neither in Helgi nor in any one else do I deem I have an over-match in strength to deal with. As far as I am concerned, the last word on this matter is now spoken if you promise before witnesses to marry me when, together with your sons, I have wreaked the revenge."

Gudrun said she would fulfil all she should agree to, even though such agreement were come to before few men to witness it. "And," said she, "this then we shall settle to have done."

Gudrun bade be called thither Halldor, Thorgils' foster-brother, and her own sons. Thorgils bade that Ornolf should also be with them. Gudrun said there was no need of that, "For I am more doubtful of Ornolf's faithfulness to you than I think you are yourself."

Thorgils told her to do as she liked.

Now the brothers come and meet Gudrun and Thorgils, Halldor being also at the parley with them. Gudrun now sets forth to them that "Thorgils has said he will be the leader in this raid against Helgi Hardbienson, together with my sons, for revenge of Bolli, and Thorgils has bargained in return for this undertaking to get me for wife. Now I avow, with you to witness, that I promise this to Thorgils, that of men in this land I shall marry none but him, and I do not purpose to go and marry in any other land."

Thorgils thought that this was binding enough, and did not see through it. And now they broke up their talk. This counsel is now fully settled that Thorgils must betake himself to this journey. He gets ready to leave Holyfell, and with him the sons of Gudrun, and they rode up into the Dales and first to the homestead at Tongue.

Chapter 61
Of Thorstein the Black and Lambi

THE NEXT LORD'S DAY a leet was held, and Thorgils rode thither with his company, Snorri Godi was not at the leet, but there was a great many people together.

During the day Thorgils fetched up Thorstein the Black for a talk with him, and said, "As you know, you were one in the onset by the sons of Olaf when Bolli was slain, and you have made no atonement for your guilt to his sons. Now although a long time is gone since those things befell, I think their mind has not given the slip to the men who were in that raid. Now, these brothers look in this light upon the matter, that it beseem them least, by reason of kinship, to seek revenge on the sons of Olaf; and so the brothers purpose to turn for revenge upon Helgi Hardbienson, for he gave Bolli his death-wound. So we ask this of you, Thorstein, that you join in this journey with the brothers, and thus purchase for yourself peace and good-will."

Thorstein replied, "It beseems me not at all to deal in treason with Helgi, my brother-in-law, and I would far rather purchase my peace with as much money as it would be to their honour to take."

Thorgils said, "I think it is but little to the mind of the brothers to do aught herein for their own gain; so you need not hide it away from yourself, Thorstein, that at your hands there lie two choices: either to betake yourself to this journey, or to undergo the harshest of treatments from them as soon as they may bring it about; and my will is, that you take this choice in spite of the ties that bind you to Helgi; for when men find themselves in such straits, each must look after himself."

Thorstein spake: "Will the same choice be given to more of the men who are charged with guilt by the sons of Bolli?"

Thorgils answered, "The same choice will be put to Lambi."

Thorstein said he would think better of it if he was not left the only one in this plight.

After that Thorgils called Lambi to come and meet him, and bade Thorstein listen to their talk.

He said, "I wish to talk over with you, Lambi, the same matter that I have set forth to Thorstein; to wit, what amends you are willing to make to the sons of Bolli for the charges of guilt which they have against you? For it has been told me as true that you wrought wounds on Bolli; but besides that, you are heavily guilt-beset, in that you urged it hard that Bolli should be slain; yet, next to the sons of Olaf, you were entitled to some excuse in the matter."

Then Lambi asked what he would be asked to do. Thorgils said the same choice would be put to him as to Thorstein, "to join with the brothers in this journey."

Lambi said, "This I think an evil price of peace and a dastardly one, and I have no mind for this journey."

Then said Thorstein, "It is not the only thing open to view, Lambi, to cut so quickly away from this journey; for in this matter great men are concerned, men of much worth, moreover, who deem that they have long had to put up with an unfair lot in life. It is also told me of Bolli's sons that they are likely to grow into men of high mettle, and that they are exceeding masterful; but the wrong they have to wreak is great. We cannot think of escaping from making some amends after such awful deeds. I shall be the most open to people's reproaches for this by reason of my alliance with Helgi. But I think most people are given to 'setting all aside for life,' and the trouble on hand that presses hardest must first be thrust out of the way."

Lambi said, "It is easy to see what you urge to be done, Thorstein; and I think it well befitting that you have your own way in this matter, if you think that is the only way you see open, for ours has been a long partnership in great troubles. But I will have this understood if I do go into this business, that my kinsmen, the sons of Olaf, shall be left in peace if the revenge on Helgi shall be carried out."

Thorgils agreed to this on behalf of the brothers. So now it was settled that Lambi and Thorstein should betake themselves to the journey with Thorgils; and they bespoke it between them that they should come early on the third day (Tuesday) to Tongue, in Hord-Dale. After that they parted. Thorgils rode home that evening to Tongue.

Now passes on the time within which it was bespoken they should come to Tongue. In the morning of the third day (Tuesday), before sunrise, Thorstein and Lambi came to Tongue, and Thorgils gave them a cheerful welcome.

Chapter 62
Thorgils and his Followers Leave Home

THORGILS GOT HIMSELF ready to leave home, and they all rode up along Hord-Dale, ten of them together. There Thorgils Hallason was the leader of the band. In that train the sons of Bolli, Thorleik and Bolli, and Thord the Cat, their brother, was the fourth, the fifth was Thorstein the Black, the sixth Lambi, the seventh and eighth Haldor and Ornolf, the ninth Svein, and the tenth Hunbogi. Those last were the sons of Alf o' Dales.

They rode on their way up to Sweeping-Pass, and across Long-waterdale, and then right across Burgfirth. They rode across North-river at Isleford, but across White-river at Bankford, a short way down from the homestead of By. Then they rode over Reekdale, and over the neck of land to Skorradale, and so up through the wood in the neighbourhood of the farmstead of Water-Nook, where they got off their horses, as it was very late in the evening. The homestead of Water-Nook stands a short way from the lake on the south side of the river.

Thorgils said to his followers that they must tarry there over night, "and I will go to the house and spy and see if Helgi be at home. I am told Helgi has at most times very few men with him, but that he is of all men the wariest of himself, and sleeps on a strongly made lock-bed."

Thorgils' followers bade him follow his own foresight. Thorgils now changed his clothes, and took off his blue cloak, and slipped on a grey foul-weather overall. He went home to the house.

When he was come near to the home-field fence he saw a man coming to meet him, and when they met Thorgils said, "You will think my questions strange, comrade, but whose am I come to in this countryside, and what is the name of this dwelling, and who lives here?"

The man answered, "You must be indeed a wondrous fool and wit-bereft if you have not heard Helgi Hardbienson spoken of, the bravest of warriors, and a great man withal."

Thorgils next asked how far Helgi took kindly to unknown people coming to see him, such as were in great need of help. He replied, "In that matter, if truth is told, only good can be said of Helgi, for he is the most large-hearted of men, not only in giving harbour to comers, but also in all his high conduct otherwise."

"Is Helgi at home now?" asked Thorgils; "I should like to ask him to take me in."

The other then asks what matters he had on his hands.

Thorgils answered, "I was outlawed this summer at the Thing, and I want to seek for myself the help of some such man as is a mighty one of his hands and ways, Thorgils and Helgi's servant and I will in return offer my fellowship and service. So now you take me home to the house to see Helgi."

"I can do that very well, to show you home," he said, "for you will be welcome to quarters for the night, but you will not see Helgi, for he is not at home."

Then Thorgils asked where he was.

The man answered, "He is at his out-dairy called Sarp."

Thorgils asked where that was, and what men were with him. He said his son Hardbien was there, and two other men, both outlaws, whom he had taken in to shelter. Thorgils bade him show the nearest way to the dairy, "for I want to meet Helgi at once, when I can get to him and plead my errand to him."

The house-carle did so and showed him the way, and after that they parted. Thorgils returned to the wood to his companions, and told them what he had found out about Helgi. "We must tarry here through the night, and not go to the dairy till tomorrow morning."

They did as he ordained, and in the morning Thorgils and his band rode up through the wood till they were within a short way from the dairy. Then Thorgils bade them get off their horses and eat their morning meal, and so they did, and kept them for a while.

Chapter 63
The Description of His Enemies Brought to Helgi

NOW WE MUST TELL what happened at the dairy where Helgi was, and with him the men that were named before.

In the morning Helgi told his shepherd to go through the woods in the neighbourhood of the dairy and look out for people passing, and take heed of whatever else he saw, to tell news of, "for my dreams have gone heavily tonight."

The lad went even as Helgi told him. He was away awhile, and when he came back Helgi asked what he had seen to tell tidings of.

He answered, "I have seen what I think is stuff for tidings."

Helgi asked what that was. He said he had seen men, "and none so few either, and I think they must have come from beyond this countryside."

Helgi spoke: "Where were they when you saw them, and what were they doing, or did you take heed of the manner of raiment, or their looks?"

He answered, "I was not so much taken aback at the sight as not to mind those matters, for I knew you would ask about them."

He also said they were but short away from the dairy, and were eating their morning meal. Helgi asked if they sat in a ring or side by side in a line. He said they sat in a ring, on their saddles.

Helgi said, "Tell me now of their looks, and I will see if I can guess from what they looked like who the men may be."

The lad said, "There sat a man in a stained saddle, in a blue cloak. He was great of growth, and valiant-looking; he was bald in front and somewhat 'tooth-bare.'"

Helgi said, "I know that man clearly from your tale. There you have seen Thorgils Hallason, from west out of Hord-Dale. I wonder what he wants with us, the hero."

The lad spoke: "Next to him sat a man in a gilded saddle; he had on a scarlet kirtle, and a gold ring on his arm, and a gold-embroidered fillet was tied round his head. This man had yellow hair, waving down over his shoulders; he was fair of hue, with a knot on his nose, which was somewhat turned up at the tip, with very fine eyes – blue-eyed and swift-eyed, and with a glance somewhat restless, broad-browed and full-cheeked; he had his hair cut across his forehead. He was well grown as to breadth of shoulders and depth of chest. He had very beautiful hands, and strong-looking arms. All his bearing was courteous, and, in a word, I have never seen a man so altogether doughty-looking. He was a young-looking man too, for his lips had grown no beard, but it seemed to me he was aged by grief."

Then Helgi answers: "You have paid a careful heed, indeed, to this man, and of much account he must needs be; yet this man, I think, I have never seen, so I must make a guess at it who he is. There, I think, must have been Bolli Bollison, for I am told he has in him the makings of a man."

Then the lad went on: "Next there sat a man on an enamelled saddle in a yellow green kirtle; he had a great finger ring on his hand. This man was most goodly to behold, and must still be young of age; his hair was auburn and most comely, and in every way he was most courtly."

Helgi answers, "I think I know who this man is, of whom you have now been telling. He must be Thorleik Bollison, and a sharp and mindful man you are."

The lad said again, "Next sat a young man; he was in a blue kirtle and black breeches, and his tunic tucked into them. This man was straight-faced, light of hair, with a goodly-featured face, slender and graceful."

Helgi answered, "I know that man, for I must have seen him, though at a time when he was quite young; for it must be Thord Thordson, fosterling of Snorri the Priest. And a very courtly band they have, the Westfirthers. What is there yet to tell?"

Then the lad said, "There sat a man on a Scotch saddle, hoary of beard and very sallow of hue, with black curly hair, somewhat unsightly and yet warrior like; he had on a grey pleated cape."

Helgi said, "I clearly see who that man is; there is Lambi, the son of Thorbjorn, from Salmon-river-Dale; but I cannot think why he should be in the train of these brothers."

The lad spake: "There sat a man on a pommelled saddle, and had on a blue cloak for an overall, with a silver ring on his arm; he was a farmer-looking sort of man and past the prime of life, with dark auburn long curly hair, and scars about his face."

"Now the tale grows worse by much," said Helgi, "for there you must have seen Thorstein the Black, my brother-in-law; and a wondrous thing indeed I deem it, that he should be in this journey, nor would I ever offer him such a home-raid. But what more is there still to tell?"

He answered, "Next there sat two men like each other to look upon, and might have been of middle age; most brisk they looked, red of hair, freckled of face, yet goodly to behold." Helgi said, "I can clearly understand who those men are. There are the sons of Armod, foster-brothers of Thorgils, Halldor and Ornolf. And a very trustworthy fellow you are. But have you now told the tale of all the men you saw?"

He answered, "I have but little to add now. Next there sat a man and looked out of the circle; he was in a plate-corselet and had a steel cap on his head, with a brim a hand's breadth wide; he bore a shining axe on his shoulder, the edge of which must have measured an ell in length. This man was dark of hue, black-eyed, and most viking like."

Helgi answered, "I clearly know this man from your tale. There has been Hunbogi the Strong, son of Alf o' Dales. But what I find so hard to make out is, what they want journeying with such a very picked company."

The lad spoke again: "And still there sat a man next to this strong-looking one, dark auburn of hair, thick-faced and red-faced, heavy of brow, of a tall middle size."

Helgi said, "You need not tell the tale further, there must have been Svein, son of Alf o' Dales, brother of Hunbogi. Now it would be as well not to stand shiftless in the face of these men; for near to my mind's foreboding it is, that they are minded to have a meeting with me or ever they leave this countryside; moreover, in this train there are men who would hold that it would have been but due and meet, though this our meeting should have taken a good long time before this.

"Now all the women who are in the dairy slip on quickly men's dress and take the horses that are about the dairy and ride as quickly as possible to the winter dwelling; it may be that those who are besetting us about will not know whether men or women be riding there; they need give us only a short respite till we bring men together here, and then it is not so certain on which side the outlook will be most hopeful."

The women now rode off, four together.

Thorgils misdoubts him lest news of their coming may have reached Helgi, and so bade the others take their horses and ride after them at their swiftest, and so they did, but before they mounted a man came riding up to them openly in all men's sight. He was small of growth and all on the alert, wondrously swift of glance and had a lively horse. This man greeted Thorgils in a familiar manner, and Thorgils asked him his name and family and also whence he had come. He said his name was Hrapp, and he was from Broadfirth on his mother's side. "And then I grew up, and I bear the name of Fight-Hrapp, with the name follows that I am nowise an easy one to deal with, albeit I am small of growth; but I am a southlander on my father's side, and have tarried in the south for some winters. Now this is a lucky chance, Thorgils, I have happened of you here, for I was minded to come and see you anyhow, even though I should find it a business somewhat hard to follow up. I have a trouble on hand; I have fallen out with my master, and have had from him a treatment none of the best; but it goes with the name, that I will stand no man such shameful mishandling, so I made an outset at him, but I guess I wounded him little or not at all, for I did not wait long enough to see for myself, but thought myself safe when I got on to the back of this nag, which I took from the goodman."

Hrapp says much, but asks for few things; yet soon he got to know that they were minded to set on Helgi, and that pleased him very much, and he said they would not have to look for him behind.

Chapter 64
The Death of Helgi, AD 1019

THORGILS AND HIS FOLLOWERS, as soon as they were on horseback, set off at a hard ride, and rode now out of the wood. They saw four men riding away from the dairy, and they rode very fast too. Seeing this, some of Thorgils' companions said they had better ride after them at their swiftest.

Then said Thorleik Bollison, "We will just go to the dairy and see what men are there, for I think it less likely that these be Helgi and his followers. It seems to me that those are only women."

A good many of them gainsaid this. Thorgils said that Thorleik should rule in the matter, for he knew that he was a very far-sighted man. They now turned to the dairy. Hrapp rode first, shaking the spear-stick he carried in his hand, and thrusting it forward in front of himself, and saying now was high time to try one's self.

Helgi and his followers were not aware of anything till Thorgils and his company had surrounded the dairy. Helgi and his men shut the door, and seized their weapons.

Hrapp leapt forthwith upon the roof of the dairy, and asked if old Reynard was in.

Helgi answered, "You will come to take for granted that he who is here within is somewhat hurtful, and will know how to bite near the warren."

And forthwith Helgi thrust his spear out through the window and through Hrapp, so that he fell dead to earth from the spear.

Thorgils bade the others go heedfully and beware of mishaps, "for we have plenty of means wherewith to get the dairy into our power, and to overcome Helgi, placed as he is now, for I am given to think that here but few men are gathered together."

The dairy was rigged over one roof-beam, resting on two gables so that the ends of the beam stuck out beyond each gable; there was a single turf thatch on the house, which had not yet grown together. Then Thorgils told some of his men to go to the beam ends, and pull them so hard that either the beam should break or else the rafters should slip in off it, but others were to guard the door lest those within should try and get out.

Five they were, Helgi and his within the dairy – Hardbien, his son, to wit, he was twelve years old – his shepherd and two other men, who had come to him that summer, being outlaws – one called Thorgils, and the other Eyolf.

Thorstein the Black and Svein, son of Alf o' Dales, stood before the door. The rest of the company were tearing the roof off the dairy. Hunbogi the Strong and the sons of Armod took one end of the beam, Thorgils, Lambi, and Gudrun's sons the other end. They now pull hard at the beam till it broke asunder in the middle; just at this Hardbien thrust a halberd out through where the door was broken, and the thrust struck the steel cap of Thorstein the Black and stuck in his forehead, and that was a very great wound. Then Thorstein said, as was true, that there were men before them.

Next Helgi leapt so boldly out of the door so that those nearest shrunk aback. Thorgils was standing near, and struck after him with a sword, and caught him on the shoulder and made a great wound. Helgi turned to meet him, and had a wood-axe in his hand, and said, "Still the old one will dare to look at and face weapons," and therewith he flung the axe at Thorgils, and the axe struck his foot, and a great wound that was.

And when Bolli saw this he leapt forward at Helgi with Footbiter in his hand, and thrust Helgi through with it, and that was his death-blow.

Helgi's followers leapt out of the dairy forthwith, and Hardbien with them. Thorleik Bollison turned against Eyolf, who was a strong man. Thorleik struck him with his sword, and it caught him on the leg above the knee and cut off his leg, and he fell to earth dead.

Hunbogi the Strong went to meet Thorgils, and dealt a blow at him with an axe, and it struck the back of him, and cut him asunder in the middle.

Thord Cat was standing near where Hardbien leapt out, and was going to set upon him straightway, but Bolli rushed forward when he saw it, and bade no harm be done to Hardbien. "No man shall do a dastard's work here, and Hardbien shall have life and limbs spared."

Helgi had another son named Skorri. He was brought up at Gugland in Reekdale the southernmost.

Chapter 65
Of Gudrun's Deceit

AFTER THESE DEEDS Thorgils and his band rode away over the neck to Reekdale, where they declared these manslaughters on their hands. Then they rode the same way eastward as they had ridden from the west, and did not stop their journey till they came to Hord-Dale. They now told the tidings of what had happened in their journey, which became most famous, for it was thought a great deed to have felled such a hero as was Helgi.

Thorgils thanked his men well for the journey, and the sons of Bolli did the same. And now the men part who had been in Thorgils' train; Lambi rode west to Salmon-river-Dale, and came first to Herdholt and told his kinsmen most carefully the tidings of what had happened in Skorradale. They were very ill-pleased with his journey and laid heavy reproaches upon him, saying he had shown himself much more of the stock of Thorbjorn "Skrjup" than of that of Myrkjartan, the Irish king. Lambi was very angry at their talk, and said they knew but little of good manners in overwhelming him with reproaches, "for I have dragged you out of death," says he. After that they exchanged but few words, for both sides were yet more fulfilled of ill-will than before. Lambi now rode home to his manor.

Thorgils Hallason rode out to Holyfell, and with him the sons of Gudrun and his foster-brothers Halldor and Ornolf. They came late in the evening to Holyfell, when all men were in bed. Gudrun rose up and bade the household get up and wait upon them. She went into the guest-chamber and greeted Thorgils and all the others, and asked for tidings.

Thorgils returned Gudrun's greeting; he had laid aside his cloak and his weapons as well, and sat then up against the pillars. Thorgils had on a red-brown kirtle, and had round his waist a broad silver belt. Gudrun sat down on the bench by him. Then Thorgils said this stave:

> *"To Helgi's home a raid we led,*
> *Gave ravens corpse-repast to swallow,*
> *We dyed shield-wands with blood all red,*
> *As Thorleik's lead our band did follow.*
> *And at our hands there perished three*
> *Keen helmet-stems, accounted truly*
> *As worthies of the folk – and we*
> *Claim Bolli now's avenged full duly."*

Gudrun asked them most carefully for the tidings of what had happened on their journey. Thorgils told her all she wished. Gudrun said the journey had been most stirringly carried out, and bade them have her thanks for it.

After that food was set before them, and after they had eaten they were shown to bed, and slept the rest of the night.

The next day Thorgils went to talk to Gudrun, and said, "Now the matter stands thus, as you know, Gudrun, that I have brought to an end the journey you bade me undertake, and I must claim that, in a full manly wise, that matter has been turned out of hand; you will also call to mind what you promised me in return, and I think I am now entitled to that prize."

Then Gudrun said, "It is not such a long time since we last talked together that I should have forgotten what we said, and my only aim is to hold to all I agreed to as concerning you. Or what does your mind tell you as to how matters were bespoken between us?"

Thorgils said she must remember that, and Gudrun answered, "I think I said that of men within this land I would marry none but you; or have you aught to say against that?"

Thorgils said she was right.

"That is well then," said Gudrun, "that our memory should be one and the same on this matter. And I will not put it off from you any longer, that I am minded to think that it is not fated to me to be your wife. Yet I deem that I fulfil to you all uttered words, though I marry Thorkell Eyjolfson, who at present is not in this land."

Then Thorgils said, and flushed up very much, "Clearly I do see from whence that chill wave comes running, and from thence cold counsels have always come to me. I know that this is the counsel of Snorri the Priest."

Thorgils sprang up from this talk and was very angry, and went to his followers and said he would ride away.

Thorleik disliked very much that things should have taken such a turn as to go against Thorgils' will; but Bolli was at one with his mother's will herein. Gudrun said she would give Thorgils some good gifts and soften him by that means, but Thorleik said that would be of no use, "for Thorgils is far too high-mettled a man to stoop to trifles in a matter of this sort."

Gudrun said in that case he must console himself as best he could at home. After this Thorgils rode from Holyfell with his foster-brothers. He got home to Tongue to his manor mightily ill at ease over his lot.

Chapter 66
Osvif and Gest Die

THAT WINTER Osvif fell ill and died, and a great loss that was deemed, for he had been the greatest of sages. Osvif was buried at Holyfell, for Gudrun had had a church built there.

That same winter Gest Oddliefson fell ill, and as the sickness grew heavy on him, he called to him Thord the Low, his son, and said, "My mind forebodes me that this sickness will put an end to our living together. I wish my body to be carried to Holyfell, for that will be the greatest place about these countrysides, for I have often seen a light burning there."

Thereupon Gest died. The winter had been very cold, and there was much ice about, and Broadfirth was laid under ice so far out that no ship could get over it from Bardistrand. Gest's body lay in state two nights at Hegi, and that very night there sprang up such a gale that all the ice was drawn away from the land, and the next day the weather was fair and still. Then Thord took a ship and put Gest's body on board, and went south across Broadfirth that day, and came in the evening to Holyfell. Thord had a good welcome there, and stayed there through the night.

In the morning Gest's body was buried, and he and Osvif rested in one grave. So Gest's soothsaying was fulfilled, in that now it was shorter between them than at the time when one dwelt at Bardistrand and the other in Saelingsdale.

Thord the Low then went home as soon as he was ready. That next night a wild storm arose, and drove the ice on to the land again, where it held on long through the winter, so that there was no going about in boats. Men thought this most marvellous, that the weather had allowed Gest's body to be taken across when there was no crossing before nor afterwards during the winter.

Chapter 67
The Death of Thorgils Hallason, AD 1020

THORARIN WAS THE NAME of a man who lived at Longdale: he was a chieftain, but not a mighty one. His son was named Audgisl, and was a nimble sort of a man.

Thorgils Hallason took the chieftainship from them both, father and son. Audgisl went to see Snorri Godi, and told him of this unfairness, and asked him to help. Snorri answered only by fair words, and belittled the whole affair; but answered, "Now that Halla's-grig is getting too forward and swaggering. Will Thorgils then happen on no man that will not give in to him in everything? No doubt he is a big man and doughty, but men as good as he is have also been sent to Hel."

And when Audgisl went away Snorri gave him an inlaid axe.

The next spring Thorgils Hallason and Thorstein the Black went south to Burgfirth, and offered atonement to the sons of Helgi and his other kinsmen, and they came to terms of peace on the matter, and fair honour was done (to Helgi's side). Thorstein paid two parts of the atonement for the manslaughter, and the third part Thorgils was to pay, payment being due at the Thing.

In the summer Thorgils rode to the Thing, but when he and his men came to the lava field by Thingvellir, they saw a woman coming to meet them, and a mighty big one she was. Thorgils rode up to her, but she turned aside, and said this:

> *"Take care If you go forward,*
> *And be wary Of Snorri's wiles,*
> *No one can escape,*
> *For so wise is Snorri."*

And after that she went her way.

Then Thorgils said, "It has seldom happened so before, when luck was with me, that you were leaving the Thing when I was riding to it."

He now rode to the Thing and to his own booth. And through the early part the Thing was quiet. It happened one day during the Thing that folk's clothes were hung out to dry. Thorgils had a blue hooded cloak, which was spread out on the booth wall, and men heard the cloak say thus:

> *"Hanging wet on the wall,*
> *A hooded cloak knows a braid [trick];*
> *I do not say he does not know two,*
> *He has been lately washed."*

This was thought a most marvellous thing.

The next day Thorgils went west over the river to pay the money to the sons of Helgi. He sat down on the lava above the booths, and with him was his foster-brother Halldor and sundry more of them were there together. The sons of Helgi came to the meeting. Thorgils now began to count out the money.

Audgisl Thorarinson came near, and when Thorgils had counted ten Audgisl struck at him, and all thought they heard the head say eleven as it flew off the neck. Audgisl ran to the booth of the Waterfirthers and Halldor rushed after him and struck him his death-blow in the door of the booth.

These tidings came to the booth of Snorri Godi how Thorgils was slain.

Snorri said, "You must be mistaken; it must be that Thorgils Hallason has slain some one."

The man replied, "Why, the head flew off his trunk."

"Then perhaps it is time," said Snorri.

This manslaughter was peacefully atoned, as is told in the Saga of Thorgils Hallason.

Chapter 68
Gudrun's Marriage with Thorkell Eyjolfson

THE SAME SUMMER that Thorgils Hallason was killed a ship came to Bjorn's-haven. It belonged to Thorkell Eyjolfson. He was by then such a rich man that he had two merchant ships on voyages. The other ship came to Ramfirth to Board-Eyr; they were both laden with timber.

When Snorri heard of the coming of Thorkell he rode at once to where the ship was. Thorkell gave him a most blithe welcome; he had a great deal of drink with him in his ship, and right unstintedly it was served, and many things they found to talk about. Snorri asked tidings of Norway, and Thorkell told him everything well and truthfully. Snorri told in return the tidings of all that had happened here while Thorkell had been away.

"Now it seems to me," said Snorri, "you had better follow the counsel I set forth to you before you went abroad, and should give up voyaging about and settle down in quiet, and get for yourself the same woman to wife of whom we spoke then."

Thorkell replied, "I understand what you are driving at; everything we bespoke then is still uppermost in my mind, for indeed I begrudge me not the noblest of matches could it but be brought about."

Snorri spake, "I am most willing and ready to back that matter up on your behalf, seeing that now we are rid of both the things that seemed to you the most troublesome to overcome, if you were to get Gudrun for wife at all, in that Bolli is revenged and Thorgils is out of the way."

Thorkell said, "Your counsels go very deep, Snorri, and into this affair I go heart and soul."

Snorri stayed in the ship several nights, and then they took a ten-oared boat that floated alongside of the merchant ship and got ready with five-and-twenty men, and went to Holyfell.

Gudrun gave an exceeding affectionate welcome to Snorri, and a most goodly cheer they had; and when they had been there one night Snorri called Gudrun to talk to him, and spake, "Matters have come to this, that I have undertaken this journey for my friend Thorkell, Eyjolf's son, and he has now come here, as you see, and his errand hither is to set forth the wooing of you. Thorkell is a man of noble degree. You know yourself all about his race and doings in life, nor is he short of wealth either. To my mind, he is now the one man west about here who is most likely to become a chieftain, if to that end he will put himself forward. Thorkell is held in great esteem when he is out there, but by much is he more honoured when he is in Norway in the train of titled men."

Then answers Gudrun: "My sons Thorleik and Bolli must have most to say in this matter; but you, Snorri, are the third man on whom I shall most rely for counsels in matters by which I set a great store, for you have long been a wholesome guide to me."

Snorri said he deemed it a clear case that Thorkell must not be turned off. Thereupon Snorri had the sons of Gudrun called in, and sets forth the matter to them, laying down how great an help Thorkell might afford them by reason of his wealth and wise foresight; and smoothly he framed his speech on this matter.

Then Bolli answered: "My mother will know how most clearly to see through this matter, and herein I shall be of one mind with her own will. But, to be sure, we shall deem it wise to set much store by your pleading this matter, Snorri, for you have done to us mightily well in many things."

Then Gudrun spake: "In this matter we will lean most on Snorri's foresight, for to us your counsels have been wholesome."

Snorri urged the matter on by every word he spoke, and the counsel taken was, that Gudrun and Thorkell should be joined in marriage. Snorri offered to have the wedding at his house; and Thorkell, liking that well, said: "I am not short of means, and I am ready to furnish them in whatever measure you please."

Then Gudrun spake: "It is my wish that the feast be held here at Holyfell. I do not blench at standing the cost of it, nor shall I call upon Thorkell or any one else to trouble themselves about this matter."

"Often, indeed, you show, Gudrun," said Snorri, "that you are the most high-mettled of women."

So this was now settled that the wedding should take place when it lacked six weeks of summer. At matters thus settled Snorri and Thorkell went away, Snorri going home and Thorkell to his ship, and he spent the summer, turn and turn about, at Tongue or at his ship.

Time now wore on towards the wedding feast. Gudrun made great preparation with much ingatherings. Snorri came to the feast together with Thorkell, and they brought with them well-nigh sixty men, and a very picked company that was, for most of the men were in dyed raiments. Gudrun had well-nigh a hundred and twenty first-bidden guests. The brothers Bolli and Thorleik, with the first-bidden guests, went to meet Snorri and his train; and to him and his fellowship was given a right cheery welcome, and their horses are taken in hand, as well as their clothes. They were shown into the guest-chamber, and Thorkell and Snorri and their followers took seats on the bench that was the upper one, and Gudrun's guests sat on the lower.

Chapter 69
The Quarrel About Gunnar at the Feast

THAT AUTUMN GUNNAR, the slayer of Thridrandi, had been sent to Gudrun for 'trust and keep,' and she had taken him in, his name being kept secret. Gunnar was outlawed because of the slaying of Thridrandi, Geitir's son, as is told in the Niard-wickers' Saga. He went about much 'with a hidden head,' for that many great men had their eyes upon him.

The first evening of the feast, when men went to wash, a big man was standing by the water; he was broad of shoulder and wide of chest, and this man had a hat on his head. Thorkell asked who he was. He named himself as it seemed best to him.

Thorkell says: "I think you are not speaking the truth; going by what the tale tells you would seem more like to Gunnar, the slayer of Thridrandi. And if you are so great a hero as other men say, you will not keep hidden your name."

Then said Gunnar: "You speak most eagerly on this matter; and, truth to tell, I think I have no need to hide myself from you. You have rightly named your man; but then, what have you chiefly bethought yourself of having done to me?"

Thorkell said he would like that he should soon know it, and spake to his men, ordering them to lay hands on him.

Gudrun sat on the dais at the upper end of the hall, together with other women all becoifed with white linen, and when she got aware of this she rises up from the bridal bench and calls on her men to lend Gunnar help, and told them to give quarter to no man who should show any doubtful behaviour. Gudrun had the greatest number of followers, and what never was meant to happen seemed like to befall.

Snorri Godi went between both sides and bade them allay this storm. "The one thing clearly to be done by you, Thorkell, is not to push things on so hotly; and now you can see what a stirring woman Gudrun is, as she overrules both of us together."

Thorkell said he had promised his namesake, Thorleik Geitir's son, that he would kill Gunnar if he came into the countrysides of the west.

"And he is my greatest friend," Snorri spake. "You are much more in duty bound to act as we wish; and for yourself, it is a matter of the greatest importance, for you will never find such another woman as Gudrun, however far you may seek."

And because of Snorri's reasoning, and seeing that he spoke the truth, Thorkell quieted down, and Gunnar was sent away that evening.

The feast now went forward well and bravely, and when it was over the guests got ready to go away. Thorkell gave to Snorri very rich gifts, and the same to all the chief men. Snorri asked Bolli Bollison to go home with him, and to live with him as long as he liked. Bolli accepted this with thanks, and rides home to Tongue.

Thorkell now settled down at Holyfell, and took in hand the affairs of the household, and it was soon seen that he was no worse a hand at that than at trade-voyaging. He had the hall pulled down in the autumn and a new one built, which was finished when the winter set in, and was both large and lofty.

Between Gudrun and Thorkell dear love now grew up, and so the winter passed on.

In the spring Gudrun asked how Thorkell was minded to look out for Gunnar the slayer of Thridrandi. He said that Gudrun had better take the management of that matter, "for you have taken it so hard in hand, that you will put up with nothing but that he be sent away with honour."

Gudrun said he guessed aright: "I wish you to give him a ship, and therewithal such things as he cannot do without."

Thorkell said and smiled, "You think nothing small on most matters, Gudrun, and would be ill served if you had a mean-minded man for a husband; nor has that ever been your heart's aim. Well, this shall be done after your own will" – and carried out it was.

Gunnar took the gifts most gratefully. "I shall never be so 'long-armed' as to be able to repay all this great honour you are doing to me," he said.

Gunnar now went abroad and came to Norway, and then went to his own estates. Gunnar was exceeding wealthy, most great-hearted, and a good and true man withal.

Chapter 70
Thorleik Goes to Norway

THORKELL EYJOLFSON BECAME a great chieftain; he laid himself out much for friendships and honours. He was a masterful man within his own countryside, and busied himself much about law-suits; yet of his pleadings at court there is no tale to tell here. Thorkell was the richest man in Broadfirth during his lifetime next after Snorri.

Thorkell kept his house in good order. He had all the houses at Holyfell rebuilt large and strong. He also had the ground of a church marked out, and gave it out that he had made up his mind to go abroad and fetch timber for the building of his church.

Thorkell and Gudrun had a son who was called Gellir; he looked early most likely to turn out well.

Bolli Bollison spent his time turn and turn about at Tongue or Holyfell, and Snorri was very fond of him. Thorleik his brother lived at Holyfell. These brothers were both tall and most doughty looking, Bolli being the foremost in all things.

Thorkell was kind to his stepsons, and Gudrun loved Bolli most of all her children. He was now sixteen, and Thorleik twenty years old.

So, once on a time, Thorleik came to talk to his stepfather and his mother, and said he wished to go abroad. "I am quite tired of sitting at home like a woman, and I wish that means to travel should be furnished to me."

Thorkell said, "I do not think I have done against you two brothers in anything since our alliance began. Now, I think it is the most natural thing that you should yearn to get to know the customs of other men, for I know you will be counted a brisk man wheresoever you may come among doughty men."

Thorleik said he did not want much money, "for it is uncertain how I may look after matters, being young and in many ways of an unsettled mind."

Thorkell bade him have as much as he wanted.

After that Thorkell bought for Thorleik a share in a ship that stood up in Daymeal-Ness, and saw him off to his ship, and fitted him well out with all things from home. Thorleik journeyed abroad that summer. The ship arrived in Norway. The lord over the land then was King Olaf the Holy. Thorleik went forthwith to see King Olaf, who gave him a good welcome; he knew Thorleik from his kindred, and so asked him to stay with him. Thorleik accepted with thanks, and stayed with the king that winter and became one of his guard, and the king held him in honour. Thorleik was thought the briskest of men, and he stayed on with King Olaf for several months.

Now we must tell of Bolli Bollison. The spring when he was eighteen years old he spoke to his stepfather and his mother, and said that he wished they would hand him out his father's portion. Gudrun asked him what he had set his mind on doing, since he asked them to give him this money.

Bolli answered, "It is my wish that a woman be wooed on my behalf, and I wish," said Bolli, "that you, Thorkell, be my spokesman and carry this through."

Thorkell asked what woman it was Bolli wished to woo.

Bolli answered, "The woman's name is Thordis, and she is the daughter of Snorri the Priest; she is the woman I have most at heart to marry; I shall be in no hurry to marry if I do not get this one for wife. And I set a very great store by this matter being carried out."

Thorkell answered, "My help is quite welcome to you, my son, if you think that if I follow up this matter much weight lies thereon. I think the matter will be easily got over with Snorri, for he will know well enough how to see that a fair offer is made him by such as you."

Gudrun said, "I will say at once, Thorkell, that I will let spare nothing so that Bolli may but have the match that pleases him, and that for two reasons, first, that I love him most, and then he has been the most whole-hearted of my children in doing my will."

Thorkell gave it out that he was minded to furnish Bolli off handsomely. "It is what for many reasons is due to him, and I know, withal, that in Bolli a good husband will be purchased."

A little while after Thorkell and Bolli went with a good many followers to Tongue. Snorri gave to them a kind and blithe welcome, and they were treated to the very best of cheers at Snorri's hands. Thordis, the daughter of Snorri, was at home with her father; she was a woman both goodly and of great parts.

When they had been a few nights at Tongue Thorkell broached the wooing, bespeaking on behalf of Bolli an alliance with Snorri by marriage with Thordis, his daughter.

Snorri answers, "It is well you come here on this errand; it is what I might have looked for from you. I will answer the matter well, for I think Bolli one of the most hopeful of men, and that woman I deem well given in marriage who is given in marriage to him. It will, however, tell most in this matter, how far this is to Thordis' own mind; for she shall marry such a man only on whom she sets her heart."

This matter coming before Thordis she answered suchwise as that therein she would lean on the foresight of her father, saying she would sooner marry Bolli, a man from within her own countryside, than a stranger from farther away. And when Snorri found that it was not against her wish to go with Bolli, the affair was settled and the betrothal took place. Snorri was to have the feast at his house about the middle of summer.

With that Thorkell and Bolli rode home to Holyfell, and Bolli now stayed at home till the time of the wedding-feast. Then Thorkell and Bolli array themselves to leave home, and with them all the men who were set apart therefor, and a crowded company and the bravest band that was. They then rode on their way and came to Tongue, and had a right hearty welcome there. There were great numbers there, and the feast was of the noblest, and when the feast comes to an end the guests get ready to depart. Snorri gave honourable gifts to Thorkell, yea and to both of them, him and Gudrun, and the same to his other friends and relations. And now each one of those who had gone to the feast rode to his own home.

Bolli abode at Tongue, and between him and Thordis dear love sprang speedily up. Snorri did all he could to entertain Bolli well, and to him he was even kinder than to his own children. Bolli received all this gratefully, and remained at Tongue that year in great favour. The next summer a ship came to White-river. One-half of the ship belonged to Thorleik Bollison and the other half of it belonged to some Norwegian man. When Bolli heard of the coming of his brother he rode south to Burgfirth and to the ship. The brothers greeted each other joyfully.

Bolli stayed there for several nights, and then both brothers ride together west to Holyfell; Thorkell takes them in with the greatest blitheness, as did also Gudrun, and they invited Thorleik to stay with them for the winter, and that he took with thanks. Thorleik tarried at Holyfell awhile, and then he rode to White-river and lets his ship be beached and his goods be brought to the West. Thorleik had had good luck with him both as to wealth and honours, for that he had become the henchman of that noblest of lords, King Olaf.

He now stayed at Holyfell through the winter, while Bolli tarried at Tongue.

Chapter 71
The Peace between the Sons of Bolli and the Sons of Olaf, AD 1026

THAT WINTER the brothers would always be meeting, having talks together, and took no pleasure in games or any other pastime; and one time, when Thorleik was at Tongue, the brothers talked day and night together. Snorri then thought he knew that they must be taking counsel together on some very great matter, so he went and joined the talk of the brothers. They greeted him well, but dropped their talk forthwith.

He took their greeting well; and presently Snorri spoke: "What are you taking counsels about so that ye heed neither sleep nor meat?"

Bolli answers: "This is no framing of counsels, for that talk is one of but little mark which we talk together."

Now Snorri found that they wanted to hide from him all that was in their minds, yet misdoubted him, that they must be talking chiefly of things from which great troubles might arise, in case they should be carried out. He (Snorri) spoke to them: "This I misdoubt me now, that it be neither a vain thing nor a matter of jest you are talking about for such long hours together, and I hold you quite excused, even if such should be the case. Now, be so good as to tell it me and not to hide it away from me. We shall not, when gathered all together, be worse able to take counsel in this matter, for that I shall nowhere stand in the way of anything going forward whereby your honour grows the greater."

Thorleik thought Snorri had taken up their case in a kindly manner, and told him in a few words their wishes, and how they had made up their minds to set on the sons of Olaf, and to put them to sore penalties; they said that now they lacked of nothing to bring the sons of Olaf to terms of equality, since Thorleik was a liegeman of King Olaf, and Bolli was the son-in-law of such a chief as Snorri was.

Snorri answered in this way: "For the slaying of Bolli enough has come in return, in that the life of Helgi Hardbeinson was paid therefor; the troubles of men have been far too great already, and it is high time that now at last they be put a stop to."

Bolli said, "What now, Snorri? are you less keen now to stand by us than you gave out but a little while ago? Thorleik would not have told you our mind as yet if he had first taken counsel with me thereon. And when you claim that Helgi's life has come in revenge for Bolli, it is a matter well known to men that a money fine was paid for the slaying of Helgi, while my father is still unatoned for."

When Snorri saw he could not reason them into a change of mind, he offered them to try to bring about a peaceful atonement between them and the sons of Olaf, rather than that any more manslaughters should befall; and the brothers agreed to this. Then Snorri rode with some men to Herdholt. Halldor gave him a good welcome, and asked him to stay there, but Snorri said he must ride back that night. "But I have an urgent errand with you."

So they fell to talking together, and Snorri made known his errand, saying it had come to his knowledge that Thorleik and Bolli would put up with it no longer that their father should be unatoned at the hands of the sons of Olaf. "And now I would endeavour to bring about peace, and see if an end cannot be put to the evil luck that besets you kinsmen."

Halldor did not flatly refuse to deal further with the case. "I know only too well that Thorgils Hallason and Bolli's sons were minded to fall on me and my brothers, until you turned elsewhere their vengeance, so that thence-forward it seemed to them best to slay Helgi Hardbeinson. In these matters you have taken a good part, whatever your counsels may have been like in regard to earlier dealings between us kinsmen."

Snorri said, "I set a great store by my errand turning out well and that it might be brought about which I have most at heart, that a sound peace should be settled between you kinsmen; for I know the minds of the men who have to deal with you in this case so well, that they will keep faithfully to whatever terms of peace they agree to."

Halldor said, "I will undertake this, if it be the wish of my brothers, to pay money for the slaying of Bolli, such as shall be awarded by the umpires chosen, but I bargain that there be no outlawing of anybody concerned, nor forfeiture of my chieftainship or estate; the same claim I make in respect of the estates my brothers are possessed of, and I make a point of their being left free owners thereof whatever be the close of this case, each side to choose their own umpire."

Snorri answered, "This is offered well and frankly, and the brothers will take this choice if they are willing to set any store by my counsel."

Thereupon Snorri rode home and told the brothers the outcome of his errand, and that he would keep altogether aloof from their case if they would not agree to this. Bolli bade him have his own way, "And I wish that you, Snorri, be umpire on our behalf."

Then Snorri sent to Halldor to say that peaceful settlement was agreed to, and he bade them choose an umpire against himself. Halldor chose on his behalf Steinthor Thorlakson of Eyr. The peace meeting should be at Drangar on Shawstrand, when four weeks of summer were passed.

Thorleik Bollison rode to Holyfell, and nothing to tell tidings of befell that winter, and when time wore unto the hour bespoken for the meeting, Snorri the Priest came there with the sons of Bolli, fifteen together in all; Steinthor and his came with the same number of men to the meeting. Snorri and Steinthor talked together and came to an agreement about these matters. After that they gave out the award, but it is not told how much money they awarded; this, however, is told, that the money was readily paid and the peace well holden to. At the Thorness Thing the fines were paid out; Halldor gave Bolli a good sword, and Steinthor Olafson gave Thorleik a shield, which was also a good gift. Then the Thing was broken up, and both sides were thought to have gained in esteem from these affairs.

Chapter 72
Bolli and Thorleik Go Abroad, AD 1029

AFTER THE PEACE between Bolli and Thorleik and the sons of Olaf had been settled and Thorleik had been one winter in Iceland, Bolli made it known that he was minded to go abroad.

Snorri, dissuading him, said, "To us it seems there is a great risk to be run as to how you may speed; but if you wish to have in hand more than you have now, I will get you a manor and stock it for you; therewithal I shall hand over to you chieftainship over men and uphold you for honours in all things; and that, I know, will be easy, seeing that most men bear you good-will."

Bolli said, "I have long had it in my mind to go for once into southern lands; for a man is deemed to grow benighted if he learns to know nothing farther afield than what is to be seen here in Iceland."

And when Snorri saw that Bolli had set his mind on this, and that it would come to nought to try to stop him, he bade him take as much money as he liked for his journey. Bolli was all for having plenty of money, "for I will not," he said, "be beholden to any man either here or in any foreign land."

Then Bolli rode south to Burgfirth to White-river and bought half of a ship from the owners, so that he and his brother became joint owners of the same ship. Bolli then rides west again to his home.

He and Thordis had one daughter whose name was Herdis, and that maiden Gudrun asked to bring up. She was one year old when she went to Holyfell. Thordis also spent a great deal of her time there, for Gudrun was very fond of her.

Chapter 73
Bolli's Voyage

NOW THE BROTHERS went both to their ship. Bolli took a great deal of money abroad with him. They now arrayed the ship, and when everything was ready they put out to sea. The winds did not speed them fast, and they were a long time out at sea, but got to Norway in the autumn, and made Thrandheim in the north.

Olaf, the king, was in the east part of the land, in the Wick, where he had made ingatherings for a stay through the winter. And when the brothers heard that the king would not come north to Thrandheim that autumn, Thorleik said he would go east along the land to meet King Olaf.

Bolli said, "I have little wish to drift about between market towns in autumn days; to me that is too much of worry and restraint. I will rather stay for the winter in this town. I am told the king will come north in the spring, and if he does not then I shall not set my face against our going to meet him."

Bolli has his way in the matter, and they put up their ship and got their winter quarters. It was soon seen that Bolli was a very pushing man, and would be the first among other men; and in that he had his way, for a bounteous man was he, and so got speedily to be highly thought of in Norway. Bolli kept a suite about him during the winter at Thrandheim, and it was easily seen, when he went to the guild meeting-places, that his men were both better arrayed as to raiment and weapons than other townspeople. He alone also paid for all his suite when they sat drinking in guild halls, and on a par with this were his openhandedness and lordly ways in other matters. Now the brothers stay in the town through the winter.

That winter the king sat east in Sarpsborg, and news spread from the east that the king was not likely to come north. Early in the spring the brothers got their ship ready and went east along the land. The journey sped well for them, and they got east to Sarpsborg, and went forthwith to meet King Olaf. The king gave a good welcome to Thorleik, his henchman, and his followers. Then the king asked who was that man of stately gait in the train of Thorleik; and Thorleik answered, "He is my brother, and is named Bolli."

"He looks indeed, a man of high mettle," said the king.

Thereupon the king asks the brothers to come and stay with him, and that offer they took with thanks, and spend the spring with the king. The king was as kind to Thorleik as he had been before, yet he held Bolli by much in greater esteem, for he deemed him even peerless among men.

And as the spring went on, the brothers took counsel together about their journeys.

And Thorleik asked Bolli if he was minded to go back to Iceland during the summer, "or will you stay on longer here in Norway?"

Bolli answered, "I do not mean to do either. And sooth to say, when I left Iceland, my thought was settled on this, that people should not be asking for news of me from the house next door; and now I wish, brother, that you take over our ship."

Thorleik took it much to heart that they should have to part. "But you, Bolli, will have your way in this as in other things."

Their matter thus bespoken they laid before the king, and he answered thus: "Will you not tarry with us any longer, Bolli?" said the king. "I should have liked it best for you to stay with me for a while, for I shall grant you the same title that I granted to Thorleik, your brother."

Then Bolli answered: "I should be only too glad to bind myself to be your henchman, but I must go first whither I am already bent, and have long been eager to go, but this choice I will gladly take if it be fated to me to come back."

"You will have your way as to your journeyings, Bolli," says the king, "for you Icelanders are self-willed in most matters. But with this word I must close, that I think you, Bolli, the man of greatest mark that has ever come from Iceland in my days."

And when Bolli had got the king's leave he made ready for his journey, and went on board a round ship that was bound south for Denmark. He also took a great deal of money with him, and sundry of his followers bore him company. He and King Olaf parted in great friendship, and the king gave Bolli some handsome gifts at parting. Thorleik remained behind with King Olaf, but Bolli went on his way till he came south to Denmark. That winter he tarried in Denmark, and had great honour there of mighty men; nor did he bear himself there in any way less lordly than while he was in Norway.

When Bolli had been a winter in Denmark he started on his journey out into foreign countries, and did not halt in his journey till he came to Micklegarth (Constantinople). He was there only a short time before he got himself into the Varangian Guard, and, from what we have heard, no Northman had ever gone to take war-pay from the Garth king before Bolli, Bolli's son. He tarried in Micklegarth very many winters, and was thought to be the most valiant in all deeds that try a man, and always went next to those in the forefront. The Varangians accounted Bolli most highly of whilst he was with them in Micklegarth.

Chapter 74
Thorkell Eyjolfson Goes to Norway

NOW THE TALE is to be taken up again where Thorkell Eyjolfson sits at home in lordly way. His and Gudrun's son, Gellir, grew up there at home, and was early both a manly fellow and winning.

It is said how once upon a time Thorkell told Gudrun a dream he had had.

"I dreamed," he said, "that I had so great a beard that it spread out over the whole of Broadfirth." Thorkell bade her read his dream.

Gudrun said, "What do you think this dream betokens?"

He said, "To me it seems clear that in it is hinted that my power will stand wide about the whole of Broadfirth."

Gudrun said, "Maybe that such is the meaning of it, but I rather should think that thereby is betokened that you will dip your beard down into Broadfirth."

That same summer Thorkell runs out his ship and gets it ready for Norway. His son, Gellir, was then twelve winters old, and he went abroad with his father. Thorkell makes it known that he means to fetch timber to build his church with, and sails forthwith into the main sea when he was ready. He had an easy voyage of it, but not a very short one, and they hove into Norway northwardly.

King Olaf then had his seat in Thrandheim, and Thorkell sought forthwith a meeting with King Olaf, and his son Gellir with him. They had there a good welcome. So highly was Thorkell accounted of that winter by the king, that all folk tell that the king gave him not less than one hundred marks of refined silver. The king gave to Gellir at Yule a cloak, the most precious and excellent of gifts.

That winter King Olaf had a church built in the town of timber, and it was a very great minster, all materials thereto being chosen of the best.

In the spring the timber which the king gave to Thorkell was brought on board ship, and large was that timber and good in kind, for Thorkell looked closely after it. Now it happened one morning early that the king went out with but few men, and saw a man up on the church which then was being built in the town. He wondered much at this, for it was a good deal earlier than the smiths were wont to be up. Then the king recognised the man, and, lo! there was Thorkell Eyjolfson taking the measure of all the largest timber, crossbeams, sills, and pillars.

The king turned at once thither, and said: "What now, Thorkell, do you mean after these measurements to shape the church timber which you are taking to Iceland?"

"Yes, in truth, sire," said Thorkell.

Then said King Olaf, "Cut two ells off every main beam, and that church will yet be the largest built in Iceland."

Thorkell answered, "Keep your timber yourself if you think you have given me too much, or your hand itches to take it back, but not an ell's length shall I cut off it. I shall both know how to go about and how to carry out getting other timber for me."

Then says the king most calmly, "So it is, Thorkell, that you are not only a man of much account, but you are also now making yourself too big, for, to be sure, it is too overweening for the son of a mere peasant to try to vie with us. But it is not true that I begrudge you the timber, if only it be fated to you to build a church therewith; for it will never be large enough for all your pride to find room to lie inside it. But near it comes to the foreboding of my mind, that the timber will be of little use to men, and that it will be far from you ever to get any work by man done with this timber."

After that they ceased talking, and the king turned away, and it was marked by people that it misliked him how Thorkell accounted as of nought what he said. Yet the king himself did not let people get the wind of it, and he and Thorkell parted in great good-will.

Thorkell got on board his ship and put to sea. They had a good wind, and were not long out about the main. Thorkell brought his ship to Ramfirth, and rode soon from his ship home to Holyfell, where all folk were glad to see him. In this journey Thorkell had gained much honour. He had his ship hauled ashore and made snug, and the timber for the church he gave to a caretaker, where it was safely bestowed, for it could not be brought from the north this autumn, as he was at all time full of business.

Thorkell now sits at home at his manor throughout the winter. He had Yule-drinking at Holyfell, and to it there came a crowd of people; and altogether he kept up a great state that winter. Nor did Gudrun stop him therein; for she said the use of money was that people should increase their state therewith; moreover, whatever Gudrun must needs be supplied with for all purposes of high-minded display, that (she said) would be readily forthcoming (from her husband).

Thorkell shared that winter amongst his friends many precious things he had brought with him out to Iceland.

Chapter 75
Thorkell and Thorstein and Halldor Olafson, AD 1026

THAT WINTER AFTER YULE Thorkell got ready to go from home north to Ramfirth to bring his timber from the north. He rode first up into the Dales and then to Lea-shaws to Thorstein, his kinsman, where he gathered together men and horses. He afterwards went north to Ramfirth and stayed there awhile, taken up with the business of his journey, and gathered to him horses from about the firth, for he did not want to make more than one journey of it, if that could be managed. But this did not speed swiftly, and Thorkell was busy at this work even into Lent. At last he got under way with the work, and had the wood dragged from the north by more than twenty horses, and had the timber stacked on Lea-Eyr, meaning later on to bring it in a boat out to Holyfell.

Thorstein owned a large ferry-boat, and this boat Thorkell was minded to use for his homeward voyage. Thorkell stayed at Lea-shaws through Lent, for there was dear friendship between these kinsmen.

Thorstein said one day to Thorkell, they had better go to Herdholt, "for I want to make a bid for some land from Halldor, he having but little money since he paid the brothers the weregild for their father, and the land being just what I want most."

Thorkell bade him do as he liked; so they left home a party of twenty men together. They come to Herdholt, and Halldor gave them good welcome, and was most free of talk with them. There were few men at home, for Halldor had sent his men north to Steingrims-firth, as a whale had come ashore there in which he owned a share.

Beiner the Strong was at home, the only man now left alive of those who had been there with Olaf, the father of Halldor.

Halldor had said to Beiner at once when he saw Thorstein and Thorkell riding up, "I can easily see what the errand of these kinsmen is – they are going to make me a bid for my land, and if that is the case they will call me aside for a talk; I guess they will seat themselves each on either side of me; so, then, if they should give me any trouble you must not be slower to set on Thorstein than I on Thorkell. You have long been true to us kinsfolk. I have also sent to the nearest homesteads for men, and at just the same moment I should like these two things to happen: the coming in of the men summoned, and the breaking up of our talk."

Now as the day wore on, Thorstein hinted to Halldor that they should all go aside and have some talk together, "for we have an errand with you."

Halldor said it suited him well. Thorstein told his followers they need not come with them, but Beiner went with them none the less, for he thought things came to pass very much after what Halldor had guessed they would. They went very far out into the field. Halldor had on a pinned-up cloak with a long pin brooch, as was the fashion then. Halldor sat down on the field, but on either side of him each of these kinsmen, so near that they sat well-nigh on his cloak; but Beiner stood over them with a big axe in his hand.

Then said Thorstein, "My errand here is that I wish to buy land from you, and I bring it before you now because my kinsman Thorkell is with me; I should think that this would suit us both well, for I hear that you are short of money, while your land is costly to husband. I will give you in return an estate that will beseem you, and into the bargain as much as we shall agree upon."

In the beginning Halldor took the matter as if it were not so very far from his mind, and they exchanged words concerning the terms of the purchase; and when they felt that he was not so far from coming to terms, Thorkell joined eagerly in the talk, and tried to bring the bargain to a point. Then Halldor began to draw back rather, but they pressed him all the more; yet at last it came to this, that he was the further from the bargain the closer they pressed him.

Then said Thorkell, "Do you not see, kinsman Thorstein, how this is going? Halldor has delayed the matter for us all day long, and we have sat here listening to his fooling and wiles. Now if you want to buy the land we must come to closer quarters."

Thorstein then said he must know what he had to look forward to, and bade Halldor now come out of the shadow as to whether he was willing to come to the bargain.

Halldor answered, "I do not think I need keep you in the dark as to this point, that you will have to go home tonight without any bargain struck."

Then said Thorstein, "Nor do I think it needful to delay making known to you what we have in our mind to do; for we, deeming that we shall get the better of you by reason of the odds on our side, have bethought us of two choices for you: one choice is, that you do this matter willingly and take in return our friendship; but the other, clearly a worse one, is, that you now stretch out your hand against your own will and sell me the land of Herdholt."

But when Thorstein spoke in this outrageous manner, Halldor leapt up so suddenly that the brooch was torn from his cloak, and said, "Something else will happen before I utter that which is not my will."

"What is that?" said Thorstein.

"A pole-axe will stand on your head from one of the worst of men, and thus cast down your insolence and unfairness."

Thorkell answered, "That is an evil prophecy, and I hope it will not be fulfilled; and now I think there is ample cause why you, Halldor, should give up your land and have nothing for it."

Then Halldor answered, "Sooner you will be embracing the sea-tangle in Broadfirth than I sell my land against my own will."

Halldor went home after that, and the men he had sent for came crowding up to the place.

Thorstein was of the wrothest, and wanted forthwith to make an onset on Halldor. Thorkell bade him not to do so, "for that is the greatest enormity at such a season as this; but when this season wears off, I shall not stand in the way of his and ours clashing together."

Halldor said he was given to think he would not fail in being ready for them. After that they rode away and talked much together of this their journey; and Thorstein, speaking thereof, said that, truth to tell, their journey was most wretched. "But why, kinsman Thorkell, were you so afraid of falling on Halldor and putting him to some shame?"

Thorkell answered, "Did you not see Beiner, who stood over you with the axe reared aloft? Why, it was an utter folly, for forthwith on seeing me likely to do anything, he would have driven that axe into your head."

They rode now home to Lea-shaws; and Lent wears and Passion Week sets in.

Chapter 76
The Drowning of Thorkell, AD 1026

ON MAUNDY THURSDAY, early in the morning, Thorkell got ready for his journey. Thorstein set himself much against it: "For the weather looks to me uncertain," said he.

Thorkell said the weather would do all right. "And you must not hinder me now, kinsman, for I wish to be home before Easter."

So now Thorkell ran out the ferry-boat, and loaded it. But Thorstein carried the lading ashore from out the boat as fast as Thorkell and his followers put it on board.

Then Thorkell said, "Give over now, kinsman, and do not hinder our journey this time; you must not have your own way in this."

Thorstein said, "He of us two will now follow the counsel that will answer the worst, for this journey will cause the happening of great matters."

Thorkell now bade them farewell till their next meeting, and Thorstein went home, and was exceedingly downcast. He went to the guest-house, and bade them lay a pillow under his head, the which was done. The servant-maid saw how the tears ran down upon the pillow from his eyes. And shortly afterwards a roaring blast struck the house, and Thorstein said, "There, we now can hear roaring the slayer of kinsman Thorkell."

Now to tell of the journey of Thorkell and his company: they sail this day out, down Broadfirth, and were ten on board. The wind began to blow very high, and rose to full gale before it blew over. They pushed on their way briskly, for the men were most plucky. Thorkell had with him the sword Skofnung, which was laid in the locker. Thorkell and his party sailed till they came to Bjorn's isle, and people could watch them journey from both shores. But when they had come thus far, suddenly a squall caught the sail and overwhelmed the boat. There Thorkell was drowned and all the men who were with him. The timber drifted ashore wide about the islands, the corner-staves (pillars) drove ashore in the island called Staff-isle. Skofnung stuck fast to the timbers of the boat, and was found in Skofnungs-isle.

That same evening that Thorkell and his followers were drowned, it happened at Holyfell that Gudrun went to the church, when other people had gone to bed, and when she stepped into the lich-gate she saw a ghost standing before her.

He bowed over her and said, "Great tidings, Gudrun."

She said, "Hold then your peace about them, wretch."

Gudrun went on to the church, as she had meant to do, and when she got up to the church she thought she saw that Thorkell and his companions were come home and stood before the door of the church, and she saw that water was running off their clothes. Gudrun did not speak to them, but went into the church, and stayed there as long as it seemed good to her. After that she went to the guest-room, for she thought Thorkell and his followers must have gone there; but when she came into the chamber, there was no one there. Then Gudrun was struck with wonder at the whole affair.

On Good Friday Gudrun sent her men to find out matters concerning the journeying of Thorkell and his company, some up to Shawstrand and some out to the islands. By then the flotsam had already come to land wide about the islands and on both shores of the firth. The Saturday before

Easter the tidings got known and great news they were thought to be, for Thorkell had been a great chieftain. Thorkell was eight-and-forty years old when he was drowned, and that was four winters before Olaf the Holy fell.

Gudrun took much to heart the death of Thorkell, yet bore her bereavement bravely.

Only very little of the church timber could ever be gathered in.

Gellir was now fourteen years old, and with his mother he took over the business of the household and the chieftainship. It was soon seen that he was made to be a leader of men.

Gudrun now became a very religious woman. She was the first woman in Iceland who knew the Psalter by heart. She would spend long time in the church at nights saying her prayers, and Herdis, Bolli's daughter, always went with her at night. Gudrun loved Herdis very much.

It is told that one night the maiden Herdis dreamed that a woman came to her who was dressed in a woven cloak, and coifed in a head cloth, but she did not think the woman winning to look at.

She spoke, "Tell your grandmother that I am displeased with her, for she creeps about over me every night, and lets fall down upon me drops so hot that I am burning all over from them. My reason for letting you know this is, that I like you somewhat better, though there is something uncanny hovering about you too. However, I could get on with you if I did not feel there was so much more amiss with Gudrun."

Then Herdis awoke and told Gudrun her dream. Gudrun thought the apparition was of good omen. Next morning Gudrun had planks taken up from the church floor where she was wont to kneel on the hassock, and she had the earth dug up, and they found blue and evil-looking bones, a round brooch, and a wizard's wand, and men thought they knew then that a tomb of some sorceress must have been there; so the bones were taken to a place far away where people were least likely to be passing.

Chapter 77
The Return of Bolli, AD 1030

WHEN FOUR WINTERS were passed from the drowning of Thorkell Eyjolfson a ship came into Islefirth belonging to Bolli Bollison, most of the crew of which were Norwegians. Bolli brought out with him much wealth, and many precious things that lords abroad had given him. Bolli was so great a man for show when he came back from this journey that he would wear no clothes but of scarlet and fur, and all his weapons were bedight with gold: he was called Bolli the Grand.

He made it known to his shipmasters that he was going west to his own countrysides, and he left his ship and goods in the hands of his crew.

Bolli rode from the ship with twelve men, and all his followers were dressed in scarlet, and rode on gilt saddles, and all were they a trusty band, though Bolli was peerless among them. He had on the clothes of fur which the Garth-king had given him, he had over all a scarlet cape; and he had Footbiter girt on him, the hilt of which was dight with gold, and the grip woven with gold; he had a gilded helmet on his head, and a red shield on his flank, with a knight painted on it in gold. He had a dagger in his hand, as is the custom in foreign lands; and whenever they took quarters the women paid heed to nothing but gazing at Bolli and his grandeur, and that of his followers. In this state Bolli rode into the western parts all the way till he came to Holyfell with his following. Gudrun was very glad to see her son.

Bolli did not stay there long till he rode up to Saelingsdale Tongue to see Snorri, his father-in-law, and his wife Thordis, and their meeting was exceeding joyful. Snorri asked Bolli to stay with him with as many of his men as he liked. Bolli accepted the invitation gratefully, and was with Snorri all the winter, with the men who had ridden from the north with him.

Bolli got great renown from this journey. Snorri made it no less his business now to treat Bolli with every kindness than when he was with him before.

Chapter 78
The Death of Snorri, and the End, AD 1031

WHEN BOLLI HAD BEEN one winter in Iceland Snorri the Priest fell ill. That illness did not gain quickly on him, and Snorri lay very long abed. But when the illness gained on him, he called to himself all his kinsfolk and affinity, and said to Bolli, "It is my wish that you shall take over the manor here and the chieftainship after my day, for I grudge honours to you no more than to my own sons, nor is there within this land now the one of my sons who I think will be the greatest man among them, Halldor to wit."

Thereupon Snorri breathed his last, being seventy-seven years old. That was one winter after the fall of St. Olaf, so said Ari the Priest 'Deep-in-lore.' Snorri was buried at Tongue.

Bolli and Thordis took over the manor of Tongue as Snorri had willed it, and Snorri's sons put up with it with a good will. Bolli grew a man of great account, and was much beloved.

Herdis, Bolli's daughter, grew up at Holyfell, and was the goodliest of all women. Orm, the son of Hermund, the son of Illugi, asked her in marriage, and she was given in wedlock to him; their son was Kodran, who had for wife Gudrun, the daughter of Sigmund. The son of Kodran was Hermund, who had for wife Ulfeid, the daughter of Runolf, who was the son of Bishop Kelill; their sons were Kelill, who was Abbot of Holyfell, and Reinn and Kodran and Styrmir; their daughter was Thorvor, whom Skeggi, Bard's son, had for wife, and from whom is come the stock of the Shaw-men.

Ospak was the name of the son of Bolli and Thordis. The daughter of Ospak was Gudrun, whom Thorarin, Brand's son, had to wife. Their son was Brand, who founded the benefice of Housefell.

Gellir, Thorleik's son, took to him a wife, and married Valgerd, daughter of Thorgils Arison of Reckness. Gellir went abroad, and took service with King Magnus the Good, and had given him by the king twelve ounces of gold and many goods besides. The sons of Gellir were Thorkell and Thorgils, and a son of Thorgils was Ari the 'Deep-in-lore.' The son of Ari was named Thorgils, and his son was Ari the Strong.

Now Gudrun began to grow very old, and lived in such sorrow and grief as has lately been told. She was the first nun and recluse in Iceland, and by all folk it is said that Gudrun was the noblest of women of equal birth with her in this land. It is told how once upon a time Bolli came to Holyfell, for Gudrun was always very pleased when he came to see her, and how he sat by his mother for a long time, and they talked of many things.

Then Bolli said, "Will you tell me, mother, what I want very much to know? Who is the man you have loved the most?"

Gudrun answered, "Thorkell was the mightiest man and the greatest chief, but no man was more shapely or better endowed all round than Bolli. Thord, son of Ingun, was the wisest of them all, and the greatest lawyer; Thorvald I take no account of."

Then said Bolli, "I clearly understand that what you tell me shows how each of your husbands was endowed, but you have not told me yet whom you loved the best. Now there is no need for you to keep that hidden any longer."

Gudrun answered, "You press me hard, my son, for this, but if I must needs tell it to any one, you are the one I should first choose thereto."

Bolli bade her do so. Then Gudrun said, "To him I was worst whom I loved best."

"Now," answered Bolli, "I think the whole truth is told," and said she had done well to tell him what he so much had yearned to know.

Gudrun grew to be a very old woman, and some say she lost her sight. Gudrun died at Holyfell, and there she rests.

Gellir, Thorkell's son, lived at Holyfell to old age, and many things of much account are told of him; he also comes into many Sagas, though but little be told of him here. He built a church at Holyfell, a very stately one, as Arnor, the Earls' poet, says in the funeral song which he wrote about Gellir, wherein he uses clear words about that matter.

When Gellir was somewhat sunk into his latter age, he prepared himself for a journey away from Iceland. He went to Norway, but did not stay there long, and then left straightway that land and 'walked' south to Rome to 'see the holy apostle Peter.' He was very long over this journey; and then journeying from the south he came into Denmark, and there he fell ill and lay in bed a very long time, and received all the last rites of the church, whereupon he died, and he rests at Roskild. Gellir had taken Skofnung with him, the sword that had been taken out of the barrow of Holy Kraki, and never after could it be got back.

When the death of Gellir was known in Iceland, Thorkell, his son, took over his father's inheritance at Holyfell. Thorgils, another of Gellir's sons, was drowned in Broadfirth at an early age, with all hands on board.

Thorkell Gellirson was a most learned man, and was said to be of all men the best stocked of lore.

Here is the end of the Saga of the men of Salmon-river-Dale.

THE END OF THE WORLD

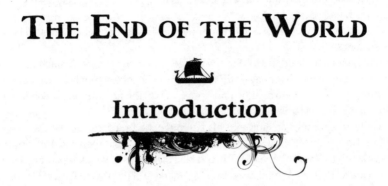

Introduction

BALDER WAS PURE OF HEART, and he represented goodness in every form. His life in Asgard was one of kindness and generosity, and while he lived the force of his righteousness would allow everyone in Asgard to enjoy peace from evil. But evil comes in many forms and not even the gods could be protected from its sinister influence forever. In Asgard, Loki was the evil that would burst the bauble of their happiness, and it was Loki who would bring about the end to the eternal conflict between virtue and corruption. It was an end that had been predicted since the earth was created, and its reality was as frightening as every prediction had suggested. Ragnarok would rid the world of evil, and leave a trail of ashes that blotted out the sun and all that had once glowed in their gilded world. But it is from ashes that new life springs, and the world of the Viking gods was no exception.

The Death of Balder

TO ODIN AND FRIGGA, we are told, were born twin sons as dissimilar in character and physical appearance as it was possible for two children to be. Hodur, god of darkness, was sombre, taciturn, and blind, like the obscurity of sin, which he was supposed to symbolise, while his brother Balder, the beautiful, was worshipped as the pure and radiant god of innocence and light. From his snowy brow and golden locks seemed to radiate beams of sunshine which gladdened the hearts of gods and men, by whom he was equally beloved. Each life that he touched glowed with goodness, and he was loved by all who knew him. Balder tended to his twin brother Hodur with every kindness and consideration. Hodur worshipped Balder, and would do nothing in his power to harm him.

The youthful Balder attained his full growth with marvellous rapidity, and was early admitted to the council of the gods. He took up his abode in the palace of Breidablik, whose silver roof rested upon golden pillars, and whose purity was such that nothing common or unclean was ever allowed within its precincts, and here he lived in perfect unity with his young wife Nanna (blossom), the daughter of Nip (bud), a beautiful and charming goddess.

The god of light was well versed in the science of runes, which were carved on his tongue; he knew the various virtues of simples, one of which, the camomile, was called 'Balder's brow,' because its flower was as immaculately pure as his forehead. The only thing hidden from Balder's radiant eyes was the perception of his own ultimate fate.

There came a morning when Balder woke with the dawn, his face tightened with fear and foresight. He had dreamed of his own death and he lay there petrified, aware, somehow, that the strength of this dream forecasted sinister things to come. So Balder travelled to see Odin, who listened carefully, and knew at once that the fears of his son were justified – for in his shining eyes there was no longer simply innocence; there was knowledge as well. Odin went at once to his throne at the top of Yggdrasil, and he prayed there for a vision to come to him. At once he saw the head of Vala the Seer come to him, and he knew he must travel to Hel's kingdom, to visit Vala's grave. Only then would he learn the truth of his favourite son's fate.

It was many long days before Odin reached the innermost graves on Hel's estate. He moved quietly so that Hel would not know of his coming, and he was disregarded by most of the workers in her lands, for they were intent on some celebrations, and were preparing the hall for the arrival of an esteemed guest. At last the mound of Vala's grave appeared, and he sat there on it, keeping his head low so that the prophetess would not catch a glimpse of his face. Vala was a seer of all things future, and all things past; there was nothing that escaped her bright eyes, and she could be called upon only by the magic of the runes to tell of her knowledge.

The grave was wreathed in shadows, and a mist hung uneasily over the tombstone. There was silence as Odin whispered to Vala to come forth, and then, at once, there was a grating and steaming that poured forth an odour that caused even the all-powerful Odin to gag and spit.

"Who disturbs me from my sleep," said Vala with venom. Odin thought carefully before replying. He did not wish her to know that he was Odin, king of gods and men, for she may not wish to tell him of a future that would touch on his own. And so he responded:

"I am Vegtam, son of Valtam, and I wish to learn of the fate of Balder."

"Balder's brother will slay him," said Vala, and with that she withdrew into her grave.

Odin leapt up and cried out, "With the power of the runes, you must tell me more. Tell me, Vala, which esteemed guest does Hel prepare for?"

"Balder," she muttered from the depths of her grave, "and I will say no more."

Odin shook his head with concern. He could not see how it could be possible that Balder's brother would take his life; Balder and Hodur were the closest of brothers, and shared the same thoughts and indeed speech for much of the time. He returned to Asgard with his concerns still intact, and he discussed them there with Frigga, who listened carefully.

"I have a plan," she announced, "and I am certain you will agree that this is the best course of action for us all. I plan to travel through all nine lands, and I will seek the pledge of every living creature, every plant, every metal and stone, not to harm Balder."

And Frigga was as good as her word, for on the morrow she set out and travelled far and wide, everywhere she went extracting with ease the promise of every living creature, and inanimate object, to love Balder, and to see that he was not injured in any way.

And so it was that Balder was immune to injury of any kind, and it became a game among the children of Asgard to aim their spears and arrows at him, and laugh as they bounced off, leaving him unharmed. Balder was adored throughout the worlds, and there was no one who did not smile when he spied him.

No one, that is except Loki, whose jealousy of Balder had reached an unbearable pitch. Each night he ruminated over the ways in which he could murder Balder, but he could think of none. Frigga had taken care to involve all possible dangers in her oath, and there was nothing now that would hurt him. But the scheming Loki was not unwise, and he soon came up with a plan. Transforming himself into a beggarwoman, he knocked on Frigga's door and requested a meal. Frigga was pleased to offer her hospitality, and she sat down to keep the beggar company as she ate.

Loki, in his disguise, chattered on about the handsome Balder, who he'd seen in the hall, and he mentioned his fears that Balder would be killed by one of the spears and arrows he had seen hurled at him. Frigga laughed, and explained that Balder was now invincible.

"Did everything swear an oath to you then?" asked Loki slyly.

"Oh, yes," said Frigga, but then she paused, "all, that is, except for a funny little plant which was growing at the base of the oak tree at Valhalla. Why I'd never before set eyes on such a little shoot of greenery and it was far too immature to swear to anything so important as my oath."

"What's it called?" asked Loki again.

"Hmmm," said Frigga, still unaware of the dangers her information might invoke, "mistletoe. Yes, mistletoe."

Loki thanked Frigga hastily for his meal, and left her palace, transforming at once into his mischievous self, and travelling to Valhalla as quickly as his feet would take him. He carefully plucked the budding mistletoe, and returned to Odin's hall, where Balder played with the younger gods and goddesses, as they shot him unsuccessfully with arms of every shape and size.

Hodur was standing frowning in the corner, and Loki whispered for him to come over.

"What is it, Hodur," he asked.

"Nothing, really, just that I cannot join their games," said Hodur quietly.

"Come with me," said Loki, "for I can help." And leading Hodur to a position close to Balder, he placed in his hands a bow and arrow fashioned from the fleetest of fabrics. To the end of the arrow, he tied a small leaf of mistletoe, and topped the razor-sharp tip with a plump white berry. "Now, shoot now," he cried to Hodur, who pulled back the bow and let the arrow soar towards its target.

There was a sharp gasp, and then there was silence. Hodur shook his head with surprise – where were the happy shouts, where was the laughter telling him that his own arrow had hit its mark and failed to harm the victim? The silence spoke volumes, for Balder lay dead in a circle of admirers as pale and frightened as if they had seen Hel herself.

The agony spread across Asgard like a great wave. When it was discovered who had shot the fatal blow, Hodur was sent far from his family, and left alone in the wilderness. He had not yet had a moment to utter the name of the god who had encouraged him to perpetrate this grave crime, and his misery kept him silent.

Frigga was disconsolate with grief. She begged Hermod, the swiftest of her sons, to set out at once for Filheim, to beg Hel to release Balder to them all. And so he climbed upon Odin's finest steed, Sleipnir, and set out for the nine worlds of Hel, a task so fearsome that he shook uncontrollably.

In Asgard, Frigga and Odin carried their son's body to the sea, where a funeral pyre was created and lit. Nanna, Balder's wife, could bear it no longer, and before the pyre was set out on the tempestuous sea, she threw herself on the flames, and perished there with her only love. As a token of their great affection and esteem, the gods offered, one by one, their most prized possessions and laid them on the pyre as it set out for the wild seas. Odin produced his magic ring Draupnir, and the greatest gods of Asgard gathered to see the passing of Balder.

And so the blazing ship left the shore, will full sail set. And then darkness swallowed it, and Balder had gone.

Throughout this time, Hermod had been travelling at great speed towards Hel. He rode for nine days and nine nights, and never took a moment to sleep. He galloped on and on, bribing the watchman of each gate to let him past, and invoking the name of Balder as the reason for his journey. At last, he reached the hall of Hel, where he found Balder sitting easily with Nanna, in great comfort and looking quite content. Hel stood by his side, keeping a close watch on her newest visitor. She looked up at Hermod with disdain, for everyone knew that once a spirit had reached Hel it could not be released. But Hermod fell on one knee and begged the icy mistress to reconsider her hold over Balder.

"Please, Queen Hel, without Balder we cannot survive. There can be no future for Asgard without his presence," he cried.

But Hel would not be moved. She held out for three days and three nights, while Hermod stayed right by her side, begging and pleading and offering every conceivable reason why Balder should be released. And finally the Queen of darkness gave in.

"Return at once to Asgard," she said harshly, "and if what you say is true, if everything – living and inanimate – in Asgard loves Balder and cannot live without him, then he will be released. But if there is even one dissenter, if there is even one stone in your land who does not mourn the passing of Balder, then he shall remain here with me."

Hermod was gladdened by this news, for he knew that everyone – including Hodur who had sent the fatal arrow flying through the air – loved Balder. He agreed to these terms at once, and set off for Asgard, relaying himself and his news with speed that astonished all who saw him arrive.

Immediately, Odin sent messengers to all corners of the universe, asking for tears to be shed for Balder. And as they travelled, everyone and everything began to weep, until a torrent of water rushed across the tree of life. And after everyone had been approached, and each had shed his tears, the messengers made their way back to Odin's palace with glee. Balder would be released, there could be no doubt!

But it was not to be, for as the last messenger travelled back to the palace, he noticed the form of an old beggarwoman, hidden in the darkness of a cave. He approached her then, and bid her to cry for Balder, but she did not. Her eyes remained dry. The uproar was carried across to the palace, and Odin himself came to see 'dry eyes', whose inability to shed tears would cost him the life of his son. He stared into those eyes and he saw then what the messenger had failed to see, what Frigga had failed to see, and what had truly caused the death of Balder. For those eyes belonged to none other than Loki, and it was he who had murdered Balder as surely as if the arrow had left his own hands.

The sacred code of Asgard had been broken, for blood had been spilled by one of their own, in their own land. The end of the world was nigh – but first, Loki would be punished once and for all.

The Revenge of the Gods

THE WRATH OF THE GODS was so great that Asgard shuddered and shook. As Odin looked down upon Loki in the form of the beggarwoman, and made the decision to punish him, Loki transformed himself into a fly and disappeared.

Although he was crafty, even his most supreme efforts to save himself were as nothing in the face of Odin's determination to trace him.

Loki travelled to far distant mountains, and on the peak of the most isolated of them all, he built a cabin, with windows and doors on all sides so that he could see the enemy approaching, and flee from any side before they reached him. By day, he haunted a pool by a rushing waterfall, taking the shape of a salmon. His life was uncomplicated, and although he was forced to live by his wits, and the fear of the god's revenge was great, Loki was not unhappy.

From his throne above the worlds, Odin watched, and waited. And when he saw that Loki had grown complacent, and no longer looked with quite such care from his many windows, he struck.

It was one particular evening that Loki sat weaving. He had just invented what we today call a fish net, and as he worked he hummed to himself, glancing every now and then from his great windows, and then back at his work. The gods were almost upon him when he first noticed them, and they were led by Kvasir, who was known amongst all gods for his wisdom and ability to unravel the tricks of even the most seasoned trickster. And as he saw them arriving, Loki fled from the back door, and transformed himself into a salmon, and leapt into the pond.

The gods stood in the doorway, surveying the room. Kvasir walked over to the fishing net and examined it closely. His keen eyes caught a glimmer of fish scales on the floor, and he nodded sagely.

"It is my assessment," he said, "that our Loki has become a fish. And," he held up the fishing net, "we will catch him with his own web."

The gods made their way to the stream, and the pond which lay at the bottom of the waterfall. Throwing the net into the water, they waited for daybreak, when Loki the salmon would enter the waters and be caught in their net. Of course, Loki was too clever to be trapped so easily, and he swam beneath the net and far away from the part of the pond where the gods were fishing. Kvasir soon realized their mistake, and he ordered that rocks be placed at the bottom of the net, so that none could swim beneath it. And they waited.

Loki looked with amusement at the god's trap, and gracefully soared through the air above the net, his eyes glinting in the early morning light. And as his fins were just inches from the water, and when he was so close to escape that he had begun to plan his celebrations, two firm hands were thrust out, and he was lifted into the air.

He hardly dared look at his captor, and he began to tremble when he saw that it was none other than Thor who had moved so swiftly to catch him.

"I command you to take your own form, Loki," he shouted, holding tight to the smooth scales of the salmon.

Loki knew he was beaten. Quietly he transformed himself once again into Loki, only to find himself hung by the heels over the rippling waters. And as Thor raised his great hammer to beat Loki to death, a hand reached out and stopped him. It was Odin, and he spoke gently, and with enormous purpose.

"Death is too good for this rodent," he whispered. "Take him at once to the Hel's worlds and tie him there for good."

And so it was that Loki was taken to Filheim, where Thor grabbed three massive rocks and formed a platform for the hapless trickster. Then, Loki's two sons, Vali and Nari, were brought forth, and an enchantment was laid upon Vali so that he took the form of a wolf and attacked his brother Nari, tearing him to pieces in front of his anguished father. Gathering up Nari's entrails, which were now endowed with magic properties, he tied Loki's limbs so that he lay across the three rocks, unable to move. The entrails would tighten with every effort he made to escape, and to ensure that he could not use trickery to free himself, Thor placed the rocks on a precipice. One false move and he would be sent crashing to his death in the canyon below.

Finally, Skadi caught a poisonous snake, and trapped it by its tail so that it hung over Loki's face, dripping venom into his mouth so that he screamed with pain and terror. He began to convulse and was such a terrible sight that his wife Sigyn rushed forward and begged to be allowed to stay beside him, holding a bowl with which to collect the poison.

The work of the gods was done. They turned then and left, and Sigyn remained with her husband, ever true to her wedding vows. Every day or so she moved from her position at his side in order to empty her bowl, and Loki's convulsions brought an earthquake to Asgard that lasted just as long as it took her to return with her bowl. They would remain there until the end of time – for the gods, that is. The end of time was nigh, and it was Ragnarok.

Ragnarok

TOO LATE THE GODS REALISED how evil was this spirit that had found a home among them, and too late they banished Loki to earth, where men, following the gods' example, listened to his teachings, and were corrupted by his sinister influence.

Seeing that crime was rampant, and all good banished from the earth, the gods realised that the prophecies uttered of old were about to be fulfilled, and that the shadow of Ragnarok, the twilight or dusk of the gods, was already upon them. Sol and Mani grew pale with affright, and drove their chariots tremblingly along their appointed paths, looking back with fear at the pursuing wolves which would shortly overtake and devour them; and as their smiles disappeared the earth grew sad and cold, and the terrible Fimbul-winter began. Then snow fell from the four points of the compass at once, the biting winds swept down from the north, and all the earth was covered with a thick layer of ice.

This severe winter lasted during three whole seasons without a break, and was followed by three others, equally severe, during which all cheer departed from the earth, and the crimes of men increased with fearful rapidity, whilst, in the general struggle for life, the last feelings of humanity and compassion disappeared.

In the dim recesses of the Ironwood the giantess Iarnsaxa or Angur-boda diligently fed the wolves Hati, Skoll, and Managarm, the progeny of Fenris, with the marrow of murderers' and adulterers' bones; and such was the prevalence of these vile crimes, that the well-nigh insatiable monsters were never stinted for food. They daily gained strength to pursue Sol and Mani, and finally overtook and devoured them, deluging the earth with blood from their dripping jaws.

At this terrible calamity the whole earth trembled and shook, the stars, affrighted, fell from their places, and Loki, Fenris, and Garm, renewing their efforts, rent their chains asunder and rushed forth to take their revenge. At the same moment the dragon Nidhug gnawed through the root of the ash Yggdrasil, which quivered to its topmost bough; the red cock Fialar, perched above Valhalla, loudly crowed an alarm, which was immediately echoed by Gullin-kambi, the rooster in Midgard, and by Hel's dark-red bird in Niflheim.

Heimdall, noting these ominous portents and hearing the cock's shrill cry, immediately put the Giallar-horn to his lips and blew the long-expected blast, which was heard throughout the world. At the first sound of this rally Aesir and Einheriar sprang from their golden couches and sallied bravely out of the great hall, armed for the coming fray, and, mounting their impatient steeds, they galloped over the quivering rainbow bridge to the spacious field of Vigrid, where, as Vafthrudnir had predicted long before, the last battle was to take place.

The terrible Midgard snake Iormungandr had been aroused by the general disturbance, and with immense writhings and commotion, whereby the seas were lashed into huge waves such as had never before disturbed the deeps of ocean, he crawled out upon the land, and hastened to join the dread fray, in which he was to

One of the great waves, stirred up by Iormungandr's struggles, set afloat Nagilfar, the fatal ship, which was constructed entirely out of the nails of those dead folks whose relatives had failed, through the ages, in their duty, having neglected to pare the nails of the deceased, ere they were laid to rest. No sooner was this vessel afloat, than Loki boarded it with the fiery host from Muspellsheim, and steered it boldly over the stormy waters to the place of conflict.

This was not the only vessel bound for Vigrid, however, for out of a thick fog bank towards the north came another ship, steered by Hrym, in which were all the frost giants, armed to the teeth and eager for a conflict with the Aesir, whom they had always hated.

At the same time, Hel, the goddess of death, crept through a crevice in the earth out of her underground home, closely followed by the Hel-hound Garm, the malefactors of her cheerless realm, and the dragon Nidhug, which flew over the battlefield bearing corpses upon his wings.

As soon as he landed, Loki welcomed these reinforcements with joy, and placing himself at their head he marched with them to the fight.

Suddenly the skies were rent asunder, and through the fiery breach rode Surtr with his flaming sword, followed by his sons; and as they rode over the bridge Bifrost, with intent to storm Asgard, the glorious arch sank with a crash beneath their horses' tread.

The gods knew full well that their end was now near, and that their weakness and lack of foresight placed them under great disadvantages; for Odin had but one eye, Tyr but one hand, and Frey nothing but a stag's horn wherewith to defend himself, instead of his invincible sword. Nevertheless, the Aesir did not show any signs of despair, but, like true battle-gods of the North, they donned their richest attire, and gaily rode to the battlefield, determined to sell their lives as dearly as possible.

While they were mustering their forces, Odin once more rode down to the Urdar fountain, where, under the toppling Yggdrasil, the Norns sat with veiled faces and obstinately silent, their web lying torn at their feet. Once more the father of the gods whispered a mysterious communication to Mimir, after which he remounted Sleipnir and rejoined the waiting host.

The combatants were now assembled on Vigrid's broad plain. On one side were ranged the stern, calm faces of the Aesir, Vanas, and Einheriar; while on the other were gathered the motley host of Surtr, the grim frost giants, the pale army of Hel, and Loki and his dread followers, Garm, Fenris, and Iormungandr, the two latter belching forth fire and smoke, and exhaling clouds of noxious, deathly vapours, which filled all

All the pent-up antagonism of ages was now let loose in a torrent of hate, each member of the opposing hosts fighting with grim determination, as did our ancestors of old, hand to hand and face to face. With a mighty shock, heard above the roar of battle which filled the universe, Odin and the Fenris wolf came into impetuous contact, while Thor attacked the Midgard snake, and Tyr came to grips with the dog Garm. Frey closed with Surtr, Heimdall with Loki, whom he had defeated once before, and the remainder of the gods and all the Einheriar engaged foes equally worthy of their courage. But, in spite of their daily preparation in the heavenly city, Valhalla's host was doomed to succumb, and Odin was amongst the first of the shining ones to be slain. Not even the high courage and mighty attributes of Allfather could withstand the tide of evil as personified in the Fenris wolf. At each succeeding moment of the struggle its colossal size assumed greater proportions, until finally its wide-open jaws embraced all the space between heaven and earth, and the foul monster rushed furiously upon the father of gods and engulphed him bodily within its horrid maw.

None of the gods could lend Allfather a helping hand at that critical moment, for it was a time of sore trial to all. Frey put forth heroic efforts, but Surtr's flashing sword now dealt him a death-stroke. In his struggle with the arch-enemy, Loki, Heimdall fared better, but his final conquest was dearly bought, for he, too, fell dead. The struggle between Tyr and Garm had the same tragic end, and Thor, after a most terrible encounter with the Midgard snake, and after slaying him with a stroke from Miolnir, staggered back nine

Vidar now came rushing from a distant part of the plain to avenge the death of his mighty sire, and the doom foretold fell upon Fenris, whose lower jaw now felt the impress of that shoe which had been reserved for this day. At the same moment Vidar seized the monster's upper jaw with his hands, and with one terrible wrench tore him asunder.

The other gods who took part in the fray, and all the Einheriar having now perished, Surtr suddenly flung his fiery brands over heaven, earth, and the nine kingdoms of Hel. The raging flames enveloped the massive stem of the world ash Yggdrasil, and reached the golden palaces of the gods, which were utterly consumed. The vegetation upon earth was likewise destroyed, and the fervent heat made all the waters seethe and boil.

The great conflagration raged fiercely until everything was consumed, when the earth, blackened and scarred, slowly sank beneath the boiling waves of the sea. Ragnarok had indeed come; the world tragedy was over, the divine actors were slain, and chaos seemed to have resumed its former sway. But as in a play, after the principals are slain and the curtain has fallen, the audience still looks for the favourites to appear and make their bow, so the ancient Northern races fancied that, all evil having perished in Surtr's flames, from the general ruin goodness would rise, to resume its sway over the earth, and that some of the gods would return to dwell in heaven for ever.

Regeneration

OUR ANCESTORS BELIEVED fully in regeneration, and held that after a certain space of time the earth, purged by fire and purified by its immersion in the sea, rose again in all its pristine beauty and was illumined by the sun, whose chariot was driven by a daughter of Sol, born before the wolf had devoured her mother. The new orb of day was not imperfect, as the first sun had been, and its rays were no longer so ardent that a shield had to be placed between it and the earth. These more beneficent rays soon caused the earth to renew its green mantle, and to bring forth flowers and fruit in abundance. Two human beings, a woman, Lif, and a man, Lifthrasir, now emerged from the depths of Hodmimir's (Mimir's) forest, whence they had fled for refuge when Surtr set fire to the world. They had sunk into peaceful slumber there, unconscious of the destruction around them, and had remained, nurtured by the morning dew, until it was safe for them to wander out once more, when they took possession of the regenerated earth, which their descendants were to people and over which they were to have full sway.

All the gods who represented the developing forces of Nature were slain on the fatal field of Vigrid, but Vali and Vidar, the types of the imperishable forces of Nature, returned to the field of Ida, where they were met by Modi and Magni, Thor's sons, the personifications of strength and energy, who rescued their father's sacred hammer from the general destruction, and carried it thither with them.

Here they were joined by Hoenir, no longer an exile among the Vanas, who, as developing forces, had also vanished for ever; and out of the dark underworld where he had languished so long rose the radiant Balder, together with his brother Hodur, with whom he was reconciled, and with whom he was to live in perfect amity and peace. The past had gone for ever, and the surviving deities could recall it without bitterness. The memory of their former companions was, however, dear to them, and full often did they return to their old haunts to linger over the happy associations. It was thus that walking one day in the long grass on Idavold, they found again the golden disks with which the Aesir had been wont to sport.

When the small band of gods turned mournfully towards the place where their lordly dwellings once stood, they became aware, to their joyful surprise, that Gimli, the highest heavenly abode, had not been consumed, for it rose glittering before them, its golden roof outshining the sun. Hastening thither they discovered, to the great increase of their joy, that it had become the place of refuge for all the virtuous.

Biographies

Abbie Farwell Brown
American author Abbie Farwell Brown (1871–1927) was born in Boston and attended the Girls' Latin School. While attending school she set up a school newspaper and also contributed articles to other magazines. Brown's books were most often retellings of old tales for children such as in *The Book of Saints* and *Friendly Beasts*. She also published a collection of tales from Norse mythology, *In the Days of Giants*, which became the common text held by many libraries for several generations.

H.A. Guerber
Hélène Adeline Guerber (1859–1929) was a British historian who published a large number of works, largely focused on myths and legends. Guerber's most famous publication is *Myths of the Norsemen: From the Eddas and Sagas*, a history of Germanic mythology. Her works continue to be published today and include *The Myths of Greece and Rome*, *The Story of the Greeks* and *Legends of the Middle Ages*.

Eirikr Magnusson
Eirikr Magnusson (1833–1913) was an Icelandic scholar who worked during his life as a librarian at Cambridge University. He arrived in England in 1862 after being sent by the Icelandic Bible Society to translate Christian texts. Magnusson's most notable work was his teaching of Old Norse to William Morris and their collaborations on translations. Together they published numerous Icelandic sagas including *The Story of Grettir the Strong*, *Volsunga Saga* and *Heimskringl*. Magnusson and Morris also spent time traveling around Iceland to visit places which were of significance to the Icelandic sagas they translated.

William Morris
Textile designer, poet, novelist and translator William Morris (1834–96) was born in Essex and studied at Oxford University. Morris is best known for his textiles work as he created designs for wallpaper, stained glass windows and embroideries that are enduringly popular. Alongside this, Morris wrote poetry, fiction and essays and after befriending Eirikr Magnusson he helped to translate many Icelandic tales. In his final years Morris published fantasy fiction including *The Wood Beyond the World* and *The Well at the World's End* and these were the first fantasy books to be set in an imaginary world. His legacy is an important one as he was a major contributor to both textile arts and literature.

Dr Brittany Schorn
Foreword
Dr Brittany Schorn is a Research Associate in the Department of Anglo-Saxon, Norse and Celtic at the University of Cambridge. She is co-editor with Judy Quinn and Carolyne Larrington of *A Handbook to Eddic Poetry: Myth and Legends of Early Scandinavia* (Cambridge University Press, 2106) and author of *Speaker and Authority in Old Norse Wisdom Poetry* (de Gruyter, 2016).

Text Sources

Many of the tales in this book come from H.A. Guerber's edition of *Myths of the Norsemen* (George G. Harrap, London, 1909) and Abbie Farwell Brown's *In the Days of Giants*, (Houghton Mifflin & Co, New York, 1902). *The Story of Frithiof the Bold* and *The Story of Gunnlaug the Worm-Tongue and Raven the Skald* are from Morris and Magnusson's 1875 edition of *Three Northern Love Stories and Other Tales* (Ellis & White, London), while their *Story of Grettir the Strong* is a version published by F.S Ellis, 1869. The *Laxdaela Saga* is based on a translation by Muriel A.C. Press (Dent, London, 1899).

Remaining contributors, authors, editors and sources for this series include: Loren Auerbach, Norman Bancroft-Hunt, E.M. Berens, Laura Bulbeck, Samuel Butler, Jeremiah Curtin, O.B. Duane, Dr Ray Dunning, W.W. Gibbings, Bethany Gooding, Jake Jackson, Judith John, Katharine Berry Judson, Charles Kingsley, Andrew Lang, J.W. Mackail, Chris McNab, Professor James Riordan, Rachel Storm, K.E. Sullivan.

FLAME TREE PUBLISHING
Epic, Dark, Thrilling & Gothic
New & Classic Writing

Flame Tree's Gothic Fantasy books offer a carefully curated series of new titles, each with combinations of original and classic writing:

Chilling Horror • Chilling Ghost • Science Fiction
Murder Mayhem • Crime & Mystery • Swords & Steam
Dystopia Utopia • Supernatural Horror • Lost Worlds
Time Travel • Heroic Fantasy • Pirates & Ghosts • Agents & Spies
Endless Apocalypse • Alien Invasion • Robots & AI • Lost Souls
Haunted House • Cosy Crime • American Gothic
Urban Crime • Epic Fantasy • Detective Mysteries

Also, new companion titles offer rich collections of classic fiction, myths and tales in the gothic fantasy tradition:

H.G. Wells • Lovecraft • Sherlock Holmes
Edgar Allan Poe • Bram Stoker • Mary Shelley
African Myths & Tales • Celtic Myths & Tales • Chinese Myths & Tales
Greek Myths & Tales • Japanese Myths & Tales • Heroes & Heroines Myths & Tales
Irish Fairy Tales • King Arthur & The Knights of the Round Table
Alice's Adventures in Wonderland • The Divine Comedy
Brothers Grimm • Hans Christian Andersen Fairy Tales
The Wonderful Wizard of Oz • The Age of Queen Victoria

Available from all good bookstores, worldwide, and online at
flametreepublishing.com

See our new fiction imprint
FLAME TREE PRESS | FICTION WITHOUT FRONTIERS
New and original writing in Horror, Crime, SF and Fantasy

And join our monthly newsletter with offers and more stories:
FLAME TREE FICTION NEWSLETTER
flametreepress.com

GOTHIC FANTASY

For our books, calendars, blog
and latest special offers please see:
flametreepublishing.com